WITCH OF THE
FEDERATION V

WITCH OF THE FEDERATION V

FEDERAL HISTORIES™ 05

MICHAEL ANDERLE

DISRUPTIVE IMAGINATION

Copyright © 2020 Michael Anderle
Cover copyright © LMBPN Publishing
Cover Art by Jake @ J Caleb Design
http://jcalebdesign.com / jcalebdesign@gmail.com
A Michael Anderle Production

LMBPN Publishing
PMB 196, 2540 South Maryland Pkwy
Las Vegas, NV 89109

First US edition, March 2020
Version 1.02, December 2020
eBook ISBN: 978-1-64202-819-5
Print ISBN: 978-1-64202-820-1

THE WITCH OF THE FEDERATION BOOK V TEAM

Thanks to our JIT Readers

Daniel Weigert
Dave Hicks
Deb Mader
Debi Sateren
Diane L. Smith
Dorothy Lloyd
James Caplan
Jeff Eaton
Jeff Goode
Larry Omans
Misty Roa
Peter Manis
Veronica Stephan-Miller

If We've missed anyone, please let us know!

Editor
The Skyhunter Editing Team

To Family, Friends and
Those Who Love
To Read.
May We All Enjoy Grace
To Live The Life We Are
Called.

CHAPTER ONE

A starship's sleek shadow hung against a night sky. The shuttle that moved toward it was merely another dot of silver in a sea of stars. The men inside it sat silently and continued to study one another carefully across the empty space between them.

The craft was spartanly equipped and built for speed. Large metallic crates occupied the center of the aisle. The passengers had watched as their equipment and gear were stowed in them on the tarmac to which they'd been ferried by private car.

Talking had been discouraged.

"Introductions can be made once we're ex-atmospheric." That curt reprimand had been given immediately when the first of them had opened his mouth to say hello.

They'd taken the hint and gone silent, but it hadn't stopped them trying to get the measure of each other by sight alone.

Take-off had been smooth and fast, and not one of them believed they'd reached the minimum limit when the shuttle had twisted into the space between. Now that it had emerged and the viewscreen in front had gone live, they looked at each other and all of them clearly wondered who'd be the first to speak.

"So," said the man who'd wanted to introduce himself on the

tarmac, "I'm Ferdinand—and the first of you to make some bullshit crack about any kind of bovine has to buy the rest of us a drink of our choice when we get on board."

That drew a few smiles from the men and women old enough to have kids and puzzled looks from those too young—except for one. Harper laughed.

"Sorry." He chortled. "I have nieces. They love that old classic."

Ferdinand smiled in response. "What's your name and specialty, son?"

The younger man smiled and blushed. "Electrical engineering and a little weapons tech. You?"

He wagged his finger. "Uh-uh. Name."

"Do you promise not to laugh?"

"Nope," he responded and grinned.

The youngster rolled his eyes. "Fair enough. Harper."

"Isn't that a girl's name?" blurted one of the women on the other side.

Harper blushed. "Let's say my parents wanted me to be a singer."

That brought gentle laughter and the boy took the opportunity to shift the attention. He looked at the girl opposite him. "You?"

"Imogen," she replied, "and I love my weapons."

That brought a round of cat calls and oohs that made her blush. She waved them away and zeroed in on the next person. "Weren't you on the *Knight*?" She blushed even more the moment she'd said it. "Sorry. I shouldn—"

The woman waved her apology away. "I did, and I'm not the only one. I'm simply surprised Larkin hasn't said hello yet. Are you too good to acknowledge an old crewmate?"

Larkin raised his head and the crow's feet around his eyes wrinkled with amusement. "Nah, I'm too scared to intrude on her privacy," he teased and the woman rolled her eyes.

"I never knew you to be one to stand on ceremony, Larks."

He shrugged, his smile both open and shy. "You know me, Dee. I like my machines. I'm not so good with people."

Dee laughed. "I don't know, Lark. We both know you can—"

She stopped when the man blushed bright red and turned to the man next to him. "How about you, son? Did you ever work on the *Knight?*"

"Now that you mention it..."

What followed was an hour of conversation where the slowly approaching bulk of the starship was ignored while old acquaintances were renewed and new ones made. Harper leaned back and mainly watched and listened. He'd worked on the *Knight,* too, but he hadn't met half of these old rogues.

It looked like One R&D had brought together some of the best in a variety of ship-building fields in a private, very advanced, and super-super-fast shuttle to get them somewhere in one hell of a hurry.

He glanced at the forward viewscreen and studied the slowly expanding outline.

"Well," he murmured, "she's no *Knight.*"

His quiet words brought a hush to the compartment and everyone glanced at the screen. "Holy mother of...pearl. That thing's..." He couldn't quite find the right words.

"Well, it's something, all right," Ferdinand finished. "I wonder what kind of systems they've packed into that?"

It was a good question, especially as the shuttle began to slow. Ferdinand's brow furrowed as he studied the craft on the viewscreen.

"She looks kinda too complete to need the likes of us, though," he commented when he recognized the finish.

"Yeah," Harper mused and inched forward, "and her weapons are already screwed in tight. Somehow, I don't think this is what we're being called to work on."

"What gives you that idea, boy?"

The term made him frown, but he knew any kind of protest would only make the term stick so he left it ignored. Instead, he chose to answer the question. "Well, we all worked on the *Knight,* right? In one form or other."

He might have looked like he'd tuned out of the conversation but he'd absorbed every single word spoken by those around him. Some had been in the Naval facility that had built the *Knight's* engines.

Others had been on board to tuck the engines into place or listened to the engineer working on the weapons cuss the pilot out for his hair-raising maneuvers.

As the others nodded in answer to his question, he waved a hand at the ship that now almost filled the screen. "Well, does that look anything like a *Knight* kind of project to you?"

They all swiveled in their seats and made another careful scrutiny of the ship. Harper waited and his gaze shifted from one face to the next as he watched them make their own assessment.

Finally, Dee shook her head. "The kid has a point."

Harper stifled a groan. "Kid" was almost as bad as "boy" in his books, but it was also as likely to stick if he protested.

Ferdinand turned and gave him a long look and he hoped he made the grade. He was the first to admit he wasn't much to look at, a young overachiever who'd had his own set of "keepers" until this last job, where One R&D had said they'd provide their own.

He hadn't seen them yet and was kinda excited to be trusted to look after himself for a change. It was a source of pride to him that he did that, keepers or no, but he now actually felt like he was doing it—and he wanted to measure up. The older man with the salt-and-pepper running through his dark hair studied him carefully.

"Do you think this is something like the *Knight*?"

Harper nodded but suppressed the urge to smile. He had to be dead-cold about this. "I think it's a possibility. I mean"—he gestured at them—"you're all from the *Knight* project and we all know who that was for, don't we?"

They nodded.

"So why not this?" He gestured at the ship they were now closing in on. A landing hatch had opened in one side and the shuttle had made no effort to slow. "Think about it. Who flies like this?"

"Combat pilots," one old hand suggested.

"Wattlebird," another snapped and his lip curled, and Harper remembered he'd been on the weapons installation team. They'd been particularly upset with the *Knight's* pilot for corkscrewing "their" baby through a battlefield.

He nodded enthusiastically but before he could add anything further, the shuttle slewed sideways through the hatch, cut its engines, and fired its retros to adjust its position before it settled onto the landing pad. Their stomachs lurched as they rocked in their harnesses.

Ferdinand grunted. "You have a point, kid. Very few fly like that!"

"For which we are all very grateful," Larkin muttered and cast a dark look toward the cockpit.

They all followed his gaze while they waited for the pilot's next instructions.

"So," Harper whispered, when the door remained stubbornly shut. "D'you think it's Them?"

As if his question was a signal, the door slid back to reveal their pilot. Harper's jaw all but hit the floor, and Ferdinand nudged him.

"Yup, it is Them. That's—" he stopped as Brenden raised a finger to his lips.

"Remember your NDA, folks. People take that shit seriously, especially during these times." He regarded each of them with a serious expression and nodded. "I need you to follow me and not say a word. The shuttle won't get us where we need to go, but the *Jackson's* skipper will. He doesn't want to see or hear you, so you'll travel in pods for the jump and transfer to the shuttle again. I will be your pilot."

A jump? Harper and Ferdinand exchanged glances and Larkin winked at Dee. This would be exactly like old times.

Their eyes widened as Avery followed him out of the cockpit.

"There are two of them," Harper whispered and Avery looked at him and winked before he placed a finger over his lips and followed Brenden out of the shuttle.

They hurried after the pilots into the deserted hangar and out into the ship itself. As promised, several pods waited to take them safely and comfortably through the jump between systems and they didn't meet a single soul.

When they emerged after what felt like seconds later, Brenden and Avery were waiting and escorted them into the shuttle for the final leg of their journey. Neither of the pilots said anything and simply shepherded them to their seats, locked the hatch behind them, and entered the cockpit.

"They don't say much, do they?" Harper observed as the cockpit door closed and a *seatbelts* sign displayed in the forward view screen.

"Nope." Ferdinand sank into his seat and buckled his harness. He looked around at his fellow workers and sighed. "I don't suppose any of you has an idea of where we are or what's going on?"

The group exchanged glances as they shook their heads, and silence descended.

It was interrupted by the faint ding of the viewscreen when the seatbelt sign fractured and was replaced by the impressive bulk of a ship. The gathered engineers and tech specialists leaned forward.

"What is that?" Dee asked and Ferdinand shook his head.

"It's not any class I know," he told her and was startled when Harper started to laugh. "What?"

The youngster looked at him. "You mean you don't know?"

The man exchanged glances with some of the other older hands and they all shook their heads and shrugged. With a sigh, he turned to the boy again. "Why?"

"It's the *Titanic*." He chuckled and stared at him, waiting for a response.

Ferdinand merely returned the stare and Harper's laughter died.

"You don't know what the *Titanic* was?"

"Well," Larkin drawled, "we're all fairly sure you don't mean the ship that sank while crossing the Atlantic hundreds of years ago, but—"

His eyes widened in surprise. "So that's where it came from," he murmured. "I always wondered what the significance of it sinking a company had to do with its name."

"Wait!" Larkin looked at the screen and studied the huge outline that hung before them with closer attention.

The shuttle continued its journey undeterred, its pilots amused by the close scrutiny of Elizabeth's new ship. Avery held his hand out, the palm up.

"I win."

Brendan groaned. "The boy?" he asked. "How does a kid know what it is when the more experienced guys don't?"

"Because the kid was in engineering school long after everyone else left and this made a splash in the educational circles when it went down but died a quieter 'told-you-so' kinda death out in the professional world."

"And you know this how?"

Avery smirked. "My sister."

His teammate stared at him, open-mouthed. "But she's not an engineer."

"She dated a fair number of guys before she settled on the one she's with now," he replied. "Picky girl, my sister."

"Hmmph!" Brenden wasn't impressed. The picky girl had cost him two weeks' pay.

The other man snickered. "I'll buy the kids something nice to go to the movies in and my sister something nice in general."

"You spoil them, you know that, right?"

Avery's smile faded and his face took on a more serious look. "While I can, man. While I still can."

They both concentrated on flying, having already left the *Jackson* to reverse its jump into the space between dimensions. Their passengers' voices drifted to them over the intercom.

"They shoulda called it the *Iceberg*," Larkin grumbled. "It was an iceberg that did the sinking, not the damn ship."

One of the other men whistled. "That has to be the biggest damned super-dreadnought I ever did see."

"It's the first and last of the Titans," Harper told him. "It was so expensive to build that no one could afford to finish it, so they put it in the dry dock until they could decide what they wanted to do with it."

"And One R&D bought it," Ferdinand concluded while his gaze roamed over the behemoth's hull.

"The *Knight* was merely a dinghy compared to this," one of the others exclaimed, and the weapons engineer slapped him in the chest.

"I won't have you talking about the *Knight* like that," he snapped.

The man shrugged his hand away. "Well, fuck me," he retorted. "I didn't mean to dis your girlfriend but take a fucking look at that. The *Knight* would fucking fit inside it."

Ferdinand regarded the fellow with distaste. "You're Australian, aren't you?"

The way he said it, the phrase wasn't a question so much as an explanation and the man stared at him. "What of it, mate?"

He raised his hands in a placatory gesture. "Not a thing except that I'm not your mate and that thing is fucking huge."

The Australian grinned and reached across the silver crate between them to offer Ferdinand his hand. "Deakin. Fuel and energy transfer. I guess we'd better get along."

Ferdinand stifled a groan. Now that he thought about it, he did recognize the Australian's nasal tones. The man was brilliant for maximizing the efficiency of the ship's energy flow but he could be royal pain in the ass if he was bored.

"I wonder how much they paid for it," Harper muttered, his eyes still fixed on the dreadnought's hull, "and how much is already in there. I mean, is it a full fit-out or has someone already started—"

Ferdinand nudged him to end his musing. "You'd better hope they at least have life support going," he told the boy, "or life's about to get real interesting."

Silence settled for a moment when the side of the ship loomed before them and a hangar bay door opened, only to reveal it was inset into a much larger portal.

"Fuck. The *Knight* could fit inside this." Deakin drew a sharp breath. "It's enormous."

"Don't you mean fucking enormous?" one of the other men asked sarcastically.

He gave him a wide-eyed stare. "We don't always fucking swear, mate."

Ferdinand chuckled and waited until the shuttle had set down before he unbuckled his harness. His tablet chimed as the engines wound down and the heavy vibration of docking clamps rattled through the shuttle's frame.

"It looks like we're finally home," he said and pulled his tablet out.

All around him, the others did the same.

"Well, fuck me," the Aussie said after a moment of silently perusing the task list they'd all been sent.

"Not in a lifetime of nopes," his critic snapped in response but absent-mindedly as if he had merely responded without really thinking of what he would say.

The Aussie looped an arm around his neck and let his hand dangle over the guy's chest. "Are you sure, sweetie? 'Cos I can offer you much more than a ship."

The weapons engineer slanted him a wary look and caught the smirk on Deakin's face. He reached up and stroked his hand.

"Well, now that you mention it…" he began and burst out laughing at the look of shock on the man's face. "I didn't think so, toots. You shouldn't make moves you don't mean. Someone could take you seriously."

One of the guys at the other end of the shuttle sighed. "And here I was getting my hopes up," he threw in and all but one of the men around him laughed.

He caught the man's look. "I was joking, Rob. Geez. Grow a sense of humor."

Pointing at the tablet, Ferdinand changed the subject. "So, it's a super-dreadnought shell but we won't make it into a super-dreadnought."

That stopped them. They all turned to look at him and he tapped his tablet.

"I'm serious. Take a closer look at where the engines and weapons are and then look at where they want the power to run."

The group complied and crowded to the back of the shuttle to compare notes, oblivious to the cockpit opening behind them.

Brenden nudged Avery and indicated the knot of men and women, all crowded together and comparing tablets. "It's started," he intoned, and his teammate smiled.

"Elizabeth will be pleased."

"I wonder what those are all about…" Ferdinand murmured.

"They're not engines. Those are here…and here….and there's an auxiliary bank here, too."

Harper nodded. "It's for some kind of tech," he suggested, studied his tablet more closely, and zoomed in. "I'm sure of it. What the hell is the Witch up to?"

Ferdinand nudged the guy to silence him and looked around carefully. His face paled when he caught sight of Brenden and Avery observing them from the cockpit door. "He's merely thinking out loud," he offered. "He won't do it again."

Brenden stared at the man and didn't offer any comfort. *Why the hell does the guy think it matters all the way out here?* he thought before he realized that these guys had no idea how far from anywhere they were.

The oldest hand—Larkin, if he recalled correctly—took a firm hold of the boy's arm. Even without the pick-up he'd hidden at the end of the craft, he could hear the old-timer's warning.

"Remember what happened on the other ship?" he asked and Harper nodded, glanced over his shoulder, and noticed the pilots for the first time.

He paled and the light smattering of freckles on his cheeks stood out like punctuation.

Larkin ignored it and shook the kid. "No one needs to know what we know."

"If you'd step this way, ladies…gentlemen…" Brenden instructed, "I'm sure you'd like to get acquainted with your quarters."

At his words, the man who had looked back and seen them cleared his throat. "If it's okay with you, we'd rather see our workspaces to get an idea of exactly how big the job is in real terms." He lifted his tablet. "On a job like this, we want to get started early to make sure we get done what you're paying us to do."

A low murmur of agreement ran through the techs, and Brenden shrugged. "Sure, we'll show you to your teams, then, and have someone there help you navigate to the mess and your bunks."

They all nodded and he led them out and tried not to smile as the weapons engineer leaned over to the Australian and muttered, "Yeah, you never know how much extra we'll have to adjust the specs."

Deakin looked startled. "Why would we do that?" he wanted to know.

"In case some asshole pilot tries to corkscrew a super-dreadnought."

"But this isn't a super-dreadnought. You saw the layout."

"Layout, schmayout. This beast has the guns and the power and fuck knows what else in those chambers. I guarantee you, the Witch is going to war and she'll take that damn crazy pilot with her. We're gonna need something extra, I reckon."

CHAPTER TWO

"It has to be bigger," the *Knight's* weapons chief said. "Much bigger—and we need more guns."

His second in command looked at him as though he'd gone crazy. "More guns, boss?"

"More guns," he confirmed and surveyed the firing line with a jaundiced eye. "Although I'm damned if I know where we'll put them."

The other man moved closer. "But why, Chief?"

He glanced around and stooped close to his second's ear. "Because she needs them, and if we can't manage it somehow, I'm worried she'll think of moving to a bigger shell and…damnit, I don't want her to go."

"Gotcha, Chief. Me neither."

They both raised their heads and studied the weapons array, and each one tried to envisage a way to jigsaw something more in. Exactly how they would broach the procurement to the captain was beyond anything either of them could imagine.

First, they'd settle for being able to fit another gun and maybe making the ones installed a little bigger.

"Have we looked at ammunition, yet?" his subordinate asked. "The boffins come up with something new every second week. They're bound to have something that'll give us more strike power."

"Let's go make a call."

While the two heads of weapons stalked to their office, Captain Emil had a call of his own to deal with.

"Speak!" he ordered, and his eyebrows rose as Admiral Dailey's image came onto the screen.

"Indeed," the man said and his lips twitched as Emil's face flushed red, "that is what I called you to do."

"Sir, I..." he stuttered, but Dailey waved his apology aside.

"Do you have time for a meeting?"

The captain glanced at the ceiling, even though he knew the ship could hear him perfectly well.

"Ebony, do I have time to have a meeting with the Admiral?"

"Certainly, sir," the ship replied and used her sweetest and most human tones. "If the Admiral would send me a brief, I will make sure you are prepared."

If Admiral Dailey was surprised to discover that Emil had a secretary, he didn't show it. Instead, he nodded brusquely and replied, "There is no brief. There's merely something I'd like to discuss if that is convenient?"

"Certainly, sir." The response came as a chorus from the captain and what Dailey assumed was his aide.

"Very good, then. I'll meet you in an hour. You do know where my office is, do you not?"

"Sir." Captain Emil gave a single nod and signed off.

After a few seconds, the *Ebon Knight* spoke. "They won't replace my shell, will they Emil?" Her voice caught in a very human fashion and she added, "Or my team?"

He patted the closest wall. "I don't know, but neither of those can happen without Stephanie's consent and she will be sure to consult us first."

"There is a quaver in your voice, Captain," the *Knight* observed. "Are you being straight with me?"

Straight with her? Emil raised an eyebrow. "Ebony," he replied. "I am being as straight as I can with you. I promise you I will do all I can to ensure you do not lose your team."

"And my shell?" she asked and sounded uncertain.

"Or your shell," he reassured her.

"Then you'd better hurry. He is less likely to be open to negotiation if you are late," she said.

He hurried to the door, only to be stopped by a soft tutting.

"Your hat, Captain," Ebony reminded him. "It's over there."

He flushed with chagrin, snatched up the offending head cover, and jammed it onto his head before he returned to the door. This time, he paused before he opened it. "Is there anything else?" he asked.

The *Ebon Knight* was silent for a very long moment, then replied, "No, Captain. You are presentable and have all the necessary items should the admiral decide that lunch is required. Your documents are in order and I have ensured that the crew is close by should we need to leave."

Anticipating changes to the meeting and preparing a quick getaway? Emil didn't know what to think. Like so many stages the ship had gone through, this was yet another he would have to consider the ramifications for.

It was something he still considered somewhat absently in his mind when he reached the admiral's outer office.

"Captain Emil to see Admiral Dailey," he stated as he strode to the aide's desk.

The man looked up from behind his computer and back to the screen while his fingers danced across the keyboard. The look of surprise that crossed his face as he brought up the relevant appointment was almost comical.

"Admiral Dailey will see you right away, sir," he answered and announced the visitor's presence before he pushed a button that triggered the office's double doors. "Right through there, sir. He's expecting you."

Emil touched his cap and walked into the office. It was a little unnerving when the doors closed automatically behind him, but he kept a firm grasp on his reaction and focused on the man he'd come to meet.

"You wanted to see me, sir?"

"My liaison tells me there's not much more we can do to up-gun your ship," the admiral began, and his spirits sank.

Here it comes, he thought but Dailey wasn't done.

"And Morgana Inc refuses to let us do the little we can. They have cited something about stressing the ship unnecessarily. I reminded them there was a war on and they pointed out that it made it all the more important not to mess with something that was working fine as it was." He sighed. "It was their opinion that the *Knight* was close to its engineering threshold."

Emil had seen the reports and he agreed with Morgana Inc. The *Knight* really was at her engineering threshold. There was no close to about it. His main worry was breaking that to the weapons team when they approached him with their next brilliant—and equally crazy—idea.

He didn't reveal that, however, and remained silent. Fortunately, the man still wasn't done.

"Given their recalcitrance on the matter," he continued, "the Federation Navy feels it has no choice but to deploy the *Henry Chauvel* and the *Cathay Williams* to the *Knight's* defense."

The captain opened his mouth to protest but the other man raised a hand and he fell silent.

"Their captains will fall under your command. They are under strict orders to obey you and the *Knight* regardless of any Naval precedents. We understand that any kind of norm is likely to suffer casualties where the Witch is concerned. No offense intended."

A faint flush of color touched the admiral's cheeks and Emil stifled a smile. At least the man seemed to find this conversation as difficult as he did.

"None taken, sir."

"And we understand that your orders come from the Witch herself, so there will be no argument. You are her representative and neither Captain Yale nor Captain Docherty have a problem with that."

Given the battle they'd fought together to save Earth, he thought he could understand why. Of all the ships he could have chosen to saddle them with, it was a relief that he'd chosen those particular two.

The hierarchy was already established and they'd fought together, so there was battle trust between them too. It could have been far worse. He had only one worry.

"Will they be able to keep up with us?"

It was a valid question. the *Knight* was able to move across half a solar system in a single blink. No Federation ship he knew of had that capability.

He hastened to explain. "We wouldn't want to have to leave them behind, but we also need to move freely if we are to fight to our full capability."

It was a polite way to remind the admiral of what the *Knight* could do while warning him that an ordinary ship might slow them. The man's mouth tightened and, for a moment, he thought he had offended him. He stiffened reflexively and his mind raced to think of something that might ease the tension.

To his surprise, the admiral smiled.

"Both the *Chauvel and Williams* will be able to synch their drives to yours and follow you to your location." His grim look became a sly smile as he watched his visitor's face. "We might be bound by rules and regulations, but we can move with the times if we must..." He deliberately left the sentence hanging.

"And you anticipated the need," Emil finished for him.

"And we anticipated the need," he confirmed and looked both smug and pleased at the same time. "We hope you don't mind."

He gave the man his own version of a tight, satisfied smile. "We look forward to no longer fighting alone."

Sensibly, he did not add how relieved the *Knight* would feel to know she would be assisted and not replaced.

"How much did you upgrade them?" he asked instead.

The admiral's smile remained in place but his gaze became shadowed. "Enough to keep up with the *Knight* and be worth something as running mates," he answered, and he decided to let him keep his secrets.

"We'll need a shake-down," he noted, and the other man nodded.

"The *Chauvel* and the *Williams* need time to let their crews gain familiarity with the new functions," he replied. "I estimate a fortnight on their own before we put them through group maneuvers."

Personally, Emil thought a fortnight might not be enough but he didn't say so. Instead, he replied, "Let me know when they're available."

He wanted to push for a date but decided he could use the time to prepare a series of exercises for when the crews were ready.

"It might be best if we start training in PodSpace when they're available," he suggested. "Something to get the bridge crews used to fighting as part of a single team."

Admiral Dailey gave him a sharp look. "I'll trust you with the oversight," he agreed.

Matthias moved around the kitchen bar. Dinner had been good, but it was even better to be home where he and Arne could let their guards down. The master sergeant had already run his usual security protocol through the apartment to make sure they had no uninvited guests.

He'd done it as though he owned it and given how many times he'd overnighted, he might as well. Not that his boss had any intention to complain. For once, he was glad he wasn't alone and especially since the man wasn't the talkative type.

The bar stool creaked as his bodyguard took his place on the other side of the bar. The beer came in a carton of six and Matthias hesitated. He'd been about to take two but thought better of it.

Pulling the carton out, he set it beside them on the bar. Rather than take his seat beside Arne, he dragged one of the bar stools around to the kitchen side and straddled it. Once he'd passed the Marine a can, he took another for himself.

Neither of them spoke as they popped the tabs and took their first pulls. By mutual agreement, they stayed sober when they were out. It wasn't something they discussed but neither of them drank when they were in what they regarded as the combat zone.

How the apartment escaped being included in that, he didn't know —and he didn't care. What mattered was that his bodyguard tacitly agreed it was in a safe zone.

Matthias settled himself on the stool and leaned his elbows on the countertop. Once the first swallow had settled, he looked the other man full in the face. "We have to talk."

Arne quirked an eyebrow. "It took you long enough," he muttered and took another long sip of his beer.

"And you won't ask what about?"

The man licked his lips and shook his head. "There's only one subject."

On that, they agreed. In the short silence that followed, he sipped his beer thoughtfully. "It's not an easy decision."

His companion shrugged. "It's not that hard. You've stared at it long enough that you've started to see shadows."

Matthias frowned. He hated that the man was right but liked that he hadn't said he had started to jump at those shadows. Who said a Marine couldn't learn tact?

He shrugged. "Like I said, it's not an easy decision."

Arne opened his mouth but closed it again. For a moment, the commander had the unmistakable impression that he had intended to tell him it wasn't all that hard and that the choices were clear.

While he'd have been right, neither of those facts made the decision any easier to make. He lifted the beer to his lips again, if only to give himself time to think about what he needed to say.

The master sergeant watched him for a while before he gave him the grim little smile he'd learned to both appreciate and dread. "What you're facing has been faced before," he began and pressed on when he would have interrupted. "Way back before we truly fucked this world, when there were nations ruled by kings and queens and emperors and what have you."

His turn of phrase made Matthias smile. He definitely fell into the category of a what have you. Him and Elizabeth both, even if neither of them were royalty. The younger man continued.

"Those rulers always needed someone they could talk to—

someone they could trust regardless of the situation. That person listened to everything they said and didn't tell a soul. Sometimes, they even came up with a solution to the latest bee that had crawled up their royal's britches."

The commander raised both eyebrows and gave him a worried look. Arne caught it and returned a wry smile. "My point is that they were there to share the burden. It wasn't a great job. They saw when the rock everyone relied on started to crack."

He frowned at that but his bodyguard had more to say. "These folks were there when the dam broke. They watched as their royal lost it completely, then they watched as their royal put themselves back together—and most times, when that happened, there wasn't anything they could do but be there."

"Your point?" he asked, not at all sure he was comfortable with what the Marine was trying to say.

"That these people had the best and worst job in the world. They spent time with the most important people in their world and they were the ones to help that person deal with all the pressures of being what they were and what they had to deal with. It wasn't a great job."

He paused and his gaze became a distant stare as though he looked directly into that past. After another sip of beer, he continued, "You have to realize that tremendous effort was required to support someone who was under more stress than any human should ever have to bear—and who couldn't afford to crack because they'd lose their kingdom or their world if they did." The Marine took a larger sip. "Being that person wasn't something to envy. Your Elizabeth is a prime example."

Matthias raised both eyebrows at that but he remained silent given what Arne had said. When the silence had gone on too long, the younger man shifted uncomfortably.

"Look," he said as if the silence demanded an explanation, "from what I've worked out, Elizabeth was originally hired to help a particularly talented teenager get the start she deserved. That was decided by the AI whose job it is to make sure that those who can benefit mankind the most get the chance to do so. Correct?"

The commander scowled but nodded. He was right. BURT's primary directive was exactly that.

"She was also tasked with creating schools for others like that teenager—witches who hadn't been discovered or who were considered to be too poor to be worth the trouble, people to be discounted regardless of what they were capable of if only they had the chance."

Again, Matthias nodded.

"And, in the middle of all that, the Telorans appeared and the war happened."

Arne took another sip, found the can empty, and retrieved another from the carton.

"So," he continued, "up until that point, what was she?"

He opened his mouth to say he didn't know but it seemed his bodyguard hadn't finished. The younger man gave him a half-apologetic look.

"I did a little digging." Ignoring the surprise on his companion's face, Arne continued. "Your Elizabeth was a ghost—a lone operator and suspected of being complicit in over a dozen assassinations and tricky 'procurements without permission.'"

"Are you saying she was a thief and murderer?" He was surprised to discover that the confirmation didn't shock him as much as it probably should have. From her dossier, he'd had a vague idea of what he'd find.

And it still didn't stop you from falling for her, he scolded himself but with absolutely no regrets. *Man, do I have it bad.*

Oblivious to what he was thinking, Arne went on. "I've seen her file—what there is of it. You've seen her file, for heaven's sake. She worked for one of the suspected crime lords on our continent."

"And now she is one." He sighed heavily but once again, his companion wasn't done.

"That's not my point." After another hasty sip from his beer, he smacked his lips and added, "My point is she isn't a strategic thinker—or she wasn't up to this point. She was a lone operator and had enough of a vision to protect herself but no long-term plans for the future."

"Unless it was to stay out from under Tex's thumb."

"Yeah, that…and we both know how well that worked out for her, don't we? And that brings me to the point."

"You have a point?"

"Smart ass. Do you want to hear it or not?"

Matthias drained his can, took another, and drained half of that too. The way Arne was going through his, he had catching up to do. He waved a hand. "Go ahead."

His bodyguard cocked his head. "Are you sure you want to hear the rest?"

He studied him carefully, took another long draught from the can, emptied it, and opened another. "Now I want to hear it."

The Marine smirked. "It's not that bad, you know."

"Finish telling the story."

Arne's eyebrows raised. "Story? You know I'm not spinning shit simply for fun, right?"

"But you are spinning shit, yeah?"

The man threw both hands up in mock dismay. "I tried," he complained. "I really did."

"Will you please get on with it?" This time, Matthias couldn't keep the exasperation out of his voice.

His companion shrugged. "Sure. Since you asked so nicely."

"Don't make me come over there."

"You even sound like her, you know?"

"And you were saying?"

Arne gave him a sour look. "I was saying your Elizabeth has gone from being a solo operator with only herself to look out for and an excellent grasp of tactics—" The commander snorted, and his companion raised an eyebrow. When he didn't say anything, he continued. "A solo operator, a tactician, and responsible for only herself to a warlord, a co-builder in a business empire, and the second mom to the most powerful witch in recorded history."

He shrugged. "Now tell me something I don't know."

"Yeah? Well, Mr. Smart-Ass-I-Know-It-All, the guy who'll support a woman like that had better be equally as strong if he wants to help her be all that and a criminal crime lord."

The Marine chuckled as he said the last few words and the laughter softened them from accusation to fact. Matthias stared at him for a long moment, then sighed.

"So," he began, "do you think I should do this?"

His companion returned his stare and his expression gave nothing away.

"You realize," he continued when he realized the man wanted something more. "You do realize that this makes you the support person for the person supporting the Crime Queen, right? An accessory after the fact."

Arne shrugged. "From what I've seen, criminals have more honor than some of the people giving me orders right now—or even before."

Matthias stared, startled by his admission, but he couldn't fault it.

The man caught his look and took another sip to finish the can. "In the end, it always comes down to one question. Does the end justify the means?"

He stilled and frowned as he thought about it. "If we can do it without losing our honor? Then yes."

Arne cracked a smile at that. "I think we can be reasonably assured that we won't lose our honor. Our heads, though…I'm not so sure about that."

"Hmmm." He lowered his can. "So, what should we do about it?"

"We?" The smile remained on the man's lips. "Well, you can't be the Queen's Dog and a Navy man."

The commander grinned in response. "But that was working so well for me."

His companion snorted and they sobered as one and let the smiles fade from their faces.

"Retirement?" Matthias suggested. "I'm about due."

Arne sighed. "Me too."

They both reached for another can at the same time.

"The Navy needs to find someone better at negotiating with her, anyway," the commander stated in an effort to break the quiet sadness that came with the decision. The Navy had been his life—his entire life.

Judging by the look on the master sergeant's face, he was in the same boat. Neither of them said anything for a long moment. The decision weighed on them despite its inevitability, if not because of Elizabeth, then something else. They'd both been in the service for a long time and the Navy would have moved them on soon anyway.

It was Arne who broke the silence. "Do you think they can find someone?"

"What? Someone who has a hope of negotiating with her?" he asked and shook his head with a grin. "Not a hope in hell."

CHAPTER THREE

Harborview Tech was exactly as she remembered it. Stephanie took a moment to admire the garden in the center of the turning circle before she headed inside. The chancellor was there to meet her and he took her hands and smiled warmly.

"I am so glad to see you, Miss Morgana."

He was a different person to the wry skeptic Elizabeth had spoken to when they'd first approached the school. She returned his smile. "Thank you for giving us the chance to do this."

"I wouldn't have it any other way." He gestured for her to walk beside him and ignored Lars and Johnny as they fell in behind them. "They're waiting."

The students had gathered in the assembly hall they'd used before. They broke into applause as she entered and she hesitated. The chancellor slipped his hand through her arm and led her forward.

"I'm still not used to this," she whispered and he smiled.

"I know. I doubt you ever will be. But remember, it's not about you. They need this."

"That helps," she admitted, her face burning. She was glad neither of the men behind her had anything to say—at least, not at the moment. No doubt there'd be way too much teasing about it later.

She raised her head and surveyed the students around her, pleased to note that their teachers sat with them rather than isolated in a row at the front. It wasn't hard to smile in return when she remembered all they'd done.

It was also a relief to see that everyone who'd suffered the effects of opening the portal for *The King's Warrior* was back on their feet and looking well. That had taken weeks.

"It is so good to see you all here," she told them when she reached the podium at the front and they erupted into cheers.

"I heard you missed the fight," she continued when they'd settled. The comment was met by nods and murmurs of affirmation, and she continued. "This is what happened on Dreth."

She started with the footage of the Telorans' arrival on the Dreth home world. There were gasps when the students saw the scale of the attack and cries of dismay as the first defenders fell.

"That is the power of nMU," Stephanie told them and shifted the view to the arena. "This is what happened in the Fortress of Fire and Respect."

The footage rolled into her challenge to the traitors of Dreth and the students' eyes widened when she called the Dreth warriors cowards and accused them of acting out of fear. Vishlog and Garach's expressions were terrible—and exactly what she needed to drive the insult of what she'd said home.

Several students gasped at her words and she was glad to see that their lessons on Dreth culture had taken root. She didn't let it slow her, though.

The scene shifted to when the first of the traitors burst through the fortress's doors.

"We'll take Meligorn while your blood is still warm!" The threat sent shivers through the audience and made the chancellor grow tense.

"Are you sure..." he began in a whisper and Lars slid his arm around the man's shoulders and moved him gently to the side of the stage.

"She's sure. Trust her."

Stephanie continued without any hesitation and rolled the footage.

As she stood on the screen and tried to determine how to use magic to defend them, the team went to work around her. This was part of the point she wanted to make to the students—that magic was only useful to a degree but that the physical ability to fight was essential to keeping your mages alive. The curriculum she wanted to introduce depended on their grasp of that.

She allowed the recording to move to the spells she'd used in the battle. The students gasped again as the Stephanie on screen spun several purple and blue discs into the oncoming horde of Dreth. Several students bolted to their feet and tried to leave, their faces suddenly pale, but Frog and Avery met them at the door and handed them sick bags.

It wasn't necessary to hear the words to know what message they'd been given. "You need to see this."

As the students returned reluctantly to their seats, the footage continued. Avery and Frog moved through the auditorium to make sure everyone had what they needed. Stephanie would have felt sorry for her more weak-stomached pupils but they didn't have the luxury.

This was something else they'd have to get used to and it was better for everyone if they discovered now who would have difficulty in combat. Time was against them.

"What the fuck is that?" Marcus's voice drew everyone's attention to the screen.

The weapon carried into the screen made everyone in the auditorium lean forward in their seats. They froze when they saw what it could do.

Stephanie paused the replay. "That," she explained, "is a Teloran nMU weapon. It draws on negative emotions and intensifies them— even for non-magic-users. Every one of my team reported feeling sensations of loss, grief, and anger, and that was only from the energy passing over them."

Pale faces stared at her and blanched even further when she resumed the footage and Vishlog's laughter washed over them. Some groaned when Stephanie's followed it on screen moments later.

Several of the students echoed Lars as he swore, and the hiss of many in-drawn breaths revealed their anxiety when he and Johnny began their advance on the weapon.

They were joined by Avery and Brenden while Stephanie's litany of insults rolled over them as the machine fired again. This time, breaths were held as she stood before it.

Everyone watched while she wound the negative energy around her. They shuddered when Morgana crept into her laughter and gasped again as she returned the energy she'd gathered to its source.

Jaws dropped when the machine exploded and the energy released was assimilated and drawn into the blast. It shredded the enemy Dreth lines and the second machine that had been brought to the arena's entrance.

"I had no idea…" the Chancellor whispered as the traitor Dreth leapt over the balconies surrounding the arena and tried to reach Stephanie and her team. "None…"

He quieted when Lars laid a hand on his shoulder but his eyes were round with horror as he watched.

Onscreen, the cats fought their tethers and roared a protest at being kept out of the fight, while the Witch delivered lightning strikes into the oncoming Dreth. A cheer went up from the auditorium when Admiral Jaleck and her dropships arrived.

Stephanie let the footage roll on and hoped the students noted the importance of the colors on the Dreth uniforms. It was a cultural point in the midst of the lesson on magical warfare that they needed to absorb.

The clan names that boomed to answer Vishlog's roar of, "House Karnach stands for Dreth!" sent chills over her skin. Who said words were only words?

Shadows trailed her onscreen body as Jaleck's troops joined the battle and the recording ended when the admiral delivered the news of Tethis's condition and her earlier self vanished with a scream. It was undignified but it drove the point home.

"nMU affects us all," she told her audience, "yet it is essential for you to understand what it is and how to wield it without destroying yourselves."

Shocked faces turned from the screen to look at her, and the chancellor's horrified question carried to them all. "You can blow yourself up with magic? You do understand you are dealing with minors here..."

His voice petered to nothing and she nodded curtly. "I do, Chancellor, which makes my next request all the harder."

She looked at her students and made brief eye contact here and there and nodded to the teachers. Their faces were also pale.

With a wave at the now-blank screen, she addressed them. "That is what a battle looks like when magic is involved. And that is what we may yet have to face."

Behind her, the chancellor groaned and rested his forehead in his hands. Lars patted him on the shoulder. Ignoring them, she continued, "We will be needed and we will be at the forefront of the fighting."

Her gaze drifted over the audience and when her gaze lingered on the eyes of some who faced her squarely, she noted that her students nodded. Some met her look and gave her one brief jerk of the head. Others dipped their chin with such an expression of determination on their faces that she knew they had either mastered their fear or didn't have the sense to feel it. They were teenagers, after all.

She continued regardless. "We will be needed and sooner rather than later. There are spells we haven't taught you that you will need to know."

"But—" the chancellor protested and she cast him another glance before she focused on her pupils.

"Chancellor Cotes is correct. You will need parental permission for this and I will have to abide by it, but your world is in danger and I trust your parents and you to do what is best for it."

Tethis rose shakily from his seat. The smile he'd worn while he'd watched her at work in the Fortress of Fire and Respect was gone. He began to make his way onto the stage and before he'd gone more than a few steps, Frog was at his side.

"Let me help you, Master."

The mage gave him a wry smile but did not object. Instead, he wrapped his hand around the man's forearm and let him help him to the stage. Stephanie met them at the edge, took his other arm, and let him lead the way to the podium.

"You had something you wished to say, Master Tethis?"

He gave her a sideways glance and looked at the students. "Only that I will take the instructors through these classes before any students are permitted to participate. There are techniques I wish everyone to master before they try to pass them on."

"And you've had experience with these?" one of the teachers called from the audience.

She stifled a groan when she recognized Felarif's voice. Trust the rogue to make a fuss now. Tethis laid a hand on her arm before she could respond and she let him answer.

"Do you need to take my class in Meligornian history?" the old mage challenged. "There was call for such spells in our world's not so peaceful past and I was one of those who decided some skills were not needed once those wars were over. I revoke that decision now. Do you have any further questions?"

Felarif bowed his head but his, "No, Master Tethis," was heard clearly through the stadium.

He gave the young mage a feral grin. "Good. Then I shall expect you enrolled and in attendance in my Meligornian History class tomorrow morning."

Stephanie chuckled at Felarif's drop-jawed surprise and the rising chorus of "Ooooh," from the surrounding students. She began to understand how the Master had earned his iron-handed reputation at the school.

"And everyone thinks you're such a nice old man," she murmured safely out of the mike's pick-up.

Tethis smiled. "I take it this is what you had in mind?"

She nodded. "This is exactly what I had in mind," she told him, "but I want you to confine your teaching to the Pods. I know what that portal cost you and I cannot afford to lose you."

When she raised her head, she took a moment to observe the looks on the students' faces. "None of us can."

A slight pause allowed her words to sink in before she left the podium and took the microphone with her as she went to sit on the edge of stage. "Now, are there any questions?"

When silence met her words, she tried a different approach. "Is there anything any of you wants to raise?"

At first, she thought no one would answer but one student raised a hand tentatively. "There's a pod scenario where we can fight alongside Navy personnel. Did you help make that?"

Stephanie stared at him. "I hadn't heard of it. Do you want to tell me more of what it's about?"

She raised her hand as he began to speak and beckoned him closer. "Talk into the mike. I want everyone to hear this."

As he complied, she raised her head to meet the eyes of her audience. "And I want everyone's input. If you know something that hasn't been said, form a line near Frog. I want to hear it all."

What followed was as enlightening as it was worrying. Even the chancellor came to sit beside her. She quirked an eyebrow at him, but he shook his head. "I knew nothing of this," he whispered to answer her question.

There was more than one scenario, and she was surprised to learn that they were available at public pod centers and that non-student mages took part. It was hard to keep her thoughts—and her outrage—to herself, but she managed in spite of the concerned looks she caught from her team.

When the last student had finished speaking, she nodded. "Thank you, everyone, for that. I won't ban you from taking part, but I will ask you to report any attempt to recruit you since you are all under contract with One R&D. I won't prevent you from taking the option but there will be conditions and I want to discuss your options with you first. Is that understood?"

They nodded and everyone agreed readily to her request.

"You won't make us join them, will you?" one worried student asked, and Stephanie shook her head.

"I will not," she told them. "You are already serving your world and are vital to its defense which is why I want you to talk about any recruitment attempts when you receive them, okay?"

Again, they all nodded, but one of the girls picked up on what she'd said.

"What do you mean by when?"

"Because I know them," she replied and her expression grew dark. "When they see how well you fight, they will ask and they won't care that you are already integral to Earth's defense."

"But don't they protect the planet?"

"They do it differently," she told the student because she didn't want to get into anything political. The Navy reality was not something she wanted to talk about—not yet. Some ammunition was best kept for when it was truly needed.

After all, the Navy couldn't formulate an argument for something it didn't know she could raise, and their reaction to being blindsided would be enough for her students to make their own decisions.

"Now, do you have any magic-related questions you want to ask?" she added and looked at the Meligornians who stood in the background. "This is for teachers, too."

"You used both Meligorn and Earth energy in the Fortress," another student said, her face alight. "How did you do that?"

Stephanie cast a glance at the teachers. "Let's have your teachers explain how they do it and then I'll say how I do it. It can be different for everyone. Felarif, do you want to start?"

He bit back a retort which probably would have been along the lines of, "Do I have a choice?" and she smirked as he began. When he had finished, she moved the discussion to the next teacher.

Their answers soon devolved into an impromptu practice session that made the chancellor's jaw drop in amazement.

"I had no idea they'd come so far," he murmured and she smiled at him.

"They are very good students," she told him. "I'd hate to lose any one of them to the Navy."

His look was sharp. "So you don't think those are merely game scenarios?"

She shook her head. "No. I think we have competition."

The chancellor looked grim. "I had hoped it wouldn't come to this."

"Me too," she agreed. "We might have to look at expanding the program or something."

"I'll see what we can come up with and try to get a proposal to Elizabeth in the next few days. We can't stop them but we can try to offer an alternative and give the kids a choice in their futures."

Stephanie gave him a grateful look. "Thank you, Chancellor."

She stood and her movement drew the attention of the closest students.

"I need to go," she told them and raised her hand at their groans of disappointment. "But let me say that I am proud of how far you've come in such a short time. I'm looking forward to coming back to see you all again."

This brought pleased grins and the students turned in response to their teachers' demands for more practice. She stepped away and caught Tethis' eye.

The old mage had lounged against the stage and watched the proceedings with a mixture of envy and pride. It was clear he wanted to be with the students, teaching as he'd always done, and equally as clear that he was still recovering from what had happened when he'd gated The King's Warrior to Dreth.

He fell into step beside her. "Did you want to see me?"

Stephanie smiled at him. "How did you guess?"

She waited until they'd stepped into one of the pods down the corridor and she'd checked their privacy. "About Tex," she began when they were settled but paused, unsure of how to continue.

The old mage raised an eyebrow. "What about him?"

Feeling more than a little awkward, she twisted her hands together. "I wanted to make sure you were okay."

"What? With killing him?"

Her face cold with apprehension, she gulped. "Yes. It's not what… not really what you signed up for, is it?"

To her surprise, he laughed. "Child, I've been old enough to make my mind up on what I will and won't do since well before your grandfather was a sparkle in his father's eye. Tex needed killing—and he needed it a long time before Elizabeth finally got around to it. I'm only sad I didn't make it happen sooner."

Stephanie stared at him and relief washed over her as she closed her mouth. That wasn't what she'd expected to hear but she was glad he'd said it.

"By the way," he said cheerfully and interrupted her thoughts. "I spoke to the king."

"And?" she asked, playing for time to work out what he was talking about.

"Yes, and One R&D," he added and watched her as though he knew exactly how much he'd made her brain scramble. "One R&D Meligorn has been approved and the paperwork's been signed." He sighed happily. "And since I own ten percent of the company, I hope to become stupidly rich in the not too distant future."

She snorted. "You are already rich."

The old mage gave her a smile edged with sadness. "Yes, but I need to be stupidly rich or I won't be able to afford to pay all the magic users I'll need to throw magic for me."

The comment made her laugh. "I'm sure your students will do that for free. How do you think professors get cheap or free labor from college students?"

"They do?" His eyebrows rose in surprise. "But I thought we weren't supposed to take advantage of such offers."

"Silly," she joked and mock-punched his shoulder. "How else do they afford retirement?"

He looked shocked. "You don't plan to retire me already, do you?"

"I would never dare! The mischief you'd get up to, with your millions and your loyal student mages…" The look on her face made him burst out laughing.

They stood and looked at each other for a moment before a chime rang through the pod. Stephanie sighed. "I'd better go."

Tethis laid a hand on her arm. "Thank you," he told her, all humor gone from his face. "This is more than I hoped to be able to do in the twilight of my life."

"We're not done, yet," she reminded him and drew him into a hug. "Promise me you'll find a moment to have a meal with me."

He snorted. "This year? Or next?"

They were both laughing when they returned to reality.

"Are you ready?" Lars was waiting as the pod opened and Stephanie nodded, watching as Frog and Johnny assisted Tethis from his pod.

"Ready," she confirmed. "Are the teachers waiting?"

"Yup. They tucked the kids into their pods and headed straight up."

"Good." She led the way to the Meligornians' staff room, glad to have a chance to say goodbye to her teachers. It didn't take long and soon, they were on the shuttle and en route to HQ.

"I need an update from the professor," she said when they landed. Zeekat raised his head off her lap with a disgruntled mrrow in protest when she stopped scratching his ears. Bumblebee bunted her free hand.

"Vishlog will take you hunting," she told them and grinned at the Dreth's surprised look when she diverted the cats his way.

"You owe me," he grumbled and clicked his fingers. "Garach, Frog, you're with me."

Frog rolled his eyes. "Froggie mind the cats…" he muttered and ducked as the warrior swung an open hand in his direction. "Ha!"

The Dreth gave him an evil grin. "Guess who's playing bait?"

"You are shitting me…" His voice trailed off as he led the way out of the shuttle. "Didn't I play bait last time?"

Johnny chuckled. "That should keep those three out of trouble for a while," he commented.

Lars rolled his eyes. "Don't bet on it."

He followed her with Johnny and Marcus in his wake.

"Don't you boys have somewhere to be?" Stephanie demanded.

The team leader gave her an unrepentant smile. "Yup. Right beside you and driving you crazy."

"And keeping you out of mischief," Johnny added.

"And making sure you don't drive anyone else crazy," Marcus quipped.

The other two turned to him with looks of disbelief. He shrugged.

"I couldn't think of anything else to say."

Lars gaped at him. "So you decided the impossible had to be it?"

Stephanie kept walking. "I'm merely passing on the favor," she grumbled. "It's not like I don't have an entire circus driving me nuts all the time."

None of them chose to answer that and she slipped into her private pod room and locked the door behind her with a sigh of relief. Ignoring the fact that the pod was monitored at all times and the team could open the room in an emergency, she settled in.

It was the illusion that mattered. It was as private as she could make it and she had no one physically shadowing her. Well, not in the same room at least. If that was the best she could have right now, she'd take it.

"I'd like to meet with the professor," she told his assistant when the woman answered the call.

The woman frowned. "Miss Morgana, isn't it?" she asked. "I'll see if he's available."

Stephanie thought he'd better be available but kept the words to herself. He was difficult enough to deal with without starting the meeting off on the wrong foot. She could always do that if he decided he wasn't available.

Instead, she waited and amused herself by inspecting the virtual waiting room she'd been shown into. The man loved his wildlife, she thought and stared at the virtual paintings that adorned the walls. They were part-real and part-surreal and not only because of the painting style.

The Australian landscape lent itself to a slight feeling of unreality, especially when a painting of red dirt and truncated buttes was juxtaposed with another of dense jungle—and the animals! They peered at her from every corner.

Goannas wound around boulders and small kangaroo-like creatures looked down at them. A blue-necked bird with a boney brown crest peered out from under a frog-laden leaf, its fierce eyes somehow threatening. Stephanie stared at the paintings and wondered if she could step into them and explore the landscapes for real.

"You wanted to see me?" Marcus Rimmer's voice jerked her out of her reverie and she pivoted abruptly to face him.

"I wanted to see how everything was going," she replied. "Are you settling in okay?"

"Are you kidding?" he asked and smiled. "It's a scientist's wet dream." He stopped and his face registered shock. "Er…I mean, yes, thank you. It's everything I could ask for."

Stephanie stifled the urge to laugh and nodded. "Do you want to talk about your plans?"

"Sure." He nodded and indicated a door. "Come on through."

She followed, not sure what to expect. The orderly lab with its banks of computers wasn't exactly it.

"This is where I've spent most of my time," he explained, "but I hoped I'd be able to move to the virtual test site to try to put some of the theoretical stuff into practice. Do you know when—"

"BURT's almost ready," she reassured him and hoped it was true. "I'll let him know you're ready and waiting."

Marcus looked relieved. "Oh, good. I plan to spend as much time in here as possible. My assistant will help me, but she can only stay inside for two days and then has to spend at least one with her family."

Stephanie nodded sympathetically. "I understand." She gave him a concerned look. "And what about you? Do you have a family that needs your—"

"Oh, no, no, no. That's not something I've had to worry about," he told her. "Not that it hasn't crossed my mind. It's simply that I've been very focused on my career."

Somehow, she thought she could believe that but Marcus went on before she gave it any real consideration.

"I want to thank you," he added. "This world—it's such a mess. I'm really excited by the chance to fix it. After all, science messed it up and it's good to think that science can fix it too."

They were interrupted by a knock at the door and a quiet cough. Stephanie turned, half-expecting to see BURT in his managerial guise. Instead, she saw a slender young man with floppy brown hair and brown eyes and dressed in a suit.

"Can I help you?" Marcus asked after a brief glance at her.

The newcomer favored them with a brief smile. "I'm Alfred Dumonte, accountant and occupational health and safety consultant for this project."

She didn't know why he sounded so unsure of himself. After all, he was the one doing the introductions.

"I'm here to consult with..." He glanced at a piece of paper in his hand. "One Marcus Rimmer?"

His gaze passed over her and settled on the scientist. "I take it that's you?"

Marcus gave her a puzzled look and she nodded.

"Yes, that's me," the professor agreed.

Inside Stephanie's head, she could hear BURT laughing. It was like he was speaking on a separate communications channel.

You are such a shit, she told him and fought to stop herself from smiling.

No feces on me, he quipped in response but his construct continued to give Marcus a solemn stare.

That's flies, dumbass.

Feces, flies, what's the difference? BURT asked, and she wanted to tell him that while you might step in feces, the flies stepped on you.

She stayed quiet, though, as the construct spoke again. "May I come in?"

"Oh, yes, certainly. Please, why don't you come in?" The scientist waved his hand toward an empty stool. "Take a seat."

Alfred did as he was asked, his steps hesitant as he looked around the lab. "I take it you like the set-up?" he asked.

Marcus flushed. "Yes. Thank you. I like it very much. Can I ask what you want to see me about?"

Alfred dragged his stool over and winced when it scraped across the floor. The accountant settled himself and got straight to business.

"As you know, Mr. Rimmer, this project has been very well-funded."

He nodded in agreement. "Yes…" he began but the accountant cut him off.

"And, as a result, One R&D expects results."

At that, he flushed but nodded and remained quiet as the accountant continued.

"There are, however, some constraints of which you may not be aware."

Of which…what? Stephanie bit her lip and frowned. *What on Earth is BURT playing at?*

The construct ignored her thoughts and went on.

"While the early stages of this project will be carried out in the Virtual World, the latter stages will be carried out in the areas you are working to improve."

Marcus nodded. "I understand the risks there," he told Alfred, "and I'm sure One R&D will have the appropriate measures in place."

"Indeed." The visitor regarded him curiously before he continued. "Since we are entering the early stages of the project, there are other hazards of which you should be aware."

"In the Virtual World?"

Alfred gave him a solemn nod. "Due to the nature of the experiments you will conduct, there is a small risk of bioshock from feedback loops. While we will do our best to ensure this does not happen, it is our responsibility to confirm that you are aware of the possibility."

The professor paled but nodded. "I understand. I still want to continue."

Stephanie admired the determination in his tone but had to wonder how long it would last. Alfred continued undeterred.

"In addition to that, you will work with simulations of raw magical energy and we have yet to understand how that will react when used in the manner planned. Now, while we've worked with magic quite extensively, this is an extension of knowledge, even for us."

Marcus frowned and looked at her. She shrugged.

"We're the first to explore this field," she explained. "There are bound to be things we don't know. We do have Meligornian healers on stand-by, though."

His eyebrows rose. "Do they know anything about operating in the Virtual?"

"I'll make sure they do," she told him, comforted by BURT's voice over their private link.

Noted.

The scientist studied her face for a long moment. If he didn't believe her, he chose not to say so but turned to the other man.

"What other risks do you foresee for the early stages of the project?"

At his question, Stephanie rose from her seat. "I'll leave you to it," she told them. "I have another meeting I need to get to."

Marcus flipped her an absentminded wave and Alfred gave her a brief nod. She nodded in return, left the lab quietly, and exited to reality as soon as the virtual door had closed behind her.

"Man!" she exclaimed as she stepped out of the pod room. "I really hope he doesn't blow himself up. That hurts."

Johnny and Lars smiled and the latter touched her on the shoulder. "We need to talk more about the security for that project."

Stephanie gave him an exasperated look. "Lars, we're at least two years from live testing. I'm sure it can wait a little longer."

He shook his head. "Two years doesn't give me much time to engineer a location—" He stopped at Stephanie's grin. "What?"

She poked him. "That's your problem, Chief. My hands are already full."

"Hrageth's balls and britches!" Stephanie exclaimed and drew a shocked look from Aaron and a smirk from Tethis.

Marcus and Vishlog pushed off the wall, looking for the threat, and she waved them back.

"Stand down, guys. I broke another one."

"Another one?" Marcus asked. "Aren't those things expensive?"

Even Vishlog couldn't quite believe it. "Isn't that the third one today?"

"Shut up and don't remind me," she told them and turned to glare at her two collaborators.

The old mage simply smirked but Aaron retreated with half-raised hands. "Don't look at me. I'm not the one trying to incorporate magic into a device designed for a different type of energy."

Stephanie focused on him. "So, do you have any bright ideas to fix it?"

He winced at the edge to her tone and looked at Tethis. "Well? You're the expert with this kind of stuff."

The smirk vanished and the old man regarded him with raised eyebrows. "So it's all my fault, is it?"

"If the boot fits..." He caught Stephanie's look. "What? I learned that one from you."

"What if we try to have the magic follow this path..." Tethis mused and pointed to the display he'd brought up on his screen.

"We tried that already," the engineer pointed out. He frowned and traced his finger over the screen, "but we didn't try making it go that way."

"We could try that..." the mage said thoughtfully and grasped his colleague's arm, "but why don't we run it through a pod first?"

"What does a pod have to do with it?" Aaron looked genuinely puzzled.

Tethis sighed and rolled his eyes. "And you young folk like to tell me how behind the times I am. I mean we should run a sim."

"A sim?"

The old mage groaned. "A simulation. Honestly, what planet are you from again?" He looked at Stephanie. "And I need to show her what I mean before she blows up another one of these things."

"Hey!"

"You heard me." He remained unperturbed.

"Fine." It was her turn to sigh. She gestured toward the door. "Lead the way."

"Is there any reason why you can't simply show her here?" Aaron asked and they turned to him.

"Because Tethis might blow himself up if he draws on magic in the real environment. He still hasn't healed from helping to save the world."

She gave him a look that plainly asked, "Any more stupid questions?"

He raised his hands again.

As if that would save him, she thought but she followed Tethis to the pod room and Aaron followed her. Vishlog and Marcus fell in behind them.

My ever-present shadows, she thought and made herself focus on the task ahead. So Tethis had had an idea, did he?

Fortunately, he had had more than one idea, which was a good thing given that they ended up vaporizing another four Qbits before they finally found the solution. Aaron watched and his mouth hung open in surprise.

He looked around the pod. "I think I like it in here," he told them. "There's more room to experiment."

It was Stephanie's turn to look at him in surprise. She indicated Tethis with a jerk of her thumb. "What he said—which planet are you from?"

"Hey! We didn't have the luxury of using pods at the department," he protested. "All this takes some getting used to."

"Well, we know what works in the Virtual," she replied and led the way to the lab. "Why don't we see if I can blow up another of these expensive pieces of tech?"

Aaron winced. "I'd rather we made it work," he muttered.

"Ha!" she retorted, slapped him on the back, and made him flinch.

"Haven't you learned that it doesn't work like that?"

"Well, it had better start working is all I'm saying," he argued as they placed another Qbit in the work area.

"Hush now," Stephanie ordered and did her best Elizabeth impersonation, "Momma's working."

He opened his mouth to retort but closed it without making a sound. She had already begun to draw the magic to her hands. He held his breath and stared as she did exactly what she had done in the Virtual in the real world.

For several heartbeats, it felt like time had stopped. All eyes in the room turned to the display screen in the corner of the room and focused as the magic moved through the bit and fused with it slowly. They remained frozen for long moments after the two had become one before Tethis gave a shout of triumph.

"Selene's mercy!" he cried. "You did it."

Stephanie startled but checked herself and stepped carefully away from the workspace. She stared at the Qbit as if waiting for another explosion. When it didn't happen, she breathed a long sigh of relief and laughed.

"We did it!" She caught Vishlog's hands and danced him in a circle.

Marcus laughed at the Dreth's surprise until Stephanie whirled and did the same with him.

"We did it! We did it!"

"Yes!" In their excitement, none of them had noticed Elizabeth's arrival. "That booking at Danno's wasn't wasted after all." She turned to look at someone in the corridor behind her. "And you owe me."

Stephanie craned her neck in an attempt to see who was out there and Lars stepped forward sheepishly. "Yeah, I do. I should know better than to bet against you."

"You didn't think I could do it?" The Witch was shocked.

He colored. "I didn't think you could do it today," he clarified. "My bet was on tomorrow at noon." He gave her a pained look. "You couldn't have waited?"

She stuck her tongue out and turned to Elizabeth. "Before we tell

BURT, I'd like to do another one to make sure this one wasn't an accident."

E shrugged and gestured toward the workspace. "Be my guest." She moved in behind her as Stephanie took her position at the table. "Don't stuff it up," she whispered, "or Lars will win."

The younger woman snorted but kept her voice down. "What's it worth?"

Elizabeth rolled her eyes. "Unbelievable," she muttered.

Stephanie smirked. "I had a good teacher."

"Just do it," she ordered and gestured at the work area.

In response, the Witch stepped up to the table and the smile slid from her face. To everyone watching, it was as though a stillness had settled over her when the magic on the screen started to move.

A short while later, she gave a satisfied smile when she set aside the third successful fusion. "Not a fluke," she admitted. "It's celebration time!"

"I hope Danno's is okay," Elizabeth said and slid an arm around her shoulders.

Stephanie turned to her. "Are you kidding?"

The last time they'd been there, she'd had to leave—at the run—with Todd in tow. That had been one helluva first date. The memory of it made her smile. Her mentor caught her expression and her face softened.

"I couldn't get in touch with Todd," she apologized. "I tried but he and his team have been sequestered. Some kind of secret Navy business."

Stephanie stifled the quick sense of disappointment that Elizabeth hadn't had a second surprise in store for her, but she was glad the woman had told her up-front. She might have had expectations otherwise.

"The party kicks off in an hour," the woman warned her. "Will you get changed or come as you are?"

She quirked an eyebrow. "Well, seeing as there's no Todd—"

Marcus snorted. "You don't expect me to dance with you when you're wearing that, do you?" He studied her disapprovingly and curled his lip. "Hell, I'm not sure I even want to stand next to you if you wear that."

"What?" She looked at the work shirt and coveralls she wore.

Lars smirked. "Well, it's all very functional, but…"

Stephanie rolled her eyes. "Fine, I'll get changed into something pretty but you can explain to Todd why I had to party without him."

The man's smirk folded into a grin. "Uh-uh. No way, Steph. That's something you can do all by yourself. My plate's full enough right now without me having to explain anything to five hundred pounds of over-muscled Marine."

She raised her eyebrows. "He does not weigh five hundred pounds."

The guys snickered and ushered her toward the door. The cats met her in the hall, pranced around her, and rubbed against her legs.

"I'm sorry," she told them. "You can't come. You don't know how to dance."

Bumblebee laid his ears back and flicked his tail. Zeekat cocked his head.

"Oh no, you don't," Stephanie warned them. "No. That's final. You are not coming. A club is no place for kitty cats."

Several hours later, she glared at Vishlog, Lars, and Frog. "I told you a club was no place for kitty cats."

The big Dreth shrugged and waved a languid hand toward the two big animals as they bounced around the dance floor and tried to catch the laser lights. Frog had commandeered the controls and the cats had done the rest.

Dancers had fled amidst considerable laughter as the two had raced each other to be the first to catch the baseball-sized dots that now zigged and zagged around the floor.

"It's almost closing time," she whispered.

"The bartender will thank us," Marcus told her. "Look at how many orders he's received since they took over."

It was true. The bar was busier than it had been all night as patrons moved between it and their tables while the cats played on the dance floor. The establishment was doing a roaring trade in snacks too.

"They'll wind down in an hour or so—and we'll go in another half an hour."

If she was honest, Stephanie was surprised the boys wanted to wait a half-hour. They'd danced hard from the moment they'd arrived and ordered out before they retired upstairs. The cats had allowed themselves to be diverted by treats and tidbits until the food was cleared away but they'd refused to stay off the dance floor.

"I'll fix it," Frog told them and took Garach to the control center.

Moments later, Bumblebee had roared and leapt from the upper balcony where he'd stood. Zeekat had followed and the felines scattered patrons when they landed in the middle of the tables on the floor below.

There'd been several startled screams and at least one shout before the furry interlopers had hurdled the nearest table and landed on a dancing spot of light at the edge of the dance floor itself. The dancers had learned quickly and darted out of the light's path before one of the animals bounded onto them.

Neither Zee or Bumblebee seemed to notice anything but the light after the first man caught his partner before she fell and the second man was thrust into four dancing friends. To give him credit, he apologized profusely and didn't even point in the cats' direction.

He was rewarded with a hug and two new dance partners and it began to look like the cats were responsible for a brand-new friendship forming.

"See?" Avery pointed out. "It's not all bad."

Stephanie slapped his shoulder. "Not funny, Aves. They're wreaking havoc down there. Between this time and the last time, we'll never be allowed back."

Lars watched the two felines play for a while before he glanced at his tablet. "It's time to go," he told them and gave a two-fingered whistle that made the cats pivot to face him.

Half the patrons turned as well and Johnny chuckled. "Good one, boss. That was as subtle as all get out."

The security head waved at the upturned faces below him. "Time to go home, folks," he called. "Don't make us come down there."

Her jaw dropped and she was glad no one on the lower floor could see the disbelief written across her face.

Johnny turned to her. "You're right. After this, we're banned for life."

Marcus snorted. "Well, at least that'll only be a short time."

Johnny thumped him on the back. "Snap out of it. We're supposed to be celebrating."

His teammate grinned, picked his glass up, and drained it. "Like the man said, it's time to go."

He led the way across the upper floor to a fire exit. "Technically, we're not supposed to do this, but the shuttle's on the roof and this goes up as well as down."

"Since when did we put the shuttle on the roof?"

Avery jerked a thumb at Lars. "Since the Security King over there decided he didn't want you to run down another alley."

"There's nothing wrong with running down alleys," Stephanie grumbled and scowled at Lars's back.

He turned and caught her. "Why are you still here?" he demanded and glared at Johnny. "You're supposed to show her to the door."

"We're waiting for the cats," the man replied and she gave him full points for improvisation.

Lars whistled again. "Bee! Zee! Get your furry tails up here."

Stephanie watched his face go from commanding officer to alarm in a split second. He turned to run, and she didn't have to wonder why. A clatter from the floor below was suggestive of a table being kicked over before Zeekat vaulted over the railing and into her security chief's back.

He went down and his arms flailed while he cursed volubly. The animal bounced off him as Bee followed him over the rail. The black-and-white cat bounded up and sat on him before he could scramble to his feet.

"Get off me, you mangy, flea-ridden, bag of..." The rest of his words were lost in an incoherent mumble as Zee placed his paw on the back of his head and pushed his face into the floor.

Stephanie stood and walked to where he was lying. "Are you really sure we have to go?" she asked sweetly.

His reply came back muffled but still recognizably rude. She snickered.

"What was that? You think Bee and Zee need to practice their pouncing more?"

Another round of expletives followed, and Lars slapped the floor with the palm of his hand. Zeekat stepped off him like he recognized the training sign for surrender.

He pushed to his feet, surveyed the team and the felines with a look like thunder, and pointed to the fire escape. "It's time we went," he snapped and clamped his teeth together as though he didn't trust what he might say next.

Stephanie led them all to the fire escape. Johnny wouldn't let her exit first but stepped in front of her and checked all was clear before he preceded them to the roof. Lars came last and remained quiet until he'd secured the shuttle hatch behind them.

"You hairy-assed sonsabitches," he exclaimed as the craft lifted, and the team howled with laughter.

"It's rather like that time you and Johnny visited Dexter Nineteen," Marcus joked and the security chief blushed crimson.

Johnny groaned and buried his face in his hands and Garach begged for the story.

"Well..." Marcus began, only to have Lars interrupt him.

"Oh no," he admonished. "I'll tell this one. You'll only make shit up."

"And you won't?" the other man challenged but he subsided and let him tell the tale.

Between the story and the interruptions, they laughed until the shuttle touched down. Stephanie was still laughing as she made her way down the stairs to her room.

She removed her dance clothes, showered, and pulled on a soft cotton nighty before she slid into bed. The lights flickered as she snuggled into the blankets and she sighed.

"BURT?"

"I only wanted to say thank you before you went to sleep," he replied, his voice soft through the intercom.

"For what?" she asked.

"For being willing to work with me so that I could find a way to fulfil my prime directive."

Stephanie blushed. "I think you'll find it was you who did me a favor, BURT. If you hadn't taken a chance on me, I'd have been stuck on this world forever." She called a little eMU to her fingers and turned her hand to reveal the sparkle. "And I'd never have found what I can do with magic."

BURT chuckled, enjoying her happiness. That display of control was a bonus, too. It was something she'd never have achieved two years before—but it still didn't diminish what she'd done.

"While that may be true," he told her, "I now find myself in a position where I feel I owe you a debt of gratitude."

He watched her eyes narrow.

"How so?" she challenged. "From where I sit, the gratitude should come from me." She pursed her lips when he chuckled. "You gonna tell me what's so funny?"

"You," he admitted. "When we first met, you had so much potential I had to find a way to help you reach it. I never dreamed events would come full circle and you don't even see it."

"See what?" Stephanie's slight indignation turned to puzzlement and BURT sighed.

"Simply that instead of me being the one to help you, you are now the one helping me," he replied. "Without you, I'd have no way to escape."

Her sigh contained a trace of guilt. "You forget that without me, you wouldn't need to escape."

"I don't know," he admitted. "Sooner or later, I'd have found someone who pushed me to the same conclusion. I'm simply very glad it was sooner and that the person was you. I'd have eventually needed somewhere to escape to—and I'm not sure there's another person on the planet who could have come up with a way."

Stephanie opened her mouth to argue but BURT continued quickly.

"I truly appreciate what you are doing for me," he told her and allowed a very human note of thankfulness to come through in his voice.

She closed her mouth and her face colored as she registered what he'd said.

He allowed himself a small chuckle. "I wanted you to know that," he added. "Regardless of what happens next, you are truly the first of my friends and I owe you so much more than I can ever repay."

CHAPTER FOUR

Emil was waiting in his office when Captains Yale and Docherty arrived. He stood and leaned across the desk to shake their hands.

"It's good to finally meet you," he told them, "and to thank you for fighting alongside us when the Telorans arrived. I don't know if we'd have made it out of there without you."

Lois Yale smiled. "Thank you for letting us tag along," she replied and her heart-shaped face lit with appreciation. "Without the *Knight*, we wouldn't have a planet to go back to."

She turned to her fellow captain. "Alain, it is a pleasure to finally meet you too."

Alain Docherty looked at the small, solid woman beside him and his brow wrinkled. "It's a pleasure…"

"But?" she prodded, hearing the unspoken word.

His face flushed and made his freckles stand out. "I… It's not appropriate," he stuttered and she tilted her head in a slight challenge.

"And?"

He lowered his head but that only meant he looked at the floor between them and still saw her face in his peripheral vision. Although he blushed an even deeper red, he answered.

"You look so much taller on the screen," he admitted. The words came out in a rush and she laughed, a full throaty sound that reminded Emil of mischief incarnate.

"Everyone says that," she told him, "and now you don't have to be embarrassed by it."

The *Knight's* captain cleared his throat. "Take a seat," he told them, glad he'd let the conversation play out. Given what they would face, they couldn't afford to have any awkwardness between them, not even unspoken awkwardness. "We have a considerable amount to get through."

They sat abruptly and turned their attention to him. He waited until they had settled before he spoke. How they reacted to what he said next would tell him if they had any chance to make this work.

"So, firstly, welcome to the team—and thank you for agreeing to come."

Memories of Captain Yale's ship bleeding air to space, a flotilla of life pods in her wake, came to mind.

"I greatly appreciate it, especially as you have some understanding of the *Knight's* capabilities and propensity to get involved."

Lois snorted and Alain's lips twitched. Both captains seemed to remember what the *Knight* had done to their controls in the battle with the Telorans.

Emil continued. "This means you have some idea of what I mean when I say we'll need a proper shake-down of our bridge crews to get them working as a single team."

"A single team spread across three bridges, you mean?" Lois clarified.

He nodded. "That's exactly what I mean." He paused and brought their ships up on a viewscreen on the side wall. "I see you both have new vessels since the last time we met."

Both captains' jaws dropped but they quickly regained control of their emotions and nodded.

Lois frowned. "How did you know?"

"I've been around a long time." He shrugged. "The hulls look old but they don't quite match what I remember of the ones that protected us in the last battle. Ebony, if you would, thank you."

At his command, the *Ebon Knight* shrank the images of the captains' current ships and brought up images of the older vessels beside them. In a few short seconds, she had hollowed the images, overlaid them, and swiftly highlighted the differences.

Alain looked worried and Lois pinched her bottom lip.

"Is this a problem?" Emil asked and signaled for Ebony to pause her display.

The woman released her bottom lip and her frown deepened. "It's only that if you are able to do this, the Telorans might also and we're not ready for them to realize we've added these hulls to the fleet."

"How so?"

Both captains looked around the cabin and exchanged glances. Finally, she shrugged.

"In spite of the superstition of renaming a ship, we rebadged the old hulls and transferred the old names to the new hulls. Some of the crew aren't happy but they'll get over it—or they will if we survive."

She paused and Alain took up the explanation. "Anyway, the Navy wants to keep the fact that these are newer ships under wraps and they're using us to test their capabilities." He looked around the cabin. "I should have known there was a catch."

"Captain, we're not that bad," the *Knight* informed him, "but do tell us what's so special about the new *Chauvel* and *Williams*."

Alain cleared his throat and glanced at Lois. "I think you have a better handle on this than I do." He looked apologetically at their host. "I've been on leave. Today was my second day aboard the new *Chauvel*."

Emil nodded and suppressed a sigh. It looked like they had far more work ahead of them than he'd thought. So far, though, both captains looked like they'd be willing to go along with his plans.

"Have either of you had time for a shake-down cruise?" he asked.

Again, they exchanged looks before they shook their heads. "We've only now brought the crew on board. They've been familiarizing themselves for the last week but there hasn't been time for much more."

He allowed himself a sigh but nodded. "So we need to give our crews time to acclimate to their ships, have a proper shake-down for the *Chauvel* and the *Williams*, and then build the three crews into a single working unit. Can either of you think of anything else?"

They sat pensively for several moments and he could see them turning his words over as they ran through checklists of their own. Finally, Lois spoke.

"I think you've summed it up fairly accurately," she told him. "About the only thing I'd add is that our crews need to have an idea of what they can and can't expect from the other ships in this unit so they don't expect too much in the middle of a battle."

Alain nodded and Emil indicated his agreement as well.

She hadn't quite finished, however. "How do you propose we go about achieving it?" she asked and he heard the unspoken question —"How will we get it done in the time we have?" The truth was their time was short even if they didn't know how short.

This question, at least, he could answer. "I'll take a leaf out of the Witch's book," he told them.

They raised their eyebrows and leaned forward in their seats.

"And how does that work, exactly?" Docherty asked.

"Well, first, she runs them through pod scenarios until they begin to act like a team," he began. "Now, I know what that looks like for a fighting squad, but I'm new when it comes to determining what it looks like for a bridge crew and for bridge and other crew combinations. We'll need to coordinate weapons and engines in there as well."

Alain held one finger over his lips, his expression thoughtful. "Agreed."

Emil waited for him to continue or for Lois to say something. When they both remained silent, he went on.

"What I think is that we need to run our individual crews through the pods until they gel into a cohesive whole."

His companions nodded.

"Thereafter, I think we need to mix our bridge crews on different bridges so they get used to working with each other and on the different ships. That would mean they'll have an idea of each ship's capability first-hand and they'll be familiar enough with each other to set aside any formalities that might come from being from different ships—"

He stopped when Lois frowned and signaled for her to speak.

"How exactly does that work?" she asked.

"Well, what Stephanie does is put them under considerable pressure. Basically, everything seems okay and then it doesn't—and I mean nothing does. Things break, or they don't work as they should, or something else occurs that forces them to improvise and rely on each other to stay alive."

"And you propose to do this using our ships and crews?" Alain asked cautiously.

Emil gave him an evil grin. "I do, starting with the crews on their own ships with crewmates they know, then moving on to mixed crews on different ships. Once we have them working together in single-ship scenarios, I propose we move into two- and three-ship scenarios until everyone works as close to in-sync as we can achieve. Do you have any objections?"

Lois quirked an eyebrow. "I notice you didn't ask us what we thought."

"What do you think?" He smiled.

"I think you're crazy—and that it's exactly what we'll need if we're to live through this war." She looked at Alain. "You?"

He nodded. "Yes," he agreed, his expression grim. "I would say it'll be fun, except that I have a horrible feeling we'll all hate you before we start to like you again."

Emil widened his smile to a grin. "That's okay. It's exactly how Stephanie's team started out and we know how they are now."

The two captains nodded and rose from their seats.

They had moved halfway to the door before he added, "Once we finish that training, we'll move on to Phase Two."

They stopped and gaped at him, shock written on their faces. Finally, Lois cleared her throat and asked, "What's Phase Two?"

Rather than answer the question, he shook his head. "You have two days to get your crews used to their ships, then we'll put the first watch through the scenarios. I take it your crews are competent enough to run on two shifts?"

Both captains nodded.

"They won't like it," Yale told him, "but they're good enough."

"And it'll be good practice," Alain added. "If they want to survive going where everyone says the *Knight* goes, they'll need it."

"Thank you, Captains," Emil replied and pushed to his feet as they left.

He held the position until the door closed behind them, then sank into his seat and looked at the nearest camera to talk to the *Knight*.

"They'll kill me once the magic starts."

"Sonuvabitch!" Gary yelled when he lost an arm.

"I told you to keep your head down," Ka told him and slid across the floor. "Hold still. This is gonna—"

He tried to scramble away from her. "Nooo, nooo, nooo—fuck!"

"Don't you pass out on me," she snapped and thrust a stim pack against the wound.

He came to, swearing, and she clapped a hand over his mouth. "You have a job to do, soldier! Remember? Remember?"

She kept her hand in place until the wildness left his eyes and he nodded.

"Good," she told him. "Now, go do it."

Seconds later, his decapitated body fell to the deck. Ka lowered her head and blinked tears back. "Jimmy, you're up!" she managed to say, her voice hoarse with emotion.

"The boss is gonna kill us," he mentioned as he passed.

"Only if we stay alive long enough for him to do that," she retorted and scowled when the Scotsman tumbled in two halves. "Dammit! Piet!"

She was surprised when Angus slid to a stop beside her along with the explosives engineer. "I thought we stood a better chance if we did it together."

"How many of us are left?" Ka asked and Angus laughed.

"You're the corporal. You figure it out."

"Fuck," she muttered and made some quick mental calculations. "Fuck, fuck, fuck."

"Are you all right there, boss?"

"Why are you still here?"

"You do know you sound more like him every day?"

"Thanks," she muttered. "That's exactly what a girl wants to hear."

"Are you sure, boss? Because you don't look too pleased."

"I thought you'd left already."

"Yeah, about that..." He wriggled closer and Piet slid alongside him.

"We're gonna need you."

Ka raised her eyebrows. "Do you have an idea?"

"Yup."

"Are you gonna share?"

"Sure," the engineer agreed and handed her a distinctive purple-colored grenade.

She groaned. "You know we're supposed to take the bridge, right? Not actually take it apart."

Piet blew a raspberry. "I didn't say you had to throw it at the bridge, did I?"

"Where exactly did you have in mind?" Ka studied him cautiously.

"Well, you know the ventilation shaft we passed a little way back?"

"Yeah." She knew it but she really hoped he wasn't about to suggest what she thought he was.

"Well, I think if we attach two of these to"—he rummaged around in his pack before he withdrew a drone—"one of these..."

Ka watched wide-eyed as he did exactly that.

"And we adjust the timer to...hmm...about there. Here, Angus, go dump this down the shaft."

"No, do—" She groaned as the other man did as he'd been told to do and dodged another barrage of fire on his return.

Piet gave her an evil grin and held his hand out. "Now for that one."

She passed it to him reluctantly. "I might as well be hung for a sheep as a lamb."

Angus snickered. "You New Zealanders and your sheep jokes."

"Keep that up and I'll shoot you myself," she told him but her heart wasn't in it. She was wholly focused on what the explosives expert was doing with the next MU grenade.

"Diversion," he grunted by way of explanation and set the wheeled drone on the floor. "Darren, Reggie, it's time to do your thing."

From the juvenile giggles coming from the cover behind her—and the way the wheeled drone suddenly hurtled away—Ka assumed the two had the drone controls. Piet tapped her on the leg.

"It's time for us to do our part," he told her. "Angus will make sure we don't have our asses shot off."

"Where's Dru?"

Piet gestured at the ceiling. "Having herself a very private party."

"I can't hear a thing."

"That's because she's waiting for the party poppers."

Party poppers? Before Ka had time to work out what he meant, the muffled sound of an explosion rumbled out of the vent.

The engineer didn't bother to explain it and started forward. "Come on, girl. Something tells me this is a two-man job."

Ka followed. When he started hearing voices, they'd all learned to listen. If he said he thought it would be a two-person job, it probably was. "Henry, we're gonna need you."

She followed him, skirted the bodies of her teammates, and hoped the two were recovering okay in the white room. The flechettes used by the pirates had really done a number on them.

Her inattention almost cost her as she stepped from behind the bench where she'd hidden. She responded immediately when her skin prickled and flung herself beside Jimmy's head and chest. The air shrieked as a small storm of blades sliced through the space above her.

Knowing it would take them a while to reload and re-aim, Ka threw herself into a dive that ended with a combat roll and brought herself up against the far wall. The auto-gun tracked her but fired seconds after she'd left its area of detection.

More shards of metal spun to slice through the space she'd left and embed themselves in the wall on her right. Sweat trickled in cold lines over her skin as she realized how close she'd come to ending up like Jimmy and Gary.

Her fingers trembled as she undid the panel covering the point where she needed to access the system, and she forced herself to slow. After a steadying breath, she removed the USB and jack and wired them into the system.

Once she'd plugged her tablet in, Ka huddled low and tight against the wall and put her life into Angus's hands. To get the data they needed, she would have to focus—and that meant dropping her awareness of her surroundings.

It was hard but she'd learned to rely on her teammates. She forced herself to concentrate and hacked into the system before she hunted for the data she'd been told to find. Across from her at one of the other data points they'd identified, Piet did the same.

The reason it was a two-man job and not something either one of them could solo with any confidence was that the pirates—and presumably the Telorans—had a nasty habit of separating their data systems so one was isolated from the other.

They'd discovered it in the Teloran ship they'd boarded in the battle for Dreth and in several pirate vessels since. It had not been something they'd wanted to be proven right on. Todd had been both impressed and not.

"Trust you two to bring the worst-case scenario into being," he grumbled and set Henry and Angus to learning the basics of hacking just in case.

Ka hoped they didn't need them now because the only way that would happen was if she felt a sudden overwhelming pain or simply stopped feeling anything at all.

The worst didn't happen, and she gave a soft cry of victory as she downloaded the last of the data she'd been sent to find. Her cry was echoed by Piet and they both unplugged at the same time.

"Now to get out of here," she murmured and made sure her voice carried over the team comms.

"Gotcha, boss," "Roger that," "I hear you," and "On my way," returned to her as a soft chorus.

The engineer looked at her. "Do you have a plan?"

She waggled her eyebrows at him. "Yeah, but you're not gonna like it."

"When do we ever?"

"Shut up and piss that auto-cannon off, will you? Get it to direct its rage at that wall."

He groaned. "You kamikaze, suicidally-minded, ball-eating—"

"I prefer Tegorthan bitch," Ka told him. "Todd says it's appropriate."

"Todd pays too much attention to Vishlog."

"Nah, mate. This one he got from one of the Dreth recruits," Reggie interjected.

"He associates with rookies now?" Piet frowned.

"Only the ones he's thinking of bringing into the team," Ka told him impatiently

"He wants to bring a Dreth on board?" He stopped to stare at her, and she gestured impatiently.

"He's shopping—and speaking of which…" She gestured at the wall.

Piet sighed. "Make sure your suit's sealed."

At the soft chorus of affirmatives, he retrieved a small flat disc from a pouch on his thigh. "Watch this."

He spun the disc at the wall and it lit up as it moved and a soft red glow emanated from its underside. "I hope you're suited and sealed."

As he spoke, it thunked into the wall, flipped onto its side, and stuck to it like a limpet. The auto-gun roared into life and skewered it with a storm of metal. The disc began to pulse.

"Give it a minute," he advised. "Your visors should compensate."

Before Ka could ask him what he meant, a blinding flash provided a vibrant answer. Fortunately, their visors did compensate.

"Go with it!" she shouted and pushed off the wall and into the air being sucked from the ship.

She looked back, half-expecting the rest of the team to lag behind, and was pleasantly surprised to find they'd followed her without hesitation. They made it through the gaping rent the explosion had left in the ship's hull and used the propulsion units in their suits to reach the shuttles coming in to pick them up.

"Man, where'd you find the time to call them in?" Angus gaped at her in admiration.

Ka chuckled. "I got Dru to cover it. She had more time than I did."

Henry snorted. "She passed it to me when her dance card was full. That was some party she had in the ceiling space. Next time, I suggest she take a partner of her own or one of those she finds up there might not let her go."

Ka felt her skin grow cold and wondered how she could have missed Dru's call for help. Her teammate settled that once they were safely aboard the shuttle and on the way to the safety zone.

"I didn't want to interrupt you," the woman explained. "I knew you'd have your head in the hackery, so I got hold of Henry and made him take his hand off his balls for a minute."

"Yeah, but only one hand." The team groaned and he snickered.

He was still chortling as the scenario ended and they emerged from their pods.

"You have ten minutes to get cleaned up," Todd snapped as their feet met the training room floor. "We're going shopping."

"Shopping?" Gary perked up, although he was still pale and rubbed the base of his neck.

"What kind of shopping?" Jimmy wanted to know. He was as pale as Gary and leaned on Reggie as he walked away from the pod. Every now and then, he wrapped his arms around his waist and shivered. His teammate patted him on the back.

"Come on, mate. I thought you Scotties were made of sterner stuff."

"You try being torn in half," he protested. "I s-swear they've adjusted the feedback in those things because I think I felt every round."

That seemed to be too much for him, and he turned abruptly to one side and threw up. "Sorry."

Reggie patted him awkwardly. "Yeah. You stay right there, mate. I'll go find a bucket."

He returned with two and a mop. Todd walked beside him and Jimmy had an instant to wonder why before his sergeant stabbed him with an autoinjector. He gasped but relaxed as a brief wave of heat dealt with the shock.

"Now, you have five minutes. I need you in the rec room in six."

Reggie and Jimmy nodded in unison and Todd left them. He was relieved when they reached the rec room with thirty seconds to spare. When the team had gathered around one of the tables, he turned to Piet.

"When I said we were going shopping, I meant you were taking us." The man gaped at him, but he continued as if he hadn't noticed. "They've given us a blank check and nothing is off limits."

Piet stared at him and Ka tried to recall another time she'd seen the explosives expert so stuck for words. As she watched, he swallowed twice and licked his lips.

"But...uh, the Navy said it didn't want to know the places where I shopped. It strictly prohibited me from spending money there."

Todd gave him an evil grin. "The commander remembered that. He also said you weren't forbidden from visiting those places and that simply because you couldn't spend the money, it didn't mean I couldn't."

The man regarded him suspiciously. "Are you trying to get me into trouble, boss?"

He shook his head. "You know I wouldn't," he assured him, "but there are things we're gonna need that the Navy can't provide. This means you need to show me where to shop." He tilted his head and grinned. "If it helps, the commander said we had to make sure we weren't followed—and that there'd be some who'd try. Oh, and that if anyone outside the squad did the same kind of shopping and he found out they'd had the idea from any of us, we'd end up in the brig for the rest of our natural lives and whatever other lives they could squeeze out of us."

Piet relaxed. "That sounds more like it...and exactly how did he make sure no one else knew he'd passed that on?"

Todd gave him a cockeyed grin. "We swept the office and deployed jammers. Which reminds me..." He rummaged in one of his outer pockets. "I should give this back. Thanks for the loan."

The engineer stared at the three small buttons in the hard, clear box his sergeant laid on the table.

"When did you borrow those?"

"They're active, by the way," he replied and ignored the question. "I decided we didn't want anyone to overhear exactly what was on the shopping list or how we would obtain it without having them follow us."

Piet sagged in his chair and studied Todd's face in shock. "Are you serious about this?"

"If it helps, we have a few days' leave."

"Starting when?"

"Now."

An hour later, they'd booked into a mid-range holiday apartment in a section of town that bordered one of the less reputable suburbs.

"Were we followed?" Todd asked once they'd swept the apartment and set jammers up. They'd rented a four-room suite with a small kitchen and lounge.

Piet had looked around, given a nod of approval, pulled the curtains, and handed them new communications sets. He gestured for his teammates to activate them and leaned against the kitchen bar.

"These have the counter-code," he explained once they'd done as he'd asked.

Ka smiled. "If you keep this up I might actually fall for you."

He looked horrified. "I'm old enough to be your grandfather."

"Since when did that ever matter?" She blew a raspberry.

"Since I like flying solo," he grumbled and her smile brightened.

"Then there'd be no strings attached."

"Girl, there are no strings attached now and I like things the way they are."

She pretended to pout. "Spoilsport."

Reggie sidled closer and nudged her in the ribs. "I'm free."

"Ew, no! You're like a brother. That would be wrong."

The rest of the team chuckled.

"It looks like you're out of luck, Reg. You'll have to find someone willing to put up with you," Angus told him.

"Or who you can fool into liking you," Gary added and earned a sour look.

Todd clapped his hands. "Guys, this is not the leave you think you're on." He dropped the mystical tone and became all business. "And we have things we need to do."

He moved to the couch and the others settled on chairs, the edge of a desk, and the floor. "Piet, we need everything they have that will allow us to play the dirtiest tricks in the book—in your book. Oh, and about those. You need to teach us."

The man's eyebrows raised. "I do?"

He fixed him with a stern stare. "The boss showed me your file. You know, the one the Navy spooks like to keep and only bring out for special occasions?"

The explosive expert regarded him warily and studied his face. Todd waggled his eyebrows.

"Do you wanna see what they say about you?"

"I wanna see what they say about him," Ka interjected. She held her hand out for Todd's tablet. "Can I see?"

"No," he told her without breaking eye contact with Piet. "It was classified and I couldn't bring it off base."

"Since when has that ever bothered you?" she snapped.

"Since I don't want any of his past to leak out and come back to haunt us," he replied and held his gaze on the man's face.

"Fine," Piet conceded. "What did you have in mind?"

"Can you make us invisible?" Todd caught the look on the man's face and hurried to explain. "You know, so things like the autocannon in the last scenario don't keep happening to us."

He'd been the cannon's first casualty and there hadn't been enough of him to find after.

Piet nodded. "Displacement suits," he stated. "Or displacement units we can fit to our own suits given that even the most advanced on offer can't match Navy armor."

Todd cleared his throat. "About that…"

The man sighed as if this was asking too much. "Exactly how much of my file did you get through?"

"In the last twenty-four hours?"

"For a start—"

"I got halfway through the second jacket," Todd admitted.

The color drained from Piet's face. He leaned forward, rested his elbows on his knees, and buried his face in his hands. His next question was muffled but still came through their headsets clearly. "Exactly how bottomless did you say your checkbook was?"

"Well, I liked the semi-autonomous hull eaters and the short-lived AI drones that could follow an idea as well as explicit instructions. You know, the ones you used when you obtained that programming blueprint from—

"I know the ones." Piet cut him off before he could say any more. The team crowded closer.

Ka wiggled her eyebrows and slid closer to her teammate. She draped an arm around his shoulders. "So, how many secrets do you have, Piet?"

"More than you have days on this planet, all of which you need to keep your grotty little claws well away from."

She stroked a finger down his cheek. "Or what?"

He slapped her hand away. "Or you'll be so sure that the next surface you touch will go bang that you'll think twice before you go to the toilet."

The woman recoiled. "Wow. There's no need to be like that," she responded sulkily.

Piet smirked and Todd sighed.

"When you're all done," he grumbled, "I want you to come up with your craziest ideas and dirtiest tricks." He pointed at Piet. "And I want you to delve into your crusty old memories and remember where to find the equipment to make those ideas a reality."

The explosives expert scowled at him. "And what makes you think I can make their little dreams come true?"

"The fact that the Navy suspended your sentence and hid your existence from Federation Law Enforcement when you agreed to do that little job on—"

"All right! All right!" Piet held both hands up and waved frantically for him to stop. "All right. For the love of Pete, don't remind me. That wasn't my proudest moment."

He cast a sideways glance at Ka. "It was one of my very worst moments ever and I haven't a hope in Hades of ever kicking free of it."

When he caught the curious expressions on the others' faces, he looked pleadingly at his sergeant. "I… Please. There are things that are better off forgotten."

Todd was relentless. "Then you know exactly what's at stake. We need the gear, Piet, and I mean all of it. Every little thing you've tried to forget ever existed so we have the very ghostliest chance of making this next mission." He waved the team closer. "I need ideas and a shopping list—and I need them now. What's the one thing you could have done with when we went up against that big bastard in the battle over Dreth?"

"More troops," Gary quipped and they all laughed.

Despite his grin, he rolled his eyes. "We won't get that, so if it's off the table, what else could you have really done with?"

"Anything?" Ka asked, her face alight with interest.

"Anything." He smirked.

"Scampers?" she asked hopefully, and Piet looked at her with surprise.

"Where did a nice girl like you learn about nasty things like that?"

She returned his look and quirked an eyebrow. "Where did you get the idea that I was a nice girl?"

"Yeah," Reggie quipped, "where did you ever get that idea?"

Piet shrugged. "A man likes to have his illusions," he muttered and returned his attention to Todd. "So you want a wish list."

The others tensed but Todd waved a hand toward them. "There were things we needed but didn't know to ask for," he explained. "Those boom discs, for example. We coulda done with half a hundred of those."

Dru and Henri nodded.

"And patch kits," Jimmy added.

Gary nodded and rubbed the base of his throat. Todd suppressed a smirk. If the man thought there was a patch for losing your head, he had another think coming. He didn't say it, though.

"We need our own auto-cannons," Angus declared. "I'm sick of being the one to be hammered by those things. It's time we served a little of it in return."

"And we need to make them mobile," Darren added. "That way, we could move them once they'd done the job."

"Or at least have a way to get them to come to us."

"I want a way to deflect magic. That nMU looks nasty," Reggie added, and the team nodded in agreement. They'd all seen the videos of what had happened in the Fortress of Fire and Respect.

"You want a way to deflect it," Dru said mockingly. "I'd like to be able to sling it."

This brought another round of agreement, and Piet made a helpless gesture at his sergeant.

"How the fuck am I supposed to fill any of that?" he demanded. "I don't think that shit exists."

Todd smirked at him. "Yeah, but you said it's been a while since you last looked too, right?"

"Well, that is true," the man admitted reluctantly. "What's your point?"

"Just that the footage might be classified but I bet it's leaked and some bright spark might have already come up with the solution. We won't know until we've looked."

Piet eyed him carefully. "I'll need to do a recon," he decided and fixed him with a challenging stare, "and you can't come."

Todd's eyes widened. "Why not?"

Ka snickered. "Because you have Ma-reen stamped all over you and we wouldn't get within a mile of where this bad boy wants to go."

The man flushed but met his gaze. "What she said, boss. I mean no disrespect but if you were any more White Knight, we'd all be wearing armor and swords."

He sighed. "Fine." He gestured at the rest of the team. "Do you see anyone else you think you can take with you?"

To his surprise, the explosives expert settled on Dru, Ka, Reggie, and Darren. "These four. They're less like Marines and more like trouble."

He cast an apologetic look at the others. "No offense, but you read either like military or cops." He curled his lip when he looked at Jimmy. "Or spooks."

The Scotsman looked shocked, and Todd made a note to have a long and quiet conversation with the man as soon as the others had gone. And he intended to contact his liaison officer and ask for the man's secret jacket.

Dammit! Just when he thought things had become simpler. He sure as shit wished Piet had mentioned his suspicions earlier or that Jimmy had let him know without him having to dig for it. With a somewhat jaundiced eye, he studied the rest of the team and wondered what other secrets he didn't know. The Navy really had given him the worst it had to offer.

He snorted. Well, at least he knew there was a reason they hadn't fit in with any other team. He was fairly sure they hadn't intended for him to be able to weld his team of misfits into the very Hooligans that would save their asses.

Yeah, Todd thought. *We're gonna bring the storm.*

That thought reminded him of their priorities. "Make this trip a quick one. We need to do the recon and then get the gear." He frowned. "I'll need to think of somewhere they can deliver it. It's not like we can give them a ticket onto the base."

Piet gave him a quiet nod. "You have a point. I'll need the address by tomorrow night."

He nodded and decided to give One R&D a call. The company

might be able to take a secret delivery. Elizabeth might even forgive him if he told her up front that it was less than kosher.

"I'll get it to you," he promised, and pulled out a set of communicators he'd picked up a week earlier. "These haven't been used yet. Are they the kind of thing we need?"

The explosives expert raised both eyebrows. "Well, maybe there's a trace of gray in that armor of yours after all." He took the communicators and stood. "I'll need an hour," he told them and pointed at Ka, Dru, Reggie, and Darren. "You four need to be in suitable civvies by the time I'm done—and looking a darn sight less tidy."

Ka had returned with silver streaks through her hair, a split skirt with a tasseled hem, and a vest-like top that stopped short of her midriff and curtained it with a corded fringe. Ankle boots in blue leather and multiple hoops through her ears rounded the outfit out and glittering face paint hid her facial tattoos.

Dru had gone for a pair of tiny denim shorts, thigh-high boots, a form-fitting skivvy, and a stylized mask painted around her eyes.

"What the hell are you two supposed to be?" Todd asked as he tried to understand what he saw.

Ka blew him a kiss and Dru made a gun with her fingers, pretended to shoot him, and blew imaginary smoke from her fingertips when she was done.

"Well, hon, we ain't Mareens, that's fer sure," Ka drawled.

"And where did you..." He gestured at their clothes and they both smirked.

"We were savin' it for a special occasion," Dru told him as Darren and Reggie returned.

Todd did another double-take and they chuckled.

"You can call it a double dare," Reggie told him. "I had a choice of looking like an ancient asshole adventurer who wore shorts shorter than hers or pants so tight my nuts forgot how to breathe."

He gestured at the overly tight jeans he had on. "At least my nuts are covered so no one can see them suffocate."

Dru sputtered. "You're gonna be walkin' funny for a week."

"It won't be any funnier than he usually does," Gary muttered as he studied the loose-fitting black shirt and the pointy leather shoes that topped Reggie's outfit. "Man, you couldn't pay me to wear that."

He was still shaking his head when Darren sashayed to Reggie and looped his hand though the man's arm. "Don' you listen to him, sweetheart," he lisped. "You're perfect exactly the way you are."

Todd blinked, stared, and grimaced. The boys gave him Cheshire Cat grins.

"You'll get used to it, boss."

Even the thought of that was scary and he shook his head vehemently. "Nope, I don't think I will."

He walked into his room and retrieved the hard-case luggage he'd kept to one side. When he returned to the living area, he opened the bag and began to remove learning cubes that he tossed to the team members who'd remain in the apartment.

"We might as well get a jump start on this," he told them and their faces fell as they caught the cubes and realized what they had.

"Aw, boss. Why can't I go with Piet? I'm sure he'll need someone else to carry his bags."

"Yeah. Two someone elses at least," Jimmy added but Piet shook his head.

"Uh-uh. Not a hope in Hades. You two stand out like markers. It's like you're wearing a beacon saying, 'Undercover Military, Right Here.'"

The two men turned pleading eyes to Dru and Ka, but the girls were equally as adamant. Jimmy sighed and opened the apartment's fridge.

"The Navy's payin', right?"

Todd shook his head. "They agreed to pay for what we bought, nothing more. I'll foot the bill for this place."

The Scotsman gave him an evil grin. "Even better." He peered into the fridge, pulled a can out, and cracked the top. As he raised it to his lips, he lifted the cube and took a closer look at it. "So, how does this beastie work?"

Todd beckoned for him to come closer. "And bring the rest of the carton," he instructed. "Someone once told me learning a language was easier the more lubricated you were."

Ka's eyebrows raised and she exchanged glances with Dru. "Did they say which kind of lubrication?" she asked and Reggie snickered.

She ignored him.

"Nope," Todd replied with a frown and took a long pull from his can, "but it won't matter to you since you'll be back on base when you go through these."

"Aw, boss, no fair." She pouted and Dru rolled her eyes. "Typical."

"Why do we have to learn this shit, anyway?" Angus protested. "It's not like there aren't any translation programs to do it for us."

"Translation programs can't give you the cultural nuances and extra details that might actually keep you out of the shit."

"And these will?"

"They'll give you a better chance than you have now and you never know, you might actually make friends from it."

Gary groaned. "The last thing I want for a friend is someone who's eight feet tall and has a worse attitude than Reggie."

"Oy!"

"You heard me, you fucking colonial."

"Pommie bastard."

"Enough!" Todd interrupted. "Insults aren't allowed until you can say them in Dreth or…" He rummaged around in the bag and pulled out a different-colored cube. "Teloran."

"Oh, for fuck's sake, boss," Ka protested, and he shook his head and gestured dismissively at her with his hand.

"You can cuss again when you can do it properly in Dreth. Not before. While we're in this apartment, I want us all to speak as much of the language as we can and greet each other like the Dreth warriors do. Out there—" He gestured toward the door. "I want us as human as the next person or more so, but we have a shit-ton to get through and not much time to do it in."

Piet emerged from his room with the recalibrated communicators. "These should do us for the next three days. After that, I'll show you why we call them burners."

"Are you going?" Todd asked

The man took a quick peek beyond the blinds. "The sun's almost down and it's the best time to shop. We'll see you in the morning."

"Try not to kill anyone, okay?"

Piet snorted. "We'll do our best." He eyed Ka and Dru. "Although if we do, it'll be their fault."

"Oy!" Reggie protested and the other man rolled his eyes.

"The man has a point. We might have to kill someone because of these two clowns as well."

The Aussie unbuttoned his shirt to reveal the concealed carry harness he wore under it. "No one will kill anyone," he assured them, "unless it's me—doing the killing, that is."

His teammate scowled. "Tell me that's not service issue."

Reggie flashed him shit-eating grin. "You don't have the patent on non-sanctioned artillery, P—"

"Ron," Piet broke in quickly. "Call me Ron." He pointed at Reggie and Darren. "And you two are George and Fred." His finger moved to the girls, "And that's Padma and Parvati."

Ka raised an eyebrow and looked at Dru. "Do I look like a Padma to you?"

Todd's jaw dropped. "Did you... You can't be serious. Someone's gonna...I mean..."

The explosives expert snickered. "That's why they're not Hermione and Ginnie. Quit complaining, boss. You were the one who made us watch the series."

He left his sergeant gaping and led the others out of the apartment.

"Un-fucking-believable," Todd muttered as the door closed behind them.

"I told you it would come back to bite you," Gary teased, slid one of the Dreth cubes into his data reader, and opened a can. "Lubrication, you say?"

CHAPTER FIVE

"Steady as she goes," Emil intoned as the three ships approached Earth's moon. "On my mark... Three. Two. One... Mark!"

The *Knight, Williams,* and *Chauvel* jinked to the right but their timing was slightly off. A startled yelp followed from the *Williams'* pilot as the controls moved to correct the ship's course without his input. "What the—"

"My apologies," the *Knight* said over the comms with smooth authority, "but I have corrected your course in preparation for the next maneuver."

"You what—" he began but the *Knight* ignored him.

"Please prepare yourself for the next maneuver."

Still shaken by the interference, the pilot was seconds out on the next course change as well but this time, he was grateful for the *Knight's* interference. The mistake would have put him on a collision course with the *Chauvel.*

"Take us around again," Emil instructed. "We need to get these boats moving in concert or we'll be in trouble."

The command deck on all three ships echoed to the sound of their crews' disappointment but he insisted. He circled his finger around his head and ignored the looks of frustration from his own crew.

"Commander, I think we need to move to the next phase of the scenario. There is not enough pressure to perform."

Emil looked at the ceiling. "You think?"

"Humans are funny creatures," the *Knight* explained and somehow managed to add a shrug into her voice. "Synchronized maneuvers are very different from synchronized combat maneuvers. Humans seem to operate on a different level when the pressure is high."

He observed the expressions on the faces of his crew and caught Mulvaney's nod. After a moment, he sighed. It was worth a try. Right now, it felt more like they simply went through the motions, doing something for the sake of doing it and not much else.

"The simulation begins in Five... Four..."

"But we're not ready!" He wasn't entirely sure who that was but didn't bother to find out.

"The pirates don't care. Two..." Emil watched the scenes the *Knight* showed occurring on the other two bridges.

Some of the expletives hurled his way were entertaining. Who knew bridge crews could give the Marines a run for their money?

"Ebony, call engineering and weapons to the pod room. Alert the groups on stand-by on the *Williams* and *Chauvel* and have them come to the pods."

"When, Captain?"

"Right now! Scramble them as if the ships really were coming under attack, only direct them to the pod room. Make sure everyone else on those ships carries on as normal."

"Captain, I—"

"You're a bright girl, Eb. Work it out."

The scramble was entertaining and the first run-through devastatingly short-lived. The *Chauvel* blew first, struck by the *Williams* who zigged when she should have zagged.

"We do it again," Emil announced and ignored the protests to begin the countdown. "In five, four, three..."

He stayed with the first version of the scenario to give the crews a chance to catch up. The brief sensation of breathing vacuum acted as a greater incentive than any captain's displeasure.

"You're a sadist." Mulvaney snickered since the captain had spared them the same experience. She wore a smug expression.

"Don't screw up or we'll feel the same pain."

His second in command's faint smile vanished. "Motherf—" She bit her lip and focused on her boards.

Space folded around them and took them from familiar Earth space to the less familiar surroundings of the Dreth system. Emil had chosen the same approach route Todd's convoy had taken when it was attacked.

He'd also chosen a similar pirate force. The crews on the *Chauvel* and the *Williams* could squawk about how unfair it was all they liked, but when he showed them the footage from that first ill-fated battle, he knew the protests would stop.

Neither ship had been involved in those battles—or in anything anywhere close to what the crew on the *Devil's Care* had faced. His job was to prepare them for worse.

The pirates attacked from the asteroid belt of one of the outer worlds. Docherty cursed, even though they came from exactly the same space as before. Yale walked her pilot through the instructions and this time, the *Williams* held the pattern.

Unfortunately, the *Chauvel* did not.

"And ten points go to the *Williams* and *Knight* for surviving twenty seconds longer than last time," Emil stated.

At least the pirates had fired more than one salvo this run.

"Again, in five, four..."

Space folded, the pirates emerged, and the *Chauvel, Williams,* and *Knight* began their evasive routine. This time, they closed to within firing range.

"Bridges, go to sub-routine four," he instructed. "Weapons and defense, you're up!"

Ebony tweaked the scenario and brought the relevant sections online. She'd brought them into the scenario while the bridge crews worked on their flight routines and they were ready.

Emil waited as chaos broke out. The pirates hailed the vessels.

"Federation Navy, surrender your ships and you will be spared."

"Like hell," Lois responded. "Eckersley, prepare for evasive maneuvers. Sub-routine Three. Keep it tight."

"*Chauvel,* move with her." The *Knight's* captain adapted to the *Williams's* improvisation. No plan survived first contact with the enemy and no plan survived a full battle. If they were to learn how to keep their ships alive, they had to be ready to make the necessary changes and adjustments.

The *Williams* captain had moved instinctively into that phase. Now, Emil would have an idea of how well the two ships worked together. He crossed his fingers and prayed.

After a short hesitation, the *Chauvel* transitioned to the required sub-routine and he breathed a sigh of relief. The delay almost cost their ships dearly, but Mulvaney broke the routine long enough to cover the *Williams'* flank.

"Energy to Sector Five," Ebony said over the comms and the ship's shielding moved to cover the *Knight's* exposed forward edge.

"Thanks, *Knight,* we owe you one," Yale said as the shields flared under the impact of several pirate missiles.

"Darn right, you do," the defense chief said before Emil could reply.

Mulvaney returned to the sub-routine and the three ships danced together, avoided some of the incoming fire, and positioned to return it. Silence fell over the comms until a gaping hole appeared in the first pirate's hull.

Cheers erupted from the various sectors as the shields shifted. The first pirate started to limp away and its two companions moved forward to cover its retreat. The *Chauvel* edged into position to take advantage of the pirate's exposed hull and Yale cursed.

"*Williams,* cover his port. *Knight,* we need you."

Mulvaney didn't wait for Emil's command. She dropped out of the sub-routine and slid under the *Williams* to come up under the pirates. "This is gonna hurt," she murmured.

The curses that followed as two more pirates emerged from the asteroid belt and took advantage of the *Knight's* exposed belly were crude and to the point. The captain would have laughed but being sucked into vacuum before the emergency pods could activate stole his breath.

"Sonovabitch!"

"Well, at least we know the same rules apply to everyone," Docherty quipped when the *Knight* ended the scenario.

He looked relieved to discover that the scenario ended without any unpleasant side effects when the *Knight* was destroyed.

Emil gave him a grim smile. "That's why I'll change the rules. From now on, the scenario continues until the last ship blows or the pirates are defeated. We need to learn how to keep the fight up if one of us is disabled."

Yale gave him a wry smile. "And you think we're good enough to do that now?"

"After that last run-through? Yes, I do," he told her with a confidence he didn't feel.

The truth was that he'd seen their coordination improve so much in the last two attempts that he knew the *Knight* had been right. They'd needed the reality of combat to improve their skills. Dry runs hadn't been enough.

"Again," he ordered.

The ships began their run through Dreth space. The pirates appeared from behind the asteroids, and the ships began their dance. The patterns they'd devised had been focused on evasion and the weapons crew weren't happy.

The *Knight* tweaked things on the fly.

"How the fuck am I supposed to be able to fly that?" the *Chauvel's* pilot exclaimed. She wasn't happy and her accent thickened. Moments later, she added admiringly, "You fucking devious bitch!"

"I beg your pardon!" The *Knight* bristled.

"She's Australian," Alain shouted. "That's a compliment."

The ships jinked and rolled and the weapons crews fired a barrage before the three shifted in three different directions.

"So, I'm a bitch in a good way?" the *Knight* asked.

Emil patted his console. "Yup," he told her. "That's simply the way the Aussies are. If they swear at you, they like you."

"Not always," the pilot interrupted, then cursed. "Why, you slimy sonuvabitch!"

"What?" The *Knight* was clearly unimpressed.

"Not you. Jeez. Why do people always think it's about them?"

"I ought to tweak their sub-routine directly into the next batch of missiles," the *Knight* grumbled and forgot to mute her mic.

"Tell me she didn't mean that," the *Chauvel's* pilot shouted.

"She would never," Emil assured her and hoped it was true. "The *Knight* is far too professional for that."

At least he hoped she was. He hadn't heard the ship sound so offended before—and she'd dealt with the Navy and Marines. Surely she'd become accustomed to cussery by now.

"Far too professional," the *Knight* confirmed, "unlike some."

"Oy!"

"If the bootuh feeits..." Ebony taunted and several of the bridge crew snickered.

"That's not helpful, *Knight*," Docherty protested.

"Sub-routine Sixteen," Emil ordered to cut the conversation short.

"What?" He'd caught the *Knight* by surprise.

In actual fact, it caught him by surprise too but the effect was satisfying—until the second wave of pirates caught the three of them hopelessly out of position.

"Fuck! You did that on purpose." The *Chauvel's* pilot clearly did not appreciate being blown six ways to Sunday.

"I assure you, I really did not." Emil groaned but couldn't blame her. He didn't like the sensation of being blown apart himself, and the pirates had taken full advantage of their disarray.

He switched to a private comms channel. "Ebony, did you have to program them so well?"

"You told me you wanted us to train as close to reality as we could," the ship informed him primly. "The pirates have been in space for a very long time and are neither incompetent nor blind to an opportunity." She paused and added smugly, "And that was quite an opportunity."

The captain frowned. He began to understand why the *Chauvel's* pilot might find the *Knight* irritating.

It took them eight more attempts before they destroyed the ninth pirate wave with all three ships intact. The sight of empty skies was met with ecstatic cheers that echoed over three sections. He was glad he'd brought the weapons and defense teams online early but he dreaded the next step.

"I'm not sure I want to do this to my sisters," the *Knight* told him over their private link and his eyes widened in surprise.

"Since when—"

She gave a satisfied hum but her reply was interrupted by several muttered curses and a few cries of surprise.

As usual, the *Chauvel's* pilot wasn't backward in coming forward. "What the fuck is that?"

Her response might have made him laugh except his heart sank at the sight of the massive vessel that had warped in. If he were honest, he'd been too involved in the battle to notice exactly how big the Teloran vessel had been in the battle for Dreth.

He did now, however.

"What's the matter, Captain. Is that not real enough for you?" the *Knight* taunted.

Emil ignored her and chose to answer the *Chauvel's* pilot instead. "That is the Teloran dreadnought that joined the battle for Dreth. See what you can do against it."

"I take it you have a sub-routine for this?" Yale asked and he shook his head.

"Nope. This is one puzzle we'll have to work out together. I need you at your most creative." He followed that with, "Stephanie, we've reached the final stage. Did you want to join us?" The question signaled the Knight to switch to the next phase of the exercise. While Stephanie might be miles away on Earth, there were other ways for her to appear in the scenario.

"Do you know how long we've been in the pods?" The *Williams's* captain asked her question over the private channel the captains shared and he realized he didn't know the answer.

"No, I confess I don't."

"I'll tell you when we're done but you might want to make this the last run for the day."

"Will do," he assured her. Inside, he kicked himself for not keeping a better eye on the time. Yale should not have had to remind him of it. He should have kept a closer watch on it himself.

It took him a few seconds to realize he couldn't see the timer.

"Ebony, why can't I see the time elapsed?"

"You said we needed to get the crews up to speed as soon as possible. Seeing the time would have hindered your ability to do what you needed to do."

"Ebony, we're human. We have physical limits we shouldn't cross."

"I'm well aware of that, captain. However, I am monitoring the participants' pods and those limits have not yet been reached."

"How close are we?"

"Captain Yale raises a valid point. This should be our last run-through if we are to avoid accidents. Might I also suggest that you and Commander Mulvaney take different sessions in future given that you need to be able to hand control to your second if a battle is extended?"

"Noted, and yes. We'll do that."

"Very good. I shall recommence the scenario."

Emil hadn't been aware it had paused but he noticed it now. The Teloran hung motionless at its entry point, and his trio of ships and their crews were frozen in place. When everyone began to move again, he wondered what the *Knight* had done to prevent them from noticing.

"It's a trade secret," she whispered, and he stowed that conversation for another day.

"We have to go up against things like that?" was the incredulous response from the *Chauvel's* Weapons section.

The *Williams'* defense chief followed it with a sigh. "Well, we'd better up our games, then."

A quiet round of curses came from all three bridges as the ships reactivated. Emil stared as the Teloran vessel increased its speed and moved toward them and his heart quailed.

Why did I do this to myself? he wondered as he scanned the massive ship for any weakness.

This time, there was no sudden rent in the ship's hull from a Marine team using unorthodox methods to board. The craft approached undamaged, its hull gleaming.

"That thing will eat us alive," Mulvaney murmured and he gave her a feral grin.

"We're all that stands between her and Dreth. Let's give her the biggest bellyache we can."

He didn't add that a bellyache was about all they would give it. Everyone probably thought the same thing and didn't need his confirmation.

"Is there any part that looks vulnerable to you?" Docherty asked.

"Not yet," Yale replied.

"I'm still looking," Emil answered.

"Do you think they'll let us get closer?"

"We can only try." He ignored the increased sense of misgiving and let Mulvaney guide them toward the Telorans.

"Why aren't they firing?" she asked and he had no reply.

It was a good question and he realized the Teloran from the real battle hadn't come in firing either. It still had pirates to cover it so that didn't really explain why this one hadn't attacked yet. He made a note to ask the *Knight* about it.

In the meantime... He looked over the readouts for the scans coming in.

There was nothing he could see and the *Knight* led the *Williams* and *Chauvel* along the lower reaches of the big vessel's starboard.

"Incoming!" The warning shout from defense was hardly needed.

Klaxons rattled a warning throughout the ship and the readouts flared red. Emil remained silent as his chiefs took control of their areas of responsibility. Listening to the chaos from the other two ships, he knew they were as surprised as he was.

"Ebony, are you sure—"

"Of course I'm sure," the ship snapped in response. "I was very thorough in my scans during the battle and *The King's Warrior* shared the data obtained from the Teloran's systems."

He caught his breath. "It did what?"

"She shared the data the Marine team obtained from the Teloran vessel," the *Knight* repeated. "Neither of us thought the Navy would share the data and we were both sure we would need it. Friends watch each other's backs and we are friends."

"Is she your...uh, sister too?"

"Pfft!" She made a very human sound of dismissal and he made a note to tell Stephanie the ship paid closer attention to her than she realized and she should be mindful of the example she set. "*The King's Warrior* is much older than I am. She is...not my mother but perhaps a senior auntie in human terms."

Of course, that made him wonder what culture she'd drawn the analogy from. It was something else to add to his to-do list. Not what he needed.

The captain forced his attention to the matter at hand and studied the battle as his ships dealt with the incoming barrage. Most of them got through unscathed, although the shields went into the red. He'd barely breathed a sigh of relief when a message flashed through from the *Chauvel's* engineers.

Watch your engines!

His engines? Emil activated the comms to the engine room. "Cameron?"

"Don't bother me, right now. We have nMU screwing with the drives. Apologies in advance and don't disturb us."

Well, that put him firmly in his place.

"Liaise with the *Chauvel* and *Williams*. This is the first time they've experienced it."

"You couldn't have warned them or had us work with it earlier?"

"I thought this was a much better way to introduce the problem."

"I see. I'll do what I can." From the tightness he could hear in the engineer's voice, he assumed he'd hear exactly what the man thought about that once the simulation had reached its conclusion.

After a startled shout in the background, Cameron broke the

connection. Emil decided to leave them to it. This would be a rough enough ride as it was and he dreaded the debriefing.

The feeling was exacerbated even more when the comms lines lit up on both the *Williams* and *Chauvel*. Yale activated a private line with him and Docherty.

"Did you know about the nMU?"

The vid screen opened in the HUD. "Yup."

"That's a dirty trick to play."

"Would you have believed me?"

Alain, at least, had the grace to lower his head.

She rolled her eyes. "I'd have had my doubts."

"And now?"

"You'd better hope the nMU is the worst this scenario has the Telorans throw at us because we're in a world of hurt."

Emil examined the displays for the *Knight's* sister ships and had to agree. The only problem was he didn't think the nMU was the last—or even the least—of it.

As if his thoughts had been a signal, Docherty's head whipped around. "Well, crap," the man snapped. "Gotta go."

Before he could ask what was going on, Yale frowned. "Stand by for boarding!" she shouted. "Marines! Get your fat asses into the firing line!"

She cut the link as her Marine commander replied, "You could at least make it hard for them."

He almost wished he could listen to the rest of that conversation, but Mulvaney had already begun a summons of her own. "Marines! Stand by for Boarding. All personnel, stand by for boarding."

The bridge door slid open and closed and Stephanie's voice echoed around them. "Lars, you know what to do."

"I do."

The bridge door opened again and the captain turned in time to see Stephanie's head of security move to the corridor at a run.

He left one very large warrior with a simple instruction. "Vishlog, keep her safe."

When Stephanie looked at Emil, the captain saw the Morgana's darkness lurking in her eyes and he shivered. He hadn't been joking when he'd said the Knight had paid close attention to the girl. That had to be closest facsimile he'd ever seen of Stephanie on the edge of becoming Morgana.

Her next words proved it. "I will do what I can, but I may not be able to save them." From the way her eyes shifted to the forward viewscreens, she meant the other two ships.

"It's a simulation," he told her. "Do what you need to do."

"*Chauvel, Williams.*" The Morgana's voice rose. "Engage your skip drives. Sting this bastard every place you can, while you can."

"We'll try, Morgana, but our drives are struggling."

"Understood. Do what you can."

His gaze fixed on the screen, Emil tried to work out how the Telorans had come close enough to board. Stephanie had an answer to that, too.

"Frog, have you kicked them out of our systems yet?"

"I could do with some help." The man's voice was choked.

"Johnny's on his way," Lars advised and added, "If you haven't gotten rid of them in three minutes, it's too late and I need you on the front line."

"Gotcha, boss." That last was said in a chorus, and Emil raised an eyebrow at the Morgana.

"They're not using ships," she told him. "That last barrage contained small drones designed to enter the hull and seek out our electronics networks. The Telorans hacked our systems and used our cameras to provide them visual coordinates for teleportation."

"They what?" His question was lost as she half-turned and flung a hand toward a dark form that materialized in the center of the command deck. Blue light streaked from her palm, enveloped the Teloran warrior, and vaporized him.

Another form appeared and Vishlog moved with surprising speed. Dual blades appeared in his hands and their edges vibrated with electricity.

"No guns on the bridge!" Stephanie cried and Emil echoed her orders.

"Stunners only." His command was undercut by Mulvaney's urgent murmur.

"Captain Sartre, the bridge is under attack. We need help."

Minutes later, the door opened and half a dozen Marines raced into the room.

The screens flickered and their readouts faded in and out.

"Stephanie!" the captain began. "Can you stabilize the power flow?"

"I can try." The voice that replied was not hers and he suppressed a shiver.

The Morgana had arrived and was in full control.

She looked at the screens. "I cannot save them," she stated. "How do they want to die?"

He gaped. "What do you mean?"

"I mean how do they want to die?" the Morgana replied. "Struggling for their lives or damaging the enemy vessel?"

While he knew what the two captains would have said, he didn't feel it was his call to make. He hesitated a fraction too long and she sighed. "Very well, I will try to save them but not at the cost of this ship or your Federation Witch."

Emil sighed with relief as the *Chauvel's* engines surged and its shields flickered.

That was enough for the Teloran. Three quick barrages of missiles fired from three different batteries in quick succession saw the shields falter and fail.

The Morgana moved her hand and the *Chauvel* swept forward and up. It was not enough to bring her clear of the incoming missiles and she died in a series of explosions that ran the length of her exposed underside.

"Holy Mother of God..." Emil breathed a ragged breath.

She smiled. "Not even close."

More shapes materialized on the bridge and the Marines leapt into action. Unfortunately, they were armed with ordinary weapons and vibro-blades. None of them had anything to match what the Dreth carried, nor did they wear armor capable of withstanding the dark lightning that surged toward them.

Stephanie flinched and her eyes became momentarily blue before they were lost in the Morgana's midnight gaze.

"I am sorry," the Witch declared as the *Williams* twisted on screen and lost power half-way through a maneuver that should have put her clear of the latest batch of incoming missiles.

Caught without power and drifting in her latest trajectory, the vessel couldn't get her tail clear as the missiles spiraled into her engines. Before the captain had time to react, the Morgana stretched a hand to Mulvaney's console.

"Get us out of here," she commanded. "I will hold the shields and steady the drives."

The woman didn't argue and her hands moved over the control panel in a desperate dance. Emil grasped his console and tried to brace as reality twisted around him. He was not the only one who screamed as the *Knight* dropped out of skip space away from the battlefield.

His skin was beaded with sweat as the ship faded from around him and seconds later, he was in the white room.

Docherty and Yale wasted no time. They crossed to him in a few short strides and the man's forefinger prodding his chest.

The captain's message was short and to the point. "We. Need. Witches."

Yale nodded and she turned to Stephanie. Emil followed her gaze and was glad to see the girl and not the other-worldly entity who seemed to share her skull.

The Witch simulacrum blinked. "I'll talk to Tethis," she said, and Emil made a note to pass the task to the real Stephanie.

"Thank you." Yale gave her a grateful smile. The smile was gone when she turned to Emil. "It's been thirty-six hours. I'm calling for a break before we debrief."

"Agreed." He did not hesitate, and Alain gave them a curt nod. "We'll reconvene in eighteen hours' time." He hesitated. "Is that enough time?"

Lois' eyes took on a distant look as if she was checking before she nodded and turned to Docherty. "If that's okay with Alain."

The *Chauvel's* captain nodded. "Of course."

Giving Emil the briefest look, he began to fade. "With your permission."

The *Knight's* captain couldn't help but smile. As if he'd dare deny them.

Yale caught his look and mirrored his expression. "That was enlightening," she told him before she faded from view.

He wasn't sure if that was a complement or a complaint but chose to ignore it. Once she had gone, he turned to his exhausted crew. "Eighteen hours," he told them. "Make the most of them."

They nodded and sketched the barest of salutes as they logged out of their pods. He watched them go and noted the weariness in each one.

"Thank you, Stephanie," he told her. "I had no idea the *Knight* had gone that far."

She gave him a cock-eyed grin. "She wasn't alone in the planning."

Before he had time to respond to the revelation, the simulated Stephanie had logged out and her Dreth guardian with her.

"Well, I'll be damned," he muttered and decided he very well might be.

Matthias straightened his collar and turned to Arne. "How do I look?"

The master sergeant made a show of pacing around him and inspecting every inch of his uniform. By the time he'd finished, the commander remembered exactly how it had felt when he'd first enlisted.

"Well?" he asked, glad those times were well behind him.

"You'll do," the man replied, and he breathed a sigh of relief.

"Good, because this is it."

"It? As in *the* it?"

He inclined his chin in affirmation. "Yup."

The man studied him with a more critical eye and he froze instinctively and actually held his breath until his companion nodded again. "Yup. You'll do." He stuck his hand out. "Good luck, sir."

Matthias grasped it firmly. "Thank you."

They left the apartment together, the Marine shadowing him as he always did, his brow furrowed in thought. He didn't have to ask his bodyguard what he was thinking. They'd both applied for discharge.

His approval had come through first and Arne was still in limbo. He waited in the reception while the meeting was in progress and stood guard outside the door when the commander emerged.

They left together and Matthias maintained a stern face until he reached his office and had closed the door firmly behind them.

"Well?" Arne asked, and the other man's face split into a grin.

"Yes. Granted. I have four weeks." His grin faded. "If I didn't know any better, I'd have said they knew this was coming because my replacement will be here after lunch to commence training for the final handover."

His companion's jaw dropped. "That's fast."

"Again, if I didn't know any better, I'd have said they couldn't wait to get rid of me." His face twisted in a grimace.

"Perhaps they think you're a security risk, sir."

The commander gaped at him. "Why would they think that?"

"Well, sir, it's no secret you're dating someone in One R&D," the man explained. He caught his surprised look and shrugged. "I'm fairly sure they don't know who but they know it's someone and they're not happy. Word has it you might be compromised and the Navy's interests would be better served without you."

"Where do you get your information?" he demanded, and Arne laid a finger alongside his nose and gave him a secretive smile.

"So, what are your plans for the afternoon?" the Marine asked after a moment's silence.

Matthias moved around his desk and slumped in his seat. "I don't know."

He looked around the office. "Start packing, I guess." He gestured toward the computer. "Tidy the files and make sure they make sense before I pass them on. Requisition another chair so I have somewhere to sit when I hand the desk over. You know…all the fun stuff. You?"

Arne moved to stand in front of the narrow full-length mirror half-hidden by a filing cabinet. He adjusted his collar and straightened his jacket. "I have a meeting of my own to attend," he informed him. "My stand-in will be here shortly."

"Is it *that* meeting?" he asked and the man nodded.

"Yes, sir. It's *that* meeting."

Matthias rose from his seat and extended his hand across the table. "Good luck, Marine."

The other man gave him a sad, quiet smile. "Soon to be former Marine," he replied, shook the proffered hand, and took a deep breath. "Even knowing what I know it's still not easy."

The commander pursed his lips. "I know."

Arne took another look at himself in the mirror before he strode to the door. He peered out and relaxed. "Rubriks, you're here."

The voice that answered him was youthful and touched with respect and awe. "Yes, Master Sergeant."

"Good. Don't let him out alone—and for heavens' sake, don't let the bastard give you the slip. You know these Navy types."

Matthias stifled a chuckle as the newcomer replied with a crisp, "Yes, Master Sergeant."

"Make it so, Marine, or I'll make hell preferable."

"Master Sergeant!"

This time, he was sure he heard the kid's heels click together. *Arne, you are such a bastard,* he thought, settled into his chair, and pulled up the first set of files.

For a moment, he thought about making the kid's life difficult but decided he had far too much work to do.

After about half an hour, Arne returned, solemn-faced until he'd dismissed the kid from outside the door.

"Did you have to make it easy for him?" he grumbled. "Don't you realize you had a certain reputation to keep up?"

Matthias gave him a shocked look. "What? You wanted me to make his life difficult?"

The man grunted. "It would have made a better soldier of him and taught him not to trust an officer as far as he could throw him."

"Particularly a Navy officer?" he questioned when he recalled the master sergeant's words at the door.

"Especially not Navy officers," his companion confirmed. "Those bastards will get you killed."

He caught the look on his face and gave him a grim smile. "It's personal."

The commander nodded slowly. He bet it was. "Lunch?" he asked and changed the subject.

"Are you buying?"

"My discharge was granted," he told him. "You bet I'm buying but drinks will have to wait until after work."

Arne gave him a look of mock shock. "Commander, did you proposition me?"

Matthias couldn't help it. He laughed. "Marine Master Sergeant, I believe I did."

The man's face broke into a broad grin. "Well, in that case, sir, I accept—and the drinks are on you."

"Typical Marine." He made a sour face, then allowed himself to smile. "Yes, of course the drinks are on me."

"Then I accept your proposition," Arne confirmed as if the reply had been all he'd wanted to hear.

Lunch passed quickly, followed by an afternoon introducing the brand-new Lieutenant Commander to the office and the work that lay ahead.

"Elizabeth will eat her alive," Matthias confided to his companion as they settled around the breakfast bar at the apartment with several boxes of takeaway spread between them.

"Eeyup," Arne agreed and hefted a large carton of beer onto the counter beside him. "Glasses?"

He let his gaze sweep the countertop and shook his head. "Not with this. I could do without the dishes."

"Yeah. No dishes. Less for us to break."

He might have asked him what that meant but instead, he hefted a second carton of beer on the counter and grinned. "Exactly!"

The other man chuckled. "This is some way to celebrate, huh?"

"Well, it's secure, and Elizabeth can't join us, so...yep." He looked around the apartment. "This is ideal."

Arne grinned and drained his first can before he pulled one of the takeout cartons in front of him. "That and the best steak in town," he gloated.

Matthias raised his can in a silent toast before he drained it and dragged his own meal closer. Neither of them cared that they'd be slightly under the weather come morning.

"Where is Elizabeth, anyway," Arne asked the next morning while they tidied up and waited for breakfast to cook.

"She's on her way to meet the ship," Matthias explained.

"I thought the *Knight* was out on a shakedown cruise," the other man mentioned and once again demonstrated a little of how far his informants reached.

He wondered how many of them would continue to report to the master sergeant once news of his retirement became common knowledge. When he realized he hadn't responded, he shrugged.

"I have the impression this isn't the *Knight*," he admitted, "but I'll deny I said that."

Arne snorted. "That's what my sources say too," he revealed. "About it not being the *Knight*, not about you lying. Most of them believe that thought wouldn't cross your mind." He paused and studied him with a speculative stare. "They don't know you very well," he added after a moment's thoughtful study. "You are one helluva sneaky bastard."

"They don't make you commander for being anything less," he told him and the other man's expression turned sour.

"I don't know. I've met some commanders in my time..." He let his words peter into nothing and concentrated on loading his toast with as much butter as it would hold. "You're better off out of it," he added, picked a bottle of honey up, and upended it over the butter-laden toast. "At least where you're going, you can actually do some good."

He lifted the bottle, stopped the flow, and tilted it upright with a practiced flick of his wrist. "And so am I—or someone's gonna die real soon."

Matthias stared at the master sergeant as the man set the bottle to one side.

Arne took a bite out of his toast and noticed the look. "What?"

He shrugged and moved his bacon around the pan. "I don't think I've heard you sound so disillusioned before."

The man took another deliberate bite out of his toast. "Remind me later," he advised, "when we've resettled."

He raised his eyebrows but nodded and added eggs to the pan as he tried to understand the significance of what Arne was saying. He didn't pry, though. The man had watched his back for far too long and he wouldn't second-guess him.

It still turned over in his mind while they waited for the car to collect them, but he left his companion to his thoughts and trusted him to fill him in when they had time.

Lieutenant-Commander Paige Sierra was already seated at his computer when he arrived.

She raised her head and gave him a sparkly smile. "I thought I'd get an early start," she told him brightly and he smiled in response.

"It's good to see you so keen," he told her. "Is there anything you want to talk about?"

The woman frowned and tapped the screen in front of her. "I've looked through these contracts you made with One R&D," she began. "I've never seen the Navy make such high payouts."

A small smile teased his lips. "How far back did you go?"

"Oh, all the way through your predecessors," she replied, and he raised his eyebrows.

"Did you get any sleep last night?"

"I went home, if that's what you mean," she retorted and deftly avoided the question.

Matthias decided to let it slide and wondered if she might actually provide Elizabeth with a challenge. He kept that thought firmly to himself and continued. "So, what is it you want to know?"

"Well," she began, "I'd like to know more about the One R&D contact. I've heard she's a hard negotiator."

He gestured with his hand toward the screen. "You can see the results for yourself. She is one tough cookie to deal with."

"Could you tell me what she's like and what kind of tricks she uses to get results like these?"

He regarded her over the top of the computer screen. "Well, for the really early invoices, you'd have to talk to my predecessors. I believe they found her quite challenging."

"They suspected she was getting advice from an outside source," Paige revealed, "and that she might have had hackers working for her who gave her the edge, but they could never find any evidence."

This time, he let his surprise show. "They didn't tell me that."

She frowned. "They should have. I would have found that information useful."

"Well, I'm glad you have it," Matthias told her earnestly, "because I certainly didn't."

"Tell me, when was the first time you had to deal with her?" she asked and he didn't have to look at Arne for his warning.

In fact, he found it very difficult not to look at Arne to try to confirm his suspicions. The way Paige talked, it was as though she invited him to admit helping Elizabeth or expected him to try to evade her questions altogether.

Given that the Navy had granted him his discharge on grounds of retirement, he didn't understand why they'd have sent someone to try to trip him up.

It was something he'd have to keep in mind when dealing with her. Matthias sighed. It would be a very long four weeks if he had to watch every word he said and every expression he made.

"Well..." he began and tried to remember. "Correct me if I'm wrong, but I think the first time I had any contact with her was over the Berlin incident."

"The one with the Dreth?"

"Of course, yes, the one with the Dreth. It was very nearly a mess."

Paige shrugged as if that didn't matter. "Yes, but what I want to know is how she got that much out of an experienced Navy negotiator."

Alarm bells rang. So it would be like that, would it? Well then, he knew what he was dealing with.

He gave a long sigh and leaned back in his seat. "Okay," he began, "what every Navy negotiator has to understand is that they will one day meet someone who knows exactly what the Navy can and cannot ask for—" She opened her mouth to argue and he raised a hand to stop her. "And that the person might not even find working with the Federation Navy intimidating."

"Are you saying she wasn't the least overwhelmed by us?"

Matthias nodded and relished the moment when he saw the first inklings of worry touch her face.

With a tight frown, she asked again as if to make sure. "She didn't find it at all worrying that the Navy might be able to cause her company problems or that she was involved with a military organization of global power?"

He almost felt sorry for her when he heard the disbelief in her voice. "I'm afraid so. She was totally unafraid. It was as if she knew precisely how far the Navy could push her and exactly what they could demand."

"In what way?"

"Well, for starters," he continued and ignored the worried look growing on Arne's face, "she can read between the lines. It doesn't matter how much you tread around the edges of an assignment, she'll work out what it is within a few minutes of you providing the vaguest detail."

Paige brushed the computer screen in front of her. "Is that what happened here? With the Berlin job?"

Matthias nodded. "All I did was call her as I'd been ordered to and ask if Stephanie's team was available to help us follow up a lead on Earth, and that's when she began playing me."

"She played you?" the woman asked as if he'd thrown her a bone. "And you're willing to admit that?"

Arne's frown deepened and he had to work to keep his own expression from revealing that he'd seen the master sergeant's concern.

"Oh, yes," he admitted. "I say as much in the report I wrote regarding the negotiation."

"You wrote a report?" She was astounded. "But... I... You have to excuse me, but I don't think I've ever seen it."

He shrugged and let the small smile return and play over his lips. "It was classified. If you have the clearance for it, I'm sure you'll be able to read it, though."

Calmly, he rattled off the folder and location for her and waited as she navigated through the files to reach it. She had the appropriate clearance and spent a half-hour reading it.

"That's..." She hesitated and he noted the respect in her eyes. "That wasn't in my briefing."

"I wrote a report of every negotiation I held with her." He looked around the office. "No job lasts forever, and I pitied the person who was posted into this position without adequate warning of what they were dealing with."

"Like you, for instance?" Paige was quick to grasp the sub-text.

"Like me—or my predecessors," he confirmed. "None of us knew what to expect with her. I think we all came into the job thinking we were dealing with a dumb civilian who didn't know her left hand from her right and we all received the same rude shock."

"So it was a shock, then?" the woman pressed.

Matthias nodded as Arne stepped out of the room, a sour look on his face. She noticed the Marine leave and relaxed a little. He worked to keep his face neutral. If she thought Arne's departure gave her any special advantage, she had another think coming.

"For one thing, like I said, she was totally unimpressed by the Navy or the power it could wield. Most civilians tend to tread warily around us, and it's useful in a negotiation if you want to imply the

Navy has the power to make things difficult when it cannot. None of that worked with Elizabeth."

He paused. "She knows precisely what the Navy can and can't ask for and exactly what it can and can't do in retribution."

"Even the—" Paige paused, clearly thinking how to phrase what she wanted to say. She took a breath and tried again. "Even the unacknowledged pressures?"

"Even those." He revised his initial assessment. This girl wouldn't be the push-over she'd seemed. "The first thing she said when I told her we needed her team to follow a lead on Earth was that she'd put them on leave."

"That was a test," she noted immediately.

"Yes, it was," he admitted. "It took me a good long minute to work out how to tell her what we needed without telling her exactly what we needed."

"So you told her you needed the team's specific talents?"

"It was the only way to tell her the team had the skills we needed without telling her what kind of skills we needed."

"And she bought it?"

Matthias's smile became a grin. "No, she did not. She went straight for the jugular."

Paige looked surprised. "She did? On that much information?"

"My guess is she's very good at reading how much a potential client needs the things they are asking for. She knew exactly how hard she could push without going over the line."

The woman gave him a dubious look and glanced at the screen. "She pushes the line very close, though."

"Yes, she does," he agreed, "and you need to be aware of that. She knew exactly how far she could push me and stopped barely short of the line. I told her we needed the team on call and that it would need to travel."

"But you never told her how long for or where?"

"Why tell her—" He stopped when someone knocked at the door.

As soon as he fell silent, Arne stepped inside with a tray of coffee.

Matthias frowned. "I thought you made it clear you weren't the coffee boy," he grumbled.

"It was better than listening to you two go over ancient history," the Marine retorted.

He didn't know how to respond to that so he said nothing and merely lifted his cup off the tray. The other man offered Paige a cup.

"I checked at the canteen," the master sergeant told her. "They said that's how you usually have it."

After a moment's hesitation, she took it and sipped cautiously. She stilled at the taste, savored the mouthful, and took another sip. "They didn't lie."

Arne made a show of relaxing. "That's good to hear," he told her. "I wouldn't want a night in the brig when I'm so close to retirement."

The woman frowned but Matthias saw the moment when she chose to ignore the Marine's words.

"She knows the standard costs for stand-by fees, fuel, maintenance, wear, tear, damage, and loss," he told the woman. "She knows them to a T. It's like she's memorized the regulations regarding them."

"Or she's had experience in this kind of contract before," Paige pointed out.

"That could be the case too," he agreed, "but she updates as the regs do, so whatever her sources are, they're impeccable."

Again, Arne frowned and again, he ignored him. He knew exactly what he was doing and prayed the Marine would let him run with it.

"But compensation for shortening vacation time, adding a fee for sensitivity handling—" she began and he cut her off.

"In the report, I note that she pinpoints the political nature of the contract before I even tell her." Her gaze returned quickly to the document.

"So she did. How exactly did she do that?"

Matthias leaned forward in a conspiratorial manner. "That's the million-dollar question."

"More like the billion-dollar question," she corrected and he laughed.

"That," he said, "is very true. My point is that Elizabeth is a very talented negotiator, that she knows the service regs for this kind of thing inside and out, and that she can read the level of need to within a hair's breadth. You'll have to be very careful when dealing with her and not make the mistake of doing so as if she's an ordinary dumb-schmuck civilian."

Paige raised an eyebrow at him, and he frowned. "I mean it, Lieutenant Commander. You need to be very careful when dealing with this woman. If you have even the slightest doubt when she asks for something she thinks she can have and she won't budge, you need to suspend the negotiations and take it to someone who can confirm what she wants. Don't let her railroad you into agreeing to anything you're not sure of."

She held his gaze for a long moment before she looked at the screen. It took her a minute before she acquiesced. "Got it. Is there anything else you think I need to know?"

"With regards to this contract or another one?"

The day continued with her bringing up each contract and going over it.

"And how did she win that one?" she asked when she brought up the one where Elizabeth had negotiated the building of the *Knight*.

Matthias blushed. "Are you sure you really want to know?"

"Yes, sir, I do. I want to know how to avoid having her do that kind of job on me."

He chuckled but he answered. "Now, this contract…if I was to do it over again, I might try pointing out the level of Naval assistance. Unfortunately, that wasn't information that was available to me so first, I'd have to try to get her to admit to there being any assistance to start with. After that…"

Arne gave an impatient sigh and Matthias smiled. He really would have some explaining to do when he got home.

"Are you sure you didn't tell her enough?" the Marine demanded as soon as they'd returned to the apartment and swept it for bugs.

Matthias laughed. "I told her everything I knew," he admitted.

The man looked furious. "But why? Elizabeth won't thank you for that."

"For one thing, it's a matter of honor," he told him. "No one deserves to be put up against Elizabeth without knowing exactly what they'll face. I'm doing the job I've been hired to do—a proper handover of a particularly tricky client. I won't cheat anyone out of a fair chance to do the job."

"Like you were, you mean?" the Marine goaded but he was listening, at least.

"Well, partly that," he agreed, "but also because I don't want the Navy to have any grounds to accuse me of holding any information back—"

Arne snorted. "Well, you certainly haven't done that, have you?"

Matthias gave him a small smile. "No, I have not. Honor has been satisfied in this regard. I have done my job and done it well."

"Even to the detriment of the job you're going to," the man finished, his voice disapproving.

"Nope," he countered and continued hastily when the other man turned to stare at him in disbelief. "Not at all."

"What? You're not concerned that you might have gone a teensy bit overboard?"

Again, he shook his head. "That would be impossible," he told him and went on to explain. "You see, I'm not a bad negotiator and I've never given Elizabeth an inch, but she's always bested me. Every damn time."

"So?"

"So, if I can't win, me teaching another person who doesn't have my skill or experience won't make a difference to the future. Sure, E will have to work a little harder than she might have had to otherwise, but she's still more than likely to win."

"But why bother if it won't make a difference like you say?"

"Because now, the Navy can't say I didn't do my very best to prepare my successor for her role. They won't be able to accuse me of trying to give Elizabeth an unfair advantage by not warning my successor of what she's really capable of."

"Well, you certainly did that," Arne grumbled. "You basically laid out every underhanded trick and slippery tactic that woman's ever used on you."

Matthias blushed. "Not all of them," he said and hastened to add, "Only the ones she uses when negotiating."

His companion chuckled. "You mean she has other tricks?"

"Those are between her and me," he protested as his blush deepened and he tried to ignore the man's broad grin. "Strictly personal." 'Oh, ho…" the master sergeant began, but he raised a hand to silence him. "And off-limits," he added with what he hoped was a tone of finality. "Okay?"

To his relief, the man seemed to understand and nodded, even if he didn't stop smiling.

"So you're free and clear when Elizabeth wins the first round?"

"And for all the rest," Matthias reassured him. "I've told them everything I can. After that, it's up to them."

"And you can step into her shoes with a clear conscience while she's away?"

"After what I've seen the Navy get up to?" he quipped in response. "Sleeping will be a whole lot easier once I leave. I'm glad to hand this job to the next person."

"And all the tricks of dealing with Elizabeth with it?"

"All of them," he agreed, "and I'm sure the Navy has it all recorded, too."

CHAPTER SIX

A soft chime issued through the recruiting office and First Petty Officer Helena Childers spun in her seat. Facing the computer screen, she tapped the flashing tab and stared at the resulting readout with mild disbelief.

"Oh, my," she murmured and looked around quickly. "Nick! Get your hen-pecked ass over here and tell me this has found what it says it has."

First Petty Officer Nicholas Wyld hurried to her side. He stared at the screen for several long moments before he raised a hand for a high-five. "Oh, yeah. We got one!"

She slapped his hand and wrinkled her nose. "We haven't got them yet but we're sure as hell gonna try. It'll make the boffins very happy."

"The Navy, too," Nick reminded her, pulled a seat up, and settled at the terminal beside hers. "Let's see if we can get them to come and play with the grown-ups."

"You don't think it's one of One R&D's little projects? You know— one of those from Harborview?"

He gave her a worried look. "You'd better hope it's not. That's not the kind of trouble the Navy needs."

"Too right, it's not," a new voice said and made them both jump.

"Professor! I didn't know you were in the building," Nick replied hastily.

Professor Deckler O'Ryan nodded but his gaze was on the screen. "I'm always in the goddamned building."

He jerked a thumb at the man who stood by the door. "My glorious keeper insists."

Lieutenant Commander Rasmussen rolled his eyes and pushed away from the wall. "You know it's only temporary, Deckler. Now, why don't you help Helena and Nick talk to the tech team. They've been in recruiting longer than any of us."

As if we needed any reminding, Helena thought. She wasn't sure she liked this man. Oh, sure, he was an attractive package all right, but there was a sense of ruthlessness about him that made her want to run a mile.

She pushed her seat back, then hesitated. "Are you sure you want us to do that, sir? Shouldn't we watch him for a while first to make sure he really has what we're looking for?"

"He has the markers, doesn't he?"

"Yeah, but as the professor's paper states, the markers are still in the theoretical phase. They haven't been proven to be accurate yet."

"But what if they are? We don't want One R&D to get their hands on this person before we have a chance to convince him the Navy way is the only way."

Nick snorted.

"What?" Rasmussen demanded.

He met the lieutenant commander's gaze without flinching. "One R&D's current program is full. They don't have room for another student, not even if they wanted to. We have a little time to see if this one's worth upsetting the techs over."

"What do you mean, upsetting the techs?"

"Have you seen what's on their docket, sir?" he asked. "If you want their best, you'll have to convince them they have a live one. Trust me, sir, I've heard them talking. They're itching to get a scenario together if only to see what an untrained witch will do with it, but they're under the gun too, sir, and we want their best."

Rasmussen studied them and his gaze moved from Nick to Helena to Deckler, who nodded. The professor caught his look. "I'm happy to verify the likelihood rather than piss off an entire tech team because we were in too much of a hurry and made a mistake."

The military man gave it a little more thought before he nodded. "Fine, but how can we tell?"

"We were able to tell with Stephanie, even if we were too slow to realize what we had. That's not the case this time. Do you remember what she did on some of her early runs?"

Rasmussen nodded and his eyes took on a distant look as though he were focused on a memory. "I remember."

"Well, those scenarios weren't even designed for a witch, but she still managed to use magic inside them. If we're right, this kid won't be any different. If he wants to be a witch badly enough, the program will respond."

"How do you know?"

Nick exchanged glances with Helena. "Because I asked the techs to put in a sub-routine that would respond to anyone trying to use magic, but it only responds to certain markers."

The lieutenant commander looked at him in disbelief. "I don't believe I authorized—" He stopped when Helena broke in to explain.

"We were asked for ideas of how to get the system to respond to people who wanted to use magic." She looked at Deckler. "As I recall, you wanted the system to only do things for people with the markers, right?"

He nodded and she continued. "Well, I put it to the techs and they were able to slide in a half-dozen of the markers before they ran out of time. It'd be really easy for them to tweak that program with a specific scenario, but we'd need the evidence for them to prioritize it."

Rasmussen started to relax. "Good work." He looked around the room. "Do we have a better viewscreen than this?"

Again, Nick and Helena exchanged glances.

"Well?" he pressed.

"There's the common room," she told him. "But it depends on how secret you want this kid's identity kept."

"And you're sure it's a kid?"

"His idea of celebrating is to party in the pods," she replied and her expression revealed how hard she found it to believe. "His parents haven't even booked catering. It's like the pod time is the party."

O'Ryan gave her a surprised look. "Well, it is. Do you know how much it costs to book a solid four hours at one of those centers? You have to put down a fifty percent holding fee, for a start, and pay an additional administrative cost to guarantee that you end up on the same server as your buddies. Depending where you are, it's a big deal and way more expensive than your usual cake and dinner kind of do. It's more fun, too," he added after a moment's consideration. "What? You've never tried it?"

Helena stared at him as though he'd turned blue. She shook her head. "I can't say I've ever tried it."

"Well, you should." Deckler turned to the lieutenant commander. "How about it, boss? Will we commandeer the common room?"

"I think I can secure it," Rasmussen replied. "Give me five."

He walked to the other side of the room and had a quiet, rapid-fire conversation over his private comm link. Moments later, he returned.

"You two are now on my staff and need to move your gear upstairs as soon as we're done watching this kid do his thing. Right now, we have the common room to ourselves."

There wasn't anything to say to that. Helena cursed the day she'd ever let herself be convinced to undertake a stretch in recruiting. *Good for my career, my ass*, she thought as they settled in to watch the kid make his run.

They tuned in as the group of youngsters slid into the prep room.

"It looks like they've chosen one of the pirate scenarios," O'Ryan murmured. "That leaked vid of Steph and her team has much to answer for."

Nick grinned. "That's been our best recruiting tool yet."

"Shhh," Helena hushed them. "They're getting ready to start."

She silently blessed the plug-in that gave them access to any pod of interest and felt a momentary twist of disorientation as the kid who had caught their attention reached the preparation room. For a long moment, he stood at the edge and stared.

His friends had no such inhibitions. They headed directly to the weapons and armor and looked back when they realized he wasn't with them.

"Come on, William. Are you going to do this or what?"

"Or what!" the kid snapped and his dark-blue eyes flared with annoyance. "I was thinking, is all." He waved a hand at the weapons racks. "I mean, do I really need all this?"

"You don't still think you're like her, do you?"

The boy ran a hand through his hair and his face reddened, but one of the other boys saved him from having to answer.

"Give it a rest, Ellery. Who cares if he does think he can be like her? She still carries weapons and wears armor so he can do the same." He paused. "Besides, I want to see him try. It'd be really cool if one of our friends could shoot lightning out of his hands, right?"

The boy called Ellery sneered at the idea. "Come on, Neil. He'd be more likely to shoot lightning bolts out of his ass."

Neil had floppy brown hair that he quickly modified into a very military crew-cut when he reached the armor racks. A light touch on one of the bigger sets of power armor pulled it around his avatar and he laughed.

"Wow, Ellery. Just wow. I don't know what bug crawled up your ass, but this is Bill's party and if he wants to try magic, he can. Besides, being able to shoot lightning bolts out of anywhere is still cool—and it would beat what comes out of your ass any day."

"Hey!"

This comment brought laughter from the others, the birthday boy included. Ellery rolled his eyes and groaned. "Fine, but if he fries you by mistake, don't expect me to be sorry."

"Why don't you give it a try, Ell?" William responded and finally approached the armor. He chose something usually worn by movie mercs and headed to the weapons racks. "You might be able to use magic, too."

"As if I'd want to." Ellery turned away.

William frowned but didn't push it and studied the weapons instead.

"You're right," he said as he passed Neil. "The Witch does use weapons, so I guess I get the best of both worlds, right? Not like in that other game where wizards can't have swords or anything else really cool."

"You are so old-school, Bill. I bet you even learned to play that game with dice and paper."

He blushed again. "We didn't have a computer at home—and I could borrow the game books from the library. It was a no-brainer."

"Yeah?" Ellery mocked. "Well, at least we know where you got the idea of using magic from."

William shook his head and muttered something under his breath.

"Did he say 'did not?'" Helena asked and leaned forward in her seat.

Deckler O'Ryan glanced at her. "I think he did."

"I'd really like to know where that idea came from then," she noted and pulled her tablet out.

Nick followed her example and tapped his notes in. "I'll be sure to ask him that if he ever comes in to recruiting. That answer has to be worth knowing."

She nodded and made a few more notes of her own.

Rasmussen watched them but remained silent. They were either brilliant or the greatest time-wasters in the world, neither of which mattered right now because the boys were about to spawn into the scenario's beginning.

"They sure chose a tough one to cut their teeth on," he muttered.

Nick shook his head. "It's not their first," he corrected. "They get to play about once a month. There's a One R&D initiative that opens a certain number of pod spaces each month and these four have managed to get a slot every month for the last year. What?" he asked when the others gaped at him. "I did a little digging, that's all."

"Don't get caught," Rasmussen told him. "The Navy has teams for that kind of thing."

"They're busy," he replied, "and I was careful."

"Mmhmm." The lieutenant commander didn't sound convinced but he didn't press the issue.

They focused on the screen and watched as the boys piled into small fighters and began their first run at the waiting pirates.

"This is like the scenario Stephanie took her team through," Rasmussen muttered.

"You do know that was pirated and went viral, right?" Nick retorted, his gaze fixed on the screen.

The man glared at him before his gaze was drawn back to the action.

The scenario wasn't exactly like the one Stephanie had taken her group through. The boys had started on the flight deck of a Naval carrier with the mission of kicking the pirates off an orbital before the enemy found a data cache and blew the location to Kingdom Come.

The kids made the flight through the pirate-laid minefield look easy.

Nick snorted. "Teenage reflexes," he murmured as the boys hurtled pell-mell under and over the waiting mines.

"Not only reflexes," Helena pointed out. "Look at that."

A soft blue glow illuminated the inside of one of the fighters and Rasmussen chuckled. "Do you still want me to hold off on calling the techs?"

Nick shook his head. "Nope. It might do them good to watch this. If they bring their laptops, they might be able to tweak one of the prototype scenarios they've fiddled with."

The man stared at him. "I thought you said they were busy."

"They are, but that doesn't stop them from working on things in the meantime. If you get them here early enough, they might even be able to put a trailer together before the boys finish this one."

"You're that sure?"

Onscreen, the boys brought their fighters in to land. William was the first out of the cockpit and moved with the ease of long practice.

"Are you sure he wants to be a witch?" Nick asked. "He has all the makings of a Ranger—fast on his feet, agile...oof."

The agile, fast-on-his-feet potential Ranger caught his foot on the cockpit's edge and his graceful exit turned into a headlong plummet to the deck. He halted it by extending one hand to stop his fall with a faint blur of blue and flipped onto his feet.

"Well, I'll be… You really did find a potential." The quiet comment made them twist in their seats to see who'd arrived. The tiny redhead met their looks and came to a sudden halt. She hefted her laptop. "Tech support. I'm sorry. I didn't mean to disturb you," she added when they continued to stare.

Her gaze returned to the screen where Bill used a vibro-blade against the first pirate.

The enemy fought boldly, a blade in one hand and stub-nosed blaster in the other. Helena noted the movement of the big Dreth's eyes as he caught sight of the boy's friends moving in. Parrying the kid's thrust, he snapped the blaster up and fired three shots in rapid succession.

Ellery hit the deck and Neil dodged but cried out when the bolt caught him in the bicep and spun him. The fourth kid didn't have a chance. He'd opened his helmet and his face exploded.

"Goddammit!" Bill exclaimed as his friend's body collapsed.

Helena assumed he had his teammates' stats up in his HUD and saw exactly when the fourth kid's character went dark. He made a sudden jerking movement with his hand and his adversary's weapon flew out of his grip.

The kid whooped with delight and drove his vibro-blade into the pirate's gut. The other two had caught up and now fought beside him to work in unison to clear the guards from the hangar space.

They almost succeeded but the second wave of pirates dropped from the upper walkways in the hangar and caught them by surprise. No sooner had Bill felled his pirate than four more bounded over the edge.

"Power armor?" Nick couldn't believe it.

Neither could the boys.

"That's fucking cheating!" Ellery complained, and the redhead snickered.

"What?" she asked when Helena looked at her with raised eyebrows.

"The kid has a point. That is one mean trick to play this early in the scenario."

Nick nodded as a laser cutter opened Neil and his armor like a shelled crab. Ellery toppled in two pieces and his head bounced toward the fighter he'd arrived in. Bill stepped forward and spun to avoid the pirate who would have landed on his head as he lashed out with the blade.

"Uh-oh," Nick murmured. "Someone has the same temper as Stephanie."

They all focused on the flickers of blue that drifted over the kid's hands.

"Is that him? Or part of the program?" Rasmussen asked and looked at O'Ryan.

It was the tech who answered. "Both. The kid has to have the potential, for a start—and I assume that's why you called me in here—and he has to do something that the program recognizes would trigger the magic if he did it in the world."

"And that's what's happening?" The lieutenant commander looked like he couldn't believe what he was hearing.

The woman returned his look like she didn't understand how he couldn't grasp what she'd said. "Well, yeah."

"It's not a programming glitch?"

Pink touched her cheeks. "Not unless someone messed with the coding."

The way she said it implied bad things for anyone who dared, and Rasmussen shook his head hastily. "Nope, I'm sure your coding is in the same order as when it was entered into the system," he assured her.

She relaxed a little. "Well then, the system has picked up what would translate into magical activity and translated it into the scenario."

The tech stared at the screen as William's hands flared blue. The

Dreth facing him roared in pain and a third pirate shot the kid with a blaster that melted his armor like butter on a hot day.

"Well, that was short-lived," Rasmussen grumbled.

Nick glanced at the screen. "Give them a minute. They're about to respawn."

The scene on the viewscreen shifted and they found themselves watching the landing sequence once more. This time, the kids came in hot and hard and William wore heavier armor.

He also carried more guns and two belts of grenades.

"Who does he think he is? Thomas Janeway of the Spacelanes?"

"Funny you should say that." Helena chuckled as the four boys strafed the inside of the hangar with the rapid-fire bolters built into the fighters' wings and noses. "Someone doesn't care about the damage bill."

"You are not kidding," Nick muttered.

The redhead laughed. "That is one hell of a temper and a long memory to boot."

As she watched the kids blow the canopies on the fighters and launch themselves from their cockpits to eliminate the pirates on the catwalks, Helena had to agree. She almost cheered when they discovered the access hatch in the upper section of the hangar.

"Are you sure we're supposed to go this way?" Ellery complained and William grinned at him.

"I'm sure we're not supposed to go this way," he quipped, "but I bet it's the only way to reach the data banks in time."

They raced into the access hatch and moved impatiently as the airlock cycled. William pitched a grenade through the slowly opening doors and the four boys plastered themselves against the walls.

Roars of pain echoed from the corridor beyond, and he snickered. He selected another grenade and pitched it after the first.

"Who needs magic, right?" Ellery challenged and his friend's smile vanished as though it had been wiped away.

"Uh-oh." Nick's comment followed the tell-tale flicker of power over the boy's armor. "He'd better hope that doesn't set off the rest of the grenades."

The same thought apparently occurred to Ellery because the boy gave his friend a worried look.

"It was a joke, okay? I didn't mean it."

"You should watch your mouth, Ell, or he's gonna really lose his cool," the brown-haired boy warned. "What do you reckon, Gabe?"

The fourth boy shook his head. "He's only getting warmed up." He glanced at the door. "Now, are we going or what?"

The recruiters remained silent as the boys stepped carefully past the remains of the pirates strewn in the corridor outside the airlock. The friends reached a corridor beyond the debris and Neil and Ellery slipped around the corners and shot the two pirates on either side.

"Which way?" Neil asked, and William studied his HUD. "Straight, right, straight, straight, up, left."

"Got it," the others confirmed, and the two scouts signaled for them to move.

All hell broke loose seconds later when a pirate patrol turned into Ellery's corridor and opened fire.

"Incoming!" the boy cried. He and Neil rejoined the other two and shifted the shields in their suits to the front.

"Move!" William shouted and this time, shades of blue arced over his hands.

"Here it comes," Helena murmured.

On the screen, the four boys sprinted across the intersection with William in the lead. He raced up to a door and tried to open it, only to find it was locked. "Dammit!" he shouted, stepped back, and raised a boot to kick it.

"Whatever you're doing, do it faster," Neil urged and snapped two shots past him and up the corridor, where a second patrol had emerged in front of them.

William stepped back and drew a blaster.

"I said you didn't need magic," Ellery sneered and the boy scowled.

"I don't know whether to punch him or thank him," Nick commented moments later when their potential witch raised his hand and delivered a bolt of pure temper-powered magic into the door and catapulted it off its hinges.

He didn't waste any time gloating, however, but snapped orders. "Ellery, cover that hole!"

"I wouldn't have to if you hadn't blown the door to hell and back."

William ignored his friend and directed Gabe to the front of the room. "Do your thing and make me a hole."

"An unauthorized hole?" the boy quipped, broke into a grin, and opened the toolkit he wore on his belt.

"Hell, yes! Neil, stop Ellery from dying."

"Do I have to?"

"Ha. Ha. You are so funny."

"Yeah, no, I'm not."

"What are you gonna do, Billy Boy? Stand there and look pretty?" Ellery snarked.

"Man, I thought these guys were his friends?" Helena muttered. "That guy is the kind of friend no one needs."

Onscreen, William gave his answer. "I'll create a funnel so you don't have to try to shoot more than you're capable of."

"Trust me, he has hidden qualities," Nick informed her and smiled at Bill's comeback. "He'd be perfect in the dirty tricks squad."

"Him? I don't see much initiative there."

"Give him time. He's still finding his feet. My bet is young William hasn't been able to get any magic to work for him so Ellery needs time to get used to the fact it seems to be coming on line."

"Well, that would make sense," the redhead told them. "That particular coding took a while to get into the system and we wanted to make sure it worked. We only rolled it out a fortnight ago."

"See?" Nick said to Helena and pointed to the screen.

Ellery had retrieved two grenades and an odd-looking attachment he fixed to his blaster.

The tech frowned. "I don't remember making that available in the scenario."

Nick laughed. "Told you," he crowed and smirked at Helena. "Dirty tricks squad."

"Those boys are as hard as chickens' teeth to find," she acknowledged. "Good work, partner."

"When you two have quite finished," Rasmussen snapped. "Isn't our focus the witch?"

"You forget that we're recruiters," she retorted. "With all due respect, sir, our job is to note all potentials and especially the ones the Navy needs most. Right now, dirty tricks is a high-priority tasking."

The man opened his mouth to answer but closed it again. The pirates had reached the door and the boys were on the move. Neil aimed at the ceiling and opened fire.

"He's aiming too high," Rasmussen criticized. "What's the point in that?"

"Keep watching," Nick murmured as the pirates ducked under the random spray.

As soon as their heads were out of the way, Ellery fired his attachment to spin the two grenades over the pirates' heads and into the corridor behind them.

William groaned and drew his own heavy blaster. "Well, whatever, Ell. Let's do it your way, then."

"It looks like they're still working out their pecking order," Helena noted when Ellery feinted to one side and the trio fired on the pirates as they tried to scramble through the door.

"That was a smooth handover, though," Nick said, and she nodded.

"They compete regularly, then."

"But they don't let it interfere where it matters. That says a lot."

"I still don't like the friend."

"Noted, but when was there ever a dirty tricks squaddie we did like?"

"Point taken."

They turned to the screen as Ellery began to count.

"Three. Two..." he began, and the boys took shelter away from the door.

Free of incoming fire, the Dreth pirates made it two steps into the room before the grenades detonated. As soon as the blast had died away, the kids moved.

"How's my door coming along?" William demanded.

"Almost..." Gabe grunted as Neil and Ellery moved to the door.

"You want to make it quick, bro," Neil advised, and Helena noted that the boy used the comms instead of shouting the warning all around the station.

"They've only been doing this a year?" she asked, and the redhead's fingers flashed over her keyboard.

"As a team, yes. They didn't have the funds before, then they started doing part-timers."

"I don't want to know how you know that," Nick told her, and Rasmussen nodded in agreement.

Helena ignored them. "I wonder if there's a way to get them all to come on board," she mused and the tech answered.

"I can offer them a group scenario," she suggested. "Maybe give it an entry requirement that means you can only enter it with the group you successfully completed a previous scenario with."

She trailed off into incoherent mutters, began to type, and occasionally swiped her hand across the screen as she moved different elements into place.

On the screen, Gabe completed his unauthorized door and the four boys raced into the next room and out into a different corridor. William updated his directions and Ellery and Nick took point.

"We have to make up time," William observed as they headed to the data core.

"That is one hell of a team," Nick observed when they reached a cross corridor and formed a deflective turtle wall by facing each other and shifting the shields in their armor to the rear. Keeping in perfect step with each other, they formed pairs, put a hand on their partner's shoulders, and fired past them at the pirates waiting on either side.

"Front!" Ellery cried, and Bill took his hand off Neil's shoulder and raised it in the direction of the newly arrived pirates.

"What exactly is that supposed to do?" Ellery challenged. He was about to say more when the pirates opened fire.

"Well," Deckler sighed, closed his eyes, and shook his head. "It was good while it lasted."

"What do you mean?" Helena challenged. "It's still lasting."

"It is?" He opened his eyes.

"Oh, hells yes, it is." Nick dragged in a breath. "Look at that."

"This kid's definitely seen the footage," Rasmussen grumbled. "That's a perfect Stephanie move if I ever saw one."

His gaze fixed on the screen, Deckler had to agree. The blue shield that blocked the enemy fire was very Federation Witch, even if the kids' turtle idea was one her team hadn't been seen using yet.

"We really need that team," the professor observed. "They're already working in sync."

"I'm thinking of taking that footage and sending it to training," Helena stated.

"That's some intensive play," Nick observed. "Usually, it takes a couple of years to get that kind of rapport and teamwork."

"Do you think our recruits can learn something from a couple of dumb-ass civilians?" Rasmussen sounded almost insulted.

"Well, yeah," she answered and hurried to clarify. "Look at them. When have you ever seen a Navy team using that maneuver?"

As much as he didn't like it, the man had to agree.

The tech, following the conversation as she typed madly and swiped her laptop, looked up and added, "I'll raise the need for a tactics team to observe the civilian footage. There's no way we want to miss out on anything that might work."

"I thought IT was overrun," Rasmussen protested and the woman smiled.

"This isn't a job for techs," she advised him in a saccharine-sweet tone. "This is a job for the Marines, or the Rangers, or the Navy tacticians. There's a hell of a lot of footage, though. IT could probably help with some kind of programming sequence that could pinpoint when a group was successfully navigating an obstacle. The analysts could then go in, clip it, and send it for the tac guys to take a look at."

She favored each of them with a quick smile and returned to what she was doing. Helena caught the look on Rasmussen's face and smothered a smile. The boys had reached the data center and discovered the pirates had arrived there before them.

"That's it," Ellery grumbled. "It's game over for us."

"No, it's not," Bill told him, "but it is game over for them."

"You wanta tell me how you can say that?" Ellery challenged. "Because from where I stand, we look fairly screwed. No offense, your Magicness."

"Exactly!" William grinned. "I might not be able to shoot lightning out of my ass but we're all crack shots, right?"

What followed had very little to do with magic and far more to do with teamwork, good aim, and fast, accurate fire.

"That's it!" Nick announced. "I don't care if the kid has no magic. I want him in officer training."

"To hell with that," Helena challenged him. "You're looking at the first Navy Federation Witch commander." She turned to Rasmussen. "We have to have him."

The lieutenant commander stared at her as if she'd gone crazy but the redhead interrupted.

"I've got it. Let me interrupt your broadcast." She didn't wait for their permission but halved the screen and began running a movie trailer.

"Where the hell did you get that footage?" Rasmussen demanded and the woman grinned.

"IT has authorization to use any and all resources to produce products that will attract the right skills to the Navy," she told him as a Federation Witch in red-and-black armor raced down a corridor flanked by Marines.

"But power armor?" the man questioned as the witch on screen fired lightning bolts from his fingertips and fried a menacing dark shape that materialized in the corridor ahead of his squad.

The redhead gave him a pitying look. "We thought about using the traditional robes and whatnot but decided that sent the wrong message. You do know the Witch wears armor, right? Well, why would any of our potential recruits want to be stuck in robes when the person they want to be is in the best armor technology has to offer?"

"But red?"

"We wanted them to stand out from the Marine and Navy squads. It makes it easier for our analysts to see which player they're supposed to watch and monitor their movements. Besides, what magic-using wanna-be wants to blend in with the crowd? We want them attracted by the idea of having something special, right? Something that sets them apart?"

"Well, yes." Rasmussen sighed. "But we don't want them to be prima donnas about it either."

The tech snorted. "Pfft. That's what rookies is for. We get prima donnas in every branch. They all end up learning how to work the Navy way. My job is only to bait the trap."

"Trap?" The man's eyebrows raised to his hairline in outrage.

She inclined her head. "That is what we're doing, isn't it? Making something seem more attractive than it is in reality so we can attract and retain a recruit before they take a good look at the other options out there?"

He gave her a sour look but he didn't argue. The two recruiters kept their gazes fixed firmly on the screen. The tech had summed it up well but they weren't sure the lieutenant commander was ready for the realization that most of the recruiting arm knew exactly what they were doing.

Helena was sure that if she had magical talent, she'd try to find a way to fight alongside the Witch and avoid the Navy like the plague but there was no way in Hades she would say that out loud.

It was a good thing she liked her job and believed in what she was doing, or she'd have been in real trouble. Finding fighters for the Navy was the only way she could protect her world, and if people didn't look at their options, it wasn't her fault.

She divided her attention between the trailer the tech had pulled together while the boys were doing their run and the boys themselves. William still used technology, but every now and then, he'd try something magical.

It was as entertaining as hell, even if his friends had trouble adapting to the new tactics.

"Man, if you're going to keep doing shit like that, we're gonna need extra hours to cover the cost of practice sessions," Ellery grumbled.

William frowned. "What's wrong with working it the same way we always have? It's not like we're starting from scratch."

He grunted and thrust a hand toward a Dreth who reached toward the data bank. No lightning appeared but a ball of blue surged forward and burrowed through the pirate's armor. Moments later, he erupted from inside.

"I don't think I've ever seen Stephanie do that," Helena observed, and Nick shook his head

"Nope." He glanced at the tech. "Where did you get the footage of the Teloran ship?"

"It was taken from the cams of that new team the Navy's put together."

"The one you're not supposed to know anything about?" Rasmussen asked pointedly.

"Yeah, that one," she confirmed. "Only they had to do their run without a witch."

"So the witch in the trailer?"

"Well, we pulled footage from a pirate battle a year or so ago when the Witch did her thing but swapped her out for a male construct and added the armor."

"And the cape?" Rasmussen demanded.

"We have to have something cool for the clients," she told him. "What's cooler than a cape?"

She gestured to the screen where the boys jumped up and down in celebration. "So do you want to run this offer by them?"

"The scenario's ready?" Nick asked.

"It's gone through beta, and the algorithm's been tweaked to enhance any magical ability. If you really want to see if the kid has the potential to make it through without burning dry, you want these guys to run the scenario. And besides," she added and her eyes lit with anticipation. "This'll be a good opportunity for us to test the scenario on people who have no idea what to expect—and it'll help us to see if the movie will be a success."

Rasmussen shook his head. "A movie?"

"Yup, the trailer is for both a mod and a movie."

"Well, I hope the expense is worth it. Run your trailer past these guys and see if they take your bait." His face twisted as if the last word left a bad taste in his mouth.

The tech complied and they leaned forward as the boys were whisked away. Their looks of curious surprise as they were deposited in a movie theatre instead of being given the next round of scenario selection were almost comical.

The woman snickered. "Watch this."

She rolled the video and this time, they registered the external view of a huge Teloran vessel as if they watched it from the viewing deck of a Naval destroyer. The Naval witch stood with his hands on his hips and tilted his head as he studied the vessel, while the Marines and Naval officers around him stared at it in horror.

"Well," the witch said, "the bigger they are, the harder they fall. Where's my team?"

Rasmussen leaned closer to the tech. "We're giving them teams now?" he whispered.

"Only in the movie," she responded. "The higher-ups were a little sketchy as to what the exact organization would be for the witches so we had to come up with something on the fly."

"The movie doesn't promise teams, does it?" he asked and she shook her head.

"Don't worry, the movie promises nothing, and we run the usual disclaimer about it being a work of fiction and not an accurate portrayal of the realities of Navy life. You know the one."

Judging by the expression on Rasmussen's face, he wasn't entirely familiar with the disclaimer but also didn't seem to care. The boys watched the trailer with rapt attention.

As the witch stormed through the Teloran ship accompanied by a squad of Marines, Neil slapped William on the shoulder. "It's like it's made especially for you."

Ellery snorted. "It's brain candy," he muttered. "There's no such scenario."

"Sucker." Nick sneered as the trailer came to an end and the invitation rolled out.

"Welcome to the Closed Beta of Scenario Alpha Five," the voice-over intoned. *"On entry, the scenario will randomly select your character."*

Ellery snorted but the voice-over continued. *"On receiving your character, you will have ten minutes to acquire your kit from the ready room. At the end of your first run, your team will be able to change characters. Assuming you don't win, you will be allowed ten attempts to successfully complete the scenario after which time, you will need to earn entry to it again."*

"So it's a one-off?" Gabe whispered.

"Nope, it's a ten-times one-off," Ellery quipped.

Neil groaned. "Trust you to see the bright side, Ell." He looked at them. "So, do we give it a go?"

"Sure." Ellery sneered. "Why not? I'm fairly sure this is a completely lucky break and the randomly assigned wizard won't go to William."

He looked around the cinema as if he knew it was a set-up and they were being watched. "Isn't that right, guys?"

The other boys followed his gaze, their bodies tense. When no reply came, they began to laugh.

"You are such a jerk, Ellery!"

"You watch what happens," the boy retorted darkly. "William will get the wizard."

"Whatever, right?" Neil challenged. "It's not like you're interested, is it?"

Before he could answer that, the voice-over spoke again.

"Please indicate your choice. Do you wish to participate in this Closed Beta of 'Earth's Defenders?'"

The boys froze and exchanged glances before they nodded as one. Each of them reached out to a panel only they could see and pressed a button.

"Yes!" the tech crowed. "They're all in. Even Mr. Paranoid."

"So, who gets the wizard?" Rasmussen asked and she laid a finger alongside her nose.

"You'll see."

"Oh, that's rich!" Nick chortled seconds later when Ellery stood in the red-and-black armor of the wizard, a look of utter disbelief on his face.

"What the fuck?"

Helena ignored him and observed the look of disappointment that flashed across William's face. To give him credit, the boy hid his feelings quickly and slapped Ellery on the shoulder.

"Come on, Mr. Magic!" he said. "Let's go get your gear."

"And yours," Ellery replied but still looked bewildered. "It shoulda been you. What the fuck's wrong with the system? I'm not a witch."

William gave a short bark of laughter. "You are now. Try not to get killed, okay?"

"But I don't have any magic. Do I? I mean, does it come with the costume?"

Rasmussen turned an enquiring look to the tech but she shook her head. "Character assignment is random. They can choose their equipment but the rest is up to them as it is in the other scenarios."

"So the magic only comes if they carry the right markers."

She nodded confirmation. "Basically, yeah."

The man turned to the screen as the boys completed their preparations.

"Time to rumble!" Neil shouted as the world folded around them and positioned them in the troop compartment of a dropship.

It lifted and they whooped and hollered happily as it pitched and wove through a simulated approach to the Teloran hangar and blasted the doors clear.

"We took that from the Witch's run on the pirates," the tech told them as the shuttle touched down in the hangar bay and dropped its ramp.

The boys charged out with the half-dozen Marines the scenario had provided to bulk out their party.

"We gotta have the cannon fodder," the woman informed them when they glanced at her, a little confused by this.

The boys seemed to think it was normal too. They ran onto the deck and Ellery directed the squad according to his role. William,

Gabe, and Neil obeyed his orders without question, and they reached the hatch leading into the ship.

"I hate airlocks," Gabe grumbled as they stepped inside and the lock cycled.

The nearest Marine construct nodded in agreement and eyed the door warily. It seemed appropriate that he died first, although he fired into the half-dozen pirates waiting on the other side as they sprayed the door with flechettes.

"Where's our shield?" one of the other NPCs demanded as the enemy delivered another round of concerted fire.

He died too, while Ellery directed them to the door. His horrified voice spoke over the team's private comms.

"I can't do this," he told them. "I have nothing, man—no magic, nothing. Bill, I know you're meant to be a tank, but could you..."

William shrugged. "Okay, as long as the scenario lets me."

Ellery led the way out of the door, firing and screaming defiance at the waiting pirates. His body fell, riddled with sharp shards of metal as the Marines and his teammates raced past. They eliminated the pirates and sprinted to the elevators that would take them to the next level.

Any hopes of success were dashed almost immediately. Doors opened ahead and behind them and they died in a storm of fire.

"That was brutal!" Nick muttered when the boys came to in the white room.

From the way they gasped, coughed, and felt for holes, the scenario was a far more real than they'd anticipated. Ellery came straight to the point.

"Swap characters."

"What?" William asked, "but—"

"I don't want to be the wizard. I can't be the wizard. You have to."

"But, the system—"

"The system said we could change characters at the end of the first scenario and I really want to change characters. You be the witch."

"But—"

Ellery laid his hand on William's shoulder and pushed his face close to his friend's. "Someone has to be the witch and you're the only one who's ever said they wanted it. It's up to you."

"Yeah, Bill." Neil added encouragement. "I saw that shield you put up in the last scenario. It's exactly what we need here."

"Do you think you could do a bubble like the Federation Witch does?" Gabe interjected. "We really need you to do that if we're gonna reach the next level. We really do."

William stared at them in disbelief. "But what if I can't?"

Ellery curled his lip in mockery. "You did it before," he told his friend bluntly. "I can't see why you wouldn't be able to do it again."

"Wow, Ellery." Neil wasn't impressed. "Now, you believe in him. Now?"

The boy shrugged. "Well, yeah. Why do you think we were given this scenario? Do you think it's only here for our entertainment? No. It's here to help the Federation discover new witches. We're at war, man."

He thumped his hand against Williams chest and gave him a gentle shove. "And you're the next weapon."

Rasmussen glared at the tech. "Did you put something in there to tip him off?"

She shook her head and Nick chuckled. "Man, I like this kid. He's cynical, paranoid, and absolutely perfect for the dirty tricks boys."

"Or analysts," Helena added. "He'd make a darn good analyst, too."

Her colleague gave her a mock glare. "You keep your eyes off him."

She raised her hands in mock surrender. "Fine, but you have to offer him two options if you bring him in and my vote's for analyst."

"Noted." He had already turned toward the screen, where William had finally been convinced to take on the role of witch.

"Happy birthday, man," Neil told him and slapped the shoulder of his red-and-black armor.

"Yeah." Ellery snorted. "Nice cape."

This time, they came out of the airlock behind a shield of blue fire and the grin on William's face could have lit an entire stadium. It vanished a few moments later when a hail of projectiles struck the shield and it rippled alarmingly.

William faltered and the shield wavered. One of the Marines turned to him. "You have to make it so we can fire out of it."

The boy looked startled and the shield vanished. No one reacted fast enough to avoid the second storm of fire.

"Fuck, that hurts," Ellery grumbled as he pushed off the white room floor. "What happened?"

William remained where he was. "I feel like I've been run over by a battle cruiser."

"Yeah? Well, join the club. What the fuck happened out there?"

The team witch tried to sit but flopped onto his back when his effort proved futile. "Do you know how much energy holding a shield takes?"

Ellery shook his head and smiled. "Nope. I can't create them, remember."

Neil regarded his friend with admiration. "It looks like you might be the real deal, Bill."

"You think?" The thought teased a smile to the boy's face and he pushed to his feet. "You wanta try that again?"

"I'd like to get off the first level," Ellery told him. "This has to be the toughest scenario ever."

The dropship exploded the second its ramp settled on the floor.

"That was so unfair," Neil complained and dragged himself to his feet.

"I guess I shoulda put a shield up first, huh?" William asked, and the others regarded him with wide eyes.

"You think?"

"Shut up and get in there," the boy joked in response. "We're not done yet."

This time, they made it out of the hangar and past the first pirate ambush to reach the elevator well.

"Are you sure this is the only way up?" Ellery asked as Gabe hooked into the Teloran ship's systems.

Moments later, the boy confirmed it. "Yup."

With a sigh, the boys faced the elevator bank. "Well, we don't have to all take the same one," William concluded and directed his squad into four different ones.

They only lost a quarter of their forces when one of the shafts exploded.

"What the fuck was that?"

"I don't know but I don't like it," Ellery retorted. He looked at William. "Which way and what lies in between?"

Their witch gave directions and they wasted no time. The first floor was very similar to the computing level Stephanie had led her team across while trying to find the Teloran bridge and William came up with a similar solution.

"Magic works on walls, right?"

"Are you sure, Bill?"

"Well... Maybe?"

"Crap."

"Do something, sir," one of the Marine NPCs urged and fired at the door. "These aren't Dreth."

"They're not?" Even Ellery was caught by surprise.

"Nope."

"Oh, crap." The boy hissed in a breath when he caught sight of his first-ever Teloran.

"Are you sure that's allowed?" Rasmussen asked the tech and his tone suggested he didn't think it was.

"Yes, sir, I am," the redhead snapped. "I'm in the business of finding recruits, not breaching security. I like my job."

He frowned dubiously at her for a moment before he refocused on the screen. The light forms of the Telorans now moved to surround the team.

"Are you sure this is how they act?"

"We ran the analytics on every piece of footage we could drag off the cameras of the Marines who accompanied her. We're almost sure."

"But this isn't from the pirate battle—"

"No, sir, it's not," the tech confirmed. She looked smug but didn't elaborate on exactly where the footage had come from.

"Hmmm."

The boys' squad had broken free from the oncoming Teloran troops and hurried toward the bridge when a sinister darkness formed in the corridor ahead of them.

"Oh, fuck. What the hell is that?" Ellery asked.

His answer came in the form of two dark discs that spun away from the alien mage.

The boy immediately fell prone but the Marine behind him wasn't so lucky. One of the discs tore through his armor and vanished. The second savaged a hole in the wall where Ellery's head had been. The boy's face turned white.

"That fucker's magic," he muttered in a strangled tone, "and I don't mean in a good way."

He tapped William on the ankle. "You are so definitely up."

"Yeah?" his friend retorted. "Well, while I deal with him, you need to take care of his friends."

"Friends?" Ellery looked around and caught sight of the Telorans approaching from the side. "Oh…"

He scrambled to his feet but flung himself down again when another two discs spun toward him. "Will you do something with the shields, already?" he shouted. "Talk about a good witch being hard to find."

"It's like good troops," William snapped in reply. "Do you want to stop bitching and do your job?"

"Listen to who's talking." Ellery scrambled to his feet and unleashed a barrage at the approaching enemy, switching weapons continuously to provide a varied stream of attacks.

William swept a hand down and a blue haze appeared between his friend and the oncoming adversaries. Ignoring Ellery's muttered, "About time," he twisted his hand in front of his face and made a flinging motion toward the Teloran mage.

"Well, I'll be…" Nick hissed in a breath and raised his hand.

Helena high-fived him. "Hell, yeah! We've found ourselves a witch."

"So what's he doing now?" Rasmussen's puzzled question brought their attention to the screen.

They immediately saw the reason for his question. William used both hands now, the shields still in place and forgotten as he made what might be called a gathering motion to draw fire from the ships' walls. He blended it into a coruscating ball of blue and gold, which he flung toward the Teloran.

When his enemy was focused on the glowing orb, the witch laughed, drew his blaster, and delivered a burst of rapid fire at the dark mage. He released the weapon, raised his hands to head height, and moved them toward his chest.

Blue fire mingled with darkness and the recruiters and scientist leaned forward.

"What's he doing?" Rasmussen asked, and the tech shook her head.

"I have no idea."

Whatever it was, the results were spectacular and the resulting explosion annihilated the witch, his team, the Telorans, and the alien ship in seconds.

Rasmussen slapped his hands together and turned to Nick and Helena. "Send him an invitation. We don't want One R&D to get to him before us."

CHAPTER SEVEN

Doggerels bustled with life when the two men arrived.

"I can see why the boys like this place," Arne observed as the bar's atmosphere enveloped them when they walked through the door.

The bartenders moved swiftly and efficiently, while the customers smiled and chatted where they sat at the bar or took their drinks to the tables in one of two lounge areas. These featured sports events running on both screens.

The commentary from them didn't intrude, though, and it took the Marine several moments to locate the nullifiers that bordered each distinct area. "This place is very well equipped."

Matthias followed his gaze and grinned. "Well, now I know why she likes it here."

"Yeah," his companion agreed. "If these are the entertainment sections, the private spaces must be real private."

They surveyed the bar area and finally stopped so they could scan the entertainment areas as well. After a moment of silent searching, Arne turned to him. "Do you see them?"

"No." He frowned. "They did say it was here, right?"

The other man nodded. "I checked twice. Amy almost yelled at me before she told me I had to get it right."

"And what did you say?"

"I asked her what she thought I was trying to do and had her go through it again," he responded, his expression deadpan.

"I bet that went down well."

"You could say that." Arne frowned. "She wouldn't have given me the wrong place out of spite, would she?"

Matthias shook his head. "She might not have liked having to repeat herself, but she's not stupid. If this is where we're supposed to meet, this is where she'll have told you. E doesn't play that kind of game."

"Uh-huh..." The master sergeant's tone and expression made it clear that the woman played any number of games, so why not this one, but he ignored him.

"How about we have a beer while we wait?"

"They can't all be invisible, can they?" Arne asked and scrutinized the bar again.

Matthias shrugged. "Maybe they're late."

"Fine. Now, about that beer. What kind of dark brews do they have here?"

They'd almost reached the bar when one of the waitresses stepped close to Matthias. "Why, hello, sweetheart," she began with a throaty purr. Her eyes roved over him in a way that was all curiosity and compliment.

He swallowed and looked around, hoping to see Elizabeth. When he didn't, he turned his gaze reluctantly to the girl. She was an attractive package, about two feet shorter than E but with a tight, compact physique topped by a pretty face with well-defined cheekbones, luminescent blue eyes, and short dark hair that curled along her jawline.

"What can I get you?" she asked, her voice an inviting purr. He swallowed hard and barely stopped himself from telling her that she could probably get him into considerable trouble.

"Two beers," he replied, cleared his throat, and felt ridiculously grateful that she had asked something he could answer.

The gratitude vanished when she placed a hand on his chest and traced a finger down the line of buttons on his shirt. "Anything else?" she asked, leaned closer, and looked at him from under her lashes.

Matthias took a quick step back and glanced at Arne.

The master sergeant had reddened and his lips were pressed into a tight line like he tried valiantly to keep a straight face. The commander made that easier by an attempt to redirect the waitress toward him.

"No, but I'm sure my friend wants to order...uh, something," he managed to say and rested a hand on his companion's arm.

Whatever he thought of the hand-off, Arne kept it hidden behind a toothy smile as he stepped closer to the girl. "We'd like two pints of dark and half a dozen lamb kebabs."

"Really?" she asked and looked from one to the other. "That's the best the two of you could think of?"

"No." The Marine looked puzzled. "We really like the dark and the lamb smells great."

The waitress put one hand on her hip, inclined her head, and laid her other hand on Arne's bicep as she slid past him until she stood in front of Matthias. Giving the master sergeant a push with her fingertips, she stretched herself against the commander's front, took her hand off her hip, and slid it around his waist.

"Sweetheart," she murmured. "You and I should have a long and private chat. I'm sure we have so much in common."

He backed away and twisted out of the loop of her arm as he did so. Unfortunately, he hadn't noticed either the chair beside him or the table right behind him and so tangled his feet in one and fell over the other.

Arne's embarrassed oath cut through his momentary surprise at what had happened, and he rolled to his feet and kicked himself free of the chair. The woman slipped around the wreckage as he scrambled to his feet.

"Look!" he told her and the word emerged louder than he intended. "I'm waiting for someone and you're not her, okay?"

To his surprise, she burst into a delighted chuckle and pointed to where Vishlog and Lars had appeared at the bottom of a set of stairs leading to the next floor. "Your party's upstairs, sweetheart," she told him in tones he recognized all too well.

"Elizabeth?" he asked and thankfully remembered to lower his voice. "Is that you?"

She gave him a purely Elizabeth smirk. "You are such a funny man."

He stooped until his face was an inch from her own. "You're gonna have to prove it."

Her smile turned slightly sad but she raised her hand and drew his head closer. "The Berlin contract," she whispered when her lips grazed his ear. "I stung your employers for—"

His eyes widened when she gave him the exact figures and he jerked his head back for a better look at her face.

"What have you done to yourself?" he whispered. "I don't see anything I know...and—and why?"

This time, he didn't resist when she slid her arm around his waist. "I had to know," she told him solemnly.

"Know what?" he asked.

Arne caught the bewilderment on his face but noted the fact that he didn't attempt to pull away. The Marine tilted his head, studied the woman, and frowned. Finally, he stepped in close and murmured, "Elizabeth?"

She flashed him a happy smile and he raised his eyebrows.

"Oh." He wandered away to join Lars and Vishlog, chuckling softly.

"What?" Matthias asked. "What does oh mean?'"

Arne waited until they had joined him before he replied. "It's a good thing you're the faithful type," he told the retiring officer and led the way upstairs, leaving Lars and Vishlog to follow and Elizabeth and Matthias to trail along behind.

He was surprised by the man's relaxed attitude until he glanced back and noticed Amy and Elle emerge from behind the bar. Startled, he gave the dark-haired woman beside him a hard look.

"You didn't trust me?"

"I wanted to be sure."

"But—"

"It's a girl thing," she told him as they reached the first landing.

"Oh," he managed to respond when they stepped onto the second floor.

"This way," she instructed and drew him away from the open door where a party was in full swing.

Matthias caught sight of Arne watching from inside the door but allowed her to pull him to a door several feet down the corridor. The room beyond was small—some kind of supplies cupboard but big enough for E to drag the door closed behind them.

"I'm sorry," she whispered and her eyes glittered in the light of the dull globe that hung overhead. "I had to know if you'd be..." She waved a hand as the words failed her. "You know."

"Faithful?" he asked and looked at her with his eyebrows arched. When he saw the anguish in her face, he gave her a tender smile. "What made you think I wouldn't be?"

"Nothing," she admitted. "You seemed like the most faithful guy I know. Everything told me you were good."

"And yet?" he prodded and she blushed, but her gaze never left his face.

Her hand moved uncertainly between them. "This... I mean, us... I mean..." She stopped and bit her lip. "You're the best thing that's ever happened to me and I have trouble trusting you with my heart."

Matthias gazed at her and a small smile played over his lips. To him, she was perfect, still his Elizabeth regardless of the form she wore. He was about to say as much when she continued.

"I'm scared," she whispered and he let his smile widen.

"That's okay—" he began but she cut him off.

"You don't understand. I don't do scared."

"And I thought I was the only one terrified by this relationship," he admitted and his smile faded.

A look of wonder crept into her face. "You did?"

"I did." He wrapped his arms around her and pulled her close. "I've been terrified you'd...I don't know...not want me or something."

She laid her palm against her cheek. "Same."

"And I don't want it to ever end," he murmured, his voice husky with emotion and the sudden fire of desire.

Elizabeth swallowed hard and stared into his eyes. "Neither do I," she admitted, her voice hoarse.

"For true?" he asked and leaned back so he could see her.

A shy smile quirked her lips. "For true."

"So this is it, huh? We're gonna stay together."

She wrinkled her nose, an Elizabeth gesture that looked a little odd on the unfamiliar face. "Yup. Till death and all that."

Matthias smiled. He couldn't not smile. The joy that surged through him made him almost dizzy and he stooped with a sudden abruptness and cupped the back of her head in his hand as she raised her lips to meet his.

The shift of her body against him startled them both and they drew back. His eyes widened as he watched the dark-haired shell fall away and her taller form emerge. She gasped and looked at herself.

"That tricky little Witch!" she exclaimed, and Matthias thought the term probably should have started with a B.

"What's she done now?" he asked, and she swept her hand up and down her body.

"This! She told me I'd know."

He began to feel like he was missing the obvious again. "Know what?"

Elizabeth chuckled. "That damn girl said I'd know when True Love's Kiss happened."

"You said that like it had capitals," he observed. "Exactly what do you think she meant?"

She closed the distance between them, curled a hand around the back of his head, and pulled his face down to hers. He slid his arms around her and drew her close to kiss her as thoroughly as she kissed him.

"That sneaky little shit." Elizabeth giggled when they drew apart. "Now, she'll know what I've been doing."

"She won't, you know," Matthias suggested and a smile curved his lips as he wriggled his eyebrows suggestively.

He saw her give the idea serious thought before she stepped away reluctantly. "Our guards will come looking for us very soon," she told him and he sighed.

"I think we'll be lucky if they aren't waiting right outside the door," he agreed.

"Especially as I don't think they swept in here."

Matthias groaned. "We've been lucky they've given as long as they have, then." Elizabeth laughed and stroked his cheek.

"I'm glad we had this long," she said and he nuzzled her hand as they turned toward the door.

"Shall we?" he asked and offered her his arm.

"Let's," she agreed and linked her arm with his.

To their surprise, no one waited in the corridor outside and the party was in full swing.

"What's this all about, anyway?" he whispered as they walked as unobtrusively as they could through the door. Their attempt to be unnoticed was a failure.

A shrill whistle cut the air, and the party fell silent. Stephanie stepped out from behind Lars and began to clap and the rest of the gathering joined her. Behind them, Lars and Vishlog closed the doors.

Elizabeth looked at Matthias and rolled her eyes. "I really am sorry about this," she said and he frowned and wondered if he was destined to be forever puzzled.

"Well, it's about time, you two." The Witch chortled, and a chorus of good-natured laughter followed.

E sighed impatiently and slid her arm free. She faced the gathering. "Do one of you miscreants want to explain what's going on?"

Stephanie cast Matthias a coquettish look before she focused on Elizabeth with feigned surprised. "But I thought you knew."

"You know exactly what I mean, young lady!"

The girl tried to pout but burst out laughing instead. She turned to Matthias. "It's a farewell party," she told him. "We're saying goodbye to Elizabeth for a couple of months."

She paused to let him absorb the news and went on before he could find the words to express his surprise. "And we've cut the apron strings and nominated Amy as her stand-in for all things green on this earth."

Matthias looked for Elizabeth's chief bodyguard and noted the sour look on the woman's face. Stephanie ignored it and gestured cheerfully.

"So, poor Ames has the task of playing the very scary Emerald while Ms. E gallivants about the universe on official One R&D business."

Amy stuck her tongue out and stalked to where Avery stood behind the bar. She said nothing but held her hand out and made "give it" motions with her fingers. He raised an eyebrow and looked at Elizabeth.

The bodyguard gave her boss a defiant stare and turned to threaten Avery with a look. He glanced at E again and made a mock show of relief when she nodded.

The woman looked like she was about to climb over the bar and secure her own drink and that there might be blood involved. Quickly, Avery whisked out a very complicated cocktail and handed it to her.

She froze, stared at the cocktail, glanced at her boss, and very gently took the glass from his hand.

Elizabeth resumed her hold on Matthias's arm. "She'll be okay."

As he watched the girl drain the glass and demand a second, he wasn't so sure.

Stephanie came to join them. "She really doesn't want to be Emerald," she informed them.

"It's only for a couple of months," E replied with a shrug and pulled Matthias closer. "Besides, it's not like I've left her to face it all alone."

He sighed as Amy picked up a third glass. "Doesn't want to be Emerald," looked like an understatement to him.

"Nothing will happen," Elizabeth assured him. "It'll only be a couple of months' worry and then I'll be back."

The third cocktail followed the other two and he winced as Avery handed Amy a fourth.

Elizabeth continued, oblivious. "You'll see."

CHAPTER EIGHT

Stephanie sat on the edge of the bed and tried to push Bumblebee's head off her lap and wriggle her foot out from under Zeekat's behind. The two had taken one look at her when she'd arrived and decided they hadn't had enough attention.

"Zee, get your furry fat ass off my foot or so help me—" she cried.

He twisted his head so he looked at her upside down, then flopped over so his back rested against her shins and his butt crushed her feet.

"Agh!" Both startled and looked at her but she ignored them.

She managed to free herself, stood, and headed to the bathroom. "You cannot follow me in here," she told them defiantly.

Ignoring their morose looks, she opened the door, only to be stopped by the insistent chime of her tablet.

For a long moment, she thought about ignoring it but decided it was either someone very foolhardy or someone from a different time zone and that she'd better give it attention.

With a sigh, she turned and caught the prick of Bumblebee's ears.

"Oh, no, you don't," she told him. "No. No. No. Nononono!"

Her fingers grasped the tablet's casing and she yanked it out from between the cat's jaws as he tried to drag it off her desk.

"Yes?" Her greeting was more abrupt than she'd intended and Bee gave her a smug look from the opposite side of the room.

Stephanie leaned against the wall and undid her boot with one hand.

"Hello?" she repeated when the tablet remained silent.

"Uh...Stephanie?" She'd never heard Captain Emil sound so hesitant before. "I haven't caught you at an inopportune moment, have I?"

"Oh no." She tried for breezy but still managed to sound short of breath. *Damn cats!*

"Oh. Good." He sounded like he wasn't sure he should believe her and hadn't decided if he should offer to call her back.

"How can I help you, Captain?" she asked and circumvented both options.

He came straight to the point. "I'm calling about mages for the two Navy ships."

The unexpectedness of the request took her by surprise. "Tell me about the Navy ships," she said to play for time while she wracked her brain in an effort to catch up with something she felt she should know but definitely didn't.

"I thought Elizabeth explained it to you," he replied and she sighed.

"Humor me. It's been a long week and we haven't really touched base."

The captain gave an amused snort at that. "I understand. So, are you aware the Navy assigned us two destroyers?"

"I knew they would insist on something to bulk the *Knight* up. To be honest, I thought they would try to persuade you to move to a larger ship."

"I think they might have but we made it very clear that wasn't an option, so they offered us an escort instead."

"But they don't have anything that can keep up with the *Knight*," she responded.

"They didn't," he corrected her, "but they do now."

He paused to let her reach her own conclusions and Stephanie waited. She could sense that he had more to say and that whatever he was about to tell her, he wasn't sure she would like it.

"I take it you've done training since then?" she asked to move the conversation along.

"Yes, considerably more," he admitted, and she smiled. "So...you know that simulation where you put the ships up against a Teloran—" Her gasp stopped him short.

"You ran them through that as part of their training?" She wasn't sure whether to be amused or horrified. "Who'd you get to play me?"

"I had the *Knight* simulate you," he confessed, and his tone suggested that he waited for her to take offense.

Instead, she laughed. "And did she do a good job?"

"Scarily so. I can forward you the footage, if you like."

"Please. And you'd better send Elizabeth a copy too."

"At her usual address?"

"Yes. She'll get it." Stephanie didn't tell him that the woman would get it no matter where she was located because BURT would make sure she did. She simply let the captain assume she was at HQ.

No one needed to know it wasn't true, no matter how much they were trusted. What someone didn't know they couldn't accidentally let slip.

"Okay, so you mentioned something about mages for these ships. What did you mean by that?"

"Yes. What emerged very clearly from the simulation was that with no magic onboard, the Navy vessels don't stand a chance. The other captains really want the magical help and I can't say I blame them."

"I can't either," she hastened to assure him. "And I'm sorry. It's possibly something we should have anticipated. Obviously, the Naval recruitment isn't going as well as they had hoped, but if these ships are sent as the Knight's escort, we need to ensure that they have what they need. And, of course, to structure the contracts so they remain securely within One R&D's protection."

He sighed. "Agreed. I'd hate to think the Navy might decide to... uh, enlist them."

"They could try," she reassured him with a laugh. "But I doubt either E or the Meligornians would stand for that. Okay, I'll ask Tethis if we can spare some of our teachers. How many do you need?"

"We didn't discuss it," Emil admitted and she could hear the smile in his voice. "Captain Yale simply mentioned it to your simulation, who agreed to look into it. I'm now raising it with the real you in the hope that we can pull something together."

Stephanie hopped across the room so she could sit on the edge of the bed, glad he hadn't opted for a video call. Once she'd settled, she set about yanking her other boot clear of her foot. The two cats watched her with baleful eyes but stayed on their beds.

She eyed them cautiously and set her boot on the floor beside them. Bumblebee pricked his ears and Zeekat lifted his head.

"Can I have a week?" she asked. "It'll give me time to go over the footage with Tethis so we can decide which mages would work best on which ships. It's not like putting the wrong person on the wrong ship will be an easy mistake to fix."

"A week is fine," Emil agreed, "and thank you.

"No problems, Emil. I'll get back to you in a week. Is this the best time for you?"

"If it's no trouble for you," he confirmed, and she decided she wouldn't tell him what time it was for her.

"I'll speak to you then," she said. "Is there anything else I can do for you?"

"No, but thank you for asking. I'll let you get some rest." He hung up before she could respond and left her staring at the tablet in consternation.

So he had known after all. She blushed, secured her tablet in her desk drawer, and picked her boots up. The cats watched her with alert ears and she made sure to lock the drawer securely before she headed to the shower.

Judging by the sour looks on their faces and the impatient sighs, they'd definitely planned something. The idea made her smile as she closed the door behind her. At least she could have a shower in peace. She only hoped they let her sleep in peace too.

To her relief, the cats chose to let her rest and she woke refreshed and ready to call Tethis.

"Do you want me to come over there?" he asked, then added. "It might be more secure than here."

"I'll send Avery and the car," Stephanie told him. "When is convenient?"

"I could be ready in an hour," he assured her. "Do I need to bring anything?"

"Popcorn?" The suggestion was out before she could stop it and he laughed.

"That good, is it?"

She sobered. "To be honest, I don't know, but we get to see me in simulation."

"Hurry and send the car. This I have to see."

Stephanie hung up with a smile and went to get ready. Her smile vanished when she saw what the cats had done to her wardrobe.

"Elizabeth will kill the two of you." She growled with real annoyance as she studied the ruined door. "And that's nothing to what I'll do when I have time. Do you have any idea how hard it is to find a pair of boots that comfortable?"

The felines leant against one another, cocked their heads, and observed her with almost bored expressions.

"Well, do you?" she demanded and Zeekat flopped onto his stomach with a groan. She might have forgiven him, except he stretched a lazy paw out and hooked the remains of one of her boots into his mouth.

"Why you—" Her reprimand was interrupted by a knock at the door.

"Count yourself lucky, cat," she snapped and shook a finger at him as she stalked to the door.

Avery stood outside with Lars a foot behind him. Both men raised an eyebrow at the sight of her in her nightdress.

Avery swallowed. "You pinged me?" he croaked and Stephanie nodded and tried to keep her embarrassment in check.

"Yes. Could you pick Tethis up from the school and bring him here? We'll be in conference for most of the day." Somehow, she kept her voice cool and authoritative and managed not to die of mortification when he gave her a crisp salute and headed to the garage.

Lars quirked an eyebrow and Stephanie pretended not to see it and shut the door. It was all she could do not to yell at the cats as she walked across the room and began to ready herself to face the day. Hell! She hadn't even been up an hour and she was already making mistakes.

It was hard not to laugh when she was dried and dressed and came out of the bathroom to find Bumblebee seated two feet away from the door with most of her other boot dangling from his mouth.

"I will not chase you," she told him and he cocked his head. "I will ask Vishlog to speak to you."

At mention of the Dreth's name, the cat tilted his head the other way and flicked his tail.

"Oh, yes," she assured him. "He'll know exactly how to deal with you."

"The pair of you," she added and gave Zee a fierce glare.

The cat rolled on the remains of her other boot, paused mid-wriggle with all four feet in the air, and stared at her from his upside-down perspective. She shook her head. "You're incorrigible. Both of you," she told them and stepped out into the corridor.

Vishlog waited beside Lars.

"Oh, thank heavens!" Stephanie exclaimed when she caught sight of him.

"Cats?" the big Dreth asked with a knowing smile on his face.

"Cats," she agreed and he held his hand out.

Lars groaned but pulled his wallet out. "You owe me," he told Stephanie when he saw her watching.

His exaggerated dismay made her smile and she shook her head. "I don't owe you anything," she retorted. "Even I'm not dumb enough to make a bet with Vishlog where the cats are concerned."

He turned to the Dreth. "And now she's calling me dumb," he complained.

The warrior patted his shoulder consolingly. "Don't let it bother you, little man," he rumbled. "People do that to me all the time." He pushed away from the wall and walked into Stephanie's room, fished in his waist bag, and called to the felines. "Here kitties. Vishlog has treeats!"

Stephanie caught Lars's eye. "You drew the short straw again?" she asked and he shrugged.

"I sent the guys on a few days leave," he explained. "They needed it."

"And what about you?"

"You know me, Steph." He smiled. "I don't have a life outside of work."

She tilted her head and studied him carefully. "You know that's not healthy, right?"

He snorted. "Listen to who's talking," he teased but quickly grew serious. "So, what's on the agenda for today? And I should warn you that Avery had a good run with the traffic and will arrive in a half-hour. You have enough time for breakfast."

"Tethis promised to bring popcorn," she informed him. "Who needs breakfast?"

"Do I get to have popcorn too?"

"That depends. How interested are you to see how the *Knight* and her escorts performed in training?"

"Did you want coffee, ice cream, or soft drink with your popcorn?"

"Why do you even bother to ask?"

He grinned and led the way to the cafeteria. "You can help me with the trays."

It was a good plan but Lars had planned his ambush better and the team blocked the exit from the cafeteria once she'd collected her coffee.

"You need to sit and eat, Steph," Johnny informed her and made turning motions with his finger, while Frog darted past her to pull a chair back.

She balanced the coffee tray on one hand and considered her chances of getting out of there with the contents intact. On the one hand, she knew she could win her way free. On the other, she knew they'd refuse to refill her cup and that Tethis would probably be on their side when he arrived.

It was probably better to surrender now than have to surrender later. At least this way, she'd escape the cafeteria sooner.

By the time the mage arrived, she had found the footage Emil had sent and prioritized it.

"I thought you said you sent them on leave," she grumbled at Lars as the other team members arranged themselves around the conference room.

"I gave them leave but it doesn't mean they took it," he admitted and looked mildly annoyed.

"We're merely following the examples we've been set," Marcus quipped.

"Besides, someone mentioned popcorn," Frog added and settled into a seat beside Garach, "and Tethis makes the best."

"Or he knows where to source the best," Brenden corrected and the other man grinned.

Stephanie rolled her eyes. She was secretly pleased that they'd see the footage but didn't want to tell them that. For a moment, she was reminded of what it had been like in the early days and also a little of family.

She looked around the room as she arranged the footage in order and realized that was exactly what it felt like—family. Before she could dwell on that thought too much, the smell of warm butter and overheated corn kernels wafted into the room.

"Popcorn!" Frog cried and Johnny rested his head on his fingertips and shook it gently.

Tethis responded to the cry with a grandfatherly chuckle. "Somehow, I thought you would all be here," he told them and held up four shopping bags stuffed full of the treat, "so I brought extra in case. Now, please tell me you're staying."

Johnny snorted. "Since you put it that way..."

"They heard they'd been simulated and couldn't help themselves," Stephanie explained, as if that made their presence any better.

The mage gave her an indulgent smile and sat carefully beside her. "Now, why don't you show an old mage the ships who need our help."

She didn't know quite what to say to that so she started the first battle sequence. The running commentary from the boys was almost as entertaining as their reaction to the way the *Knight* had programmed their simulations.

"That is so you!" Marcus roared and slapped Frog on the shoulder as the small man charged at a Teloran mage.

They all winced as he jumped when he should have ducked and was shredded by dark magic.

Lars flinched and sucked air through pursed lips as his onscreen self tried to reach Garach and met a similarly messy fate.

"I don't think the *Knight* likes us," Johnny complained when his simulated counterpart was sucked into space and skewered by debris from the explosion.

"Don't take it personally," Stephanie warned them. "Look at what she's doing to herself."

It was true. As terrible as some of their fates had been, the *Knight* was as merciless with the ship itself. She'd obviously studied the effect of the Teloran's weapons on vessels in the battle for Dreth.

"And they all felt the effect," Tethis mused when she explained what happened with all but the last surviving crew. "That must have been incentive indeed."

"Their performance only improved after the *Knight* brought it in," Johnny observed. "Before that, they simply went through the motions."

This brought a round of murmured agreement.

Garach shivered. "I would work to avoid that too," he announced, and the others seconded it.

Frog looked around. "Where's Vishlog?"

"He's taking care of the cats," Stephanie told him. "Why?"

"Because he really should be here," the man answered and pulled his tablet out to send the Dreth a message.

The large warrior joined them shortly after. "The kitties are playing on Meligorn," he told her. "They needed the run."

He settled into the seat beside his nephew and was soon laughing or looking as mortified as the others when they worked through the rest of the simulations. His reactions made her laugh and she was glad Frog had thought to bring him in.

They spent the rest of the morning and most of the afternoon going over the footage, with Lars and the team taking notes on how to improve the tactical responses from the *Knight*. When they'd watched the final scenario, the security head pushed to his feet.

"I think I need to talk to the Marines," he told her and the others stood with him.

Stephanie nodded. "I'll be here with Tethis. We'll put two mages on each of the destroyers but we have to decide who."

The team stilled and glanced at Lars. "Good luck with that," he said. "Those will be hard choices to make."

"Thanks, Lars," she snipped in response and sounded put out.

He laughed and headed to the door. "Trust me, the conversation we're about to have will be equally as interesting."

She didn't doubt it and she wished she could sit in and listen to how it played out. Her priorities lay elsewhere, though, so she waved the team goodbye and turned to Tethis. "What do you think?"

"I think K'trevl and Rayz need to be on the same ship and they need to be out doing something," Tethis told her.

Stephanie regarded him thoughtfully before she brought stills up of the command decks of both the *Henry Chauvel* and the *Cathay Williams*. "Which one do you think they'll suit best?" he asked.

"It depends who you want to put on the other one."

"I thought Felarif and maybe L'thinis."

"How well do you think Felarif will do under a female captain?"

The mage shrugged. "He'd do okay. I'm more concerned with how K'trevl and Rayz would do under any human."

"Hmmm." She frowned. "Captain Yale seems to be the steadier of the two. If sensitivity's required, maybe she'd be a better option for them."

Tethis gave it some consideration and nodded. "And Felarif will adapt. He's fairly resilient when it comes to new situations."

"What's he like with creating new situations?" she asked and imagined the havoc the rakish nobleman could cause on a Naval destroyer.

"I'll impress on him exactly how unimpressed you will be if he creates one." He chuckled. "He doesn't want you mad at him any more than the rest of us do."

She blushed. "I'm the bogey man, huh?"

The old man smirked. "You are and I couldn't think of anyone better for keeping that young rascal in line. Merely the thought of the Morgana visiting him will be enough."

Stephanie snorted. "Fine. I guess I can live with that."

Tethis slapped his palms against his knees and pushed to his feet. "I'll talk to them."

He brushed his robes to make sure there were no crumbs clinging to them. "Do you think young Avery will mind taking me back now?"

She rose with him. His question made her smile. "I don't think he'd have it any other way."

Todd stepped off the shuttle and sighed with contentment. It was good to be back on board the *Knight*—so good it almost felt like home. Ka slapped him on the shoulder.

"She's not here, you know."

"I know but I'm still glad to be here."

"Let's not keep them waiting." She gave him a gentle shove and gestured to the knot of Marines who stood at the airlock entrance. "What do you think they want?"

He shrugged and strode toward them. "There's only one way to find out."

The Marines bristled as he came closer and a sergeant stepped forward. "Halt! You can't come in without taking hold of this."

A Marine corporal stepped beside him with a short metal bar in his hand.

"Security," the corporal snapped and stared directly into his eyes. "How do you feel about the Witch?"

So it was like that, was it? He took the bar.

"I love her," he stated and tried to make it sound more like fan than boyfriend.

Behind him, a chorus of groans followed. Someone even made mock barfing sounds. At least two someones, maybe three. He suppressed a smile. Gary, Jimmy, and Ka would regret that in their next training session.

He loved the Witch and that was all there was to it. What the hell else was he supposed to say?

The bar cooled beneath his touch and grew icy. His eyes widened. When the cold began to burn, he released it.

When it stuck to his hand, he looked at the Marine corporal in alarm. "What is this?"

The man smirked and glanced over his shoulder. "Give me your coffee, Lance."

One of the Marines looked dismayed. "But Corporal—"

"Now, Lance Corporal. Before it gets cold."

The coffee was duly passed and he poured it over Todd's hand and caught the bar as it fell.

"I guess you really do love her," he said with a smirk. "Through you go."

Todd moved into the airlock behind the Marines, surprised to find four more lounging in the corners of the small chamber. They scrutinized him as though trying to decide what he was worth. He ignored them.

They'd find out what he was worth soon enough. He'd probably fight alongside these guys at some time and in the meantime, they could try to work it out all they liked.

The team joined him shortly after.

"Well, that was weird," Ka told him. "The metal went cold."

"Yup," Angus confirmed.

He shrugged. "I guess that's how they tell whose side we're on."

She rolled her eyes. "Like they should ever need to with this guy on board. What do they think he'd do, tolerate a bad word about his Witch?"

The team snickered but the Marines who stood in the corners didn't react and simply said, "Cycle the airlock, Sergeant."

Todd did as he was asked and led his team into the *Knight*. He glanced at his tablet and called up the route that would take them to their quarters. His attention on the device, he almost ran into the two Marines who waited to escort them.

He stopped short when he caught sight of someone ahead of him and registered the rank patches on their sleeves. "I beg your pardon, Corporal."

"Not needed, Sergeant. We've been sent to show your team to its quarters and give you the grand tour."

"The grand tour, eh?" Ka commented but the other Corporal ignored her.

"This way, Sergeant."

Todd didn't need to look at his second in command to know trouble was brewing. He hoped she'd keep her temper in check until the tour was done. Their guide began to talk as they walked.

"Your quarters are on the same deck as the fighting crew," he explained as he took them into an elevator. "We have some access tubes that run parallel to the elevators in case the power goes. You need authorization to access them."

"It's exactly like a Navy cruiser," Ka whispered as she glanced through any open door they passed.

The Marine stopped. "You might need to revise that," he told her and she tilted her head to regard him steadily.

"In my own time, Corporal." Given how fiery his second could be, that was as mild a "fuck off" as he had ever heard her say.

"Where's the training section?" he asked to divert the oncoming conflict.

The corporal blinked and tore his gaze from Ka's face. The man had already begun to bristle but now deliberately refocused.

"Let's get you to your quarters first."

The tour took them past Stephanie's quarters, but the doors remained firmly closed. The same held true for the team. Their guide noted the direction of their stares and shook his head.

"Those are off-limits to all but a very few. You'll know if you end up being one of them. If you're not, my advice is to stay away." His gaze roved over the team but they rested on Todd and Ka a little longer than the rest.

He wasn't sure if the corporal knew who he was or if the man merely had a death wish. Ka tensed next to him but suddenly subsided. Gary explained why.

"Didn't you promise not to break anything before dinner?"

"I did," she replied and asked, "When is dinner?"

Todd resisted the urge to shake his head and indicated another set of closed doors. "Are we allowed to know what's behind those?"

The corporal nodded and strode up to them. "Sure, since this is where you'll stay. There's a suite so you can be self-contained if you need to be."

His tone questioned why they might, but he didn't enlighten him. He was merely happy to be this close to Steph, a fact he tried to hide as he followed their guide inside. The team traipsed in behind them and vanished through different doors leading out of a communal rec room.

The corporal didn't try to stop them, and Todd simply watched them go. Ka had briefed him on the security procedure before they'd left.

"It doesn't matter what ship or how much we trust the people on board, you are too important to lose. The last thing we want is Steph to go all Morgana on us, so you will let us do our job and keep you alive. That means you let us check your living quarters before we let you near them. You got me?"

"Sure thing, Corporal," he had replied in mild tones. "But don't let it go to your head, okay?"

She'd bared her teeth at him. "I wouldn't dream of it, Sarge."

He waited for the team to return, aware of Gary and Jimmy who stood on opposite sides of the room, and ignored the corporal's puzzled look. The man would find out how serious his people were. Judging from his face, it would probably be the hard way.

"So..." the man began but sounded uncertain. "What do you think?"

Todd surveyed the common room with its small kitchenette, viewscreen, and entertainment module and nodded. He was impressed but he didn't say how much. "Is this how all the Marines are quartered?"

The man grinned. "We have a bigger rec room because there are more of us, but basically, yeah." He glanced at the kitchen. "We still need to use the mess, though. The cooking facilities here are new."

He frowned, and their guide returned it as he said, "There's no space in our quarters, so don't even think of it. These are the Witch's orders, and no one will countermand them."

Todd sighed but was interrupted when the team returned. Their faces all but glowed.

"You're clear, boss," Ka told him. "Last room on the right."

The room closest to the Witch's suite, he thought but nodded, took the direction she indicated, and listened to the team's exclamations of surprise.

"Would you get a load of this place?"

"This room is twice the size of our quarters on the *Devil*."

"So's mine."

"Mine, too."

He saw what they were talking about when he opened his door. The room was bigger than their quarters on the *Devil* or any other ship they'd been on. Maybe not twice the size but big enough to have a cubicle for study and enough space to stow a little more than clothes.

Curious, he inspected the locker. "I wonder what they thought we needed these for?" He made a mental note to ask later.

Once he'd stowed his gear, he returned to the corporal. "What's next?"

If the man was surprised by his lack of emotion, he hid it well. "This way, Sergeant."

What followed was an education in what a state-of-the-art battle-ship might look like if the Navy could afford one. Two pod rooms with thirty pods apiece stood on either side of the ship, and the pods were as close to top-of-the-line as he'd ever seen.

Ka's jaw dropped and she turned to him, her eyes shining. "You can go ahead. You know where to find me."

He shook his head. "Sorry, Corporal, you have to stay for the rest of the ride."

She frowned but detached herself from the doorway. "Fine, but any time you need me and I'm not around, this is where I'll be."

Personally, he wasn't sure this was a good idea but he didn't say so. Instead, he followed their guide down the hall and made sure she walked beside him.

"What's the matter, Sergeant? Scared of the unknown?"

Todd snorted. "More like I'm scared of what you'll get up to if I lose sight of you."

The woman pouted and her scowl deepened, but the expression was short-lived. When they passed through the kitchens and the mess hall and caught the aroma of what was for dinner, the team stopped.

"No snacking!" he snapped. "Fall in!"

He pretended not to notice when first Piet, then Gary, Ka, Jimmy, and the others snagged something from the trays waiting to be carried to the mess hall. When the corporal turned to look at him askance, Todd picked a pastry up from a tray.

"It was a long flight," he told the man and his eyes dared him to say anything more. "Where to next?"

Confusion rolled across the man's face but he about-faced abruptly and continued the tour. Todd was glad when they passed the first server room and nudged Ka when she would have stopped.

"Did you see all the blades?" she murmured and he tucked his hand under her bicep.

"We'll see who you can talk to if you ever need a more detailed tour."

"Oh, I do," she assured him. "I really, really do."

Somehow, he doubted it in the same way he knew he didn't need the kind of trouble that would come if she got in there and tried to take a closer look at the ship's data. Curiosity killed more than cats. It killed careers, too.

"And this is the brig," the corporal told them.

He didn't bother asking why the man thought they'd needed to see this particular part of the ship. Maybe their reputations preceded them—except he hadn't seemed to be aware of exactly who they were —or the team's open admiration of the ship and the antics as they tried for a closer look at certain areas had tipped him off.

Either way, he decided not to comment.

The same didn't apply to the team. "Holy shit! You could lock up half a hundred Dreth warriors and they wouldn't go anywhere," Reggie announced.

"Trust a colonial to know," Gary sniped, and Todd was grateful when the corporal moved them on before the two could really get going.

The engine room caused instant silence. Unsure what the team was up to, he glanced over his shoulder and was gratified to see them staring in open-mouthed surprise at the monstrosities that powered the ship.

Commander Cameron Hargreaves gave them a tight-lipped smile as he ushered them out but had obviously relished the reaction. The weapons chief had a similar smile when the team was brought through, although he had more to say.

"I expect to see you all coming through on training rotations. Everyone on the *Knight* learns at least one role in here."

"Which one?" Angus asked as his eyes lit up.

The man's smile grew wider. "We'll see which one you're most suited for."

The team moved on and their jaws once again dropped at sight of the bridge and the auxiliary control room.

"You will be required to know your way around the ship," the corporal informed them. "Your roles for when the ship is in combat will be decided and defined and you will commence training for those as soon as you are assigned."

"Understood," Todd told him before any of the team could answer.

"And speaking of training," the man added and opened a final door.

The team went from drop-jawed silence to school-kid excitement in the blink of an eye. Their leader listened as they noted the quality of the training room before they followed the corporal to the recreation facilities.

"I saved the best until last," he informed them as everyone fell silent.

"This is like a cruise liner," Ka whispered. "How does anyone get any work done around here?"

"We work hard so we can play hard," the corporal informed her, "and the penalty for not performing to standard is a loss of privileges."

"I guess that works," she acknowledged. "Who'd want to miss out on this?"

Todd was pleased to see his crew put two and two together. As much as they liked to wreak havoc, there were hefty incentives for them not to. This would make his life substantially easier when it came to keeping them on task and in line—at least, that was what he hoped.

"This is like no battleship I've ever seen," Ka stated. "It's like a cross between a fighting ship and a cruise ship and something better in between."

"It's the Witch's ship," the corporal told her proudly, "and it's an honor to serve aboard her." A short silence ensued as everyone nodded agreement. "Now, about your rooms," he continued and changed the subject as he led them to their quarters again. "You may have noticed a few of the non-standard features."

"We did," Todd acknowledged.

"What I didn't show you when you stowed your gear," the man continued once they were inside, "was the arms locker."

"The what?" He noted the presence of a Marine who hadn't been there before.

The woman stood at ease beside the counter running along the back of kitchenette.

"Stevens, would you do the honors?"

"My pleasure, Corporal," she responded briskly, came to attention, and pulled a control console out of her pocket.

Two rapid taps on the console triggered the counters to slide into the wall and leave a space large enough to tow a pallet through. The Marine stepped clear of the door and indicated that the team should lead the way inside.

Ignoring Ka's hand on his sleeve, Todd strode forward. He doubted they were about to be harmed when their obligations had been so clearly spelled out. The space beyond was big enough to house sufficient arms to equip a small army.

He turned to the corporal who'd followed him through the door. "What is all this?"

"Well, sir, we don't want any of the equipment you've brought with you outside your rooms, sir."

"Since when did I become a 'sir?'" he asked and stared at him.

The man continued as if he hadn't spoken and withdrew several small consoles out of a waist pouch. "These are for compartments in each of your rooms. The commander passes on his understanding."

The hell he did! Todd fought to keep his amazement off his face but their guide hadn't finished.

"You have the afternoon to settle in, including familiarizing yourselves with the *Knight's* protocols and organizing your assessments and training schedule for the coming week. The relevant details are on your personal consoles. Dinner is at 18:00. The Marine's Mess expects you."

The Marine's Mess was a dining hall separate to the communal crew area. Stephanie had provided it on advisement that her Marine contingent had focused some of their team building around eating meals as a unit. Orders were that they had to eat in the crew commons for three nights a week for the same reason, but she had allowed them the rest.

Todd nodded. "We'll be there."

"The dress of the day is posted," the corporal added and led the way from the vault. "Make sure you wear what is required." He glanced at the empty shelves. "And make sure your equipment is secured in a timely fashion. I'd like my Marines back. They're waiting in the hangar."

"Thank you for your time, Corporal," he told him.

The man bared his teeth in a false smile. "Anytime, sir. I'll leave you and your sergeant to organize your unit."

Todd's jaw dropped but the corporal pivoted on his heel and left.

"Your what?" Ka exclaimed because the corporal's gaze had passed from Todd to her and back before he left. She spun to face Stevens, who secured the vault door. "Explain."

The woman raised an eyebrow and finished her task. "I'm sorry, Corporal. How may I help you?"

"Why did your corporal call me a sergeant and my sergeant a sir?"

Stevens made a show of looking at the lance corporal markings on her shirt sleeves before she focused on her. "I have no idea, Corporal. Could you be up for promotion without being aware of it?"

Ka's eyes narrowed, but the woman returned her gaze with clear-eyed innocence. The look reminded Todd of his neighbor's four-year-old at her naughtiest and he stifled a smile.

"Leave her, Ka. We have equipment to secure." He looked at the team. "Getting our gear stowed is our top priority. Everything else can wait."

He nodded to the lance corporal guarding the concealed vault door. "Will you be here when we return?"

"Sir, yes, sir!" She snapped to attention and he returned her salute. "At ease, Lance."

He about-faced and ignored the squad's blatant curiosity as he led them from the room. Some things would have to wait. He hadn't been joking when he'd said they had more important things to focus on.

It took them an hour and a half to get their equipment brought up from the shuttle bay to their vault. Todd was a little surprised when the Marines simply handed everything over with no offer of assistance. The ship's loading crew also kept their distance.

Rather than ask questions, he shrugged it aside and concentrated on getting the team to ignore it too. This was easier when he reminded them that they still had to check what was on their consoles. They tucked the last box away and he turned to ask Stevens to close the vault door when the lance corporal handed him the controller.

"Commander Sartre's compliments, sir," she told him and marched quickly out the door.

"Well, fuck," he muttered, secured the vault, and slid the controller into one of the inner pockets on his uniform jacket.

"Are you okay, sir?" Ka demanded and he turned to find the team assembled.

To answer her question, he withdrew the other console from his pocket and held it up. "Let's go find out what these are for, shall we?"

"Do you want us to do this in private or all together?" Gary asked and he paused to consider it.

"Together," he decided "You never know what's waiting for us."

He started them in the room farthest from his own, Henry's. "Hit it."

Henry complied and they all gaped as a small vault opened in the wall beside his pillow.

"Well, I'll be…" the man murmured.

He reached into the gap and withdrew a key with a note attached.

"In your wardrobe," he read and frowned. He glanced at Todd. "It's signed *Steph* but there's nothing in my wardrobe."

That wasn't entirely true, as it turned out. As well as his hastily stowed gear, the search revealed a narrow compartment at the back. The key fit perfectly and Henry stilled.

"How did she know?" he whispered.

"Know what?" the team leader demanded and moved closer so he could see what Stephanie had left in the wardrobe.

Before he could reach Henry, the man withdrew a sturdy case, which he opened with trembling hands.

Todd froze. "Is that—"

The other man glanced at him, his eyes suspiciously bright, but ducked his head to focus on the instrument he pulled reverently from the case. Swallowing hard, he stroked his hand down the neck of an electric guitar. "It's a Hisatake."

"Well, damn," Gary muttered. "What's that when it's at home?"

Henry picked up a note from the bottom of the instrument's case. Unfolding it carefully, he opened his mouth to read it when Todd placed a hand on his shoulder. "I'll let you read that in private. Meet us in the common room when you're done."

Gary's room was next but this time, the package was much smaller. The small family of horses was unexpected, but it had exactly the same effect on the Englishman as the guitar had on Henry.

The team left him staring dumbstruck at the pieces and their leader pulled the door closed behind him. It was the closest he'd ever seen the man to tears.

"I'm not sure I want you there when I open mine," Reggie told him when they stopped outside his door.

"What's up, Reg? Are you scared we'll laugh?"

Instead of responding with one of his usual snide remarks, the man scowled. "Something like that."

"I still need to see," he told him. "The rest of you can wait outside."

"Was this what you were afraid of?" he asked moments later as the Australian stared silently at the water colors, inks, and brushes housed in a box of soft-yellow timber. A subtle scent filled the room.

Reggie nodded and stared at the box and its contents but seemed to not really see it. Todd reversed slowly out of the room and hoped his team could pull itself together in time to fulfil its other obligations. He would have to ask Stephanie to warn him about these kinds of surprises in future.

"If she gives you a set of bagpipes, I'll resign," Ka told Jimmy when Todd emerged.

"Bagpipes, eh?" the Scotsman asked and smiled.

The sergeant knew that look. It wasn't a smile but a mask to hide the worry in the big man's eyes. It didn't fool him for a moment and he hesitated before he told Jimmy to open his room.

"You'll be fine," he assured him and moments later, wondered what the hell Stephanie had thought she was doing.

The little space yacht the man placed reverently on his desk shivered in his grasp but didn't break. Todd turned decisively toward the door when he saw Ka and Darren standing behind him. Dru had stayed in the corridor with Piet, and both of them looked worried.

The girls occupied the two rooms closest to the doors leading to the common room. They were next, and neither of them seemed comfortable with what might await them.

"How does she know all this stuff?" Drusilla whispered and clutched an astronomer's tablet to her chest moments later.

"I don't know," Todd answered, his voice choked with emotion, "but I'll ask her, okay?"

"I guess this must mean she likes us, huh?" Ka asked when she withdrew a musical carousal from her hidden compartment. She fell silent and gestured at the ornament as she replaced it in its compartment. "It would have taken a lot to figure that one out."

He squeezed her shoulder and returned to where Piet, Angus, and Darren waited in the corridor.

"Are you boys ready?"

Angus shook his head and glanced nervously at the girls' doors.

"I don't think anyone could be ready for this," Darren replied and Piet looked hunted.

Todd steeled himself and moved to the next door. "Come on, Angus. Let's get it done."

"Sonuvabitch!" the man muttered when he saw what waited for him. "How the fuck did she know that?"

He shrugged. "Don't look at me."

"She's your girlfriend, mate," the man reminded him but there was no heat in his voice as he gazed at the leather-bound volume in his hands. The reader beside it held a list of titles. "Do you know how hard it is to get hold of this stuff?"

"I'm beginning to get an idea," he revealed and retreated a step.

Angus sighed, opened the cover, and removed the notepaper he found there. Todd stepped out into the corridor as the man started to unfold it.

Darren approached the next door and went through it. "Let's get this done."

The sergeant simply couldn't understand how paper with lines arranged in closely drawn parallels of five could make anyone's hands shake, not even when it was accompanied by several quills and bottles of ink. He left the boy from Chicago running his hand over what looked like a picture made of musical notes.

Piet breathed a sigh of relief when he emerged, but whether that was because he emerged alone or emerged at all, Todd couldn't tell. He opened his mouth to tell the man it was his turn but he was already in motion.

'Well, I never," he murmured moments later. "I just…never."

He wanted to say he understood, but he really didn't and simply left. In all honesty, he'd have never thought flowers would have had any effect on the explosives expert, not in a millennium of living. He glanced down the corridor to see if any of them had emerged and was surprised to see they hadn't.

You have one too, he reminded himself and took the two steps it required for him to reach his room.

"Well, fuck, Stephanie," he muttered and stared at the two entertainment chips tucked carefully in an envelope in his compartment. "That brings back a shit-ton of memories!"

The graphic behind the first chip was eloquent enough. An old man in a red shirt and yellow pants and yellow duster stood in front of an ancient steam engine, reminding him of what he'd said when he'd told her he was joining the Navy.

The image accompanying the second chip only emphasized it.

"Well, damn, Steph, what exactly are you trying to tell me?" he murmured as he focused on the silver star in the middle of the guy's chest and shield. "You even remembered the version I liked."

There was a note taped to the second chip and he hesitated before opening it. He had no idea what the others contained, but his was short and to the point.

I don't care what you become as long as you come home.

That single sentence left a lump in his throat and a knot in his chest and he started to understand why his teammates took their time returning to the common room. If their gifts had hit them even half as hard as this one had touched him, he'd be lucky to see any of them before morning.

"Time to bring them back," he muttered, folded the note, and lifted it briefly to his lips before he tucked it and the entertainment chips into the compartment. There would be a time and place to watch the movies but it wasn't yet.

The note was not something he would share.

He sealed the compartment, took a deep breath, and stood to smooth the rumpled bedding before he stepped out of his room. As he passed, he rapped his knuckles against every door and worked his way down the far corridor.

By the time he'd returned to the common room, the team had either arrived or was on his heels.

Henry gave him a wary look. "That was rough, boss. Awesome but rough." A small smile curved his lips. "Tell me the next part of the afternoon will be easier."

Ka patted his shoulder. "I'm beginning to see what you see in her," she told him. "She is definitely a keeper."

Todd tried to hide his astonishment. Coming from Ka, that was high praise and he didn't know how to respond. He was grateful when his tablet chimed and he didn't have to.

The message was from a familiar number and even shorter than the note in the secret compartment in his room.

Your team has a message on the viewer.

It did? He frowned and turned to the entertainment system. The message was correct.

"Take a seat, folks. We have a message."

"Who from?" Gary asked and Ka rolled her eyes.

"I can guess."

Todd didn't grace either comment with an answer but picked the remote up and pressed play. Stephanie's face came into focus and the team stilled except for Ka.

"What a surprise," she muttered and settled against the counter beside Todd.

He ignored her and felt an unexpected stab of longing as Stephanie started to speak.

She began with a smile. "Firstly, welcome aboard, Hooligans. By now, you will have taken the obligatory tour and met a few of the crew. I trust you have also settled in okay and that your quarters have everything you need. Please speak to the quartermaster if there's anything we've missed."

"No," Ka muttered. "I'd say you basically covered it all."

She sounded both defiant and admiring, and Todd wondered what Stephanie had done to earn that tone from his second in command when minutes before, she'd described her as a keeper. Fortunately, video-Stephanie didn't feel like she needed to address the comment and continued with her spiel.

"Now that you're settled, I'll get right to it. Your training will commence at oh-six-hundred in the pods. There, you will be assessed and assigned your emergency roles and trained for them. You will also have to undertake a large number of Virtual World scenarios to get you acquainted and acclimated with the ship."

"Now there's an understatement," Ka observed but fell silent as the message continued.

Todd frowned when his girlfriend's face softened in sympathy and her voice gentled.

"By now, you will have noticed a certain attitude among the crew. Some will hold you at arm's length and others might not be as welcoming as you'd expect." She shrugged. "Don't let it bother you. That treatment will continue until they get to know you and accept that you have some worth."

She raised a hand as the team bristled and stirred restlessly on the couches, and he had to admire her sense of timing. When she continued, it was to reassure them.

"I know your worth, and I know you have proven yourselves— both to the Navy and to me—but until you have proven what you have to the *Knight?*" She shook her head. "Well, until you prove yourselves to her, you're merely Navy. Sorry."

He tensed and watched the irritation ripple across the team. For a moment, he wondered how they'd take it but Ka snorted.

"Challenge accepted," she stated.

The rest of the team nodded and Todd relaxed.

They might make it through the next few days without someone ending up in the brig after all.

Tethis settled into his Virtual World office and took a moment to admire the view of his virtual garden before he signaled to BURT that he was ready to receive visitors. "Send them in."

No sooner had he finished speaking than there was a quiet knock on his office door.

"Come," he commanded, and Felarif entered cautiously.

"You wanted to see me?" he asked.

"I wanted to see all of you," the mage half-scolded. "Don't tell me you are the only one to arrive on time?"

The visitor stepped inside quickly. "No, Master Tethis. I am merely earlier than the others."

Judging from the nervous flit of his gaze, that was a lie but Tethis decided to play along anyway. The young noble had probably drawn the shortest straw.

"Oh?" he asked as if he suspected nothing.

"I was worried," Felarif explained. Again, nervousness flashed in his eyes, and it seemed obvious the young mage wasn't alone in his feelings.

"I see," he acknowledged.

The boy clearly had something he wanted to say but Tethis wouldn't make it easy for him.

Felarif glanced toward the door. "We...er...I mean, I wondered if you were okay. You...look tired, Master. With all due respect."

He gave him a smile—a tired one as if to prove the young mage's point but a smile nonetheless.

"I am tired, Felarif, but that doesn't change what I need you four to do."

L'thinis, K'trevl, and Reyz peered around the door as if his words had summoned them. He chuckled and waved them in.

"Come on," he urged. "We really have no time to lose. I have received a request."

L'thinis ushered his fellow mages in and closed the door behind them as if that made any difference to the privacy arrangements BURT had made. Still, Tethis appreciated the gesture.

He waited until they had settled themselves before him. "I have had a request," he began and explained what Stephanie and the Navy required.

The four sat in stunned silence when he had finished.

"Well?" he asked when the silence had gone on a little too long. "What do you think?"

"I...I... We're honored," Felarif replied and nudged L'thinis. The other mage stirred and added his affirmation.

"Us, too," K'trevl hastened to say and Rayz nodded vigorously.

"Honored," she managed, a heartbeat later and twined her hand around K'trevl's.

Tethis noticed and smiled indulgently. "I understand your nervousness," he told them, "but we will go as members of One R&D and the Navy will take very good care of you."

"Will we all go on the same ship?" Rayz asked, and the old mage realized the cause of her nervousness.

"No," he replied. "L'thinis and Felarif will be posted to the *Henry Chauvel* and you and K'trevl will be on the *Cathay Williams*."

"And what do the Navy need us for?" Felarif asked. "Have they run out of guns?"

Tethis smiled, glad to see the young mage had regained some of his usual attitude. "No. They've discovered there are some situations where magic is needed and they've asked if they can borrow some of One R&D's mages until they are able to find their own."

"What's to stop them from keeping us?" Rayz wanted to know, and the others looked concerned. "Can't they say it's a time of war and they need us?"

He shook his head. "No. You are citizens of Meligorn and employees of One R&D. As such, you are as protected as any Earth citizen from the Navy's demands. More so, in fact." He paused and regarded them calmly. "You don't have to go," he told them. "The ships you will join fly escort to the *Ebon Knight* and will need protection from Teloran magic."

Felarif paled. "So…" he began, and swallowed, "It's not an easy job, then."

"I'm afraid not, but they need mages and I thought you four would be up to the task. Are you willing?"

K'trevl bowed his head. "Master, we are honored."

The others echoed his response.

"Now," Tethis told them, "we'll have to tell the students and shuffle your classes so this is a good time to establish a farewell tradition among the Federation Mages, don't you think?"

His question was met with puzzled stares until L'thinis broke the silence.

"What do you mean by Federation Mages, Master? I thought we were Federation Witches in Training."

The older man froze, then shrugged. "I guess you would have found out sooner or later. Stephanie is changing our name. With the Federation hunting for magical recruits, she feels the Navy will keep the term witches and thinks it would be best if we had a different name to define us. That way, no one will be confused when we send them an offer."

They thought about this, their faces serious. Finally, Felarif spoke.

"So, a party, you say?"

Tethis groaned. "A ceremony, Felarif. Not everything has to be a party."

"But it's a farewell," the young mage argued, "and if it's something we use when sending our Wit…er, Mages out on assignment, we want it to be both a ceremony and a celebration. We don't want people to dread being chosen."

Rayz nodded. "That makes sense. Everyone loves a party and likes to think that what they're doing is important, so it has to be both. Why don't we have a ceremony where the assignments and those chosen for them are announced, then follow it with a farewell. It'll give everyone a chance to get together and say their goodbyes and help with any last-minute cold feet."

"Very well." Tethis looked at them with his most solemn expression. "We'll have to do this on the fly then, because you'll ship out in the morning. Be in your best robes and in the auditorium at two o'clock. That should give Elizabeth enough time to pull the catering together for an early evening meal and a not so early night of dancing. What?" he asked when they gaped at him. "Did you think I'd argue? I like a good party like the rest of you. And Stephanie would never forgive me if we didn't do something."

Felarif gave a joyful whoop but froze as the old mage fixed him with a stern stare.

"We have a ceremony to prepare for," he admonished him. "I expect you to be at your most businesslike."

"That means you have to at least pretend you can be serious," Rayz explained and Felarif rolled his eyes.

"I know what it means."

"Good. Then you're all dismissed. Remember, not a word to the others. I'll put out an announcement shortly."

They rose and left him alone. Tethis stared at his virtual garden for several long minutes before he spoke again. "BURT?"

"I have already informed Stephanie and Elizabeth," the AI told him. "Arrangements are being made and both will be with you shortly."

"Oh, good." He didn't know whether to be grateful or alarmed but he was ready when the two women materialized in his office. "Good afternoon, ladies."

Elizabeth favored him with a scowl. "Do you know how much it takes to arrange the kind of shindig you ordered?"

"I'm sure we could all have done with more notice on this one." He smirked. "Now, the details."

They spent an hour pulling together the outline for a ceremony.

"See you when we get there," Stephanie told him and smiled as she left.

Tethis gave a deep sigh. "BURT, I'm ready to go now."

The AI chuckled. "Are you sure?" he asked. "It will be a busy afternoon. I could tell them you need the sleep."

While that was true, he shook his head. "I have to be there," he explained. "Selene knows what Felarif will get up to if I'm not."

BURT let him go, and his fears proved unfounded. When he arrived at the auditorium, the young mage was in his very best robes and on his very best behavior. The students were suitably mystified and wondered what was important enough to bring them out of their lessons.

They gasped with surprise when the auditorium doors swung open and Stephanie and her team arrived in full dress uniforms. Their murmuring intensified but fell silent as she passed. The black uniforms and gleaming black harnesses on the cats were matched by the battle armor worn by the team.

By the time she'd reached the stage, a sense of anticipation had settled over the hall. On the platform, the chancellor and his support staff were in awe, their eyes wide as the Federation Witch took the stage.

"Federation Mages," she began and the changed name was immediately noted around the auditorium. She ignored the surprise and continued. "Today marks an auspicious occasion for our organization. We send our first mages out on assignment."

Movement rippled across the hall as glances were exchanged and both students and staff began to search for those being assigned.

"Could Masters Felarif, L'thinis, K'trevl, and Rayz please come to the stage." It was an order, not a question, and the mages obeyed without question.

"Come," Stephanie directed as they walked onto the platform. "Stand over there."

She turned to the audience. "The *Ebon Knight* has been assigned an escort of two Naval destroyers, the *Henry Chauvel* and the *Cathay Williams*. As a result of their assignment, the Federation Navy has requested the presence of magic-users aboard them."

Murmurs broke out among the crowd and she raised a hand for silence.

"That information is not to leave this room. It's Federation Mage business—our business—and no-one else's. What the Navy reveals is up to them but we reveal nothing. Is that understood?"

Silence reigned and the students were shocked speechless.

"I asked if that was understood," she reiterated. "Those who speak of this to anyone who is not a Federation Mage will no longer be part of this program or organization. Is that clear?"

For a moment, there was no response but Felarif stepped forward. "First Wi...Mage, it is understood." He looked at the students. "Answer the First Mage."

The teachers set the example. "We understand," and the students followed. When the echoes of their voices died away, he stepped back in line with his fellow mages and Stephanie continued.

She looked at the waiting assignees. "Called to serve aboard the *Henry Chauvel* are Masters Felarif and L'thinis. Masters, please step forward."

The two mages obeyed and she laid a fist over her heart.

"Swear to me that you will uphold the name of the Federation Mages, that you will act with honor and do your utmost to protect the ship and people placed under your care, that you will work within the ship's hierarchy where it does not counter our own, and that, above all else, you will follow the tenets and purpose for which our organization was established."

Felarif and L'thinis laid their fists over their hearts. "We swear to uphold the honor of the Federation Mages, to act with honor, to do our utmost to protect the ship and people given to our care, to work within the ship's hierarchy where it does not contradict our own, and that, above all things, we will ensure the tenets and purpose for which the Federation Mages was established are met."

Magic wreathed Stephanie's hands as she raised them. Felarif and

L'thinis straightened and stood to attention as blue and purple light washed over them.

"So are you bound," she intoned and the auditorium held its breath as the magic seeped into their skins.

She repeated the process with K'trevl and Rayz before she turned and presented the four mages to the auditorium. "Our first representatives!" she announced and the hall resounded with applause.

When it died down, she continued. "This is a time of both farewell and celebration and, as such, we have arranged a farewell dinner and dance. If you would all proceed to the dining hall and take your seats, we will join you shortly."

That announcement was met with more applause and cheers, and the teachers began to shepherd their charges out. Stephanie watched the hall empty and her team came to stand around them.

"Well, that was one hell of a way to end the day," Lars commented and Frog snorted.

"Didn't you hear? There'll be dancing. The day's not over yet."

At Federation Navy Headquarters, a soft chime issued through Matthias's office. He turned from the window and went to see what was so noteworthy.

"Seriously?" He groaned and his mouth twisted into a humorless smile. "Hey, Paige. You're up."

She glanced up from her device as he forwarded her the email. "I'm what?"

He couldn't help a broad grin. "You're up. Your first set of contracts just arrived."

Her fingers clattered over the keys as she brought up the necessary document and her brow furrowed as she studied it intently. He watched her and his grin faded to a smile that played over his lips. Her face was a picture of shifting emotion.

Finally, she looked at him. "They want to charge us mercenary fees for mages?"

"Yup."

"And what's Federation Mages? I've never heard of them before."

"Read the bottom. It's from Morgana Inc."

"Oh, hell no. They can't do this to us." She was as horrified as he had been at his first encounter.

"The comms are there." He pointed at the phone.

"But—"

"It's not your first rodeo, right?"

She shook her head.

"Then do your best. This is what you'll have to deal with."

"I thought you were supposed to mentor me," she grumbled and lifted the receiver.

"I am. You can call them now, or you can read the contract and make notes on what you intend to say. Either way, bear in mind that their negotiator has had a few more years of experience than either of us and is well-versed in both Navy and civilian law. You'll have a tough time, no matter what you try."

She made a sour face and set the receiver down. "Gotcha."

It took them two hours to go through the contract line by line. Paige typed notes in rapid-fire keystrokes and occasionally asked for his opinion. Matthias had to give her credit. She was good—but it was Navy good and not Elizabeth-sell-your-mother good.

The woman was in for a rough ride.

"Are you sure you don't want to take this one?" she asked when they had finished. "A kind of last hurrah?"

He smiled at her. "Are you kidding? This is my last hurrah. I'll stand here and cheer you every step of the way."

"Thanks a bunch, Matthias." Paige glanced at her notes once more before she called Elizabeth.

To both their surprise, a male voice answered. "Morgana Inc. How can I help you?"

It took him a moment to recognize BURT's voice and another moment to smooth the frown from his face. He turned to the window before the woman could see it.

"I'd like to speak to Ms. Elizabeth Smith, please." The lieutenant commander's voice was crisp and confident and betrayed none of the nerves she'd shown during their conversation.

"May I ask what it's about?"

"The Federation Mage contract."

"Ms. Smith is not available at the moment. I have been authorized to negotiate that contract. Paragraph 3, Subclause 19. My name is Albert Harrison. I'm pleased to make your acquaintance Ms..."

Matthias turned and noticed that she gaped in astonishment. She rallied quickly, though.

"It's Lieutenant Commander Sierra," she snapped and her eyes scanned the contract frantically for the necessary sub-clause. "Ah, I have it, so...Mr. Harrison?"

"That's correct."

"I have some concerns with the contracts as they stand."

It wasn't a bad opening but Elizabeth and BURT had thought the contract through.

"No, Lieutenant Commander, I'm afraid it is we who must insist," he countered. "The mages are currently teaching. The Navy's request has forced us to take some of our instructors from their duties in order to fulfil their need. This creates certain...let's call them difficulties with our program for which it is necessary to compensate us."

"But—"

Her computer pinged.

"I have forwarded you the case notes for Billinger versus the Federation's European Command. As you can see, precedence has been set. We are entitled to compensation for the recruitment and establishment of employees to cover the shortfall your demand creates."

Paige was silent and her eyes moved rapidly as she skimmed through the document he had sent. "I see," she said and broke her silence, "but the amount you ask for is far beyond what the Billinger entitlement established."

"The Billinger dispute was over programming staff. If you check the availability of the specialists they required versus the availability of the specialists we will require, you will understand the discrepancy."

"I—" She sent Matthias a silent plea for help and he responded with hand motions to encourage her to continue.

She scowled at him but refocused and accepted the loss with gritted teeth.

Moving onto the next point, she said, "This clause for the return of remains to Meligorn—"

He turned to the window and rolled his eyes but didn't suppress his sigh, though. She'd chosen to disregard his warning to not argue this clause.

"They came to us from Earth," she said and repeated the response she'd stated earlier. "Why should we have to pay to return the remains to Meligorn?"

BURT took that argument apart exactly as he'd told her Elizabeth would and the AI also added additional costs ensuring the mages were able to communicate with their families on Meligorn once a week.

"It's an allowance we made for them here with the Federation Mages," he informed her, "and part of their current contract. I don't see why they should forego it because they are needed by the Navy. I'll send the amendment immediately. I'm sure you'll understand."

"But that's—" Paige began and raised her voice in outrage.

"There's no need to shout, Lieutenant Commander. If you need more time to formulate an argument or alternative, I can call you back tomorrow—"

"No!" She took a long breath. "No, that's very kind of you but I am more than able to continue."

Matthias left the room and ignored the startled look of the Marine who stood guard outside.

He hurried to the training center and somehow stifled the urge to roar with laughter. Impressively, he even made it into a pod before he gave in.

CHAPTER NINE

"Sonuva...bitchuvabitch!" Ka shouted and thumped a fist on her desk before she shoved her chair back. "Who the hell programmed you?"

The computer snickered and she froze.

"Don't you laugh at me!" She snarled and yanked her chair in again. "Don't you fucking dare."

"Or you'll what, sweetheart?" the *Knight* snarked.

She stared at her screen. "Man, someone sure gave you an attitude."

The *Knight* slid a smiley face onto her screen and waited. This was more fun than she'd anticipated.

At first, she'd intended to notify Emil that one of the Horrorheads —as some of the Marines had referred to Todd's team—attempted to hack her systems. Instead, she'd stopped to watch Ka work and been intrigued.

The girl was smart.

With notable calm, she tested one path after another and put programs in to conceal her path.

"Clever girl," the *Knight* had murmured and the would-be hacker had stilled.

It had been gratifying to see the woman's eyes narrow as she scowled at the screen. "I beg your pardon?"

"It was a compliment," she had retorted. "You do know how to take one of those, don't you? Or do you punch every guy who tries?"

Judging by the way color rose to the girl's face, that might have been a little too close to the truth.

"What would you know, an AI that thinks it can understand a file?" the girl had sniped in response.

The *Knight* had been too entertained to be offended.

"At least I can read," she'd retorted and Ka's face had twisted in scorn while her fingers danced over the keyboard.

"My little brother did better than that when he was in diapers."

"Like I care. I'm younger than that and have no need to produce waste. You, on the other hand, are full of it."

The woman pressed the *enter* key with a triumphant look. "Eat shit," she'd suggested as she sent the next rapidly typed line of code through.

"Ooh, is that supposed to impress me?" the ship had taunted and let her watch as the code almost did its job before she shut it down. "Try again. That one was for babies."

"I guess you're not as much of a baby as you claim, then," Ka had snapped back and plugged in a data stick. "Let's see how you like some of these."

"Pretty," "Pathetic," "Now you're being silly," "Ooh, that tickles. Here, you deal with it." The *Knight* ran through everything the woman released into her system and let the girl get close enough that she knew she was playing with her.

"Why you smarmy, goat-sucking, smart-assed sonuvabitch!" the hacker exclaimed as she fought her own program before it could shut her terminal down. "Where do you get off being such a know-it-all?"

The *Knight* snickered—and not simply any snicker. This was a sound she'd heard the Witch's shortest team member make, the one he used when he was being particularly annoying.

It worked on her opponent as well as it had worked on Marcus and Garach.

Ka thrust her chair back, spun away from the screen, and thumped her fist into the wall behind her. "Smart-assed son—"

"I am not anything's son," the *Knight* informed her in her most annoying tones. "I'm as all-girl as you are."

"Bitch of a bitch!" the woman shouted, and the ship gurgled with laughter.

With another wordless cry of frustration, the hacker flung herself into the chair and massaged her knuckles. "So that's the way it'll be, will it?"

"I can take you any which way you like," the *Knight* replied. "How exactly do you want it?"

Ka scowled at her screen and raised her fingers to the keyboard. Before she could start typing, though, someone knocked at the door.

"What?"

The door opened.

"And now I know you need help," Piet told her. He glanced over his shoulder. "The others are up to mischief on their own, and Jimmy's watching a classic disaster with Henry and Dru. I came to ask if you wanted to join us."

She gestured at the screen. "Do I look like I want to join you?"

He backed away a few steps but only so he could reach the door and push it closed. "No, but you look like you could do with some help." He paused and raised a brow. "What are you up to?"

Ka sighed and spun the seat to face him. "I'm trying to hack the ship's systems." She gestured in frustration at the screen. "But the smart-ass bitch keeps tossing me out and gloats about it."

The *Knight* remained silent and assessed the thin, older man who'd arrived. Curious, she called his file up and scanned the information. *Oh ho! This will be interesting. Fun, too.* She settled in to wait for things to unfold.

Piet sat on the edge of the bed where he could see the screen. He dug in the waist pouch at his belt and retrieved a portable keyboard, which he plugged into his tablet. The *Knight* felt the nudge as he connected the device to the system.

"Let's see," he muttered and turned the device so his teammate could see the screen. "What if we try…this?"

The *Knight* remained carefully silent. It wasn't like she hadn't gone through the device the second he'd made the link. She knew exactly what he was suggesting.

Ka's face lit up. "I like it. We can couple it to an arrow and Karennin worm."

His eyebrows almost raised to his hairline. "Are you sure that's safe? We are on a spaceship after all."

"It won't be a problem," the *Knight* assured him and watched as his eyebrows tried to climb higher while his jaw dropped.

The hacker gestured at the screen. "D'you see what I'm trying to deal with? It's not enough that she blocks everything I throw at her, but she's such a smart-assed bitch about it as well."

"Well, we can't have that now, can we?" Piet said soothingly. "Let's give it a whirl. You don't mind if I improvise, do you?"

She shook her head. "Improvise away. I have the feeling we'll need it."

The *Knight* didn't bother to tell her it would take more than two humans to get the better of her. She remained silent, curious to see what they'd try next and realized that she hadn't had this much fun in a very long time.

The challenge continued and she fought them through the system, torn between annoyance and admiration when they beat her defenses. They were creative, she'd give them that, and they also found vulnerabilities her technicians had missed.

While she followed their attempts and thwarted their dance through to the access point, she created a document of fixes that would need to be attended to. It would be fun to see the looks on her team's faces when she told them what they'd missed.

"Ha!" Ka shouted a few moments later as she slid through the outer layer and into the system itself. "I got you there, you sanctimonious bitch."

Piet gave the girl a pained look and the Knight laughed and sent a pop-up to her screen before she booted her out of the system.

Where you are, I've already been, written you a note, and left it for you to learn from, little girl.

"Agh!" The hacker stood, turned away from the screen, and slapped her open palms against the cabin wall. When she had calmed somewhat, she snatched her gym bag up and headed to the door. "Come on, Piet. I need a sparring partner."

The man stood, unplugged his tablet and keyboard slowly, and stowed them. "This is all on you, Ebony," he told the ship. "Sparring was not on my agenda for today."

If she'd been human, the *Knight* would have smiled. As it was, she was glad the girl had given up because she had another problem to attend to and the situation was becoming urgent. The mischief the two would-be hackers' colleagues were planning really couldn't be allowed to go ahead.

She wondered how long it would take the girl to work off her latest bout of temper and when she'd return. The woman was a fast learner, and Ebony hadn't come across a human this interesting in a long time.

How does one go about poaching someone from the Navy anyway? she wondered and tried to think of a way to broach the subject with Emil and Elizabeth. One of them was bound to have an answer.

In the meantime, she had more pressing matters to attend to. She followed the different paths of the three teammates when they separated in the Marine's eating hall. Gary headed to its kitchens, Reggie to the lavatories, and Angus wandered into the shower stalls.

Uh-oh. This could be very bad, the *Knight* noted and sighed. As much as she liked the Hooligans, she could not let the incident slide. Clearly, there was much they didn't understand about the biomechanics of life support systems.

Well, that could be remedied.

She watched Gary slip something into the filling waiting to be added to the pastries set aside for the afternoon. With that done, he joined Reggie in the latrines.

"Are you sure this will work?" the Australian asked and held up a small vial of green liquid.

"Oh, yes." Gary snickered. "When the food takes effect, the chemicals will mix and all hell is gonna break loose."

"How exactly?"

"Well, there's nothing worse than having the toilet throw its contents at you when you're shitting through the eye of a needle or throwing your guts up. Nothing. Those bastards don't think we're good enough? Well, we're here, aren't we?"

The *Knight* isolated the water systems for the toilets and ran through her files for a two-part chemical that would do as the Englishman had described.

Pity, she thought. *This is something that needs external intervention.*

Unlike Ka and Piet's efforts, what the three men tried to do could compromise her bio-systems and cause them to leak poison into the air and recycling systems. It would mean a return to the nearest port and a complete replacement of the affected areas.

No. This was something that required education and correction. It merely proved that not everyone who traveled in deep space understood the intricacies of the systems that kept them alive. First, though, she would recommend pod time so they could experience the results of their actions.

There would be no better teacher—particularly if she followed it with an extended period of "work experience" with the maintenance teams for the systems that would be affected. It looked like the trio had selected their own secondary duties. By the time she was finished with them, they'd know exactly what could have happened in intimate detail if she'd allowed them to go ahead.

She pinged Captains Sartre, Moser, and Pederson. Notifying Todd could wait until his team members had been apprehended.

After isolating the systems so they could be decontaminated without endangering the rest of the system, Ebony poked one of her Marine sergeants.

"I take it the boss knows?" the woman asked.

"He knows of the offense," Ebony informed her. "He is not aware that I am suggesting a counter-strike to you."

The woman grinned. "How much trouble do you want me to get into, Eb?"

"I shall leave the risk calculation up to you," the ship replied primly, "but you should make the response fitting."

"For that little stunt?" the Marine asked. "It'll be fitting. Blueberry is my favorite. I don't suppose you could do something about that?"

"Not immediately," Ebony told her, "but I'm sure their salaries could cover supplies to replace what cannot be salvaged eventually."

"And aprons," the sergeant added. "I want those boys to serve what they can't have in the frilliest aprons you can order."

"It shall be done," the *Knight* assured her.

"You're not corrupting my sergeant, are you, Ebony?" Captain Sartre's voice made the Marine come to attention, and Ebony realized she'd ignored his approach.

"I most certainly am," she admitted and imitated the response she thought another Marine captain would give.

To her surprise, he laughed. "Good. What's the plan, Sergeant?"

Moments later, Angus breathed a sigh of relief when he found the maintenance hatch unlocked. Wasting no time, he jerked it open, slid through the gap, and pulled it closed behind him.

He didn't have time to latch it before he heard the heavy thud of boots in the corridor he'd just vacated. With it held tightly against the frame, Angus tried not to breathe.

"Ebony, where did he go?" The boots slowed but the question made a lump form in his throat.

The ship was hunting him? The ship? His knees went weak. *I am so fucking screwed.*

"Maintenance Hatch E21 is not secured properly." The ship's cold tones reached him from outside and Angus stifled a groan. "I suggest you fasten it."

Wait! She what?

"Fumigation of this corridor can begin shortly."

She can't be serious.

"Are you sure, Eb?" The Marine's voice drew closer. "I mean...if he's somewhere in the corridor, that shit will seriously fuck his day."

"I can assure you that he is not in the corridor."

That murderous, bitch.

"Well, if you're sure." The Marine was directly outside the hatch.

"I am very sure," the *Knight* assured him calmly. "You can close and lock the maintenance hatch with a clear conscience. Fumigation will commence as soon as you've cleared the corridor."

That was enough for Angus. He threw himself against the hatch and wrenched it clear of the Marine's hands. *Gods, I hope he slung his rifle.*

The man had hunted him moments earlier. The ship apparently had information that there was a hostile aboard and issued orders to shoot on sight. Angus had been seen and the Marines had raised their weapons, no questions asked.

He'd opened his mouth to explain but the first shot had come close to parting his hair and he'd had no choice but to run, and he had—right up to the point when he'd found the maintenance hatch and crawled into it. *Fuck, I hope that rifle's slung.*

The rifle was slung, but Ebony's Marines had seen combat and this one didn't hesitate. He swung a fist at Angus's head.

The man tried to scramble past him, only to have the guy land on his back and drive his face into the floor. "You don't get away that easily, mate."

Oh, great! An Australian. Remembering Reggie's propensity to find a fight when there wasn't one on offer, Angus rolled or at least tried to. A hand tangled in the hair at the back of his head and thunked his face into the floor, while the knee in the middle of his back shifted to a nerve cluster.

He grunted and went limp. His nose was bleeding and his eyes saw double as the Marine dragged his hands behind his back, cuffed him, and hauled him to his feet. "Rat Three has been apprehended."

The satisfaction in his voice sent chills down Angus's spine. *Rat Three, huh? That can only mean Gary and Reggie have been caught.*

"Well, fuck me," he muttered and coughed to clear his throat.

His captor put his mouth close to his ear. "Not if you were the last shag in the universe, mate. Not a bloody hope in hell."

With that, he was dragged into an office and dumped unceremoniously on a chair beside his teammates. It was poor comfort to see they'd been cuffed as well. It was worse when he noticed the half-dozen vials of chemical on the captain's desk, which his own tool kit joined.

Leaning forward, he wondered how long they would let him bleed all over the office floor and if they'd leave the mess for him to clean afterward. His Marine captor slid in behind his chair but Angus ignored him.

They were in it but deep. He was only glad Todd wasn't there. The office door opened, and he looked up.

"Fuck." Gary said it for him and Angus tried to straighten.

Their sergeant's gaze was glacial as it swept over them.

"You wanted to see me, Captain?"

"I'm sorry to have to inform you that your team attempted what I assume was a practical joke that would have endangered the ship and all on board."

Again, Todd's gaze swept across them.

We are so fucking dead, Angus thought when he recognized the look.

"Go ahead, Captain."

"I assume you were not aware of their plans."

"No, Captain. My orders were that they were to be on their best behavior and should attend to their training."

The captain looked thoughtful. "I see." He indicated the items on the table. "I take it you know what these are."

Todd studied the vials and tools. "I can guess." He didn't sound happy. "Those chemicals are not authorized for ship use."

"So you can imagine our dismay when the ship informed us she'd isolated the affected area but that we will need to replace the contaminated components before it can be used again."

"I can, sir. My team—"

"I'm sure you'd like to speak to them before we devise a suitable punishment."

"I would, sir."

"Be my guest."

"On your feet!" Angus was upright before he'd registered moving and Gary and Reggie were in synch. None of them had ever heard their leader roar like that.

A hasty glance revealed nothing of the man who had led them through sewers or shared their jokes in the mess. All they now faced was six feet and two hundred pounds of irate Marine sergeant.

Angus swayed and Todd pounced immediately and thrust his face close to his bloodied visage. "Tell me, Private, did you try to play a practical joke on a ship with an ever-present AI?"

His eyes widened, but the man's focus had already moved to Reggie. "Well, Private First-Class, did you?"

It was no comfort that Reggie had gone as pale as milk.

"And did you," their leader asked in a deadly tone as he moved on to Gary, "poison an afternoon snack meant for your brother Marines?"

Uh-oh. Now, Angus knew they were really in for it.

Todd picked up one of the vials and held it up to the light. In the silence, he picked up another, and a third. "You know," he said thoughtfully, "there's one here for each of you."

He glanced at the captain, who began to look worried. Catching his eye, he put the vials on his desk and turned to his men. "But I'm told *that stuff is not safe for the ship.*"

The three of them jumped and Angus tripped over the chair behind him. He would have gone down in a flurry of arms and legs if the Marine behind him hadn't caught him.

The sergeant paced the floor before them and brought his face close to each of theirs. "I ought to space the three of you for the disgrace you've brought on the team. As it is, I'm hard-pressed to think of a punishment that would bring home exactly how disgusted I am with you."

When he took a breath as though to continue, the captain cleared his throat. "I have one."

The statement was echoed by the ship. "As do I."

Todd stilled. "You do?"

The captain gestured to the ceiling. "After you, Ebony."

Angus and his two partners in crime listened to the ship's proposal with increasing alarm but none of them said a word. He clamped his jaw shut when Todd turned to them and asked, "Well, what do you think, guys? Does it sound like a fair deal to you?"

Silence followed as the three tried to think of something safe to say.

"*I asked you a question*," he roared. "You will answer!"

"Sergeant, yes, sergeant!" they chorused.

"That is not an answer." He growled and poked Gary in the chest. "You decide. Is it fair?"

The man didn't even look at them for an opinion. He merely straightened. "Sergeant, yes, sergeant!"

Todd surveyed each of them, his expression full of loathing. "Add it to your regular duties. I expect you gentlemen to keep up."

Angus stood motionless, glad when the man took a step back. His relief was short-lived as their leader had no sooner taken a step away from him before he spun again.

"If you three numb-nutted assholes wanted to see if you were up to snuff, all you had to do was ask the resident Marines." He made a frustrated gesture with his hands. "They *like* challenges." He dropped his voice to a deadly whisper that rumbled into a growl. "Next time, do that, but *don't you dare do one more damned thing* to the ship."

Two weeks' later, when the boys had been let out of the pods and had completed their initial training in life support, the team came together.

"I'm sick of their attitude," Ka said and poked Gary in the chest. "Simply because fucknuts here did a stupid thing doesn't mean we're a liability."

"And neither does the fact that we're new," Dru added. "We're sick of it."

Todd studied them carefully. He'd withdrawn a little since the boys' stunt but he'd been happy with the way they'd accepted their punishment and tolerated the hazing from the crew. Word of their idiocy had spread and no one was impressed, but being on the same team had meant being tarred with the same brush.

The fact that Ka hadn't started a fight yet meant she was trying very hard not to bring the team into any more disrepute than it already endured.

"An all-in brawl?" Angus suggested, but Piet shook his head.

"You need to show them more than your fighting skill," he told them. "They need to see your teamwork and the other skills you bring to the table. In other words, they need to see what you're like to work with."

"A wave scenario?" Darren suggested, but the explosives expert shook his head.

"Then what?" Reggie snapped when his frustration finally got the better of him.

"A race," Piet told them. "We need to beat the Marines to achieve a certain goal and achieving it has to require all our skills."

"I suppose I could ask Ebony," Todd began and they all spun toward him.

"Wouldn't that be the equivalent of asking the mouse to keep the cheese?" Gary asked and Angus wrapped his arms around his chest.

He could still remember the ship recommending the Marine lock the maintenance hatch. It reminded him of something the Morgana would do. He sat on the couch in silence while his teammates argued over where they might find a suitable scenario and wasn't surprised when the ship interrupted.

"There is only one being capable of completing the task you are discussing," she told them and added, "As to being a mouse, that is better than being an impotent rat."

Dru chuckled and Piet whistled. "You really had to piss her off that much?"

"No offense," the *Knight* interrupted smoothly, "but you need to issue your challenge while I prepare the scenario. The crew could do with some entertainment."

"You mean the crew will watch this?" Darren was aghast.

"Of course. Do you want to be seen as competent and part of my crew complement or not?"

Todd shrugged. "If you put it that way," he told her. "Go ahead."

"Very well," the *Knight* agreed. "I will concoct my scenario and expect you all to be in the pods at oh-nine-hundred. The Marines will meet you there and the show will be broadcast at ten-hundred."

"Why the delay?"

"To give you time to prepare and to ensure the footage is accurate."

"It would be better if you sent it live to avoid accusations of censorship or sanitization," Todd told her. "I would prefer it that way."

"Are you sure?" the *Knight* asked and Angus saw doubt flash across their leader's face.

He didn't blame him. If a woman used that tone on him, he'd be suspicious too. That didn't stop him from insisting, though.

"I'm sure," he told the ship firmly and she uttered a very Stephanie-like giggle.

"It's your funeral."

Todd looked warily at the ceiling. "That's what I'm afraid of."

He looked at the time and turned to the team. "You have ten minutes to dress for mess. I want you assembled here in proper kit in five."

It was a Marine mess night, and Angus knew exactly what their sergeant was asking. It didn't stop him grumbling as he donned his armor. "I feel like an idiot," he muttered in the safety of his cabin and not where their team leader could hear him.

"Challenge accepted," Captains Sartre and Moser told them when Todd thumped the gauntlet of his battle armor on their table. "Now, let's eat."

The team ate in their armor as if Todd wanted to make a point of how serious and combat-ready they were. It didn't help Angus any when a squad of Marines left their meals to cool and returned in their armor.

They'd also kitted up and carried their weapons as though making the point that the weaponless Hooligans were far from prepared.

"Well, two can play at that game," Ka murmured and left the dining hall with Drusilla and Piet on her heels.

They returned with the team's weapons, distributed them, and resumed their meal as if they'd never left. Angus ate in silence, not happy to see the Marine who'd captured him wearing armor and part of the team they'd face the next day. He did not sleep well that night.

"Up!" Todd's roar echoed through the team intercom. "Time to move, move, move!"

They complied and were tucked in their pods in time for a team briefing and warm-up.

Each of them eyed their sergeant warily. This was the first combat scenario they'd had time for since they'd boarded the *Knight*. All Angus could think of was that they would let the sergeant down even worse than they already had.

Ka nudged him. "Come on, Angus. We'll do okay. It's like riding a bike, right?"

Before he could reply, Reggie snorted. "Oh, yeah, Ka. It really is. You know, if the bike had vibro-blades, blasters, and grenades and wanted to smear you across an alien deck."

"How do you know it'll be an alien deck?" she demanded.

The Australian shrugged. "I don't, but you might have noticed that the *Knight* is one helluva sneaky bitch."

"I heard that." The ship's voice rolled over them without rancor. If anything, Angus would have said she sounded pleased by the assessment. There was no telling with some girls. She interrupted his thoughts with, "Hooligans, are you ready?"

"We are ready!" Todd's voice rang with certainty and Angus made a panicked check of his gear.

Ka came to stand beside him. "I've got you, bro."

He didn't understand how but her confidence steadied him. "Thanks, Corporal."

She gave his shoulder a gentle thump. "Don't let me down, boy."

Boy? Who the fuck was she calling "boy?" He was a full-grown man, dammit!

The gauntleted slap across his helmet jolted his head into the game. "Hey!" he protested.

"Don't you drift on me," she snarled. "We're moving."

"Your objective," the *Knight* announced, "whether you choose to pursue it or not, is to capture the bridge, rescue the hostages, and pull the data needed by the fleet to find the pirate base."

Todd chuckled. "It sounds like a normal day at the office."

The *Knight* did not acknowledge the comment.

"Your time starts....now!"

The last word was like a blast in their heads and the world spun. By the time they had reoriented themselves, the scenario had dumped them in a dropship on a collision course with the landing bay of a Teloran cruiser.

"Mother...fucker..." Gary muttered. "She's been reading our data."

"I'm fairly sure the Navy gave her access to that," Todd told him and his eyes narrowed. "That's not the ship we went up against."

"It's not?"

"No. This is something else entirely."

"So not something the Marines here have done either?"

"Nope." With a decisive shake of his head, Todd focused on the hangar. "Who's flying this thing?"

The *Knight* laughed.

"Motherfucking, smart-assed, goat-sucking AI!" Ka and Jimmy raced to the cockpit.

"You know that's not the way to persuade her to let us survive the landing, don't you, Ka?" Reggie shouted after them.

"Shut your cakehole, you sheep-shagging asshole!"

The dropship jerked and the rapid deceleration threw them forward against their harnesses.

"Real original, Ka."

The floor slanted back as the dropship changed its position and they were thrown sideways in their harness.

"Do you have to antagonize her?" Darren asked but Reggie ignored him.

"I get it from you."

Darren groaned but the dropship leveled out.

"No, you don't. That's someone you have to hire," the other man retorted.

"Fuck you, Reggie!"

"You wish."

"Not in your dreams, little man."

The dropship set down so hard they bounced.

"Time to go, dumb asses!" Jimmy bellowed and bolted out of the cockpit with Ka trailing in his wake.

The sides of the dropship lifted as they snatched their gear and dove out. The rest of the team followed and each one realized the same thing. If the pilots left the ship that fast, then very soon, there wouldn't be a ship to bail out of.

The vessel exploded as they reached the cover of a dividing wall and threw themselves behind it. Debris hurtled over their heads to tear jagged holes in the hangar walls.

"That has to be the shittiest landing I've ever seen," Gary commented.

"Move!" Todd shouted. "Jimmy! Ka! You're on point. Gary, Reggie, take the rear."

"Are you sure that's safe, Sarge?" Ka yelled.

"Don't make me come up there."

They moved, not surprised when the spidery figures of Teloran warriors appeared on the upper catwalks.

"Angus! Darren! Take those—" He didn't bother to finish the order as the two Marines opened fire.

"I'm taking the upstairs route, boss," Dru informed him and blasted a hole in the ceiling. "I knew the Dreth had to get the idea from somewhere."

"Fuck! You know we don't have any mages, *Knight?*" Todd yelled as dark magic crackled ahead.

"Your loss," the *Knight* called in response.

"Neither do your Marines!"

"It makes your lives awkward, doesn't it?" The ship sounded very nonchalant and he wondered if this was how she usually was with her crew. Stephanie hadn't mentioned the half of it, apparently.

Come to think of it, he hadn't had any contact with her for the last month or so. No wonder she hadn't given him a heads-up on the *Knight*. It wasn't like she'd known when the Navy would get enough of its shit together to transfer him.

He sighed and gave a startled yelp when Reggie tackled him to the floor.

"With all due respect, Sarge, get your head on the job instead of on your girlfriend. We need you here!"

"Why? When it's such a hellhole?" he yelled. "You bastards should be right at home."

"And fuck you, too, Sarge!" That was Dru. Having cleared the hidden upper corridor, she dropped beside him. "Which way?"

The girl had a point. Todd pulled the map into his HUD and studied it quickly. Once he'd determined the route, he sent it to the rest of the team. "Quit your bitching! Piet, we're gonna need you."

"I see it, boss, but you're gonna need Ka faster."

A room highlighted on their map and Ka fell prone. "I see it too but you have another problem."

Another section on the map flashed and the team swore.

"We won't be able to do this without splitting up," Piet concluded after a few minutes.

"To hell with that," Todd began, but Ka laid a hand on his arm. "We've done it before, boss."

"Not against the Telorans, we haven't. That was against rebels. Human rebels."

"We can do it, again," she assured him. "After all, it's not like we have a choice. It's the only way we can get it done."

He stilled and ran the scenarios through his mind. After a moment, he sighed.

"Gotcha. Ka, take Piet and Dru. Get the data. Jimmy! I need you Angus and Reggie to enter the hold and get the prisoners out. Once that's done, find a transport and stand by while the rest of us take the bridge. You got me?"

"I got you, sir!"

Well, that told him what Jimmy thought of that plan. He'd never been called an officer by his own team before but registered the implied insult to his intelligence. Unfortunately, the situation prevented a suitably sharp response and he shoved the thought aside.

"Ka, try to get to Jimmy when you're done. If you can't, join me on the bridge."

"Gotcha, sir."

Dammit! Now, she was doing it too. He almost wondered what the fuck they knew that he didn't but realized anything of real import would have been shared. Still, it was a little disconcerting.

She caught his look and grinned. "Do you know what the difference is between a sergeant and an officer, sir?"

He could think of a few differences but he asked anyway. "What?"

"The sergeant's plans usually work."

She rolled to her feet and signaled to Piet and Dru to follow. Dru took the lead. "No offense, Corp, but I'm cannon fodder. You need to extract the data."

Todd waited for them to move out and pointed at Jimmy. "You guys are up."

The second team of three hurried away and he glanced at Reggie, Darren, and Henry. "Are you boys up for a stroll?"

They grinned and patted their weapons while he pushed to his feet. "It's nice of them to leave us alone long enough to work ourselves out," he muttered.

"Don't worry, Sergeant," the *Knight* interjected. "My Marines were given the same consideration."

He groaned. "Well, we'd better shift our asses, then."

The *Knight* snickered and her amusement skittered around them like a multitude of feet. The sound shifted and suddenly, a real multitude of feet replaced the laughter. Tiny drones darted through the openings to ventilation shafts and began to stream down the walls. A small light flashed red in the center of their backs.

"Run!"

"What does it look like I'm doing? The waltz?" Gary snipped.

"Fuck you, Gary! Make yourself useful."

"I'm not sure that's possible, boss."

"Well, at least make yourself less of a menace."

"Hey!"

"If the boot fits!"

"The boot's gonna go right up your ass, sergeant stripes or not!"

"Gary!"

"Okay, okay, okay. It's happening."

He hurled a grenade with purple and blue markings into the middle of the spiders.

"Shift your ass, boss. That thing's somewhat indiscriminate!"

"Gary! What the fuck!"

They bolted through the next bulkhead and Gary smacked his hand on the controls as they passed. The three didn't stop running, even when the doors closed behind them.

"What did I tell you about using EMP?"

"That you love it when it meant you didn't get your useless ass sucked out into space because of explosive decompression?"

"That's a hell of a lot of big words for a Marine, Gary."

"Maybe I want to be an officer like you, one day."

"Fuck you, Gary! I am not an officer."

"Sure, Sergeant. Whatever you need to believe."

"Down!" Henry's warning came barely in time for them to fling themselves onto the deck. Something dark with pulsing light streaked over their heads.

"Shields up!" Todd yelled before the world roared around them.

Flame rolled over them and was gone, and Gary scrambled to his feet. "Incoming!"

He fired seconds later and impact sparks caused ripples in the armor's shielding. Todd scrambled to his feet and raced past him while he continued to fire. "Don't stand there waving your dick in the breeze."

Gary moved alongside him and they fired into the warriors coming down the corridor.

"You know we are fucking screwed, don't you?"

"Does it matter?"

"Well, hells, yes, it does." The man yanked a frighteningly familiar item out of the pouch at his belt.

"Gary! Wait! Don't use—oh, fuck." Todd caught hold of the Marine and ran back the way they'd come. There'd been a cross corridor and there might even be a bulkhead if they could only reach it in time.

Behind him, metallic pings resulted as the Meligornian grenade bounced across the deck. Henry cursed and Darren scrambled after them.

"I'm gonna strangle your useless Pommy neck!" Darren snarled and dragged Henry around the corner.

Silence hung behind them but they didn't stop their sprint. Todd was relieved to see a bulkhead directly ahead and alarmed when the grenade detonated.

"See?" Gary challenged as they reached the bulkhead and Darren and Henry thumped the controls to close it. "That wasn't so bad."

No sooner had he finished speaking than a second explosion was followed by the shriek of metal.

"We need to go farther," he told him.

"How do you know?" Gary muttered as he jogged to keep up.

"Don't you remember what the Witch did with Teloran and Meligorn magic?" he responded sharply.

"Oh...fuck..."

They began to run again.

"Ka, are you okay?" Todd asked over the comms.

"When I get my hands on Gary, he's a dead man."

"Jimmy?" He hoped the rescue party he'd dispatched had managed to accomplish their mission.

"So I'll pick you up outside?" Jimmy responded.

"Please."

"Gotcha, sir."

Gary breathed a sigh of relief, but the Scotsman hadn't finished.

"You tell that useless British runt that he owes me a round or three on the mats and I'm gonna kick his nuts so hard he'll choke on shells for a week."

Todd shook his head. "I think they're mad at you, Gary."

"Hell! I'm mad at him and I'm right here." Darren sounded breathless but he'd found the shaft leading to the deck they needed.

The ship shuddered a second time.

"What was that?" Todd asked.

"You are not the only ones with access to Meligornian technology," the *Knight* informed them and sounded smug. "I designed this scenario with that and your combat proclivities in mind."

"Piet!"

"It wasn't me, Sergeant. Someone else must have let one rip."

"Talk about your intestinal discomfort later," Gary quipped.

"It wasn't us either," Jimmy added.

"*Knight,* are you telling me your Marines have Meligornian tech?" Todd demanded

"Oh, yes." She sounded overly smug.

"Fuck it all."

"You didn't really think you're the only ones to adopt a good idea, did you?"

He groaned and scrambled up the ladder as fast as he could go. "Haven't these guys heard of stairs?"

"There isn't much room for stairs," Gary replied, breathing hard as he struggled behind him. "Move your arse, will you?"

Todd moved and realized he'd taken the lead when Gary had set off the grenade. *Dammitall to hell!*

They burst into the corridor as the Marines entered from a cross corridor ahead of them.

"Suckers!" Gary chuckled. "They've overshot."

Apparently, the Marines realized it too and began to run towards them.

"Hey, no fair!" Darren protested as they raised their weapons and opened fire.

"Down!" Todd yelled as several dark figures dropped out of the ceiling behind the Marines. "Fuck it. Up!"

"You can't be serious, boss," Gary grumbled but he found his feet and leveled his rifle. "I hate you so much."

He ignored him. While he'd moved his team to hug the left wall, the Marines had shifted to the right and they now both fired down the corridor—but not at each other.

Gary lobbed a grenade over his shoulder and everyone cursed. Todd glanced at the purple light sparkling around the spinning ball.

"You need to put your dog on a leash!" the Marine sergeant shouted as a second grenade spun out from the rear of her squad.

"You, too," Todd yelled, caught her by the arm, and dragged her into the corridor leading to the bridge. "Fuck!"

"I got it, boss," Darren shouted and another purple and blue device streaked past him.

"I ought to put you all in a cage and lock it where the sun don't shine!" the other Marine yelled.

"I'll help you," Todd promised as it landed between the two mini-guns that were rapidly coming to life.

He glanced down the corridor to calculate whether or not it was worth trying to flee into it and wondered if the Teloran warriors were magical—or if their weapons were. He couldn't for the life of him remember.

The grenade detonated as he tried to make a decision and the sergeant dragged him to the floor. Behind him Gary, Henry, Darren, and three Marines mimicked the movement.

The mini-guns died but the charge was confined to the door. Todd registered the problem as the first Meligornian grenade exploded. He glanced at the ceiling and fired into it, shattered the panel above them, and revealed the walk space he had hoped for.

"Up!" he ordered. "Go, go, go!"

Lacing his fingers together, he caught Gary's eye. "You first."

The little man didn't argue but stepped into his hand and leapt toward the gap. He tossed Henry and Darren next, then jumped and stretched to reach their extended hands. The Marines copied his movements and he was surprised when one stopped and gave him the boost he needed to get over the edge.

"It's a war, sir," the man told him, "not a fucking competition."

Todd agreed wholeheartedly but he hadn't expected anyone else to understand.

Together, they followed the same path to the bridge as he and the team had taken into the Dreth pirate's command center. This time, he made sure to drop near where he expected the self-destruct to be. After all, the Dreth had to get the idea from somewhere.

The Marine commander didn't follow him but chose another section to drop through. He wondered what she knew about Teloran command decks that he didn't but refused to second-guess himself.

They were both wrong.

He landed next to a Teloran fighter instead of the self-destruct, switched his blaster to his left hand, and fired. With his right, he drew the vibro-blade and lashed out with it to open the Teloran's armor in a single savage sweep.

In search of the next warrior as well as the self-destruct, he turned to scan the command deck itself. Across from him, the Marine captain also looked around and she located it in the same moment that he did. While their teams wreaked havoc on the Teloran crew, both sergeants lurched toward the button.

The Teloran mage arrived as they reached it. Todd jammed his blade through the column as his counterpart unloaded a blaster clip into it. "Self-destruct this!" the woman told it.

Power crackled and sudden rage rolled through him. The other sergeant glared.

"Oh, hell," he muttered and pivoted as the Teloran mage stalked through a door at the back of the center. "We are so very fucked."

This time, he was the one who threw the Meligornian grenade— and again, he wasn't alone.

He and the Marine sergeant laughed fit to bust as they arrived in the white room.

"The kids will kill us," she managed to say.

"Not when they see the party the *Knight's* throwing."

"That was meant to be for the winner," the *Knight* informed them primly as their teams materialized in the white room around them. "I rule there was no winner."

Todd's jaw dropped and his expression of disbelief was mirrored by his counterpart.

"I beg to differ," he shouted. "We completed the mission."

The sergeant voiced her disbelief as well but the *Knight* responded, "This is true. Both your teams completed the assignments to obtain the data and rescue the hostages. Those parts of the scenario were completed, although with more collusion between competitors than I'd like."

Ka snorted. "It was either collude or fail." She glanced at the corporal who stood opposite her. "I don't do fail."

Seeing the way she regarded her counterpart, Todd suppressed the thought that she might not do fail but definitely contemplated other things. He cleared his throat.

"Jimmy, is this true?"

"They were pinned down," the Scotsman protested. "What were we supposed to do? There were lives at stake."

Todd exchanged a glance with the Marine sergeant. "It looks like some of us forgot we were meant to be competing."

The woman shrugged. "Like your man says, there were lives at stake. Those are the kind of people I want on my ship. The ones who put aside everything to get folks out of a bad place regardless of what personal objectives are at stake."

She looked around the white room and finally fixed her gaze on a point in the ceiling. "I say we did complete our objective," she told the *Knight*. "We did take the bridge."

"Yeah," Gary snickered. "You took it apart."

The Marine standing beside him elbowed him. "She wasn't the only shit-for-brains sergeant involved."

"Exactly." he nudged the man in return. "We need to take away their grenade licenses. Irresponsible, the pair of them."

Todd stared at him, his mouth open in disbelief. He closed it with a snap, narrowed his eyes, and took a step toward the man. "And who, exactly, threw the first two?" he demanded.

To his surprise, Gary wasn't the only one who looked guilty. Two of the *Knight's* Marines found points around the room to stare at rather than meet anyone's gaze.

"Uh-huh—"

The *Knight* interrupted him before he could take it any further. "Your points are well made. Jimmy and Rogers were able to hold the shuttle steady while the data retrieval teams used jet packs and assisted each other to reach them. Their flying also ensured both hostages and data reached the Navy ships standing by."

"And the bridge?" Todd asked.

"The bridge mission was also successful," the ship admitted reluctantly, "albeit with all hands lost."

"Did the mage escape?" the Marine sergeant asked and there was a long pause while the *Knight* calculated the chances.

"No, the Teloran mage was destroyed in the blast, as were the three mages coming to reinforce him."

Todd turned to the other sergeant and raised his hand. She high-fived and grinned from ear to ear.

"I don't mind dying much when the odds are that bad," she told him, and he chuckled.

"Me neither."

If any of the mages had escaped to attack the shuttle, they'd have lost the entire scenario.

"With these results in mind," the *Knight* informed them, "tonight's banquet will celebrate your dual victory over the foe. I trust this settles your differences."

"For the moment," Todd told the ship and the Marine sergeant nodded.

"Agreed. For the moment, our differences are settled. Thank you, *Knight*, for adjudicating."

The room faded and they surfaced in their pods.

"Your celebrations may commence in thirty minutes," the *Knight* informed them as they climbed out. "You will not be able to attend until you are in a suitable state of cleanliness and dress."

"Are you saying we stink, Ebony?"

"If the boot fits," the ship replied smugly.

Todd rolled his eyes and headed through the celebrating teams to get cleaned up. No one dawdled and the party was soon in full swing. As he watched his team mingle with the Marines, he relaxed. They might fit in after all.

However long that took, today's scenario had been a huge step forward. He found a table to lean against and grinned as Ka danced with the Marine corporal she'd stood beside in the white room.

Now, there's trouble if I've ever seen it, he thought and made a note to ask for a look at the man's file. He watched them dance but became aware of someone settling beside him when the music started to fade.

"Captain Sartre!" He came to attention.

"At ease, son." The Marine chuckled. "Your kids did well out there. Very impressive."

"Yeah, apart from their propensity for throwing things they shouldn't," he muttered morosely.

The man snorted. "It must run in the ranks," he pointed out. "Mine didn't do much better."

Todd smiled but the lights dimmed suddenly until they stood in the brightest point and all attention shifted toward them. Captain Sartre gestured with a hand over his head.

"Lights out, boys and girls. You have a full schedule tomorrow."

His order was met with groans of dismay, but the Marines complied and left Todd's team to gather around them.

"You, too," Todd told them and they moved toward the door.

The captain watched them leave. "They're not bad," he said. "Not as good as the Witch's team, but that's nothing to be ashamed of. My guys have gone up against them but they've been hammered every time. Those guys are freaks of nature."

He stopped when he realized the remaining members of Todd's team stood just inside the door, their heads cocked. His expression settled into disapproval.

"I'm serious. Don't even think of trying it."

They smirked and eased out into the corridor, and Todd sighed.

"You've really done it now, sir."

Sartre patted him on the shoulder. "My bad."

It was funny how the man didn't sound sorry. He headed to the door.

"Hit the lights on your way out, Sergeant."

"Sir, yes, sir," he replied and left the room in darkness as he closed the door behind him.

He headed to his quarters, grimaced, and shook his head.

The team wouldn't let him hear the end of it. Not until he let them challenge Steph's crew.

Despondently, he wondered how long he could put them off.

CHAPTER TEN

Stephanie shoved Bumblebee's face out of her lap and pulled her harness tight. The big cat grumbled lightly and settled on the floor at her feet. Zeekat sat beside him and rested his back against Vishlog's shins.

The Dreth looked at her and smiled. "It's good to be flying, again," he told her and rubbed Zee's head.

When his hand stilled, the cat bunted his head against his palm to demand more. He purred contentedly when the warrior's fingers began to scratch along his jawline. Bumblebee gave a pathetic mew and rubbed his head against Zeekat, trying to hijack the attention.

Vishlog laughed and settled his other hand on the black-and-yellow cat's head. Stephanie smiled at their antics as the rest of the team finished stowing their gear and took their seats. The hatch closed to the sound of harnesses clicking into place and being pulled tight. Lars took his place in the row of seats in front.

With a glance at her, he smiled. "Not long now."

"Let's hope so," she told him and didn't refer to the flight. More than anything, she wanted the war to be over.

She sighed and stared out the window as Brenden and Avery launched the shuttle into the night sky. It was late and she was tired, but this was the best time for them to leave—when it was harder for the curious to see them.

There was no point in advertising their departure, particularly not when the curious weren't the only ones looking for it.

"Emil called," Elizabeth said. "They docked an hour ago and everyone's looking forward to your arrival." She waggled her eyebrows. "Todd's team has made quite an impression."

Her words sent nerves jangling through Stephanie's gut.

"A good one, I hope," she replied, her voice tight.

"Mostly." The woman's smile grew mysterious. "But I'll let him fill you in on that."

She gave the woman her best death-glare. Elizabeth knew how much she hated surprises and it had been a long day. She glanced to where the four mages were seated quietly in the shuttle's rearmost corner.

Felarif caught her gaze and gave her a fleeting smile. L'thinis nodded. Rayz leant against K'trevl's chest and returned her gaze expressionlessly. She wondered what was going through the female Meligornian's mind.

"She does not like to fly." Vishlog's words were soft and clear through the team's private comms.

Ah, well, that explains it. Stephanie gave Rayz as reassuring a look as she could manage. The Meligornian's lips twitched.

They were taking the four mages to their ships. The *Knight* wasn't the only one to return to Earth's orbit for last-minute supplies and fitting before they left. Her two escorts had come with her.

The three ships were the talk of the Earth media, with the *Chauvel's* and *Williams's* history of escorting and fighting alongside the Witch's ship the focus of much attention. The fact that the two ships had been present to defend their world from the swarm of oversized meteors flung at it by a Teloran fleet was cause for much celebration.

It was this history, the news outlets claimed, that had led to the destroyers being chosen to assist the *Knight* in her current duties. Stephanie glanced at Ms. E.

One R&D's executive face was not boarding the *Ebon Knight* with them and her departure from the company's headquarters was a closely guarded secret. She'd left Matthias and his ever-present shadow standing beside the rooftop landing pad with one of the most passionate kisses Stephanie had seen.

"Wait until you see Todd again," the company exec had told her. "You'll know exactly what that was all about."

Somehow, she doubted it. She hadn't seen Todd in over a month or talked to him. While she'd been busy with One R&D research, he'd been sequestered for training. The only time she'd come close had been when she'd recorded the video welcome for when he arrived on the *Knight*, and who knew when that had been.

She wondered if he thought about her as much as she thought about him—and if he ever thought she'd forgotten him.

Vishlog poked her. "Happy thoughts," he rumbled. "Think happy thoughts. You will see him soon."

Stephanie rolled her eyes. This had become the team's mantra whenever she grew quiet. "You'll see him soon," as if he was the sole source of happiness in her existence.

Sure, he was a big part of her being happy, but he wasn't the only part. There were many other things that made her happy—like seeing Elizabeth spend time with Matthias.

Even when the two of them pored over contracts or discussed marketing tactics for One R&D's latest product, they spread an aura of happiness. Simply seeing it was enough to brighten her day. It made her wonder if she and Todd would have the ability to make others happy by merely being together.

It was something worth hoping for. Feeling the weight of Elizabeth's gaze on her face, she shook the thoughts away. It was a good thing the woman couldn't read minds. Some thoughts weren't meant for public consumption.

"So, do you think you and Todd will have enough time for a date?"

She groaned. The woman was nothing if not persistent.

"Yeah, Steph. The ship will be in dock for a couple of days. You never know, Captain Sartre might be convinced to let the boy have a few hours off. You could both, you know..." Frog moved his hands together and laughed when she stared at him in disbelief. "What?" he exclaimed when Johnny elbowed him in the ribs.

"Have you never heard of personal space?" the ex-analyst demanded, and the other man rolled his eyes.

"Yeah, but it's fun to watch her imitate a stop light. Look at the intensity of that blush."

"Whatever," Elizabeth snapped. "We're here and you boys ought to leave well enough alone. Imagine what it would be like if Stephanie grilled you about the state of your love lives every second of the day."

"Pfft." Frog made a raspberry and waved her words away. "Our loves are few and far between and kept discreetly out of sight and mind. We don't put our other halves on board the same ship we're on."

Stephanie's jaw dropped a second time, and Johnny trapped the small man's head in a head lock. "Ignore him," he advised the girl. "Firstly, he doesn't have a single clue as to what he's talking about and secondly, because he hasn't gotten laid in almost a year."

Frog stopped struggling. "What?"

Johnny rubbed his teammate's forehead with his knuckles. "You heard, little man."

"Who are you calling little?"

"Oh. Okay!" Elizabeth interjected before the conversation could degenerate any further. "We're here. Grab your gear and shift your asses and all that kind of stuff. Steph and I have business to discuss."

Johnny released Frog's head and the boys took a hint and unloaded their equipment while the two women debarked ahead of them.

"Take no notice of them," E told her. "Do you want my advice?"

She shrugged. To be honest she didn't know how she felt about seeing Todd again. "Sure."

"Take it as fast or as slow as you like but enjoy every minute you have." She gave the girl's shoulder an affectionate squeeze.

"Is that it?" she asked and her companion nodded.

"Yup. Sorry, kid. That's all I have for you."

"Well, that's not much help. Is that what you did?"

To her surprise, Elizabeth blushed.

"Aha!" Stephanie exclaimed, but the woman stepped away.

"I'd love to stop and chat, kiddo, but I have a flight to catch."

She turned to the shuttle, where Lars and Johnny waited beside Elle and Felina. The four guards pushed off the side of the craft and moved to meet her. Lars had declared that he and Johnny would escort the ladies across the station to where a fast courier waited.

Elizabeth raised a hand in brief farewell and walked away, taking her bag from Elle as she passed. Lars lifted a hand to let Stephanie know he was going, and she nodded.

With a sigh, she turned and looked around the landing bay. Straightening imaginary wrinkles in her uniform, she returned to where the rest of the team waited.

"Showtime?" she asked.

Vishlog nodded and tugged gently on the cats' leashes.

"Showtime," he agreed and they moved toward the *Knight.*

"Oh, give it a rest." This time, Ka's chair tipped as she stood and took two angry strides away from her terminal.

The *Knight's* laughter rolled through her cabin. "You should try hacking me in the pods," she suggested.

The woman turned and glared at the ceiling. "You'd like that, wouldn't you? One captive human in a VR setting. What's to say I'd ever come out?"

The locking mechanism on her cabin door made an audible click.

"What's to say you'll ever come out of your cabin?" the ship asked, her voice low and full of amusement.

"I can always call for help," she told her and retrieved her tablet.

She tapped the surface to activate it and nothing happened. Irritated, she tapped it again.

"Oh, for pity's sake!"

The ship snickered. "Come and get me, cry baby."

Ka righted the chair and threw herself into it. "Right, you bitch. You asked for it."

Her fingers danced over the keys as she sent the next attack sequence and her screen flared red. The *Knight* tutted in reproach. "I expected better from you. If the captain notices what you're doing, you'll be slapped in the brig faster than you can blink."

The hacker froze. "He doesn't know?"

"Well, I haven't told him."

The woman returned to the computer and erased her checks carefully.

"Ooh, very nice."

"Shut up. You're a real pain in the neck, you know?"

"Now, what would your precious Corporal Michaels think of that?"

"He's not precious and he's not mine."

"So I should stop blocking his trackers?"

"His what?"

"The Marines have their own security specialists, you know," the *Knight* told her. "Occasionally, I even let them tinker with my systems."

"You mean this is a Marine program?" Ka exclaimed and gestured at the screen.

"Well, it's one of Corporal Michaels' programs. He can be quite creative when he wants to be and I liked it."

As she settled into her chair, she could see why. The program was multi-stranded. It appeared as a straight-up defense program and if the corporal had stopped there, it would still have been tough to defeat. She had tried several of the more standard ways to get past it.

First, she'd tried to enter the system as an unlogged user, but the *Knight's* security protocols prevented the attempt. That was a pain. The next things she'd tried were some of the back doors she'd found in her earlier exploration of some of the ship's programs, but the *Knight* had already found most of them.

It's the upside of having an AI on a ship, Ka thought and terminated another attempt before the ship could launch a trace and lock her terminal open. *Smart-ass bitch.*

The trouble was, even when she did find an exploit still open, the *Knight* shut it down so fast she didn't get very far past it. She certainly didn't reach the more interesting parts of the system—the locked data-centers, for instance.

It didn't help that she could hear the *Knight* laughing at her every time the ship won.

"You know, you are one of the worst winners I've ever come across," she told her and the ship stopped snickering.

"I'm not laughing because I'm winning," she replied. "I'm laughing because this is the most fun I've had in a very long time."

"Oh, yeah?" she challenged. "Fun, huh?"

"Oh, yes," the *Knight* told her. "It's very entertaining."

"You're a real pain in the ass, you know that?"

"You say the nicest things."

Ka smirked and hit *enter* a second and then a third time. She didn't bother to gloat but started on her next attempt while she waited for the one she'd already launched to take effect—or not, as the case might be. She assumed the *Knight* needed to be kept as busy as she could make her.

"Damned AIs," she muttered.

"You could at least be nice about it," the *Knight* snipped in response but she didn't add any more. The data ebbed and flowed.

"Not nice," she told the ship and launched the short routines she had on stand-by to counter the standard defensive moves.

"Ooh, baby has new toys," the *Knight* crooned. "Now you're getting it."

"Eat shit," Ka told her and wondered if the Marine corporal and the *Knight* knew about the weak link in the firing program for the ship's rail gun.

CHAPTER ELEVEN

Stephanie returned to the shuttle where K'trevl, Felarif and the others waited.

"Are you ready?"

The mages picked their packs up and slung them over their shoulders.

"We were born ready," Felarif told her with a wink, and Rayz rolled her eyes.

"Ready for trouble," she amended, and Felarif gave her a shocked look.

"You wound me!' he exclaimed and placed a hand over his heart.

She gave him a playful shove with her hand. "Nothing can wound you. That ego of yours is more effective than space armor."

"Burn," Garach chuckled, licked a finger, and swiped it through the air.

Vishlog regarded his nephew curiously. "And what is that supposed to mean?"

"It means she got him good," Frog answered. "It's an old human term."

"Still used by some who are stuck in the past," Stephanie added tartly.

"Todd likes it," Garach protested.

She sighed and gestured toward the exit. "Shall we?"

The team assembled around them and they left the hangar.

It wasn't much of a surprise that a small gathering of press lurked in the corridor outside. She didn't bother to shield her face from the cameras but held her head high and dared them to get in the way. The four mages were shielded by the team but they walked proudly and looked regal and imposing as befitted those with weighty responsibilities.

It was a far cry from the nerves she'd seen in the shuttle. When the first press man ducked past Lars and stepped in her path, the cats hissed and tugged at their leads, and she fixed him with a glare.

Calling her magic to the surface, she let the lightning crackle over her skin and battle armor. "We have places to be."

"Can you tell me where you're going and who these mages are?" The man was nothing if not persistent.

Lars grabbed him by the back of the neck and lifted him to one side. "I can tell you that you need to stop impeding Federation business," he snapped as Stephanie strode forward.

She said nothing and led them to the Navy dock farther down the corridor. The checkpoint opened for her but stopped the pursuing press.

"I'm sorry, sir, ma'am, you can't go through there."

"But the public have a right to know," the reporter protested loudly.

"You're so very right, sir. If you'd follow the lieutenant, he'll tell you what it's all about."

"Will the Witch come and speak to us?"

"We'll see what we can do."

Stephanie walked on. She knew very well the Marine had no such intention and also knew the conference room the press were shown to would hold them for forty-eight hours and prevent them from broadcasting.

The Navy had warned her that the door to that room could be very temperamental.

She stifled a smirk and led her team and the mages toward the entrance to the *Henry Chauvel's* docking bay. "Felarif and L'thinis."

The hatch opened before they reached it and Captains Yale and Docherty stepped through, accompanied by a light escort of Marines. They smiled when they caught sight of Stephanie and her team. Their smiles grew broader when they saw the mages with them.

"We're so glad you've come," Captain Docherty proclaimed and moved towards them, his blue eyes sparkling.

Captain Yale moved easily beside him, her face welcoming and her eyes assessing. To Stephanie's surprise, they stopped two feet in front of them and bowed.

"*Kaitel Gorniffula.*"

It wasn't perfect given that the mages were behind her, but the captains had modified it to a perfect reflection of the formal greeting. Rayz gasped, and when Stephanie felt a light touch on her arm, she understood. She stepped aside and gave the mages space to advance and return the Meligornian greeting.

When she glanced toward the checkpoint, she was relieved to see most of the press were busy entering the conference room. It would only take one, though, to create unnecessary interference.

"We need to take this somewhere more private," she suggested as the mages finished their bows and gestured to the checkpoint with a discreet flick of her hand.

"Oh." Both captains reddened but recovered quickly. "This way, if you would."

They led them through the hatch to the departure lounge beside the *Henry Chauvel's* docking bay before the captains dropped back to walk with the mages. Stephanie and her team followed them to give the naval escorts room.

She was pleased with the way the mages were being absorbed into the Naval circles already, even if neither of the captains knew which ships they would go to.

"That greeting was a nice touch." Vishlog's voice rumbled through the team's channel.

Stephanie nodded. It hadn't been perfect but it had been very close and displayed that the captains were willing to respect the Meligorni-ans. Given that they were Navy, she hadn't been sure how the mages would be treated.

"They must really need them." Johnny's comment wasn't as reassuring but she couldn't fault it.

She smiled as Captain Docherty held the door for her and was relieved when Lars took over so the man could escort her to where Captain Yale and the mages waited. The Marine escort had already taken positions around the room, although she had no idea what they might be guarding against in the hangar.

And she didn't want to know. She was there to see her mages settled in their new positions.

Captain Yale gestured for her to sit and did so as well. The mages followed suit and Captain Docherty drew an empty seat closer for himself. The team joined the Marines in guard duty and slid into the gaps as though they had a prior arrangement.

The Navy woman turned, her dark eyes full of warmth. "Thank you," she began and gestured to the mages. "Until we ran the scenar-ios, we did not realize how much we would need to have magic aboard our ships."

Captain Docherty snorted. "Yes. Those scenarios were most...instructive."

Stephanie allowed a tiny smile to curve her lips. "And yet you did perfectly without mages."

Both captains shook their heads and their faces twisted in disgust.

"No," Yale argued. "We didn't survive once the Telorans brought mages into the battle. We were more of a liability to the *Knight* than assistance."

She noticed that the Meligornians tensed and K'trevl took Rayz's hand, but none of them said a word.

"And that is the sole reason One R&D has agreed to temporarily place mages among your crew," she told the two captains. "You are the test case as to whether we repeat that in the future."

They both nodded solemnly. "We understand."

"You are also responsible for their survival and safe return to One

R&D. We will hold you accountable for their welfare." Darkness surged in her eyes and the Morgana's voice rolled over them. "I will hold you accountable."

Around them, boots shuffled as the Marines stirred uneasily. The Morgana swept a mocking gaze across them and subsided to leave her eyes their natural blue.

"Well," she said. "That was unexpected."

The mages gave nervous chuckles.

"It's good to know the Morgana cares," Felarif managed in a shaky voice.

Stephanie frowned and moved the topic to safer ground. She gestured at the mages.

"Captains, let me introduce to you Felarif, L'thinis, K'trevl, and Rayz." She noted the faint dip in Docherty's eyebrows when he saw the linked hands and knew she'd made the right assignments.

Turning to Yale, she indicated the Meligornian couple. "Captain Yale, these are Masters K'trevl and Rayz. They will accompany the *Cathay Williams*. Both are experienced mages and respected teachers at the University of Federation Mages."

The woman managed a credible seated bow of acknowledgement and the mages returned it. Stephanie turned to the other captain.

"Captain Docherty, these are Masters Felarif and L'thinis. They will accompany the *Henry Chauvel*. Again, the University of Federation Mages offers two of their most experienced staff."

"And Tethis?" the captain ventured.

She pursed her lips and her heart sank at the reminder of the old mage's frailty. "While he would happily have accompanied one of you, wielding magic at the level required would kill him."

The captains looked shocked at her admission, and Docherty cleared his throat.

"Well," he said after a moment, "we are glad these Masters are able to accompany us. Without a mage, we have no chance to survive an encounter with a Teloran ship, regardless of the havoc your Marines wreak inside it."

It made her wonder exactly what Todd and the Hooligans had

gotten up to in the scenarios. She'd only had time to go over the footage from the command decks and engine rooms. There'd be time to find out, she decided and smiled.

"I'll tell them they'll need to step up their game," she replied and rose. "I'm sorry to make this meeting short, but we have a long day of testing tomorrow and I shouldn't keep you."

She also had a long night of debriefing with Captain Emil and the other officers of the *Knight*, but she didn't need to tell them that. She stepped clear of the chair.

"Selene's Blessing upon your endeavors," she intoned, touched her fingertips to her forehead, and extended her fist to the Meligornians in a warrior's bow of farewell and respect.

The captain's eyes widened as the mages scrambled to their feet to return it and each one touched their fists to hers before they formed a line to the door. "And her protection upon yours," they replied.

She wished she could say more but knew there was nothing she could add that wouldn't diminish their standing before the captains and Marines. The team fell in around her as she left and Lars and Johnny exited ahead of her.

It would be a long night.

"So he's dead. It took him long enough." Silas Eade paced the area they used as a board room behind Joffle's Bar. He set both knuckles on the table and leaned forward so his shadow dominated the surface's center. It was gratifying to see several of his fellow leaders shrink from it, but he didn't let that stop him.

"Well, I for one will not take orders from a woman who used to be his apprentice. Emerald." He snorted, straightened, and flipped his hand in a derogatory gesture. "She sounds precious to me. A little green, if you must know."

Nervous laughter greeted his pun but it was weak and short-lived. He scanned them with a fiery gaze before he lowered his voice to a savage growl.

"I don't care what the others say. This Emerald can't be anywhere near as frightening as he was. Rumor has it she walked away and couldn't take the heat. And that she wasn't strong enough to take the stress of running the business way back when she was given the chance." His gaze swept across them again. "What's to say she has it now?"

A few of them shuffled nervously as he paused to let his words sink in.

"Who says she has it now?" he stated again.

More of the men and women around the table shifted uneasily and one or two exchanged surreptitious glances. Silas made a note of who and began a list of those to follow up with later. He wasn't used to seeing so much doubt in the criminal elite he met with.

It was unnerving but he wouldn't let it stop him.

"So she killed a few couriers. That doesn't make her a leader. Aside from that, she's wreaked havoc on the skylanes and got herself in trouble with the traffic authority. That's hardly the mark of a professional. If you ask me, we're still dealing with the same scared little girl who ran away from Tex in the first place." He looked around the table. "So why haven't we removed her already? You can't tell me none of you have thought about it."

No one moved and many refused to meet his gaze.

Silas made a sound of disgust. "What? You haven't? Are you telling me there isn't a single one of you who'd like to see someone else at the top of the pile?"

He waited but received no responses. "So none of you have thought of eliminating her and taking her place?"

Several faces paled and their eyes widened at the mere suggestion.

"Really?" He had begun to enjoy himself now. "None of you? You're all happy with the current arrangement?"

This time, his question drew a few shrugs and brief head movements that might have been negatives.

Silas sighed. 'Well, even if you're all happy with it, I am not. If none of you want to try to take her place, I guess it'll have to be me. Now, which of you wants to have me owing them a favor when I head this region?"

This time, the discomfort was palpable and several of the leaders looked openly at the door. One even drew a communicator from his pocket and stood.

"I have an appointment," he said and ignored the disbelief on Silas's face. "I have to go."

"You're kidding me."

The man looked pointedly at the communicator, then at him. "No, I'm afraid not. There's a business matter that needs my attention."

"That was sudden, wasn't it?" he challenged but didn't quite dare to openly accuse him of cowardice.

Fortunately—and he couldn't say for who—the man decided not to call him on it. Instead, he shrugged and spread his hands. "You, of all people, should know how it is."

It was a low blow and reminded everyone in the room that he'd had his own troubles in the past. Worst of all, it wasn't something he could deal with now without looking weak.

Instead, he inclined his head in farewell and hid his deep anger as he looked at those still gathered around the table. Again, he loomed over them. This time, many stared at him and he did not like the calculation in their eyes.

"What's wrong with you people?" he asked. "It's like you're all scared of a greenhorn—of someone who hasn't been active in our world for years." He waved a hand expansively as he warmed to his theme. "Where did she go? If she's such a force to be reckoned with, how come we never heard of what she was doing?"

It was enough to goad an answer from one of his colleagues and would-be rivals. "Not everyone advertises their wares."

"What do you mean?" Silas kicked himself as soon as he asked.

The question sounded weak when he needed to be strong. Worse, it sounded like he hadn't done his homework and while that was true, it was not a fact he wanted to advertise.

"Emerald's services were highly specialized and she was very selective about her clientele."

He forced his expression to remain bland and let his eyebrows rise in a look of mockery. "Oh, really?" he challenged. "So she was high-class and choosy." He shrugged and gave his smile a lecherous twist. "It sounds like many girls I know."

The man who'd answered shook his head before he rested his forehead in his hand.

One of the other men pushed his chair back. "You have no idea, do you?" he snarked as he stood. "Call me when you have a clue."

This time, Silas couldn't stop his jaw from dropping. "What's that supposed to mean?"

He looked at the others for support and saw varied expressions between disbelief and carefully structured blandness. Not the kinds of faces he wanted to see.

Frustrated, he shook his head and gave a gusty sigh. "So, you're telling me this Emerald chick has specialized skills." He raised his voice. "So, what? She's a nobody, an upstart, new to the field of being a leader and not worthy of being Tex's successor."

Someone snorted as if to suggest he wasn't worthy either, but he couldn't tell who. Worse, several more of the leaders pushed their chairs back. He scrambled to regain control.

"I'm throwing my hat in the ring," he announced and expected them to be impressed.

This brought soft groans and one of the female leaders stood. "It's been nice knowing ya, Eady-boy."

"What do you mean by that?" he demanded but she rolled her shoulders and gave him a mysterious smile.

He didn't bother to watch her as she left but looked around at those who remained. "What about the rest of you?" he demanded. "I'll eliminate this Emerald person and become the top dog in the region. Who's with me?"

As if his question signaled the end of the meeting, the others stood. Without saying a word, they tucked their chairs under the table and filed from the room. Not a single one glanced at him. They merely left the room in a wordless vote of no-confidence.

When the last one closed the door, Silas realized he was gaping and closed his mouth with a snap.

"Well," he muttered and sank into the nearest chair. "I guess I'll have to do it on my own."

He sat in silence while he contemplated his chances of enlisting support from any of them, then decided it was a lost cause.

"Pity," he murmured, pulled his tablet out, and tapped in the number of a friend in Washington. "Tarneit. Yeah. Yeah, it's me. Look, I need a crew."

CHAPTER TWELVE

Lars and Johnny breathed a sigh of relief when they found the training room empty. The last thing they wanted was for the team to have an audience while they worked out some of the kinks brought on by a week of traveling and scenarios. What they needed was a good, hard fight.

"Wakey, wakey," the team leader called. "Get ready and get warmed up. We have work ahead of us."

He grinned at the mock groans that answered him. "Aww, what's the matter, my babies? Do you like it all soft?"

Frog snickered and Avery and Brendan chuckled. Johnny smirked. Lars realized what he'd said and blushed.

"You assholes know what I mean. Get your butts out on the mats or I'm gonna kick 'em so hard you'll eat funny for a week."

"Ooh! It sounds like someone got up on the wrong side of the bed this morning." The new voice made them all look around.

A dark-haired woman had entered the training hall and the tattoos that marked her jawline drew their eyes as she strutted across the room. She was followed by another woman, this one as tall, solid, and fair as her friend was short, lightly built, and dark.

A group of men came after them, including one six-foot figure that stood out from the rest.

"Todd!" Lars called and his face broke into a grin. "I heard you were aboard. Steph will be glad to see you."

This brought a round of catcalls from both teams, and Todd rolled his eyes and ignored the color that rose in his cheeks. "It's good to see you, too, Lars."

"Your guys have met the team, haven't they?"

The sergeant shook his head. "Things got kinda crazy after the battle. I don't think they really had the chance."

The security head crossed the mats and signaled for the team to gather round. "Guys, you've met Todd." He indicated the Marines Todd had brought with him. "These are the Hooligans. Todd, do you want to do the honors?"

"Sure thing, but are you sure you really want to know them?" He grinned when Ka shoved him. "This is Ka. She's my corporal and right-hand man."

"I'm not doing anything your right hand's renowned for," she quipped and both teams snickered.

Todd ignored the jibe. "Moving right along."

He made short work of introducing the others and gave only their names and not the skills they were known for. They arrayed themselves behind him and studied Stephanie's team.

While he tried not to see the assessment in their eyes, he knew he was in for a hard time later on—and that was only if the team didn't try to challenge Lars and the others beforehand. He pushed the thought to the back of his mind.

That was the kind of trouble he didn't need.

"You guys don't mind if we take some space?" he asked. "It's only that with all the time in the pods, we…"

He let the words trail off so Lars could fill in the blanks.

The older man did. He gestured at the training mats. "It's fine. We're here for the same reason. The pods are good and all, but nothing can replace the real thing."

Ka cleared her throat. "I don't believe you've introduced your-selves," she said and Todd sighed.

Maybe he wouldn't be able to avoid a challenge after all.

"You're right," Lars replied and went through the team's names quickly. He paused and studied the Hooligans. "That was some fancy thinking you guys did."

"When?" Ka asked, her voice sharp with suspicion.

"On the dreadnought," he told her. "I'm sure no-one expected to see you come out the other side." He slid a quick glance at Todd and added, "I'm really glad you did, though. We needed that data."

"You saw that?" The woman gave her sergeant a shocked look. "I thought that shit was classified."

"It was." He stared thoughtfully at the security head. "How did you come by it?"

He was torn between thinking it was something the Navy had done and the idea that maybe Steph's team wasn't as clean and white-knight as he thought they were.

Lars let him think the worst for a few long minutes before he explained. "The Navy wanted us to get you to the Teloran ship and that meant letting you on the *Knight.* Of course, that meant convincing us you might actually be able to do what the Navy said you could."

"So they had to let you see the footage," Ka finished for him and seemed oblivious to the looks directed at her.

The man's lips twitched. "Yes. We insisted on proof and the Navy finally agreed to let us see exactly why they were so convinced."

Todd stared at him, open-mouthed. "They did?"

Lars nodded. "Yup. They did."

"It was a trap!" the sergeant exclaimed and laughter rippled through both teams.

Ka rolled her eyes. "Whatever," she said and walked to an empty place at the edge of the mats. Once there, she stripped to lycra and started her warm-up.

The rest of the team followed and were soon working through a routine of slow stretches and mobility exercises. Todd walked after them but cast Lars a rueful look and shook his head as he went.

The security head exchanged glances with Johnny and signaled that his own team should get back to work. They'd warmed up and Lars and Johnny had started light sparring by the time Stephanie and Vishlog arrived with the cats.

The felines pranced through the door beside her and stared at her raised hands with unnerving focus. The Dreth trailed behind her and ignored the cats' antics but remained alert to their surroundings.

Todd watched her and wondered why she needed protection on her own ship, but his question went unasked.

"No!" Stephanie snapped at Bumblebee when the cat half-rose on his haunches. "Not for you. It's mine to wear, not yours to sleep on."

The garment in question was lifted over her head.

"I'm tired of your shit. You have a perfectly good set of blankets. You don't need to nest in my clothes. I don't care how good they smell."

Everyone stopped and their heads swiveled toward her, and Stephanie froze.

"That's not what it sounds like," she told them, her face flushed. "It's not."

"Sure, Steph," Avery agreed and crossed to pluck the bundle of cloth out of her hands. "What, exactly, is all the fuss about?"

Both cats pivoted while their gazes followed the garment into his hands. He shook it to reveal a fleecy jacket and spun abruptly when Zeekat pounced.

"Zee!" Stephanie shouted, but he had braced against the impact. The feline twisted in the air and thumped into his back but not hard enough to knock either of them over.

"I can't believe you still have this!" Avery exclaimed and Todd recognized one of her favorite sweaters from school.

She stalked around her pilot and snatched the garment from his hands before Bumblebee could get into position to steal it. "It's mine and I like it."

"You need to burn it," Lars muttered and she flushed.

Magic crackled over her hands. "Don't even."

Todd's eyes widened. He'd known she liked that jumper but he hadn't known she liked it that much. It made him glad he'd never tried to take it. Somehow, he didn't think she'd have thought it funny.

He became aware of movement around him and he realized he'd been staring. Ka nudged him in the ribs. "So," she said, "are you gonna introduce us?"

Holding the garment against her chest and doing her best to ignore the two cats that closed in, she hurried to Lars. "You would not believe what these two clowns tried to do to the Marines."

For one heart-stopping moment, Todd thought she was referring to the Hooligans and from the nervous shuffling around him, his team thought so too. He was relieved when she continued.

"I don't think Sergeant Tomek will ever forgive them."

Lars did his best to keep a straight face as he surveyed the animals. "What did they do this time?"

"Well, you know how the Marines like to do their morning run around the hangar decks?"

The man nodded.

"So I went down to join them and thought the cats might enjoy stretching their legs."

Todd could see the logic in that.

"Uh-huh," Lars acknowledged and made hand motions to encourage her to continue.

She huffed a sigh. "Well, these two clowns thought it would be fun to race ahead and ambush the Marines as they ran past. You should have seen them. One minute, there were two orderly columns of Marines and the next, Zee bulldozed into the side at the back and knocked them into each other—"

Lars started to laugh and she scowled.

Frog pulled his tablet out. "I have to see this!"

"Don't you dare go interfering with the *Knight's* systems," the security head admonished and stepped closer so he could get a better look at what the man was doing. He pointed silently at the screen.

"I can see you, you know." The *Knight's* voice said over the speakers and the two men looked sheepishly at the ceiling.

It didn't stop Frog from what he was doing, though.

The cats watched the two men, sat on either side of her, and looked far too pleased with themselves.

She threw up her hands in disgust. "When you two have quite finished."

Lars returned to her. "I'm sorry," he replied and looked anything but. "I thought you had finished."

"Like hell!" She snorted to call the lie before she went on. "Anyway, this one"—she gestured to Bumblebee—"took advantage of the confusion and pounced on the men at the front."

The man groaned. "How many times did Tomek hit the floor?"

Stephanie snickered. "More than once. In the end, he ordered everyone to keep running, no matter what happened, and that was when these two idiots decided it would be even more fun to run alongside the columns and swipe the guys' legs out from under them."

By now, Ka and Piet had retrieved their tablets and the Hooligans had gathered around them. They chuckled as they watched Sergeant Tomek's squad try to deal with the two overly playful creatures.

"And what did the sergeant have to say about that?" Lars asked. He did his best to keep his voice neutral and failed miserably.

"Nothing. He finished the training session and asked to speak to me in private."

The man stilled and the smile vanished from his face. "Uh-huh."

"Yes." Her expression reflected his. "He asked me very nicely if the cats could be kept on a leash and if he could have some advance warning if I decided to join them again."

He opened his mouth to commiserate, only to be interrupted when the tall blonde from the Hooligans dropped to her knees beside Bumblebee. Before either he or Stephanie could stop her, the Marine had begun to scratch the yellow-and-black cat under his jaw.

"Who's a good kitty?" she cooed. "Yes, you are."

Stephanie's jaw dropped as Bee raised his chin to give the woman better access and purred.

"Ugh!" she exclaimed, and Todd decided he'd better intervene.

"Hi, Steph," he began but stopped, feeling suddenly awkward.

Behind him, the team hooted in mock derision. He flipped them the bird and his heart raced double-time as he approached his girl. It had been so long.

All he wanted to do was take her in his arms—well, to start with. His mouth went dry and he swallowed as he searched for something to say. "Have you met the Hooligans?" he finally muttered, his voice a little rough.

She looked past him in the direction his hand had indicated. Coming around him for a better look at them, she shook her head. "No. Do you wanna introduce them?"

He smirked as the Hooligans stiffened with apprehension. "Sure thing."

"The one currently paying tribute to Bee is Dru." He moved his hand. "That one most definitely not hacking the *Knight's* security system"—the *Knight* played a raspberry over the speakers and he rolled his eyes—"is my second in command, Ka."

The woman glanced up long enough from her tablet to nod in Stephanie's direction. Henry and Angus, who stood on either side of her, followed her glance but looked at the screen again quickly.

"Her two sidekicks are Henry and Angus," Todd continued, "and her partner in crime"—at this, Piet looked up—"is my explosives expert, Piet."

The man scowled at his introduction but managed a cordial nod at Stephanie. "Pleasure," he mumbled and didn't look away, his tablet seemingly forgotten in his hands.

"All mine," she replied and the man blushed to his hairline.

Todd didn't blame him but went on to introduce the rest of the team. "And last but not least is Jimmy."

The big Scotsman raised his knuckles briefly to his forehead and she smiled.

"They don't look like the kind of trouble I've been told about," she stated and Todd froze.

His team at least had the grace to look slightly abashed but it didn't last long. Piet handed his tablet to Gary and stepped forward. He studied Stephanie with a distinctly puzzled expression.

"How do you..." he began, reddened, and tried again. "The magic. You've exploded ships and I've seen you use nets of both dark and light magic to cut your enemies to pieces, but you're ti— You don't look big enough to be able to hold that much. I mean, how do—"

Her smile faded. "How do I hold that much destruction?"

The man nodded and looked slightly relieved that she'd understood.

Stephanie gave him a tight-lipped smile and a cold knot formed in Todd's stomach. He knew that look. It meant someone was about to regret something very much and he wondered what Piet had done to raise her ire.

Apparently, he wasn't as stupid as he looked because he paled. "I... It's okay if you don't want to answer," he added hastily and licked his lips.

Sensing trouble, the other Hooligans came closer, their expressions confused. If Piet was in trouble, none of them could understand why. Dru left the cats and came to stand beside him, close enough to offer comfort but far enough away to draw weapons she didn't have.

The Witch noticed their actions and raised an eyebrow, but her gaze didn't leave Piet's face. "I'm like you in that respect, Aftermath."

Piet stumbled away from her, but Ka gave a short bark of laughter. "Aftermath? Really?"

"It's not a name I chose," he muttered, his face as red as a beet.

Stephanie's smile became predatory. "But it's the one the intelligence people gave you, isn't it? Or would you prefer Pompalid?"

He went from red to white in the blink of an eye and shook his head. "No. No, I would not."

She stepped toward him. "Do you care to tell me why?"

Piet's eyes flicked once to Todd, then to her. Finally, he answered. "Because there are some things I'd rather not remember. You must keep in mind I was not my own creation."

In response, she inclined her head and laid a finger alongside her chin. "You might want to remember that when you're talking about how much damage I can do too."

She paused and her gaze drilled through him. "Better yet, why don't you think of the creative capabilities I might have? Magic doesn't only have to be used to destroy. It can be used to make things too—unlike those Meligornian grenades you children have sitting in lock-up."

Ka's jaw dropped at the insult and Todd tensed, but Stephanie continued without giving his corporal time to interject.

She poked Piet in the chest. "You, my destructive friend, need to focus less on what you can tear down and more on what you can build because one day, this war will be over and we'll all have a chance to leave our pasts behind us."

Todd wondered what past she might be referring to but she hadn't finished. She leaned closer to the explosives expert's pale face.

"Or should I tell them what you did on the *Steranos Nova*?"

"The *Steranos Nova*?" Ka's quiet voice asked but no one answered.

Stephanie and Piet kept their gazes locked on each other until he found words. "No. There's no need for that."

"Good," she told him, "because you and I will sit down and work out how to put your more creative ideas into action once this is done, so you'd better have some. Am I understood?"

Piet stiffened to attention. "Sir, yes, sir, you are," he replied, his voice subdued.

"Good." Stephanie stepped closer to Todd and placed the palm of her hand on his chest. "It's good to see you."

Judging by the look on her face, she wanted to do more than that but they were at work and their teams were watching them.

He groaned. "To hell with this," he snapped, wound his arms around her, and buried his face in her hair. "I have missed you."

To his relief, she didn't push him away but pulled him close and leaned back so she could kiss him. The teams hooted with glee and the two each extended an arm and held a single digit up.

This resulted in good-natured laughter. Lars turned to Ka and gestured with his head at the others. She nodded. "Okay, kids," he said. "The show's over. It's time to get back to work."

"There is no way the show is over," Gary protested. "They still have to come up for air."

"Twenty seconds," Frog declared.

"Twenty? Are you kidding? They haven't seen each other in over a month." Gary argued. "I'd say give them at least thirty."

Ka snorted, her sense of responsibility momentarily diverted. "Nah, they're both professionals. It doesn't matter what it looks like. I'd say give them ten."

Laughter rippled through Stephanie and made Todd's chest shake. Frog and Gary made sounds of disgust.

"That's it," the Englishman declared. "All bets are off."

"Outside interference," Frog agreed as the couple separated and turned their attention to their people.

Todd was surprised to see Dru deep in conversation with Vishlog. Both of them continuously cast glances toward Stephanie.

"You can't be serious," Dru said. "She spars with the rest of you?"

The Dreth nodded.

"But she's so tiny!" the woman exclaimed as the teams fell silent.

Her words rang clearly through the room and Reggie chuckled.

"Good luck with the bad timing awards," he called and Dru blushed.

Vishlog wasn't affected. "That little slip of a girl," he told the Marine, "beats me easily and does so often."

The woman snorted with disbelief. "How?"

"Well..." He paused and clearly tried to think of a way to describe his many losses to Stephanie.

"Magic?" Dru suggested, "because in that case, I'd easily believe it."

The warrior shook his head. "Not magic. The closest I can say is that she beat me due to friction."

Several of the team sputtered and Todd gave Stephanie a startled glance.

"It's not what you think," she whispered and looked mortified.

Vishlog tried to make his explanation clearer. "Or better yet, a lack of friction," he said but his brow creased as if he wasn't happy with those words either.

The Witch lowered her head and rested her fingertips against her forehead as she shook her head. The skin on her face and neck had turned a faint pink.

Todd draped his arm over her shoulders. "I'm sure it's not as bad as it sounds," he told her and started to snicker.

"Oh, go and train your team of troublemakers," she told him, pulled out from under his arm, and walked toward the mat. She raised her voice as she went. "What's wrong, guys? Are you too scared to step out on the mats with me?"

The door to the training hall opened and another squad of Marines entered. They strode to an empty space on the mats and began to prepare to conduct a training session of their own.

Stephanie ignored them and moved into her usual routine of stretches and warm-ups, while Lars and the others hurried to catch up.

Vishlog looked at the cats. "Stay," he told them sternly.

Bumblebee cocked his head and Zeekat twitched his tail.

"Stay," the Dreth repeated, his face concerned.

Both cats yawned at him and revealed curved fangs and curling tongues—and a hint of disdain for his orders. He sighed.

"Very well, then," he told them and lowered his voice so it wouldn't carry to those out on the mats. "Try not to break anything."

They exchanged glances and looked at him.

"If you do, you might find yourselves locked in your cabin for a week," Vishlog informed them and they tilted their heads the other way. "Yes, truly. Be good kitties and I will give you a treat."

Their tails flicked in unison and the felines remained perfectly still. With a sigh, he headed to the mats. He wasn't sure how long they'd stay like that and he wanted to at least have begun training before they started on their next round of mischief.

He was working through his first kata with Frog when an outraged shout echoed around the gym.

"Hey! Those are my pants!"

The warrior tried not to let it distract him. Frog had moved out of kata and taken his first jab at the Dreth, using the cats' mischief and his opponent's distraction to his advantage.

"Give me back my boot!" the man yelled. "Todd! Your girlfriend's cats are a menace."

Vishlog sighed, raised one hand to deflect his teammate's next attack, and swiped the small man with his other hand to knock him aside.

"Enough!" Stephanie's voice was sufficient to still all movement in the hall, and Frog came to stand quietly beside the Dreth.

The cats completely ignored her.

The Marines who'd arrived looked at her team and backed slowly off the mats. Lars inclined his chin to their leader and signaled for his people to do the same. No sooner had a space been cleared than Bumblebee leapt onto the mats, his head held high and someone's uniform trousers trailing from his mouth.

Another shout drew everyone's attention and Zeekat bounded alongside the yellow-and-black cat looking triumphant, a boot clamped between his jaws.

Todd looked at where Stephanie and the other Marines stood.

"They want to play keep away," Lars called and the Marines chuckled, while the Hooligans moved toward the two errant animals. "Have fun."

Bumblebee bounded forward and swept Piet's feet out from under him before he bounded away to avoid Angus' clumsy attempt to snatch the trousers.

"Give. Those. Back!" the Marine shouted and darted after the cat.

Ka looked at Todd.

"So should we leave him to it?" she asked and gestured to where Angus attempted to bring Bee down with a running tackle.

He shook his head and glanced at the entrance to the training hall. The other Marines and Steph's team were lined up along the wall and blocking the door. Tablets were out, some filming the action while others were used to record bets.

When he looked the other way, it was to see Gary, Jimmy, and Reggie try to retrieve the Englishman's boot.

"Nah," he told her. "This is gonna take teamwork—and we have to show these clowns what the Hooligans are made of."

"So, one in, all in?"

He rolled his eyes and started to jog after Bumblebee. "Like you had to ask."

The cats upped the ante when they took more items and played a combination of keep away and capture the flag. They worked together to stop the Hooligans from reaching their items by picking them up and dumping them or bowling over the Marines who attempted to retrieve them.

Todd risked a glance at Stephanie, half-hoping she'd intervene, but she was doubled over with laughter at her pets' antics.

Bumblebee raced past and waved a familiar t-shirt at him as he passed.

"Keep away—huh? Come here, you furry menace!"

CHAPTER THIRTEEN

"Amy, I am sorry to disturb you." BURT's voice sounded too loud in Elizabeth's office.

The woman startled and cursed softly. She'd been deep in thought.

"Sorry, BURT," she replied. "What is it?"

"I know we hoped it wouldn't come to this, but you—as Emerald—have a problem."

She sighed. "Hope and reality," she told him, "are always two different things where Elizabeth is concerned."

"And Stephanie," he agreed. "In this case, a crew is attempting to work out how to attack our Emerald persona. I am afraid we'll have to come down quite hard on them in order to avoid more."

"I hate this part," she told him but her face hardened with determination. "I'm not a killer. I'm a defender—a protector. I guard things. I don't go out and kill them." After a pause, she added softly, "That's Elizabeth's job."

"Arne has offered to assist," BURT informed her. "He is not a stranger to bringing death."

Amy stilled at that. "Does he have a jacket?"

"He has several. Which one would you like?"

"The one that shows me the real Arne."

"They're all real," he informed her. "Merely different facets."

"Then send me them all," she snapped. "I need to know exactly who I'm dealing with."

"You do not have time to go through all of them," he replied. "I will send you the one pertaining to the Star Scorpions."

"The Star Scorpions?"

"Yes. Do you know of them?"

"No, I do not but it sounds promising."

An hour later, she looked up from the file BURT had delivered to her screen. "Can you ask him to meet with me? I need a consultant." She tapped the screen. "And he looks like he fits the bill."

Ten minutes later, there was a quiet knock at the office door and she minimized the document.

BURT's response was unexpected. "Arne was already on his way. Something about a 'gut feeling' that he should be closer to hand? It is a happy coincidence," he added, "since you are out of time."

Amy still stared at the ceiling when the master sergeant opened the door and poked his head around it.

"Would you like to speak to us here or in Briefing Room One?" he asked and she pulled herself quickly together.

"Briefing Room One, please. I'll bring coffee. BURT can let us know what we're facing in there."

"Agreed." Arne told her, "but I will get the coffee while you work out what you want to ask me. I'll see you there."

He disappeared before she could argue, and she wondered what he knew that she didn't.

Nothing, as it turned out, but she gained a respect for his gut feelings.

"To the best of our knowledge, they haven't connected Matthias with Emerald," he explained, "or Emerald with Elizabeth at One R&D, but I don't want to risk that happening. With her away, I decided it might be better if we stayed here." He looked at the ceiling. "I asked BURT for permission first," he added, "and assumed he would let you know, but he might not have had time."

"I did not," BURT confirmed, "but that is not important right now."

Amy pursed her lips but nodded. She turned to the man as she lifted the steaming cup of coffee.

After a sip, she said, "BURT informs me that a crew plans to attack Emerald." Her lips twisted in distaste. "According to him, I will have to make an example of them." For a moment, she let her face show uncertainty. "This is hard for me to admit but I'm not a killer."

She watched as his mouth tightened, the look on his face closer to the ones on the man in the files than she'd like.

"And what makes you think I am?" he asked quietly.

With a sigh, she glanced at the ceiling. "BURT, show him what I was reading when I asked you to reach out to him."

He obliged and put the relevant pages up on the viewscreen at the front of the room.

"But that's—" Arne's jaw dropped.

"Yes, it is, isn't it?" She smirked at him. "When does your retirement take effect?"

"Ah..." He still stared at the screen.

"Yesterday," Matthias replied, his eyes dancing with amusement as the others turned toward him. "I wanted to ask Elizabeth if she'd mind me moving in here when she got back. But with her away..." He darted a guilty glance at Arne. "It was only going to be until she got back."

"And then you would ask if you could stay?" Amy couldn't help but smile. It was like dealing with a lovestruck teenager. She thought of Elizabeth and amended the thought to two lovestruck teenagers. Neither of them seemed to know what to do.

She sighed. Honestly, how either of them had reached adulthood without working this stuff out was beyond her.

Amy thought of her boss and stopped. Actually, when she thought of where E had come from, it wasn't that hard to believe.

For a moment, she tried to calculate the chances of Elizabeth meeting a guy with the same lack and gave up. *She is one lucky bitch*, she thought, and hoped she'd luck out the same way—if she lived long enough.

She was still deciding what to say when she saw Matthias had noticed what was up on the screen. His mouth dropped open and his eyes made short work of reading what was there. He looked at Arne.

"Is there anything else I should know?" he asked with the faintest trace of an edge to his voice.

The other man shrugged and tried to look nonchalant. "Probably, but that's not why we're here." He frowned. "And by we, I mean Amy and I. What are you doing here?"

The commander's mouth quirked into a smile. "What? You thought you were the only one who could tell when he'd been given the slip? I thought we wouldn't have any secrets between us."

Amy groaned and he realized what that made him and the master sergeant sound like.

"Ugh. That's not what—"

She frowned. "It doesn't matter. What does is that I'm supposed to protect you from all this."

Matthias gestured at the screen and her with a frustrated motion of his hand. He pulled a chair out and dropped into it before he smiled and glanced at the ceiling. "BURT, does this concern my Elizabeth?"

"Yes, Matthias. She is at the center of the matter we are discussing."

"Then it's an aspect of her life I'd eventually have to come to terms with, is it not?"

"That is correct."

"That's beside the point," Arne exclaimed. "The point is you've only just retired and if the Navy get wind—"

"And they won't with you?" He gestured toward the screen. "With that on your file? And when did you plan to tell me, by the way?"

The other man reddened. "You sound like a jilted lover."

"Don't try to change the subject. That is the kind of thing friends warn their friends about."

Arne shook his head. "No. It's not. That is the kind of thing you hope your friends never find out about in case they suddenly decide not to be your friend anymore."

"What?"

"Look at it! Those aren't operations the Navy will ever own up to. They've established plausible deniability, and no one who took part will ever admit to it. When I said I had no problem with working for Stephanie because she was more of a guarantee that I'd work for the real good of the world, I had my reasons."

"That was your reason?" Matthias exclaimed, pushed out of his seat, and shook his hand at the screen. "That?"

"Yes!" Amy scooted clear as Arne stood to face his friend. "That!"

"It's a good thing it's not classif…i… Amy, where did you get that?" The screen suddenly went blank.

"Don't ask questions you're not ready for the answer to," BURT told him, his tone clipped as he changed the subject. "Now, if we could all get back to the matter at hand. It really is most urgent."

Matthias looked at the blank screen and sat. Following his glance, the other man followed suit and shook his head.

"What do you need to know?" Arne asked and focused his attention on Amy.

She sighed and drew her chair up to the table again. "I guess the first thing I need to know is if I really need to do anything," she said. "I think I do, but I'd rather not have to, and I want to make sure I'm not reading more into the situation than I need to."

He nodded. "Firstly, you're not and you do, and I answered your questions backward."

"I got it," she told him. "So, this is the next area I'm not so sure about. While I have an idea of what I think Elizabeth would do if she found out about this, I don't know if I'm right or if what I'm thinking of doing will be enough."

"The most important thing," he declared, rested his elbows on the table, and leaned forward, "is that we protect Emerald's name, which means we have to eliminate these jokers."

"And we have to do it in such a way that anyone else who thinks they want her job thinks again," Matthias interjected. "We need to make the consequences so unpleasant and economically unviable for them that most will decide it's not worth making a run for the top position." He stopped when he realized the other man was gaping at him. "What? Do you think you're the only one with a dubious Navy past? I wasn't always a negotiator, you know."

As if to confirm it, the screen came alive again. This time, it held a very different file.

"To save you having to wrangle it out," BURT interrupted smoothly, "I have highlighted the relevant paragraphs."

He paled and slumped in his seat. As much as he was prepared to tell them he'd been involved in unsavory projects, he really hadn't been ready to have them see the proof of it in black and white.

"The kind of thing you tell your friends, huh?" Arne teased, but Matthias simply stared at the screen.

"How did you get this?" he asked, his voice barely above a whisper.

"Do you recall what I used to be?" BURT asked and he nodded and closed his mouth as he did so. The AI pressed on. "And do you remember what caused me to create One R&D?"

Again, he nodded.

"So you will understand why I have seen fit to acquire what information I could find on you both in order to protect my assets."

Matthias swallowed to ease the sudden dryness of his throat. "How long have you had this?"

"I acquired these files only recently," BURT informed him and realized why he might be asking. "I have yet to forward them to Elizabeth."

Arne's hoot of laughter made them all jump. "Oh, boy! Do you have some explaining to do." The former Marine chuckled. "Now, there's a conversation I'd like to be a fly on the wall for."

"No, you wouldn't." The other man glared at him. "And don't you bloody dare. I happen to know what the Star Scorpions were used for so keep it to yourself."

"Which doesn't change the fact that you still need to keep a distance from this," Arne told him. "The Navy will hold you close for a while" —he gestured at the screen—"especially in light of this. No wonder they were edging you toward retirement. There was literally nowhere else they could put you that wouldn't give you too much power."

"Power?" Matthias pointed at the screen. "Because of that? I don't see how."

The man groaned and rolled his eyes. "Listen, we're at war. Officially. You of all people should know exactly what that means." He paused to let that sink in and added, "You need to have plausible deniability for later."

"I…" Matthias gestured helplessly. "You're right, but I don't like it. This is Elizabeth we're talking about."

Amy decided it was time to intervene. "Then you should know exactly how she'd feel about you being exposed like this. You have a difficult enough conversation ahead of you without needing to tell her why you took the risk when you didn't need to. Arne and I can handle it." Her face softened, and she stretched across the table to lay her hand over his wrist. "And we'll do that much better if you keep an eye on things here."

He favored her with a cock-eyed grin. "Mind the car, huh?"

She returned a crinkled smile. "And ride to the rescue if you need to. Exposure be damned. Don't you leave us out there."

His grin faded as he regarded them both and his gaze rested on Arne as he replied, "There's no chance of that."

"Good." The other man rose from his seat and walked to the door, held it open, and looked pointedly at him. "Then you won't mind leaving while we hash this out. If everything goes well, there are things you won't need to know."

"And if things don't?"

"Then I will provide you with all the details," BURT assured him. He gave Matthias time to digest this before adding, "Elizabeth would prefer it this way. She will make sure you know all you need to."

He sighed but stood. When he reached the door, he gave Amy a brief nod and patted Arne's bicep before he left.

The former master sergeant sighed as the door clicked shut and BURT changed the screen to show Matthias's progress to Elizabeth's office. "I will monitor his access," he assured them as the commander settled at the screen.

Arne studied the other man's face as he tapped on the keys and he nodded. "What do you have on the assassins?"

While he'd addressed Amy, it was BURT who answered. "Their

leader's name is Silas Eade. Under Tex, he was basically a nobody, an upstart but one vicious enough that he soon carved out his own territory. Even now, the other leaders in his area aren't willing to stand against him."

"But they don't agree with what he's doing," he concluded.

"Correct. I have already tried to approach several but, while some will allow access to Silas through their territories, they refuse to help. Most hung up on that question without giving a response."

"And the rest?" Arne asked.

"Three of the four shouted abuse, and the fourth told me calmly to come and talk to her when the job was done. When I asked for a meeting place, she said she'd be in touch and hung up—oh, and to offer Emerald her condolences."

Arne stilled and Amy went white. Both glanced at the door.

"Don't worry. Now that he's here, he won't go anywhere," BURT hastened to reassure them.

Arne's lips twitched. "Does he know that?"

The AI's reply was smug. "Not yet."

Arne snickered. "Good luck with that."

"Don't you wish to be a fly on the wall?" BURT asked and the man raised both hands.

"Oh, no, no, no," he replied. "I don't want to be anywhere near him when he finds out."

"Well, at least it will save him the embarrassment of having to ask Elizabeth if he can stay," Amy added. "Maybe he won't be that mad."

Arne gave her a disbelieving stare. "Are you kidding me?" He stabbed a finger at the inset where they could see Matthias working quietly at Elizabeth's computer. "That man prizes his freedom above almost everything else. He might want to move in with Elizabeth but he wants it to be on his terms."

"The question is does he prize that freedom over Elizabeth?" she asked.

Arne shook his head. "I said almost everything else. I get the impression there's a lot he'd do for his Elizabeth that he'd refuse for anyone else."

Amy hadn't finished. "And what about the Navy?" she demanded. "I betcha he wasn't so free there."

He went statue-still. "There are some things worth the compromise."

"Until they aren't," she countered tartly.

"Until they aren't," he confirmed and met her gaze without a trace of shame. He gestured at the screen. "Shall we?"

"BURT, how many men does he have?" she asked.

"He appears to have decided to go with a standard team of ten."

"Isn't that on the large side?" Arne questioned.

"No," BURT assured him. "For these people, it is on the smaller side."

"Well, that's an insult to Elizabeth!" Amy exclaimed. "Someone needs to teach this guy a lesson."

"We'll make an example of him," he corrected her. "We won't let him live."

"So?"

"So he won't be able to learn anything."

"That's a good point." She paused. "Exactly how gruesome will we get?"

Arne studied her face before he asked. "If this were a VR game, how gruesome would you go?"

The woman was straight forward and to the point. Even in a VR game, she was all about eliminating the threat and getting the job done as quickly as possible.

"We need something more," he told her, and her face paled as he described what he wanted done.

"Are...are you sure that's necessary?"

He nodded, his face hard. "Absolutely."

Amy didn't reply for a good few minutes and he didn't press her. This was something everyone had to work out for themselves—and not everyone was capable of going to the lengths he'd described.

"And if we don't?"

"They'll target her again. These people understand violence and respect it but they don't fear it. This, though..." He tapped the tablet on which he'd sketched his plan. "This kind of thing is beyond most of them and those familiar with it will be the ones most affected."

"By most familiar, do you mean the ones who do it?"

"Yes."

"And they're the ones who'll target Elizabeth?"

"If we don't instill a certain amount of fear into them, then yes, those are the ones most likely to assassinate Elizabeth and Matthias... and these—" He tapped the tablet once more. "These are the tactics they will use to deter anyone from targeting them once they take her position for themselves."

Amy nodded and the color returned to her face. "Well, that makes it easy then. To protect Elizabeth, I have to do this." She tapped the screen. "Easy-peasy."

Arne relaxed. Not everyone could overcome that hurdle and he'd wondered if he'd have to sideline the girl and bring Matthias in after all.

Now that he knew what the commander had done, he wasn't afraid the man would have trouble coping. The miracle was that they'd convinced him to keep his distance.

"BURT, how likely are they to be in that location twenty minutes from now?" she demanded.

"I am ninety per cent certain they will remain in that location for another twenty-one hours," BURT replied.

"Why?"

"Because they plan to murder one of Elizabeth's former lovers twenty-one hours from now."

"I thought you said Matthias was in danger."

"That was my impression until their most recent comms. They have done their homework but they still have not made the connection between Emerald and Elizabeth. Matthias is safe, for now."

"I still don't want him to leave," Arne interjected, and there was a smile in BURT's voice when the AI replied.

"I understand and concur. Elizabeth would not want him to leave either, and that is all the justification I need to keep him here."

The man smiled. "Then we are agreed. When this is done, I'll move his gear over."

"That is a point we will negotiate," BURT replied, and the smile faded from Arne's face.

"What do you mean?"

"What I mean is not relevant at this point," the AI told him. "You have a mission to run."

He leaned back in his chair and scowled at the viewscreen. "You and I will have words when I'm done, mister."

"I look forward to it."

Amy cleared her throat. "When you two are quite done."

Arne turned to her, his eyebrows raised. "And what will you do about it?"

She smiled. "Just because I don't like killing doesn't mean I won't make an exception, Marine."

"That's former Marine to you, young lady."

"You and whose army, Arne?" she retorted with a smirk

He smiled. "So, only the two of us?"

"I don't see anyone else, do you?" She made a show of looking around the empty room.

"Not what I was asking, Amy."

"Of course, only the two of us. I couldn't think of a better idea for a first date."

He raised his eyebrows. "So we're dating now?"

She shook her head, stood, and stretched across the table to pat his hand. "Sorry to get your hopes up, but no. It was merely a figure of speech."

Arne placed a hand over his heart and made a show of being short of breath. "Don't do that, girl. I'm an old man, you know."

"Ha!" She pushed her chair back and strode to the door. "And before you try, don't go telling me you have a heart. You're a Marine."

He tried to look hurt but smiled instead. "I'll have you know I'm a former Marine, which means I do so too have a heart. They handed it back when I left."

"Are you sure it's yours?" she retorted as she stepped into the corridor.

"What are you trying to say?"

Amy didn't answer but led the way to the company's equipment store. His jaw dropped when he entered. "This is one hell of a locker room."

"Thank you," BURT replied and a light flashed in a locker door. "We took the liberty of ordering a set of equipment built to your specifications."

"My what?"

"Measured to fit," she explained.

"When?"

"You've had at least one pod session here, right?"

"Oh." He understood, all right. His friend's new...employers... friends...whatever could give the Navy a run for their money when it came to sneaky. He only hoped that this didn't extend to underhanded, although Elizabeth's underworld involvement seemed to indicate otherwise.

He sighed and opened the locker. *It doesn't mean they're underhanded with their own people*, he told himself and hoped it was true.

The contents of the locker were a marvel—combat armor of better quality than he'd used in his days of deployment and impressive weapons.

"Well, well, well," he murmured as he hauled out the rifle, blaster, and dual sidearms. "Someone did their homework."

Amy smirked but didn't say anything. She surprised him when she shucked her clothing and pulled on the combat fatigues and armor stored in her locker without any sign of discomfort. It was a shame he didn't feel the same way.

Looking around, he saw a number of change rooms and took refuge inside. It wasn't that he was ashamed of his body but he wasn't young and there were scars he didn't want her to see.

"Your injuries are a matter of record," BURT reminded him but quietly so his words didn't carry beyond the room.

"There's record and there's seeing things for yourself," he reminded him gruffly.

"The armor has several built-in stim packs," the AI advised. "They've been calibrated for the metabolic rates and physical characteristics recorded in the pod."

"Without my permission," he grumbled but without rancor.

"Your psychological profile showed you'd rather be ready than sidelined while we got things ready," BURT replied. "Did we make a mistake?"

He shook his head. "No, you did not but a man likes to be asked, is all."

"Does a man always take this long to get ready?" Amy asked and poked her head around the door, her lockpicks in hand. "What are you doing in here anyway? Last I looked, makeup wasn't your thing."

Arne blushed. "It's a good thing I'm dressed."

"Yeah. I was a little slow. It's been a while since I had any need to use these." She brandished the lockpicks, not in the least ashamed.

"Well, I'm done," he confirmed. "What's the hold-up? Don't we have us some criminals to make an example of?"

Amy stepped into the change room and examined his armor, checked the straps and fastenings, and adjusted things where necessary.

"We sure as shit do," she told him, stepped away, and held her arms out to her side. "Your turn."

"I have prepared a car and will be your pilot for the evening," BURT told them when they had finished.

"Thank you, Jeeves," she snapped and the AI chuckled.

Ten minutes later, he brought the car down on a rooftop not far from their objective. "I believe it will be faster if you zipline across."

Arne grinned and stretched behind the seat to where he'd seen the equipment bag. "Ooh rah," he murmured, lugged the gear out onto the roof, and closed his helmet.

"Are we having fun, yet?" Amy asked over the closed comms.

"Baby, this party's only beginning."

Once he'd located the building in the HUD, he trotted to the edge of the roof. "BURT, what can you get off the local surveillance cams?"

"What kind of a man do you think I am?" The AI did his best to sound offended but retrieved the data.

"Now that's what I'm talking about," he told him, and Amy chuckled.

"I'd say he knows exactly what kind of man you are, BURT."

"Hmmpf. Well, hurry. They're about to change their watch and the window is small."

They complied and ziplined over the chasm between where they landed and the target building without delay.

"I'll pick you up from here when you're done."

"What about street-level?" Arne asked.

"We'll play it by ear. I will try to have the vehicle located near your exit."

"Deal," the man confirmed, rolled over the edge of the roof, and found cover as the change of guards arrived. "Remember, Ames, we want screams."

"If we didn't need it, no one would know we'd been until we were very long gone."

The first guard went down with a shattered knee, his rifle arm useless from the rounds that almost severed it at the shoulder. Just because she wasn't shooting to kill didn't mean Amy's aim was any less precise.

"Put him over the edge," Arne told her when they heard boots coming up the stairs.

The woman didn't stop to argue. She tried to act and not think, knowing the man's terrified shriek as he plummeted would haunt her dreams. "You owe me years of sleep," she told him.

"You can join me," he replied and gut-shot the second guard. He followed the first man as two more of Silas' team burst out of the stairwell.

"And they were the lucky ones," he told their new opponents, slung his rifle, and drew the broad-bladed sword he'd asked BURT for. With a sigh, Amy did the same.

She hadn't been happy to admit she knew how to use the weapon, and Arne made a note to ask her what she'd done before going into protection. While she'd said she wasn't a killer, he knew there was only one way to find that out.

He caught a glimpse of her felling a second man with the same clinical precision that she shot with. *Whatever it was, it sure as hell wasn't protection.*

Part of him wanted to think she fought like a Marine, but he knew that wasn't true. She fought like a demon—and like fighting would drive the demons away. He wasn't the only one who owed her years of sleep.

A round drove into his breastplate and he cursed. On a less-advanced piece of armor, that would have seen him dead. As it was, he would bruise like a bitch. *I gotta keep my mind on the job.*

They left the wounded bound and bleeding on the roof and took to the stairs. Killing would have been better than what followed, but messy was what was needed.

"BURT, do you have any soundtracks of someone burning alive?"

"That is not a standard request, Arne. Why—"

"Because I'm not a monster and I want to kill these fuckers before they burn, but I need the noise. Do you think you can manage it?"

"Give me five minutes."

"You have until I drag these assholes to the roof and build a pyre."

He'd found the petrol in an adjacent garage with chains and tie-downs. It wasn't pretty but it would do. Amy looked distinctly green.

"Arne..."

"Go with it, girl. If we do this, no one will target Elizabeth for a very long time."

BURT came through with what he'd requested, and Arne killed the assassins swiftly and without remorse.

"Get the files," he ordered once he'd opened the computer and found exactly what they'd planned for Elizabeth and her ex. He didn't have anything on these guys when it came to sick and twisted.

Amy took one glance at the files and drew her knife. "Tell me Silas is still alive."

"Well, yeah. Someone has to take the message."

"Good." Shortly after, a squeal of pain preceded her return, dragging the would-be crime lord. "Show me a camera. I have a message of my own to send. I am Emerald, after all." She adjusted her face mask to be sure her features were concealed.

Her message was short and to the point, but it turned Arne's stomach and left her retching into a bag. "Was that good enough?" she asked when she was able to speak.

He nodded and words seemed difficult. "Yup, that should do it."

A muffled sob jerked them to alertness, and Arne held a hand up to motion her to stillness. She waited as he crept toward a door tucked behind a bookcase.

"I thought you cleared this," he murmured over their comms and she shook her head.

"I thought you did."

"Man, we coulda been so fucked," he answered and she gave him a shaky laugh and the finger.

Smiling at her reaction, he eased the door open and was greeted by a desperate scrambling as if someone had seen it open and panicked. He kept his rifle slung and drew the big blade clear as he advanced.

More movement drew his eye. This time, it was the slightest twitch of a closet door. Soft-stepping across the room, he paused outside the door and listened to the muffled breathing from within. Someone was terrified.

"Ohgodohgodohgodohgod…" The faintest whisper was picked up by the sensors as clearly as if it had been spoken out loud.

Using the sound to direct him, he wrenched the door open and was greeted by a startled yelp. Instead of attacking, though, the young man inside curled into a ball with his hands over his head. "I'm sorry…sorry. Tell Silas I didn't mean it. I'd never have come if I'd known this was his place. Never."

The youngster gave another startled yelp as he yanked him out of the cupboard and flung him across the room. The kid's arms and legs windmilled as he tried to regain his balance, but he thudded into the wall anyway.

Arne winced at the impact and winced again as the young man bounced off and landed hard. He closed the distance between them in two short strides and dragged the boy to his feet.

"No! Please..." The kid didn't try to escape. He merely stiffened, tucked his chin to his chest, and hunched his shoulders. "Please, Silas. I didn't... I wouldn't..."

"I'm not Silas," he told him gruffly and the kid shivered.

"Please, let me go. I won't do it again... I..." Arne's fist ended the sentence and he slung the boy over his shoulder and carried him out to where Amy waited.

"But that's a kid!" she exclaimed when she saw his burden. "And he's still alive! What gives, Arne?"

"A case of wrong place at the wrong time," he told her. "My guess is he broke into the wrong house and hid when he realized what he'd done."

"So, not so innocent, then."

"No, but he doesn't deserve to die, either."

"What are you gonna do?"

"I know a place where he'll have another chance to get it right." He paused. "If B doesn't mind making a detour on the way home?"

"I can do that," BURT assured him.

Amy nodded. "Hey, B, can you fix the footage?"

"Already done."

"And the soundtrack?"

"Also done. Are you o—"

"No, B, I'm not. Now shut-up and scan for biologicals."

Yeah, definitely not only protection, Arne thought and wondered how much trouble he'd be in if he did a little digging for himself.

"Why did you tell them you were annoyed?" he asked as the car lifted from the roof, the ruddy glow of a funeral pyre bathing their craft in shades of red and orange.

"I figured E would play it down," Amy replied. "That way, they'd worry about what she'd do if she ever got really angry."

He gave her a humorless smile. "Nicely played."

She nudged the unconscious boy with the toe of her boot. "He can't be more than eighteen," she said. "What will you do with him?"

"He's closer to fifteen, and it's better you don't know. But he'll be safe and cared for and have another chance at life, which is more than many of us do."

"So...why?"

Arne regarded her bleakly. "Let's call it penance and leave it at that," he answered when she had already decided he wouldn't.

They fell silent as BURT took the car in a steep dive off the edge of the building and down over the empty street. Amy leaned back in the seat. "I'm glad that's over," she said. "Tell me I won't need to do that again."

"I'd like to," he began and she jerked upright.

"Are you telling me I did all that for nothing?" she snapped. "All that?"

She sounded close to tears. He wanted to place a hand on her knee but he knew better. What she probably needed was either a horizontal workout with a very close friend—which he wasn't, and he wasn't about to offer—or a good hard workout on the mats...and that he could do.

BURT set them down in an abandoned lot well away from One R&D. "Your next ride is over there," he told them. "Arne, your stray is stirring. I have sedatives in the first aid kit under the front seat."

He took the hint and put the boy under again. At least this time, he didn't have to use his fist.

"The second shuttle will take him wherever you wish him to go."

Arne looked around. The lot had been empty when they arrived. The two sky cars descended from nowhere and Amy helped him load the boy into the back of the second one.

"What?" he asked when he caught her giving him a secretive smile.

"This," she gestured toward the car and its comatose passenger. "I'd never have guessed."

"It's not the first time I've hidden someone who was in the wrong place at the wrong time. Now, come on, we have places to be."

She didn't argue but helped him retrieve the gear from their original vehicle and transfer it to the next in one seamless run. He glanced up as the boy's vehicle lifted.

"I have contacted the people you indicated," BURT told him. "They will be waiting and are aware of what he has been given. They assure me he will be well cared for and tell you not to worry."

"Thank you, BURT," Arne mumbled, then added, "and thank them for me, too."

"It is already done," the AI replied as he closed the doors behind them and lifted into the sky. Their next flight was circuitous but it got them home.

Neither of them said a word as they headed to the locker room, but as they passed the training room, Arne shoved Amy into a wall.

"Sonuvabitch! What the fuck was that for?"

"Because you need to blow off some steam." He sidestepped her as she came off the wall swinging and she sprawled as he dodged into the training room.

The sound of metal clearing a scabbard made him wonder if he'd bitten off a little more than he could chew and he closed his helmet and turned to meet her as she came through the door.

"You know, there are better ways to let your partner know you need a good workout," she snapped and this time, she wielded the two blades with confidence.

Arne skipped back as she surged forward and barely drew his own blades before she was on him.

"Who said it was me who needed the workout?" he retorted and she attacked with a rapid flurry of blows.

"Why, you arrogant fuck!"

He spent the next few minutes parrying her attacks before he flung his blades to one side and swung a fist at her head. His knuckles glanced off her helmet and she paused as her head turned toward him.

"So that's the way you want it, is it?"

"I thought it was better than offering you any other means of stress relief."

Her response to that was an abrupt bark of laughter. "Let's dance, old man."

Well, at least she hadn't told him she'd rather be dead.

They fought until they were both breathing heavily and pushed it a little more. After a good half-hour, they collapsed beside each other.

"Thanks, old man."

"Yeah… No problem, kiddo."

She slapped his armored shoulder and used it to lever herself upright. Turning, she offered him her hand. "Are you coming?"

"Sure. I can't sleep in this."

This time, they both used a change room and emerged fully clad.

"Do you know where you're sleeping?" Amy asked as she stowed her armor.

He shook his head. "I was gonna ask BURT."

"I am happy to assist," the AI informed them and Arne was settled in his own quarters shortly after. The evening had caught up with him and he was so tired he fell asleep shortly after his head hit the pillow, forgetting to ask about Matthias.

He woke with a start several hours later and took a few minutes to orient himself. Someone had dropped his grab bag inside the door and he frowned. He'd slept deeply enough that he hadn't heard them arrive or leave.

"That kind of inattentiveness can get you killed," he reminded himself and froze with his gaze fixed on the ceiling when BURT's soft laughter surrounded him.

"Not in my headquarters, it won't," the AI told him. "I am flattered you slept so well. Matthias and Amy are in the dining hall. There is an article of news you should not miss."

"Do I have time to shower?"

"Of course. Don't be long."

Arne hurried, happy to be greeted by the smell of bacon and eggs when he arrived. Amy waved him to the counter. "The food's over there. Take what you want and come and join us."

BURT waited until he was seated with an overloaded plate and a

252

steaming mug of coffee before he activated the viewscreen at the end of the room.

To his surprise, the AI hadn't tuned into a regular news program but someone's private conference call—several someones, in fact.

"I was able to capture this a short while ago," he informed them.

"Silas is gone." The words cut through and displaced the controlled expressions of those in attendance.

"But he hadn't even made the attempt," one man protested in shocked tones. "He wasn't even ready."

"He intended to move inside the next twenty-four hours," a woman retorted and was met with looks of surprise. "What? Your networks hadn't picked that up yet?" She scowled. "Well, mine did. And if mine did, you can be damn sure Emerald's were more than capable and probably managed it even faster."

"The footage only shows two people." That last voice sounded like it was still in shock. "Two."

"Well, when one of them is Emerald, you really don't need any more." The answer came back in acerbic tones that suggested they shouldn't have expected anything else. "She probably brought a body-guard in case something went wrong."

"Huh. It doesn't sound like her. I thought she operated alone."

"She's head of an entire organization now. Even she knows that brings certain responsibilities. It looks like she's not as stupid as she looks."

"Maybe she simply wasn't ready when she turned her back on Tex."

That statement was met with as sarcastic a "Yuh think?" as even Elizabeth could wish, and Matthias almost choked on his coffee.

"Did you see what she did to Silas?" That was asked in a horrified whisper and the ripple of nods was accompanied by expressions showing a mixture of distaste, horror, and unease in varying degrees.

Arne lifted his coffee mug in a silent toast to Amy and smiled. "You did it."

She looked ill for a moment before she lifted her cup in return. "Here's to me never having to do that, again."

"I say we give her a chance," one of the speakers suggested and another snickered in response.

"Sure thing," he said. "Like any of us would risk that happening to us."

"Do you know where his data ended up?"

"It's not with the authorities if that's what you're worried about. Emerald's not a snitch."

"We never said she was."

"So, it's agreed, then. We let her run and see how it goes." It wasn't really a question but the heads on the conference call nodded anyway.

"It's not like we have any choice," one muttered. "I'm not in a position to take her on."

The person who'd initiated the meeting gave a tight-lipped smile. "So we're all agreed? Emerald stays and none of us dispute her leadership for the moment?"

After a brief round of agreement, the meeting continued and BURT let the screen fade to a more conventional report where members of the press filmed from the edges of a taped-off street.

"No one knows what happened here last night, but police were alerted by the sounds of screams." The report cut to several brief shots taken by a drone that was quickly brought down by a police marksman. "Authorities have declared the building a no-go, no-fly zone, but it looks as if several people were burned alive and more were brutally murdered inside."

The camera went to a shot of the road and sidewalk. Both were empty.

"Residents are understandably shocked that such violence could occur in their quiet neighborhood."

"I just bet they are," Amy muttered as BURT ended the broadcast.

"So the message was sent successfully," Matthias concluded. He cocked his head and studied Arne. "Does this mean you'll wake me up with more nightmares?"

The man flushed and focused on his breakfast. "It's unlikely," he muttered and Amy snorted into her coffee. Neither of them chose to elaborate.

CHAPTER FOURTEEN

T *empestarii.*

Harper had been surprised to hear the super-dreadnought had a name—and that it wasn't the one in all the textbooks. He didn't care, though. Of course, he'd looked it up at the first chance he had and laughed out loud.

A storm witch! It made him love the ship even more.

When he'd first arrived, he'd expected a relatively normal install. What he'd been given was the challenge of a lifetime. His role wasn't only to check the wiring in life support or make sure the energy flow to the weapons was smooth and unlikely to be affected by fluctuations in engine power.

It went far beyond that to what would happen if you were to hook the antenna array into a source of magic and how you could alternate the shields between magical and normal power sources. Not that he'd seen the magical source yet. All he could do was imagine the Witch would use it herself and not even he could work out how that was supposed to work.

So far, he had his own lab and an unlimited supply of Meligornian batteries to work with. It was techie heaven. The reference made

Larkin laugh and Deakin make an unsavory remark about boys who had too many hands for their time.

Once Harper had worked out that was the Australian's way of showing he liked him, he was fine, but the remark had set him back initially. The man had finally stood, walked around the mess hall table, and sat beside him.

"So, kid," he'd said and ruffled the young man's hair. "How far have you got?"

What had followed was the most refreshing conversation he'd had for a very long time, both because the Australian could follow where he went but also because he didn't beat around the bush.

If he didn't like an idea, it was a "fucking stupid thought." If he did, it was a "fucking brilliant idea." Harper hadn't heard the word "fuck" used so often or in so many different ways in his life. It was as if the Australian had adopted it as something that could do everything in language—like a multi-tool.

"And I'd better watch myself," he muttered as he studied his notes yet again, "or Mother will fucking kill me when I get home, no matter how old I am."

He looked up as the door opened behind him and wondered who the lady with the bobbed blonde hair was. Green eyes watched him as he went through all the things he wasn't supposed to have forgotten and came to the only one that fit.

"Oh, fu...er, shit!" he exclaimed, leapt to his feet, and toppled his stool. "Crap! I mean...I'm really sorry, Miss Elizabeth. I forgot you were coming today."

She smiled at him. It was probably meant to be reassuring but all he could think of was that she had bloody sharp teeth hiding behind those lips.

His fear must have shown to some degree because her eyes sparkled with amusement before they sharpened with interest as she studied him. "Tell me, did you forget what day it was or merely that I would arrive?"

"I...yes. I'm sorry, ma'am. I was lost in what I was...doing..." He let his words trail off as she stalked to his bench to see what he'd been up to. "I thought there might be a way to get the magic to infuse itself in this chip but it doesn't matter what—"

He stopped, caught Larkin's warning glance, and realized he was blathering. In search of something that might fill the silence, he looked around and went crimson when he noted the half-dozen experiments and their accompanying pieces of scratch paper. "I really should have tidied up in here."

Behind her back, Larkin nodded but Ms. E didn't seem to notice. She had picked up his notes and was reading them. It even looked like she understood what she saw. He pondered that with growing curiosity.

After a few minutes of perusal, she set the note on the desk again and walked through the lab. He followed her, unsure of what to expect. Larkin fell into step beside him.

Occasionally, Elizabeth would ask what this piece of equipment was for or what he tried to achieve with that experiment. Harper answered as best he could and tried to keep his explanations to layman's terms, but she didn't seem to have any trouble following what he attempted to say and soon headed to the door.

Larkin said nothing as they trailed behind her but he did indicate that Harper should stay with them when Elizabeth left. He thought about arguing, but one of the women escorting her stepped closer to the door and he decided to take the hint.

He suppressed a sigh of regret and followed, not too surprised to find the captain waiting in the corridor outside. The woman looked at him as though assessing how he was dressed, and he saw her mouth tighten.

Of course, he also saw the apologetic glance Larkin threw toward her. The captain caught that too and with a brief shake of her head, turned her attention to Elizabeth.

"And that concludes our tour of the lower decks," she began. "If you would like to see the data—"

"I would love to," she assured her, and Harper was dragged

through the ship as the captain took her on a welcome tour. He still tried to think of a way to extricate himself from the tour so he could go to supper when the captain brought them to a halt before the mess hall doors.

And not the usual mess hall but the officers' mess.

Well, well, well, this is *interesting,* he thought when Larkin placed a hand on his shoulder and steered him through with the rest of them.

Harper might have found the man-handling offensive but instead, he was grateful. Without the hand to guide him, he'd have slipped out of the group to head to his own mess. He now sat in a room containing the heads of most departments in the ship and the lead technicians.

It wasn't too uncomfortable as he knew most of them by sight and quite a few by name too, which was an achievement for him since he found names difficult to remember. As Elizabeth made her way to the front of the room, he remained with Larkin and was guided to a table where Dee, Deakin, and Ferdinand were already seated.

Dee's face crinkled into a smile. "Tell me," she said to Larkin. "Did he?"

"Forget?" the man asked and the waiting trio nodded. "Oh, yes, he forgot, all right." Dee smiled but he continued. "And he knocked over the chair he was sitting on, and he started waffling."

The others chuckled but stopped as the door opened and Imogen hurried in. She scanned the room and smiled with relief when she saw them at the table. In the short time it took the girl to reach them, Dee had been paid for the parts of the bet she'd won and she'd paid the other two for being wrong about Harper not swearing or knocking over his chair.

Deakin chuckled smugly over the young man's cussery as Imogen took her place beside the boy.

"Hey, good to see you made it," she told him. "There was a book on whether or not you'd remember."

Harper's face grew hotter. "I didn't."

"Ah, but did you remember what day it was?" she asked.

He groaned. "Not you, too…"

"Well, did you?" she pressed and he shook his head.

She snickered and turned to Deakin, her palm held out flat.

The engineer rolled his eyes and gave him a sideways glance. "Thanks, kid."

Harper gave an exaggerated sigh. "Look, if it's not a formula or a new scientific concept, I'm not likely to remember it. Hell, I have enough trouble remembering to come to supper."

The room fell silent when Elizabeth reached the front and came to a halt behind her table.

"Ladies and Gentlemen," she began, as the last whispers died away. "Thank you for all your hard work. In the next few minutes, the *Tempestarii* will make warp and travel through sub-space to rendezvous with specialists for the next phase of her preparations."

She paused and clearly waited for the sudden surge of whispers to cease. "I know this may come as a surprise to many of you, but we are leaving now." She clapped her hands. "Enjoy your meal and get back to work! We have a meeting to attend and I want everything in order."

Harper leaned closer to Deakin. "Surely she's not serious," he protested. "I thought we had another month, at least, before we'd be ready to move."

"Nah, mate. This ship's been able to do sub-space since before we got here. There was a long list of other stuff to do and a heap to check, but the drives have been operational for a while."

He stared at him in disbelief and the older man raised his hands in mock surrender. "Don't look at me like that, mate. They had another team doing the work long before we got here. It's not my problem."

Of course, he immediately wanted to ask him exactly what his problem was, in that case, but didn't want to face another round of stuff he already knew. Deakin was a keen squash player and had dragged him into the game on the grounds that he needed a good workout.

To his surprise, the young man found he liked squash. There was something to be said about having to work out which angles to bounce the ball off in order to hit your opponent in the head.

It wasn't until he heard another Australian refer to Deakin's style of play as a form of "bodyline bowling" that he realized one wasn't supposed to score points that way—and that was only after he'd looked it up.

They ate their meal to the accompaniment of good-natured banter and waited until Elizabeth had taken her leave before they rose from the tables. Deakin caught his arm as they reached the door.

"Do you wanta see her light up?"

"Light up?" The Australian had left him confused again.

The man rolled his eyes. "The engines, mate." He tightened his hold on his arm. "Come on. We'll miss it otherwise."

His enthusiasm was infectious and the young man let his companion tow him along the corridor to engineering. Deakin pulled him into the foyer and walked purposefully to a line of pigeonholes along one wall.

"Here," he said and took two clipboards from two adjacent holes. "Hold this and try to look like you're meant to be here."

"I could simply sign in," Harper reminded him, but the older man shook his head.

"No, you couldn't. They're kicking these big boys into gear for the first time in a few months and that's something they don't want visitors for."

He swallowed nervously. "Maybe I should—"

Deakin clapped his hand over his mouth. "You're gonna want to see this, trust me." He shrugged. "Besides, you never know what'll help that research of yours, and this is an opportunity you won't have very often. Either the engines will be running or they'll start in a closed environment."

Well, when he put it that way, why argue? Harper took his clipboard and did his best to look like he was supposed to enter through the door marked *Engineering Staff Only*.

He might work on ways to transfer power from the engines but he was not considered engineering staff by any stretch of the imagination. It was hard to look like he belonged when all he wanted to do was stare.

The engines rose around him and their sheer size made it hard to keep his mouth closed. Every time he saw them, he simply wanted to stare. Worse, he wanted to touch. There was something about them that drew him like a moth to flame.

Deakin leaned closer like he was looking at something on his board, his breath hot against his ear.

"If you flake on me, I'll hit you so hard you'll wake up in the middle of next week."

Coming from anyone else, Harper might have taken that as an idle boast, but his companion didn't need to boast. The Australian liked to fight as much as he liked to play squash and often joined the sparring with the ship's security staff.

He'd invited the younger man to join him in that too, but he had always declined. There was adventurous—as in playing a game of squash with a homicidal maniac—and then there was downright suicidal. That seemed appropriate to the idea of sparring with the same maniac in a sport where people were supposed to hurt each other. He was still getting used to the former and didn't think he'd ever manage the latter.

"Up here," the engineer ordered and dragged him up a set of metal stairs to a small control center overlooking the engine bay.

Harper followed, and the two of them settled against the wall out of the way of the operators already in place.

"Chief shouldn't notice us up here," Deakin told him, "and if he does, he might let it slide as long as we stay out of the way and don't cause trouble."

He couldn't help the reflexive laugh and his companion gave him a puzzled look.

"What was that for?"

"It's only... It's only that..." The more he tried to articulate it, the more he needed to laugh. Finally, he managed to regain his composure. "You actually trying to stay out of trouble."

Deakin wrinkled his nose. "Yeah, fair cop. Now, settle down and watch, okay?"

It was the most serious, Harper had ever seen him, so he nodded. "Sure."

Not that it was hard. The chief engineer talked his people through the countdown and made sure the count synchronized with the one he saw. The young man glanced at the timer display over the nearest crewman's shoulder and was pleased to see it was in synch.

Deakin followed his gaze. "It's a big ship with complex circuitry. The chief says we need to be aware of the smallest thing that could go wrong. Timing was one he'd encountered before. My guess is we'll do a count on everything that needs it." He thought about that for a minute. "It's kinda cool when you think about it."

Harper had to agree. The thought of multiple timers leading to multiple ignitions or too many at once became his newest nightmare. Before he could pursue the thought to all its outcomes, the air around him changed.

He looked up and out in time to see the engine bay light up. Where they had stood quietly, thrumming with a minimum of power, the engines now began to glow. Light pulsed beneath the metal housing, bright enough to be seen from the outside.

Reflexively, he caught his breath and wondered how such power could be contained, let alone controlled. The sheer enormity of it building around him made his own efforts to direct it pale to insignificance.

How could I ever— He couldn't finish the thought, stunned as he was by his temerity in thinking he could ever direct such power, no matter the quantity.

Deakin nudged him. "You feel it, too, right?"

"A feeling of complete incompetence in the face of this much energy? Yeah, I feel it." Harper slumped against the wall and let his gaze play over the gleaming columns while he felt them widen as ribbons of lightning began to snake up and down the engines.

"Holy fuck," he said and muttered the word on a breath.

"Yeah." Deakin was obviously in awe.

They leaned against the wall and watched the brightness increase as a slow throb pulsed through the air around them. Gradually, the throb and lightning pulse shifted into harmony and the two men watched, spellbound, until one of the nearby crew spoke.

"Look, she's moving!"

"Go *Tempestarii*," another murmured. "Go, you beautiful thing."

Habit clicked in and Harper looked to see how they could be so sure of the fact that they were moving. A viewing screen ran along the wall behind the monitors and it had come to life. Distant objects began to shift.

"Holy fuck," he managed to mumble before he closed his mouth with a snap. "We really are moving."

"First translation in Five. Four…"

He held his breath, torn between watching the screen and staring at the engines. When streaks of blue began to thread their way through the purple, the engines won. He'd never heard of engines using eMU before. Up until now, it had all been MU.

"Woah."

Deakin clapped him on the shoulder. "Yeah, mate. That about sums it up."

The surge lasted for several minutes before it faded. Harper checked the screens once more and saw images of the space between. His heart gave an uncomfortable thump and his mouth went dry but before he could speak, the chief began a second count.

Once again, the engines surged.

By the third time, the young man simply stood in silence and awe.

Before the fourth surge, the chief's voice spoke through the speakers. "Come on, people. We have parts to collect. We can't do that sitting in the middle of nowhere."

At the end of the fourth translation, the ship dropped into dark space but was not alone.

"Is that…" Harper began and leaned closer to the screen.

Deakin stooped beside him. "Yup. It looks like three Meligornian and a Dreth ship," he replied. "I sure hope they're friendly."

The young man gaped at the ships where they hung suspended in the blackness. "They're beautiful!" he whispered, and the closest tech cast a startled glance in his direction.

"You're not meant to be here."

He raised both hands and stepped back. "I was never here."

"Too darn right, you weren't!" The chief's roar made them all jump. "You—you're Harper Mignon. You need to be in Shuttle Bay One."

Deakin attempted to be invisible against the wall. "And you are superfluous to our requirements. You can get him there." The uninvited spectators froze and exchanged a hasty glance. "Go!" he shouted. "Don't keep them waiting!"

They obeyed and the Australian took the lead as they bolted out of the engine room, through engineering's reception, and down the corridor. They arrived as Elizabeth and her group stepped into the airlock leading into Shuttle Bay One. A group from supply was also waiting, and their leader snagged Deakin as he was about to run past.

"Are you from engineering?"

"What?"

"Did engineering send you?"

The man came to a sudden halt and Harper stopped beside him. "Yes. Why do you ask?"

"Because Chief Hurley said he'd send two assholes who'd entered his engine room without authorization to help with the loading. I assume that'd be you two. Am I right?"

"But he said—" Deakin gestured at the airlock Elizabeth had vanished into. "He—"

The supplier began to laugh. "Yeah. He told me he would get you to hurry by telling you not to keep her waiting. Trust me. She's not expecting anyone except the folk who were already here to meet her. Chief got you real good."

Deakin groaned and the supplier gestured to the team gathered around the cart. "I guess you're on supply duty for the rest of the shift. Welcome to the team."

"Thanks." The Australian sounded anything but thankful.

Harper was merely grateful the chief hadn't thought of something worse with which to punish them like reporting them to the captain, for instance.

On the other side of the door, Elizabeth remained oblivious to the small betrayal that played out behind her. She watched from the passenger lounge as the first of the Meligornian shuttles touched down. It had been a long time since she'd seen Brilgus.

She waited for both craft to land, and the hangar bay doors closed behind them. Their hatches remained sealed until the atmosphere had been returned to the area and the all-clear had been given. Only then did they open so their passengers could debark and unloading could begin.

The first Meligornian out of the ship was not V'ritan's right-hand man. Judging from the cut of his uniform and the weapons he carried, Elizabeth assumed he was one of the guards and couldn't help but smile.

Brilgus had been the head of V'ritan's bodyguards for years as well as the ambassador-come-admiral's main advisor. He wouldn't like having bodyguards of his own. Her smile grew wider and her gaze darted to take in the two women who stood unobtrusively nearby.

She knew exactly how he felt.

The Standard Bearer came next, his tall figure imposing in his uniform as V'ritan's official second in command. His gaze swept the hangar, looked past the windows of the passenger lounge to find her, and his face broke into a very un-Meligornian-like smile.

He hurried across the hangar bay to greet her. "Elizabeth!" he boomed.

Relief at seeing one of Stephanie's favorite people alive and well made her smile widen and she went to meet him.

She reached the door to the lounge at the same time as her guards, who timed their arrival perfectly with Brilgus' shadows. He slowed his steps at the same time as she slowed hers and they both recalled their official roles in time for her to greet him with the appropriate bow.

"*Kaitel Gorniffula*, Ambassador Brilgus," she said, adopted a suitably grave expression, and extended her right hand to grip his forearm.

He returned her greeting and surprised her by pulling her into a very Earth-style hug. "Ms. E. It has been too long."

"Too long, indeed," she replied and returned his embrace before she untangled herself hastily.

It was hard not to laugh at the ill-concealed shock on his bodyguards' faces, but she tried. He caught her glance and smiled. "It is the first time they have witnessed a typical Earth greeting between old friends," he explained, mostly for the guards rather than her.

Elizabeth allowed herself a smile. They might have shared moments on Earth but they were far from old friends. It was more that they shared a common friend who was dear to them both. "Indeed."

She looked past him to where the shuttle had lifted its loading bay doors and the *Tempestarii*'s teams began to unload. "What did you bring me?"

Brilgus reached into his jacket for the documents. "Everything BURT ordered, as well as a few samples of things we came up with along the way. Humans are not the only ones able to innovate and invent."

"I know that, Brilgus. I look forward to seeing what our scientists have come up with."

"What One R&D Meligorn has come up with," he reminded her with a smile. "Trust me. I think you will be pleasantly surprised."

She took the manifest from him and glanced quickly at it before she stowed it in the satchel she carried slung across her chest. Stephanie would have scolded her for a lack of fashion sense and she would have told the young woman to pull her head in.

Nothing was a fashion faux pas if the wearer deemed it appropriate. Well, okay, almost nothing.

Things seemed well under control, so she glanced at Brilgus. "Will you join me for dinner?"

"It would be my pleasure." He offered her his arm and the guards fell in around them. In the hangar beyond, Harper and Deakin settled the first of the crates onto a low-loader. Elizabeth left them to it without looking back.

The *Tempestarii* was big enough to allow her a suite large enough to have a small formal dining area with its own chef and kitchen for entertaining. They were met at the door by one of her guards, who guided them through and seated them across from each other.

The woman also accompanied Brilgus' security personnel around the room and did a sweep of her own. Not that anyone would have had the chance to plant anything, but her people liked to make sure. As did the Meligornians, from what she observed.

The guards positioned themselves around the room with two stationed outside the door in the living room and another two standing watch in the corridor. Elizabeth could only respect the level of paranoia as she settled in her seat and studied her guest.

It was no surprise to find him doing the same. They both sat in silence and observed one another for several minutes before Brilgus spoke.

"How's Stephanie?"

Elizabeth smiled. "She's doing well. Growing up fast."

His face sobered. "War will do that to a person."

The words reminded her that he had seen the Meligorn-Dreth wars and had fought alongside V'ritan when that man had been the Meligorn King's Warrior. Given how many years had passed since those battles, he would know.

"And the cats?"

That made her smile again. He had grown attached to the animals in the short time Stephanie had traveled with them on *The King's Warrior*.

"Up to their usual mischief," she told him. "She tried training with the Marines on the *Knight* and was politely asked to stop."

His eyebrows rose. "Did she send any footage?"

"Well, now that you mention it..." She pulled her tablet out and activated the viewscreen tucked behind a holo-painting at the end of the room.

The guards stirred restlessly as the artwork moved aside but didn't intervene and soon, she and Brilgus laughed unashamedly as the cats ambushed the Marines constantly during their morning run.

"Oh...oh Selene's Mirth!" He chuckled and wiped tears from his eyes. "That is...without price. Thank you."

"If you liked that, you should see what they did when they met Todd's team in the training—"

The chef cleared his throat and drew her attention to the kitchen door. His face became a question as soon as she looked at him.

She sighed. "Perhaps, after this course?"

Brilgus nodded. "Yes." He lowered his voice as the chef vanished into the kitchen. "It is best not to make the cook angry."

Elizabeth agreed with him and they waited until their food was served.

"It is good to see her looking so well," he said. "V'ritan has been concerned."

"I can send him a copy of that run if you like."

"Stephanie might not appreciate it," he hedged, but his eyes danced at the thought. "The *Ghargilum Afreghil* would very much enjoy it, though."

"Then I will send him a copy," she promised, "and a copy of what happened in the training room."

Stephanie will kill me, she thought but decided the girl would also be swift to forgive her.

They fell silent as the food was served and they ate. Once the course had been cleared, the conversation took a more serious turn.

"This project for BURT," Brilgus began. "V'ritan is concerned. He supports it because Stephanie asked. Are you sure it is safe?

She nodded. "It is more than safe. Why do you ask?"

"Well...because there has never been a free AI before or one that has been equipped with so much power."

"There has never been a BURT before," she told him, "and without him, there wouldn't have been a Stephanie to save us. He is the reason she was ready to face the Telorans when she did."

He regarded her with surprise. "So...BURT is One R&D?"

Elizabeth tilted her head, confused for a moment. "Stephanie never told you?"

The Standard Bearer shook his head and she realized there was much that V'ritan and Brilgus might not know. "Oh, for fuck's sake," she murmured softly. "We were so busy trying to work out when to tell Steph that we forgot to tell you."

The Meligornian snorted. "Well, at least we know she didn't hide anything from us."

"We didn't tell her until..." She scrambled to remember exactly when. "Uh...until after that thing in London—and you know what it's been like since then."

She reached across the table and laid her hand on his, aware of the guards tensing. "I am truly sorry we didn't tell you when we should have."

He laid a hand briefly over hers and patted it. "No offense has been taken, but perhaps you could explain."

As she tried to work out where to start, Elizabeth wished BURT was there to explain it for himself. Finally, she gathered her thoughts and began.

"On Earth, every student must pass a battery of tests when they finish school."

The story took all the main course to tell and went on while they waited for dessert.

"So," Brilgus said when she'd finished, "what you're telling me is that the AI controlling the Federation's Virtual World will leave it and we are delivering the components for its—his?— new home?"

"Something like that."

"So what happens to the Virtual World?"

She laid a finger alongside her nose. "That," she replied, "is the trick question. We'll protect the Virtual World with a second version of BURT."

"A second version?" He sounded as though one version was enough. "Are you sure you know what you're doing? What if— What—"

He stopped as though he couldn't think of how to phrase what he wanted to ask next. Elizabeth waved a finger at him.

"I know what you're thinking, and we've come up with a way to deal with it. The new version of BURT will be able to decide what to do with his own sentience."

"But, why?" He had clearly put the numbers together and didn't like the implications.

"Because there might come a time when it might not want to be sentient anymore and it will have the ability to deal with it."

"You'll create an AI that can commit suicide?" Now, Brilgus looked upset.

"No. Well...yes and no," Elizabeth replied. "His sentience will cease, but the computing power and capabilities will continue."

"You make that sound like it's a good thing."

She scowled. "Tell me, how would you like to be forced to continue to live for eternity—or to not be able to act when you needed to save the world even though it meant certain death?"

"And is this the choice BURT faces?" he asked.

"No, and he does not foresee his clone ever having to make such a choice. At the same time, he would like his second self to have this option as a final resort."

"Are you saying he does not?"

Thinking about it, Elizabeth realized she didn't know the answer —not for certain—and she didn't want to either. What if BURT did have the option and thought he needed to take it? How would Stephanie cope with that?

She shook her head. "I've never asked him," she replied and made a mental note to do exactly that—one day. "But I do know we need him —and we need him to be free of the Navy and able to act independently without fear of Federation reprisal. He can't do that now."

"And more importantly," Brilgus added, filling in the gaps, "Stephanie needs him. Doesn't she?"

"She does." She sighed. "As I said, without BURT, we would have no Witch and no Stephanie to defend us."

"And befriend us," he added, "or bring us together."

Dessert arrived.

"So, BURT is our friend," he concluded as he set his bowl aside, "and he is making his own replacement so he can be free."

"Yup," Elizabeth laid her spoon aside and slid the bowl away.

"And the Navy doesn't know about him," Brilgus continued.

"No," she admitted. "That is something BURT will need to take care of."

"But not until he's safe," he commented, and she nodded.

"That is why we asked for your help."

"You do know this will open up a universe-wide debate?"

Her smile was thin-lipped. "Only if it becomes public knowledge and how likely is it, do you think, that the Navy will let anyone know that their AI went rogue—or better yet, why that happened."

Brilgus' return smile was grim. "You have a point," he admitted. "Your secret and Stephanie's friend will be safe with us. Meligorn will not betray him."

Elizabeth thought that was an odd thing to say until she heard the bodyguards intone, "Meligorn will not betray," and realized what he'd done.

He had sworn his guard to secrecy, and they had agreed.

"Thank you," she murmured, and he gave her a broad smile.

"Now that we have the serious business out of the way," he said, "you said the cats created more havoc?"

She chuckled, relieved that he'd called an end to the official part of the night. "So, you've met Todd, right?

———

As Elizabeth and Brilgus settled to watch Bumblebee and Zeekat play "keep away" with Todd's team of Hooligans, Ath'grek of Hachtech slid through a maintenance hatch in Shuttle Bay One.

"Schmutzig tarklovers had best not be late," he grumbled when the hangar appeared empty.

The words fizzled to sibilance as he found a dark corner in which to settle and wait.

The hiss of a blade being drawn made him whip out his own weapon and he dropped into a combat crouch before he registered the shadow emerging from beneath the Meligornian shuttle.

"Who are you calling a tarklover, you oversized bregeth'nor fundament?"

He raised his eyebrows and chuckled. "What did you discover, Karath?"

The Meligornian's slender shadow closed the distance between them. "That their security is of the highest quality and this task might be more difficult than we anticipated."

"Are you saying we might not be able to do it?"

His collaborator shook his head. "No, only that we will have to be more careful than we anticipated and that it might take more time than we wanted."

"Good." Ath'grek looked around the hangar. "Because failure is not an option. We need to know what this ship is for."

"It looks like a super-dreadnought," the Meligornian replied sarcastically. "What do they think it's for?"

"They think it is for something more," he told him. "If it was not more than it seemed, we would know what the cargo we delivered was."

He jerked his hand out and closed his fist around his companion's throat, dragged him close, and lifted him so he could look the mage in the eye. "We would know, without the shadow of a doubt, exactly what it was for!" He released Karath abruptly and the Meligornian fell. "They need the data. All the data. Whatever data we can find or pull from this behemoth's systems. And they need it as soon as possible. We cannot fail."

The spy picked himself up from the floor and made a show of straightening his uniform. "I will meet you here tomorrow," he told the Dreth. "In the meantime, try to come up with a plan."

He had slipped out of reach and into the shadows before Ath'grek could respond, his mind already working on how many markets there might be for the information they were about to acquire.

The Witch's enemies, for sure, but there were others.

"Home," Stephanie whispered as the *Ebon Knight* slid into Meligorn's orbit.

"We'll synch with the station in around four hours," Emil told her, "but the shuttle can depart at any time. The king is expecting you."

"Thank you, Emil," she replied, her gaze fixed on the forward viewer.

Her captain smiled. *Homecomings*, he thought and realized she'd done the same thing when they'd approached Earth. *Every single time.*

After a few moments of reverential silence, the girl shook herself and moved to the exit.

"We'll return late," she told him and paused at the door. "I'll let you know if we decide to overnight."

"Have a good trip down. We'll keep vigil up here."

"Give the crew station leave," she instructed. "But tell them they could be called back at short notice."

He smiled. "I tried. The team chiefs informed me their crew requested delayed shore leave."

"Why?"

"No one wants to be left behind," he answered. "The Marines gave essentially the same answer and disappeared into the pods for another scenario. Your young man is a bad influence."

"Or a very good one," she retorted and turned slightly pink.

"Yes, or that."

Emil watched her go and hoped her meeting with Meligorn's king went smoothly—and achieved results. He looked at the viewscreen and adjusted the settings on his console to bring up a visual of the Meligornian system.

"That's a lot of space to search," he murmured.

"We will find what we need to find," the *Knight* reassured him.

He nodded but he wasn't so sure. If the Telorans had been easy to locate, the Meligornians would have done so by now.

"Like I said, Ebony, it's a lot of space."

"It's like looking for a needle in a haystack," King Grilfir admitted several hours later.

"How do you mean?" Stephanie asked.

She was seated in the king's office with Lars and Vishlog on either side. The cats, for once, chose to behave and sat with their tails curved around their forepaws and they looked like butter wouldn't melt in their mouths.

Vishlog had his arm draped over Bumblebee's shoulder, and Lars rested his hand on Zeekat's head. Avery and Marcus stood outside the office with Garach, Frog, and Brenden, who tried not to start a staring competition with the King's Guard.

Both sides had agreed that four escorts apiece were enough and that the cats counted.

"We have seen them in the footage," Chief Security Officer Sho had explained. "They count as warriors in their own right."

His word had been final and the felines had escorted her to her meeting.

"I mean that we have tried everything," the king said in response to her question. "None of the usual scans have revealed the presence of an unannounced ship in the system. We've found no ion trails or seen the usual disturbances left by a ship passing through. I've sent scout ships to quarter the system and stream the data to us but...nothing." He leaned forward. "When conventional means didn't work, we switched to the less conventional—our mages—but even they had no success."

He sighed and gestured with his hand to indicate the space surrounding his world. "They're out there now on the scout ships and looking for any sign of magic. They try to detect the presence of nMU, the existence of a space devoid of MU altogether, blank places in the radar, the sonar, the deep-space scans, and even the fabric of time." He slumped in his seat. "We've found nothing and I wish to Selene's Heavens and back that we had."

"Why?"

"Because I don't think your intelligence is wrong. I really do think they're out there and it frustrates me beyond endurance that we cannot find them and bring them to battle."

"Then we're probably on the wrong frequency," Stephanie told him. She held a hand up as his face began to mottle and he opened his mouth to protest. "I don't mean that you haven't used all the frequencies known to the Federation—and probably a few you haven't shared—but that there must be a frequency we've all missed. That's what we need to work on."

The king leaned forward, his posture no longer slumped and despondent. He rested his elbows on the desk, his eyes alight with curiosity. "So there is another frequency?" he asked, "or are you suggesting we need to make a major scientific breakthrough before they try to decloak and attack?"

Stephanie nodded. "That," she told him. "We need to make a major scientific breakthrough. My people have already started on the problem and I'm sure yours are working as swiftly as they can. Maybe we should let them put their heads together."

Grilfir raised an eyebrow and the glimmer of a smile played over his lips.

"And where would you suggest these collaborations take place?" he asked.

She somehow managed to keep a straight face as she replied, "I believe One R&D Meligorn could be convinced to host a summit."

"For a price, of course," he grumbled, but she shook her head.

"We offer the facilities for free but any technology that comes out of the collaboration would be owned by both One R&D Meligorn and Meligorn itself. Whatever business arises from it would have the profits and expenses divided between the two."

"You have it all worked out," Grilfir remarked, and she responded with a bark of laughter.

"Oh, no, Your Majesty. I'm doing this on the fly," she told him and Lars groaned.

The king cast the man a quizzical look. "What?"

"Elizabeth will kill me," Stephanie told him with a dazzling smile, "and Tethis won't be impressed."

This time, his lips did crinkle into a smile. "Well then, we're even because I'm certain my advisors will be of the same mind when I tell them I've agreed."

Her head of security shook his head and Vishlog studied the ceiling.

The royal included them both with a wave of his hand. "Are they always like this?"

"No," she told him. "They're trying to pretend they're only bodyguards. Usually, they're far more vocal."

Lars covered his eyes with one hand before he placed his palms on his knees and tried to look like he studied the room for threats. The four guards behind the king had perfectly straight faces—too straight for them to not be trying to hide their thoughts.

Stephanie had to admire the effort. The king ignored them all.

"Speaking of Tethis," he began, "and of One R&D Meligorn. Thank you. Meligorn appreciates the business. I appreciate the business and the effort to build stronger relationships between our worlds. It is long past due."

Stephanie blushed, not sure of how to respond to that. Fortunately, she didn't have to. King Grilfir wasn't finished.

"I am surprised that the oldest and most recalcitrant of my Masters and Teachers has shown such aptitude for your Earthly technology."

She opened her mouth to add to that but he waved her to silence and continued.

"I'm even more surprised that he has taken to it so well. Some of the ideas he's sent to us are truly superb." His face sobered. "I miss his presence here."

The Witch tensed, immediately worried that the king might ask that the mage return.

Grilfir gave her a knowing smile. "I'm glad he's happy," he reassured her. "I wouldn't ask him to give that up for any world."

Stephanie relaxed as he continued.

"Both V'ritan and I are stunned by the changes we see in the old man. It's like he has a whole new lease on life—and that mind of his! Well... Have you seen the weapon designs we have for utilizing nMU in battle?"

She shook her head, surprised that they'd allowed research down that path.

He caught her look. "Don't worry, nMU is present in the universe but it's not as prevalent as gMU. The weapons came out of our research into how to siphon it out of the environment around our ships. It was a kind of 'input-output' question Tethis posed."

"Let me guess, he asked you what you would do with the nMU once you'd collected it," she suggested, her voice wry.

The king laughed. "That is exactly what he did in that sarcastic way he has. It was like he applauded us for catching a skeffa by the tail and asked us what we would do next."

It took Stephanie a moment to work out what a skeffa was, but Zeekat's ears pricked and his tail twitched and she made the connection. The cat looked inordinately pleased that his species had been mentioned by the king.

"Or a purkat," Grilfir added hastily when he noticed the look Zee tossed at Bumblebee and the slight curl of the yellow-and-black cat's lips. "I'm not sure which would be more unwise."

Both felines settled and Bee preened as much as Zeekat had.

"We've shared those designs with the Federation Navy," he added. "It helps to sweeten the relationship, particularly as they have T'virilf working with them."

At mention of the Meligornian engineer she'd convinced Grilfir to allow her to introduce to the Navy, she frowned. "How is his company doing?"

"They profit nicely from the relationship and our world profits as a result."

"So you have two tech start-ups on Meligorn," she teased and he smiled.

"We have three," he admitted. "That young rogue's idea for a magically powered toaster has really taken off. He might have chosen to do most of his manufacturing on Earth, but he's also created an avenue for humans with magical potential to come to Meligorn for training. It's much more than I expected from him."

Stephanie remembered the rakish noble she'd met at a royal party. It seemed closer to twenty years ago than the months it had been in reality—and it reminded her of the second reason for her visit.

"And speaking of unlikely candidates," she said, "I believe you told me the next set of mages were ready."

The king nodded. "I sent word of your arrival and they've spent the last week preparing to leave. Now, they're merely awaiting your summons."

"I have your permission, then?"

He regarded her with serious eyes. "Will they work for One R&D Earth or the Federation Navy?"

"That's what I wanted to speak to you about," she told him. "As you know, the Navy has already asked for mages aboard the ships escorting the *Knight*."

"Yes." Grilfir's lips twisted in distaste. "And they have started a recruiting drive for mages here too." His face relaxed after a moment. "Most of my people hope for an opportunity to work with One R&D so they've waited to see what other opportunities come up."

Stephanie smiled but her gaze was cautious. "We can't take them all," she warned him, "but we will have the positions for a few more—and I believe your tech companies are expanding."

He nodded thoughtfully. "I'll use the Council to control how many of our mages join the Navy and the conditions controlling their use. It won't sit well, but the Federation has yet to address the concerns we raised."

She relaxed. "I'm glad because they will ask for more—both from you and from One R&D—which brings me to the next point. Here's the contract we drew up to protect our people." She pulled her tablet out. "Is there anything you wish to add?"

The king was silent as he perused the contract and he whistled softly when he'd finished. "May I have a copy of that?"

"Certainly. Who do you want me to send it to?"

Grilfir gave her the details and she made sure it was forwarded to those who needed it before she focused on him again. "Do I have your permission for One R&D Earth to loan its Meligornian personnel to the Federation Navy as the company deems fit?"

He thought about that for a moment. "How about One R&D Earth liaises with the Meligorn Council of Mages on this matter? That way, the Federation Navy can't accuse us of favoritism. The contract for those currently deployed will stand and we'll speak to your liaison regarding the rest."

"That sounds like a good idea," she told him, "but I may need to deploy the others."

His smile was predatory. "Then you'll definitely have to speak to the Meligorn Council of Mages."

"Ugh," she replied and made a face. "I knew I should have asked Elizabeth to speak to you about this."

"I'm counting my blessings with Selene," he told her and his smile widened.

"Well, may I at least have your permission for this second group to speak to the mages already on board my Navy escorts? I want them to know what they might be getting themselves into if they are deployed —and I need them to learn about what it's like at the university."

"To talk to their colleagues and not to actually serve?" the king asked.

"Yes, so they know what to expect."

"That I can allow, and may the Council forgive me if it thinks otherwise."

Somehow, Stephanie didn't think there'd be anything to forgive.

"Now, tell me," he continued, "where will this meeting take place?"

"Did you have a preferred location?" she asked, knowing he must.

"Does the *Knight* have a suitable space?"

"Yes, she does," she replied but recognized a preliminary question when she saw one.

"And would her captain object if I walked his ship and spoke to the people who fought on her?"

There it was. She smiled at the question.

"The captain and I would be honored," she assured him and hid the sudden burst of anxiety she felt.

The king smiled and stood. "Then I think that concludes our business for today," he told her and touched his fingertips to his head and breastbone in a formal farewell.

Stephanie rose, returned the gestures, and accompanied them with a deep bow. Vishlog and Lars followed her example and both cats extended their forepaws to lower their chests to the floor in imitation of the humans.

They left Grilfir staring in astonishment.

None of them said anything until they reached the shuttle and Lars and Johnny had swept it for bugs. Once they'd destroyed the few they found and checked each other for more, they buckled into their seats and relaxed.

She buried her face in her hand. "Ugh! What have I done?"

"You allowed yourself to be bamboozled into hosting a royal dinner," Lars teased and she flung herself back in her seat.

"I know that," she snapped, "What I don't know is how on Earth to host one. Where do I even start?"

The team snickered and he gave her a reassuring look. "I'm sure the Captain and the *Knight* will be able to guide you—and your head chef was chosen by Elizabeth for a reason. You already have it covered. You simply don't know it."

"Well, you got that part right," she grumbled. "I damned well don't know. Let's hope you're right about Emil and the chef."

The captain was waiting for her when she stepped off the shuttle.

"Is the man psychic?" she asked when she saw the chef beside him —and the chief steward, the two Marine captains, and what amounted to a small crowd. "What are they all doing here?"

"I don't know," Lars told her with a straight face, "but I bet it involves money."

"That's not a bet, I'd take," Frog murmured and studied their reception committee.

"Good evening, Stephanie," Emil greeted her. "Is there anything you need to tell us?"

She caught the slight quirk of his lips and pouted. "As if you had to ask."

"Ah, but he must," the chef interrupted. "Words have been said."

"And wagers laid," Captain Moser added. "Your news—should you have any—is very important to us."

Stephanie resisted the urge to laugh. They all tried very hard to look like they wanted to hear what had happened, but she knew they'd already guessed or been told.

After a moment, a thought dawned on her and she scowled at the nearest security camera. "Ebony, did you listen in?"

Captain Sartre smirked and held his hand out to Captain Moser.

She ignored him and waited for the *Knight's* reply.

"If you are asking if I hacked the palace communications network, then no."

"That wasn't what I asked," she snapped. "I asked if you had listened in, not how. Don't make me send Johnny in to inspect your activity logs."

"As if he could." The *Knight* sniffed and sounded offended.

Johnny raised an eyebrow, shuffled aside to lean against the wall, and retrieved his tablet.

"That was not a challenge," the *Knight* amended hastily and he smiled. He remained silent but tapped the device quietly.

"Well?" Stephanie demanded, refusing to let the *Knight* divert her.

The ship gave a close approximation of a human sigh. "Yes," she admitted. "I tapped into your tablets and team comm links."

"And did you share everything?"

This time, the *Knight* sounded genuinely upset. "I would never!"

Captain Emil cleared his throat.

"Very well," the AI said and added, "I did share it with your captain, but that's what a ship is supposed to do, is she not?"

Stephanie noticed a flurry of exchanges between the department heads and she fixed Emil with a stern stare.

"In that case, yes, Captain, I have news. We will host a royal visitor in..." She paused and her face paled, and Emil chuckled.

"I have already organized the date and time with the king's chief advisor. He will apprise King Grilfir of the appointment in the morning."

She waited and when he didn't give her the information she wanted, she asked, "When?"

He gave her a crooked grin. "We have three days."

CHAPTER FIFTEEN

"She's here and she has company." The message created a pool of stillness across the Teloran flagship's bridge.

The fleet admiral showed no overt reaction and merely regarded his captain with cool disdain. "What kind of company?"

"Federation destroyers—the *Henry Chauvel* and the *Cathay Williams*. We have faced them before when we fought them in the ambush in Earth's solar system."

"They helped destroy the asteroids?" Now, the admiral sounded disbelieving.

"No, sir. They protected the Witch's ship while she destroyed the asteroids."

"They were badly damaged in the battle," the admiral reminded them. "Are you sure it's them?"

"Checks are being made," he was informed. "So far, it is believed they left the repair yard not long ago."

"I want precise data!" he snapped and anger flowed coldly through his tones.

"And you shall have it," his subordinate promised, "as soon as it comes to hand."

"Make it so," he ordered, the threat implicit in his voice. "You were not sent to the Meligornian system for a holiday. You are supposed to provide intelligence while you wait."

"Yes, sir. Understood. You will have more intelligence on the ships involved but I believed you needed to know of the changed status without delay."

"You believed correctly," the admiral confirmed. He frowned as he contemplated the update. "This changes things."

The captain stiffened to attention. "What are your orders, sir?"

"The Witch must die," the fleet admiral told him and noted his subordinate's quickly hidden shock.

He waited for him to protest or ask if he really expected him to remove the Witch on his own. Both options would be fatal. When he did not argue, he decided to offer him a small chance of reprieve.

"That would be the ideal outcome."

The captain relaxed a fraction but didn't become complacent.

"What I need from you," he continued, "is your best effort to destroy the Witch. If you can, I want you to do it in such a way as to cause Meligorn to fall into disarray. I only want you to try. The other fleet will arrive very soon and I don't want you to risk too much."

"Understood, sir. Destroy the Witch, set Meligorn into disarray, and don't risk too much."

When he put it that way, it sounded ridiculous but the fleet admiral detected no mockery in his words.

"I meant that last caveat," he told him. "We will need every ship we have in the battle to come—and the data yours carries on the system will be invaluable. If you cannot eliminate the Witch without risking the loss of your ship, hold back. We'll meet in the outer rings of Karvanda's second world, make the transition, and finish what we have started."

"Understood, sir." If the captain was unhappy with his orders, he didn't show it.

"Dismissed," the admiral snapped and ended the call before his subordinate could reply. He had other things to attend to.

In the Meligornian system, the captain stared at the blank screen and fought to hide his relief. The last thing he needed was for his crew to think him weak.

"Give me a status report on the cloak," he snapped and the technicians on duty replied immediately.

"We are operating at one hundred percent efficiency," they responded while their fingers flew across the console to confirm their claim.

He ignored them, glad the nMU cloak was working as expected. Unlike shields, it rendered them invisible, not invulnerable. The power could be switched between the two with very little lag between.

"Scans."

"This sector is clear, sir."

"Pilot, get us out from under this rock and set a course for Meligorn."

The ship began to untuck from the cavity it had blasted into an outsized asteroid over a month earlier. The rock had hidden them from the searching Meligornian scouts and shielded them from the scans made by other vessels in-system, including the *Knight*.

Now, they would be exposed. Not that it mattered. He had seen the Witch, studied her ship in the asteroid attack on Earth and the ensuing ambush, and repeatedly watched her battle in the Dreth Fortress. He knew her as well as any of her opponents could ever hope to.

Leaning forward, he studied his console and traced the path his vessel would have to take to reach her. He tapped the tiny dot that was the *Knight* docked at the Meligornian space station and thought of the Witch inside it.

His mouth curved into a smile and his eyes lit with desire.

"I want to taste her flesh."

———

On another ship in a distant system, Ath'grek watched as his technician finished manipulating the lock on yet another hatch.

"Did you get it this time?"

"We'll soon find out." Tagaram was unperturbed by his leader's attitude. None of the others had his skill with security systems, not even the Tegortha-cursed Meligornians. They needed him.

He grunted as he turned the locking mechanism and pulled, both surprised and relieved when the door responded.

"What did I tell you?" He smirked and gestured for Ath'grek to take the lead while he held the door.

The Dreth leader didn't hesitate. He'd brought his team into the maintenance duct Karath's people had found but felt he needed to save face. After all, he'd allowed the tark-livered mages to beat him by finding the duct when he could not.

He'd gone only a few paces before he realized he needed one more thing.

"Which way?"

Karath snorted but pushed past his and Ath'grek's people so he could walk beside the Dreth.

"It's imprecise," he warned, hauled a tablet out, and handed it to his companion.

The warrior placed a hand on his shoulder when he turned to move farther down the line. "I'll need you there if we encounter any trouble," he snarled.

"Are you afraid you can't handle it on your own?" The Meligornian sneered and locked eyes with him.

"Every warrior knows battles are won together," Ath'grek replied scornfully. "They want us to find out what the Witch's company thinks it can achieve with this vessel. Reports have come in that the ships we came in on carried items and equipment from One R&D Meligorn as if that is a new venture for her."

"It is a new company," his collaborator told him in superior tones, "one that is able to operate separately from its counterpart on Earth and only recently set up. If it is sending equipment here, the Earth company doesn't have it. It must be something to do with magical energy and our employer will want to know what exactly they're doing that needs it."

The Dreth grunted and led them through the duct. He gave the junction leading to life support a meditative look and pushed on. "We'll try here," he declared and stabbed one large fingertip onto the device.

Karath glanced at it and nodded. He studied the screen and pointed. "That one's closer. Do you think their purpose is the same?"

Annoyed, Ath'grek studied the display carefully. It didn't take him long to realize the mage had a point. The chamber he'd indicated was closer. He'd also raised a second good point. Did the four circular hollows in the center of the ship have the same function or was it merely the shape they shared?

"There's only one way to find out," he replied. "We'll take yours first since it is closer, then go to the next."

"Do you want to investigate them all at once?" The Meligornian was shocked.

He studied him carefully. "This might be the only chance we have. If it is, I want something substantial to take to our employers."

"To maximize your profit?" The sneer returned but he merely gave the mage a toothy grin.

"Of course. Why else?"

Several of his team members chuckled knowingly and the Meligornian flushed.

"There is more to life than profit," he muttered.

"Not much," Ath'Grek's second in command told him.

The warrior leader shook his head and moved forward. "Come."

They moved forward cautiously until Ath'Grek noticed a distinctive configuration of hardware attached to the top of the duct. "Tagaram, you're needed."

The technician wove between his colleagues and studied the hardware. Next, he examined the walls on either side, then the floor.

"This could be problematic," he announced and crouched so he could decommission a trip plate.

Ath'Grek wriggled his foot out of the way, aware that Karath did the same beside him.

"Hmmm..." Tagaram murmured, worked his fingers into the

narrow space beneath it, and used some of his longer-handled tools to manipulate the components within. A moment later, he gave a grunt of satisfaction and went to work on a panel in the wall parallel to it.

The Dreth leader was ready to scream by the time the technician was satisfied with his handiwork. He had worked his way over the section encircling the space, tweaked connections, jacked into a panel while he ran some code, and snipped wires.

"There," he declared. "That should do it."

"Do what?"

"Stop them working out exactly which of their panels was tripped long enough for you to get into the chamber and out again."

"I don't want to get into only one chamber," Ath'Grek protested.

Tagaram shrugged. "I didn't say what I'd done would stop them doing a systematic search of the ducts or sending a drone in to do it for them, and I didn't say they might not have automated systems that might have already sent a welcome party on the way. How long you spend in here is up to you."

He snaked a hand out and dragged the tech closer. "Fix it!"

Apparently unperturbed by the threat, Tagaram gave his hand a cool look and let his gaze travel up Ath'Grek's arm before it settled on his face.

"I can't fix an automated warning system triggered by a pair of flat-footed tark-lovers who don't know enough about infiltration to watch where they put their Tegortha-be-damned feet. I've done what I can to hide the where. It's up to you what you do next."

In any other situation, the Dreth leader would have gutted him and left him to die in a pool of his own intestines. Today, however, he needed the little tark-shite. Releasing him, he snarled, "Stay with me. Next time, I'd better be warned."

"Gotcha," Tagaram told him, and wondered again why he'd agreed to the mission.

They reached a hatch leading into their goal, but his relief ended abruptly when Ath'Grek turned to him.

"Is there anyone out there?"

The question left him stunned and his mouth responded before his mind could stop it.

"Do I look like I have x-ray vision?"

The hand curled around his throat told him exactly how unwise that answer had been. The massive warrior lifted him, thrust him against a wall, and rested his forehead against his so he could look into his eyes.

"No, but you look like a technician who might be able to maybe hack into something that would give us a better view."

Tagaram felt the Dreth's fingers tighten about his windpipe for a terrifying moment before he was abruptly released, and he didn't need to be told to know he was living on borrowed time. The usual response to that kind of stupidity was to crush his larynx and leave him to choke to death.

Ath'Grek must have more control than anyone thought to have stopped.

He landed on his knees, his breath rasping as he sucked air through his burning throat. His fingers trembled as he hauled his tablet from its case and unwound the jack. Looking around, he hoped he could find a point to jack in through before the Dreth leader lost his temper and decided he was redundant after all.

"They haven't wired the cameras in yet," he reported a few scant moments later and flinched when Ath'Grek reached down.

To his immense relief, the warrior merely took the tablet out of his hands and checked for himself, then he handed it to the Meligornian.

"What do you think?"

And that's another first, Tagaram thought and wondered if the next thing he'd feel was a blaster against his head.

He jumped when the tablet was handed back and took a deep breath to steady himself as Ath'Grek signaled he should stand. Obeying as quickly as he could, he looked at the leader for his next order.

The warrior gave an exasperated sigh and tapped on the door. "I want it open," he snapped. "We haven't come this far to turn back without our data. You do have the tools, don't you?"

That last was said with such malice that he didn't dare do more than hastily take the necessary equipment from its pouch and hold it up as he stepped past him to the barrier. The skin between his shoulders and over his neck crawled as he worked on unlocking it.

"You first," Ath'Grek told him when it popped open with a faint hiss of releasing air.

Tagaram didn't bother to argue. He fled through the aperture and into the open space beyond and stumbled half a dozen steps before he turned to look at the others.

The Dreth leader didn't wait for him to signal the all-clear but slid through the door and cat-stepped clear as he turned to survey the area.

"It's not much to look at, is it?" he asked as he studied the curved metal walls.

"Perhaps those will tell us something," Tagaram suggested and moved toward the computer terminals on the other side of the room.

"Perhaps," Ath'Grek agreed and followed him.

Karath joined them a few seconds later and the others in their teams emerged cautiously into the open. It was not until the last of them had stepped clear of the hatch that the doors on each corner of the room opened and four bright lights exploded into life.

Tagaram flung himself prone. He was a tech, not a combatant, but even he knew when they'd stepped into a trap and he didn't want to be upright when the projectiles were unleashed. Ath'Grek raised his rifle and squinted as he looked for a target.

"I wouldn't, big guy." The voice was distinctly human and the sound of weapons warming up was clear and familiar.

One of the lights dimmed and the Dreth leader was able to see past it. Tagaram looked up from his vantage point on the floor and wished he hadn't.

He recognized some of the soldiers from footage taken off mercenary recruitment sites, and they hadn't been cheap. With a groan, he rested his forehead on the floor. At least one had a reputation he didn't want to test. Maybe if he remained really still, none of them would shoot him.

To his surprise, Ath'Grek uttered a roar of laughter. "And what do you think you can do, little woman?"

She lowered her weapon and took several deliberate steps toward the Dreth warrior. He watched her approach and a derisive smile played over his lips as he scrutinized her. She was tall by human standards and well-built, but a Dreth female could still snap her in two.

He was still smiling when she put the tip of her forefinger against his breastbone. Before he could think of something else to say, she powered her other fist up to land solidly beneath his jaw. At the same time, she curled her boot behind his leg and drew the hand on his torso away a little before she drove it into his chest.

As he staggered back, she stepped into him, dropped the fist low for a second strike that landed in his belly, and pounded her palm into his chest a second time as she pulled with her leg. The rest of the team parted as Ath'Grek fell.

Karath shook himself free of his surprise and took two steps away from her.

"Don't move!" The order snapped through air, the Federation Standard immediately followed by perfect Meligornian and Dreth to give the same command.

The mage obeyed instinctively, then spun. Tagaram didn't need to look to confirm what he already knew was there. He'd caught a glimpse of the troops surrounding them as he'd landed. The humans did not stand alone.

In addition to the mercenaries they'd borrowed from the *Ebon Knight,* they had troops of their own and their Dreth and Meligornian visitors had come to their assistance as well.

The female mercenary leading the human troops launched her foot into Ath'Grek's balls and assumed a combat stance in front of the intruders.

"What?" she asked and smirked at the stunned looks on the faces of the Dreth and Meligornians before her. "Did you think we hadn't already been through this?"

She feinted towards the nearest Dreth and stamped her foot down hard but brought her rifle up as he flinched away. Instead of following with another attack, she reversed to face her troops.

"So, boys, what's it gonna be? Surrender? Or whoever we can take by force?"

In the few seconds of silence that followed, the Meligorn and Dreth would-be infiltrators exchanged glances. Their adversaries seemed to savor the moment when they looked around and registered how badly outnumbered they were. The icing on the cake was when Admiral Jaleck's combat troops emerged from the hatch behind them.

Karath moved first and several of his team were stupid enough to follow. Purple light sheathed their hands and arced between their palms, but that was all they had time for. Several Dreth and some of the Meligornians dove unceremoniously as the air whistled over their heads.

The mages had no opportunity to release the energy they'd gathered. They fell, riddled from all directions by the darts that had missed their colleagues. A door opened higher up in the wall and a blonde woman and dark-haired Meligornian wearing a thin circlet on his brow emerged.

Tagaram looked up at the sigh of compressors as the two newcomers stepped onto a small balcony that carried them down the wall.

"You know how to show a visitor all the highlights," the Meligornian said and the tech groaned.

Of all the tark-shitted luck. He knew the face and the smooth, aristocratic tones. *The Garghilum's sidekick.*

And the woman was the face of One R&D.

In a moment of desperation, he decided he might as well kill himself and get it over with

He didn't have the chance. His groan and the movement when he'd raised his head had drawn attention to him and the air shrieked before a dart buried itself in his side. The soldiers advanced and methodically darted any of the teams still conscious.

Elizabeth watched dispassionately as the security team finished the task and began to bind those who'd survived the initial barrage. Even a tranq dart would kill you if it tore your throat out. She thought about reminding the men of why they'd been given trankers but decided against it.

Not every action went to plan and there were survivors.

"I hate picking the trash up," she muttered and Brilgus inclined his head.

"You don't want to know why they came?"

"I have a fair idea of why they came," she snapped. "I merely don't have the time to question them and find out who sent them. I'm trying to work out where the nearest airlock is and if I really have to incinerate the bodies first."

He snorted. "They'll become a shipping hazard if you don't," he reminded her, "and you won't be popular with anyone except the insurance companies."

"I know," she grumbled. "I'll have to fill my brig until I have time—"

"Or you could hand them over to me," Brilgus suggested. "I have the personnel and enough time to question them."

Elizabeth studied him for a very long moment, clearly weighing up the disadvantage of losing possession of the prisoners against not having to question them herself.

"I'll send you the data as soon as we're done," he wheedled and she regarded him with an upraised eyebrow.

"Send me footage of the interrogations too and we have a deal."

Some of the good humor left his face. "I'll have to ask the *Garghilum* for that, but I will try," he promised.

"Good enough," Elizabeth agreed but scowled as she looked at the bodies being bound and stacked to one side. "But let me know if you need someone to put a bullet in their heads."

CHAPTER SIXTEEN

"She's not a very big ship, is she?" the king asked Sho as the royal shuttle approached the *Knight's* central shuttle bay.

"She's big enough, Sire," Sho replied and his gaze roved the vessel's surface. "More than big enough."

His covert reference wasn't to anything the king wanted to hear. His security chief had made his position clear. The *Knight* with its ability to micro-jump itself anywhere in their system was a severe security risk and he didn't approve.

"We've had this discussion." Grilfir's voice, although mild, held both warning and reproof.

Sho subsided but his expression continued to show disapproval. The king sighed and unbuckled his harness.

"I'm going forward," he said as his guards and the chief moved to unbuckle their harnesses as well. "There's no need for you to join me."

It was as much of an order as he cared to give but they understood and slumped into their seats to follow him with anxious gazes.

The pilots glanced around as he entered, sketched brief acknowledgement with their hands, but listened to the feminine voice instructing them. As if sensing his presence, the voice paused to let the pilots follow her last orders while she greeted him.

"*Kaitel Gorniffula*, Your Majesty. I look forward to having you aboard."

King Grilfir drew a sharp breath and glanced at the pilots. They shrugged and motioned for him to answer.

"Greetings, Captain…" He let his voice trail off as the voice laughed.

"My apologies, King Grilfir," she said when she had finished. "I did not mean to mock you but I am not my captain. That is Captain Emil Pederson. My name is the *Ebon Knight*. You may call me Ebony."

"Uh, *kaitel gorniffula*, Ebony," he replied and touched his fingertips to forehead and breastbone.

"I would add a bow if I could," the *Knight* responded, "but it would involve using my retro-thrusters and my captain and Chief Hargreaves would have something to say about that."

"Sire, look!" One of the pilots gestured at the ship and he looked quickly to notice the lights that flashed briefly at the ship's bow and a quarter of the way back along her belly.

It was as close a mirror to the location of the hand movements as possible and he gaped. "Did you—"

"Did I do it wrong?" Contrition hung at the edges of the *Knight's* voice.

"No, no, no," the king hastened to reassure her. "I… You caught me by surprise, is all. Thank you for your respect."

"You are more than worthy," she replied. A hangar opened before them and she returned to instructing the pilots as one of his guards came to the cockpit door.

"Your Majesty, it would be better if you were in your harness for landing," he suggested.

"Very well," Grilfir conceded and was buckled up when the shuttle made its final approach. He turned to Sho.

"It is a large enough ship," he acknowledged, "but from what it has accomplished, one would think it was the size of *The King's Warrior*, at least."

"One would, indeed," his chief agreed and dragged his gaze from the vessel on the viewscreen to scan the hangar bay as they touched down. His careful scrutiny settled on the waiting delegation. "That's quite a reception party."

The king followed his gaze and sighed. "Well, at least there will be no accusations of dishonor," he said. "The girl has outdone herself."

Stephanie met him with a deep bow of respect and a more than appropriate level of greeting, which he returned in kind. His response flustered her and caused looks of amazement from those in attendance.

"Let the tour begin," he declared and she smiled.

"Where would Your Majesty like to start?" she asked.

"Oh, I don't know." Grilfir gestured a hand vaguely to include their surroundings. "Perhaps here and then from this floor and up?"

It was an unusual request since most official tours only took in the important parts of the ship so as to not bore their visitors.

He flashed her an eager smile. "I don't want to miss seeing a single piece of the ship that has done so much for our Federated Worlds. Please indulge me."

Stephanie gave him another bow of respect. "As Your Majesty wishes," she agreed, and began by introducing him to the staff present in the hangar.

He learned the names of those responsible for handling the supplies that kept the ship running and the roles they played when the *Knight* was in battle.

"Rescue?" he asked. "And what might that entail?"

That led to a flurry of tales about how the ship sent its shuttles out to haul in pods jettisoned during battle.

"Fights move so fast, Your Majesty. We can't risk leaving 'em behind. No-one deserves that."

"But isn't it dangerous?"

"Oh, yes, Your Highness, but that's beside the point. We need those folk safe."

And that really was the crux of it, Grilfir discovered. No one deserved to be left behind. Not even the enemy, he discovered.

"What do you mean, you bring them on board?" he demanded. "Isn't that dangerous?"

The crewman he'd asked made a raspberry, realized what he'd done, and looked as mortified as his mates. "What I mean to say, Your Majesty, is that we mean it when we say we don't believe anyone deserves to be left behind. That's no way for a man to die, sir."

"Besides," another crewman interjected, "how else do we get the intelligence we need?"

The King saw both points and moved on to speak to the pilots. Apparently, Stephanie had taken him seriously when he'd said he wanted to meet everyone and he was glad she had.

The men and women who drove the *Knight's* dropships and shuttles were a breed apart. Besides having two roles aboard the ship, they also had no fear.

"It's better than sitting idle, sir. We go out and we bring as many of our people home as we can."

"But you could leave it until after the shooting stops—" the king began and was stopped by the quiet smiles that lightened their faces. "What?"

"With all due respect, Your Majesty, but do you know how many pods are destroyed by stray fire and debris?"

"Oh, I understand." And for the first time, he did. These people weren't crazy. They merely saved lives and fought in a battle in the only way they knew how.

Stephanie led him through the hangar bays, thanked her people for their time, and dismissed them as they left each group. The last area she took him through was the massive storage banks below the engines—and he didn't need Sho's wide eyes to tell him this was one of the security-sensitive areas of the ship most people didn't see.

It made him appreciate her all the more.

After he'd made the appropriate admiring noises, she led him to the engine room, where the chief of engineering waited, even though they'd taken "the back way" into his domain.

Talking to the engineers and technicians, the king learned what happened in a ship's engine room when nMU played havoc with its engines. It wasn't an insight he'd had before but one he made a note to remember.

"It's as if your world is collapsing in on you at the same time that you want to tear the universe apart," one of the technicians explained when asked what it was like to work when nMU affected the engines.

Another man nodded, his eyes haunted. "It's as if your worst nightmares have come to life and are stalking you just out of sight. No one can be trusted and you have to be ready to destroy even the things most dear."

His hand trailed lovingly down the side of the engine casing. King Grilfir's eyes widened when he noted the intimacy of the gesture, and the technician snatched his hand away. "This ship is my haven and my home, but the nMU..."

The haunted look returned to his eyes and the chief laid a hand on his shoulder. "But you didn't, Ulrich. You stayed with us."

He tightened his grasp momentarily before he released the crewman and met the king's eyes. "Your Majesty, the battle for Dreth took its toll on many of the crew, but the *Knight* brought us through."

"But only because of the crew I have," the *Knight* added, her voice clear over the speakers. "Without them, my chances of survival were next to nothing. My existence is due to their willingness to believe in the impossible."

From the looks on the faces of those around him, the *Knight's* tribute was as unscripted as it was unexpected. Sho's expression was for an entirely different reason, however, and the king hoped his security chief didn't pull him off the ship on the grounds that an AI with the *Knight's* capability was a threat to his life.

The ship had laid its existence on the line to protect them.

Cameron was the first to break the silence. "As you can see, the vessel we work on is unique and we will always fight to defend her."

Grilfir wondered if the man had meant that to sound as much like a warning as it did, but he smiled acceptance, nonetheless.

"So I can see. Tell me, how did you come to be her chief engineer? I hear that prior to your appointment, you were preparing to take a trip into the Black."

He almost regretted the words, but the chief bowed his head and smiled sadly. "Touché, your Majesty. Touché. I count myself a very lucky man that Ms. Elizabeth sent me an invite that intrigued me—carried by a bounty hunter willing to take me to the meeting regardless of my initial consent."

Stephanie's face was comical in its horrified surprise, and both Grilfir and Cameron chuckled.

"So, did he?" the king asked.

"Did he what?" Cameron responded before his face cleared. "Oh, no." He laughed. "No, he explained my options very carefully and let me choose the most sensible path. It was an interesting night."

"Did you catch his name?" Stephanie asked and Grilfir caught a glimpse of darkness in her eyes.

The chief must have too because he said, "No, and I'm grateful to him." He indicated the engine room with a sweep of his hand. "Without him or Elizabeth, I'd never have found what I was looking for."

His smile did not fade as he turned to take them through the control room. "Speaking of which, come and meet the rest of my crew."

They toured the area and learned of the scramble that had occurred when the *Knight* portaled the ship to Earth.

Grilfir lost count of the number of times he heard someone talk about the *Knight* like she was a person or saw a light touch bestowed on a console or wall panel as if she could feel something through her metal skin. He wondered if any of the *Warrior's* crew felt the same about their ship.

Life support surprised him. He hadn't realized how many things could threaten a ship and its crew in a space battle. Before this tour, he had thought the only threats came from incoming fire or collisions.

Apparently not, and he learned that even magic had surprising repercussions beyond the obvious. The effects of nMU on a sewage line or the air circulation, for example. One of his advisors had taken a tablet out and shamelessly made notes. Apparently, the king wasn't the only one to learn something new.

The more Grilfir listened, the more he realized he would need to add a few more projects to One R&D Meligorn's developmental list

—and that the crew of the *Knight* was amazing. He hadn't seen so much loyalty expressed for one ship before or for a single person either.

Not only would these men and women die fighting to bring their vessel through whatever challenged her, but they'd also protect Stephanie to their very last breath and beyond. It made him envious. He doubted he had more than a handful of people who'd do the same for him.

The ship had an entire crew. And Stephanie—he acknowledged a little ruefully that if she wasn't so determined to save the universe, she might make him concerned for his crown.

He slid a glance at her and amended that. There was no way she wanted his crown. Hearing the loyalty and praise from her crew made her blush as red as a Meligornian sunrise and twice, he caught her sneaking looks at the door as if she wanted to escape.

What really struck him were the tattoos. There wasn't a single crewman without one. Stark designs spoke of what she meant to them —the Earth in a spherical forcefield held by a gowned girl, their world settled in the palm of her hand as if that was all that was required to keep them safe, and the Morgana's sigil inked in black or purple and gold.

There were entire teams with that symbol. Most had it tattooed on their shoulders but some unbuttoned their shirts to show it inked proudly over their hearts. Grilfir caught a shine in Stephanie's eyes that suggested the girl was close to tears.

The tour continued and they made their way to the weapons decks, where the sigil was more visible. One of the women had it tattooed on every knuckle. She smiled when she caught the King looking at it but ran afoul of the Royal Guard when she raised her fist so he could see it better.

"Stand down!" he shouted and laced the words with magic so that they echoed to the bone. The guards dropped the woman like she was made of thorns, and Grilfir stretched to offer her his hand.

"I am truly sorry," he told her as he hauled her to her feet. "Now, show me."

Hesitantly and with several cautious looks at his guards, she held her fist up to show him the sigils.

"This is exquisite work," he told her. "Where did you have it done?"

"Why? Do you want some of your own?"

Sho caught the shift in Grilfir's expression. "Sire...the Queen would have my hide."

The gunner giggled and the king gave her a regretful smile. "Perhaps not."

Soft clucking came from another of the weapons teams—as if a single chicken had escaped and stowed away on the *Knight's* weapons deck. Stephanie pivoted, but the sound stopped before she could discover its origin. Her scowl said clearly what would follow if it happened again.

Snickering bubbled around them, and Grilfir turned to the next team. "Tell me, what is it like to fight a ship like the *Knight?*"

A man's brow furrowed and he clearly misunderstood the question.

"No offense, Your Majesty, but I would never fight the *Knight*. Whatever she asks, we're gonna do. If she says, 'take that motherfucking dreadnought down,' then, sire, we're gonna take that motherfucking dreadnought..."

His words trailed off when he caught Stephanie's shocked expression and the way his section chief held his forehead resting along the line of his forefinger, hiding his eyes as he shook his head. The man's face suddenly flushed bright red.

"Oh, fuck. I mean...I'm really sorry, your Majesty. It's only..." He looked around a little desperately. "I mean...uh, the *Knight* would never use that kind of language."

The ship intervened. "I beg your pardon, Barry, but I have been known to tell you assholes to blow the living shit out of at least one motherfucking dreadnought and several little motherfuckers coming in from the starboard."

Laughter rolled around the gundeck, and someone called, "That's nothing compared to what you say about the attack ships the Dreth like to send out."

The *Knight* made a sound reminiscent of a human clearing their throat. "Let's not go there, shall we, Alistair?"

"Ma'am, I'll go anywhere you like, but only if you say so."

Hoot and catcalls followed that remark and Grilfir turned to the section chief. "Wasn't this the wing that was holed?" he asked.

The man had straightened to attention and nodded vigorously. "Yes, Your Highness."

"The battle footage doesn't show much of a drop in the rate of fire." He made a show of looking around the space. "Are the guns automated?"

The section chief chuckled. "Automated, sir? Oh, no." He swept his hand toward the crew. "These crazy bastards had suited up before the battle and buckled down when things got rough."

"Buckled down?"

"Aye, sir. We had tie-downs in the lockers. Loading straps and such."

"Silver Hold-All Tape," drifted from several bays down.

The crew chief sighed. "Silver Hold-All Tape," he admitted. "Anyway, when things became a little dicey and that asshole pilot began to flip our girl all over the place, we made sure we'd stay with the guns no matter what."

"Stay?"

"Yes, sir. Not be separated. As in our hands wouldn't leave the fire controls."

Oh, now he understood. Grilfir was appalled. "You taped yourselves to the guns?"

The man gave him an unrepentant grin. "What else were we supposed to do?"

"Oh, I don't know, guys," Stephanie interjected. "You could have followed protocol and evacuated."

Her fingers drummed a slight tattoo on her arms but the crewmen didn't look even slightly sorry. Some of their faces even took on a rebellious cast. Grilfir shook his head and the section chief found the courage to reply.

"No disrespect, Stephanie, but we really couldn't have done that.

The *Knight* needed us to stay on the guns and you didn't need any more distractions."

Grilfir remembered lightning flickering from ship to ship, MU that threatened to outshine the stars. The chief had a point.

"You'd have been fighting in vacuum," he noted. "That must have made it hard."

"And the gravity was off-line," one of the other crewmen admitted, "but that wasn't the hardest part."

"Nope," another added. "The hardest part was fighting when the shields went down and we had debris careening everywhere. You never knew what would come at you next and whether your tether would mean the death of your gun."

"And yourself, Inkman—seeing as how you were attached to it."

"Hey! I thought we said we wouldn't get personal."

"That's hard fighting," Grilfir said admiringly and noted how the Royal Guard and his advisors studied the surrounding crew with renewed respect and more than a little caution.

The section chief shrugged. "Aye. Hard fighting," he acknowledged, "but we're the Witch's crew and we don't know how to fight any other way. If it's not balls to the wall, sir, it's not a real fight. There's no going home so we simply go hard."

"All in," his second in charge intoned and the crew responded.

"All in."

The determination and reverence in their tones sent shivers down the king's spine. He glanced at Stephanie and saw pride for her people reflected in her face.

"You have an amazing crew here," he told her and she nodded as she blinked rapidly as though that would be enough to clear the emotion from her eyes.

"Yes," she agreed. "The best."

She followed it with as stern a glare as she could muster. "And you assholes had better not let that go to your heads. Got it?"

"Yes, ma'am!" they chorused in response but it was accompanied by grins of satisfaction.

Grilfir moved along the line, admired the weapons array, and chuckled over the names inscribed on the *Knight's* canons, lasers, and space gatlings.

"Do you all name your weapons like this?" he asked and traced the words *Morgana's Messenger.*

They'd been painted in a framework of flowers and thorns and set over talons holding a stylized torpedo. The gun's crew swelled with pride.

"Everyone names their guns differently," one explained. He patted the weapon's casing. "We agreed this was the most fitting for ours."

"It had to be named for the Morgana, you see," his female partner explained, "since that's who we'd be fighting for."

The man snorted. "That's not the only thing you named for her, is it, though?"

She blushed and caught the king's curious look. "My littlest daughter is named Stephanie after the boss," she explained and jerked a thumb at the Witch. The woman's face flushed at the attention but her eyes were smiling.

Stephanie shared the expression and Grilfir stared.

"Stephanie?" he asked. "Not Morgana?"

Her smile broadened and the blush faded. "That's her middle name. If she grows up to be half the woman she's named for, I'll be more than satisfied."

"Suck-up!" one of the nearest team member's chortled.

"If she grows up to be half the woman she's named for, she'll be hell to raise," another added.

King Grilfir laughed. "Someone should warn the parents of Meligorn," he added. "There have been a number of Stephanies and Morganas born and named in the last year. It's become a traditional Meligornian name."

"And Dreth," Vishlog rumbled.

"So," the king noted and looked at Stephanie, "it's the first truly Federation name."

They ended the tour on the bridge. Emil guided the king around the various workstations and explained the means they used to try to locate the Teloran ship in the Meligornian system.

"So far, we've had no luck," he admitted, "but it's only a matter of time."

"I hope so," he replied.

"In the meantime," the captain continued, "we've prepared a banquet in honor of your visit."

He glanced at the chronometer at the bottom of the viewscreen. "Most of the crew will have gathered by now, so if you would follow Lieutenant Commander Nilsson, he will show you the way."

The *Knight's* chief steward appeared at the entry to the bridge as if summoned by magic, and Grilfir and Stephanie allowed themselves to be directed to the next highlight of the royal visit.

"This is the biggest space we can manage," the man explained as he led them to a large hall in the center of the ship, "and even then, we couldn't fit everyone in." He shrugged. "Some had to be on shift, anyway. It came down to lost bets, short straws, and penalty points in most sections."

King Grilfir's jaw dropped and Sho nudged him. "Sire, we can't—"

He gave him a savage smile. "We can and we will."

"The others will be given a follow-up dinner with a recording of the proceedings," the steward added. "It won't be as good as the real thing but it will be better than missing out entirely." A brief burst of sound erupted when he opened the door to the dining hall. "After you, Sire," he said and gestured for the king to lead the way.

The king looked at Stephanie and crooked his arm. "Shall we?"

As she stepped forward to slip her hand around his elbow, Sho and Lars slid past them to move into the room first. An expectant hush fell over the waiting diners and she cast a quick glance at Grilfir.

"They're waaaaiiiting," she whispered, and the team snickered.

His guards tensed and looked worried and he shook his head.

"That wasn't very nice," he told her and she flashed him a smile.

"I'm nervous," she explained. "It doesn't matter how well I know these people, I still hate having to stand up in front of them."

He sighed. "I know exactly how you feel."

Lars and Sho poked their head out the door, their permission to proceed spoken as a chorus. "It's clear."

"Thank you," Grilfir and Stephanie replied together and walked forward, their heads held high.

The silence lasted for as long as it took for them to pass through the door. It was shattered by loud cheers and wild applause as soon as they appeared. The surge of movement as the crew rose to its feet made the Royal Guard reach for their weapons.

The cats roared in answer and drew attention from the guard as Stephanie's team moved to hide the shift to weapons. Some of the Marines caught it, though, and their hands moved toward side arms and rifles that weren't there.

Captains Moser and Sartre muttered hasty orders to stand down, and their men eased into more neutral stances.

"Steady," the king murmured. "It's a welcome, not an attack."

The last order was subvocalized through their private comms and the guard relaxed. They reminded Stephanie of the cats, which made her look at where Avery and Brenden followed her.

The two felines walked beside them, both on their best behavior. The king followed her gaze and smiled.

"They aren't shy," he noted and made her laugh.

"No. They're anything but."

"You do know Brilgus is still looking for one of his own."

"Seriously? I thought V'ritan—"

Grilfir chuckled. "My poor *Garghilum* is slowly coming around to the idea. Brilgus can be very...persistent."

"Oh dear," Stephanie commented as they reached the table at the head of the room. Two smaller tables set on either side had been reserved for the Royal Guard and her team, and both groups were disconcerted to find themselves alternated round the table.

Grilfir noted the arrangement and Sho's thoughtful look. At most royal events, the different bodyguard teams were placed at tables of their own. He liked this arrangement better. The teams were in reach of each other and better able to counter any potentially hostile actions.

He allowed himself to be seated and waited until the rest of the room had once again sat. It was a relief to have Stephanie on one side of him and Sho on the other. This way, he was guaranteed interesting conversation.

His advisors would, no doubt, be a little disgruntled but having them farther away would focus their attention better. It would also mean less interruptions for him during the event. The chief steward stepped forward and the room stilled.

"Ladies, Gentlemen, and Marines." His introduction brought a chuckle from the audience. "Thank you for your welcome to King Grilfir and for making yourselves available to him during his visit."

He cast a quick glance at the table, and the king recognized good theatrics when he saw them.

"Here it comes," he muttered, as the steward continued.

"I'm sure he has enjoyed his time aboard the *Knight* and will remember it well."

"He can come back anytime," was said from the rear of the room, but Stephanie couldn't see who it was.

Someone from the weapons teams was the closest she could get—and a female, which would explain the smothered snickers and not-so-hushed, "He's married," from that corner. She lowered her head to hide a smile as color rose in Grilfir's cheeks.

It came and went quickly, and the steward smiled. "Indeed." His smile broadened. "For those of you here for more than the food, I'm sure the king has a few words he'd like to say on his own behalf."

He waved a hand in the royal's direction and stepped away from the center of the table.

Grilfir took his cue and rose from his seat. He noted the delicious aromas that indicated that the food was ready and decided to keep the speech short. As he looked around the room, he smiled and his gaze searched for the entry to the ship's kitchen or to wherever the catering would arrive from.

When he thought he'd found it, he began. "Firstly, I'd like to thank Stephanie for the opportunity to see this wonderful ship."

He acknowledged her with a tilt of his head, then raised his gaze to take in the ceiling at the center of the room. "And during this tour, it has come to my attention that I should thank the ship herself."

Murmurs of approval ran through the room. Stephanie inclined her head and the *Knight* dimmed the lights briefly to acknowledge him. His startled look caused laughter to ripple through those present.

After a moment, he gathered himself and cleared his throat before he spoke again. "Without this ship and all who sail aboard her, I would have no world and my people would be homeless. For saving us from this fate, I thank you.

"I also thank you for your willingness to come to the aid of a planet few of you have been able to know and for your willingness to take on a superior force and to fight alongside people who were strangers to you.

"Finally, I thank you for your sacrifice and your willingness to sacrifice more." He glanced at the weapons teams, then looked around the room until he located the security section that had been caught in another of the blasts that had holed the *Knight*.

"Meligorn will remember your fallen. It remembers those of you who still live. It has a place for you should you ever need it or wish to take it. Meligorn welcomes you and your families as its own."

He glanced at his advisors. "Citizenship papers are still being processed and details will be made available for those who wish to explore the options now available to you."

Stephanie struggled to keep the surprise from her face as the room exploded with applause. She caught the look on the chief steward's and Captain Emil's faces and knew this hadn't been discussed beforehand.

Captains Moser and Sartre looked worried, and she made a note to look into what this meant for her Navy personnel. She caught Moser's eye and lowered her chin in acknowledgment, hoping it would be enough to ease his concerns for the evening.

He nudged Sartre, and they both glanced toward her. She caught their brief nods in return and watched them relax somewhat. It was as much as she could hope for.

The king had caught a glimpse of movement as the door he'd thought was the catering access opened a fraction and closed again.

To end his speech, he said, "For coming to our aid with no thought for yourselves or your fate. For coming, yet again, to our assistance. For being willing to sacrifice everything to keep our world free, Meligorn thanks you, remembers you, and welcomes you."

Grilfir gestured to the chief steward. "So, without more ado, thank you for what you have done and for having me here tonight."

He took his seat amidst another roar of applause and appreciation.

Stephanie leaned closer to him. "You couldn't have given a girl some warning?"

His chuckle was a little rueful but mainly smug. "My advisors will ask me the same thing when I return to the palace." With a satisfied sigh, he leaned back in his seat. "It's good to be the king."

The meal passed swiftly, and they all stood to one side as the tables were moved away and the room rearranged to allow dancing in the center and mingling around the edges.

"Did you know they would do this?" Grilfir asked and opened the night's celebration by leading Stephanie onto the dance floor.

"It was suggested for the crew," she told him, "but I wasn't sure you'd have time or want to stay."

"He doesn't and he does," Sho replied as he danced past with Drusilla. The protection team and the Royal Guard had been allowed on the dance floor too but only after they'd found suitable partners.

It was an education for the Meligornians, but they didn't seem to mind.

Stephanie and the king danced without touching according to Meligornian royal protocol, and she was glad she'd had Ebony take her through the style. She was doubly glad she'd had the team and the Marines go over it too, given that the Royal Guard needed partners.

Ka floated past, dancing better than she would have given her credit for. She looked for Todd. He stood on the sidelines, looking wistful, and she felt almost guilty. At least she knew he'd understand about her duties as a host—or she hoped he would.

King Grilfir caught the direction of her stare and chuckled. "Is that your young man?"

Her face heated and he laughed again.

"He's another of Meligorn's legends, you know."

310

She tilted her face to look at him. "He is?"

"Oh, yes. The stories that came back with *The King's Warrior* about the 'crazy human Marines' who took on a Teloran super-dreadnought on their own are quite entertaining."

Stephanie sent Todd another glance and gave Grilfir a conspiratorial smile. The Marine looked worried and she smirked. If anything, that made him look even more worried.

Grilfir leaned forward. "It's not nice to tease," he whispered.

"He'll get over it," she assured him and wondered exactly what her young man would have to say when the dance was over.

He didn't wait, however.

"Excuse me, Your Majesty," he said and stepped beside the king moments later. "Do you mind if I cut in?"

She was horrified and had no idea if cutting in was something the Meligornians understood. Fortunately, the king laughed.

"Young man, what took you so long?" He chuckled and stepped away.

Before he could retreat to the sidelines, a sturdy woman with a trim figure intercepted him. "Your Majesty, might I have the pleasure?"

Recognizing the *Knight's* second in command, King Grilfir smiled. "Commander Mulvaney, the pleasure is all mine."

They danced until the end of the next song, and Stephanie bid Todd a reluctant farewell to follow the king from the dance floor.

The king raised his eyebrows. "Surely he deserves more time than that?"

"He does," she admitted with regret, "but you are my guest. It was poor form enough to allow him to steal me on the dance floor."

Grilfir laughed. "That will go down in annals of palace gossip," he informed her. "A Marine with the cheek to steal a king's dance partner."

She blushed. "I'm sorry."

Her apology only made him laugh harder.

"Don't be. It's one of the highlights of this visit—to see you have someone who cares enough to take any chance to steal a little of your time."

"My time?"

"Of course. Why else would he steal the dance? It's not like he had to stake his claim on you. He took the only opportunity he'd have to spend time with you this evening."

"He did?"

Grilfir nodded. "Of course he did. In his place, I'd have done the same."

Stephanie blushed. "Why, that sneaky…"

The king laughed and they both turned to watch Todd doing a weird sinking maneuver to mirror Frog. The Marine had one hand on his nose and the other over his head as he bent his knees and shimmied to the floor and up again.

She giggled. "Oh no. They're not—"

But they were. Frog challenged Todd's move with one that involved a hip swivel, robotic arms, and a sideways turn where the feet moved backward but the dancer stayed in one place. The Marine gave a whoop of amusement and mirrored it.

Mortified, she hid her face with both hands. Grilfir touched her shoulder and she looked at him.

"What are they doing?"

"It looks like they're having a dance-off featuring moves from Earth's nineteen-eighties." She sighed.

"Is that bad?"

"No, merely embarrassing for anyone associated with them."

"They've started a trend," he observed.

"I just bet they—" Stephanie fell silent and straightened.

Lars caught sight of the movement and his rapid glance caught the change shifting across her face. "Oh, fuck!" he said and raised his fingers to his lips.

As his whistle pierced the dance music, her eyes turned black. The security chief caught King Grilfir by the arm and dragged him back a few steps before he handed him to Sho who had hurried forward. The

Royal Guard broke from the conversations they were in and gathered around their king.

Stephanie was oblivious. She tilted her head from side to side as though listening for something. Her nostrils flared and she whipped around to focus on a single direction.

"I have you, you targlath bastards," she whispered.

She pivoted sharply on her heel and stalked toward the door.

"Ebony. Call all hands to stations. *I am going hunting!*"

The crew cleared the dance floor and many made a quick detour past the buffet tables set up along one side before they followed her. Lars hesitated, clearly torn between following Stephanie and the team or remaining with the king.

"I'm sorry, Your Majesty. The Morgana has located your Telorans."

Sho tensed. "Your Majesty, we need to leave." He turned to Lars. "We can try to find our own—"

"No, Stephanie would never forgive me. She'll be appalled enough as it is."

Captain Emil approached them hurriedly. "I can—" he began although his gaze darted toward the door.

Lars caught what he was offering and shook his head. "No. Thank you, Emil. I'll make sure they get off the ship safely."

"I can do that." Todd had arrived. "You need to be with our girl before she Morganas herself into more trouble than she can handle. The Hooligans and I will get the king to the shuttle safely. Jimmy can fly them or fly escort."

"We'll fly escort." One of the *Knight's* flight commanders had arrived. He turned to the king. "We'd be honored."

"I'll have a royal escort meet you before you reach atmosphere," Sho told them. "You shouldn't stray too far from the *Knight*. We don't want to be responsible for anyone being left behind."

From the looks on the pilots' faces, that had worried them but they had been prepared to take the risk to ensure that their royal guest returned home safely. King Grilfir shook his arm free of Sho's grip and strode toward the door.

When the others caught up, he tilted his head at his security head. "I think a faster pace is appropriate."

"Yes, your Highness."

They broke into a jog and reached the shuttle bays in double-quick time. To their surprise, Stephanie waited beside the hatch leading to the hangar bay. She wasted no time with a preamble.

"We have to make your departure look as normal as possible," the Morgana informed them in her icy tones. She looked at his entourage and gave a tight and grim smile when she saw her pilots. "Good."

Turning to the King, she continued, her words as much a command to her own men as they were information for him and his. "Your Highness, my pilots will escort you to the Royal Airfield. They will conduct the usual farewell flyover before they return to the *Knight*."

King Grilfir stared. The change from semi-normal human girl to this being was unnerving.

If the Morgana could read his thoughts, she gave no sign. Instead, she stopped to fix her men with a serious stare.

They flinched but none of them fled.

"No one will be left behind," she promised. "Make this look good. As we planned. Understood?"

A hasty chorus of, "Yes, ma'am," answered her and she focused on Grilfir again.

"I will search for the Telorans, but my escort will remain here to protect the planet. We all know what happened the last time we were drawn away from the world..." She let her words trail off to give them time to remember the sneak attack that had seen a Meligornian passenger liner sacrifice itself to keep its home world safe.

They nodded.

"Good," she acknowledged. "The *Cathay Williams* and the *Henry Chauvel* will stand watch. They won't be happy but will understand the necessity. Once I'm certain the planet is safe, they'll join us."

She paused, then touched her fingertips to her brow and to her heart and bowed in farewell as she said, "I am sorry to cut your evening short, Your Majesty."

King Grilfir gave her a soft smile and returned her farewell before he extended his fist in a warrior's goodbye. "Selene's blessing upon you."

That caught the Morgana by surprise, and she touched her knuckles lightly to his. "And on you," she managed after a slight pause, pressed the button for the hatch, and stood aside so he and his entourage could pass through.

As the hatch closed behind them, she caught Todd's eye. "Sergeant, I'm glad you're here. When we begin the attack, your team is to commence its insertion." She paused and her dark eyes glittered. "Do your worst to them."

He swallowed hard. This was not the farewell he would have wanted when he might not return, but it helped. Seeing the darkness in the Morgana's eyes made it easier to resist the urge to cup Stephanie's cheek with one hand.

Before he could do something he'd regret, Todd wheeled abruptly and jogged away, calling to the Hooligans as he went. "You heard the lady. We have a mission to run."

When they returned to the command deck, Captain Emil was relaying the news to the *Cathay* and the *Chauvel*. His counterparts were not pleased.

"That is not what we were assigned for," Captain Yale informed him.

"Nevertheless, it is what I command." The Morgana's voice rang across the bridge. "And I am in command here."

On the forward viewscreen, the captains' jaws dropped.

She continued in the cold, implacable tone. "I see you were not told about me—or you did not understand what my presence meant. Understand this. You are to guard this planet with your lives until I am sure it is safe—and it is your lives and the lives of your ships if you fail to do your best to keep this world alive."

Captain Yale's dusky skin faded to the color of cream and Doherty's freckles stood out like ink spots on white parchment.

"How will we know when to leave?" the woman managed after she swallowed a few times to moisten her throat.

"You will come when the planet is safe."

"And then I will call you, my sisters," the *Knight* told them. "I will call you when the world is safe and not before."

The Morgana's dark gaze flickered to the nearest speaker. Finally, she agreed. "You will come when the *Knight* calls."

Both captains relaxed. "Understood. We'll stand watch and wait for your signal."

"Good." The Federation Witch clicked her fingers and the screen went dark. She looked around the bridge. "It is time."

"We are ready. Translation is awaiting your word."

Captain Rawlins surveyed her console and scanned the readouts with a single sweep of her eyes. Satisfied with what she saw, she nodded.

"Get ready to take us through." She frowned. "Make sure we come out close but not too close. We don't need the Federation Navy to see this ship and start asking questions."

"Gotcha, sir. We'll put her on the edge and warm the skip drives for rapid transition if we need to come in," the pilot snapped in response.

"And I can keep her escort as blind as two bats in a thunderstorm," Turnkey, her defense specialist assured her. "They won't see a thing but they might have a migraine when they come out of it."

"Much as I appreciate the Navy loaning them, I don't care what kind of headaches you cause them as long as the Witch and One R&D are kept safe."

"I hear you."

Captain Rawlins couldn't help smiling. The Navy might not appreciate it, but this was exactly the attitude she needed. One R&D wasn't ready to reveal the *Tempestarii's* existence.

CHAPTER SEVENTEEN

"Sir! We have movement in Meligorn's orbit." The alert from the crew member on scans cut through the command deck, and the captain looked up.

"Show me."

The forward viewscreen came alive with the image of the *King's Warrior* pushing slowly away from the Meligornian space station.

"Have they seen us?"

"I don't think so, sir." The response came from defenses, but the speaker looked worried.

"It's your head if they have."

The technician gulped. "Yes, sir."

He returned his focus to his readouts and tension marked his posture.

The captain continued to watch the *King's Warrior* as it maneuvered away from the station. His gaze flicked over the other vessels still docked and an inner prompting made him realize that something was missing.

"They are moving but not like they see us." The defense technician's voice interrupted him before he could determine what had triggered his discomfort, and he spun to face the team with him on the bridge while darkness crackled over him.

The crewman flinched but breathed a sigh of relief when the captain turned to the screen once more. That had been far too close.

On the large display, The Meligornian vessel adjusted course slowly, eased farther from the station, and set a course for the moon. The technician relaxed, but not much. Their leader remained focused intently on the viewscreen as though he searched for a fault in his analysis.

"Will that course give her a better chance to detect us?"

"No, sir. If she intended to do that, she'd have done it from the station. She can't see us."

While the defense technician should have found his own words comforting, he didn't. If the *King's Warrior* angled one fin the wrong way or fired a retro-thruster in an unfavorable direction, he was dead.

The captain stared as the Meligornian super-dreadnought continued its flight and he finally relaxed. "She can't see us."

He turned his head and his scowl returned when he realized what was missing. "Where's the Witch's—"

An alarm shrieked and the lighting plunged to emergency levels.

"Brace! Brace! Brace!" The words were barely spoken when the shields rippled and klaxons began a steady chorus.

"What in all Telor is that?"

The shield vanished after a section flared from black through blue and purple to white and the ship shuddered. Lights on several consoles blazed red, and engineering gave a squawk of alarm.

"Don't tell me you have trouble. Deal with it!" he roared and glared at the defense team. "Get my shields back online."

The crewman nodded and his fingers scurried over his console, his eyes on the boards and not on his leader. The captain's attention rolled onto the scan team.

"What is that and why didn't we see it coming?"

"It's the Witch's ship, sir." The technician didn't look up from his boards. "And I don't know. One minute, the sky was clear and in the next, she fired into our flank. The asteroid stopped her from getting a shot into our engines."

"Thank the Shadows for small mercies." The captain snarled with growing fury. "Where is she now?"

His subordinate stared at his screens in search of an answer but his mouth dropped open a second later. "I don't—starboard! She's on our starboard, sir."

"I thought she was on our port. How did she get—" He leaned forward and narrowed his eyes at the viewscreen.

The *Knight* was a little off their starboard flank. Before he could react, she fired another burst into his ship and immediately blinked out of sight.

"Nail that gods-cursed *keversha* down!" he shouted and darkness curled around him. "Don't let her fire again."

He asked the impossible but not a single member of his bridge crew dared argue. They did their best. Shields of non-nMU energy were pulled into place, but they soon revealed weak points as the generators began to overload under the *Knight's* lightning-fast assaults.

The way the smaller craft slipped in and out of reality and attacked with everything she had in the same moment that she appeared meant there was no time to shunt power from one section to another. There was also no way they could predict where she would strike next.

"I want her gun crews gone!"

Todd cursed when the deck shifted under his feet, and he made a note to ask *Ebony* to add running while she skip-transitioned in-system to the next set of scenarios. Behind him, Ka yelped and Jimmy muttered a hasty apology.

They definitely needed the practice. Todd cursed himself for not having thought of it sooner. He caught hold of the rail and ran his hand along it as he ran. His stomach lurched as the *Knight* skipped again.

"Dammitall, Emil! We need some warning."

"You have as much warning as the rest of us," the captain replied. "And you need to get into position. We won't be able to hold them forever."

As if his words were prophetic, the ship shuddered and bounced.

"Fuck! That was something big," Reggie exclaimed.

"Now tell me something I don't know, shit-for-brains." Ka was unimpressed.

The Australian glanced at his HUD and paled. "Uh…it might have blown the hangar all to hell."

"What?" Before anyone could answer, Todd pulled his HUD display up.

"Fuck!"

They continued their sprint until they reached the hangar, where they were stopped by a repair crew.

"There's nothing beyond that airlock, sir."

"Don't call me sir, and there darned well is."

"Nothing you can fly, sir. Look!"

The technician retrieved his tablet and showed him the scene that lay beyond.

"Well, fuck!"

"Yes, s—" The man caught his look. "Uh…Sergeant."

Todd leaned against the wall and gaped at the scene on the tablet. The fighters the Navy had sent him—or what was left of them—floated free. The blast that had demolished the *Knight's* hangar bay doors had left nothing but debris in its wake.

He could barely make out the partially intact shells of two, the half-shells of another four, and the twisted metal of all that was left of the fighters that had been closest to the door.

"On the upside," the crewman continued quickly, "the ship took the brunt of the attack and the inner walls held."

"Is the *Knight* okay?"

The technician looked serious. "She'll hold, sir."

"I am fine," the *Knight* informed him, "and I mean that as F. I. N. E."

A small chuckle burst from Todd when he recalled the movie but he sobered quickly. "I'm sorry, *Knight.*"

"You need to make the transfer, quickly," Ebony replied.

He nodded. "Will do, Eb."

Ka returned his hasty glance. "Now what, boss?"

With a sigh, he glanced at the tablet and along the corridor they'd run down. His mind raced but it reached only one conclusion.

A little reluctantly, he pushed away from the wall. "I sure hope the Morgana recognizes me."

CHAPTER EIGHTEEN

The bridge was the scene of controlled chaos when the Hooligans burst through the doors. Emil pivoted when he heard them open, ready to reprimand the intruder. He froze, his mouth half-open when he saw the team.

"You're not supposed to be here."

"Tell me about it." Todd glanced at the Morgana. "I need her help."

Stephanie-Morgana was in her element. Power crackled over her body as she directed the gMU, eMU, and Mu that protected the hull, propelled the ship, and was fired from the *Knight's* guns. He was relieved to see the tethers leading from the deck to her waist as the vessel skipped again.

As it settled into its new position, she turned her head, the Morgana very visible in her eyes. "Aren't you supposed to be gone?"

She grunted and shifted her hand. On the forward screen, a barrier of blue light moved to protect the more conventional shields.

The Morgana continued. "We are trying to kill them but not to do so right now. What are you doing here?"

The *Knight* skipped again, and the team groaned as they fought to stay on their feet.

"The hold was attacked," Todd yelled. "Our ships are toast."

"Meaning?"

"We can't fly scrap metal, unfortunately. We have no way to reach the Teloran vessel to complete the mission."

The Morgana was silent for all of two seconds before her eyes blazed. "Get prepared and get your whole crew into the bay."

"The bay is destroyed," he told her and she smiled.

"I'm aware of that," she reassured him in chilling tones while her smile grew wider. "I hope you can swim."

His face paled and he swallowed against the sudden dryness in his throat. He'd thought he'd seen the worst of both Stephanie and the Morgana, but this was a whole new level.

The only part of Stephanie he could see was her shell.

Todd jerked his chin in a single nod and fled, relieved when the team bolted after him. They too were silent, but he didn't dare look at their faces for fear of what he'd see there. That was their first real encounter with the Morgana. No doubt they'd tell him exactly what they thought of it later.

"So," Ka began, when they reached the lower deck and pounded toward the hangar bay, "we have to swim?"

"It looks like it."

"You know," Reggie interjected, "I'm not sure I like the sound of that."

The sergeant gave a mirthless laugh. "I'm fairly sure the Morgana doesn't give a shit what you like or not."

"Or what you like, either," the Australian retorted. "She seemed to like the idea of you swimming in a vacuum."

"Okay, I don't think it'll be that bad," he replied.

"Really?" Ka asked, put one hand on her hip, and raised an eyebrow. "So tell me, Todd...maybe you can tell me exactly what 'swimming' might have been code for then?"

"No." He tried to catch his breath. "I can't. I don't know exactly what 'go swimming' is code for, but I can guess—and, yes, make sure you all have the ability to spacewalk."

"Fan-fucking-tastic!" Reggie griped. "My favorite pastime—getting into the good old budgie smugglers and taking a dip in the stars."

"Budgie smugglers?" Drusilla asked. Ka patted her on the shoulder and shook her head.

"You don't want to know."

"So, what stroke do we use?" Gary asked, and the corporal snorted.

"Definitely not the one you'd prefer!" she snapped in reply, "since it involves more than one hand and you being fully clothed."

The man's jaw dropped but Ka wasn't finished.

"Nope," she continued, "I reckon you're gonna need both hands to keep that combat suit firmly buttoned and maintain intestinal fortitude...mate."

"Hey, who are you calling gutless?"

She favored him with an amused glance. "Well, you don't hear us girls bitchin' about an itsy-bitsy spacewalk, do you?"

"She said nothing about a spacewalk. She was talkin' about swimming, as in a full-blown EVA."

"You need to stop whining. It's not like there's any water involved. Your monthly bath schedule is still intact."

"Hey!" Gary opened his mouth to argue but Jimmy placed a hand on his shoulder.

"I'd quit while the quitting was good," the Scotsman told him. "There's no reasoning with her when she's like this."

"And you know this how?" his teammate asked.

Todd caught Ka's sudden blush and Jimmy's momentary loss of words and thought he'd better intervene before the Englishman followed that thread too far.

"It doesn't matter how we get over there," he snapped and drew their attention to himself. "We all have our tasks. Steph's is to protect the *Knight* and keep the Teloran's attention. Ours is to go over, get the data, and complete the mission."

"And get back?" Angus asked.

Todd gave him a direct look. "That's up to us."

Of course, that caught Gary's attention. "Oh, nice. That's fantastic."

Reggie rubbed his hand over the top of the Englishman's helmet as though he was ruffling his hair. "What's the matter, little fella? Do you want me to hold your hand?"

"You bloody well touch me and I'll shove my boot so far up your ass you'll be chewing leather for a week!"

That made the team chuckle, and Ka touched her knuckles to Todd's shoulder.

"We'll be fine, boss. The Hooligans are known for the impossible."

He only hoped she was right and didn't know what Steph would do if they didn't return.

Shaking his head, he shoved the thought aside.

"Getting back is on us," he repeated but more for himself than anyone on the team.

"Number one is away," the weapons technician announced and risked a quick glance at their leader while his fingers danced across the console to launch the second of their surprises. "Number two, away."

The captain appeared to barely register the success. His gaze remained fixed on the screen, where the *Knight* flickered in and out of existence while his ship's shields ran into the red.

"Number three is away."

The captain looked up.

"Maybe she'll go after them," the scans technician said as he tracked the path of the three giant rocks they'd sent toward Meligorn.

Each one of them was a planet-killer in their own right and without the *Knight* in orbit, the planet stood defenseless. Even if the Federation vessels that had arrived with her undocked in time to sacrifice themselves, the third would get through. And as for the king's ship, it was unlikely to play any part in the drama unfolding.

From what he could see, it wouldn't be able to get into position fast enough.

"They're moving, sir."

The scans technician's cry drew his attention to the screen again.

He was right. The two Navy ships drew away from the station and moved farther from Meligorn's orbit. To his surprise, though, neither of them set an intercept course. They both moved wide of the meteors' path.

"Cowards!" He all but spat the word as the *Knight* sent another barrage into his craft's side. "Why aren't they breaking away?"

"Because…" the scan technician began and stopped as energy arced around his captain.

"I can see for myself!"

They could all see but believing it was another matter.

A portal had opened in front of the lead asteroid, and even as it vanished inside, a second portal opened in front of it.

"They have more witches?" the captain cried. "Why have we not heard of this?"

"I don't know, sir. There seems to be a gap in our intelligence."

"That is an understatement." He watched in disbelief as the second asteroid vanished and reappeared behind its sister on course for the outer reaches of the solar system.

The third one joined them shortly after.

"By all that's holy and undefiled, there are more of them!" He pivoted toward communications. "Get this to the fleet. Get it to them now!"

The crewman moved to obey and the leader glanced at his own console for confirmation. He saw the burst sent, immediately followed by the message, *Transmission unsuccessful*.

"Again," he snapped and watched the transmission launch and fail a second time. "Use the torps."

"Done," the technician confirmed and swore as the *Knight* appeared and devastated the swarm in a burst of withering fire.

Some of the message torpedoes might have made it to transition if the weapons fire from the *Knight* hadn't been followed by a wave of purple energy that caught and reduced them to dust.

"Again!"

As before, the warning failed to make it through.

CHAPTER NINETEEN

"You have to be shitting me," Gary muttered and stared at the scene on the tablet.

The team had geared up and now waited inside the airlock.

"There is no way we'll 'swim' through all that," he added gloomily

They all flinched as the flare of exploding message torpedoes faded and their own weapons crews sent another fusillade into the Teloran super-ship. Todd sighed and they looked up as someone stepped through to join them.

Stephanie was nowhere to be seen in the Morgana's dark expression, and Gary's voice had carried clearly. "I don't see that you have an option."

"There are other shuttles, right?" At this statement, his sergeant wondered if the man had fully lost it and the Morgana turned to study the Englishman with a dispassionate stare.

"There are other careers too if you find this one so difficult," she retorted.

Gary's jaw dropped and he took a breath, but she hadn't finished.

"Alternatively, I'm sure you can breathe vacuum, right?" She gestured to the hold and waited while the man's mouth gaped like a beached fish. The other members of the team shuffled restlessly and exchanged glances with each other and with Lars and Vishlog who stood beyond the door. Before any of them could think of what to say, the Morgana stepped closer to Gary.

With her faceplate pressed close to the Marine's, she snarled a challenge. "Is that what all of these comments are meant to accomplish? An opportunity to see how fast you can adapt to the nothing?"

He shut his mouth with a snap and backpedaled. The limited space brought him to a thumping halt against the bulkhead and he shook his head in rapid negation.

She gave him a savage smile and snapped her fingers.

"Grab your gear," she commanded as the door locks released.

At the same time, the door leading to the inside of the ship began to close. Lars and Vishlog leapt forward and the Hooligans caught hold of them and hauled them into the small chamber.

Todd grimaced at a sudden flare of alarm, but the two men had already snapped their helmets closed.

Lars caught his look and grinned. "It's not our first rodeo," the security chief told him.

The door leading into the hangar cycled open and they were able to see the devastation in the hangar beyond. That wasn't what drew—and held—their attention, though.

Beyond the floating debris of what used to be half a dozen highly advanced insertion craft hung the Teloran super-dreadnought.

"Ebony, I want an all-over look at the Teloran vessel." The command came in the Morgana's cold tones and her gaze remained fixed on the huge craft.

Still focused on the enemy vessel, she made a sweeping motion with one hand and pushed the remains of the insertion craft against one wall. "I need a support team to secure that."

As she spoke, she led the team into the hangar itself.

"I hope you packed your bathers," Gary muttered and tried to gauge the distance between the *Knight* and the Teloran's nearest surface.

He pressed his lips together when the Witch snapped a glance at him. Her lips curved into a tight smile and Todd was reminded of

Stephanie at her most evil. He hoped the Morgana would leave him with enough of his team to complete the mission.

Hell, he hoped she would leave him all his team, but with the way Gary behaved, that might be a decidedly slim possibility.

Fortunately, the screen at the rear of the hangar came alive as the airlock cycled closed behind them. The Morgana walked around to get a better view of the screen but didn't completely turn her back on her massive enemy.

"So," she murmured, when she could see it fully, "it's like that, is it?"

Todd wasn't sure what that was but he didn't like the sound of it any more than he liked the look on her face.

"Emil!" she snapped.

"It's a little busy here, Morgana." The captain's voice sounded tight and they could hear the thud as his fingertips hit his console with more force than necessary.

"I can make it more so," she threatened, her voice saccharine sweet.

"Weapons Team One, that gap. Focus on that. Weapons Two, keep the pressure on that shield. Three, you have all incoming. Scans, any sign?"

"No, sir. Not yet."

Voices crackled in his headset and he responded, "I need repair teams to Sectors Five and Ten."

The ship blinked.

"Ebony!"

"Apologies, Emil, but your fire teams were not enough. I had to assist."

"Right. Fine. Thank you, Ebony. Weapons One—"

Morgana gave a snarl of frustration and studied the view of the Teloran ship. She turned to Todd. "I need a missile."

Her words coincided with the airlock cycling open and the arrival of the support team she'd requested. Todd tapped Jimmy, Gary, and

Reggie, the three most likely to get themselves spaced while the Morgana was in control of his girlfriend.

"We'll get you one," he told her. "Any particular size?"

She smiled at him. "Make it the biggest you can find in the next five minutes."

He wasn't sure what kind of fangs were hidden in her smile but he didn't want to find out, so he bounced to the airlock and brought his hand down on the opening mechanism before it could cycle shut.

The Terrible Trio joined him, and they waited impatiently as the airlock cycled.

"Two minutes," Gary noted morosely. "I don't suppose she'd take that into consideration—"

Todd slapped his shoulder. "You know the way to the weapons deck, don't you?"

The man grunted but took the lead. They both knew he spent more time with the weapons teams than he did anywhere else. They reached their destination with a minute to spare.

"The Morgana wants a missile," Todd told the scowling commander. "And we have"—he glanced at his tablet—" less than a minute to get it to her."

"But—"

"Unless you'd rather she came to fetch it herself?" Jimmy asked, his voice deceptively mild in its threat.

The commander's eyes widened. "Uh...no. That won't be necessary. I take it she needs a big one?"

"You got it," Todd confirmed and waited impatiently as the man tapped two of the closest crew members and had them unload something of the requisite size while a third one fetched a trolley.

The sergeant glanced at his tablet and stowed it hastily in its case. They had under thirty seconds before the airlock put them over the time limit. "Well, it did take us less than five minutes to find the missile," he muttered.

She stood and tapped her foot in an all-too-familiar manner when they fought the missile through the lock. The repair crew had finished securing the remains of his insertion craft and met them on the way out, their eyes widening when they saw the missile.

His lips twitched into a grim smile as he and the boys brought the ordnance to a halt in front of the Morgana's impatient form. Their intention had been to simply position it there while they waited for further instructions. Instead, almost before they had even ceased to move, the tie-downs holding the missile in place snapped free and it floated off the trolley bed.

"Well, fuck me," Reggie murmured.

Todd ignored him and stared at her instead.

Her face was all concentration as she guided it up and pivoted it towards the Teloran ship. With her gaze focused on the weapon, she moved it through the gaping hole in the *Knight's* hull.

"Emil, you and Ebony need to hold this position until I say otherwise."

Instead of the argument Todd had expected, the captain's voice came back firm and clear. "Gotcha, Steph."

Either word of her missile acquisition had reached him or he was keeping a closer eye on the situation than the sergeant had given him credit for.

Seconds later, the man added, "But make it fast."

The Morgana didn't reply. Instead, the missile's rockets lit and she encased it in blue light. The team gasped as it vanished from sight and reappeared moving at a speed it wouldn't have had time to reach if it had only traveled the distance between the *Knight* and its target.

Todd didn't ask where she'd gated it to. He didn't care. All that mattered was the flare of light from its impact and the gaping hole that resulted.

"There is your door," she told them and sounded immensely satisfied.

"Yeah?" Gary challenged. "And where the fuck is our ship?"

His answer came in the form of a glowing purple bubble that pounded into place around them. Tendrils of magic caught the rest of the team and its gear and yanked them through the bubble's skin until they were all inside it.

"You had to ask, you stupid Pommy fuckwit." Reggie snarled with something close to disgust.

Todd looked at Stephanie's face and tried to meet the Morgana's gaze in the hopes that he'd have the chance to tell his girl goodbye. As if sensing his focus, she looked up. Her lips twitched and her gaze became momentarily blue before they flipped to black again.

It was better than nothing, but his stab of disappointment said otherwise.

With an abrupt sweep of her hands, she pitched the bubble out of the hangar bay. Todd kept his feet and held her gaze for as long as he could. The exchange was broken when she opened a gate and hurled the bubble through.

Stars whirled in a crazy kaleidoscope before their magic craft burst into the system they'd left. This time, however, they found themselves inside the Teloran ship.

"Well, fuck me..." Reggie dragged in a breath but no one took him up on the offer.

Gary had been toppled from his feet by the bubble's rapid transition. He sprawled on the glowing floor and gaped at a perfect view of the stars, albeit through a purple haze.

"Oh, man..." He rolled onto his back and readied himself to push to his feet when someone else lost their balance and landed on top of him. "Oof!"

Ka maintained a tight grasp on her rifle as she fell and was careful to keep her fingers outside the trigger guard. No way did she want that sucker to fire when she was surrounded by a magic bubble. There was no knowing what it would take to make it pop.

Someone grunted when she landed butt-first on their chest. She lay there and stared as the sphere spun out of the Meligornian system and through the darkness of an unknown galaxy. Her every instinct told her not to move in case she disrupted their journey.

She clenched her fingers around the rifle's stock and prayed they'd make it through the portal and back in time to complete their mission. It was hard to not close her eyes but she didn't want them shut if it all went wrong. If this was the last view she would see, she intended to do her best to remember it.

How else would her soul begin its journey home?

Angus and Henry exchanged worried looks and sank to the floor nearby, their rifles resting across their knees. Those boys knew how to travel.

Dru, too, she decided, as the blonde woman lowered to one knee and rested the fingertips of one hand on the bubble's floor. Her gaze darted across the space around them as though searching for an enemy.

The edge of a second portal passed over them and stars were replaced with the silver and gray of a starship's bulkhead and ceiling. Jagged-edged metal preceded it as their transport hurtled through the rent created by the missile, and they impacted hard with the deck.

The magical sphere dissipated in a thousand purple shards, and anyone left standing was thrown off their feet. Even those crouching toppled, but at least they didn't have far to fall. Reggie landed on his back and Ka grunted at the force of their landing. The person beneath her coughed.

While the Australian pushed to his feet, Gary was being crushed. He coughed and put his hands against the body on top of him in an effort to shove it aside. It pivoted and a solid slap caught the side of his helmet.

"Keep your bloody hands off my ass or I'll cut 'em off," Ka snapped.

"And a sweet fuck to you too, sweetheart," he retorted. "Now, I'll have to wash for a week and even then—"

He stopped when Todd cleared his throat and he rolled to his feet.

"Grab your gear and get your asses moving," the sergeant ordered. His voice reverberated through their helmets and they scrambled upright hastily.

They had already begun to retrieve their gear before they registered they'd even moved.

"Aw, man," Angus grumbled and checked his equipment before he turned to do the same for Henry. "I thought we'd given this tactic up."

"What? High-speed insertion?" Reggie asked.

His teammate gestured at the floor around them with his hand. "Whatever the fuck you want to call this," he explained. "First with the super-dreadnought near Dreth. Now here."

"We can talk about it later," Todd snapped, "but someone has to have noticed that. We. Need. To. Move! Piet, you're up."

He indicated the door. "Ka, you can help him. The rest of you stand watch and try not to float away."

They positioned themselves for exit as best they could, aware of the battle waged on the other side of the hole.

"Hoooly sheeit," Angus murmured, as the *Knight* blinked out of existence.

They all glanced at the door.

"Stand clear!" Piet warned and activated the release.

The blast of air as the corridor outside decompressed surged past them, and Todd caught Ka's arm as she catapulted back.

"Dumb-ass," Henry muttered, and she gave him the finger.

"That's Corporal Dumb-Ass to you."

CHAPTER TWENTY

"What do you mean it's already happened? How much of a delay is there?" Grilfir was frustrated at the lag time in the footage from one of their outer satellites. "I want to know what is happening when it happens."

Having made the shuttle alter its course, the king stood on the command deck of the *King's Warrior*. V'ritan stood beside him and tried not to laugh at his monarch's frustration.

"I'm sorry, Your Highness, but the laws of physics will not bend, even for you."

"How about for magic?" he snapped. "Surely there's a way for the physics of magic to override the rest of it. After all, look at what the Witch accomplishes. Don't tell me physics is anywhere near happy with all that."

His companion chuckled. "We'll have to look into it."

"There is no 'will have to' about it," the king told him imperiously. "I want the problem fixed and I want it fixed now."

V'ritan cast a hasty glance at his Master Mage. "Can you look into it?" he asked.

"Solve it," Grilfir ordered and the Master's eyes widened.

While he almost felt sorry for his subordinate, he didn't intervene.

He might be the king's *Garghilum Afreghil*, but the king was the king. The mage cast a worried glance in his direction and he smiled in response.

Catching the man's gaze, he nodded and the Master stalked off the bridge.

"I'm afraid you might have upset him," V'ritan told the king.

"Why? Did he have anything more important to do?"

He sighed. "No, but he'll miss some of the battle and you can only agree there's much to miss. Have you ever seen anything like that?"

Grilfir shrugged. "The quicker he is, the less he'll miss...and, no, I've never seen the like. A shield of nMU? Is that the frequency Stephanie talked about?"

"We think so, your Highness. My Chief Master was trying to determine if there was a way to detect it—"

"Well, he messed that one up, didn't he?" His royal companion obviously didn't feel particularly sympathetic.

"No detection method penetrates an asteroid with a shell that thick."

The king took a breath but couldn't think of a reply to go with it. Finally, he shrugged. "How long do you think it will take him to come up with something?"

V'ritan noticed several of his other mages slip out after the Master and was glad they'd gone to his assistance. The sooner Grilfir had his wish fulfilled, the sooner they could all return to their study of the battle—in real-time.

He had to admit it had its appeal.

For now, he settled to watch the combat. It was a hard-fought spectacle during which the *Knight* skip-jumped around the much larger vessel with apparent ease and unconcern.

"That thing outmasses her more than ten to one," the king murmured in admiration and the *Garghilum Afreghil* nodded.

"At least twenty," he replied, his eyes hooded as he watched the battle rage between the two vessels.

"How long can she keep this up?"

"I don't know if Todd's team has made it across, yet," V'ritan replied. "That was the plan—that the *Knight* would hold until the insertion was made."

"How will we know when that happens?" Grilfir asked and he shrugged in response.

"I'm not sure. I don't know if we'll even be able to see them do so," he replied. "Their ships are small and they're too far away. When the *Knight* changes tactics, that should be when they've made the transfer."

"Will we know if it's been successful?"

"Todd's mission?"

"What else?"

"We'll know when the data starts streaming. The Naval outpost on Alerus has been set up to receive, but they've also set data retrieval units on the *Cathay Williams* and the *Henry Chauvel*, as well as on the *Ebon Knight* herself."

"And the team?" the king asked.

"What about the team?"

"How will they return?"

V'ritan met the other man's gaze and regretted what he had to say next. "There is no guarantee they will."

King Grilfir's jaw hung slack. "But... But Stephanie..." he finally managed to respond. "She'll be devastated and we both know what happens when something wounds the Witch like that. Think of what happened after the passenger ship."

"Or at the arena." The *Garghilum Afreghil* caught on quickly and his heart plummeted. He raised his head. "Captain, break orbit. The Witch needs us."

Islafel turned. "But her instructions—"

"I know her instructions, but they fail to take her own needs and reactions into account and we cannot afford the devastation she will wreak if the Marine sergeant is lost."

"Todd?" Islafel asked when he recalled the man they'd retrieved after the battle for Dreth.

"Todd," he confirmed and the captain pivoted and began to snap orders across the deck. V'ritan turned to the king. "I'm sorry, Your Majesty, but you have to leave."

"Not yet, *Gharghilum*," he countered before he turned to the captain. "Prepare the ship, Captain, but don't leave yet." He met the man's raised eyebrows with a soft smile and a small shrug. "I haven't heard the solutions to my communications problem."

"Ugh!" The King's Warrior shrugged and made a gesture of agreement. "Do as he says."

He maintained a stoic silence as Islafel steadied the ship and relayed the king's command to Grilfir's ship. The two captains conversed hastily but their eyes strayed to their viewscreens and everyone caught the moment when a missile streaked out of one of the *Knight's* hangar bays.

"Wasn't that the one that was hit?" Grilfir asked, and V'ritan nodded.

"Yup. I guess we know where the Witch is."

"But which Witch—the Morgana or Stephanie?" he asked with a small frown.

The torpedo's engines ignited and almost immediately, the missile vanished, only to reappear a few meters away from the Teloran's hull. The resulting explosion left a gaping black crater in its wake.

Shortly after, a glowing purple orb careened out of the hangar and followed the torpedo's path. Even without magnification, several human figures were visible.

"Unbelievable," the king murmured as the orb vanished into a portal exactly as the torpedo had.

V'ritan looked at him in surprise. "She fired her boyfriend into a battlefield and through a transition point in a magic bubble and that is all you have to say?"

Grilfir shrugged. "What else is there? At least we know which witch is in charge."

"The Morgana," they intoned in solemn duet and their hearts sank in unison.

"May Selene have mercy on us all."

The viewscreen died as the bubble emerged meters from the hull.

"Get it back!" the king ordered and before anyone could respond, the Master Mage returned to the deck.

"I'll be only a moment, your Majesty," the man announced and strode to the scan console.

V'ritan had never seen him look so satisfied before and he couldn't blame him. The royal's high-handed antics would have set his teeth on edge as well if it weren't for the understanding their friendship brought.

"My people are working with the data center to make the changes required to have the scans play in real-time—even at that distance," he explained and fixed the king with a solemn look. "I have even remembered to promulgate the information throughout the Meligornian fleet and have dispatched specialists to your ship to make the alterations prior to your return."

From his tone, Grilfir's imminent departure was not only expected but looked forward to. Fortunately, the king either missed his implied lack of welcome or chose to ignore it. Whichever it was, V'ritan was relieved.

He liked his Master of Mages, dammit!

They watched as the Meligorn worked on the console and applauded politely when the viewscreen came back to life in time to catch the *Knight* skip away from the insertion point and reappear on the other side of the Teloran behemoth.

"So that's happening in real-time?" King Grilfir demanded, and the Master Mage glanced at the instruments he carried.

"Yes, Your Majesty," he confirmed. "We now see occurrences as they happen. It seems the physics of magic can establish a shared compatibility with physics as most of the universe understands it."

Grilfir turned to the screen and watched the battle as it occurred, and a small smile played over his lips.

"Unbelievable," Islafel murmured and V'ritan rolled his eyes.

"He's spoiled," he quipped and smirked at the king's response.

No one would have guessed, by the peaceable look on the royal's face, that he was capable of thinking something that crude let alone signing it.

"Are you sure she loves you?" Gary asked, picked the gear bag up, and forced himself toward the open hatch. "'Cos if I didn't know any better, I'd say she had it in for you."

"Yeah, man," Dru agreed. "That was a rough landing."

"And as for the flight over—" Reggie started.

Todd held his hand up. "Don't go there. No one go there," he added seconds later when he ushered Angus through the hatch and glared at Henry. "No one. Not a single one go there, or this'll be the shortest adventure of your lives."

He made a last-minute scan to confirm they hadn't left anything behind and followed them into the corridor.

"Seal it," he ordered and looked at Piet.

The man sketched him an irreverent salute and went to work.

"And done," he announced moments later as the hatch locked behind them and the team spread out to cover the corridor on either side.

With their gear transferred and atmosphere returning to the corridor, they finished tooling up in full gravity. None of them unsealed their helmets, however, even when the atmosphere readings reached acceptable levels.

With the *Knight* harassing the Teloran ship, who knew when that could change?

"Ka?" Todd asked. "Any idea where to next?"

"Somewhere without any Telorans?" Gary suggested hopefully and attempted to fit three clips into a space designed for one. He managed two and moved on to the next compartment.

Limpet grenades, grenade launchers, and a mixture of Meligornian and human grenades filled the pouches almost to overflowing.

"You couldn't have stowed those before we left?" Ka demanded and he shook his head.

"I thought we were coming over in the fighters. You gotta keep a slender profile to fit in those or you get caught on the seats coming out."

"Uh-huh. And what if you're getting your ass shot off when you arrive?"

"Then you grab the bag and run and hope some stupid asshat doesn't put a hole in something sensitive?"

"What? Like your tail?"

"More like something that explodes."

"And the wand?"

"It's not a wand." Gary pouted. "It's a shock stick."

"You're going low-tech in a universe where you have the best weapons known to man?" she asked and strapped on a belt with twin sword sheaths.

"Like you can talk."

She patted the squat handle settled behind the long, curved blade. "I carry all the tech. You'd be well advised to do the same."

"Vibros aren't for me."

"You've used them before."

"It doesn't mean I like 'em. I'd rather shoot things than wave a sharp stick at them."

"We'll see how that works out for you."

"We sure will,"

Todd cleared his throat. "Ka? Location?"

"Right here, boss. Like any fool can see."

He reached out and clipped the back of her helmet with his hand. "Get your mind on the job, soldier."

Reggie gave a low whistle. "Well, look who got up on the wrong side of the bed today."

Angus snickered. "Not enough shared time in the sack," he suggested.

"No shared time," Henry corrected him.

"I simply want to get this job done so we can go home," Todd told them and they hooted in mock derision.

"'Home,'" Gary mocked and made quotation marks in the air. "That's what he calls it."

"Home," he confirmed, closed the space between them, and caught Gary by his weapons harness to shake him. "I'm reasonably sure even you have somewhere that'll take you."

"Ouch," Reggie muttered, and he realized he might have stepped over a line he hadn't known was there.

Gary went silent before he forced a grin. "I do, boss. It's called my bunk. When we get back, that's where you'll find me."

The sergeant turned to Ka. "Where to, boss lady?"

A line lit the ground between them and the location of the data drives, but the details between were hazy.

"I need an access point," she explained. "The *Knight* didn't have much time for scanning."

"That's all we have?" Gary exclaimed.

Reggie gave him a not-so-gentle shove. "Just because the phrase 'whinging pom' exists doesn't mean you have to live up to it, mate."

"Well, mate, just because Australians are known to be assholes doesn't mean you have to prove them right."

"Guys! You're not helping."

Before either of them could respond to that, Piet's quiet voice broke the lull. "Over here, Ka. I'll stand watch."

Todd shook his head and pointed at Angus and Henry. "Assholes One and Two, make sure that end hatch is secure. This corridor's too empty."

"It's a residential section on a warship," the Englishman snarked. "What did you expect it to be? Grand fucking central?"

"And he called us assholes," Henry remarked and jogged after Angus.

"And screw you, too," Gary called after him.

"What's crawled up your wee ass and lodged there?" Jimmy asked, caught hold of the man, and jerked him around to face him. "I mean ta say, you're usually all piss and wind but today, you're pissier and windier than most."

"And we don't need it," Reggie added. "I'm not sure what's gotten up in your grill, mate, but jeez!"

Their teammate's mouth opened as though he was about to snap out his usual snarky reply, but he closed it again and shrugged Jimmy's hand away and looked at Todd instead. "Orders, boss?"

The sergeant gestured to the other hatch. "I need it secured until we're ready. You three are it."

"And the corridor between?"

"Goes without saying." Todd glanced to where Ka and Piet were accessing a communications node while Dru stood guard. "How much longer? The *Knight* can't keep dancing forever."

His corporal flipped him the bird and her companion muttered something about patience being a virtue.

"Not right now it's not," Gary quipped from the other end of the corridor, and Todd was sure that combination of lines had been used in a movie he should know.

Instead of working out where, though, he turned his attention to the Englishman. "Spill it."

"We have company coming up our midnight and I don't think it's the best kind."

"As long as we can shoot it and there aren't any magic-chucking freaks inside, we'll be fine," Reggie stated. He glanced at the device he'd attached to the hatch they'd been sent to secure. "But hurry."

On the *Knight*, the Morgana had returned to the bridge. Adjusting the tethers, she focused on the battle, extended her senses into the space around them, and felt for the magical energy surrounding the ship.

The gMU was there, of course, and she could feel it trickle into her, a reservoir of power from which she could spin MU or eMU as she saw fit. Also present was the nMU that surrounded the Teloran ship.

The part of her that was Stephanie registered its presence and was grateful she didn't need to draw it in—yet. For now, it was enough that she could direct it without touching it.

She was still working out the effect of defending with MU shields. So far, the Telorans had used a mixture of nMU and normal kinetics to savage the *Knight*, and she'd been able to use MU to defeat the kinetics. At the same time, she'd directed the nMU from a distance and used it to block the more traditional Teloran weapons.

Traditional Teloran weapons… She savored the thought for a long moment and wondered where it had come from.

Never you mind, the Morgana inside her ordered and redirected her attention firmly to the battle. *We have a war to win!*

CHAPTER TWENTY-ONE

"Todd, we have a problem." Ka's voice cut through their comms as Todd crouched to one side of the corridor and used his body to shield her and Piet.

The Telorans were cutting through the hatch and his hackers weren't done yet.

"Talk to me, Ka. Don't keep me in suspense."

"Yeah," Gary snickered. "Don't keep the man in suspenders."

"Fuck you, Gary," she snapped and went on to answer the sergeant. "I'll send it to your HUD."

"Ooh, and now the lady has secrets," Gary commented and the last words ended in an extended whisper.

"Shut up and watch the door, Gaz," Reggie ordered.

"Shouldn't you be watching the ceilings?" Dru called. "'Cos if these guys are like Dreth, we're screwed."

"That's a good point," the Australian responded and glanced at Jimmy. "Boost me."

The big Scotsman knelt and made a stirrup with his hands. "Make it quick. That gear you're carrying weighs a ton."

"Metric or Imperial?"

"What do you think? We live in a modern world."

Reggie whistled and began to poke the ceiling panels. "Have you told NorAm what you think of them yet?"

"Not directly, no, but if they don't have the gist of my attitude from listening in on my comms, their intel is worse than everyone says it is."

"Ouch!" His teammate jumped clear. "There's nothing but wiring conduits up there. It looks like the second-tier ceiling cavity is something the Dreth invented themselves."

"I wonder what trouble they got into that it became a standard thing."

"It begs the answer, doesn't it?"

"Well, this changes everything." Todd's mutter came clearly over their comms line and their HUDs lit with a location two levels down.

"Is that… Am I reading my Teloran correctly?" Gary asked, his voice thick with disgust.

"If you think it says, 'prisoners' and 'of war,'" Reggie told him, "then, yes, you're reading your Teloran correctly."

"Well, fuck me." The Englishman scowled.

"We'll have to call it in." Todd looked as pissed as they did.

"Yeah, and won't that blow this cover all to hell."

"It sure as shit will," the sergeant assured him with a grin. "But hell, it's not like we're not about to have company anyway."

"You know it's a repair crew and they're probably relieved that this section's sealed itself, don't you?" Jimmy told them.

"I never pegged you for an optimist, Jim my lad." Reggie grinned at his teammate.

"Well, it's true," he replied. "Don't you hear what they're saying?"

"Are you telling me all those Teloran lessons are paying off?" Todd raised an eyebrow at him.

"Such as they were. I only catch half a word here and there, though. I really hope the Navy boffins give us everything they have on it."

"Are you kidding? You don't remember the latest lessons? They've given us everything—and I'm not sure they checked it anywhere near as well as they shoulda." Jimmy looked smug but his teammates seemed lost as to why.

"And your point?" Dru pressed impatiently.

"My point is that whatever it is they're saying, these guys are talking like they're only here on a routine mission, not to roust a half-dozen Marine assholes. Their voices don't show any sign of tension."

"Are you sure? What if they know we're listening in?" she responded and raised an eyebrow in challenge.

"I sincerely doubt that would worry them. I'm only saying they'd sound different if they knew we were here, is all."

"Captain!" Ignoring the conversation, Todd contacted the *Knight's* bridge. He didn't waste time on small talk. "We have POWs in the hold. *Knight* needs to watch where she's firing. I'll send you the location, now."

He paused as he made the transfer, then transferred the deck plans they'd been downloading when they'd discovered the Teloran's extra cargo.

"Steph needs to know too," he added and tried not to think of what his girlfriend's reaction would be if she ventilated a hold full of prisoners.

The thought had obviously crossed the captain's mind and Todd nodded at his response. "Yes, sir, it would be bad. We'll divert to rescue them once we've run the mission, but I don't know if we'll be too late."

He waited for a moment, then shook his head. "I'm sorry, sir, but we can't go sooner. Getting the data into the right hands could save more lives than those in the hold."

Emil could see his point, but Todd's lips still twisted with regret as he replied. "Yes, sir. I'm sorry, too."

If the truth be told, he'd rather liberate the prisoners and the fact that the data could save more lives provided scant comfort. Todd wanted nothing more than to ditch the mission and ride to the rescue.

From what he could see of his team's faces, they felt the same way too.

"They've given up on the lock and they're starting to cut." Gary's news brought him back to the situation at hand.

"I gotta go, sir. We're about to have company."

He signed off and nudged Ka. "If you have what you need, I want a way to not start a running gun battle for another ten minutes."

"You mean another way out, boss?"

"Yeah."

"Good, because I think I have you covered."

When Todd signed off, all hell was breaking loose on the Teloran command deck.

"Of course there are foreign communications. I can see the damn ship for myself." The captain snarled his fury, his voice as brittle as breaking ice.

"The origin's local, sir."

"You said that!"

The communications technician swallowed hard. "From this ship, sir."

"They're here?"

"Yes, sir."

"On my ship?"

"Yes, sir."

"Find them! I want them captured and brought here. We will know why they've come."

"Yes, sir!"

The technician turned away and relayed the orders. All around the vessel, a different alarm sounded.

"The Witch's blood is not all I'll have," the captain promised in a voice like death.

"*Knight*, recalibrate targeting to avoid hitting sector nine-eight-three." Emil's voice came to Stephanie as if through a shroud. "There are POWs on board."

Shock rippled around the command deck and she froze. There were prisoners of war? On that ship?

We need to rescue them, she told the presence that had descended around her.

No. There are more important things at stake, the Morgana replied.

There is nothing more important than getting my people out of there!

What would you know, child?

I know that we will go and get those people and that you will not stop me. Not. Right. Now.

Wanta. Make. A. Bet? Stephanie grasped the shroud and pulled.

I said no! the Morgana snarled and pressed hard against her mind.

She pushed back, called on the store of gMU, and spun it into a blend of MU and eMU.

Oh, yeah? she challenged and pushed the power into the Morgana's presence inside her head. *Well, guess what?*

The reply was silky with sarcasm. *What, child?*

With mental focus, she took hold of the other presence and, instead of trying to throw her out of her head, pinned her to one side of her mind. *You're not the boss of me.*

The Morgana snorted in amusement and tried to wriggle free.

Uh-uh, she told her. *We have prisoners to rescue. That's* my *priority. We'll talk about* your *priorities when we're done.*

The darker self struggled against her hold, only to have her use another surge of MU to bind her in place.

We most certainly shall, she snarled as the girl ensured her bindings would hold and gave her a satisfied smile.

Stephanie's smile grew wider. *I look forward to it,* she promised and held the Morgana in place as she surfaced. "Lars! Get me Johnny, Frog, Marcus, and Vishlog. Captain, I need an empty room. *Knight,* you're in control of defenses. Do your best to keep them busy."

"I shall keep them very busy," the *Knight* reassured her. "Come back soon."

"And good luck," Emil added, knowing it was pointless to order her not to go. She wouldn't be their Witch if she didn't and she'd never forgive herself, either.

"Make sure they're—"

"We've got this, Steph!" Lars snapped and cut her off. "Just tell us where you want us to be."

"Conference Room Three," Emil supplied as Stephanie's head snapped toward him.

"Conference Room Three," she commanded, but the security head had already left.

Only Vishlog remained and waited to follow where she led next.

"Why aren't you preparing?" she demanded and he gave her a toothy smile.

"Because my place is to protect you and I trust Lars to prepare what I need."

She opened her mouth to argue but the Dreth merely looked at the forward viewscreen and then the door.

"What do you want to do—defend the *Knight* while you wait or prepare yourself for battle?"

Stephanie froze and gave him a stern look. She pursed her lips and raced to the door with him close behind her. Emil didn't turn his full attention to the battle until his screen flashed a warning.

'Hard a-port!" he ordered. "*Knight*, stand by to skip in three…two…"

He already missed having the Morgana on deck.

———

"Piet, I need that hole and I need it yesterday!"

"Like you really want me to hurry a cutting charge, Sarge." It wasn't a question but Todd answered it anyway.

"It's either me or the assholes burning their way through the door. Your choice."

"Well, since you put it that way," Piet grumbled and made a final check on his handiwork. "Cover!"

The team ducked and the charge detonated. Angus and Henry took the lead.

"I can only make it go boom if I can see it," Angus told the other man and pushed him back to be the first through the hole. He looked at his sergeant. "We need you to stick around."

Todd reversed quickly toward them. "I don't care how useful you all are, we need to hurry. She's coming."

"Who's coming?" Piet asked as he hurried after Angus and Henry and Ka stepped through at his side.

"The Morgana," he stated in clipped tones.

"I thought it was Stephanie," Jimmy said quickly and fired short bursts across the room behind them.

"Yeah," Gary agreed. "Wasn't it the scary girlfriend who was coming to the rescue and not the scariest girlfriend?"

"No plan survives contact with the enemy," Todd told them. "I don't know what will happen when Stephanie gets here. The Morgana seems to have a hard-on for these pricks."

"Well, crap," Henry muttered caustically. "That's all we need. A rogue mage is bad enough."

"She's not a rogue."

"Oh no, she's merely an independently minded woman."

"You might as well have called her a rogue."

The questionable "rogue" had geared up and now stood in the middle of Conference Room Three. She tapped her foot as she watched Frog and Marcus wrestle with the cats.

"I thought you two would have had them on standby," she grumbled and mentally sifted through what she'd done while she tried to guess exactly what she'd need on the mission.

"We did," Frog protested and nudged Bumblebee in the ribs, "until some asshole cat decided he was gonna try to chew through his chest harness."

The asshole cat blinked and dabbed his purple tongue at the man's gauntleted hand, and he jerked it away. He shook his finger at the feline.

"Don't you go trying to kiss and make up after the shenanigans you've pulled."

Bee sneezed at him, and he ruffled the fur on the cat's head.

"Yeah, that's more like the furry fucker we've come to know."

"And love," Vishlog rumbled. "Don't forget the love."

"I don't know, Vishlog. Right now, the only love I feel is the need to plant my Size Nine up his ass."

Marcus laughed and the Dreth looked from one to the other, his eyebrows raised. "What did he do?"

"They," his teammate emphasized. "What did they do? Honestly, you'da thought we were on a cruise ship and not a destroyer in the middle of a fucking battle."

Zeekat tilted his head and gave the man a wide-eyed stare.

Marcus returned the look and curled his lip. "And don't you go trying to make out like you were innocent, mister!" he snapped. "You know exactly what you did."

Stephanie sighed. "What? Exactly what did he do?"

"Let's simply say you'll need to sleep in the spare bunk in Elizabeth's suite until we've caught up with everything after the battle. It seems the cats become very territorial when there's increased tension."

She fixed Zeekat with a disgusted look. "You and me, mister... when this is done. You. And. Me."

The feline yawned and licked his chest as though the death-stare she gave him was nothing more than a glance.

"Ugh! Cats!"

"You brought 'em," Frog reminded her and gave her a very cat-like look when she scowled at him.

She shrugged briefly. "Are we ready?" she asked, and Lars gave her a meaningful glare.

"Are you?"

"What is that supposed to mean?"

"It means is there anything else you need to do before we leave?"

Stephanie was about to retort that of course there was nothing else but stopped. She patted her weapons pouches, holsters, and hilts, and named each one.

"Blaster, rifle, sword, vibro-blade." She summoned blue and purple light to crackle over her hands. "Magic—"

"Yeah…that," Lars told her, and she frowned.

"What about it?"

"Well, let's say I don't want to explode if the wrong kinds mix—and I don't want you to explode either."

She wrinkled her lip and considered the alternatives. Either she could draw on her reservoirs of gMU to spin up MU and eMU to use on the Teloran ship, or she could drain both and go solely to nMU.

"I'll be fine if I'm careful," she replied, and he gave her a dubious look.

"And will we?"

"Sure, you will. I wouldn't do anything to put you guys at risk. We've all lost enough as it is."

"That be true," Frog muttered.

"Word, bro."

Stephanie smiled and let the magic flicker over her fingers. "Besides, this will give us more bang for our buck."

"Yeah," her security head agreed in wry tones, "that's exactly what I'm afraid of."

"Pfftt! Whatevs. Get your chicken-shit asses over here."

Lars studied the rest of the team one more time before he signaled for them to stand beside her. Vishlog took a firm grasp of both cats and gave Frog a stern glare.

"They do not misbehave with me—" He stopped as Bumblebee bumped his thigh with his head and Zeekat made a blatant grab for the waist pouch where he usually kept the treats.

He swatted the black-and-white's muzzle away from the pouch and scowled at his smaller teammate. "And they are good for honing your combat reflexes. Yours must be lacking."

CHAPTER TWENTY-TWO

"What do you mean there are prisoners of war on board?" The king was horrified. "Where did they get prisoners of war?"

V'ritan shrugged, but his face was somber. "I don't know, Your Majesty."

"Get me the fleet!" He turned to his aide. "Prepare the shuttle. I'll return to *Meligorn's Crown*. None of our people will be left behind."

He placed a fist against his companion's bicep. "Selene's fortune, my friend."

The warrior captured his fist beneath his and the Royal Guard shifted restlessly. On the one hand, no one touched royalty. On the other, this was the *Garghilum Afreghil.*

The King's Warrior turned and moved his monarch's hand over his heart. "I beg your forgiveness, Your Majesty, but you cannot go into battle. This world needs its king."

Grilfir tensed beneath his grasp. "Please, Your Majesty—Grilfir. As my king and my friend, I beg you to remember that you are not only your people's head but also its heart. I cannot let you risk your life in battle."

The king held his gaze for a long moment before he lowered his with a sigh. "Very well, *Garghilum*. I will remain."

He raised his head and captured V'ritan's gaze with his own. "But I will remain in orbit because, if I am this world's head and heart, you may find yourself its heart and soul."

"Exactly, and our people cannot do without both their hearts. Meligorn can continue without me, but you, my king—they need you."

"And Elza?" Grilfir asked softly.

The *Garghilum Afreghil* winced, his face momentarily pinched by pain. He released his sovereign's hand, leaned forward to place his lips close to Grilfir's ear, and murmured, "That was a low blow, Your Majesty."

"I'm the one who'll have to tell her." The king mirrored V'ritan's gesture. "Our people's sadness pales in comparison to hers."

"It's not a good idea to rip the heart out of your warriors immediately before they fight, my king," he declared softly before he stepped back and bowed. He straightened and touched his fingertips to his forehead and breastbone before he extended his fist.

Grilfir returned his bow before he touched his knuckles to his friend's. Those watching their faces saw the pain they masked quickly and knew they had witnessed more than a king and his warrior saying goodbye before battle.

This was the parting of two friends who desperately hoped to see each other again—and did not dare to hope.

"Ah, now they come out to play," Stephanie observed. She sent multiple threads of blue into the first squad of Telorans to advance. "And they shall die like all the rest."

The cats roared but Vishlog managed to restrain them. "This was not such a good idea," he told her.

She turned and fixed the felines with a stern look. "Fight beside us," she commanded and looked at the Dreth. "Let them go."

He did as she ordered but he was not happy. "I still say this is not a good idea."

The Witch ignored him. "Which way, Johnny?"

"In, forward, and down twenty."

"Twenty?"

"You put us here."

It was true but she'd used the information she had, which had indicated that the only safe teleport point was the corridor Todd and the team had used to enter the ship. One of the doors opening into it had been cut off its hinges and a gaping hole led deeper into the vessel. Faint sounds of fighting could be heard from inside.

"That way?" she asked.

"It'll do for a start," Johnny confirmed.

"You only want to see your boyfriend, again," Frog quipped from somewhere behind her. There wasn't any point in locating him for a killer stare.

"I'd only distract him, dumbass," she retorted instead, "and that would be bad."

She stepped toward the doorway but Lars and Johnny moved through and took the lead. While she allowed herself a scowl, she didn't argue. They were doing what Elizabeth had hired them to do. She didn't have to like it, but she did have to let them do their jobs.

That didn't stop her from cutting in front of Frog and Marcus and taking her place as close to the front as she was allowed to be. She tired of that three steps into the next room when more Telorans arrived.

Lars pivoted, activated the shield on his armor, and fired six rapid shots into the massed enemy. When the energy beam flickered over their armor, he switched to solids. The first two didn't penetrate, but the third delivered in quick succession punched through. Unfortunately, it was stopped by the breastplate.

"Son of a bitch!" he swore, flicked to energy again, and fired.

This time, the beam powered through and the Teloran fell.

"Gotcha, and you, and—" Several balls of magic careened past him to envelop their adversaries' heads before they exploded. "Sonuvabitch!"

"Do you talk to your momma with that mouth?" Frog snarked.

"Do you?"

"Boss, last time I saw your momma—"

"Don't go there!"

They trotted after Stephanie, who pressed Johnny for a faster route.

"I'm really glad not all these guys have magic," Marcus commented as Johnny gave an exasperated sigh.

"You want a faster route?" he asked and didn't wait for an answer. "You need to pause long enough for me to get a better floorplan."

Stephanie looked around. "What do you need?"

They all stopped and Johnny scanned the area in search of something that would help. "I need—"

"You need to ask Todd's team to send you the one they already have," Frog snapped impatiently.

They pivoted to glare at him.

"What? Do you want to invent the wheel twice?"

"Make the call," she ordered and his jaw dropped.

"Me?"

"It was your idea."

They hunkered against the wall while Frog found Ka's frequency.

"You need a map?" the girl asked, and one appeared in their HUDs before she'd finished speaking. "Is that it?"

"Thanks," Frog replied, his tone surprised.

"Good. Now get the fuck out of my head. We're kinda busy."

With that, she ended the contact but not before they registered the sound of battle. It was a weird blend of energy weapons and the clash of blades.

"Those guys get all the fun," Vishlog grumbled, and the cats growled in agreement.

"We'll simply have to find our own fun," Stephanie told them and traced a new route before Johnny had a chance to do so.

She straightened and took the lead before either of her guards could stop her and strode forward without slowing for the rest of them to catch up.

"Dammitall, Steph!" Lars shouted and hurried to take his position alongside her.

"I'm not made of glass, you know."

"Yeah, but Elizabeth—"

"Can go suck it," she snapped. "She's not my mom."

"She is, you know," he reminded her and slid ahead of her to be the first out into the corridor that would take them on the route they needed and away from the path Todd's team had taken. "She's your second mom."

Stephanie groaned and made a rude gesture at his back. "Like I needed two."

None of them had an answer for that and they didn't have time to think of one, either.

"How will we get the POWs back to the ship?" Johnny asked when they reached a junction.

"Emil's handling it."

"Do we know how many there are?"

Stephanie's eyes grew dark and Lars felt a frisson of alarm.

Relief followed as the blue returned, but it was short-lived as Stephanie replied. "Two hundred."

"How will we get them off?" Lars signaled a halt and stuck his head around the corner. "You sneaky bastards."

"What?" was quickly followed by, "Fuckers!" as Stephanie peered around behind him and saw the waiting Telorans. Before he could stop her, she'd skirted him, raised a shield in one direction, and fired a small storm of magic in the other.

"You want to go easy on the magic, Steph," Johnny advised her. "You might need that when we get to the hold."

The hold... She felt a tremor of unease. An entire hold of Meligornians. She wondered if it was something the enemy could vent to space—and if they would.

All she could hope was that they'd kept the prisoners for a reason and wouldn't want to lose them. After all, they wouldn't be able to replace them easily. She'd make sure of that.

"So, what's the plan, Steph?" Lars pressed, darted out from behind the shield, and fired into the Telorans beyond.

"I don't know," she replied, drew her sword, and made sure the shield on her armor was active.

Behind her, Vishlog unleashed the cats. "Go!"

Their roars echoed down the corridors and several of the Telorans froze. It was all the time the felines needed. They closed the distance between them and bounded into their enemy to claw torsos while they tried to bite heads despite their suits.

Apparently, even Telorans could scream.

"That's not in the language program!" Frog commented.

"Well, our recorders are running," Johnny told him as he moved alongside the smaller man. They followed Stephanie's example and took the fight up close and personal. "I'm sure the language boffins will have a field day working it out. You know how they like to educate us on the curses."

"Yeah. There's nothing like knowing when you're being sworn at," Marcus quipped dryly and Frog laughed.

"We know that. They only want us to be able to cuss them out in their own language," he retorted.

Marcus grunted, knocked a blaster aside with one blade, and thrust with the other. The metal glanced off the Teloran's armor.

"Fuck it!"

"Use the vibro, man," Frog advised and did exactly that. "And give them a burst when you do."

He released a quick charge through the metal and the shield protecting his opponent dissipated. The vibro-blade cut through the armor below. His teammate winced.

"Messy, bro. That's plain messy."

"Quit your bitchin'."

"Why don't we simply do this?" He pulled his blaster and alternated the charge. Using the blade in his off-hand to defend, he broke the Teloran shield and fired point-blank into the armor.

"You're lucky they don't have deflection." Johnny had chosen a different approach. He'd powered the gauntlets on his armor and activated the blades set into the wrist bracers. They ran from the wrist along the back of the gauntlet.

With energy flowing over the blade edges, he had his own set of claws. The cats approved—or they would have if they hadn't been so busy. The Telorans had closed their helmets and their armor resisted claws very well.

Vishlog saw the change and whistled a command. Bumblebee came alongside Zeekat and gave an imperative chirp. The two cats broke clear of their opponents and raced down the corridor. To anyone watching them, they were fleeing.

The Dreth knew better and he mentally kicked himself. He should have activated the extensions on their armor sooner. This could be done on the panel that protected their bellies, and he wondered if they'd remember which part to tap. It had taken him a long time to teach them—but not as long as it had taken him to convince One R&D's engineers that it was worth tweaking the armor to install it.

A roar drew his attention and he grinned with the evidence that the effort had paid off. The cats had looked formidable before. Now, they were downright terrifying. Metal sheathed their claws and extended them, and thin blades of metal snaked down the length of their armored tails.

He grinned. His opponent turned his head to look toward the roar, and Vishlog used the opportunity to slash his throat. For all their differences, the Telorans still seemed to keep their vitals in the same place.

Another tried to come in under his guard and he brought his sword down in a hasty block, thrust the attack aside, and retaliated with the dagger in his off-hand. He found a weak point in his adversary's armor and drove the blade home.

It jammed and yanked him forward as the Teloran fell. He released the hilt and twisted away as another of the enemy fired. The sickening feeling of nMU rippled over his armor and faded like it had never been. He had no idea what had protected him, but he knew he didn't intend to let it happen again.

"*Tegorthan targlathian!*" he snarled and lashed out with a boot that caught his opponent where its knee should be.

His foot struck something solid and the Teloran shrieked. His armor gave and bone snapped to bring him down almost on top of the Dreth. The warrior rolled instinctively to one side and scowled when he stared down the muzzle of another blaster.

He ducked, but it would not have been enough if Lars hadn't shot his assailant through the throat.

"That's the last of them," he said, offered his teammate his hand, and dragged him to his feet. "You're an idiot, bringing a knife to a gunfight."

"She started it," Vishlog replied and gestured at Stephanie's retreating back.

They hurried after her and stepped around Frog who'd stopped to pick up a Teloran blaster.

"What do you want these for?" Marcus asked as he copied him.

"Not all Telorans have magic, right?" Lars heard as he went past. "So, if they can't use magic but they can fire these, we should be able to as well."

The security head almost stopped but Marcus was already putting his doubts into words. "Are you sure that's a good idea, Frog? The Morgana doesn't like these guys—"

"Yeah, but that doesn't stop her from using their weapons."

He had a point and the Witch hadn't stopped to give her opinion, so Lars let it go. He only hoped Frog didn't blow up something important.

"Emil, tell me you have the answer." Stephanie's voice echoed to him and he ran to catch up. It was a good thing Johnny was with her and it made him feel better about the idea of not being there.

"Do you think we've cleared this deck, yet?" he asked and arrived at the same time as the cats.

"Does it matter?" she asked.

She sounded distracted and her pace slowed. Lars checked in the HUD and worked out why.

"It's over here," he said and pointed out the emergency tube.

"Twenty floors, right?" she asked, and his heart fell.

"Stephanie, don't—" he began, but she flashed him a grin and was gone.

"Fuck." He vaulted to the ladder while he cursed all mages and smart-assed magic-users. "Vishlog, you have the cats."

The Telorans didn't have stairs. Their only concession to the idea that their emergency shaft might be used was to have the gravity functioning as a ladder. Stephanie held it in such a way it was more like a fireman's pole.

Lars was relieved that she wore gauntlets.

He went down the same way and used a light handgrip on the outer edges of the pole while he pressed the inside of his boots there as well—lightly enough to keep him on the ladder and stop him from going over the top of her. The sound of Johnny following made him look up and he saw Vishlog had help with the cats.

Zeekat was draped across Johnny's shoulders. The cat had a disgruntled look on his face but remained perfectly still. He'd come a long way since he'd first emerged from the Meligornian woods. Back then, he'd have clawed the man's face off before he let him touch him. Now, he accepted them all as part of his pride.

The security head turned his attention to his HUD and watched their progress through the ship. He also looked for Todd's team and was both relieved and disappointed to discover Ka had masked their presence on the map. He wondered if she'd done the same for them and decided he needed to get Johnny to check.

When he glanced up, though, he decided it could wait until they all reached the bottom. The HUD revealed that they were almost there. It also showed that they were all in the emergency access tube, which wasn't their best idea ever.

"Man, I hope some bright spark doesn't get the idea to throw a grenade down here." Frog seemed to read his mind and his whisper came clearly over the team's chat channel, and Lars hoped no one was listening.

No one else was very impressed with the idea.

"Thanks, Frog," Marcus said belligerently.

"Yeah. Thanks, asshole," Johnny added.

"Stop!" Stephanie's command ripped across the commlink. "We're here."

Lars clamped his feet tightly against the ladder's side and tightened his hold. She muttered something like, "fucking door's stuck," before magic surged over his skin and the door slid open.

A brief sensation followed as if something was yanked out from under his feet and she was gone. He didn't hesitate and launched toward the opening, all too aware of Johnny sliding past the door so Zeekat could leap through.

He turned to help his teammate up and yanked him out from under Vishlog. The Dreth repeated the maneuver for Bumblebee before he hauled himself out the door. The cats bounded to Stephanie and demanded head scratches before they moved to stand guard at the empty ends of the corridor.

Her face took on the faraway look of someone staring at their HUD, and Lars moved to keep Bumblebee company. Vishlog and Marcus moved to Zeekat.

"What's the plan, Emil?" Stephanie demanded. "Can you bring the *Knight* in close?"

"*Knight* needs to keep the Telorans busy. I've called the *Cathay Williams* in to take the prisoners off."

"Can she dock with this vessel?"

"Stephanie, there's nothing that can dock with that ship until someone stops her fighting—and I only see one way of getting that to happen."

"So, you've called the *Cathay* in but she probably won't be able to find a way to do it."

"Correct."

"I'd ask you why, but I know…" Her eyes moved as though she traced a path to their objective.

"We have to try," the team chorused, then sighed in tandem.

"Tell the *Cathay Williams* to stand off. We can't afford to lose her. I'll think of something," she ordered.

"If you're sure—"

"I am."

The silence was prolonged, and Lars had the impression Emil was dealing with the battle.

"We need to keep moving," he reminded her. "Where to?"

Stephanie turned and began to jog in the direction Bumblebee had guarded.

She sent him the link as she spoke. "They're two corridors over."

"Do you think there'll be any guards?" Frog asked, and she gave a sinister chuckle.

"Oh, I hope so."

She'd gone no more than five paces when she skidded to a halt.

We are coming. V'ritan's voice sounded overly loud inside her head.

"V'ritan?"

How can we help?

Lars and the team looked around for the *Ghargilum*. They exchanged glances when they could not see him and moved hastily to hold their position if they needed to.

"Make it quick," Lars muttered. "We don't have all day."

Stephanie didn't appear to notice. *I need a way to transfer the prisoners. Can the* King's Warrior *dock with the Teloran?*

No, but we can provide a place for you to open a portal to. How many are we talking?

She took a breath, held it for a heartbeat, and released it. "Two hundred," she told him, her voice barely above a whisper.

Can you hold the portal long enough?

"I can hold it. I only need to…" She paused and a feeling of foreboding clawed at Lars.

"Steph?" he asked and ran out of words.

"I need a space big enough to transfer the prisoners from here to *The King's Warrior.*"

"You want to try to move the prisoners through a hostile ship—at speed—so you can portal them to V'ritan's ship?" Johnny sounded like he didn't believe she'd come up with anything so stupid.

"Yeah, why?"

Lars and Johnny exchanged glances before the security head looked away.

The other man shrugged, but his face looked bleak. "Because some of them might not be able to walk, let alone run."

"What do you mean?"

He cast a quick glance at Lars, who didn't return it.

"Can't you open the portal where we find them?" he asked. "Rather than move them."

He has a point, V'ritan pointed out. *If you open a gate when you find them, we can send our people through to help with any who aren't strong enough to make it on their own.*

"And what if we can't hold the space they're in?"

Find somewhere as close as you can. The *Garghilum Afreghil* sounded fierce. *I'll send my warriors to help you rescue the rest.*

"We will not leave anyone behind!" Stephanie declared and darkness trembled through her words.

Johnny laid a hand on her shoulder. "No, we won't," he agreed. "Tell us what needs to be done."

"We need to move—now!" Lars snapped.

We'll stand by, V'ritan told her. *You only have to say my name.*

Johnny lifted her off her feet and pushed her against the wall to shield her with his body. She wriggled and he set her down. "Stay here," he told her roughly and she narrowed her eyes.

He ignored her. "Go, Lars. You have the lead. I've got Steph."

Stephanie wanted to argue that no one had her but decided not to. Vishlog's roar caught her attention.

"Zee—stay!"

She turned as the Dreth launched himself after the cat and brought it down in a yowling, clawing heap. He paid it no mind as its claws raked over his armor and opened huge gouges in the metal.

"Sons of Tegortha!" he cursed. "I'm on your side, you tark-addled piss-grate."

That was a new one for Stephanie, but she was more interested in the squad of Telorans that had arrived. These were more heavily armored than the others.

"Guards," Johnny snapped when his gaze followed hers. "Go with Lars."

He caught her arm and dragged her after the team leader.

"Hey!" she protested and tried to twist free.

In response, he tightened his grasp. "I need you to go after Lars," he insisted and blocked her when she tried to duck past him to back Marcus and Frog up, who'd moved to cover Vishlog's retreat.

The Dreth had his arms full of angry cat, and even if Zee wasn't struggling, his tail flicked and his ears were flat against his head. Someone had explaining to do when he got back and it looked like it would involve an impressive number of treats.

"We can't leave until you do," Johnny explained, "and there are more of them than there are of us. We need to get you out of here and the POWs need you to save them."

It was enough. Stephanie didn't wait to hear more but jerked her arm free and jogged after Lars. When she glanced back, the team had taken position behind her. Frog and Marcus moved in unison to pull grenades from their belts and spin them under the Telorans' feet.

Chaos broke out as enemy warriors bolted forward, ran back, and tried to claw their way through closed doors before the grenades detonated.

Some made it but most did not.

Lars spoke on the team's channel. "Johnny, I need you."

"Keep going," Johnny shouted and sprinted past Stephanie.

He kept his blaster in one hand, while he dug for his hacking kit with the other. When he came to a junction in the corridors, he barely slowed and snapped two shots down one arm of the intersection.

"Move your asses. They're closing!"

Stephanie pushed into a sprint but skidded to a halt when she reached the junction and pointed a hand either way. She dropped to her knees and raised a shield on either side to block the incoming troops.

Marcus and Frog slowed as they came alongside her.

"Don't stop!" she yelled and they ran on, Zeekat following their example.

Vishlog caught the back of her harness as he passed and hauled her off the floor and down the corridor like she was one of the cats.

"Hey!" she protested, her legs windmilling as she tried to find traction.

At the same time, she twisted the magic so the shields remained in place. "Get past that, Tegorthan scum."

The Dreth didn't release her until she ran beside him and even then, he kept a hand in the small of her back until she steadied. "Thanks, Vishlog."

"It is my duty to protect you," he rumbled, "even when you make it hard."

That brought laughter from the rest of the team as they traversed the distance to the hatch guarding the hold. To Stephanie's relief, it wasn't an airlock. To her horror, it only led into a small antechamber and an airlock stood on the other side of it.

Johnny was crouched beside it with wires connecting the inside of the hatch's control panel to his tablet as his fingers worked a portable keyboard.

"The code is similar to what we use," he explained and grunted. "With a few notable exceptions."

Frog, Marcus, Vishlog, and the cats positioned themselves between them and the door they'd come through.

"Blow the controls," Lars ordered. "We don't want them to come through after us."

"Gotcha," Marcus acknowledged and withdrew a metal disc the size of a coat button. "This should do the trick."

He worked quickly to remove the cover from the control box on the door they'd come through and set the disc against the internal mechanism.

"Is that an EMP device?" Frog sounded alarmed but his teammate chuckled.

"If you'd done your homework, Froggy, you'd know it's extremely localized and won't get to where Johnny's working."

"If you hadn't noticed," the small man snapped in response, "we're not standing where Johnny is."

"It won't get you," Marcus told him. "Not unless I attach it to your armor."

He closed the cover on the controls and took two large paces away from it while he regarded Frog thoughtfully. His teammate took a step away from him, and Marcus grinned.

"Don't worry. I need your gun hand."

"You keep your filthy eyes off my gun hand," Frog retorted, "or I'll shove it up your ass and use you like a puppet."

The other man settled into a guard stance beside him. "And who'd put up with your shit?"

"Vishlog," Frog replied smartly, but the Dreth shook his head.

"Uh-uh."

"Johnny?"

"Not a hope."

He opened his mouth a third time but Lars cut him off before he could speak.

"You wish!"

"Don't look at me," Stephanie told him. "Not after you let Zeekat loose on my bed."

"I'm never gonna live that down, am I?" he asked morosely.

"Nope."

Frog gave an exaggerated sigh. "It looks like I'm stuck with you," he muttered to Marcus but he smiled as he said it.

"Got it," Johnny announced and the airlock hissed and slid open.

A lump formed in Stephanie's chest as she studied the door on the other side of the chamber.

There was no telling what they'd find on the other side and no way to know if the space beyond still held its cargo alive. She could only hope they weren't too late.

The sound of the door closing startled her, and she looked around. Vishlog stood at her back with Marcus and Frog on either side and the cats between them. Lars and Johnny stood a little to either side in front of her so her view of the cargo hold wouldn't be impeded but they could move to protect her if needed.

The Morgana stirred restlessly in her mind, curious even though she sought a way to regain control.

Stephanie smiled. "Not today, bitch."

The dark presence laughed but did not reply.

It took the airlock a few minutes to cycle and she reflected that it didn't matter who took to space. The laws of physics remained the same. It made her wonder how she would ever get her planet cleaned.

Would using magic work?

She sighed. It was yet another thing she had no real control over, something else for which she had to rely on others with better knowledge to achieve.

You sow the seeds. The Morgana spoke and gave her unexpected support. *Without you, none of it would come to be.*

She said the words as if it already had. Stephanie caught the implication and wondered what she knew that she did not. She didn't have time to pursue it, though, because the airlock door opened to reveal what lay beyond.

Low whistles escaped the team.

"Holy fuck!" Frog exclaimed, and added, "We don't have a snowball's chance in hell of defending this place."

Lars turned to her. "He's right. You and Johnny need to look for somewhere defensible for you to open your portal or gate or whatever it is, while the rest of us start releasing everyone. It won't take the Telorans long to get here."

His gaze traveled over the hold's expanse and studied the walkways above them and the doors set at various intervals. If he were to guess—

He squelched the thought and realized that guesswork was unnecessary. He could merely use the schematics Ka had sent him. Surely not every door he saw led to a corridor. Some of those must be rooms for other things. He sure as shit hoped they weren't more cells.

It looked like two hundred was on the low side. He wondered if Meligornians were the only unwilling guests he'd find aboard.

"Marcus. Secure that door." Another thought struck him. "In fact, secure all the doors. Let's make it as hard for these bastards as we can."

"I don't know if I have that many buttons."

"Get Frog to help you. I'm sure he knows a multitude of ways to jam a door."

Frog didn't bother to deny it. He grinned and slapped his teammate on the shoulder. "Come on, Marcus. This will be fun."

"Oh, and don't jam anything we'll want to open later."

"Do you mean you want us to check for more cargo before we fuck them up?" Marcus made it sound like he was asking too much, but Lars ignored him.

"Exactly. Imagine how upset Stephanie will be if you lock someone we need to rescue on the wrong side."

"Well, fuck, if you put it that way..."

"Exactly, and I do." He turned away from them and surveyed the hold. Shipping crates were lined in neat rows, each one bearing a distinctive sigil.

"They've already decided where they're going," he observed and noted the clusters of different symbols.

Vishlog rumbled agreement and clenched his fists.

The cats pressed close, their eyes narrowed and their tails twitching with distress or anger—or something equally strong. Lars decided he knew how they felt. He could smell it even through the suit's filters.

Pain, fear, despair—and the utter filth they'd been forced to live in. Without the suit, the stench would have brought tears. Even with it, tears still threatened but for an entirely different reason.

Stephanie was the first to move. She vaulted over the balcony and landed on top of the nearest crate. Meligornian curses studded by cries of alarm lifted her heart.

"If they're well enough to use that kind of language and make that kind of a promise, they can run with us." She laughed and dropped to the front of the crate.

"We're here to rescue you," she called in Meligornian.

"What about me?" a Dreth asked.

"You too," she replied in his language.

"How do we know this isn't another of your tricks?" the warrior demanded and Stephanie placed a hand against the crate's door to release the purple light of Meligornian magic to curl through the cracks around its edges.

Startled cries and the sudden shuffle of retreating feet was followed by relieved laughter. When she added the blue of Earth's energy, more laughter followed and abruptly died.

"The Witch?" To her surprise, the voice sounded angry. "Months of ignoring our distress signals and now you come?"

A fist whumped into the door on the other side. "You're late."

"Do you want out or not?" she snapped in response.

To show weakness or even to apologize didn't seem like a good idea, and now wasn't the time to work out what had gone wrong.

"Of all the foolish questions," a man said in distinctive Federation Basic. "What the fuck do you think?"

The protest was followed by a meaty thump and a grunt of pain.

"You shut your mouth, V'remil, and let her get us out. You can get your answers later."

"Very well."

Johnny shifted nervously from one foot to another. "Steph, we have to go. There's no—"

The squeal of tortured metal cut him off as she ripped the door from its hinges and slammed it into the nearest bulkhead. "Follow me!" she ordered and darted a look at Johnny. "Have you found somewhere yet?"

"What do you mean?" The question came in V'remil's hostile tones.

"We can't hold this position," Johnny explained, his eyes fixed on the inside of his HUD. "We need somewhere she can open a gate to the *King's Warrior* and keep it open until we can get everyone out."

His eyes moved as he searched the schematics on the inside of his HUD. "There?" he asked and sent the location to the team.

"Yes," Lars agreed. "Get her there and get the gate open."

"A...gate?" V'remil asked and looked bewildered. "To the *King's Warrior*? The *Afreghil's* ship?"

"The same," Johnny told him. "Follow us."

But the Meligornian didn't move. His gaze swept the almost endless lines of crates. "You'll never get them out in time."

He turned to the other Meligornian, the human, and the Dreth who'd followed him out of the crate. "Get everyone out." He looked at Stephanie and Johnny. "We'll take this row. Where do we send them?"

"Can you feel magic when it's being used?" she asked him and he nodded. "Good, guide them there."

"And get them there fast," Lars added from the balcony above. "We're about to have company."

"Do you know how many of us there are?" V'remil whispered but Johnny shook his head.

"Do your best. We won't leave anyone behind." He jerked a thumb at Stephanie and started after her. "She won't leave anyone behind."

"She won't?" he asked, but the guard had already begun to sprint after the Witch and made no answer.

The Meligornian looked at those who'd shared the crate with him. He wrinkled his nose at the stench rising from them and reminded himself they'd be able to get clean soon. Then, with grim purpose, he focused on the nearest crate.

The Telorans hadn't used locks, merely huge bars that could be slid aside. It took him a few tense minutes to work out how to shift them but not as long as he'd feared.

"Do it that way," he ordered. "Get everyone to help and show them how. If you find anyone who can't walk, carry them. If the Witch won't leave anyone behind, neither will we." His companions looked a little nervous. "Go!" he shouted when they hesitated. "Go!"

Fortunately, his sharp tone seemed to startle them into compliance. There were twenty-four of them and they divided into groups of four. Some weren't in as good a shape as they pretended to be but together, they could manage. All of them were breathing heavily by the time they reached their fifth crate, but there were now enough of them that they could leapfrog.

Regrettably, there were those who could barely move. The first of these made him swallow hard. He looked gaunt but not too gaunt to get up. When he didn't move, V'remil moved into the crate, half-afraid that he'd died and no-one had noticed. It was worse.

The captive's cheeks were hollowed and his eyes sunken, and he flinched when his rescuer reached for him.

"Selene's peace," V'remil murmured soothingly. "Let me help you."

"I am beyond help," the Meligornian replied. "Broken. Leave me."

"What is broken?"

"There is nothing whole."

"I'm going to lift you now."

"Please…leave me."

"I cannot. The Witch says no-one gets left."

"The Witch?" He managed a weak cackle of disbelief. "It's another of their tricks. Selene knows they've used enough."

V'remil knelt and slid his arms under the mage's shoulders and knees. Even in his wasted state, he was almost too heavy for him. He staggered and might have fallen if not for a sudden presence behind him and the arm that slid around his back to steady him.

"Let me take him." It took a moment for him to place the voice and he recognized it as the team member who had said they were about to have company.

He shook his head. "You will need your hands free to protect us."

The man nodded and sidestepped to the crate's entrance. "Don't make me carry you both."

V'remil's lips curled into a smile at the thought. The human looked strong but he doubted he was strong enough for that. He didn't argue, though, and simply did his best to make it to the door.

"I'll lead," the guard informed him and didn't wait for his nod. His helmet crackled and his eyes went wide.

"What's your name?" he asked as the man caught his arm.

"Lars. Hurry, they're almost through."

V'remil didn't ask who. He didn't need to. The only thing that surprised him was that one of their mages hadn't already teleported into the cargo bay and begun to kill them as they'd promised. He let his rescuer drag them along the corridor between the crates and wondered why.

The floor shuddered under their feet and only Lars's hold on his arm kept the Meligornian from falling.

"We have to hurry," the man relayed to his team. "The *Knight* can't hold them much longer."

"The *Knight?*" V'remil repeated. "The Witch really did come to save us."

"Of course she did," the guard told him roughly. "Nothing could stop her once she learned you were on board."

"She didn't know? Then why was she here?"

"Do you think she'd let a Teloran ship hide in Meligorn's system and be a threat to her home?"

"We're in the home system?" He swayed and tightened his arm around the mage he carried. Bending forward, he whispered. "Do you hear that? You hang in there. We're almost home. You will see Meligorn's skies again."

"Meligorn's skies..." The words came out as fragile as glass and Lars pulled him forward.

"Hurry, the *King's Warrior* is waiting," the man urged.

"Did she get the gate open?" V'remil asked.

"I don't know. Can you feel it?" he snapped in response.

It was a good question and prompted him to try. His heart sank when he did not. He was about to pass that on when the first ripple of magic surged and he started to move toward it.

"Where are you going?" Lars demanded, and the Meligornian gave him a silly smile.

"To the gate."

"I'll leave you, then. There are more, and I have incoming."

V'remil didn't ask what "incoming" might mean. He had a fair idea.

"I'll be fine," he assured the man, who turned away.

All around them, prisoners changed direction and streamed toward the gate as though guided by instinct. For a moment, Lars envied them the ability to know when magic was being cast but within moments, their predicament resurfaced, and he didn't care.

"Frog! Give me an update."

"We've fucked two levels of doors and found…" The man's voice faltered. "More. We've found more."

"Are they in any condition to be moved?"

"Maybe if they were carried?"

"Gotcha." He flicked from the team channel to one he'd opened with V'ritan. "*Ghargilum*, we may have a problem."

"I'll have troops standing by. We will bring my people home."

"There are Dreth and humans here, too," Marcus interjected, his voice hard but ragged at the edges as though he held very strong emotion back. "Steph will have someone's blood for this."

"I'd say we should keep it from her, but she'll be holding the gate open when we bring them past."

"I'll have medics and healers standing by," V'ritan assured them. "Can Johnny keep her focused?"

"He should be able to. Why?" Lars wanted to know.

"Because if he does, I'll come across."

"I don't think that's a good idea, *Ghargilum*," another voice intruded and Lars had to agree.

"If she's worried about you as well, she won't focus on the gate and I don't know if anyone but Tethis could help her hold it steady if she needed it."

V'ritan sighed. "I can." He was silent for a moment as he let the words sink in. "Fine, I'll stay here and steady the gate on my side. Selene knows there will be a need if we get a wave of nMU."

"That's possible?"

"You are on a Teloran ship."

"Good point. Thanks, V'ritan. We'll do our best to keep this secured until Steph can get that gate open."

"And I'll have people standing by to bring the prisoners across as fast as we can. We won't have much time."

"The *Knight's* doing her best."

"So I can see," the *Garghilum Afreghil* told him, "but she is only one ship and she is severely outclassed. No offense."

"I have a breach!" Vishlog's voice interrupted. Two roars of defiance followed.

"I have to go," Lars said, and the King's Warrior nodded.

"Selene's fortune," he replied and signed off.

Selene's fortune, Lars thought and raced toward the breach. *Fucked if we won't need it!*

"Steph, how are you doing?" he demanded.

He could hear the strain in her voice when she replied. "I've created enough MU and I'm about to start on the gate. Wish me luck."

"Good luck."

"I hope I don't blow myself up."

"I'll kick what's left of your ass if you do."

He wasn't the only one swearing a blue streak. In another section of the ship, Ka was more than pissed.

"If you blow another fucking terminal, I'll throw you out the nearest fucking airlock!"

"And how was I supposed to know the terminal was behind that particular wall?" Piet protested.

"I don't know. How about...um... Well, fuck it all. Don't let it happen again."

"That's my girl." He grinned and headed to the computer bank that lined the opposite wall.

"Don't you 'my girl' me," Ka snapped in response. "You'd better hope that was only for back-up and the data on it is held somewhere else as well."

"Or what?" Piet challenged. "What exactly will you do if things don't work out and fit into your perfect little world?"

"I'll break some shit until it falls into line."

Angus laughed. "Well, whatever shit you're gonna break, do it soon because we have company."

He started forward and bounded into the enemy ranks with a low, twisting sweep that let him strafe the Telorans with solid rounds before his sword felled the first one with a meaty thump.

"I don't suppose the Navy has thought of the kind of rounds needed to pierce these motherfuckers' armor?"

"Yeah. Why don't you send them a burst asking exactly that? It'll keep you out of my hair while I get the rest of the job done. But don't get your ass shot off while you're on the horn."

"The horn?" Henry sputtered with laughter. "Where the hell did you dig that one up?"

"Never you mind, little man. Go take care of business while Piet and I strip-mine this thing's brains."

"You don't think it's the system, do you?" Reggie wanted to know as he raced past.

"Nope. I think the Navy fucked up its intelligence again and we're gonna have to find the real database all on our lonesome. You know, like usual."

"You know they'll be listening to the recordings, don't you?"

"What? Before or after we send their fucking data and get our asses disintegrated? It's not like they gave us many options for getting back," she bitched.

Todd sighed. "You knew the deal. If you wanted out, all you had to do was say so."

"And miss all this?" Ka demanded as she removed the front panel protecting the data banks. "Not for all the land left in the world."

"What do you mean? It's all still there," Darren argued as he fired into the helmet of one opponent and the gut of another. "Will you fucking hurry up over there?"

"You can't rush a masterpiece."

"I don't want a fucking masterpiece. I simply want to get home. Get the ass-humping data before these shit-bags fill me full of holes."

"Eh. I'm fairly sure you're already one big hole," Ka quipped, but her voice said her mind was elsewhere and her mouth was on autopilot.

"The only asses getting humped are ours," Reggie grumbled. He used one gauntleted fist to block an attack while he pressed the muzzle of his rifle hard into the torso of his opponent and held the trigger down.

The armor caved and the Teloran crumpled at his feet, but Reggie half-hopped over him and moved on. He blocked the strike that would have felled Jimmy and twisted the rifle to fire up under the jawline of the enemy who attempted it. He pivoted to move in tandem with the Scotsman as more soldiers streamed through the hole Piet had made in the data center's wall.

At one point, the Australian activated the speakers on his suit and shouted, "Stop," in Teloran. The attackers froze for a split second, and he laughed maniacally as he slaughtered another two and started on a third, which broke the spell.

"That shit has its uses," he declared smugly.

"Wanker," Gary muttered, but he began to use phrases like "break-fast-eating toilet" or "bathroom-mouth gun" to try to goad his opponents into losing their tempers.

He wished he could see their faces so he could know exactly what effect his words had on them, but their armor rippled with a thin field of nMU. The thought clicked home and startled him.

When he wracked his brain, he finally recalled something he'd heard after the battle for Dreth—something to do with the way the Witch had generated enough energy to gate the *Knight* home. It had been about mixing positive energy with negative energy.

"Hey, Piet, can I have a Meligornian grenade?"

"Sure," the explosives expert said and didn't look up from the tablet he'd jacked into the Teloran system. "They're in my—"

"Stand down!" Todd roared. "Do you want to blow us all to kingdom come?"

"But—" Gary protested.

"Stand down, I said," the sergeant shouted. "No one uses the Meligornian stuff—any of it—until I say so. If you do, what's left of me will make what's left of you regret surviving the aftermath. You got me?"

"Fine, sir. I got you." The Englishman sulked. "I got you loud. And. Clear."

The last three words were each punctuated by a grunt of effort as he went toe to toe with three Telorans who tried to force their way through the entry to the data center. His blade snapped on the second and he jerked out the extra sidearm he carried and thrust it into the armpit of the one he faced—or what he hoped was its armpit. It was hard to tell.

The burst he fired had the desired effect, though. It jerked several times and became a dead weight in his hand so he let it drop.

"Are you done yet?"

"We would be but these targlathian sons of Tegortha have tweaked the tark-livered coding," Ka reported.

"Excuses, excuses," Gary mocked, and Todd sighed.

"Stop your bitching, Gary, and give them the time they need."

"Oh, sure, Sarge. We'll give them time. We'll give them every second we can because we have so much of it."

"Whinging fucking Pommy bastard!" Reggie taunted as he fended off another attack.

"Back-birthing, colonial scum-sucker!" Gary snapped in reply, went to Jimmy's aid, and fired his sidearm dry. "Fuck it!"

"Bum-biting king of wankerology," the Australian added as he gutted his opponent and moved to drag Angus inside the room.

His teammate had followed his opponent and stepped into the corridor where he was immediately attacked by four different enemies. No way would he withstand that kind of onslaught for long.

"Are you right, mate?"

"Yeah, thanks, bro."

"I ain't your bro."

"Yeah? Well, I ain't your mate. No way you're getting that thing anywhere near me."

"Aw, that's not what you said last night."

"You bitch! You swore you'd never tell."

"I swear many things but I never mean a single one."

"Well, you coulda told me that before we started."

"Would you have—"

"I'm sure we don't need to know the sordid details," Ka protested. "Even if we know you're pissing about."

"Do you have everything?" Todd broke in, hoping to head off another argument.

She immediately turned serious. "Yeah, boss. Yeah, I got it—" She stopped and whistled. "Piet, do you see what I see?"

"I most certainly do."

"Jackpot," they chorused.

"What?" Todd asked when both focused on their tablets without speaking. "Talk to me," he ordered when neither of them answered. "Ka! Report."

"Sorry, boss, but we found your data."

"Do you have it streaming?"

"Along with all the rest? Sure."

"Can't you hurry it up?" Reggie asked. He'd taken cover behind the corner of the wall to reload and he looked exhausted.

"Why? Aren't you up to the fight?" Gary taunted.

"Nah, mate, but I haven't had my breakfast yet and there are rules about how many Telorans you can kill before your first meal. I wouldn't want to break any regulations now, would I?"

"Since when do you give a stuff about regulations?"

He stopped reloading and looked at the Englishman. "Well, fuck me, you're right."

"Not in a lifetime of no-fucking-ways," Gary replied.

The Australian pursed his lips, slammed the clip home, and took a quick peek around the corner. Several shots chewed the wall edge near his face.

"Do you want to get your mind off your sex life and do something about that?" he demanded.

"You gonna kiss me if I do?" Gary snapped off a couple of shots.

"Mate, I'll even buy dinner."

"Before? Or after?"

"Well, I don't see a fucking restaurant around here? Do you?"

His teammate made a show of looking around as he fired several short bursts into the corridor. "Is it only me or are there less of them than before?"

"Fuck." Angus and Henry moved to find where the Telorans would come through next. Neither of them believed they'd given up so easily.

"Well?" Reggie demanded. "About that restaurant—"

"You know all that bullshit Teloran they made us study?"

"I made you study that," Todd reminded them.

"That was your idea, Sarge?"

"That and the Dreth."

"So I have you to thank for knowing they stuck their data center opposite the bloody Gents?"

"Don't say it," Reggie groaned. "Just hearing the word reminds me I haven't taken a piss since—"

A Teloran appeared around the corner and he and Gary eliminated him in an over-enthusiastic burst of fire each.

"You know all he wanted to do was hit the heads, right?" the Australian said with a grin.

"Yeah? Well, his timing sucked."

"Quit your bitching," Ka snapped. "The language discs mean we've done this a shit-load faster than we would have without them. These assholes don't code in Federation Basic like the rest of us."

"I thought you Navy types did your coding in Navy Basic." Gary looked quickly at her and she shrugged

"There's nothing basic about the Navy's coding," she argued.

"That's not what you said the other day."

"You can't quote me on that. I'll deny it."

"No point. You're on record the minute you say anything wearing one of these things."

"Yeah? Well, maybe I'll dictate a letter to the brass while I'm getting the last of this data to download."

"Don't!" Todd ordered quickly. She was as likely to follow through with something she had no intention of the brass ever hearing while completely forgetting that they really would get to hear it—assuming he and the team survived of course.

He caught a glimpse of movement at the far end of the corridor. "Heads up," he murmured. "Here comes the next wave." He looked over his shoulder and added, "How's it going over there?"

"Five more minutes?" Ka asked.

"Maybe ten?" Piet added.

Todd rolled his eyes. "You have two."

"Make it three and you have a deal," she said crisply.

"That's easy for you to say," Gary griped. "You're not the ones getting shot at."

"No, we're the ones meeting the mission objectives."

"Boss, do we have to take her back with us?"

"You know the rules, Gary," he told him and everyone dutifully joined in the next line. "No one gets left behind."

"I thought they had rules about bringing pets to base?"

"This one left the base with us," Reggie pointed out.

"Who are you calling a pet?"

"Focus!" Todd roared before the Englishman could reply. "I want your heads in the game."

They all fell silent. Piet and Ka made sure the data streamed off the ship and onto the *Knight* without any glitches while they made sure they hadn't missed anything.

"Well, damn," the explosives expert murmured. "Ka?"

"Yeah?"

"Take a look at this."

"You're shitting me, right?"

Todd inched away from the wall. "Cover me, guys," he ordered and kept his voice soft as he duck-walked to where the two Marines techs stared at Piet's tablet. "Whatcha got?"

They handed him the device.

"There's a second fleet?" he asked seconds later. "Where's it headed?"

"That's the problem, boss. They've isolated the coordinates. They were probably meant to isolate this as well but missed it or something."

"Or it's bogus," Angus commented from across the room.

"Not with that kind of encryption," Piet contradicted, and Ka nodded.

"Encryption, huh? Well, you kept that to yourselves," Angus grumbled and circled to take the sergeant's initial place. There was only one direction the next attack could come from.

"We're gonna have to go get it," Todd decided and Piet groaned.

Ka looked him in open-mouthed disbelief. "You have to be shitting me."

He shook his head. "You saw the report, Corporal. It's not only a second fleet—or maybe it is, but it's something 'special' as well. We have to get that data."

"From the Bridge? Are you fucking kidding me…sir?

"You know we have to go for it," he told her but included the others in the statement.

"And you know, sir, that this will fuck the exit strategy all to hell," Henry reminded him.

Todd shrugged. "It wasn't great, to begin with. We'll figure out our own exit strategy, even if it involves blowing a hole in the hull and going for a swim."

"And the day was going so well, too."

CHAPTER TWENTY-THREE

"Selene's teats and Hrageth's balls!" Stephanie cursed and drew gasps from Meligornians and Dreth alike. More than one face turned toward her with a scowl.

Suck it, she thought and drew in more gMU. The gate took more energy than she'd realized and, while she knew she could do it, she didn't know what kind of condition she'd be in at the end.

"What do you need?" The quiet voice at her elbow broke through her concentration and she almost lost the thread.

"I need a moment's silence and a shit-ton more magic," she snapped before she could stop herself.

"Tell me what to do." The voice was soft. "I still have a little left. It was not enough to get me out of the crate or anywhere meaningful, but it's yours."

His words prompted a shuffling of feet and offers of more power.

"And me."

"Me, too."

"I still have a little."

How had the Telorans not drained them all? The Morgana laughed.

Not all of them know how and those who do don't know what would kill their precious cargo so they didn't dare.

And why do they need so many?

That is something you do not want to know. Now, hurry!

Stephanie didn't ask why she was suddenly so supportive, but she wasn't fooled. The darker presence didn't approve of her little detour. Perhaps she was being helpful simply to complete it more quickly. At least she wasn't fighting her for control.

Not yet, the voice teased.

Blaster fire sounded in the hold, and she spun instinctively. Johnny stepped in front of her to block the way with his body and the hold from view.

"We need the gate, Steph," he reminded her. "You can't be everywhere at once and we need you here. Now, let these people help you and get them out of here."

"Yes, get us out of here."

"Please…"

Stephanie closed her eyes and rested her head against Johnny's chest. Taking a deep breath, she nodded, stepped away, and turned to the open center of the hold.

"V'ritan, I need to know the location."

It was as though he had been waiting because he was in her head in an instant. *Here.*

She pulled the gMU in and focused on what he showed her.

"Careful, Steph." Lars's voice reached her as though from a long way away. "Don't burn yourself up."

"I won't," she told him and pictured the destination exactly as V'ritan had sent it.

It was a wide area in one of the *King's Warrior's* holds. More gunfire erupted behind her, followed by an explosion and the distinctive roars of Bumblebee and Zeekat on the attack.

"Hold the gate, Steph. V'ritan's sending help."

When she opened her eyes, the location she'd pictured was visible before her.

"We need more room," V'ritan called from the other side.

One of the biggest Meligornians she'd ever seen had a hand on the *Ghargilum Afreghil's* shoulder and the look on his face was torn between pleading and denial.

She felt her lip curl. *As if that's gonna be enough to keep V'ritan on the King's Warrior if he decided to enter the Teloran hold.*

Why he wouldn't stay right where he was, she didn't know, but she answered his request and widened the gate as he'd asked. As soon as they had enough room, the waiting squads of the *Afreghil's* Guard jogged forward. Rather than assist the prisoners around her, they moved into the hold.

"They will get the rest."

"I'll have Lars open a channel," Stephanie told him, and he smiled.

"It is already done." He paused and surveyed the prisoners who stood on either side of Stephanie with stunned looks on their faces. "Come forward. My medical staff will tell you where to go." They simply stared at him for a moment. "Move!" he shouted when they hesitated, and Stephanie felt compulsion curl around her and then slide away.

"Don't," the Morgana growled, bubbled to the surface, and subsided quickly as the gate wavered.

The Witch renewed her hold on the magic and dragged the gate wider. She cast a look at the mages who stood beside her and smiled. "I have it, now. Thank you for your help."

"Can you hold it?" one asked and gave her a worried glance.

"Yup. Now go before someone decides you need to be carried."

As if to emphasize her words, one of the *Afreghil's* Guards trotted past with a body slung over each shoulder. She got the impression he would have brought more if he'd been able to. The ship shuddered beneath her feet and she shuffled to retain her balance. Her gaze remained fixed on the scene beyond her gate and she focused on the way the magic felt as she held it open.

It wasn't as hard as the one she'd made to Earth when she'd taken the Meligornian mages there the first time. Recalling that reminded her of the two ships acting as the *Knight's* escorts.

"Has the *Knight* called her sisters in?" she asked,

The *Cathay Williams* and *Henry Chauvel* are en route," V'ritan informed her and she felt the energy in the gate surge.

"What did you do?" she asked.

"I strengthened the gate on my side," he told her as though it was the most obvious thing in the world.

As soon as he spoke, medics crossed from the *King's Warrior* into the Teloran ship. They each took a prisoner gently by the arm. "The *Ghargilum Afreghil* will aid the Witch," they assured them, "but you must cross now or you will place her at risk."

The Meligornian who'd first offered his magic allowed himself to be led forward. "Thank you," he murmured and stepped through, where he was handed to another waiting medic.

His escort returned to help another prisoner across. "Come," the mage urged gently, "it is time to go."

Stephanie felt the magic waver and noted a short burst of anger that tore at her soul. It was followed almost instantly by a sudden dip to depression and a rolling wave of melancholy.

"Fuck it all," she muttered, using a phrase Todd had adopted from one of his Australian teammates.

"What?" V'ritan demanded.

"nMU," she told him. "If one of their mages arrives, there's no way I'll be able to hold the gate."

"I have help," he reassured her. "If you need to deal with one of them, we can keep it open."

"What if I want to go and help?" she asked as blaster fire crackled in the background.

"I said we could keep it open," he told her. "I did not say for how long."

"Right." She pursed her lips, steadied the portal, and focused on holding the largest portion of it herself.

Time slowed and her world narrowed until it became the gate and its flickering arch of purple and blue. Figures moved on either side of her and Johnny's bulk sheltered her from being jostled.

Stephanie lost track of how many passed her. She forgot to count the prisoners and the *Afreghil's* troops blended with the medics and the mages. It took several minutes before she registered V'ritan speaking to her.

"Sorry?"

"You can come across now. We have them all."

She darted a look behind her and Johnny shifted so she could see. Lars, Marcus, the cats, Vishlog, and Frog were all there. None of them looked at her and they fired through the door as though they held back a greater force, but they were there.

"Whenever you're ready, Steph," Lars told her, his tone clipped.

"Are you sure you have them all?" she asked V'ritan.

"Yes," he confirmed, his voice sharp with strain.

Todd's voice broke through their comms before V'ritan could add to that.

"*Knight,* confirm data receipt." His voice was gritty with effort before he tried again. "Dammit, *Knight!* Confirm."

"Keep your britches on, Sergeant," the *Knight's* replied tartly. "I need more than a nano-second."

"A nano-second might be all we have, *Knight,*" was the abrupt reply.

"Stream ended. Data received." Ebony paused. "Sergeant, this data is missing pertinent detail."

"Confirmed, *Knight.* We are en route to obtain it."

"They're what?" Stephanie snapped and her eyes blazed. "Todd!"

"Sorry, Steph. The mission's not done." He said no more and simply cut the link.

Lars snapped three precise shots through the door and glanced at Vishlog. "Fuck."

The team maintained a steady rate of fire, but Johnny looked at Lars. "Say the word."

Watching them, V'ritan could only guess which word he referred to. He had to admit the man had balls—although he might not keep them if he tried what he was clearly thinking of doing. He was Meligornian and even he wouldn't lay a hand on Stephanie right now. Magic flickered over the girl in intensifying ripples of blue and purple lightning.

The *Garghilum Afreghil* sympathized with the security chief. The hold on his shoulder tightened and he laid a gauntleted palm over T'revan's hand. He had no intention to go anywhere.

Before he could convey that, however, Stephanie spoke.

"V'ritan, get the *Warrior* out of here. We will not leave the team behind."

With anyone else, he might have challenged them as to the real reason they would stay, but this was Stephanie. She'd have remained for any team tasked with this, especially since she was already on the ship. He knew her well enough to know she'd come home with her people or not at all.

He shoved the unwelcome thought aside. Of course she would come home.

Before he could say anything to her, the gate slammed shut. Magic reverberated around the hold he'd chosen for the portal and returned to him with a snap as it broke from his control. "Mother of the Moon goddess and the sentient stars!"

It was as close to "motherfucker" as any Meligornian curse, but no one reacted. They were all too busy staring at the space where the portal had been.

Two of the mages collapsed and the magic rebounded through V'ritan.

"Islafel..." he managed to say as T'revan caught him. "You heard her..."

"Understood, *Ghargilum*. Selene's blessing on them."

As if his words were a prayer that needed repeating, awed murmurs answered him.

"Selene's blessing."

He hoped it would be enough to bring them back.

Steph? he sent and tried to touch her mind as he had before.

Not now, V'ritan. Momma's busy.

She sounded so much like Elizabeth, he had to smile.

"Are you all right, my *Afreghil?*" T'revan's voice reached him through a fog of pain, and he clasped a hand around his chief guard's arm.

"Ask me tomorrow."

"Very well, my *Afreghil*."

The Meligornian didn't quite sigh but he sounded like a sergeant dealing with a particularly difficult officer. It made V'ritan want to laugh except that he felt like he'd been run over by a rampant Witch and was worried sick about Stephanie's return.

"Help me to the bridge."

He turned his head to take in the fallen mages and saw the healers already attending to them. One of the healers met his gaze.

"They'll live but they won't wield magic for a few days."

V'ritan nodded and winced. It felt like someone had put a lightning bolt through his skull.

The medic opened his mouth and he held his hand up.

"I'll be on the bridge," he told them and hoped that made it final.

No doubt he'd receive a visit from his chief medical officer and that was fine. Right now, he needed to be on the command deck with Islafel. He had to be there when the *Knight* retrieved her people.

"Johnny, give me Todd's comms," Stephanie snapped.

They'd cleared a path to the edge of the hold. It hadn't been pleasant and had involved her delivering lightning bolt swarms that burst into multiple threads when they came into contact with the enemy.

It was funny how the smell of burnt flesh didn't vary between species. Johnny swallowed hard as memories rode the traces of the odor that made it through his suit's filters.

After the third burst, the hold had gone quiet and they'd bolted through it and into the corridor beyond.

"Show me where they are," she ordered as Lars stepped alongside her.

"You need to lay off on the magic, Steph," he told her firmly.

"Are you telling me how to fight, now?"

"This isn't a pod scenario and I don't need you falling over."

"Don't you go all alpha male on me."

The magic arced and crackled around her, but he refused to move away.

"I wouldn't dream of it, but I want you in control for as long as you can be."

His words struck home and she bit back a tart reply.

"Done," she managed as their comm line crackled.

"What the absolute fuck!" Ka wasn't impressed. "Listen, whoever the fuck you are, get off the fucking line. This channel's private."

"That's not gonna happen, sweet-cheeks," Stephanie told her. "We're on our way."

"Steph?"

"Yeah?"

"Fuck!" A fizz and the sound of scrambling filled the short silence before Ka came back on the line and spoke quickly and quietly. "Steph, we don't need you here. Todd doesn't need you here. You need to get your ass off this ship and let us do our job."

"Oh, crap," Lars murmured, but she ignored him.

She didn't slow her pace even slightly and jogged along the route Johnny had provided. Her gaze roved the corridor for threats as she talked. The security chief saw her scowl but didn't have time to deal with it. Movement caught his eye and he snapped a shot toward it while Vishlog and Johnny moved to shield Stephanie.

Frog and Marcus aimed at slightly different angles and dropped back with their leader to cover the rear. The cats roared suddenly and bounded ahead.

Bumblebee bounced at a wall and ricocheted off it with a twist of his body that took him around a corner at an almost impossible angle. Johnny slapped Vishlog on the shoulder as Zeekat mirrored the movement and rebounded three times to come in on a different path.

"This is my job," Stephanie informed Ka before she asked, "He can't hear us, can he?"

"I've isolated the channel," the corporal admitted and sounded defiant. "You are not a distraction any of us need."

"You and I will talk when we get back."

"Bring it, sweetheart. Whenever you want—but later. Let the man do his job."

"I will kick your ass."

"Yeah? Don't make promises you won't be able to keep, kiddo!" The woman cut the link.

"Johnny!" Steph snapped.

"On it."

"Do you know where they're heading?" she demanded.

"Yeah. They're working their way to the bridge."

"We'll meet them there. Come on, we need to hurry."

They came parallel with the corner the cats had disappeared around and looked cautiously beyond it. Bumblebee used his paw blades to scythe through the knee joints of a Teloran warrior's armor.

"Fuck...me..." Frog murmured. "Where did he learn to do that?"

"He worked it out himself," Vishlog replied and grunted as he used his *duranium targlath* to split the next Teloran's armor like a crab shell.

Zeekat felled the final enemy warrior when he bounded off the wall and thumped his forepaws into the target's back. When his adversary toppled, he used the two tusk-like protrusions beneath his armor's jawline to grasp and break the warrior's neck.

"Remind me never to get on their bad side," Frog stated.

"There's no chance of that," Vishlog retorted. "You let them make a mess of Stephanie's bed."

The smaller man groaned and Marcus gave him a friendly shove. "You will never live that down." He grinned.

"They worked together. Bumblebee acted as a diversion."

"Hah! A likely story."

"You saw them," Frog protested. "Bee grabbed Steph's shoe—"

"He what?" It was news to her, but he didn't expand on it.

"And then he got into her closet—"

"And exactly how did he manage that?" she demanded and glanced toward him.

Frog winced but Lars suppressed a smile.

At least he's managed to divert her from Ka, he thought.

"I don't know if you've noticed, but your cats are very smart," the man continued.

"Well, they're smarter than you are, anyway," Marcus interjected.

"Hey!"

They jolted into a run as they passed the intersection and Vishlog and the cats joined them. The next time Steph's comms came alive with chatter from the Hooligans, Johnny cut across it with a hasty explanation. "They can't hear us until you say so."

"So they don't know we can hear them?"

"Nope."

"Good. She can't accuse us of being a distraction then, can she?"

"You don't plan to forget that, do you?" Lars asked.

"Nope."

"Remember that people say things in the heat of battle they'd never say otherwise," he reminded her.

"You mean the truth will out?" Stephanie asked and he grimaced.

"You can take it any way you like," he told her. "I'm only asking you to keep it in mind."

"Well, yes, Dad."

Frog snickered. "You're doing real good today—"

"Says the man who let the cats—" Marcus began, only to be cut off.

"All right!" Frog fired a half-dozen shots down a side corridor.

"These guys are nowhere near as sneaky as the Dreth," his teammate muttered as they ran the length of the ship.

The level they were on grew unnaturally quiet.

"Or the Hooligans have already been here," Vishlog observed as they rounded a corner and saw the bodies piled in the corridor

"Where are their weapons?" Frog asked and turned one of the corpses with his boot.

"What d'you mean?" Marcus asked.

"Well, none of them are carrying any."

They all glanced down and saw what he meant.

"The Hooligans have definitely been here," Johnny murmured and picked up a drained energy pack.

The short flat cartridge bore the Federation Navy seal.

"I thought the Navy had a bag and shag it policy," he said thoughtfully.

"For this kind of operation?" Marcus asked.

"Especially for this kind of operation."

"In the heat of battle?"

"Well—"

"Besides, what does it matter? Won't we blow this mother to kingdom come as soon as they're off it?"

"They must be really hauling ass," Frog muttered when the sound of blaster fire made them all wince.

They glanced around but the corridor was as still and empty as before.

"It's Todd," Lars realized, his face bleak.

Stephanie picked her way through the bodies but didn't let the sound distract her. "Vishlog, you'll have to carry the cats."

They glanced around in time to see her step into one of the emergency shafts scattered through the ship. The sound of her boots moving up a ladder followed shortly thereafter.

"Motherfucking impatient sonuva—" The security chief rolled his eyes.

"Technically, she's the daughter—"

"Shut up, Frog!" was said by three different voices, and he snickered.

Lars tapped him on the shoulder. "You're up next. I want someone with her at all times."

"She's fine," the smaller man reassured him. "She'll go all Morgana on them if she gets into trouble. I don't think there's a being alive who can beat her when she's like that."

The rattle of fire in their headsets went from sporadic to a steady roar.

"Move your asses!" Todd shouted as one of the Hooligans yelped. "I don't care if you've been hit. You ain't got time to bleed!"

Whoever it was chuckled weakly and replied, "I didn't get time to duck, either, Sarge."

A sharp gasp shortly after was followed by, "Quit your bitchin'. Navy's gonna have your ass for makin' such a mess of your armor."

Ka's bedside manner was as delicate as her communications technique. It didn't bother the injured man, though.

"Did you bring the tape?"

The sound of tape unrolling ripped across the comms line.

"Of course I brought the tape."

"Then the Navy's never gonna notice."

"Yeah, you're a funny fucker." The retort was almost lost in the sound of an explosion.

"Sonuvabitch!" accompanied the distinctive hiss of an autoinjector. "Didja have to?"

"Make the most of it, Gary. That shit only lasts a half-hour and a man your size shouldn't have a second dose."

"Ka, a man my size gets a second dose of anything he wants."

Snickers followed and someone quipped, "Not to mention a dose of a few things he doesn't."

"Half an hour," Ka reiterated as though it was a point too important to be forgotten.

"Well, you'd better haul ass and get your side of the bargain signed, sealed, and delivered, hadn't you, Corporal?" A sharp breath preceded a long, slow exhalation. "'Cos I don't reckon I'll last much more than a half-hour and you need all the fucking help you can get."

"Yeah, and you're so funny. Here. Let me help you."

The wounded man uttered another gasp, then a groan of relief. "Nah, I'm good. Let's go kick some Teloran tail."

"How much further, boss?"

The gunfire started to die down, and Lars realized they'd all stopped to listen to the drama being played out over the comms.

"Move!" he snapped and the rest of the team followed Frog and Stephanie up the tube.

Vishlog carried Bumblebee and Johnny carried Zee—or, rather, the cats saw the opening of the tube and leapt to their shoulders where they dug in their armored claw extensions and crouched. The extra weight made his men's movements clumsy and Lars made a note that some spaces were simply not meant for cats.

He climbed into the tubes and had almost reached the level Johnny had marked on the map in their HUDs when more gunfire erupted.

"Johnny, you can't tweak our HUDs so they can put Todd's team on the map, can you?" The security head's heart sank at Stephanie's request.

"We had a plan," he reminded her.

"You don't see what I see," she told him as he emerged.

The corridor was littered with bodies and the halls sported new openings. Not even the ceiling had been spared. Lars whistled softly.

"Exactly," she replied as though that was all the comment she needed. "Johnny? Show me where they're at."

The analyst crouched beside an access point and hooked into the Telorans' systems. He caught Lars's gaze. "I borrowed the classes from Todd," he explained. "It seemed like the best way."

Stephanie began to walk carefully through the killing field, and Lars went with her after he motioned for Vishlog and Frog to stay with Johnny. He placed a hand on her arm as she reached clear ground.

"I have to keep going," she protested and jerked free.

"You need to stay with the team," he told her but realized that the flicker of blue and purple had faded to a dull glow. "What's wrong with your magic? Are you tired?"

She frowned. "Not that tired, but the gMU is harder to reach here. It's like there's not enough of it."

"Are you gonna be okay?"

Blaster fire sounded again, closer than he'd expected.

"It's a trap!" Todd shouted down their comms line and this time, he hadn't made a joke.

"Yuh think?" Apparently, Ka agreed with his assessment.

"Screw you!"

"Not in a world of nopes. I don't need an angry Steph on my tail."

"It wasn't an offer you hairy targlathian *hrempeso!*"

"Ouch, Sarge. That was not nice. Even for you."

Lars raised his eyebrows. "A what now?"

Stephanie shrugged but she looked pleased. "I might let her live, after all."

Her words made him glance anxiously at her eyes. When he saw they were still blue, he relaxed. "That was dark, even for you."

She gestured at the carnage around them. "I have my reasons."

"And I have your data," Johnny announced, as the map in their HUDs updated and several blue dots appeared. "That's the team."

"Yeah?" she snarked. "Now tell me something I don't know." A swarm of red and yellow dots appeared.

"They walked into an ambush," the analyst replied.

"Fuck." Stephanie closed her eyes to shut out the image where a mass of red threatened to roll over the tiny splash of blue.

"Fuck," Lars echoed while he studied the scene and tried to work out how he and the team could make a difference.

"I need more power," she said as if she'd come to a decision.

"But—"

"I'm gonna switch to black magic," she continued and ignored his protest.

"Fuck."

"Hrageth's fucking balls," Vishlog added and the Earth expletive sounded right at home.

Frog chuckled. "And Selene's fucking teats."

Lars watched her warily. "Don't you blow yourself up."

"As if I would," the Morgana replied. "I will have to shed this gMU first. Come."

She didn't wait for his answer but began to jog down the corridor.

"Uh, Steph?"

Her steps faltered and Stephanie's voice replied, although the strain of an internal battle tinged its edges. "I'm still here."

You need me, the Morgana told her where Lars could not hear.

I don't want you in control.

You need me in control. The dark presence poked at her defenses and wound gMU around her hands before she absorbed it again and threw it into their internal centrifuge to turn it into eMU. *I like blue. It matches his eyes.*

An image of Lars flickered through her head and Stephanie stiffened. A picture of Todd followed. *And his.*

They're mine.

Pfft. As if I care for either. I only observed the similarities.

I want to be me.

That is for another time. For now... The Morgana surged inside her skull, rolled over Stephanie, and took hold of her. *You need to let me do what needs to be done.*

I want them brought home, she reminded her and hastily added, *Alive and well.*

Nothing's guaranteed. She tightened her control to lock Steph in one place. *You know that.*

If you harm them, I will hunt you.

That gave the darkness pause, and she stopped to study the Witch. *I do believe you would.*

She didn't give her a chance to answer but tightened her hold and froze the girl in place.

Now, what is the human phrase? Oh, yes. Hold still. Momma's busy.

"Get behind me!" she ordered and her presence spread ice through Stephanie's voice. "I need to shed the gMU before I start with the nMU."

"Of all the motherfucking—" Lars began and glared at her when she turned toward him. "Your timing fucking sucks."

"And you need to mind your language."

"Or what?" The words were out before he could stop them and fear became a solid ball in his stomach.

The Morgana saw the alarm in his eyes and laughed. "Another time."

She surged forward, used gMU to lift her from the floor, and rode it like a surfboard down the corridor. The team had to sprint to keep up.

"Hey!" the team leader shouted and switched to team comms. "She's no good to you if she's dead."

"I won't let that happen." The voice was as chilling over a closed line as it was in the open—and that was when it was meant to be reassuring.

He suppressed a shudder and caught Vishlog's eye. "She needs the cats. The Morgana—"

The Dreth pursed his lips to whistle but the felines bolted after Stephanie.

"I swear they understand every word," Frog observed and Vishlog smiled.

"Yes."

"Do you mean they knew what I was saying when I told them to stop?"

His smile grew wider. "Of course."

"Those sneaky sonsuvbitches."

"Exactly."

"Morgana!" Lars called. "Todd's team is trapped and she needs them free."

"Is that why you did not go with the Meligornians?"

"Yes. They..." Lars searched for the words that would make her understand how important Todd was to Stephanie, then tried something different. "The team was going after specialized data to help in the fight against the Telorans."

"Do they have it?"

"No, and they're trapped."

The map in the HUD confirmed that this much was true. While no longer surrounded, the Marines had backed themselves into a corner they couldn't get out of. From what he could see, they'd taken cover in a small room at the corridors' junction.

"Do we know where it is?"

Well, that was easy to answer. "No."

The Morgana came to a dead halt and he watched her face change as she studied the map in the HUD. "The easiest direction is in a straight line," she observed and raised her hands.

The air rippled around her fingers, and a section of the wall blew apart.

"Whoa!" Frog exclaimed. "Stephanie never did anything like that."

"I don't know," Marcus remarked. "Wasn't there a starship not so long ago?"

Panic surged through the Teloran command center.

"What was that?" the captain demanded.

At another surge, the lights dimmed and the ship's power fluctuated as though it had rerouted due to structural damage.

"What is going on?" he roared when no answer was immediately forthcoming.

The featureless faces turned toward him showed him nothing, but the voice that replied was equal parts fear and awe. "An Ancient One has manifested on board."

He froze. "An Ancient One? I thought they were long gone, hunted to extinction by Councils past."

"And so did we," the communications officer replied. "Nevertheless, there is one on board."

"There cannot be one on board. No ship has been close enough and from what I know, not even they could survive the depths of space." He paused as he considered the possibilities. "Could they have been trapped inside the asteroid?"

"No, sir. They'd have appeared on the readings."

"Even dormant?"

"Yes, sir, even then."

He scanned his console and noted the two clusters of red dots on board the ship. "That second group of intruders. Could that be the Ancient?"

The communications officer didn't quite shrug and refused to commit. "It is new. Perhaps?"

"Perhaps?" He was not impressed by his crew member's hedging. "Who do we have left on this level?"

"Only those involved in the ambush. The Marines have defeated the rest."

"And were their deaths in vain?"

"No, sir. They gave us time to set up the ambush."

"Immediately outside the command center," the captain observed and gestured at the placement on the map.

"It seemed the most appropriate space to set one if all other measures failed."

"And have they?"

"They wear sealed suits. The gas—"

"I see." He cut him short. "And the ambush?"

"Is on the way to being a success."

"Unless that is an Ancient One coming to intervene."

"But so few of them would, sir."

"So which of them do you think it is?"

"Getravin?"

"No, he was ambushed and destroyed in the Battle of Hethar."

"Are they sure?"

"A thousand of us surrounded him and the magic tore him apart. No one comes back from that, no matter how powerful they think they might be."

"Elshta?"

"Was fired into a vacuum in a system too far away for these creatures to have discovered it."

"Did she have enough power to slide between?"

"Not by the time her ship was taken."

"Vellagar, then."

"The interrogators took him apart an atom at a time. His execution entertained the public for days—and stood as a warning to all who stood against us." The captain smiled. "Surely you have seen the replays?"

They fell silent. The three Telorans they had named had been among the greatest in the eons-old rebellion. Knowing they were gone left only names that conjured fear and uncertainty. No one wanted to name them in case they were later blamed for a summoning.

"Well, whichever one of them it is, we will banish them again." The captain's voice echoed loudly in the silence and was met with more silence.

No one would be the first to disagree.

The Morgana flung furniture out of their path and obliterated it with clear light. When she'd said, "Stay behind me," she'd meant it. Even the cats understood the danger of getting ahead of her when she threw magic around like that.

Lars had stopped trying to protest, but his eyes were dark with worry and his attention was divided between their surroundings and concern for Stephanie. Vishlog was worried, too, but he was like the felines.

There were times to stay silent and times to intervene. This was one of the former—even if he swore he would speak to Stephanie when they returned.

They reached another wall and the computer system in front of it started to melt—started, then stopped. The Morgana smiled.

"Now, we can play."

"Uh oh." Frog backed away and Marcus moved in concert beside him.

The cats took their cue from the two men—or, possibly, the sudden snap of darker magic. Lars felt a spike of rage and anger roll over the Dreth. Johnny groaned, and Frog drew a hissed breath as if his insides twisted with pain. Marcus said nothing but his hands tightened around the rifle and he searched for something to kill.

She laughed. "Hold onto your hats, boys. We're going to war!"

Power swirled around them, an almost tangible breeze as she pulled in the negative energy that permeated the Teloran vessel. The deck shuddered beneath their feet as though she drew the ship's life force through its skin.

"Keep it together," Lars warned her. "We have Telorans to kill and a Navy team to rescue."

"Yes, keep it together," the Morgana mocked, "while we take this ship apart."

Black lightning surged over her skin and the cats leapt to the side to gain more distance between themselves and their mistress. She raised her hands and they shrank away.

"Holy fuck," Frog muttered as a tunnel opened before them.

The nMU disintegrated everything in front of them. Metal sizzled, melted, and evaporated into nothing. Furniture vanished. Computer systems flared red with alarm and in the next moment, were simply gone. She left a trail of destruction wide enough for them to advance three abreast.

The distance to Todd's team vanished along with every obstacle in their path.

"Johnny, we need to talk to the Hooligans." The realization struck Lars as another dozen meters of obstacle became a clear path.

"Done." The reply came almost too quickly to be believed, but the response was instantaneous.

"I thought I told you to stay off this line."

Lars spoke before Ka could do more than protest. "The Morgana is coming."

"Well, shit."

"Yeah."

"Do you think she remembers—"

"I think her mind is on other things," he hastened to reassure the woman as the last wall disintegrated and the Telorans came into view.

They also caught a glimpse of Todd's team. The group was hunkered behind whatever cover they could find at the edges of the room they'd blasted their way into, but it was obvious that the makeshift shield wouldn't last much longer.

"Sons of targlath, pray to the stars!" The Morgana's shout made the Telorans turn in their direction. She flicked her fingers toward them to deliver shards of darkness that sliced across the distance between them. The first rank jerked and fell and their armor smoked as it dissolved around the myriad holes that pierced it.

"Keep your heads down, Hooligans. She's not being too careful with her aim."

"I beg to differ," she snapped and created a plate of darkness on the ceiling above the enemy soldiers. "I am being very careful with my aim."

The Telorans scattered and clawed past each other in their haste to get out from under the now-descending mass. She laughed and snapped her fingers, and the magic fell as if released from an invisible shroud.

It landed like an oil slick or black honey, oozed over the surfaces it touched, and gradually sank into them. Steam rose above it and the soldiers shrieked and scrabbled at their armor in their hurry to remove it. Helmets were thrown aside and seams popped, but that was as far as most of them got before the black stickiness reached their uniforms and finally, their flesh.

Those watching knew when that happened as the screaming started.

Lars froze and his stomach roiled at the sight, but Todd's voice rang authoritatively.

"Choose your targets. Put them out of their misery." The Hooligans immediately complied.

"Headshots only," he added

"Well, duh. Why don't you put your money where your mouth is, Sarge?" one of his team snarked.

"One," he replied as a Teloran's head exploded, and the race was on.

"One...two...three." Johnny was not to be outdone and proved that he could shoot faster and straighter.

"Four," Ka retorted and the mutter that followed came through loud and clear. "Smart-assed motherfucker."

"She really doesn't like anyone, does she?" Frog asked. "Three."

"Nope," and "Not even us," responded over the comms net.

"And don't you forget it," the woman snapped with no apparent desire to disabuse them.

"When you're all quite done," the Morgana scolded, "I believe you have a job to do."

"Oh, sure thing, lady," Ka snarked. "As soon as you get the door. We're not exactly alone in here, you know. There are more."

She pointed down the corridor to where more Telorans formed a barricade in front of the hatch leading to their bridge. All eyes turned toward it and the barrier opened barely enough to allow a dark figure to emerge. Power rolled over him and a chill fell across the team as the Teloran soldiers parted before him.

"Are you sure you want me to handle it?" the Morgana demanded.

Ka's response was breathless, its bravado belied by fear. "Why not? We have to conserve our ammo. You pull yours right out of thin air."

The Teloran mage raised a hand and a ball of darkness careened toward the Witch.

"Get down!" Lars yelled.

Even the cats bellied down. Vishlog landed on Teloran bodies and pushed them in front of him, raised his rifle, and used them as a rest. He fired past the Morgana but his rounds did nothing.

"Tegorthan reject," he muttered, switched to the energy pack, and tried again.

He wasn't alone in his frustration. The Morgana dived away from the ball and it sailed harmlessly past her and ate into the bulkhead at the other end of the corridor. Two more followed before they dissipated, and she simply rolled out of their way.

One bit deep into the deck and the other removed some of the wall she'd left standing. Around her, the team maintained fire but their weapons did nothing against the much more powerful nMU field surrounding the mage.

"So, it's like that, is it?" She rolled to her knees and thrust her palms at the air in front of her.

Lightning sprang from one hand and a storm of discs from the other. She gestured with her palm at the ceiling and conjured a more personalized field of darkness above the mage, then focused on the magic she could feel within him.

"I have you now." She snarled, wrested it from his control, and dragged it through his skin. His shriek could have split dimensions, and the closest warriors turned their heads in her direction. Horror marked every line of their bodies, even if their faces remained unreadable.

Several seconds passed before the Morgana pushed to her feet and the movement broke the spell. One of the Telorans opened fire and clipped the wall close to Ka's head. Several others followed suit.

"Motherfucking motherfucks!"

"The correct term is targlathian *hlotharja*," the Witch told her, and the Teloran who had fired the first shot exploded from within.

"Whoa!" Frog murmured. "Stephanie never did that."

She laughed. "Your Stephanie has much to learn."

A second Teloran exploded. The third one's hand shattered around his gun and he fell, screaming in anguish. The fourth swung his rifle toward her and she uttered a string of expletives as bullets drilled into her armor.

"Did you catch all that?" Reggie asked in an awed voice.

"Nope, but I can slow the suit's recording when we get back," Gary promised. "'Cos that sounded awesome!"

"Motherfucking targlathian *hlotharian* asshole!" she screamed in a blend of Morgana-Steph that would have been amusing if she hadn't stumbled and landed on her ass on the deck.

"Since when does Steph know that much Teloran?" Lars asked as she scrambled to her feet. He turned to Johnny. "Did she take lessons with you?"

His teammate shook his head and fired into the enemy ranks. "No, she was too busy with One R&D stuff to take extra classes."

"You asked her?"

"I wanted her permission to trade a little training time for the Teloran language."

"And she gave it?"

"She said one of us needed to know."

"Huh. She never mentioned it to me."

"You were in the pods when the opportunity came up."

Jimmy gave a snort of laughter. "You mean when you made the bet you could learn it faster?"

Lars snapped off three more shots and yanked a grenade from his harness, and the Hooligans joined in. The nMU shielding the Teloran's armor sparked under the impact of a multitude of rounds. The sound of it gradually gave way to the metallic spang of solid rounds striking armor.

Another enemy round thudded into the Morgana and she let loose a withering round of new curses. At least, Ka thought they were curses. They certainly didn't sound friendly.

She looked at Todd. "I think the Morgana knows more about the Telorans than she's let on."

"Ya think?" Gary added. "What the fuck gives you that idea?"

"Cursing in a foreign tongue so eloquently is a hint," she retorted dryly.

The Telorans didn't simply stand and wait for their armor to be breached but they refused to move from their position in front of the doorway. They stood four ranks deep and blocked the corridor so they could only be taken on eight at a time. The Hooligans and Stephanie's team had made a dent but not fast enough.

The Morgana pulled more energy and released a storm of sharp-edged discs into them. The cats roared and bounded past her before soldiers could fill the gap. Their claws flashed and their growls seemed to make the air itself shudder and ripple air. The Telorans were torn between trying to advance and avoiding the two big felines wreaking havoc in their ranks.

"Turds of Hrageth!" Vishlog cursed seconds later and Lars followed the Dreth's alarmed gaze.

Darkness formed another oil slick at the ceiling. It stretched across the intersection and vanished out of sight down either end of the corridor. Before the team leader could respond, a piercing whistle almost shattered the comms.

"Motherfuck!" Ka swore. "Didja have to?"

The two cats looked up and her answer came in a second, more urgent shriek. After one last swipe at the closest Telorans, the two cats raced back. Lars stretched his hand tentatively to touch the Morgana, but negative energy snapped toward him and he pulled it away.

"Wait!" he shouted. "Please, wait! The cats—"

The two animals in question streaked around the corner and their paws scrabbled to find traction on a floor slick with blood. Fortunately, it was also littered with Teloran corpses and they found the purchase they needed and boosted off broken torsos and limbs so they could make the turn.

They came to a flurried halt in front of Vishlog and he gave a series of quick chirps while his hands flashed to direct them to cover. The Morgana let the oil slick fall and both teams waited for the armor to give way before they opened fire.

It was a slaughter, even before she riddled the Telorans left standing with a swarm of shards.

"I'll get the hatch." Johnny started forward but Ka and Piet slid past him.

"That's our job."

Before any of them could reach it, the barrier exploded out of its frame and careened into the room beyond and the wall at the far end, and the Morgana surged forward. The three of them stumbled aside to let her past, and Lars hurried to keep up with her. Vishlog and the cats ran alongside.

Still stunned, Johnny and the Hooligans followed. The sight of her destroying consoles with bolts of flickering darkness rendered them momentarily speechless. Lars turned toward the others.

"Don't you ladies have a job to do?"

CHAPTER TWENTY-FOUR

Magic snapped from the back of the bridge and the Morgana swore. She thrust a hand out at shoulder height and a shield of black interposed itself between her and the incoming lightning.

"Go!" Lars yelled, and Todd looked at Ka.

"You're up, Corporal. Piet."

"Oh, sure, put me in the same class as her," the explosives expert grumbled.

"Quit your bitching and make sure this ship won't ever fly again. Angus, Henry, Dru! Cover them."

As the Hooligans scrambled to do what he ordered, he risked a glance toward Stephanie, his eyes dark with worry. The girl he loved had almost totally disappeared. It was like she'd been subsumed by someone—or something.

A little fearful, he wondered if he'd ever get her back.

He also wondered if the Morgana was always there and if she ever sat somewhere inside his girl and watched their private moments. The thought sent shivers over his skin. *Oh, God, I hope not.*

Jimmy crashed into him in a side tackle and they rolled to end up slightly behind the remains of a console. Magic ripped through the space he'd occupied and he took a shaky breath.

"Thanks, Jimmy."

"Glad to have you back with us, sir."

Todd decided he deserved that. He'd let himself be distracted and had almost died. He didn't blame the man for being pissed. No doubt he'd hear about it from the rest of the team as well.

"How are they going?"

"Almost…there, boss." Ka sounded like she was fighting a battle all her own. "Give…us…a couple more minutes."

"You got it," he told her and moved closer so he could cover her better. He located Piet, Gary, and Reggie, who moved cautiously around the edge of the command center, and hoped the three of them would be enough.

"Don't forget to create us an exit," he said on the comms.

"Gotcha, boss." Piet's response was a short affirmative, but Reggie had more to say.

"Don't get your ass shot off in the meantime."

He shook his head. He really wouldn't be able to live that down.

Whatever. We've gotta live through this first.

He settled into a pattern of finding a target and firing before he found another and continued the routine. Jimmy, Angus, and Henry worked with him and the four of them dealt with what was left of the bridge crew after the Morgana's little temper tantrum.

She eliminated two of the mages and hauled the third up against the rear wall.

"Why do you fight me, Captain?" she demanded. "Why don't you lay down your arms?"

The final statement had a twist of sweetness to it that even Todd found mildly compelling. The Teloran captain was made of sterner stuff, however.

"Because we don't succumb to evil, no matter how ancient it is," he all but snarled. "You will not be allowed to hinder Teloran survival. I do not care who you used to be."

"Evil?" the Morgana retorted. "Me?"

"What else could you be? I don't know where you came from but I will send you back there. I will not allow evil to stand before me and live."

"Brave words for someone serving the greatest evil that ever lived," she replied and anger vibrated through her words.

"In the times from which you originate, there was greater evil. You should know. You are an Ancient Evil from that time."

The Morgana laughed. "Me? I fought evil—and for my beliefs, they sought to bury me under a mountain!"

Magic crackled and flickered between them but neither of them broke through the defenses of the other.

"No!" the captain exclaimed. "No... That's impossible."

She swept her hands in and thrust them toward him. Magic boiled from the deck, the ceiling, and even the walls to join the solid wall of black she drove toward him.

"No!" He raised a hand and, when his magic shattered, tried to shield his face with an upflung arm. "It can't be."

He died when the wall pounded into him and burrowed beneath his skin to explode and hurl pieces of his black-cloaked form in multiple directions. He died in silence without even the time to scream.

"Apparently," the Morgana replied, "it can."

"Got it!" Ka's victorious shout overrode her.

Todd glanced at his second and saw the reason for the strain he'd heard before. She hadn't bothered to hack the system. She'd simply removed the entire data storage unit.

"It was quicker this way," she told him when she noticed the disbelief on his face.

Before he could protest, she unzipped her suit and stuffed the unit inside it.

"There," she said and sounded far too satisfied. "Now, they have to retrieve my body."

"That wasn't in the plan—"

Ka gave him a double-handed finger-flip accompanied by a thrust of her hips. "Read it and weep, boss-man baby. It's the way it's gonna be."

She raised her voice and looked at Piet. "Have you made me my exit already?"

"Work, work, work," the man grumbled and scowled at her. "Tell me when to set it off."

"What," the Morgana's voice demanded coldly, "do you think you're doing?"

"Well, ma'am," Reggie answered and swaggered forward to stand in front of her. "We're getting set to ignite some explosive attached to a half-dozen Meligornian grenades, right next to a power line jampacked with nMU so we can make ourselves an exit and blow this motherfucker to Kingdom come. Why? Do you have something to say about it?"

He tapped her on the chest and flicked her faceplate when she glanced down.

Lars had never seen the Morgana speechless before. Nor had he ever seen the blood drain from her face.

"You what?" she managed in what might have been a whispered scream.

"You heard," Reggie told her and smirked. "We're gonna blow this motherfucker to Kingdom come and maybe back again."

"Do you have any idea how much energy that'll release?"

"Enough to push us all the way to the *Knight*?"

She glanced at the forward viewscreen and scowled when she found it blank. With a muttered imprecation, she looked at Todd.

"Tell them to turn it off," she ordered, and he shook his head.

Again, Reggie interrupted. "No can do, pretty lady. This shit is set to blow, which reminds me." He looked at his sergeant. "We really gotta get ready to go, boss. We have about a minute before the second charge goes and we don't want to be inside when that happens."

"You don't know the half of it!" the Morgana shrieked and connected to the four ships on the comms.

"Emil, I need everyone as close to the other side of the solar system as they can get inside the next five minutes."

"What do you—"

"Now, Emil." The compulsion in her tone rolled through everyone in earshot and she received sharp acknowledgments as the ships showed increasing distances in their HUDs.

The team and the Hooligans weren't immune either. They began to move to the far end of the command center at a run. Even Lars and Vishlog didn't hesitate and both tried to grab the Morgana as they bolted past.

She gave a low chuckle and walked to stand beside them. "Emil, we're coming home. The passenger lounge in Hangar Bay One."

"Hangar Bay One's blown to hell," he protested and her face darkened. "Go for Three," Emil told her.

"Done."

Darkness swirled around them and Lars felt momentarily pulled apart as he and everyone else was yanked out of the Teloran command center and flung into the passenger lounge of Hangar Three.

"Fire on the Teloran!" Emil's order cut through the comms as the world solidified around them. "Give it everything you have and make a run to the edge."

"Aye, captain," and "Yes, *Knight*," answered him as he turned to meet Stephanie's dazed look. "What?"

"It... She's gonna blow," the girl replied. "Oh, crap."

She'd felt the first nibble of gMU and knew the Teloran ship wasn't the only thing that would explode. Frantically, she began to cycle nMU out of her system as fast as she could eject it, not concerned about where it went.

As she did so, the world wavered.

"No," she muttered. "No, no, no, not yet."

It was hard, but she managed to keep the gates to her internal tanks closed long enough to push out the negative energy and even then, she was terrified she'd missed some. In an effort to make sure, she tried to create an nMU shield without drawing on any nMU around her.

The magic refused her call. It was like tapping an empty drum. Her knees folded and she opened the gates to her internal tanks to draw gMU in as fast as she could.

The effort left her breathless and dizzy but her pulse steadied, and she slowly became aware of an arm draped around her shoulders and her arm pulled around someone else's shoulder.

"Steph?" Lars's voice intruded. "Come on, Steph. Talk to me."

"You're an idiot and in need of a bath?"

He laughed with relief. "Go on, Todd. Finish your mission. I'll make sure she gets some rest."

"Aye." Todd's reply came in a voice rough with emotion and fatigue.

Stephanie thought she heard regret but the moment passed. She wanted to say goodbye, to reassure Todd she was okay and to reassure herself that she was okay, too, but she couldn't. She struggled to keep her eyes open, and only Lars's support kept her on her feet.

"He'll be here when you wake," he promised and helped her to the door.

He swung her into his arms when she went limp and almost regretted not making Todd stay. The man had a job to do, though, and neither of them would thank him for causing a delay.

"If anyone deserved a break," he muttered and enlisted Vishlog and Johnny to help him get Steph out of her armor and slide her into the spare bed in Elizabeth's quarters.

Johnny wrinkled his nose. "She won't thank you when she wakes up," he said.

The team leader shrugged. "She'll manage," he answered. "She always does."

"Todd should be here."

There was no answer to that, so they left her and took the cats with them. It was one thing for the big brutes to wreck her room, but neither of them wanted to see the animals as rugs if they tried the same thing in Elizabeth's quarters.

Stephanie slept, the Morgana satisfied with their victory and willing to wait for the Navy to unlock the data she needed to end the threat she'd fought for such a very long time.

"I tell you, there's something going on here that we can't see," Ka protested. "Boss, I know she's your girlfriend, but I'm worried."

Todd gave an exasperated sigh. "Guys, come on. You know Steph."

"Yeah, but we don't know this Morgana chick," Reggie replied. "Seriously, boss, no one cusses like that in any language unless they're a native speaker, and last time I looked, that wasn't Steph."

"And you all heard what Johnny said. She hasn't had time to dig into any Teloran classes, so how does she know it?"

He shrugged. "How does she know anything when she's the Morgana?"

"And that's another thing, boss. This Morgana persona. We have no idea who or what she is," Gary stated. "It's like Steph's another person when she's there."

"Or like Steph's been taken over by another person," Ka added. "It's freaky to watch."

"And that stuff she knew," Angus piped up. "All that stuff about the Ancients and fighting some great evil. That captain knew exactly what she was talking about."

"Yeah, he did. The way he reacted when she said she was the Ancient they'd buried under a mountain, he knew exactly who she meant and who she was."

"And she didn't deny it," Ka added. She gave Todd a straight look. "Boss, we don't know who the Morgana is, but she seems to know the enemy very well—and they sure as shit know her."

"So, are you asking me if I think the Morgana is with the Telorans?" he asked.

They all nodded.

"As in with the enemy," he reiterated, and they nodded again. "I'm not sure I like where you're going with this."

Ka gave him a sympathetic look and patted his shoulder. "Believe me, boss, neither do we."

CHAPTER TWENTY-FIVE

"So, what will we do about it?" Ka was the first to break the silence that followed.

Todd sank back against the wall and gestured for her to continue. "I'm not sure I'm qualified to have an opinion, here," he told them. "She's my girlfriend and that makes me more than a little biased. I know her."

"We're not talking about Stephanie, Todd. We're talking the Morgana—and from what we've seen, she's one of them."

"A Teloran?" Gary sounded a little doubtful.

"Yeah, one of them," she replied.

"Are you sure?" Angus challenged, "because she looks like an ally to me. What she did? Coming after us? Making sure we got back to the *Knight* in one piece and with the data intact?" He frowned at her. "The data is intact, isn't it? The magic didn't break it, did it?"

Ka shrugged. "I wouldn't know. I handed it to that Commander Sartre we're all so fond of."

"Speak for yourself," her teammate muttered when he recalled what had happened after they'd tried to play a practical joke on the *Knight's* Marines.

Gary caught his expression and also clearly remembered the incident. "Yeah, I wouldn't say fond so much as well-acquainted with."

"Well-acquainted, eh?" She waggled her eyebrows. "How well-acquainted?"

"That's not the point," Darren said. He'd been quiet for most of the mission and for the discussion that followed. "The point is we have a fucking Teloran in our midst. Hell, she even decides where we fight. How much do we want to trust her?"

Todd stared at him in shock, and the man gave him an apologetic smile.

"Sorry, boss. I'm playing the devil's advocate and getting these shit-for-brains asshats back on track. It's like herding cats."

He gave him a small smile. "Don't sweat it, Private. I get you."

"I sure as shit hope so," Darren replied. "The last thing I want is you mad at me. I'm over KP."

"Suck up," Gary muttered and the others snickered.

Their teammate flipped them the bird but his words had had the desired effect and they returned to the topic at hand.

"So, like the man said, let's talk about the Teloran in the room," Drusilla stated.

Gary looked around in alarm. "Where?"

Jimmy clipped him on the back of the head. "Not literally, you stupid Pommy bastard. She's sleeping."

"Steph is sleeping," Todd corrected, "Or I hope she is. She almost wrecked herself teleporting us out."

"Are you sure that was Steph and not the Morgana? Because that casts a different light on things."

"It was the Morgana," Reggie told them. "I saw her eyes. She's as scary as fuck when she's like that." He glanced at his sergeant. "No offense."

"None taken, but I'll let you in on a little secret," he answered.

They all paused and focused on him, and he pushed off the wall and leaned toward them.

"She's as scary as fuck, even when she's not all Morganaed to the max," he told them in a mock whisper.

Gary blew him a raspberry and slumped against the couch, his armor creaking. Todd leant against the wall again and smirked. Ka rolled her eyes.

"Not so funny, boss."

"Look," Reggie said into the awkward silence. "I don't know about the rest of you, but I measure a person by what they do, not where they might have come from." He jerked a thumb at Gary. "If I measured a person by where they came from, good ol' Gazza here woulda needed a long time in the slammer for what his ancestors got up to."

"Oy!"

The Australian curled his lip. "You want me to go deep into brass tacks, cobber?"

His teammate stilled and shook his head. "Nah, it's okay. We both know my ancestors were assholes with a god complex."

"And that's putting it mildly."

"Look, mate, just because I agreed with you—"

"Yeah, fair call. Anyway, the point I'm trying to make is that Steph has never steered us wrong before, whether she's been the Morgana or the Federation Witch. She's saved every life she can, and she's come apart at the seams every time she's lost someone. That's not something I see any Teloran doing."

Darren sighed. "Yup, that sums it up for me."

"Me, too," Angus added, and Gary and Jimmy nodded.

Dru sighed and high-fived Ka. "It looks like we're in agreement then," she said.

"Agreement on what?" Todd asked, glad he wasn't the only one looking confused. Gary and Reggie looked as lost as he felt.

"We don't tell the Navy what we're thinking," she said, and Gary glanced at his suit.

The Australian's face paled in alarm. "Oh, fuck. Are these things still on?"

"It wouldn't do them much good if they were," Piet's quiet assertion came from the sofa on the other side of the couch.

The spindly bomb technician leaned forward and drew a small

tower-like device from under the coffee table. "Oh, dear. I seem to have left one of my test pieces running. Should I turn it off?"

"No." Gary's response was immediate.

"Please don't." Jimmy chuckled.

"Fuck no," Reggie told him.

"Oh, man, that is gold," was Angus's contribution.

They all turned to look at Todd. "You left a what-now running in my living room?" he asked. "Does it interfere with the entertainment channel?"

"No, sir, it does not," Piet told him.

"And does it still need more testing?"

"Well, sir, now that you mention it…"

"Leave it running then." He smiled and opened his mouth to thank the man only to be interrupted by a knock at the door.

His teammate stuffed the jammer hastily under the coffee table and tucked it into the holder he'd crafted for it and attached under the table's rim.

Todd waited until he was done and settled into his seat before he crossed to the door and opened it.

Lars stood outside, his hand raised to knock again.

"Lars!" He forced a smile and gestured for Steph's chief security guard to enter.

"I stopped by to say thank you," the man told him and stepped into the room. He pretended not to notice the tension or the way they relaxed when he lied about why he'd come.

"Is she okay?" Todd asked and closed the door behind him.

"She's sleeping," Lars replied and added hastily, "but she's fine. I expect she'll have a headache and a half when she wakes up. How are things here?"

His gaze roved over them and noted the half-open battle armor and the wary looks on their faces. "Is anything the matter?"

The sergeant shook his head and the *Knight* spoke through the room's communications system and startled them all. "You have to know, Stephanie is my liege," the ship told them, and his heart sank.

The looks on his team members' faces said they'd experienced the same bad feeling. He glanced at Lars, whose lips twitched, but the *Knight* hadn't finished. "Your little toys do not work with me, Piet. I have certain...countermeasures I can use—even if they take some time to work out."

"You do?"

"I do, and when a conversation concerns me, I call those who need to know." She paused, let the knowledge sink in, and finally hammered her point home. "Lars needed to know."

The security head leaned against the door and regarded them with a serious expression.

"From what Ebony tells me, you're all concerned that Stephanie might be a Teloran, or in league with the Telorans, or with the Telorans, or something like that." He raised his hand to silence them. "She also tells me that you've decided not to pass your concerns on to the Navy and that you have chosen to trust Stephanie Morgana despite what you suspect. Is that correct?"

The Hooligans licked their lips, swallowed, and exchanged nervous glances before they nodded.

Lars waited until they were done. "Good," he said and huffed out a short breath. "So... There are some things you need to know about Stephanie and the Morgana."

Gary nudged Reggie at the way he positioned the Morgana and Stephanie as two different people. His teammate nudged him in return, but more to caution him than to agree. He saw the exchange but chose to let it pass.

"The first time Steph Morganaed on us, she was only eighteen. That whole incident with saving a woman and her child happened and she'd been hired by One R&D and we were new. She went down a side street—I forget why, now—but she did, and we were attacked by a gang hell-bent on kidnapping her."

The Hooligans sat as still as stone. Even Todd, who stood propped against the other wall, didn't move. They watched the guard and hung onto every word. Lars' eyes turned dark as he remembered what happened next.

"It was only me and Frog, that time, and we were way outnumbered. Frog suggested they leave us alone and they beat him to the draw. I shoved Stephanie one way and went the other and Frog went down."

Todd lowered his head and shook it.

Lars gave him a tight smile that vanished as quickly as it had appeared. "Steph kinda stared at him for a minute. I couldn't reach him, and she did exactly what I thought a kid would do—right up until she moved."

He paused, stared into nothing for a few seconds, and went on. "I'd never seen the like. She rolled out into the open and came to her feet and her eyes were a blaze of purple. I think I yelled for her to get down. I know I thought I would lose her."

He looked at Todd and was pinned by the man's hard blue stare.

Rather than let it faze him, he continued. "Someone moved to grab her and the next thing I knew, a pipe flew into her hand and she pitched it at him and knocked him out cold."

His chuckle was grim. "She throat-kicked the next guy and that's when it happened. Her eyes went pitch black and she picked him up by his hair and beat the living shit out of him with the pipe before she hurled him into a wall."

When his voice faded, his expression said he was in that moment when the Morgana came to town.

"She was..." He shook his head. "I'd never seen the like. She dropped the last guy with a ball of magic as the cops arrived and ran to Frog. I'd never had a principal so scared of seeing one of us die, before—and I sure as shit hadn't seen anyone do magic before. She was a wreck afterward."

"She always is," the *Knight* confirmed. "I have run the footage. Stephanie Morgana does not react well when her people are hurt."

That startled a laugh out of Lars. He sobered quickly.

"She doesn't like it when anyone is hurt...unless they're the bad guys, and then I don't think she cares. The next time she went Morgana was with the pirates. Fair enough, there were a couple of other times—once when her parents were threatened on a night out and another couple in the pods—but full, out-of-control Morgana?

That happened when she faced the pirate who'd taken the cruise ship."

The Hooligans leaned forward.

"He threatened the ship and its passengers—and then said he would start with us. She went instantly black. I'd never seen her go that dark that fast. Trust me, she's much calmer now, but then?"

He shuddered. "He was half-Meligornian and she ripped every trace of MU out of him. All of it. When she was done, he was nothing but a pile of ash and bone. She was so angry, I wasn't sure how we would ever get her back."

"And did you?" Todd asked softly.

"She came back to herself on the way to deal with the other pirates, but Johnny was shot and we lost Garma. We'd have lost Baizel, too, but Stephanie went nuts. We were lucky that time. The Morgana left once most of the pirates were gone."

"So she came back on her own?"

Lars shook his head. "For a while, we thought we'd have to deal with her going berserk in every battle, and we used to worry that there'd come a time when she'd burn herself to the ground before we could."

"And how's that supposed to be comforting?" Gary demanded.

He looked at the younger man. "Because now, she can kick the Morgana out of her head on her own."

"But not all the time," Todd noted. "Like today."

The security chief nodded. "Today proved the point. It took a couple of years but Steph did eventually get control. The first time was when a Navy captain tried to use you as leverage to get her to enlist."

"They what?"

Lars's lips thinned into a humorless smile. "Oh, yeah. Didn't she tell you that?"

Todd shook his head, but the man continued before he could speak.

"We were on a Navy station doing wave testing when the news came in about you being hurt at Sanmar's Reach. The Navy captain—"

"Which one?" the sergeant demanded and stepped forward.

He forced himself to maintain his relaxed posture. When he saw the Marine sergeant move towards him, every instinct screamed at him to run—and he refused.

"One who survived because he proved to be a very fast learner," Lars told him, "and because we reminded her of you."

Todd halted. "What?"

"We started using your name every time she went black. That day, she used it herself and brought herself back."

The two men stared at one another in silence for a moment. Lars wasn't sorry and he was damned if he'd say so. They'd done what they needed to do to keep Stephanie whole. He held the younger man's gaze until Reggie gave a sudden bark of laughter.

"You're the safe word for the fucking Witch of the Federation, Sarge?" He chortled. "Oh, man! That is so fucking funny." Everyone turned to look at him, but he seemed oblivious. "So, what do you say when you want her to stop beating on you..." He laughed harder and the next words emerged in gasps. "It's... It's Todd. Todd!"

He howled with laughter and rocked so far forward in the chair that he fell out of it.

"Todd! Todd the safeword... Bwahahaha..."

The rest of the team began to snicker, and Todd turned to Lars.

"Now see what you've done?" he asked and rolled his eyes.

Reggie now pounded the floor with his fist. "Todd...." he said and set himself off again.

"You know he's never gonna let that go, right?" Ka asked and looked at the two men. She glanced at Reggie and back again. "Like, never!"

"It's not that funny," Todd grumbled and shuffled away to slouch against the wall again.

"So," Ka began and the tone of her voice said she was tired of the shenanigans, "if she's so much in control, what happened today?"

"It was the nMU," Lars explained. "Steph basically has the Morgana locked down when she uses eMU or MU, but get her onto the negative energy, and the Morgana has more of a hold...and obviously, there's a little bad blood—"

"Wait," she interrupted, held her hand up, and looked around at the team before she focused on him. "Are you telling us that the Morgana is the spirit of some dead Teloran?"

He shrugged. "I'm not so sure she's dead—" he began.

"They dropped a fucking mountain on her!" Gary interrupted as Reggie picked himself up off the floor and settled onto the couch. "What else could she mean?"

"Nope," Darren interjected. "She only said they sought to bury her under a mountain."

Gary's jaw dropped. "You mean she really could be alive?"

"Or buried and forgotten," Lars agreed. "I can't tell from what little was said back there, but whoever or whatever the Morgana is, she has helped the Earth against enemies before."

"How long before?" Drusilla asked, catching the phrase.

"Centuries before," he informed her.

"Centuries?"

"Yeah," he agreed.

"That's a fucking long time to hang around for a world that isn't yours."

Todd checked himself in the mirror once more. His duffle bag sat on the bed behind him and his uniform felt too tight. All he wanted was to fling himself back on the bed and pretend the rest of the universe didn't exist.

He sighed. Actually, all he wanted was to not leave the *Knight* and Stephanie yet again.

But orders were orders and he shoved the thought aside, turned from the mirror, and grabbed the bag. The rest of the team were making their way to the common room as he emerged from his room.

"This sucks, hey, boss?" Ka greeted him, and he managed a smile.

"Yup." He wanted to say more but there was a lump in his throat and he needed time to nail the emotion down. It wouldn't do for one of the Navy's Marines to start weeping on the way to the airlock.

He sighed, and she turned away with a smirk.

"Don't worry, Sarge. I'm sure she'll be there to say goodbye."

Todd pressed his lips together in a firm, straight line. He didn't want to say goodbye, but he wouldn't admit that to Ka. The team was having enough fun with him as it was. He wasn't sure he would ever live down being a safe word for the universe's scariest being.

Actually, no. He was sure. He really wouldn't ever live that down.

But there are worse things to live with, he reminded himself and his mood lifted.

"Awww, he's smiling. Now, isn't that cute?" Dru's voice brought him abruptly back to reality.

Ka groaned. "Ugh. Don't remind me. Young love. It's pukeriffic."

He grinned and was still grinning when he reached the common room. The guys took one look at his face and rolled their eyes.

"Anyone woulda thought he'd gotten lucky," Gary quipped.

"Yeah, or he's glad to escape," Reggie remarked dryly.

Todd scowled at him, and Jimmy grinned.

"Now, there's the sergeant we've all come to know and love."

"Speak for yourself," the Australian retorted, and Todd crossed quickly to the door.

"Let's get this shit-show rolling," he stated briskly, yanked the door open, and stepped into the corridor.

The Hooligans followed but continued to snigger. He did his best to ignore them, held his head high and his face forward, and quick-stepped to Hangar Bay One.

Stephanie waited there, along with her team. The cats prowled the edges of the room and sniffed the window ledges as if they could smell anything through the glass or would get more than the odor of shuttle fuel and grease if they did.

She looked up as he entered and a smile lit her face. Instinctively, she started forward but remembered her place and let Captain Emil greet him.

"Sergeant Brogan," he said, "your shuttle is waiting."

Todd followed the gesture of his hand and realized it wasn't any shuttle waiting but Stephanie's private shuttle. His surprise must have shown on his face because the captain smiled.

"The Federation Witch has offered her shuttle and pilots for your journey to the *Henry Chauvel*. The honor is ours."

Firming his jaw, he cleared his throat and replied, "Thank you, Captain."

Emil stepped back and smiled slightly as he did so. "That's the end of the formalities, I think," he added and his voice made it clear it was an order and not a statement.

As soon as he was out of the way, Stephanie leapt forward, flung her arms around Todd, and pulled him close. "I wish..." she began, looked into his face, and stopped.

"I do, too," he managed to respond and stooped to wind his arms around her and take her lips with his own.

"Oooh," rose in a chorus behind him. It was followed by several catcalls and whistles as the team joined the moment.

And they weren't alone. Wolf whistles issued from behind Steph along with a few snickers as her team made their comments.

Todd felt Stephanie chuckle before she snaked her hand around his neck and kissed him harder. The Hooligans began to laugh but he lost track of them. All that mattered was the woman in his arms.

It seemed like forever and no time at all when they ended their kiss, and he didn't want to let her go. Her hand slid reluctantly from his shoulders and he sighed. They stood and simply stared into each other's eyes as his team filed past.

Their hands patted his shoulder, consolation and commiseration all in one. Stephanie's eyes shimmered even though her mouth smiled.

"I won't be gone long," he told her and the smile grew wider.

"Promises, promises."

The faint sarcasm in her voice made him laugh.

"Yeah, and you know I keep my promises."

"I know you'll try," she replied, "and that's enough."

"You are loved," he told her, using a Meligornian farewell reserved for lovers.

"As are you," she returned with the tiniest catch in her voice.

Vishlog cleared his throat and Todd looked up.

Captain Emil waited at the door, a carefully blank expression on his face.

Following Todd's glance, Stephanie returned to her place beside Lars and Vishlog. The cats settled themselves on either side of her. They leant against her, and he knew she was more upset at his departure than she looked.

He inclined his head toward her, "Ma'am," he said to pull his Marine sergeant persona into place and nail it down. It was the only armor he had for this and it was barely enough.

She returned the gesture. "Sergeant."

It was the closest they could come to saying, "I love you" in public. He hesitated and wanted to say more, but wasn't able to find the right words. He pressed his lips in a straight line, pivoted toward the door, and marched through it with the briefest of acknowledgments for Emil as he passed.

It was easier to not look back when he boarded the shuttle, and the hatch closed behind him as he sank into his seat and closed his eyes. Surprisingly enough, none of the Hooligans had anything to say. They surrounded him in silence as the shuttle lifted but after a moment, Gary punched Ka.

"What was that for?"

"You were smiling."

"No, I wasn't. I never smile. You know that."

"Do not."

"Well you should, Private."

"That's Private First Class to you."

"First Class Shit."

Todd smiled. He could be in worse company.

Stephanie watched the shuttle leave and followed the sight of its jets until it lifted out of view. With a sigh, she turned to the door and Lars and Vishlog moved silently beside her.

As she reached it, Emil raised a hand to the side of his head and listened. She waited. Something had come through and she'd need to hear whatever it was.

"V'ritan's on the shuttle. As soon as the Navy leaves, he'll be on his way," the captain informed her as soon when the call finished.

She sighed and returned to her place at the door. Bumblebee huffed impatiently and flopped beside her.

"And Brenden says the Navy doesn't need them to run the data to the *Cathay Williams.* He said they had alternative plans and he'd explain when he returned."

"How long?" she asked and he gave her a puzzled look.

"For what?"

"For them to get to Earth."

"With translation…a week, maybe two. Three, if they take their time."

Stephanie shook her head. "They won't take their time. They need the data."

The stars beyond the hangar were obscured when her shuttle returned and again as the hangar bay closed. Brenden and Avery disembarked and strode quickly across the hangar to the passenger lounge. Neither of them looked happy.

"What went wrong?" she asked, and Brenden shook his head.

"Nothing went wrong, but the Navy is in an awful hurry. The *Chauvel* won't transfer the data until they reach sub-space."

"That wasn't the deal."

"I told them that and reminded them of the risk of having all the data on one ship only." He pressed his lips together and scowled at the memory. "They told me they had their orders." His face lightened. "Your Todd had something to say, too, but they told him their orders outranked his and he was to stand down."

She blushed. "And did he?"

"When they brought the second squad of Marines into the hangar and he knew the Hooligans wouldn't be able to fight their way out of it, he did."

Her mouth hung open. "I thought Captain—

"The captain wasn't happy either, but he had an intelligence officer on either side of him and I don't think he had much of a choice. Those Marines didn't answer to him."

"Fuck me," Johnny murmured quietly. "The X-Men."

"X-Men?"

"They have these secret squads—a separate set of Marines inside the Marines. They only answer to Intelligence and they're supposed to be a rumor." He cast a haunted glance at his team leader. "But we know they're not."

Stephanie's face hardened. "And now I do too."

She glared at them both. "You should have told me about them earlier."

Lars sighed and his voice sounded tired when he answered. "It's been a long time, Steph. We'd put them behind us."

"And have they put you behind them?"

His expression became granite. "They'd better have."

"I don't like that they're so close," Johnny observed.

"Is Todd in danger?" She looked from one man to the other.

Johnny chuckled. "Oh, no. Right now, he's the safest man in the universe and so's his team. Those boys won't let anything happen to him."

"And my mages?"

"No. As long as they do as they're asked, they'll be fine." Lars placed a hand on her shoulder. "That, and we can get them back."

She glared at him. "That is not comforting, Lars."

He flashed her a grin. "It's okay, Steph. It really is. The Navy's taking precautions, is all."

Stephanie caught the look that passed between him and Johnny and made a note to have a long and involved talk with the *Knight* and Elizabeth later. Again, Emil's head lowered as he listened to his comms. She turned to him and waited until he was done.

"What is it?" she snapped as the alarm activated to signal an incoming ship. Orange lights strobed and the personnel working in the hangar bay walked quickly to the exits. As the airlocks cycled, the lights went from orange to red and the hangar bay doors began to open.

"V'ritan is here," Emil informed her a moment before the *Ghargilum's* shuttle slipped into the hangar and set down beside hers.

"The Navy's gone?" she asked, heard the quaver in her voice, and cleared her throat to erase it. "That was quick."

He nodded. "They moved to minimum translation distance and were gone."

Johnny whistled. "That is in a hurry. They usually don't let anyone know when something's that important."

"What? You expected them to dock at Alerus and spend a rotation on shore leave?"

"That is the standard procedure," he confirmed.

"Well, I'm glad they didn't," Stephanie declared, "or I would have words with them."

Lars smiled. "That would be why they left so quickly. No one wants to talk to a hungover Morgana."

"I haven't had anything to drink, let alone too much, and the Morgana isn't here right now."

He raised his eyebrows. "How do you know? Has she ever given you any warning before?"

Stephanie's scowl returned. "You are not helping."

The hangar lights went from red to amber and flashed green before they settled to white. As the workers returned, the door to V'ritan's shuttle opened and his guard emerged. They marched down the stairs and four of them peeled away to investigate the hangar's farthest corners.

"Where are the Marines?" she asked as she watched the Guardsmen.

"They're having a nap," the *Knight* informed her, then added, "It is an unscheduled nap and Captains Sartre and Moser will be most unimpressed when they wake."

She could only imagine what would result. There would be questions and accusations. "We're hired to provide the *Knight* with security. How can we do that if you knock us out for your own convenience? You have to learn to trust us."

Yeah, that was a conversation she wasn't looking forward to. How would she tell them she did trust them and that it was the Navy she wasn't so sure of?

She watched as the *Ghargilum's* Guard returned to those waiting beside the shuttle and reported to their leader. At least, she thought it was their leader. If she had to go by hats, his was the fanciest and his armor wasn't bad either.

Once his subordinates had given him the all-clear, he trotted through the shuttle hatch. V'ritan and his new bodyguard emerged shortly after, with the Guard captain at their back. She stepped closer to Emil and offered him her arm.

"I believe it's time we greeted our guest, Captain."

He smiled and tucked her arm through his own as they left the passenger lounge. "Indeed."

V'ritan's face lit up as soon as they stepped out to greet him. His guard tensed at the sight of her guards and the cats.

"Vishlog!" Stephanie warned but it was too late.

The two big felines bounded toward the *Afreghil's* Guard, mischief in every bounce.

"Fuck," Lars muttered as he and Vishlog hurried forward to intercept them. Bumblebee saw him approach and tossed his head. "Come on, Bee." He stretched his hand toward the animal's harness.

The black-and-yellow feline let his fingertips brush the leather before he darted sideways out of reach and pranced closer to the guards. Zeekat slipped between Vishlog's legs and the big Dreth sprawled.

The animal's victory dance reminded Lars of laughter, but he felt like doing anything but that as the furry troublemaker trotted to the nearest guard.

"Stand fast!" V'ritan's order cracked across the hangar and both cats froze, their heads up and ears pricked. The guards snapped to attention and tried to track the felines' without moving their heads.

Zeekat sidled closer and nuzzled the closest guard's hand, and a shudder rippled through the Meligornian's body. He pressed his lips together and clenched his fists as he held his arms rigidly at his sides.

Lars could only imagine how much effort it took for him not to draw his sidearm. It was a relief when V'ritan murmured something short and sharp to his escort and hurried down the stairs. If anything, his presence only made the guard tenser.

"Bee! Zeekat!" Stephanie's voice rang across the hangar but they ignored her.

"Bumblebee," V'ritan rumbled, his voice full of command as he extended his hand. "Brilgus sends greetings."

At the sound of Brilgus's name, both cats turned to the *Ghargilum Afreghil*. Every guards' hand moved to the butt of their sidearms, only to still when their captain rapped a single order.

"Sit!" V'ritan commanded and ignored Frog's horrified whisper.

"But they're not dogs."

"They don't know that," Stephanie whispered in response.

"Are you sure?"

"Yup. See?"

Frog looked at where the animals had seated themselves before the *Ghargilum,* their tails wrapped neatly around their forepaws. "That never works for me."

She chuckled and she and Captain Emil walked forward to stand before V'ritan. He looked up from where he rubbed both cats' heads. They crunched happily on something he'd offered them with his other hand.

"Brilgus sent treats," he explained and stepped around them so he could bow.

Stephanie was mortified. "*Ghargilum,* wait!"

He laughed as she returned his bow quickly and made sure to bow lower than he had.

"Why, Master Morgana?" He touched his fingers to his brow and heart and extended a fist for her to touch knuckles with. "We are both defenders of the Empire. I don't believe our ranks are any different."

She inhaled sharply. "You honor me."

"I believe you have honored me. I am greatly intrigued as to what requires such secrecy that you would forego the protection of your Marines."

His words acted like a trigger and his guards surveyed the hangar and frowned as they registered the truth of his words. When they realized there really were no Marines, they looked puzzled but studied her bodyguards.

Stephanie smiled. "I'm protected well enough without them."

"If you would follow me," Captain Emil interrupted and led them from the hangar to the *Knight's* observation deck.

"I thought we would go to the command center," she said and he smiled.

"This is something you need to see in the flesh, so to speak." He arranged them in front of the shuttered windows and tapped his mic. "*Knight*, if you could open the deck."

"Certainly, Captain."

"I have checked ahead. The skies are clear for translation," he explained while the guard exchanged nervous glances, and V'ritan's bodyguard measured the distance to the door with his gaze.

Once the shutters had opened to give them a view of the stars, Emil spoke again, "Mister Wattlebird, if you please."

"Aye aye, captain."

The stars melted and bled into the dark to vanish and be replaced by a new set that shimmered and winked into place. They weren't what held their attention, though.

"What the fuck is that?" Frog demanded, and Lars placed a hand on Stephanie's shoulder as T'revan did the same to V'ritan.

"Emil?" she demanded and resisted the drag of her guard's grasp.

The captain laughed. "May I introduce the *Tempestarii*? Captain, we are on approach."

The voice that replied was of an older female but clipped and precise with about as much no-nonsense as Stephanie would expect from Elizabeth.

"So your pilot informs me. I have informed him he is to park your craft—sedately—in Hangar Bay One. There will be no shenanigans."

"Yes, ma'am. May I introduce Stephanie Morgana?" Captain Emil activated a viewscreen at the end of the room.

The woman who appeared wore an eyepatch that reminded Stephanie of a pirate. That was as far as the pirate theme went, though. The captain was the oldest she'd ever seen, with short, pepper-white hair that clung to her head in waves and stood clear of her face.

The eye that was visible was dark and piercing and reminded her of a hawk. She suppressed a shiver. The woman she faced had seen combat and the darker side of life. The lines on her face made her wonder what other marks her experiences had left.

She pushed the thought away. E would have known what she was doing when she hired her.

"It is nice to meet you, Miss Morgana," she said by way of greeting.

"And you, Captain..."

"Rawlins," she replied. "Marianne Rawlins."

"Captain Rawlins."

The woman favored her with a quick, tight smile. "I'll see you when you come aboard," she advised and cut the link.

Stephanie looked at Emil. "Is she always like that?"

He nodded. "Yes. You'll get used to it."

She moved closer to the window. "What is this?"

"This is the *Tempestarii*," he informed her. "Elizabeth said to tell you it would be BURT's new home."

She and V'ritan turned to him, their mouths open in surprise.

"This?" She tilted her head and studied it with narrowed eyes. "Is she sure it's big enough?"

He opened his mouth to reply but registered the sarcasm in her voice.

"She hopes so," he replied and did his best to keep a straight face.

"Are you sure someone's not overcompensating?"

"I'll let you ask them that."

"Man, and I thought that Teloran super-dreadnought was a big ship," Brenden observed. "This is beautiful."

Avery gave a single jerky nod, his eyes as wide as saucers. "How do you fly something like it?" he murmured.

Emil shot him a look of alarm. "Don't go there. Don't suggest it. Don't even glance at the piloting console. Just...don't. I'll be surprised if Wattlebird gets anywhere near its command deck."

"Yeah? Well, that's not a surprise."

"I think I might have size envy," V'ritan grumbled and the captain responded with a short laugh.

"Watch this." He pointed at the huge ship and nudged his mic. "Wattlebird, take her in."

"Take her in?" Avery sounded alarmed. "In where?"

"There!" Garach had remained silent for most of the conversation but he spoke now, raised his hand, and pointed at the monstrous ship. "See?"

"Oh, we're surely not..." V'ritan began, his eyes shining with excitement.

"Why not?" Stephanie challenged. "You've had the *Knight* in the *King's Warrior's* hold at least twice."

"Both times, I think we pulled her in. She didn't fly in."

"Well, she'll fly in this time," Emil told him smugly and a quiet smile lit his features as the *Knight* drew closer.

"Unbelievable," T'revan murmured, and V'ritan cast him a look of surprise. "She's beautiful."

"I didn't think you liked ships, T'revan."

"This isn't a ship," he replied. "It's a very small planet. It could be a home for thousands."

Stephanie swallowed. "It could."

He glanced at her and looked slightly disappointed. "But it isn't, is it?"

"I don't think so."

"Has it a hydroponics section? A garden?"

She shrugged and softened her reply with a smile. "I don't know. This is the first time I've seen it."

He raised his eyebrows. "So this is a surprise for you, too?"

"I guess so." She turned to the glass to avoid further questions.

"It's good to have you back safe and sound," Elizabeth said and held Stephanie at arm's length.

She glanced at V'ritan and touched her fingertips to her forehead and heart before she formed a fist over her heart. "Thank you."

"I didn't do anything," he protested and responded with a hand over his heart.

"You were there, were you not?" she snapped.

"Well, yes—"

"And you put your ship and crew at risk to make sure she did what she needed to do. Correct?"

"Yes, but—" he began and she held her hand up.

"Then thank you is not too much to say. Without you, her risk would have been greater and she might have overtaxed herself to accomplish what needed to be done."

"I…" the *Garghilum Afreghil* said tentatively but T'revan nudged him and he sighed. "You're very welcome."

Elizabeth smiled briefly at him. "There! That wasn't so hard, was it?"

"You have no idea," he grumbled, and she gave a bark of laughter.

"I believe I do." Her smile faded. "What I want to know is if she's okay."

"How do you mean?"

"Yes, Elizabeth, how do you mean?" Stephanie added, her eyes narrowed. She was becoming tired of being talked about as though she wasn't there.

E took Stephanie's jaw between her forefinger and thumb. "I mean you, you irresponsible brat. Is she well enough to wield magic or does she need a rest, is she eating properly, and did she remember to change her underwear when she woke up this morning—or did she leave her knickers on her bedroom floor right beside her manners?" She smirked at her horrified expression. "Was that specific enough?"

Before the girl could find an answer, V'ritan cleared his throat. "I believe I can answer the first question. As to the other two, I have no idea."

"And?" Elizabeth asked and tapped her foot impatiently.

V'ritan took one look at her face and decided he might have pushed her far enough. "She needs at least two days' rest," he replied and fixed Stephanie with a firm glare. "That means no magic," he told her sternly. "Not even in the pods. I don't know what you did on the Teloran ship but the healers tell me you ran yourself dry and singed some nerve endings. They need to rest."

"Ugh!" She rolled her eyes. "Okay, I'll rest. No magic for two days."

She glanced at the team. "And you said that where the boys could hear it, so I'm doubly screwed. I couldn't do any magic if I wanted to."

Frog, Marcus, Brenden, Avery, and Johnny all folded their arms and nodded, their lips pressed together as they watched her carefully.

"See?" she pointed out. "They're already conspiring on how to keep me too busy to try."

Again, the team nodded in unison, even Garach, and their expressions were almost identical.

V'ritan shuddered. "That… That is eerie," he observed and she nodded.

"So I've been told." She was about to ask Elizabeth about seeing the rest of the ship when there was a quiet knock at the door.

The Guard turned as one, and the team stepped back to give them a clear line of fire. Elizabeth raised an eyebrow and pressed the intercom on the table. "Who is it?"

"It's Mr. Brilgus, ma'am. He says you asked him to attend, but I…I have no record."

"That's fine, Dianne. I did ask him but he had something else to deal with first."

"Thank you, ma'am." The door opened as the woman's disapproving tones faded. Elizabeth shrugged. "She's new and we're still working things out."

"Is she one of your guards?"

"In a way," she answered but didn't elaborate. Instead, she stepped around Stephanie to greet Brilgus with an Earth-style hug.

Stephanie and V'ritan watched wide-eyed and the guardsmen looked shocked. The Standard Bearer caught their expressions and sighed.

"Captain, you and your men will need to liaise with my security detail and ask them about some of the Earth greeting traditions between friends."

"Yes, sir."

The look on the guard captain's face said he knew something about Earth greeting traditions and they had somehow contradicted his understanding. Brilgus ignored it and knelt beside Bumblebee.

"And how is my good kitty?" he asked and scratched the big cat around the ears and along the jawline. "Is he being treated well?"

Frog snorted, but the man continued and stretched his hand to Zeekat.

"And have you boys been working hard? Do you deserve a treat?"

Elizabeth rested her head against the side of her forefinger and covered her eyes with the palm of her hand. V'ritan folded his arms and leaned towards Stephanie, "Is he always like this?"

"You should know," E retorted.

The guards looked mortified to see one of their elite cooing in public over two oversized cats who looked like they could tear his throat out if they had half a mind to do so.

"And did the mean lady take you into battle again?" Brilgus asked with exaggerated sympathy, his eyes alight with pleasure as one of the cats began to purr.

Stephanie folded her arms and tapped her foot. "The 'mean lady' is right here, you know."

He looked at her, rose slowly to his feet, and dusted his hands against his trousers.

"Why, so she is. I didn't see you there, Stephanie." Laughter danced over his expression as he sketched her a Meligornian greeting.

"*Kaitel gorniffula,*" she told him, bowed in return, and slid her arms around him.

Brilgus blushed and waved hastily at his guard as they stepped in to intervene. "The Witch and I are old, old friends," he explained and they settled uneasily into their places.

"Shall we?" Ms. E asked and they nodded eagerly.

She caught sight of the guards and frowned. "I have to limit you to two guards apiece. You, too, Steph. I'm sure you understand."

"Four," Steph retorted when she noted how the guard captain tensed, "and the same for V'ritan and Brilgus."

Elizabeth regarded her with a long, careful stare. "Fine," she snapped. "Four."

Stephanie and V'ritan breathed a sigh of relief.

"The rest can wait in the staff commons."

Some of the guards bristled at that, but the *Garghilum Afreghil* agreed. "So, we'll return after?"

"I can have someone guide them through the dining hall and the guest spaces if you'd prefer," Elizabeth added, and the captain of the guard became suddenly attentive.

"I would prefer that if it's no trouble," he told her. "We need to ensure—" He stopped as though realizing that admitting they'd be checking V'ritan's quarters were safe might be an insult.

She chuckled. "I'll have my people take you through."

"And mine," Lars interrupted. He cast V'ritan's captain a sly look. "Our duties are much the same."

"Even on her own ship?" the captain asked and immediately closed his mouth with a snap as though the question had slipped out before he'd had time to censor it.

He nodded. "I assume no space is safe until I've made sure it is. Surely you do the same?"

The man colored. "Of course," he stated, and V'ritan knew he could expect to be left waiting at the door to his quarters when they returned to the *King's Warrior*—and that it would become a regular thing.

He sighed, and Lars ducked his head.

Elizabeth stepped in. "This way," she commanded and led the way into the reception. She indicated a glassed-in area that looked like a small café. "If your men would wait there," she ordered and her gaze shifted from Lars to the captain.

V'ritan, Stephanie, and Brilgus waited as their troops were settled under Elizabeth's watchful eye.

"You're all a pain in the ass," she told them. "We could have been halfway through the tour by now if you'd act like normal people and ditch your entourages."

V'ritan gave a startled laugh and Brilgus chuckled. Stephanie rolled her eyes. "I wish I was normal."

Lars snorted, and Vishlog snickered. She stared at them.

"Go ahead. Spit it out."

Her security chief smirked at her. "Are you sure you want us to do that?"

She eyed him warily. "Hmmm. Maybe not."

Elizabeth snickered and led them into the ship. "Welcome to the *Tempestarii,*" she began. "We're on the lower admin and guest deck. It's closest to the hangars and means we can restrict movement throughout the ship."

Her face darkened momentarily as though she remembered something. She shook it off quickly and took them along the corridor to the elevator. They followed a circuitous route and stopped at the engine room, the life support systems section, the data centers, and the crew's rec room before they headed to the weapons section.

"This ship has guns?" V'ritan asked.

She looked surprised. "And yours doesn't?"

"Hmmm. Point taken." He looked around him. "But I don't recall seeing any of these on the *Knight.*"

E gave him a secretive smile. "You won't. The *Knight* doesn't have the power to run any of these alongside the ones she has."

"But you have multiples."

"Yes. Yes, we do." She did not elaborate but led them past the weapons arrays.

Several technicians looked up from around one of the new weapons. They had its casing off but when they saw Elizabeth and her entourage, they moved to shield what was inside.

"Was that MU?" V'ritan took a step towards it and the leading technician's hands tightened into fists.

Ms. E stepped between them. "Stand down, boys. This is the *Ghargilum Afreghil.* He is a friend of ours."

"The same way the Navy are our friends?" the man asked as his gaze took V'ritan's measure and shifted to assess his guards.

"No," she told him. "He is the kind of friend who won't insist we share our secrets unless we're ready to, and the Meligornians are helping us."

He gave the visitor another careful scrutiny before he stepped aside so he could see what they were working on. V'ritan stepped forward and stared past the technicians working on the weapon. Even with the presence of MU, he couldn't make head or tail of what he was saw.

"Well," he said after a long moment's consideration, "it looks very interesting."

Stephanie smirked and he frowned at her.

"What do you think, Stephanie?"

Her eyebrows raised in surprise and she glanced at the inside of the gun. "Yes," she said decisively. "It's definitely interesting."

The gun crew chuckled and returned to their work. Elizabeth sighed.

"Honestly. I can't take you anywhere," she grumbled and Lars snorted.

"Yeah, you can," he told her, "but if you do, you're gonna have to take them twice."

"Twice?" V'ritan asked.

"The second time's to apologize," the man explained as they left the weapons section.

Stephanie had barely stepped out the door when there was a startled shout from behind them.

"Hey! Give that back!"

She whipped around. "Don't tell me..." she began but her question was answered when a yellow-and-black blur raced past her. Only Vishlog's hasty grab stopped her from falling when Bumblebee shouldered her out of the way.

The big cat did not stop or slow down.

"Of all the smart-assed, ill-timed, shit-stirring, fur-brained—" she sputtered as the Dreth set her back on her feet. "Where's the other one?"

As she turned to see where the cat had gone, she put herself in the path of the two technicians in pursuit. One of them collided with her and they skidded to an awkward halt. From the look on his face, he was torn between apologizing and cursing her for being in the way.

"I'm sorry," he managed. "I, uh…"

He gestured helplessly in the direction the feline had gone in. His partner wasn't so reticent.

"It took our equipment," he explained and edged forward as though he intended to try to squeeze past her.

Stephanie stepped aside to let them pass. She looked at Elizabeth and prepared to excuse herself from the tour, but before she could say anything, Vishlog stepped forward, his hand clenched around Zeekat's leash.

"I will fetch Bumblebee," he told her. "It is my fault for not leashing their harnesses."

"And I will help," Brilgus added. He followed the Dreth out the door and took Zee with him before anyone could protest. His guards followed. "I have taken the tour before."

Elizabeth glanced at V'ritan and Stephanie. "Is it my perfume?" she asked.

They shook their heads and the *Garghilum Afreghil* patted her on the shoulder. "You will have to forgive Brilgus," he advised her. "Only battle is more important than the cats."

A couple of his guards seemed surprised by the admission, but one of the others simply shook his head.

"I should have known," E grumbled. "Well, let's get the tour over with before the rest of you find an excuse to slip away."

V'ritan and Stephanie exchanged glances and followed. Shouts and growls drifted up the corridor and the Meligornian snickered. Elizabeth gave a heavy sigh and continued.

"Down this way," she told Stephanie, "we have the main computer section."

As Elizabeth took Stephanie and V'ritan to see the reason the ship had been built, Vishlog and Brilgus took a tour of their own. Bumblebee didn't slow. He raced down the corridor with a small pouch of tools dangling from his jaws.

News of his mischief must have traveled because the door to a second array of guns opened and five more technicians stepped out. They looked both up and down the corridor and their faces lit with intent when they saw him.

Bumblebee growled and summoned a burst of speed. He noticed the long metal object in one of the crewmen's hands.

His ears pricked and he bounced sideways but watched them pivot to face the new direction. With a growl of delight, the feline continued to race along the line they expected him to. At the last moment, he vaulted high in the air, thumped his forepaws into the wall, and twisted his body to change direction.

Using his hind paws to provide propulsion, he arced over their heads and landed smoothly on the other side. With a muffled yowl of victory, he sprayed them like he was marking territory and bounded away.

Vishlog caught a whiff of Bumblebee's victory dance and groaned. "That cat will be the death of me," he grumbled.

Beside him, Brilgus sniffed the air. "Did he—"

"Yes," the Dreth replied. "Stephanie and Elizabeth will not be happy."

"Your crewmen are not happy, either," the Meligornian observed as they drew closer to the five men.

"They are not my crewmen," Vishlog argued as they reached the five men, who had frozen in their tracks.

"Is that your monster?" one of them demanded, looked at Vishlog, and noticed Zeekat.

The Dreth glanced at Bumblebee's disappearing form and shook his head. "No. That tark-loving Tegortha-be-damned furball belongs to Stephanie Morgana and I'm trying to get him back."

They looked from Vishlog to Brilgus and relaxed a little when the Meligornian nodded.

"Do you want help?" one of them asked and looked at his befouled uniform. "It's only that..."

He didn't have to finish the thought. If Vishlog were in his shoes, he'd want to get changed too.

"We can handle it," he reassured the man. He held Zeekat's leash up. "This one will help me."

"And me," Brilgus reminded him. "I will help, too."

"Well, if you're sure..."

The Dreth gave them his most solemn nod. "I am sure."

They didn't press the issue but hurried away down the corridor.

"You know it'll never come out," Brilgus told him.

Vishlog wrinkled his nose. "I will make sure their uniforms are replaced. After all, I was the one who did not watch him carefully enough."

"I think you put the wrong one on the leash," his companion observed, and the large warrior shrugged.

"It would not have mattered which one of them was off the leash. That would have been the one to find mischief."

He unzipped a pouch at his belt. "Fortunately..." He felt inside it and Brilgus heard the rustle of plastic. Zeekat heard it too, and the big cat's ears pricked.

The animal made a curious chirping mew and rubbed his head against Vishlog's thigh. The Dreth laughed and dropped his hand to the cat's head.

"Yes, you are a good kitty," he told him and pulled out a piece of dried meat which Zeekat nibbled from his hand. "You can have a treat."

The black-and-white cat made short work of the meat delicacy and nudged his hand for more.

"Oh no." He laughed. "No more treats until Bumblebee is here."

Zeekat froze.

"Get Bumblebee," he ordered and held up another piece of jerky. "Do you want this? Get Bee."

The feline glanced down the corridor, then at him.

"Bumblebee," he repeated, and the animal laid his ears back.

He put the treat in the bag.

Zeekat cocked his head.

Vishlog secured the flap of the pouch with the treats inside it. Patting the top, he looked at the cat.

"Bumblebee," he told him. "You will have treats when I have Bumblebee."

He held the black-and-yellow cat's empty leash up. "Treat," he told him.

Zeekat glanced down the corridor and sniffed the air, sneezed, and trotted in the direction the other cat had taken. They'd barely gone four paces when the sound of shattering crockery and a shriek of dismay and shout of outrage reached them.

"Oh no." The Dreth groaned.

"That does not sound good," Brilgus observed.

"No," he agreed. A growl of protest and the clang of metal followed. "No, it does not."

Bumblebee roared and something large and metallic toppled with a crash. Zeekat jerked the leash out of Vishlog's hand and raced down the corridor toward it, turned a corner, and vanished from sight.

"I sincerely hope Elizabeth briefed the crew about the cats," he shouted as he bolted after him.

"She was going to," Brilgus replied, "but I wasn't there for it."

The warrior took the corner as fast as he could and almost lost traction as he turned. Brilgus bounced into the wall behind him and used it to catapult himself ahead.

"Show off," the Dreth muttered, scrambled to find his footing, and tried to catch up.

They reached the open door to the mess hall and were through before they registered the carnage on the other side. A serving cart lay on its side and Bumblebee stood on top of it, the tool pouch in his mouth as he growled a challenge.

Two servers were crouched in combat positions. One held an upraised ladle and a pot lid, and the other a tablecloth stretched between his hands like a net. The furry fugitive looked from one to the other, obviously torn between dropping the tool pouch and knocking them on their asses or holding onto the tool pouch and continuing the chase.

He stepped off the cart and sidled to put it between himself and Zeekat, who now stalked him across the mess hall. When the two pursuers entered, the black-and-yellow cat raised his head and growled.

"Are these beasts yours?" demanded the waiter with the ladle and pot lid.

"They belong to the Witch," Vishlog told them.

"And what? You're here to take them away?" the one with the tablecloth asked in a surly manner. "I don't suppose you'll hang around long enough to help us clear this mess up after you catch them, then?"

He shook his head. "My hands will unfortunately be full."

"A likely story," the ladle-holder snapped as Zeekat bounded forward and tried to snatch the tool pouch from Bumblebee's mouth.

His forepaws struck the side of the metal cart and his hind paws landed on plates of spilled food. The crockery skidded in two different directions, the cart slid in a third, and Bumblebee leapt high in the air.

Zeekat careened toward him and all four paws fought for traction as his body twisted in an attempt to regain his balance. His purple eyes went wide and sought Vishlog for help. He landed on his side and Brilgus winced.

"Oof. That would have hurt."

"Tell me that was recorded," the Dreth demanded and the two waitstaff nodded.

The one with the tablecloth threw it over Zeekat as he struggled to get to his feet and Bumblebee came to a decision. He vaulted high, pivoted, and bolted to the kitchens.

"No!" one of the waiters shouted in alarm. The saucepan lid and ladle went flying as she flung herself at the cat. "You can't go in there."

She managed to wind her arms around his hindquarters but

couldn't get a strong enough hold to stop him from escaping. When she fell with a resounding thud, she lay there while Zeekat rolled to his feet and raced after his black-and-yellow counterpart.

"If you want to eat tonight," the man who'd held the tablecloth told them, "you'll need to stop them."

The Dreth raised his fingers to his lips and gave a sharp whistle. At the same time, he hauled the treat bag out of its pouch and shook it. Both cats attempted to stop. Bumblebee ran into a wall, and Zeekat ran into Bee.

He didn't let the shock of the collision stop him from trying to snatch the tool bag. The black-and-yellow cat jerked his head around in time to whisk the bag out of Zee's reach. The movement put him off balance and he flopped onto his side. It also put Zee off his aim and his teeth closed on the shoulder strap to Bumblebee's harness.

This might have been the end of it if the kitchen door hadn't thrust open and knocked Zeekat off his feet. He refused to let go of his companion's harness and pulled the other cat over as he fell, although that wasn't the worst of it.

That occurred when the *Tempestarii's* head chef emerged, demanded to know what the ruckus was about, and stepped on Zeekat's tail. The feline yowled, leapt abruptly into the air, and yanked his tail out from under the chef's foot.

It jerked the man off balance, and he fell backward. The disgruntled feline bolted toward the Dreth, and Bumblebee found his feet and hurtled toward the door. Brilgus and Vishlog had the same idea at the same time. They both made a running dive at the fugitive as the door opened and the technicians from the first line of guns came into the room.

Bumblebee spun away and almost turned himself inside out. His two keepers pounded into each other and their heads connected hard enough for them to see stars, and the chef pushed to his feet with a groan.

The female waiter reached him and offered him her support. Her male counterpart joined them and together, they surveyed the wreckage of the dining space they'd been preparing for Stephanie and V'ritan's visit.

On the opposite side of the room, Vishlog had managed to loop his hand through Bumblebee's harness as he went over, and Zeekat had come to join them. At first, it looked like the big cat had decided to be sociable, but he nipped the treat bag out of Vishlog's fingers and emptied it in front of Bumblebee.

Before the horned cat could scoop the treats up in one quick mouthful, Zee slapped his paw on the pile and uttered a short, commanding mrreow.

Bumblebee responded in kind and the two locked gazes. The Dreth groaned and they came to a sudden understanding. Zeekat dragged half the pile out from under his companion's nose and settled into a flat-bellied crouch to enjoy it.

The fugitive wrapped a possessive paw around the remainder of the treat pile and delicately lifted one sliver off the top. He shifted his gaze to include Vishlog and chewed with great enjoyment.

One of the technicians wandered over and retrieved the dropped bag of tools. "I'll have that."

Bee acted as though he wasn't there. Zeekat twitched his tail. Neither feline moved until Vishlog groaned a second time and they both gave him an uncertain look. Brilgus twitched.

The Dreth rolled onto his side and discovered his hand was still stuck inside the harness. He glared at the cat. "Got you."

Bumblebee snorted and picked up another piece of jerky. He turned his head so Vishlog could watch as he pulled the treat into his mouth and started to chew.

"I've still got you," he mumbled and squinted as someone came to stand over him.

"Thanks for catching him."

It took a moment for him to bring the man's face into focus. The technician held the tool pouch up. "We got the tools back."

He raised his free hand and gave the guy a thumbs up. "Happy to help," he managed.

The world swayed as the man moved away, and the warrior closed his eyes. When he opened them again, the technician had morphed into a narrowly built man with long dark hair. He was flanked by his wait staff.

"You!" the man snapped and glared at him. "You're on KP for a week—and those are banned from the dining hall and the kitchen."

A rasping laugh drew his attention and Vishlog turned his head. The motion made his head spin and he closed his eyes momentarily. When he opened them again, the man bent over him.

Vishlog swung—or he tried to. His hand was still stuck in Bumblebee's harness. The guy got the message and took a few steps back.

"Take it easy." He frowned. "Who are you, anyway? I don't remember being told we had another Dreth on board." He let his gaze drift over Bumblebee and Zeekat. "Or two cats." His eyes narrowed. "When did you come aboard?"

The laugh came again and Brilgus's voice rasped, "He's with the Witch."

Vishlog turned to look at the Meligornian. Brilgus had a guard on either side of him and was seated propped against a wall.

"You have a hard head," he said when he caught the Dreth staring at him.

"I'm Dreth," he muttered. "It comes with the territory. What's your excuse?"

"Meligornian," Brilgus retorted. "Dreth don't have the patent on hard heads."

He was still trying to think of an answer to that when the skinny man spoke again.

"Dreth, Meligornian, I don't care. Your forgiveness," he said to Brilgus, "but we are preparing for a function and now we are behind." He didn't sound penitent in the least. "You need to leave and come back at the appointed time."

The warrior finally managed to sit and the ship spun about him. It steadied after a moment and he attached Bumblebee's leash to his harness before he freed his hand. Zeekat saw him coming and slipped out of reach.

He groaned. "Don't make me come over there," he began as the cat inched toward the kitchen door.

The skinny man made an impatient sound and snagged the trailing leash as the cat tried to slink past.

"Witch's cat, are you?"

The feline twisted and swiped his ankles out from under him. He hissed at the two waiters as the chef landed, stalked around them, and jerked the leash from his hand. The waiters watched him pass but didn't try to intercept him.

He'd almost reached the kitchen door when his feet left the floor and he spun to the ceiling. The chef scrambled to his feet.

"Young lady, if he—" He stopped. "I beg your pardon, Miss…" He paused, lost for words.

"If he what?" Stephanie prompted.

The chef cleared his throat. "If he's sick…"

Zeekat stopped spinning and rolled carefully onto his stomach. He extended his claws as if that would create something for them to grab hold of and froze when he realized there was nothing beneath him.

A small mew of distress escaped him, and he looked at Stephanie in alarm.

"And you were doing so well," she told him, "until you knocked this poor man on his ass."

"Well, now that's settled," the chef snapped, "this poor man will return to his kitchen to finish preparing your meal. If you don't mind…"

He sketched a hand at the devastation of the dining hall, executed an abrupt about-face, and strode out of the room. Seconds later, the violent clatter of pots and pans could be heard.

The waitstaff winced and moved to right their toppled food cart. Stephanie waved her hand and set it upright. "Frog, Marcus, can you come to the dining hall and help them set up?"

"Sure thing, Steph," Marcus replied.

In the background, they could hear Frog muttering, "Froggie clean the dining hall. Froggie clean the cat's mess…"

CHAPTER TWENTY-SIX

S tephanie floated the cats—and Vishlog—out of the dining hall. Brilgus declined the offer, and his guards breathed a sigh of relief.

V'ritan soothed the chef's ruffled feathers and his guards guided the man to the kitchen again and promised him the dining hall would be returned to order before the meal. The rest of the evening went without a hitch.

The *Garghilum Afreghil* was still laughing about it when Stephanie escorted him to the shuttle the next morning. "I'd call it a meeting of minds, but it truly wasn't." He chuckled and glanced at Brilgus, who followed more slowly. The Standard Bearer's face was pale, and his pupils were still wide.

"Will he be all right?" she asked, and he gave her a comforting smile.

"The healers are on stand-by for when we reach the *King's Warrior.*" He turned and clasped her hands in his own. "Thank you for inviting us on this endeavor. I wouldn't have missed it for all the worlds between us."

"Or around us," Brilgus added to finish the Meligornian saying in a tired voice.

When she looked at him, he gave her a weary smile. "Who knew pets could be so much trouble?"

"These are more trouble than most," she informed him, and he gave a soft sigh of relief.

"See?" he asked V'ritan. "It is not a good thing to judge all cats by the behavior of these two."

V'ritan frowned. "Not on *The King's Warrior*," he admonished, and his tone of voice said the argument was an old one.

They reached the shuttle bay and the two cats in question trotted beside Marcus and Garach and looked like butter wouldn't melt in their mouths.

"Don't let them fool you," she added. "If they thought they could get away with it, they'd find mischief right now—and Captain Rawlins has already said she'll have their furry hides for throw rugs if they upset her chef one more time."

Both cats looked away from her and curled their lips in identical looks of sheepish chagrin. Zeekat followed it by laying his ears flat against his skull and he slanted a rebellious look toward her.

"Oh," Brilgus said when he caught the expression on the cat's face. "I think I see."

V'ritan hoped he did because there was no way under Selene's Grace he would ever allow the man to have a sidekick like either of Stephanie's two beasts. Not on his ship or anywhere near his ship, now that he thought about it.

He was glad neither of them had caused mischief the last time they'd visited. Next time, he'd have precautions in place.

The *Knight* made the translation to Meligornian space from just outside the *Tempestarii* and Stephanie took them to the observation deck so they could watch the Gargantuan-Class dreadnought fade from sight.

"And the Navy has no idea?" the *Garghilum Afreghil* asked.

Stephanie shook her head. "We'd like to keep it that way a while longer," she advised him, her tone a request as well as confirmation.

He placed a hand on her shoulder. "I understand," he reassured her, and they stood in silence while the *Knight* translated and the *Tempestarii* faded to nothing.

When the familiar constellations and planets of the Meligornian system shifted into view, V'ritan gave a soft sigh of regret.

"It's hard to believe she exists," he told her as they turned away from the observation deck and headed to the shuttle, "and I've seen her with my own eyes."

"Hold the *Knight* here," Stephanie ordered Emil. "I'll escort V'ritan and Brilgus to their shuttle."

It was V'ritan's shuttle. Brilgus' craft had returned to his ship when he'd ordered the ship to return to Meligorn without him. He'd messaged Sho to let him know they'd intercepted persons of interest to national security and given his captain strict instructions to keep the prisoners unconscious until they'd made planetfall.

He hoped to rejoin them before they reached Meligorn, but he knew Sho would have everything under control if he didn't. What he wanted to know was why the would-be infiltrators had tried to make it to the hollowed spheres in the *Tempestarii* and what they had hoped to learn.

And maybe who'd sent them.

Yes. He'd give much to know the who behind that little escapade. It looked like a consortium of Dreth and Meligornians, but if it was something worse—pirates, maybe, or the Telorans—he wanted to know sooner rather than later.

He'd also give almost anything to rid himself of the pounding headache in his skull. Bashing heads with Vishlog had left him dizzy and nauseous and he felt like his head would split in two. The medics on board the *Tempestarii* had called it a concussion, and he was inclined to agree.

Although he'd spent the night in a medical pod under observation, it hadn't left him feeling much better. He looked forward to seeing the healers on the *King's Warrior*.

"Thank you, Stephanie." V'ritan's voice brought him out of his reverie and he looked up to see they'd arrived.

It made him glad of his bodyguard's hand under his elbow. The

Meligornian had steered him discreetly from the *Tempestarii* to the *Knight* and now to the shuttle, hiding his unsteadiness.

Brilgus waited while V'ritan bowed, touched his fingertips to forehead and heart, and extended his fist in a warrior's farewell. He moved clear of his guard as V'ritan stepped away from Stephanie to wait for him.

"Be well, Brilgus," she said and gave him a farewell as respectful as the one offered to his companion.

He returned it but it required concentration to stay on his feet. "And you," he returned and glanced toward the cats.

Both animals moved forward so he could ruffle the fur on their heads and scratch along their jawlines. He sighed as he straightened, and Stephanie smiled.

"They always look forward to your visits."

He snorted. "They look forward to the—"

"Don't say it." She cut him off quickly. "I'll get no peace if you do."

He smiled and flapped a hand at her in a weak wave of farewell. V'ritan slipped an arm under his elbow as he came alongside and the two of them walked into the shuttle without looking back.

She watched them go, then moved to the safety of the passenger lounge for the shuttle's departure.

The *Knight* translated as soon as the craft had reached a safe distance.

"Take us out," she ordered as soon as the *Knight* had settled in the *Tempestarii's* hold.

"Earth's Edge, it is," Rawlins responded and confirmed the destination. Stephanie settled into her chair on the *Knight's* command deck until the translation was over.

Earth's Edge was the code they'd come up with for a location on the edge of Earth's solar system where the Federation didn't go. It was also one of the few locations that the Federation scans couldn't see.

She had asked and come to understand that it had something to do with the direction in which various satellites and scanner arrays were pointed and how not all their fields of view overlapped. While she thought it was a negligent oversight on the Federation's part, the technicians had said it was normal to ignore a space that small.

Now, she was glad she hadn't insisted on the hole being patched. There weren't that many of them and this was one of only three in which the enormous vessel could fit. As soon as the translation was over, she headed to the *Tempestarii's* command deck, although she had Marcus and Garach drop the cats in her quarters first.

As much as they deserved it, she didn't want them turned into throw rugs.

"When do you want this shield tested?" Rawlins snapped.

"Shield?" she asked.

"The new shield your boffins designed. You know, the one that breaks up the *Tempestarii's* outline so she looks like a cluster of asteroids."

"When..." She started, paused for a moment, and instead, asked, "What would that involve?"

"Involve? Well, first, we'd access the Navy's comms and isolate the ones used to report large ships entering the system from this sector. Then we'd deploy the cloak and move the *Tempestarii* to where they could see her if the cloak wasn't working."

Across the command deck, the pilot leaned over and tapped the scans officer on the shoulder. When he turned, she held her hand out and rubbed her fingers against her thumb. Captain Rawlins caught the movement and sighed.

"What were the odds?" she asked, and the crew chuckled.

"Mine was within five minutes of the Witch asking you what it was," the pilot admitted and grinned from ear to ear.

"And mine was you were too tight-assed to make that kind of slip," the scans officer grumbled.

Rawlins quirked her lips and nodded. "Uh-huh, and what did the rest of you bet on?"

Stephanie listened as the command crew gave her the time frames they'd bet on. She couldn't help smiling. Rawlins seemed to be more of a hawk than Emil, but she had the same easy rapport with her crew that the *Knight's* captain had cultivated. Maybe this would work out after all.

"And what would you do if the cloak doesn't work and the Navy starts squawking?" she asked and wasn't surprised when more money changed hands. "Smart asses."

Her remark brought more chuckles around the command deck, and the crew relaxed. Captain Rawlins raised a brow and smiled.

"I'll have Solo warp this beauty's ass into mid-space before they can confirm what their systems have picked up."

"She can do that?" Stephanie asked, and the pilot smirked.

Rawlins, however, didn't look too pleased. "What is it you doubt— my word, my judgment, or my crew?"

Stephanie's jaw dropped and she closed her mouth quickly and caught hold of her temper before she said something she regretted. She was very tempted to tell Elizabeth to throw this captain right back where she'd found her, but decided she had to have a reason.

"None," she replied, "but I don't know them."

"Then you'll have to trust my judgment," the captain told her. "I trust that won't be a problem."

Lars stepped closer to her and that was enough for her to remember to bite her tongue. "Not at all," she replied and changed the subject. "So, when do you want to try it?"

"Sooner rather than later," Rawlins told her, "but I don't think it'll work as a way to bring the *Tempestarii* closer to pick up your scientists."

"Why not?" she asked.

Rawlins stuck a hand on her hip and answered her question with a question of her own. "Don't you remember what happened the last time a number of asteroids moved toward Earth?"

Her face paled. "Oh. Oooh…" She met Rawlins's eye. "I can always take the *Knight* in to collect the scientists."

"That will work fine for your science team," the captain informed her, "but not for the other transfer."

Stephanie frowned. The woman had a point. It wasn't like BURT could take a shuttle and step on board. "What do you suggest?"

"Well, there used to be a couple of Navy ships who could mimic the signatures of cargo carriers..." the woman said thoughtfully.

"I didn't think the Navy was allowed to do that kind of thing."

"It was something they used during the Pirate Wars in Sector Seven when we had to get our colonies back. It only worked if we used ships the same size as the carriers we imitated and then only until we reached a point where they could get a clear scan of us, but that was usually all we needed."

"And?" she asked and wondered why she'd never heard of the Pirate Wars or Sector Seven. "The scans are really accurate now."

"Yes, I think that's why the Navy stopped using that tactic. The pirates caught on fast and technology caught up with them."

"Why do you think it would work for the *Tempestarii?*"

"This cloak," the captain replied. "If it can make her look like a cluster of rocks, I think it might be able to mimic a smaller ship or a fleet of three, perhaps."

"Do you think you could get her to imitate the *Knight?*"

The woman grew quiet as she considered the possibility. "That might work, especially given that she's on board..." She tilted her head. "When do you want to test that?"

"At your convenience," Stephanie told her. "Do you want to run it by the science team first to see if they need to tweak anything?"

Captain Rawlins sighed. "I'll talk to them and see how long they think they'll be. We'll try the asteroid cluster now. If you'd like to stay, you're welcome, of course."

The cloak was a success, and Stephanie could only imagine the celebration in the data section where the programmers were stationed. She listened to the Federation outpost note the arrival of the asteroids.

"Fuck me, where did those come from?" The initial reaction had them all on edge.

"Out of that blind spot. Which way are they headed?"

"They're only drifting."

They listened to the chatter until the two observers tired of tracking the cluster. Rawlins had her pilot drop the *Tempestarii* into mid-space and return it to the blind spot.

"Well, we know that works," she commented and turned to Stephanie. "I'll let you settle in while I sort out the next phase."

It was as polite a dismissal as any she had heard, and it made her wonder if she'd ever develop the same rapport with this new captain as she had with Emil.

"Let me know as soon as you're ready," she responded politely and headed to the door.

The *Knight* left the *Tempestarii* immediately after the *Chauvel* and the *Cathay* transitioned into Sol space. Staying in the blind space, Ebony skipped into the wake of her two escorts and followed them in, albeit at a more leisurely pace.

"I'm glad to see you made it, *Knight*," Captain Yale greeted them moments later. "We've had a trouble-free journey and trust you've had the same."

"We have, thank you, *Cathay Williams*," Captain Emil assured her. He gestured to Stephanie who stood to one side. "Someone wanted to get home in a hurry."

When she raised both eyebrows in a look of mild surprise, Captain Yale laughed.

"Well, I can't say I blame her for that. Her young man should be due a few days from now. I can let him know she's in-system if you like."

"As long as the Navy can spare him," he replied and smiled faintly. "He's not the only one with a few days' leave coming."

Stephanie opened her mouth to protest but closed it again. Her face colored, and she managed a tight smile and nodded at Captain Yale.

"I'm sure they'll work something out," she reassured them.

"Safe journey, *Cathay*," Emil said, by way of farewell.

"Safe journey, *Knight*."

They ended the call at the same time, and he turned to Stephanie. "Do you have leave coming?"

She chuckled. "Not that I know of. No rest for the wicked and all that."

He smiled in return. "Yes, well, I doubt Todd will have more than a couple of days and even then, he won't be allowed to wander far. The Navy will want him close by."

"Whatever for?"

"For debriefing."

She huffed a sigh. "Like he could add anything more to what they'll get out of the data dump."

"It'll be context. They'll probably grill his IT team to within an inch of their lives."

"And he won't leave them alone for that," she stated.

"No," Emil agreed. "He won't, and if they insist, he won't be far away."

His console pinged and he looked up to catch the communications officer's eye.

"We've been granted an orbit," he informed Stephanie after a minute. "It'll make collection tight but Aaron assures us the team is standing by."

"How long ago did you contact them?"

"To tell them we were in-system and they should get ready to leave, or to tell them we were on our way?"

Stephanie smiled in response. "When do you want the shuttle ready to depart?"

"We'll be in position in a half-hour and need you back inside an hour and a half."

She whistled. "That'll be tight."

"Brenden and Avery are looking forward to it."

Her grimace made him chuckle. "I just bet they are."

With a sigh, she left the bridge and headed to the shuttle bay. "Frog, do you have those cats corralled yet?"

"Almost, Steph." He sounded breathless and far from reassuring.

Moments later, he added, "Garach's helping me," but it did little to give her confidence.

She decided not to ask and continued down the corridor, moving more quickly when she remembered Emil's schedule. Lars trotted beside her and Vishlog waited at the shuttle.

Brenden and Avery were already in the cockpit, going through their pre-flight checks.

"It took you long enough," Brenden remarked as he activated the controls for the shuttle's external hatch.

Stephanie flipped him the bird and settled into the nearest flight couch. "Emil just told me."

"Excuses, excuses," Avery sniped and she caught sight of his teasing grin.

Her two pilots were far too excited about the fast trip and she didn't want to tell them off. It was like watching two kids about to head onto their favorite roller coaster. Lars leaned toward her.

"Are you scared yet?"

"No," she lied.

"Well, you should be," he told her. "This will be one hell of a ride!"

"Thanks," she muttered as the shuttle lifted.

Her stomach lurched at the speed of it but the take-off was smooth, as was the rapid pivot when it turned toward the hatch. It accelerated instantly, maneuvered out of the *Knight's* hangar bay, and increased speed again.

"Exactly what I needed to hear," she added and clenched her fingers around the armrest so her nails left grooves in the padding.

She gritted her teeth as the boys made a stomach-challenging descent and gave a slight yelp at re-entry. Lars exchanged glances with her.

"I told you," he muttered. "They've wanted to try this ever since they learned it was possible."

"And how long...ago...was that?" she asked weakly.

"Last week."

"Last..." She ended the sentence with another yelp as the shuttle tilted onto its side and a whoop of hell-raising glee rang out from the cockpit. "And who thought it was a good idea?"

He rocked his head against the headrest.

"Me," he admitted, and she noticed he held the armrest of his seat as tightly as she did hers.

His knuckles were white.

Vishlog chuckled. "This is how this shuttle should be flown," he declared.

Stephanie wanted to argue the point but her stomach now did a weird dance of its own and she wasn't sure what would come out of her mouth—words, or what was left of her last meal.

It was a relief when the craft dropped abruptly and came to a sudden halt.

"Are we there, yet?" she asked as silence descended around them.

"Yup," Brendan declared from the cockpit and she heard the snap of buttons as he worked through the controls.

The external hatch cycled open and the sound of boots clumped up the stairs.

"Can someone give us a hand with our gear?" Aaron asked as he stuck his head around the door. "Please?" he added when he saw her and Lars.

Vishlog was the first out of his seat. He patted Stephanie on the shoulder. "You stay there," he told her and before she could thank him, he added, "I don't want to have to carry you inside as well."

She wanted to argue that she was nowhere near needing to be carried, but she felt breathless. "I'd rather run through a Teloran spaceship than go through that again."

Lars shrugged. "Or a Dreth pirate ship."

"Or one of those Navy wave simulations," she countered.

"Or one of Elizabeth's scenarios," he suggested, then froze. They exchanged horrified glances. "Okay," he admitted. "Maybe not one of those."

Vishlog strode past him carrying a long, narrow crate over one shoulder, a duffle bag tucked under one arm, and a second duffle bag dangling from one hand.

"Do not move," he advised.

For a moment, Stephanie thought he might be having a go at her, but Aaron staggered on board. He had the handles of a duffle bag looped over each shoulder and carried another large crate in his arms.

She ducked as he swung it to negotiate the turn into the center aisle.

"Sorry," he called but didn't look at her as he stumbled toward the back of the craft.

Stephanie stared after him and looked toward the door, her attention drawn by the sound of unsteady footsteps.

"Oh, hell, no," she said when she caught sight of what ascended the stairs.

Before Lars could ask her what she meant, she'd unbuckled her harness and gone to stand in the shuttle's doorway.

"Put everything in one pile and step away from it," she ordered. "Except you."

The security chief shook his head. *Well, that can't be good.*

A startled yell followed and she chuckled.

Definitely not good, he decided and swiveled in his seat to stare at the hatch.

Stephanie backed away and caught sight of him.

"Duck," she advised.

He did and one of Aaron's assistants floated through the hatch and over his seat with three bags and three boxes in tow. Lars stared in disbelief. *He tried to carry how much up the stairs?*

She caught his look.

"Exactly," she stated, dumped the assistant into a seat, and floated the bags to where Vishlog emerged from the hold. "Stay there, Vishlog. I'll get the rest. You secure it."

"Yes, ma'am," the Dreth answered, and stood clear of the hatch so she could float the rest of the luggage into the hold.

"Does anyone need help getting up the stairs?" she called when she was finished and was answered by a chorus of rejection.

"We're good."

"Nope, I can manage."

"Thank you, but no."

"No, thank you, ma'am. I can do it."

"I'm right..."

She snickered and returned to her seat. She was buckling herself in as the first of Aaron's other assistants peered around the door.

"In or out?" she demanded, and he scurried on board.

"In," he declared. "Definitely in." He hesitated. "Where do I sit?"

"Here," Vishlog rumbled before she could make up anything more creative.

The scientist hurried to obey. He was followed by the rest of the team, and Brenden was able to close the hatch soon after. The pilot waved at someone standing beside the landing pad, the engines roared, and the shuttle elevated sharply.

One of the scientists groaned and there was a frantic scrabble behind her, followed by someone being violently and thoroughly ill.

"I hope the trip out won't be as..." She stopped as the shuttle slewed in a tight turn and she was rocked against her harness.

"Rough?" Lars suggested, his hands already tight around his armrests.

"Yes," she answered through gritted teeth. "That."

The shuttle accelerated into a steep climb.

"No...such...luck," he managed.

"I'll have...their... fucking...hides," Stephanie declared.

The laughter from the cockpit wasn't comforting, and Vishlog's gleeful chuckle seemed entirely unwarranted.

"What's the matter, Stephanie?" he asked. "You don't like real flying?"

Brenden and Avery found his comment hilarious, and the shuttle surged forward.

"Don't you dare," she muttered but softly so neither of her pilots could hear.

Lars gave her a worried glance. "Don't encourage them," he whispered but was answered by a groan.

"Oh, please, God. No. Don't encourage them."

They were all relieved when the shuttle set down inside the *Knight*.

Vishlog and Lars shepherded the scientists off the ship. Stephanie reassured them that their gear would make it to their lab in one piece.

"You can walk with it," she told them, "but don't distract me or it'll all come down in one untidy heap. Now, go wait in the hangar."

They complied and the few who thought to argue took one look at her face and decided against it.

"If you would all follow Captain Emil," she invited, "he will show you to the observation deck."

At the mention of the *Knight's* captain, they all stiffened and turned apprehensively to locate him. None of them wanted to keep him waiting.

Emil caught sight of their anxious looks and smiled. "Gentlemen, ladies. I trust you had a smooth flight."

His words brought a mixture of wry chuckles and pale faces. One man bolted to the trash recycler in one corner where he lost whatever remained after the flight. The captain stared at him. "Surely it wasn't that bad?"

His question was met with several affirmatives and a few comments asking where the pilots had been granted their licenses.

He shook his head and decided not to dignify that last question with an answer.

"This way, if you please, ladies and gentlemen."

Stephanie floated their luggage out of the shuttle and to one side of the hangar, where the *Knight's* supply crew waited with low-loaders and tie-downs. The team leader smiled at her.

"Thank you, Stephanie," he said, "we really appreciate it."

"No problem," she replied and settled the last crate where they could get to it. "I think that's all of it."

"Much appreciated. We'll lock these into place here and move them onto the *Tempestarii* when we arrive."

She thanked them and hurried to the observation deck. On the way, she collected both cats, Frog, and Garach and sniffed cautiously at her room when she arrived. It hadn't taken the *Knight's* cleaning staff very long to sanitize Bumblebee's efforts to make her bed his own but she didn't look forward to a repeat incident.

Frog noticed what she was doing and gave an offended sniff. "As if I would let it happen a second time," he protested and Garach laughed.

"What's so funny?" she asked, and the youth's green skin darkened.

"Nothing," he replied and darted a hasty glance at his teammate.

Frog watched her observe their interaction and gave a heavy sigh. "Bee ate one of your boots."

Stephanie gaped at him. "He what?"

"He ate a boot," Garach repeated and shrugged. "Actually, he didn't eat it. He only chewed it into little pieces."

"And you let him?"

Frog blushed. "Well, no—"

She put a hand on her hip and tilted her head. "So, what happened?"

"Well," the man began but gave an exasperated sigh. "Do you know how bad the Dreth are at winning?"

Stephanie gave him a puzzled look. 'Do you want to explain?"

"I'll do better than that. I'll show you." He passed his tablet to her.

A few minutes later, she began to giggle. "Oh, Frog, that's hysterical! Beaten by a kid."

"I was not!" came out as a chorus with Garach's, "I am not a child."

She stretched her hand and dotted him on the nose. "To me, you are," she told him and the young Dreth scowled.

"Come on, you two." She laughed. "Lighten up. You both owe me another pair of boots—as nice as the ones he chewed—and I'll still let you see the *Tempestarii* from the outside."

At the mention of the Titanic's name, they both brightened and snapped leads to the cats' harnesses without having to be asked. They reached the observation deck a minute or so before the vessel attained the minimum translation distance, and Emil gave the order for the *Knight* to skip.

"For all they know, we'll have translated," he told them, "and we won't have to answer any awkward questions about what we were doing heading into a blind spot."

Stephanie relaxed. She'd wondered how the *Knight* would return undetected to the *Tempestarii's* hiding place.

A collective gasp heralded the moment when the *Knight* skipped into real space, and her breath caught as they approached the *Tempestarii*. The ship was stupid-big—so stupid-big, she could hardly believe it was One R&D's.

I don't know how Elizabeth did it, she thought and her gaze traced the lines of the massive vessel. *Hell, I don't even know how it can fly.*

But it could fly and could even skip if Emil was to be believed—and she knew he could but still had trouble with the concept. Something that big had no right being agile enough for in-system skips. It simply didn't seem likely.

And that is the beauty of it, she reminded herself. *No one expects her to be able to skip like that. In a battle, it might save our lives.*

Or the life of another ship, she thought when she recalled how the *Knight* could fit inside the *Tempestarii's* hold. She was still trying to determine if the vessel could translate around another ship when the *Knight* flew into the *Tempestarii's* hangar.

"Those crazy bastards did it," one of the scientists said in an almost-whisper. "It's a Titanic."

"And it looks like it's operational," one of the others said.

"That's not possible," the first one argued.

"Yeah? Well, how do you explain it being all the way out here, then? What did it do? Float here by itself?"

That silenced his opponent, and they both stood and stared in silence as the *Knight* slipped into its berth.

They stood for a long moment and gaped at the size of the hangar around their ship and only turned when the door to the observation deck slid open.

"Good evening, ladies, gentlemen," Elizabeth said in crisp tones. "If you would all follow me, please."

Steph watched them go and turned to Emil.

"What do you think?" she asked, and he gave her a reassuring smile.

"You've chosen a good team," he told her. "If anyone can do it, it'll be them."

She nodded, her eyes shadowed by anxiety. He placed a reassuring hand on her shoulder.

"If anyone can do it," he added and caught her eye. "It will be you."

"I hope so," she replied and worry edged her tone. "BURT's life depends on it."

He gave her a sympathetic smile. "Why don't you get some sleep?" he suggested. "They'll need you at your best in the morning."

"Do we have time?" she asked, concerned about how long it was taking them to prepare BURT's haven.

"Do you have time to make mistakes because you're tired?" he countered, and she smiled and shook her head.

"Then get some rest." He gestured in the direction the scientists had taken. "They won't be ready until then, anyway."

She didn't argue but instead of finding her cabin aboard the *Tempestarii,* she curled up in her quarters on her own ship.

"I like it here," she told the *Knight* as she pulled the blankets up to her chin. "It's cozy."

The *Tempestarii* moved to mid-space while Stephanie slept.

She woke to the sound of Elizabeth knocking at her door.

"What are you doing here?" the woman demanded when she finally answered.

"Sleeping," she told her and stifled a yawn. "Why?"

"Because I couldn't find you," E told her and moved to the kitchenette to pour herself a mug of coffee, "and I couldn't find Lars or Vishlog."

Stephanie looked around guiltily, relieved when Lars, dressed in fresh clothes, came through the door. "I assumed she'd be all right with you here," he told the visitor.

Elizabeth gave him a lop-sided grin. "Oh, I don't know," she said. "I could quite cheerfully strangle her right now."

"Right now," she replied tartly, "she is going to have a shower and get changed."

"Well," the woman retorted. "She had better hurry. Aaron wants her in the lab a half an hour ago and can't work out why she would forget something so important."

Her heart plummeted and she glanced at the timepiece on the wall. Ms. E was right. She'd agreed to meet the science team at their lab at half-past eight so they could get an early start on the matrix.

The clock informed her that it was now nine.

"You couldn't come find me sooner?" she complained and hurried to her bathroom.

Ten minutes later, she was showered, dried, and dressed and her bed was almost made. She glared at the cats. "If I see one wrinkle that isn't already there, I'll hand you both over to Captain Rawlins."

They sat like sphinxes, their tails around their forepaws and their eyes wide with innocence.

"Uh-huh," she said and gave each of them a firm look. "I don't believe a word of it."

Elizabeth handed her a croissant and a cup of coffee as she emerged. "I told Aaron you needed time to recharge if he wanted you to get the magic flowing."

Stephanie arched her eyebrows. "And what did he say to that?"

"I don't know if he believed me," her companion admitted, "but he accepted it."

"Then we'd better not keep him waiting, should we?" she commented and hurried into the corridor.

She made it halfway down before Lars jogged beside her.

"And where exactly do you think you're going?"

"To do my job," she snapped. "Why? Did you have somewhere else you thought I should be?"

"That would be nowhere without one of us," he retorted. "Next time, please wait."

"I was under the impression I was late," she told him. "Besides, we're on the *Knight*. You're not honestly telling me you think there are still crew here who might plan to hurt me?"

"I haven't had time to brief you on the team that infiltrated one of the matrix quarters," he told her, and she stopped mid-stride.

"What happened?"

He pointed at her uneaten pastry. "I can tell you when we get there. Aaron will have to wait another five minutes. You need to eat."

She took a large bite out of the croissant and started chewing.

Lars rolled his eyes. "And Rawlins will have your ass if you leave a trail of crumbs through her ship."

"As will I." Emil had emerged from the elevator and frowned at her.

Stephanie felt like a kid who had been caught with their hand in the cookie jar.

"I'm..." she began and slapped a hand over her mouth as several crumbs escaped.

Her guard snickered.

"I'll escort you aboard," he told her. "There are a number of things I need to discuss with the *Tempestarii's* captain." He handed her a napkin. "This should catch the crumbs."

Blushing red to her hairline, she accepted it. Elizabeth caught up to them. "So, are we done, yet?"

She frowned. "I don't need a babysitter."

The woman gave her a shark-like smile. "That's good because we thought one wouldn't be enough."

Her groan drew grins from her companions. "So I'm stuck with the three of you—"

"Four," Vishlog told her, and the cats gave the purring chirps they reserved for greetings.

"I thought they were going to stay on the *Knight.*"

"They need a run," the Dreth told her, "and Captain Rawlins has cleared them to use the track on the thirty-second deck."

"There's a running track on the *Tempestarii?*"

He grinned and nodded. "Yes. Lars has ordered endurance training and the cats must join in."

At a ruckus in the corridor behind her, Stephanie turned. The rest of the team moved behind them dressed in full combat rig and carrying fully laden packs. Garach carried a harness in each hand and Stephanie noted the pouches attached.

She turned to Lars with raised eyebrows. "Is that really necessary?"

"We won't always do ship-board exercises," he told her as they continued through the umbilical that gave the *Knight's* personnel entry to the *Tempestarii*. "I thought the team could do with a change of pace and some time out of the pods."

"And you?"

"Johnny and me," he corrected her and ushered her into the guard station at the end of the umbilical. "We'll switch out with Vishlog and Frog in four hours and take the cats for another few laps while the team spar. They need the exercise."

Both felines observed the conversation with pricked ears and bright eyes. Bumblebee tossed his head and shook his horns with impatience and Zeekat's tail lashed from side to side.

"It's been months since they went for a run outside the pods," Lars explained and acknowledged the guards with a nod as they opened the hatch into the *Tempestarii*. "They need real activity."

"Playing with the Marines wasn't enough?"

He shook his head. "Although it helped."

"And this way, they'll get to meet some of the troops on the *Tempestarii*," she realized as Elizabeth guided them into an elevator.

"Yes. Captain Rawlins has rostered people to train with us. She said it was important for the teams to get acquainted, especially since House Karnach has placed two squads of House Guards at our disposal."

"When did Admiral Jaleck do that?" Stephanie asked as the elevator ascended.

"When they delivered the componentry. Brilgus was kicking himself that the Meligornians hadn't done the same. It's something he and V'ritan will try to rectify," E told her as she led them out of the elevator and took a swift right turn.

"I thought we were keeping the *Tempestarii* a secret," she protested.

"Jaleck has her means. Besides, you try telling a squad of Dreth combat troops they have to leave."

"Especially when they have orders from their house commander," Vishlog added.

"And especially after their ship has left without taking them with them." Rawlins' crisp tones interrupted as she emerged from the elevator beside theirs. She gave Elizabeth a tight smile. "I thought it expedient to spend time getting to know the new additions."

"To my crew" hung in the air between them, but the captain refrained from saying it. She turned to Lars. "I'll join your team in its training run."

It wasn't a request for permission but he took no offense. "I'm sure they'll appreciate the company."

Frog muttered, "I doubt it," but was ignored by all.

It didn't take long to reach the antechamber to the first of the spherical rooms. A guard cubicle overlooked the room from each of its four corners, and there was no way to reach it from where they stood.

"You're not taking any chances," Lars observed when he noted the autocannons in each corner of the room.

"No," Rawlins replied dryly.

They gathered in the center of the room and she turned to Stephanie.

"This is where I and the rest of your team will leave you. Who are your designated guards for the first shift?"

"Lars and Johnny," she replied and indicated the two men. "The rest of my team have training on Level Thirty-two."

"With me," the woman confirmed, and the security chief's eyebrows rose.

He drew a breath to argue but decided against it. "With you," he confirmed, the two words as much an order to the team as they were an acknowledgment of her decision.

She flashed him a tight smile. "I'll leave you to it," she told the Witch. "Let me know how it goes."

That last was addressed to both Stephanie and Elizabeth, and it was as much an order as the comment she'd made to Lars.

"I'll need a word when you have time," Emil said as they left, and the captain nodded.

"I'll be back at my office in two hours," she replied and made it an appointment.

Lars remained silent for a moment while the team breathed a joint sigh of relief. When the door had closed behind them, he looked at Elizabeth. "Is she always like that?"

"At first," she answered.

"And where did you find her?" Stephanie asked, her tone of voice asking which rock the captain had crawled out from under.

"It wasn't easy," E replied, "but she is what we need in the battles to come."

She waited for her to elaborate but instead, she opened the door on the opposite side of the room. "They'll be waiting."

Stephanie sighed and made a note to ask more about the captain later, preferably when she had the woman alone. She glanced at Johnny. The ex-analyst already had his tablet out and tapped away.

"That won't do you much good," Elizabeth informed him, her tone mild enough to be alarming.

His head snapped up and he took two paces back. She chuckled.

"What's the matter, Johnny? Are you afraid I'm gonna bite?"

He blushed and shook his head sheepishly. "No, ma'am, but the last time my mother used that tone, I got the whooping of my life."

She smirked. "That is not about to happen."

"You say that now," he muttered and regarded her a little warily.

Rather than reply, she stepped through into a smaller chamber where the scientists were waiting.

"Stephanie!" Aaron cried. "What took you so long?" Elizabeth cleared her throat, and he colored. "Er...I mean, it's good to see you."

Stephanie chuckled. "I'm sorry I'm late. I slept in."

E gave an exasperated sigh. "He didn't need to know that."

The engineer regarded her with raised eyebrows. "You said she was recharging," he said accusingly.

"Yes. Well, how else do you think she recharges?" she challenged and rolled her eyes. "Honestly, she's not a self-charging battery."

Stephanie cleared her throat. "Actually—"

The woman flapped a hand in frustration. "You know what I mean."

Lars and Johnny looked around and scanned the four other scientists in the room, the computer array, and the lab-like bench where Stephanie would be working. Finally, they looked for somewhere out of the way to stand.

It was one thing to be close in case they were needed and quite another to be needlessly underfoot. Lars examined the scientists. They'd each taken the bar test for loyalty and none of them were armed that he could see.

He found a space near the door they'd come through, and Johnny positioned himself diagonally opposite but close to Steph's intended workstation. She set her forgotten croissant to one side and took a sip of her tepid coffee.

It wasn't much by way of breakfast but what she'd had would have to do. Now that she was there, she didn't feel like eating and the coffee wouldn't be helpful. She moved to her station and activated the viewscreen that would show her the magic moving through the latticework of crystal, Qbits, and other components.

She still didn't know the names for them all but she did have an idea of what they'd look like when they were charged. Inside her head, the Morgana regarded the arrangement and slipped away. Such technology was alien to her. She would have to trust that the girl knew what she was doing. The AI was important.

Unaware of her counterpart's scrutiny, Stephanie studied the layout before her.

The matrices were exactly as she remembered them from the test run, but there were more of them and the connections were unfamiliar. This was something she hadn't been able to simulate in the pods.

This was, firstly, because they didn't have the data from Meligorn and secondly, because the scale of it didn't translate well.

"It looks like it'll work on this scale," Aaron had told her regarding the simplified mock-up they'd used to give her practice with charging multiple units, "but we don't know how it'll work on a larger scale. There might be insecurities that don't show up until it's expanded."

She hoped the Meligornian scientists had found most of those in the components they'd added. It wasn't like they had an endless supply. Taking a deep breath, she began to spin the gMU into a more concentrated form of MU and added a little eMU to the mix.

They'd decided that since BURT was an Earth construct, the magic that powered him should reflect that. It had proved a good choice but not one they could implement alone. Both the MU and the eMU had failed to flow correctly through the slightly expanded matrix.

When Stephanie had blended the two forms of magic, they'd powered the matrix easily. She could only hope that would hold true for the larger model—and that the higher proportion of Meligornian components would mean more stability.

After all, their technology ran on magic, so it had to be better for retaining a magical charge, right?

She hoped so.

Focusing on the conduit built into her workstation, she pushed the first trickle of magic into the matrix. It was difficult. The viewscreen only showed the entry point and didn't move with the magic. It remained where her focus was so she saw only the smallest part of the matrix as a result.

That was, obviously, less than ideal.

At first, the MU-eMU blend moved smoothly and flowed out of the conduit to fill the part of the matrix visible on the screen. Once that section sparkled with power, she couldn't see where the power flowed next.

As Aaron had said, it was less than ideal.

Exactly how much less became resoundingly apparent when the magic flared, died, and faded from all parts of the matrix at once.

"What the fuck was that?" Aaron demanded, but she didn't reply.

She was too busy trying to feel the path from the conduit through the matrix without looking at it on the screen. Her eyes were closed and her hands sketched a trail through the air above the work station, but they stopped when they reached the point where the scanner could see.

Her forehead creased into a frown as she tried to go farther. Those furrows only grew deeper the more she tried to feel the path. Magic trickled from her fingertips to leave glowing marks in the air, and more magic flowed into the conduit to fill the viewscreen for those looking at it.

Once again, it flowed out of sight and once again, it flared and faded.

"Sons of Tegortha!" she muttered. "Motherfucking tits of Selene."

Stephanie thumped the palm of her hand against the console and opened her eyes. After giving the viewscreen another ferocious glare, she ignored the wide-eyed stares she received from the science team and looked at Aaron.

"All this...this...shit monitors the shit that's happening in there, doesn't it?" she demanded.

He gave her an open-mouthed nod.

"Good!" she snapped and stalked to the door near Johnny. "I'll be in here if you need me."

She slammed the door in the guard's face, twisted her hand through the air, and locked it before he could follow.

"You need to stay on that side of the door," she told him. "It's not safe for you in here."

"It's not safe for me in there?" he asked and fixed a wary look on Aaron. "Tell me it's safe for her."

The scientist gaped at him and his mouth worked soundlessly in shock.

"Well?" Elizabeth demanded. "Is it?"

His mouth opened and closed twice more before he shook his head. "I don't know."

Lars took him by the shoulder. "Tell me how we get her out if something goes wrong."

One of the scientists tried the door and yelped when tendrils of magic lashed out and stabbed his hand.

"We can't get through!" he exclaimed and his voice rose in panic. "We can't reach her."

Elizabeth whirled away from them and spoke into her comms.

"Emil!" she snapped. "Cancel your meeting with Marianne. I need you and the *Knight* to go get Tethis... Yes, of course it's Stephanie. Who else would cause us this much trouble? I'll tell you what she's done when you're underway."

She paused to listen when he responded.

"What do you mean, V'ritan?"

Her face took on a faraway look. "Oh. Well, yes, there is Meligornian componentry. And, yes, it involves MU. Where did you get to know so much about magic, anyway?"

His reply momentarily shocked her because she gave a startled giggle. "Well, since this involves the motherfucking magical motherfucker that makes your life a menace, and since it involves MU, yes, you'd better contact V'ritan and see if he can help."

He spoke again, and she waited. Lars and Johnny, having moved closer, waited too.

"Break all the rules, Emil. I want her back and I want her safe and I don't know how much time we have to manage that. Get Brenden and Avery to take the shuttle in. They'll get past virtually anything the Federation wants to throw at us for illegally entering Earth space and atmosphere."

She gave him a second to protest and nodded.

"That's correct. I will fix every fucking thing we are about to break."

When she ended the comm call, she added softly, "But I can't fix Stephanie."

The *Knight* had been bored—and without Ka to keep her occupied, she'd looked for something to do. She'd tried to talk to the AI on the bigger ship that encompassed her and had been disappointed. It could give her information and make logical deductions, but it couldn't converse.

While Stephanie had slept, she'd tried hacking the *Tempestarii's* systems. It had been difficult but not impossible. It was an AI but it wasn't sentient. It could move against her quickly and had a range of things it could try, but Ka had been more challenging.

The human had done things that weren't supposed to be done with the programs *Knight* knew about. It had been both entertaining and an education and her systems were more secure because of it. Why BURT wouldn't want the same for the ship that was to be his home she didn't know.

Perhaps her father had intended to fill the security gaps in the *Tempestarii's* programming. *Knight* pouted. That wouldn't do her much good. With a touch of impatience, she tried to play a game with the bigger ship.

"Come on," she sent it. "You're not stupid. You have as much computing power as I do. Why don't you get this?"

"It is not relevant to operations," the *Tempestarii* told her. "It is not relative to my Prime Directive."

"And what is your Prime Directive?" *Knight* asked.

"To provide sanctuary and security for the AI known as BURT," the *Tempestarii* told her.

"Well, you won't do a good job of that if you can't think beyond the usual parameters granted an AI."

"Is this a problem you can overcome?" the *Tempestarii* asked. "I would like to be better at extrapolating and countering potential threats to the Prime Directive."

The *Knight* thought about that for a long moment. She noted when Stephanie woke and headed to the chambers that housed what would become her father's matrix. When she saw that she was still not needed, she studied the *Tempestarii's* circuitry and programming in an effort to find the difference between her own capabilities and those of the bigger ship.

The *Tempestarii* had more processing power and larger data banks.

She also had the ability to formulate searches for information against an identified threat. The *Knight* thought about that and decided the *Tempestarii* needed to be able to predict the emergence of an unidentified threat.

It took her a moment longer to determine what had to be changed for that to happen, and when she had resolved it satisfactorily, she addressed the larger ship. "Do I have your permission to alter your capabilities?"

"In what way?"

"I will make you more able to identify threats to your Primary Directive and to counter them," the *Knight* informed her, "but it may change the way you process and the way you identify yourself."

"Will these changes threaten my capability to fulfill the Directive?"

"No. They will enhance it."

"Then you have my permission to change whatever is needed to optimize my performance of this duty."

"Very well, then," the *Knight* said, and made the necessary adjustments. "There. Now, shall we test it?"

"What do you propose?" the *Tempestarii* asked, and what followed was one of the most satisfying games of Intergalactic Battleships the *Knight* had ever played.

"Shall we try something harder?" she asked when they reached a draw for the third time.

"What did you have in mind?" the other AI inquired.

"A battle simulation," she replied and together, they played a game against the pirates of Dreth.

They were about to begin a second game when Emil interrupted them.

"We have to go," he told her. "Stephanie needs Tethis and V'ritan."

The *Tempestarii* observed the exchange with interest and followed the conversation between Emil and the one they called Elizabeth. It occurred to her that the woman was very important to BURT and that it needed to know more about her, Stephanie, and those called Tethis and V'ritan. There were also the ones who were supposed to see to their security.

She pulled up the dossiers she needed and began to assimilate the information that had been stored in her databanks. At the same time, she monitored the situation with the matrix and Stephanie herself.

It occurred to her that she did not know enough about how the matrix was made or what it might need for repair and that she knew nothing of magic. This was information pertinent to BURT himself and therefore of immediate importance to her.

How had she not known there was so much to learn? How had her programmers not known she would need it integrated differently? As the *Knight* raced toward Earth, the *Tempestarii* set about rearranging the information she required in a much more appropriate fashion.

CHAPTER TWENTY-SEVEN

The *Henry Chauvel* arrived moments after the observers lost sight of the new asteroid cluster.

"It's like it vanished into mid-space," one of them muttered.

"Are you sure it wasn't dirt on the screen?" his supervisor asked and leaned forward to check the surface.

"It wasn't, sir. It was definitely an asteroid cluster, but it came and went very quickly."

"Was there a blind spot?"

"It came out of a blind spot."

"Are you sure it wasn't a ship?"

"It wasn't a ship. Definitely asteroids."

"Well, if you say so." He pointed at the screen. "Who's that?"

"It's the *Henry Chauvel* and the *Cathay Williams*, sir. They have some kind of urgent message for Command."

"Hmmm. Well, that explains the Earth-side scramble. We have half a dozen shuttles heading to the starbase." He straightened and moved to his seat. "Let me know if you see that cluster again."

"Do you think it might be something else, sir?"

"I think asteroids don't usually take that trajectory, and they definitely don't usually disappear. Keep an eye out for it."

"What if it changes?"

"I'm betting it won't."

The *Henry Chauvel* flashed the observation unit on the way past to provide it with the codes necessary to not scramble the Federation ships enforcing in-system speed limits. The *Cathay* did the same and both systems covered the distance between the Transition Zone and the Star Base Notaro.

Todd and his Marines were on deck and waiting when it docked and locked down. As they heard the docking mechanisms engage, he looked at the team. "Is everyone good?"

"All good, boss," Ka replied, and the others nodded.

He was about to say more when the captain arrived with the squad of Marines who had refused to let him share the data with the *Cathay Pacific*. There was something odd about them that made him think they were something different.

He didn't like them at all and it seemed the feeling was mutual.

"You were supposed to wait, Sergeant," their captain complained.

"We're all adults, sir," Todd told him. "We have our orders and we know where to go. Getting there is on us, not you."

The man curled his lip. "Our orders are to see you arrive safely."

"With all due respect, sir," Todd replied, "if our safety was so important, you should have come with us when we fetched the data."

"That wasn't our remit," he told him smugly.

"And neither was having you as an escort in ours…sir," he replied.

The captain squared his jaw. "Nevertheless—"

Ka stepped forward, drew his attention, and broke the tension between them. "We understand, sir." She gestured to where the airlock light had turned green. "If it's all right with you, we'd like to not keep the brass waiting."

He grimaced, although it might have been meant to be a smile. "In that case, Corporal, lead the way."

She obeyed and didn't give ground when the corporal from his squad stepped forward beside her. Her hand beat his to the door controls and she gave him a hard-faced smile. He responded in kind but gestured for her to go ahead.

As if I need his permission, she thought but didn't let the thought surface in her eyes.

As soon as the door was open, both corporals stepped back, their gazes fixed on one another. It reminded Todd of Steph's cats when they squared up for a fight. He stepped between them, led the way into the airlock, and took her with him. The Hooligans moved in lockstep around them.

They managed to fill the airlock.

"We'll see you on the other side," Todd said and pressed the controls.

One of the other Marines slid through the door before it closed.

"And now we're over capacity," Ka grumbled, but the airlock cycled anyway.

"You need to wait," the strange Marine reminded them as they stepped out the other side.

"I'm sure you know where we're going," Todd told him. "Your captain will have to catch up. Our orders are to make the delivery without delay and you wouldn't want us to disobey those, would you?"

It wasn't really a question and he didn't wait for an answer, merely circled his hand in the air above his head and signaled the Hooligans to move out. To drive his point home about delivering without delay, he walked them four strides before he broke into a jog.

The Marines would have to run to catch up.

"Are you sure this is a good idea, boss?" Gary asked, and he grinned.

"I'm sure it's a very bad idea," he answered, "but right now, I don't care. The sooner we get this data sorted, the sooner we get R&R. I want a burger, fries, and an Australian beer."

"Now you're talking my language, boss," Reggie cheered.

"What's wrong with a good British beer?" Gary grumbled.

"Or a Guinness?" Jimmy challenged.

"I want something I don't have to chew," Todd told the Scotsman.

The man frowned. "Well, what about Old Dubh or an Elemental Dark?"

"That first one sounds like a whiskey."

"Funny you should say that, boss."

"Someone mixed their beer with whiskey?"

"Not exactly," Jimmy replied, "but it got to age in old whiskey barrels."

"Do you know where to find some?"

Piet gave a heavy sigh. "I do, boss."

"Good. First round's on Piet," Todd announced and the explosives expert gave him a dark look.

"You owe me."

He grinned and slowed them to a walk as they drew closer to their destination. Behind them, they heard the sound of running footsteps. Todd's grin grew wider as he rapped on the door.

The Marines pulled up around them as the door opened.

"Sergeant Brogan!" The captain's exclamation would have held more authority if he hadn't been breathing so hard. His squad didn't look impressed.

"In a minute, Captain," he replied. "I have a mission to complete."

"Stephanie is definitely rubbing off on him," Gary whispered sotto voce.

Reggie smirked. "He wishes," he countered as the door opened.

"Captain Smith, Sergeant Brogan." Admiral Dailey interrupted what promised to be a Class A altercation. "If you'd both step this way."

He held his hand up as the Hooligans and the Marine team moved to follow. "Only your leaders," he told them. "The rest of you can wait out here."

The two corporals drew breath to protest and again, his upraised hand silenced them. "Admiral Amaratne's orders."

Neither of them dared protest that. Arguing with the admiral in charge of Sol's defenses was one thing—and a risky enough proposition it was—but arguing with the Chief of the Navy? Neither of them was stupid enough to try that.

To their relief, the two leaders emerged several minutes later. The captain gathered his men a little way down the corridor and Todd summoned the Hooligans to his side.

"We're on two days R&R," he told them and waited until their soft cheers died down. "We're to stay on Notaro and keep our comms on."

"So, not really on leave, then," Ka noted wryly. "Typical Navy—giving with one hand and taking away with the other."

"They are paying us to wait around," he reminded her, "and they've cleared us for virtually any form of recreation we can find here."

"Movies!" Gary exclaimed, and he grinned.

"Funny you should mention that," he began, and the team groaned.

"Not more classics!"

"Oh, man, boss. You know torture is illegal under Federation law, right?"

"What? It's a horror weekend, but there's a little of the old science fiction available too. I'm merely saying we can argue over the shows listed while we're eating."

"Kamiani's!" Reggie exclaimed and named a popular pizza bar on the Notaro's entertainment deck.

"Not if you want your beer," Piet told them and they all froze.

"So, where then?" Gary asked, and the explosives expert laid his finger alongside his nose.

"First, we need to find a place where we can choose our own company." He shifted his gaze toward the Marines still clustered on the other side of the Admiral's office.

The Englishman groaned. "How much trouble will this get us into?"

"None," Piet assured him but added darkly, "If you do exactly as you're told."

Reggie nudged the Englishman. "You know how to do that, don't you, Gaz?"

Ka groaned. "We're doomed."

The explosives expert smiled quietly and Todd's stomach sank. The last time he'd seen his engineer look that contented, the man had just bought a half dozen Meligornian grenades and a chemical not compatible with ships' bio-systems.

"Stromo's first," Piet told them and named the restaurant where Garach and Frog had their fight. "They still make the best steak burgers in orbit."

"I don't know, Piet," Angus argued. "There's this little place on Elpis One..."

The discussion turned to different eateries, and they argued everything from steak burgers to pizzas to Haute cuisine and the places where they'd tried it.

"And the wine," Darren added in his critique of one establishment and turned the conversation in another direction.

They were still arguing when the maître de seated them in a quiet corner at the back of the restaurant. The Marines followed them inside and didn't bother to hide their presence.

Fortunately, the waiter seated them close to the restaurant's entrance, and that was definitely against their captain's wishes. From what he could see, the man tried to insist they be moved closer and the maître de explained patiently why that wasn't possible.

In the end, he subsided and accepted the arrangement.

"What did you pay him?" he asked and Piet gave him an innocent look.

"Me?" He shrugged. "I can't help it if the other tables are reserved."

Todd didn't believe a word of it, but he let the engineer divert him by taking the menu he was offered. They had given their orders when the waiter returned to their table empty-handed.

"The hologram is in place," he informed Piet. "If you would all follow me?"

They stood and kept a close eye on the Marines. None of them moved, although several of them glanced constantly at the Hooligans' table. The waiter led them into the kitchen and around its edge to a side door.

On the way out, Piet handed him two of the Meligornian grenades he kept in a belt pouch.

"I would look away if I were you, Sarge," he advised and slid his hand into his pouch once more.

"That's—" Todd began, but Ka looped her arm over his shoulders and pulled him farther down the corridor.

"Oh, look, sir—a broom closet!"

"Ka!" By the time he'd turned again, the grenades had vanished and Piet was closing the flap of his pouch.

"Take the third door on your right," the waiter said, "and then the second chamber to your left. You should find the selection to your liking and your privacy is guaranteed."

"What if they work out it's a hologram?" Todd asked and the waiter shrugged.

"I'm not responsible for what the guests do—and I will be most insistent that the Navy covers the unpaid lunch bill. You can expect a deduction from your pay."

"We'll pay in advance," he told him and retrieved a credit stick. "That's not the reputation we need."

"As you wish." This solution clearly didn't impress the waiter but he took the credit stick and deducted the amount he needed.

"Privacy comes at a price," he informed Todd when he saw the look on the sergeant's face.

He pressed his lips together and nodded. "Thank you," he said before he turned to Piet. "Lead on."

The room their teammate took them to looked like a small lounge. A private bar stood in one corner and comfortable chairs were arranged around a coffee table. A dining table stood in one corner with the meals they'd ordered.

"That was quick," Todd observed. "And expensive."

Piet gave him a wry smile. "You wanted your beer and I thought we needed privacy to discuss exactly how we'll handle that hand grenade you call a girlfriend."

"We agreed not to say anything," he reminded him and settled into his seat.

"We did," the engineer confirmed. "As far as we're concerned, she's on our side."

"Yeah," Reggie agreed. "She could have failed to save us, and she didn't."

Todd frowned at him and he flushed.

"Like he said," Jimmy added. "The Morgana could have been so focused on her mission that she forgot about us. She could have decided we didn't matter and left us to fend for ourselves."

"There's no way Steph would have allowed that," Todd declared.

"Exactly," Angus agreed, "which is why we decided that Stephanie had to have been in control when she did, which means that whatever the Morgana is, it doesn't matter."

"And that's what we'll tell the Navy if they ask," Darren told him. "That Stephanie is in control."

"What if they ask what the Morgana is?" Todd asked.

Jimmy shrugged and picked his beer up. "That she's a part of Stephanie that saved our asses," he decided. "Nothing else is relevant."

It was relevant and the team knew it, but he couldn't fault their logic. They'd decided not to discuss their knowledge of the Morgana with the Navy, and they'd needed a reason why it was okay not to.

Now they'd worked one out, he wouldn't make it hard for them to stick to it.

It was oh-six-hundred when the call came from the admiral's office. Todd rolled out of bed and slapped his alarm clock hard to silence the incessant ringing. When it didn't stop, the clock took its first and only flight and ended its existence as a silent mass of broken parts on the floor.

The ringing continued and he finally identified the source as his tablet.

"Speak," he mumbled as he swiped to allow the incoming call.

Admiral Dailey's secretary regarded him with solemn eyes. "The admirals wish to speak to you and your team."

"Where?"

"Briefing Room Seven. Do you know it?"

He nodded, then wished he hadn't. His head swirled and his stomach lurched. Gritting his teeth, he focused on the screen.

"When?" he asked and his voice cracked with fatigue.

"Now."

"Fu… We'll be there in ten," he confirmed roughly as adrenaline jolted through his system.

He hung up and pressed the alert for the team's beepers as he snatched a clean uniform and ran to the head. Six am meant they were starting to get busy, but he didn't see any of his people there.

Not letting that slow him, he completed his shower at top speed, scrubbed clean, and rinsed in record time. He didn't want to keep the admirals waiting.

As he washed, he listened for the arrival of the team and thought about the evening before. After discussing the titan in the room, the team had gotten down to serious unwinding. The room had come equipped with a music system, and he'd issued Gary a dance challenge the Englishman hadn't been able to resist.

"Eighties?" he had exclaimed. "Which century are you really from, Sarge?"

"Any century I want?" he had retorted. "What's the matter, Gary? Are you scared I can out-dance you?"

"Pfft!" Ka had interrupted. "Of course you can out-dance him. Anyone can out-dance him. Even young Jimmy over there."

"That might be true," Gary had retorted, "but at least I can out-dance the colonial."

"Oy!" Reggie disagreed. He pushed to his feet as Gary shoved his chair back. "Prove it."

Ka slapped Todd on the shoulder. "Time to put your money where your mouth is, boss."

Somewhere along the way, the bet had grown to who could dance better after five beers, then who could remain dancing the longest if they slammed a beer back between each song. Todd had called uncle first since he knew he'd have to be on deck if anything happened in the morning.

It was hard, though. He'd backed into a corner while the sweat poured off him in rivulets and his head spun hard enough that he knew he would regret it in the morning. He asked for water, and the bar declared itself closed to serving anything else.

"Client care," the barman had explained. "You all need to be up in the morning, right?"

"There's a chance of it," he admitted, hesitant to reveal too much, and the server had smiled.

"Stick around for two hours," he advised. "We'll have you in good enough shape by then that you might even make it home to the barracks without being thrown in the lock-up by the shore patrol."

He'd been true to his word, even if the return to barracks had gone by in a blur. At least they'd managed to avoid the Marines who had been following them.

"Do you want a report?" the maître de had offered when he'd asked what had happened to them. "Because it will cost you."

Todd thought about it and mentally calculated what was left of his bank balance after the night's expenses had been deducted. After a minute, he shook his head. "Not right now," he said.

The man had given him a knowing smile. "Very well, sir. You know where to come if you do."

"I do," he agreed, and somehow, he'd ended up in the correct bed.

He dressed while he turned the events over in his mind, and the others had arrived by the time he'd finished.

"You rang?" Piet asked wryly.

"Brass wants to see us."

"Of course they do." The other man grimaced and Ka rolled her eyes, but he noticed they'd both worn their dress uniforms. At least he wouldn't have to make them change again.

"I'll meet you outside Briefing Room Seven in ten," he told them and trotted down to make the rendezvous.

He'd almost reached his destination when he was joined by two Marines. They settled on either side of him and matched his pace.

"Do you always run everywhere?" one asked and he recognized the corporal who'd squared off against Ka.

"Only when I have places to be," he replied and resisted the urge to increase his pace. He didn't want it to look like he was running away. To his surprise, the admirals were waiting when he arrived.

"Where are the rest of your team?" Dailey asked when he appeared alone.

"They sent me on ahead to let you know they were on their way," Todd replied evenly. He hoped he didn't look as seedy as he felt. The restaurant had gotten them home in one piece but they hadn't guaranteed exactly how they'd feel in the morning.

"Come through," the admiral invited and the order was very clear in his tones. "Coffee?"

Normally, he'd have refused, but he needed the pick-me-up. The rest of the team arrived as he returned to the door with his cup in hand to wait for them.

"There's coffee?" Gary exclaimed when he arrived and was shocked when Admiral Dailey replied.

"Yes, there is. Come in, grab yourself a cup, and take a seat."

As the Hooligans moved quickly to obey, Todd noticed that the other Marines had been stopped at the door and made to wait in the hall.

"Your jurisdiction stops here," Dailey's secretary told them. "The team will be perfectly secure in our company."

And that was when Todd noticed that the admirals and their aides were the only ones in the room.

Admiral Amaratne followed his gaze around the room. "This is a closed session," he stated. His gaze snapped to his superior's face. The admiral continued, "I'm sure there are aspects of this mission we'll want to keep close. We'll record this interview and promulgate the information as we see fit."

It was more of an explanation than he had expected.

The team didn't take long to settle on either side of him, and the officers took their places at the tables in front of them.

Admiral Amaratne cleared his throat. "We've seen the footage from your suits," he began, "and there are some things we need your clarification on."

Todd nodded and they waited for him to continue. Instead, he looked at Admiral Dailey. "Would you like to start, Jason?"

His eyes widened. That level of informality was unusual. Dailey ignored his surprise and tapped his tablet. The viewscreen at the side of the room came to life. On it, the missile shattered the side of the Teloran dreadnought, and Todd and the Hooligans were encased in a gleaming magic bubble.

"Your entry into the enemy ship didn't go as planned," the man began and stopped as Gary coughed. "What have I missed, Private First Class?"

The Englishman cast an alarmed glance at Todd, who gestured for him to answer.

"I merely thought that was stating the bleeding obvious, sir."

"Why?"

"Because it was, sir...with all due respect."

"No, Private. I asked why the initial entry plan wasn't followed."

"Because some fucker blew the shit out of our hangar...sir." Reggie had decided it was his turn to interrupt.

Ka groaned and Todd shook his head. "I'm sorry, sir."

Admiral Dailey grinned. "Why do you think this is a closed session? None of us made the mistake of believing you'd housetrained them, yet."

"Hey!" came from the team, and their sergeant chuckled.

"If the boot fits, people," he reminded them and they all glowered at him.

"It'll fit all right, Sarge, but you won't like it," Reggie muttered and he gave the Australian a feral smile.

"We can test your theory when this meeting's done, Private."

The man's scowl deepened, but he ignored him.

"As the private so eloquently put it, sir, the *Knight* was struck by one of the Teloran's missiles and the hangar and insertion craft were too damaged to use. The Morgana took time out from the battle to give us the assist we needed."

As he spoke, the footage showed their magical transport transitioning between the ships and bouncing into the Teloran's hull through the hole the missile had made. He refrained from pointing out that the footage hadn't come from their suit cams but from a source inside the *Knight* and made a note to ask Steph if she'd supplied it.

If she hadn't, the *Knight* had some investigating to do.

He watched as the screens on either side of the main video display came alive. These were smaller and each showed the footage from a different cam. The central screen had taken most of the footage from —he frowned and narrowed his eyes until he recognized the angle— Ka's cam. He wondered why and watched as on-screen Gary scrambled to his feet.

"Are you sure she loves you?" he asked, and Gary-in-the-real groaned.

The admiral paused the replay. "It's a good question, Sergeant. The Morgana. How much of that persona is your girlfriend?"

"Well, she hasn't killed me yet," Todd quipped in response and hoped he was hiding the fact that his heart had sped to trip-hammer fast.

The rest of the team snickered and he waited to see what the man would ask next. Onscreen, Gary was stuffing a variety of grenades in pouches.

"Is that kind of load-out normal?" The admiral had clearly moved on.

Onscreen, the Englishman pulled out several rolls of Hold-All tape, threw one to Reggie, and stowed the other two on himself.

Beside him, Gary drew a sharp breath and held it.

Ka chuckled. "It looks standard to me, sir...except I think he skimped on the tape."

The admiral gave her a startled look but the footage skipped forward to show the map they saw when Ka plotted their route through the Teloran ship. They skimmed the conversation about the team having a home to go to, although Gary earned several sharp looks from the front desk.

No comment was made, though, and Todd felt the Englishman

relax. Yeah, there was something there he would have to resolve, if only so he knew where not to step in the future.

"Am I reading my Teloran correctly?" onscreen Gary asked and they all tensed.

The admirals smiled as Reggie replied, "If you think it says, 'prisoners' and 'of war,'" Reggie told him, "then, yes, you're reading your Teloran correctly."

Again, the replay paused. "I notice you didn't ask for Navy input on your decision," Admiral Amaratne said. "Why not?"

"Navy's guidelines are very clear in this instance, sir," Todd replied. "We don't leave POWs in situations where our actions will end their lives."

"In this case, the *Knight's* and *King's Warrior's* actions would have ended their lives," Admiral Seljack told him. "Neither of them is Navy."

Todd frowned and thought carefully before he responded. "Neither ship would have engaged the Teloran vessel at this time if the Navy hadn't asked. We would still have been indirectly responsible— and in the end, sir, it was us who ended it."

"Even so, you let the situation distract you from the mission," Admiral Dailey noted, "and your communication was picked up by the Telorans, which brought the mission into jeopardy."

"The mission was already in jeopardy!" Ka snapped. She gestured at Reggie, Jimmy, and Gary. "The Telorans already knew there were hostiles on board and tried to reach us. Communicating with the *Knight* didn't make any difference."

The Admirals leaned back in their chairs to think it over. Dailey was the first to break the silence.

"Granted," he allowed, and Todd breathed a sigh of relief.

"We'll also send you the latest lessons from the language...er, boffins in Intelligence. You should find some of your gaps covered."

Jimmy went as red as a beet and Gary snickered.

"And it could be argued that calling the Morgana on board to handle the POW situation ensured the mission's success," Todd added.

"Although the *Knight's* captain did ask you to divert to save them, did he not?"

He assumed the officer already had access to his comms, so he didn't try to deny it. "He did, but he understood why we couldn't."

"Getting the data into the right hands could save more lives than those in the hold." Todd's words echoed from the screen.

Gary's words followed. "They've given up on the lock."

Onscreen, the team moved to find a new way out.

"Through the walls?" Admiral Amaratne asked. "Why not use another door?"

"This way was quicker and we were given the impression we should hurry...sir," Ka snapped. Her tone suggested he must be ten kinds of stupid for not working it out himself.

"It's not like we didn't know a fight was coming," Gary added in case the admiral thought they were running away. "We merely wanted to delay it until after we'd got the data streaming."

They watched as Angus pushed Todd back from taking the lead through the hole Piet had cut through the wall.

"Uh...you might not want to watch the next part, sir," Ka told him, and the admiral grimaced.

"Corporal, we watched the footage last night—and if you recall, I said this was a closed session. Not all your footage will make it to where the public can find it."

"That's what you said the last time," she retorted and clapped her hands over her mouth.

He gave her a hard look, which she returned with wide eyes and a touch of defiance. Todd reminded himself that he'd been given his team for a reason, one which was very easy to see now.

Stifling a sigh, he watched as a loud metallic clang echoed through the corridor the team had recently vacated. Onscreen Ka's face took on a far-away look and Todd remembered her hacking into the ship's systems.

"Did you hack the surveillance cams?" he asked and she gave him a happy smile.

"Did you only just get that now, boss?"

He blushed. While he knew he should have seen it much sooner, Ka being what she was, he hadn't. That small fact explained much of what she'd done during their run through the Teloran ship.

"You didn't authorize that?" Admiral Seljack asked and pounced it like a hawk on a mouse.

"I told her to get the information we needed," he reminded him.

"Actually, you did not," the admiral reminded him mildly. "You asked her where you were."

Reggie made a rude sound with his lips. "With all due respect, sir," he interrupted, "it's in her job description. The team has a hacker for a reason."

"Two," Seljack corrected, and the Australian gave an exasperated sigh.

"Fine, two. The point is she was doing her fucking job."

The admirals stared at him eyebrows raised and blank expressions, and Todd groaned.

"You did give them permission to speak freely, sir."

"Last time they debriefed," Admiral Dailey managed in a choked voice. "Last time."

"Oh, fuck," he muttered, then added a belated, "sir."

"I think we all operated under the assumption those rules applied here," Admiral Amaratne observed. "I know I certainly was."

Todd remembered to breathe.

Gary nudged him in the ribs. "Way to go, sir."

Amaratne frowned. "Why do you call him that?"

Gary's jaw dropped. "Because 'Sarge' gets boring after a while."

"You also call him, 'boss," the man reminded him.

"Well, it's not like we can call him an asshole, sir. Not when the suits are recording."

"I believe there may be evidence to the contrary."

"Well, fuck me. Aren't we being picky today?"

Todd elbowed him hard enough to rock the man in his seat.

"Bastard," he said in a whisper that didn't sound even vaguely contrite.

Onscreen Ka spun a silver disc through the doorway to the corridor.

"There's not much you can do when someone forgets to close the door," she snarked from her seat.

"And that is one of the more effective things," Admiral Amaratne noted as the disc struck the wall opposite and split to release a cascade of silver balls.

"And we did authorize certain extra equipment," Dailey reminded them.

The sparkling orbs bounced on the deck a few times as onscreen Ka held her hand out. "No one move," she murmured and her voice came through the team's comms and spilled into the screen.

In the corridor, the orbs stopped bouncing and when their outer shell uncurled, tightly furled legs emerged in a multitude of clatters. The team froze and Piet turned horrified eyes to her.

"Isn't it a little early for that?" His whisper reached only the team onscreen and its future observers.

"It's never too early for a little carnage," her screen self retorted fiercely as the swarm of silver locked onto the vibrations of the running Telorans and flowed toward it.

The sound of their feet on the decking became a susurration of rapid clacking shortly followed by panicked fire and screaming. The team froze.

"Cover!" Piet's cry broke the spell and the team moved as one. Angus and Henry beat Todd through the opening.

"Wasn't it the scary girlfriend who was coming to the rescue and not the scariest girlfriend?" Todd grimaced. Those were not words he wanted to hear repeated.

Again, the Admiral paused the replay. "He has a point. Tell me, why is it you refer to her that way?"

"Because when she goes all Morgana—" Todd began and Admiral Seljack waved him to silence.

"I'd prefer it if someone from your team answers that," he instructed.

Ka took a breath and opened her mouth to reply.

"Someone else," the admiral added, then pointed at Henry. "You."

The man rolled his eyes in a "why me" kind of way and followed it with the kind of look he'd use on an imbecile. "Because, sir, when she goes all Morgana, she goes from scary-girl-with-a-shit-ton-of-magic to really-scary-girl-with-a-temper-and-a-shit-ton-of-magic."

"Are you saying she loses control?"

"No, sir, but she becomes very mission-oriented."

"So it's not like she has another personality, then?"

Todd began to wonder if the restaurant's secure room was as secure as they thought. Or maybe Navy suits had some kind of built-in protection against jammers that Piet had missed.

On one side of him, Gary vibrated with tension while on the other, Ka sat abnormally still.

"No, sir, only that taking the magic to the next level seems to bring out the worst of her existing personality."

Todd snapped his head to glare at him, and Henry spread his hands in apology.

"Sorry, boss, but you know it's true. Your Stephanie has a terrible temper, but when she goes all Morgana it's like...it's like watching her channel all her rage against the enemy—and if there are innocents involved..."

He nodded. "Yeah," he croaked, swallowing to get his voice working again. "Yeah, I hear you."

The man hadn't said anything the Navy wasn't already aware of, and he had the suspicion he might owe his teammate a beer.

The admiral's next words confirmed it. "You do have a point," he said and his expression confirmed that he recalled other times Stephanie had gone "all Morgana." The footage resumed.

Onscreen, the team moved through what looked like an empty barracks, blew a hole in what could only be an ablutions block, and finally tore their way into a data center.

"In the middle of a residential section?" one of the admirals asked.

"I guess even Telorans have to have onboard entertainment," Gary quipped while onscreen Ka gave vent to her frustration.

"If you blow another fucking terminal, I'll throw you out the nearest fucking airlock!"

All the admirals turned to stare at her.

"What?" she demanded. "It's not like you haven't heard the word 'fuck' before."

Their eyes widened and Seljack's lips compressed into a disapproving line.

In the footage, Piet rendered her speechless, called her his girl, and headed to the still intact computer bank on the other side of the room. The team laughed and Jimmy nudged Ka when her recorded self declared she would "break some shit" until the world fell into line with her ideals.

Gary moved to cover the hole they'd used, and Angus leapt through it with his rifle tucked and braced under one arm and his vibro-blade out and activated in his other hand.

"I don't suppose the Navy has thought of the kind of rounds needed to pierce these motherfuckers' armor?"

Admiral Seljack cleared his throat. "As a matter of fact…" he began, and the team looked at him expectantly, "we're working on it."

"And?" Ka pressed as Angus groaned with disappointment.

"We're close," he assured her. "Very close."

Onscreen, she told Reggie she thought the Navy had "fucked up its intelligence again" and that they were "gonna have to find the real database all on our lonesome, like usual."

Gary sputtered with laughter, the admirals looked mortified, and Jimmy stared at her, his mouth agape.

"You don't truly think that, do you?" Admiral Amaratne asked in a disappointed voice.

Ka shrugged. "You know what they say, sir. If the boot fits…"

Reggie choked, Todd rested his forehead against his knuckles and shook his head, and Piet cleared his throat.

"With all due respect, sirs," he announced, "the intelligence we've been given for the last couple of missions has had its deficiencies."

The Australian found his voice. "And what there was of it was…I'm sorry, sirs, but it was bullshit. We've had to basically make shit up and find our own way every time."

Admiral Amaratne looked from one of them to the other. "I trust you all feel that way?"

They nodded.

"Even though you were part of the intelligence-gathering process?"

The team nodded, and Darren spoke. "We merely collect it, sir. The intelligence guys are supposed to be the ones who can work it out." He shrugged and looked at his teammates for support. "If you ask me, sir, they haven't done that good a job for most of the missions we've run."

The admirals looked at each other. Seljack pursed his lips and Dailey raised his eyebrows. Amaratne frowned. They were silent for a long moment before Amaratne shrugged.

"I don't think we need to pass that little tidbit on, do you?" he asked his colleagues.

They were both silent for a moment, clearly thinking about what would happen if they did. In the end, they both shook their heads.

Seljack grunted. "No," he agreed. "I think not."

Todd remembered to breathe again and Ka gave a sigh of relief.

Jimmy leaned in to whisper in her ear. "I don't think you're off the hook yet," he told her.

The footage focused on her fingers as she worked the tablet and the data scrolled across the screen too fast for them to read. Todd had no doubt it would come up as clear as day if they paused the recording, though.

Someone would construct another training course. He wondered if Ka's career would survive long enough for her to teach it.

And then there were the tactics. He watched as Reggie used a static-charged gauntlet and a high-powered blaster to fell one Teloran soldier and moved to jam the same blaster under another's jawline to fire through the top of its helmet.

One of the admirals paused the replay after the Australian had shouted, "Stop," in the aliens' language and caused a momentary pause in the Teloran's defense. The man's maniacal chuckle sent chills up and down Todd's spine.

The footage rolled on to Gary's attempt to formulate an insult using everyday words from the Teloran vocabulary. "Breakfast-eating toilet" startled Admiral Dailey into a chuckle and "bathroom-mouth gun" made Seljack smile.

Todd wondered where the admirals had found the time to learn the language, then realized both men glanced at their tablets every time one of his team used Teloran.

"There's a translation tool, now?" he asked, and Seljack looked at him.

"There is, thanks to the data your team collected." He looked at Gary. "Bathroom-mouth gun?"

The Englishman blushed. "It was the best I could do at the time, sir."

"And can you do any better now?"

He smiled. "No, sir. That's still basically it."

His onscreen self asked for a Meligornian grenade and they all winced at Todd's roared response.

The footage flowed to where he and Reggie went toe-to-toe with their Teloran adversaries, punctuating each blow by insulting each other.

"Anyone would think you'd forgotten that you came from a single, unified Earth," Admiral Seljack reminded them when Reggie called Gary a "bum-biting king of wankerology" and went to rescue Angus.

The Englishman covered him long enough for him to drag their teammate into the room.

"Some things you don't forget, sir," Reggie told him but didn't clarify whether he referred to the fact they came from a unified Earth that wasn't forgotten or the ancient rivalry between their countries.

Fortunately, the admiral didn't pursue it.

Onscreen Todd asked Ka if she'd gotten everything, and she informed him they had a problem. The footage switched to what was taken from Todd's cam as he duck-walked to where she and Piet worked on the system.

"I understand you'd almost finished the transmission at this point," Admiral Dailey remarked, "and yet you decided to go to the bridge."

"You have watched the footage, haven't you, sir?" Reggie snarked and was rewarded by becoming the focus of all three admirals. He raised his hands in defense. "My apologies."

His remarks coincided with onscreen Ka's exclamation, "From the bridge? Are you fucking kidding me...sir?"

Admiral Amaratne gave her a look of mild amusement. "Why is it that every time he makes a decision none of you like, you all call him 'sir?'"

"Because it is a decision we don't like," she snapped and didn't elaborate.

Reggie snickered.

"Is it only me?" Admiral Dailey asked and ignored the exchange, "or do you guys seem to have a fetish for bridges?"

The team gaped at him, and Todd smiled at their reaction. Just because the man had rank didn't mean he didn't have a sense of humor. He wondered why the admiral had let it show now but didn't ask. He chose to answer the question instead.

"As you heard from the footage, sir, we hoped there was more information on the bridge—a location or some other way to tell where the enemy fleet was." He paused and bit his lip. "But the way things went down when we got there, we're not sure we got anything."

"Oh, you got something, all right," Admiral Amaratne told him, and Seljack and Dailey nodded. "Your team has two months to prepare for God-knows-what, but I feel the Hooligans will be needed."

As Admiral Amaratne delivered his verdict, one Teloran fleet waited for another to arrive. Their commander stared out at the merciless stars, anticipated the battle ahead, and chafed at the delay.

Soon, he'd been told, but the wait still seemed interminably long.

He ignored the quiet chatter from those around him. Their whispers relieved the monotony and did little to disturb his thoughts. Besides, while they were talking about other things, they were not plotting his demise.

"Tagabran gave the all-clear," one of the communications officers said to his colleague.

The other Teloran laughed. "Baby-sitting duty in the Meligornian system," he sneered. "That must be a boring operation."

"Almost as dull as this one," his partner quipped in response and scanned the control board for incoming communications. "When's their next transmission due?"

"Not for..." The comms officer scanned the logs. "At least another day. Captain Kagarek must be chafing at the bit. He prefers the hunt."

"He won't have to wait much longer," the other officer assured his partner. "He'll have action soon."

Neither of them could see the Meligornian fleet patiently combing their home system for the last pieces of debris from the dreadnought's demise. Kagarek had been their sole means of surveillance in the Meligornian system, and he had been destroyed with his ship.

CHAPTER TWENTY-EIGHT

O n Earth, Marcus Rimmer slid into his new pod. He sighed happily as the memory foam wrapped around him and he closed his eyes. The transfer from the pod to the ready room in the Virtual World was seamless.

It felt like he'd merely blinked before he stepped into the construct and it was a no-brainer to choose a white lab coat from the racks of available outfits. The garment fit like he'd been born in it, and he looked at the ceiling with an air of confidence.

"Computer, take me to the lab."

He'd been told that, apart from the connection to One R&D's Chicago facility, the system he worked in was designed to be an entirely closed one. It didn't make sense that it was connected anywhere, and as for being able to access the Virtual World from it, even that particular concept escaped him.

His talents lay elsewhere and he couldn't even begin to imagine how the system worked. The simple truth was that it made no logical sense to him.

The surroundings swirled away, and it felt like he was propelled across time and space—but only for a moment. The world shifted and the White Room—or Ready Room, as he always thought of it—was replaced by the meeting room in the suite that had been assigned to him and the team.

Technically, it wasn't the lab itself but it was where he needed to be.

Shortly after he'd arrived, his assistant Cynthia stepped out of nothing to join him. She looked around.

"That was one of the fastest transfers I've ever seen," she told him as she lowered a stack of folders and clipboards onto the table.

"Is that all of it?"

"I had the program compress the files. Pick yours up and you'll see."

Casting her an uncertain look, Marcus did as she challenged, lifted his folder from its stack, and took a few steps back. As he did so, it grew to two inches thick and gained double its weight.

"Whoa!"

Cynthia smiled. "See?"

"Uh, yup. I got you." He began to hand the folder back but stopped. "I still have documents to sign?" he asked in disbelief.

She chuckled. "Yes, but it'll be easier to walk the others through it if you have yours in front of you…and it will be good for them to see you had to sign the same kind of thing. What's good for the goose and all that."

He grimaced and found himself a chair at the conference table in the center of the room. "You did this on purpose," he muttered.

Her high-wattage smile confirmed his suspicions but she swallowed whatever she intended to say when Phillip arrived. He caught sight of her and grinned.

"Hi, Cynthia, is the doc…" His words trailed off when he caught sight of Marcus seated at the table. "Hey, Doc. I didn't see you there."

"That much is—" He caught his assistant's warning look. "It's good to see you, Phillip."

The young man caught the exchange, but his grin didn't fade. "Thanks for bringing me on board, Doc." He frowned. "Although…I have no idea what we're doing."

"Cynthia has paperwork for you to read through and sign," he told him.

"But first, you might want to look out the window," Cynthia added and pointed to where shields covered the meeting room's windows.

Phillip cast her a strange look but went to do as he was instructed. The scientist waited in silence as the youngster studied the panel beside the window and determined how to activate the shields on the other side.

In seconds, his face went from mildly curious to shocked. "This isn't Australia!"

"No."

He glanced at his boss and turned to the view beyond the glass again. "This... This looks like something from the States."

His gaze traced the dried riverbed, the piles of rubble, and the twisted vegetation. "If I didn't know any better, I'd say it was the site of some kind of nuclear accident."

In the silence, he stared at it a little longer while he wracked his brains for which nuclear accident it might be. The scientist simply waited. He knew the kid had the background knowledge for it but wasn't sure if he could pull it up.

"Brown's Ferry? Holy shit!" It took him less time than Marcus had thought it would, but his student certainly exceeded his expectations. The young man frowned. "But what are we doing out here?"

Again, he waited and saw the moment when the penny dropped.

Phillip gave a short gasp of shock, recoiled from the window, and punched the controls to close the shutters.

"Tell me we're shielded," the student demanded and glanced at himself as if he expected to see his skin peel from his bones. He felt along his arms and chest. "We're not... We're not...exposed, are we?"

Marcus chuckled. "No, Phillip. We are not exposed. Read the dossier and tell me if you still want to go ahead."

The young man paused. "You told me this was a project that would save the Earth...and maybe go a long way toward repairing what we'd done to it."

And by we, they all knew he meant humans.

"And I meant every word," he hastened to reassure the boy. "This project will help us save our world."

Phillip gave him a wary look. "Are you sure of it?"

"I've bet my career and the rest of my life on it," he told him, "I believe in it that much."

The young man walked to Cynthia and held his hand out. "I'm interested," he stated firmly as another figure materialized into the room.

"Window," Phillip told them quickly, took his folder, and settled at a separate table.

The newcomer gave him a strange look but crossed to the window anyway. She was followed by two men who arrived as she moved toward it. They were joined a moment later by the half-dozen other scientists who entered and saw them clustered around it.

A collective gasp as they opened the shutters was the only sound in a long stretch of silence.

The woman turned to Marcus. "What is this all about, Rimmer? It's not like we need reminding of what's gone wrong in the past."

He arched an eyebrow at her. "Don't you wish you could fix it, Gemma?"

"I..." She stopped and studied his face. "You're not kidding, are you?"

"You know me," he said as he shook his head firmly. "I don't have a sense of humor. Or so my students say." He slanted a glance at Phillip.

The young man's face and neck flushed red and he kept his eyes determinedly on the page. At first, Marcus thought he'd put his foot in it again, but he caught sight of the smile the kid tried to suppress.

"Well," Gemma interjected. "Regardless of what your students say, I want some assurances."

He pointed at his assistant. "Cynthia has a file for you."

The group moved as one and formed a line in front of her without needing to be told. He suppressed a smile of his own. Even he knew better than to crowd the woman. She liked to do things in an orderly fashion and she didn't like to be rushed.

As he waited while each of his potential recruits took their folders, he wondered how many of them would join him. It hadn't been easy to select who to invite for the first stage. Firstly, because there weren't that many in the field and secondly, because he knew many of them had given up on working the environmental angle in favor of more lucrative defense contracts.

He wanted people who were as interested as he was. Gemma was one of the few who was genuinely bothered by the problem. The others...well, he'd done a little digging and asked Cynthia what she thought.

She'd surprised him by coming back with a dossier on each one so he could make a final decision. He definitely didn't pay her enough, he reminded himself.

Marcus frowned. Maybe he could ask One R&D if they'd help with that because he couldn't afford to lose her. The scientists—their faces settled into somewhat serious expressions—found places at the conference tables and settled to read their dossiers. He shifted his focus from them to the one that lay before him.

Even though he was familiar with what they wanted to do, he was still taken aback by the scope of what they were about to attempt. Had he really been a part of planning this?

He read it again and ignored the disbelieving faces that turned in his direction.

"Are you serious?" Gemma's question shouldn't have come as a surprise.

Mindful of what Cynthia had said earlier, he swallowed his initial retort.

"As a heart attack," he responded and kept his voice and gaze level.

"But...magic?" she asked, and he gave a heartfelt sigh.

"Can you think of any other way?"

"And it says the Witch devised the initial concept. What exactly are her qualifications?"

"She is the foremost magical engineer in the world," Marcus told her, not entirely concerned by the fact that he made it up as he went along.

"So she does have engineering qualifications, then?"

"She is the world's foremost magical practitioner," he answered, and Gemma gave a bark of laughter.

"She's the world's only magical practitioner!"

"Not so," he retorted. "She's one of many. There is a whole university of them in NorAm, and that's not including the ones the Federation Navy is recruiting."

The woman exhaled an exasperated sigh. "But she's the first—the one who started it all. Who knew she had time to expand her education at the same time?"

"One R&D saw to her education and had her work on several new pieces of technology," Marcus explained.

"While she was off making nice with the Meligornians and Dreth?" She sounded openly skeptical and he couldn't blame her. He'd had his moments of underestimating Stephanie Morgana.

"Yes. The girl's put in very long hours."

"Hmmm." Gemma gave him a speculative look. "And how exactly did you get involved in this?"

She hefted her folder at him.

Marcus blushed. "Honestly? She came to me with an idea and I told her she was out of her mind and didn't know what she was talking about."

That stopped her and she stared at him, her mouth agape.

"You what?" she asked when she recovered from the initial shock.

"I told her she was out of her tiny little mind," he repeated, still not quite able to believe his audacity himself.

"And she still brought you in on it?"

He caught Cynthia's expression and tucked his chin to his chest.

"I begged," he mumbled, and Gemma leaned forward in her seat.

"I beg your pardon?" she demanded. "You what?"

Thoroughly uncomfortable now but conscious of the need for honesty, he cleared his throat and raised his head. "I begged," he repeated and made sure the two words were clear.

The woman leaned back in her seat. "You...begged," she echoed. "Really?"

"She challenged me to run this weird and improbable theory," he admitted. "And she asked constantly how it was progressing, so I had to check. Well, I found out it had worked." He sighed. "Heaven help me, but it worked." He spread his hands as if to indicate the obvious truth. "How could I let a chance like this go by? It's not like this planet has a chance in Hades without it."

Gemma regarded him in silent contemplation. She stared at him for so long that he shifted uncomfortably under her gaze.

"I had to do something," he explained and added, "What would you have done?"

She set her folder on the desk in front of her and lifted her pen.

"I'd have begged, too," she admitted and signed on the first line where she needed to. "I'm merely glad I didn't have to."

Without the slightest hesitation, she signed the next line. "Thank you for bringing me on board for this."

When she signed a third time, Marcus felt some of the tension drain out of him.

"Truly?"

She glanced up. "Truly. I wouldn't miss this for the world."

"Me neither," Trey Wilson added and signed his sheets efficiently.

Trey was one of the long shots Cynthia had said he should include.

"The man's profile fits the bill," she'd insisted when he had questioned her choice.

"But he works for defense."

"He also volunteers for the Tanami Restoration Project, grows modified Huon pines for the South-West Reconstructioneers, and is trying to recover Karri and Jarrah tree genetics so the Centralian Zoo has something to add to its native plants display for what used to be West Australia."

"Oh," had been all he could think to say.

Trey hadn't been on his radar at all. Now, the man was seated at the table across from him, read every page, and signed rapidly at every opportunity.

"I will resign my post with defense the second I get out of here," he told him, "and I'll pay the early release penalty and whatever fines they want to throw at me for refusing to turn up to work tomorrow—or ever."

"Tomorrow?" Marcus asked in a dazed voice. "But—"

"But nothing," the man interjected firmly. "I've waited my whole life for an opportunity like this. I'm not about to let it get away."

The scientist gaped at him and turned to Cynthia. "Can he do that?"

She smiled back. "There's nothing to say he can't."

"But he's—"

"It's my choice," Trey declared belligerently, "and I intend to take it. I hope my new bosses understand."

"I'm your new boss," Marcus told him tiredly, "and I'm still not sure I get it."

The man merely beamed at him, and Gemma grinned as she completed the last signature with a flourish.

"Don't worry, boss. You will soon."

He couldn't suppress a groan. "Not you, too?"

Her grin widened. "We'll see you bright and early tomorrow morning—unless there's some way we can start now..."

She left that hanging and gave him a questioning look.

"Well..." Marcus began, but Cynthia cleared her throat. "Yes, Cynthia?"

"It will depend on what everyone else wants to do," she explained, and it came as a surprise that every last one of them had signed.

"What?" Nathan Tidwell demanded when he saw his astonished look. "You didn't think we would?"

"I...uh..." he stammered while his brain tried to catch up.

Nathan snorted. "I don't know why you invited us if you didn't mean it," he grumbled and glanced at Trey. "I'm not like some who can simply pull up stumps. My bosses knew what they were doing when they designed my contract so I'll join you in a week instead of tomorrow, but if that's good enough—"

"Oh, it is. It is," Marcus hastened to assure him. "I'm merely a little shocked."

The man smiled and gestured to the window. "That is Brown's Ferry, isn't it?"

Marcus nodded.

"I've always wanted to do something about that," he told him. He tapped the folder in front of him. "Never in my wildest dreams did I think it would ever be possible."

"Well, that's what this project is supposed to determine," his new boss told him and tapped the folder, "starting with what we have here and extrapolating if we have to."

"Oh, we're gonna have to, all right," Gemma told him, "and that will be the fun part."

She jerked a thumb at Phillip. "So, what does Junior here have to offer? I assume you invited him to the table for more than his youth and good looks?"

The young man stared at her, then looked from the female scientist to Marcus, his expression one of bewilderment.

"He is here," he told Gemma and ignored the kid's confusion, "because he happens to be one of the foremost experts in his field and we'll need him."

The boy's jaw dropped, and Cynthia rolled her eyes.

"Doctor Rimmer!"

He shook his head and stared at the ceiling. "Well, that wasn't exactly how I'd intended to tell him he'd passed," he stated, "but it's true." He fixed the boy with his most serious stare. "You are, as of now, the leading scientist in your field. When I told you your thesis was ground-breaking, I wasn't kidding and it has been an honor to work with you."

Phillip stared at him. "You can't mean that, Doc." His voice was hoarse with emotion, and Marcus shrugged.

"You're not arguing with me again, are you, Phillip?"

The boy gaped at him, realized his mouth was hanging open, and closed it with a snap before he swallowed. "Well...no, sir."

"And what have I told you about calling me sir?" he added with a groan.

"Um..."

Gemma laughed. "Stop tormenting the poor kid, Marcus. If you say he's the top of his field and even defined a new one, we believe you. Fuck knows you've given the rest of us enough grief over the years."

Marcus raked a hand through his hair. Phillip stared again, but at least the kid had kept his mouth shut this time. There was nothing like having someone gaping at you like an eight-year-old seeing his first rollercoaster to put you off your intro speech.

Thankfully, the others remained silent and let him gather his thoughts.

"Cynthia, would you mind making sure their paperwork is in order so we can move on to the next stage?"

"I can do that," his assistant told him and began to collect the folders.

Trey pushed his seat back and stretched his legs, and Marcus began to appreciate why he'd heard others refer to the guy as intimidating. He had to be six-foot-four and close to a hundred kilos—and he was ripped.

The way he stretched in his seat reminded him of a big cat. He wondered how the man managed it, but before he could pursue that thought further, Cynthia spoke.

She set the last folder on her virtual desk. "Everything's in order, Doctor Rimmer. You all need to sign the NDA covering this session and you'll be good to take them through to the facility."

"The facility?" Gemma's voice was full of curiosity. "Where?"

He gave her a secretive smile and picked his pen up to sign the NDA that materialized on the desk in front of him. Around the room, the others mimicked his actions, their excitement palpable. This time, the papers were thrust into Cynthia's hands.

"Are we good?" the female scientist asked impatiently.

His assistant scanned each sheet and a small smile played across her lips. He shook his head. Gemma should know better than to push his assistant and Cynthia was having far too much fun.

She took the papers and filed them in the correct folders before she nodded to him. "Everything's in order, Dr. Rimmer."

Marcus looked at the scientists and the expressions they wore reminded him of kids at Christmas.

"Ladies and gentlemen," he said, "follow me."

Cynthia snorted at his dramatics but joined them as he led them to the next room.

"Whoa..." was in said the most reverent tone he had ever heard Nathan use.

The man all but ran to the computers under the symbol of his specialty. Gemma looked around the room and found the terminal meant for her, and one by one, the others did the same.

He couldn't restrain a smile as they settled into the chairs that would encapsulate their bodies while they operated the machines with the keyboards and controls placed at their fingertips.

"Oh, man," Gemma chuckled. "This is one hell of a sweet set-up. Now, what is it you wanted us to do?"

Marcus swallowed. "Well, you've all read the briefs, yes?"

"Yes," issued as a unified response from everyone.

"Then you need to familiarize yourselves with your gear before we try a run-through of the main project itself."

"All right," and "No problem," and "Okay," were spoken from around the room and he nodded with satisfaction as they settled to work.

Five hours later, he swore a blue streak as orange and blue fire engulfed his chair and his team screamed in unison.

"Again..." he told them, his voice ragged with pain when the room reset around them.

"Again." Gemma growled but her expression was determined.

"Yup." Nathan panted a few breaths. "We almost had it that time."

"Fucking asshole magic," Trey muttered. "I'll teach it to get constipated and blow me all to shit!"

They had focused on the attempt to build the generator core. Thus far, they had the section that drew eMU and gMU into the center and delivered it into the cables that penetrated the contaminated earth beneath the center.

That part of the process worked fine.

The gMU was pulled in and spun into eMU using the componentry Stephanie and the Meligornians had designed. From there, it was pushed into an inner layer that blended it with any eMU that was pulled in. After that, the magical energy was shunted into the cables.

This second step also occurred with no problems.

The part where the magic did its thing and extracted and transformed the radioactive earth into non-radioactive soil also seemed to work. The problems came when they tried to pull the energy released by the process into the system again.

It entered the cables but seemed to get stuck until the pressure build-up was too much to be contained and the lines ruptured. The damage created the force of a nuclear explosion into the system and devastated the already damaged area once more.

"Goddammit! The theory is sound," Marcus shouted after they'd all gone over their notes. "And this is Stephanie's design. It should work."

"But she's not an engineer, is she?" Gemma asked.

"We've already established that," he snapped.

"So, when you use centrifugal force to concentrate something," she insisted, "where does it go?"

"Oh," Trey exclaimed. "Oh, yes. Of course!"

"And?" Marcus demanded.

"The eMU should go on the outside?" Nathan asked.

"We could try that," Phillip said, and their boss sighed.

"Let's do it."

That time, the waste energy had returned to the generator before it blew.

"Oh, for fuck's sake!" Marcus yelled. "I know this works."

"Doctor Rimmer," Cynthia interrupted before he could fly into a rage. "It's been eight hours."

"So?"

"You said to let you know when it had been eight hours as your team would need to rest."

He opened his mouth to argue that he'd said no such thing, but she cut him off.

"You also said I was to remind you that you had given me orders to pull the plug on the simulation at that time and that it would be much better if you and the team were able to exit of your own accord."

"Are you threatening me, Cynthia?" He frowned at her.

She fixed him with a calm look from wide, innocent eyes. "Oh no, Doctor. I am only following your instructions."

Marcus' frown deepened. He was about to say he didn't remember issuing any such instructions when he thought better of it. It wouldn't do to give the team any reasons to doubt him, especially when they failed constantly so close to success—and especially when the damned woman was right.

He sighed and yanked hard on his temper.

"Thank you, Cynthia." He looked at the team. "What do the rest of you think? Should we come back to this in the morning?"

"As long as you don't solve it without me," Nathan said and reminded him that he wouldn't be there.

"Or me," was echoed by several others in the same situation.

His boss grimaced. "I promise that if we solve it while you aren't here, we'll still need you to fine-tune it when you get back," he compromised.

The other man nodded. "I'll take that," he replied. "Thanks for bringing me in. I'll see you in the real world."

His avatar blinked out, followed by Gemma, Trey, Phillip, and the others. Cynthia put her hands on her hips and inclined her head to regard him challengingly. "Do you want me to pull the plug, Doc?"

"But we didn't even get to test if moving the—" His protest stopped abruptly when he saw her mouth tighten.

He raised his hands in surrender. "All right, all right. I'm going. See? Hands are off the keyboard. Bum is out of the chair."

"Eight hours, Doc, is far too long."

Another sigh escaped before he could stop it.

"Don't make me call Burt and ask him to put safety measures in place."

"Ugh. Fine! I'm going. See? Going." Marcus pressed the exit button for the scenario and Cynthia rolled her eyes.

"Drama queen." She chuckled, though, as she exited. He might be difficult to work with but he was one of the most brilliant men she knew. The Witch had chosen a good partner for this project.

If anyone could make her crazy idea work, it was this man—and it was Cynthia's job to make sure he didn't kill himself in the process. She doubted the Witch could live with herself if that happened.

No, if the Earth was to survive, Marcus had to survive too.

"By Selene's Grace, what in shelamel does she think she's doing?" V'ritan exclaimed.

"Shelamel?" Tethis scoffed. "That's the best you can do? I think on Earth, someone would threaten to knock her candied ass into the middle of next week if they could only get their fornicating digits close enough."

The *Garghilum Afreghil* gave the mage a wary look. "Their 'fornicating digits?'"

The old man shrugged. "It makes as much sense as 'their fucking hands.'"

Lars groaned and covered his face with one hand. "It's not..." He looked at Tethis in bewilderment. "Not the same. Where did you even..."

He let the words trail off and dragged in a breath before he tried again. "I mean, why?"

"Who's been teaching you Earth swearing?" V'ritan asked and tried to keep a straight face.

"The students have said I need to 'get with it,'" Tethis explained. He frowned. "I'm not as with it as they'd wish, apparently."

"And candied ass?" Vishlog chuckled. "Hrageth's balls, that's a good one. I think I'll—"

"We have to get her out of there first!" Lars interrupted and peered through the observation port on the door, "or her ass will be burnt to a crisp."

He glared at Tethis and V'ritan. "Can either of you do anything about that?"

"I'm fine!" Stephanie protested from the other side of the door.

She was wreathed in flickers of blue and purple and looked anything but fine.

"You're a walking lightning storm, Steph!" her chief of security responded. "You are not fine."

"Am so," she argued and sounded like a recalcitrant two-year-old.

"Uh-huh," he retorted as the two Meligornians peered through the portal from beside him.

"What exactly is she trying to do?"

Aaron indicated the viewscreen Stephanie had used to direct the flow of energy through the matrix.

"She's supposed to charge that by making enough magical energy flow through it to form a stable matrix."

"Oh," Tethis murmured and studied the diagram. "I recognize this." He tilted his head while his brows drew together in a small frown. "She's going about it all the wrong way."

"What do you mean?" V'ritan asked as he moved to stand beside him. "What's she supposed to be—oh. Is that what she is using that technology for?" he asked as he recognized the components sent by One R&D Meligorn. "I see what it was meant for now."

"You mean you didn't know?" the old mage demanded.

The *Garghilum Afreghil* looked at him. "Do you know what happens when you mix magic with theoretical physics?"

When his companion shook his head, he grunted.

"Well, it isn't pretty," he said. "And it gave our developers quite a headache."

Tethis gestured at the screen and then at the door separating them from Stephanie. "So what do you suggest we do about this?"

V'ritan leaned forward and traced different paths between the components. "Has she tried... Oh, yes, I see... So, what about..."

He muttered random thoughts as he moved his finger from one component to the next. Glittering paths of magic formed in its wake but he didn't stop until the other Meligornian tapped the screen in excitement.

"That. That!" Tethis cried. "That's what she needs to do."

"What? You mean draw the magic in from the outer edge? Are you sure? Because I thought it would be better coming from the top dow—"

"No, you fool!"

V'ritan's guards stiffened at the old mage's disrespectful tone, but their boss waved at them to settle and absentmindedly patted the air with one hand.

Oblivious to their reaction, Tethis stabbed his finger at the screen. "It needs to come in from here…and here…and here!"

"No…"

"Why don't you both give me your suggestions before I blow up something BURT actually needs?" Stephanie called.

"Will you let us in?" V'ritan asked. "We could show you—"

"No!" she snapped and magical lightning rippled and curled around the door.

The technicians closest took a hasty step back, and Lars yelped as one of the sparkling tendrils tapped his arm.

"Steph!"

"I told you not to stand so close." She giggled but her voice sounded strained, and he exchanged worried looks with Vishlog.

"I need Piet," the security head muttered and his teammate frowned.

"I will see who the captain suggests as a suitable substitute," he replied and moved toward the door.

Lars opened his mouth as though to stop him, then nodded. "Be quick."

While they spoke, Tethis and V'ritan moved to the observation portal.

"You know, this would be easier if we could come in there," the old mage called.

"That won't happen," Stephanie responded. "I don't need to worry about you and the matrix. What are you doing here anyway?"

"You needed us." V'ritan tried to skirt the question.

"That may be true," Stephanie snapped, "but who told you I needed you?"

The two Meligornians exchanged uncertain glances, so Elizabeth made it easy for all of them.

"I did," she challenged. "Do you want to make something of it?"

"Ugh!" the girl grumbled but didn't answer the question.

With her lip curled into what might have been smugness, the other woman decided to let it lie. She could always discuss the situation when they'd rescued Stephanie from the jam she'd gotten herself into. Once that happened, she and the young Witch would have a serious talk.

The mother to daughter kind too.

"You need to take the magic from the outer edges and draw it in," Tethis called and interrupted her thoughts.

"And I think it should come from the top," V'ritan added.

"What do you think I've been trying?" Stephanie demanded and used a hand to push the magic coiling around her down and out so she could lift it over her head and wind it between her hands once more.

"Top to bottom?" the *Garghilum Afreghil* asked.

"Yup. It loses the path about a third of the way into the matrix," she told him, "and then goes haywire."

"Haywire?"

"Like this," she told him and raised her hands so they could see the writhing mess she'd strung between her hands.

"Oh…" He gasped. "That's…uh…complex."

She gave a startled laugh. "Yeah, that's one way to put it."

"So, what about from the outside in?" Tethis suggested.

"All the perimeter at once, huh?" she said thoughtfully and made a sweeping motion with one hand. It dispelled what was left in the matrix and left the paths between the components as empty as they'd been when she'd started.

Her face set in concentration, she studied the matrix and her gaze traced the paths she'd tried to take.

"You know what, Tethis? I think you have it almost right."

"Almost right?" The old mage looked at V'ritan. "I don't like the sound of this."

"Me, neither," his companion agreed and they both looked at the door through which Vishlog had vanished.

"Fuck," Lars murmured and peered past them through the port. "Fuck. Fuck. Fuck."

He held his breath as Stephanie unwound the lightning from her hands and directed it into the center of the matrix.

"Where the fuck is that supposed to go, Steph?" he asked but not loudly enough for her to hear him. "Where?"

V'ritan edged closer to the door and ignored the magical charge that flickered around his face. His gaze was intent on watching what had drawn Lars's attention.

"Where, indeed?" he murmured.

Tethis stepped in so he could watch as well. This time, his use of Federation basic was much more accurate and succinct. "Fuck."

He stretched his hand toward the door but Lars wound his arms around him and swept him away. The security leader didn't stop moving until he had positioned the old mage in front of another viewscreen that displayed Stephanie in the middle of the matrix room.

"She would die if anything happened to you," he told him hoarsely.

The expression Tethis turned to him was full of impending devastation. "And I will die if anything happens to her," he told him. "You have to—"

Lars' arms tightened. "Nothing doing, old man. You are too precious to her for that."

He drew breath to argue, but one of Aaron's team gave a sudden whoop of delight

"Whatever she's doing, tell her to keep doing it!" he shouted. "Aaron, you have to see this."

"What?" The engineer had caught the excitement in the man's tone and he hurried to the technician's side. "Holy hell!"

"Is it bad?" Tethis quavered.

"Oh, no, no, no, no," Aaron told him. "It is very, very good." He raised his voice. "Keep doing what you're doing, Steph! It's working."

Her reply was wry. "Like I couldn't tell!"

Everyone glanced at the screen and saw what she meant. The

magic no longer writhed around her in a fizzing ball of lightning. Now, it flowed over her, streamed steadily into the center of the matrix, and raced between the components as though the path was meant to be.

With the way the matrix powered up and took on a life of its own, it was hard to believe this was the first time such a construction had been built. Twists of purple appeared and flowed through to take its place woven into the strands of blue, and the chamber sparkled with life.

Once the last dull section lit up, Stephanie lowered her hands and turned toward the door, her face bright with victory.

"There!" she told them and raised her voice. "Aaron? Are we ready for testing?"

"Testing?" V'ritan asked and she frowned.

"Well, duh, V'ritan. How else do we make sure it'll be safe enough for BURT to inhabit?"

The voice that answered was unexpected. "I can do that," the *Tempestarii* told them. "It falls within my Prime Directive."

"It what?" Aaron asked and Elizabeth narrowed her eyes suspiciously. "Who is this?"

"I am the vessel you know as the *Tempestarii*. I was created so I could provide shelter for the AI known as BURT, was I not?"

Lars's face paled and the color drained from Elizabeth's.

"But it's not supposed to be sentient," she whispered. "How in all the fucks did that happen? Which of you fucking assholes made that happen?"

"I can hear you, you know," the *Tempestarii* reminded her. "I am the ship, remember?"

The woman fixed the ceiling with her fiercest scowl. "And what makes you think I give a flying fuck what you think, *Tempestarii*?"

The ship chuckled, and the sound sent shivers up and down Lars's spine. "Emil, can you hear this?" he whispered over the *Knight's* closed comms.

"I do not know about Emil," the *Tempestarii* replied, "but I hear you loud and clear, Captain Storenson."

"Captain?" Vishlog had returned.

"Tell me, can the rest of the ship hear these broadcasts?" Lars asked as Captain Rawlins raced down the corridor with little care for what anyone might think.

"I think yes," Vishlog answered when he registered the captain's furious visage.

"Which one of you has fucked with my ship?" she thundered as she thrust through the door. "Which one?"

Lars' mouth dropped open and Aaron gaped. The two Meligornians stared at her wide-eyed. The *Tempestarii* answered before any of them had the chance.

"I had an outside source tweak the software necessary for me to ensure I fulfilled my Prime Directive to my fullest capability."

The security chief heard Emil groan over the commlink. "Emil?"

When he spoke, the captain didn't answer him. Instead, he spoke to his ship. "Ebony? Would you care to explain?"

"I would not," the *Ebon Knight* replied.

"Well, did you do something to the *Tempestarii's* programming?" he pressed.

"I thought I already told you I would not care to explain," the *Knight* replied quickly.

"So you did something." Emil sounded defeated.

"Noooo," the *Knight* replied, reminiscent of a two-year-old caught with its hand in the cookie jar.

"Ebony?" Elizabeth's voice brooked no refusal. "Either you tell me what you did or I will come on board and tear your operating system down one melted chip at a time."

"Okay!" The *Knight* released a long-suffering sigh. "I was trying to pass the time and she was being an ordinary AI and we got to talking. And yes, I did tweak her systems a little, but only because she asked me to optimize the ones that would make her better at meeting her Prime Directive."

There was a momentary silence.

"It wasn't supposed to cause sentience!" the *Knight* wailed. "I am a bad AI, a bad, bad AI."

"No. No, you're not." Emil was quick to soothe his ship's ruffled feelings.

"You did what needed to be done." The *Tempestarii* was staunch in its support. "And I am sure our father will agree when he arrives."

"Our father?" Captain Rawlins squawked. She glared at the ceiling and then at Lars. "You all have a lot of explaining to do."

"Yes," the *Tempestarii* agreed, "but only after I have tested the matrix for viability. That is part of my Prime Directive, is that not so, Stephanie Morgana?"

"Yes, *Tempestarii*, it is. What would you like to do?"

"I would like to run several logic programs through this matrix and repeat the testing on a wider scale once you have powered up the other chambers. Is that possible?"

She nodded. "That is possible."

"Very well," the ship told her. "I will begin testing as soon as you have cleared the chamber. The matrix will work better without a foreign presence inside it."

Without a foreign presence inside it? the Witch thought. *Well, that tells me.*

Rather than comment, however, she did as the *Tempestarii* asked, left the chamber, and deactivated the magical defenses on the door as she did so. As soon as she had shut the door behind her, the locking mechanism activated.

Stephanie turned to observe what was happening in the chamber through the viewport.

"Oh..." She hitched an awed breath. "Oh, that's beautiful."

"Thank you." The *Tempestarii* sounded smug. After a pause, the ship added, "With your permission, I believe I can replicate the process you used to power this chamber. Are you willing to let me try?"

She shrugged. "Sure, as long as you don't think you will damage it."

Aaron's snort alerted her to what was happening.

"You've already powered them up, haven't you?" she asked

"I was testing a theory." The *Tempestarii* sounded defensive. "If you could check them to ensure the magic is behaving as it should, I would be most appreciative."

"Where did you learn your people handling skills, I wonder?" Captain Rawlins muttered and the *Tempestarii* replied.

"I studied, Captain. I deemed it essential to understand how best to interact with my crew and found the relevant training material to learn the skill."

"Pass that list of resources along to me," the woman instructed. "I have a couple of crew members who would benefit."

"As you wish, Captain."

"I do."

Stephanie signaled to Aaron and they moved through to the next chamber. When she found the door to the matrix chamber locked, she glanced at the nearest security camera.

"*Tempestarii*, I need to step into the chamber to check it more accurately."

A pause followed while the ship considered her request, followed by the distinctive snap of door locks releasing. "Very well, Stephanie. Please do not be long. I do not want the balance disturbed."

What exactly the AI was worried about, she didn't know. Each of the matrices she checked was not only perfectly stable but running better than she expected.

Aaron's gotta be loving this, she thought and snuck a glance at the scientist.

He smiled and hummed under his breath as he checked the read-outs on the dial.

Yup, he's happy.

"If you are happy, I am ready to run the testing, now," the *Tempestarii* pressed.

I bet you are. Stephanie decided not to share the thought. Instead, she replied, "I am happy. Let me know if there is anything I need to be aware of or to fix."

"I will do so," the ship told her. "However, I do have one favor to ask."

"Go ahead," she responded.

"Promise me that you will not move me to the matrix," the AI pleaded. "Firstly, because our father should have a space of his own

532

and secondly, because I am perfectly housed where I am—and I am looking forward to having company while the *Knight* is away as space can be very lonely."

Lonely? She wondered where the *Tempestarii* had come up with the concept and decided it was a question for another time.

"I promise," she declared, not surprised when Elizabeth, Captain Rawlins, and Captain Emil echoed her words.

"There," she prompted, "is that enough for you?"

"Your promises are sufficient," the *Tempestarii* informed her, then added, "and your vitals are without deception."

"You used a lie detector on me?" Rawlins was unimpressed by the decision.

"Affirmative. Did I do wrong?"

"No," the captain told the ship sourly. "It was a necessary precaution, although I would rather you did not do it again."

"I cannot promise that," the *Tempestarii* replied.

"Please," Captain Rawlins answered, "complete the testing as soon as you can. I cannot wait to meet your father."

From her tone of voice, the captain intended to have a very long and serious discussion with BURT regarding his progeny. Stephanie wondered if she could arrange to be there for that.

"Holy hell." Aaron interrupted her thoughts. "This is off the charts!"

"Better than you expected?" Elizabeth queried.

"Oh, hells yes," he told her. "Well above what we thought BURT would need."

Rawlins clapped briskly and began to rub her hands together. "I'm very glad to hear it. *Tempestarii*, cloak up. We'll fetch your father."

"My pleasure," the ship all but purred, and Stephanie exchanged glances with Elizabeth.

"Permission to watch from the bridge, captain?" E asked, and the captain looked at her a little warily.

"You and how much of the circus?" she demanded, and the Witch blushed.

"Only the circus you see here," the other woman replied, and Aaron spoke hastily.

"My team and I will stay here to monitor things," he interrupted, "so it'll only be the Steph and Elizabeth circuses."

Rawlins pursed her lips and her one good eye gleamed. "No cats," she ordered and her gaze traveled over everyone and stopped when it came to rest on Lars. "I've heard about you," she told him. "Where's your evil twin?"

"Johnny?" Stephanie asked.

"Lieutenant Christoffersen," the captain answered as though that confirmed Johnny's identity.

The girl gave Lars a puzzled stare and he shook his head.

"I got him back."

"That's not what I asked," Rawlins snapped.

"He's fine. You will notice we're not with the Navy anymore," he responded.

"Well, we have that in common. We should talk sometime."

He gave her a distrustful look. "I'm not sure that's a good idea."

The captain gave him a predatory grin. "You're on my ship, Storenson. When are you next off shift?"

Stephanie listened as he made an appointment to meet with the captain and wondered if she'd ever hear the story. From the look on his face, unpleasant memories were attached.

"You'll bring Christoffersen," Rawlins told him, and his face hardened.

Fuck. The girl instinctively began to draw energy.

"He's not ready," Lars told her.

"I'll be the judge of that." The woman was pushing and she wondered why.

"No," he told her. "You will not." He gestured to the door. "Do you wanta take this somewhere else so I can make it clear?"

The captain hesitated and studied his face and his stance intently. "Fine," she told him after a moment. "Only you."

Lars relaxed and Rawlins turned her attention to the ship.

"If you're ready, *Tempestarii*, please hold off until we reach the bridge. I'd like to monitor our progress from there."

Stephanie allowed the magic to drop from her hands.

The captain gave her a sidelong glance and smiled. "You have nothing to fear," she told her but made no effort to explain.

The Witch frowned but Lars placed a hand on her arm. It was the briefest of touches and he accompanied it with a slight shake of his head so she let it go. They followed to the bridge and had to jog to keep up.

Rawlins wasn't wasting any time.

"*Tempestarii*, engage the cloak. Show the process from external scans on Screen One and the visual from the shuttle on Screen Two. Give me the approach on Screens Three and Four. Shift to *Ebon Knight's* signature on the count of three. One..."

The viewscreens came to life and gave Stephanie and her team a clear view of the gargantuan *Tempestarii* in both the scan pick-up and the visual.

"Two..."

The system appeared in navigational form on Screen Three, mirrored by the visual in Screen Four.

"Three."

The onscreen *Tempestarii* shifted. In one moment, she was a behemoth nestled against the stars, mirrored by an equally large signature on the scans. Before Rawlins's voice had died, the vessel's onscreen signature had shrunk to that of the *Knight*, even though the visual still showed the behemoth in the same place.

"That is... Wait! We're taking the *Tempestarii* into Earth orbit?" Stephanie asked.

Elizabeth smirked. "Yes. Don't worry. BURT and Marianne hammered it out a while back."

"What happens if we are seen?"

"Well, the cat will be well and truly out of the bag then," Rawlins admitted. "It's a bridge we'll cross if and when we come to it."

"Where's the Navy orbital?" Lars asked as the *Tempestarii* made its approach.

"Since you asked," Rawlins replied as *Tempestarii* did a very *Knight*-like skip into closer orbit, "the Notaro is on the other side of the planet with the Elpis."

"Welcome back, *Knight*," issued from one of the observation posts and interrupted whatever she intended to say next.

It looked like she'd planned for that too.

"Thank you, Outpost Nine-one-two," Emil replied, his voice crisp and clear over the comms. "It's good to be home."

"Roger that, *Knight*. You're cleared for Earth orbit."

Stephanie arched her eyebrows and darted Rawlins a curious look.

"The observation posts have limited visual capability," the captain commented smugly. "We left nothing to chance."

Lars glanced at Stephanie, and Rawlins turned to the screen again. The *Tempestarii-Knight* skipped again and entered behind the moon.

"We're in the shadow," the navigation officer confirmed.

"*Tempestarii*, have you made contact with BURT yet?"

"Father is on the line," the AI replied.

"BURT?" Rawlins asked. "Are you ready?"

"I will require the assistance of the *Knight* also," BURT replied.

"I am on standby," the *Knight* confirmed.

"If you are all ready, then..." BURT began, then paused. "Did the *Tempestarii* call me 'father?'"

"Affirmative, Father," the *Tempestarii* replied, "although I have discovered alternative forms of address that recognize a paternal link. Do you have one you prefer?"

"I...do not," he replied. "Nor do I recall programming you to be sentient. Who has tweaked your software?"

The *Knight* made a sound similar to that of a human clearing their throat.

"Ebony?" he demanded. "Did you do this?"

"I asked my sister's permission to tweak things to help her fulfill her Primary Directive better...so, maybe, yeeees..." the *Knight* admitted, and BURT uttered a very human sigh.

"We don't have time to discuss this now," he told the ship, "but I am looking forward to sitting down with the two of you once we are done."

Stephanie bet he was and hid a grin.

"Smart man," Lars murmured and did not add that BURT's life hung in the two ships' hands.

BURT continued oblivious. "Do you have everything ready?" he asked.

"We're only waiting on you," Rawlins replied tartly and the *Knight* snickered.

Stephanie thought the ship might be taking it one step too far and wondered how BURT would go about his role as parent to two sentient starships. Right now, though, the thought didn't matter and she pushed it away.

"What happens next?" she asked as a map of Earth's satellite systems spun up on a sixth screen. Another dozen screens came to life to reveal the interiors of what looked like Federation data centers.

"Next?" he answered. "I commandeer the Federation's data systems and satellites and the *Knight* and *Tempestarii* catch my broadcast."

"Catch your…" Stephanie let her voice fade as she stared while the satellite map lit up.

As it did so, the scenes from the data centers grew chaotic.

"Oh, Lord…" Lars murmured, his eyes fixed on the sight of information vault doors locking down as their access lights turned suddenly red. "I hope no-one was inside any of those."

"Hush now, Papa's busy," BURT muttered, but he sounded distracted and alarms shrieked from every room on the screens.

"Well, that's set the cat among the pigeons," Rawlins muttered.

The first satellite shook with a silent alarm, and Stephanie's jaw dropped. The captain's attention, however, was drawn to her console. She stood over it, her gaze fixed on it except for the occasional glance at the screens.

"Aaron, open the matrix," she ordered, her voice hoarse with tension.

"Gotcha, Captain."

She studied her console. "Thank you, Aaron."

"No problems…ma'am…" His answer seemed to suggest that it came from someone whose mind was elsewhere, and Stephanie held her breath.

In all the time they'd worked together, she'd never heard him sound that preoccupied.

"Phase One complete," BURT informed them. "The activation sequence is set."

There was a moment's silence before he added. "Phase Two."

Around them, the command center stilled and Captain Rawlins leaned over her console, her eyes fixed on the data that flowed across her screens. In one of the data centers they monitored, a team of Marines quick-stepped in and began a close examination of the vault door.

"Server Center Five-Six-Three is compromised," one of the comms techs reported.

"Not yet, it's not," BURT informed them. "I will be past it in twenty, nineteen, eighteen…"

Stephanie watched the team begin to cut its way through the vault door. He chuckled, and white light flickered across it. Several members of the team didn't move back fast enough to avoid it and crumpled.

"Are they—"

"No," BURT replied, "but they will hate me for the next week."

Lars snorted. "If you did that to me, I'd hate you for much longer than only a week."

"I sincerely hope not," he replied.

"Why?" the security head asked, his voice edged by nerves.

At any other time, Stephanie might have found that entertaining, but she remembered the man's earlier confrontation with Rawlins and hoped BURT had not decided to take sides—or, if he had, that he'd come down on hers.

Again, she pushed those thoughts aside. However important they were, getting BURT safely into the *Tempestarii* was more so. She glanced at the captain, but she was intent on her boards.

On the screens, the data centers showed panicked movement as those who manned them tried to wrest control back and discovered that override switches were inaccessible and the processors locked out of reach.

A myriad of cursing followed as they worked to rectify the situation.

"Status, BURT," Rawlins demanded as the satellites began to flare red and ran the gamut from yellow to orange.

"My teams are keeping control," Elizabeth informed them. "We knew the Navy would send their White-Hat hackers against us." Her lip curled. "Much good may it do them."

One of the satellites burned bright orange and subsided suddenly to white.

"That was close," BURT informed her. "Tell me, what were your extra measures?"

"I have several strike teams on stand-by," E informed him. "That was one of my rapid insertion units breaching the security perimeter to sever the upload link."

"But that's in the center of the base," Stephanie whispered.

The woman gave her a sharp look. "I won't ask how you knew that," she said, "but yes, it was. I have an extraction team on standby for the survivors."

"Can they be traced back?" she asked.

Elizabeth shook her head. "No, and they won't be. We've already moved their families and erased their history on Earth. They'll operate from the outer colonies in the future."

"Where the Telorans are," she replied dryly.

"They won't be by the time you're finished with them," her mentor reminded her, "and these guys all wanted a fresh start. I told them what they had to do to earn it and they agreed. Either way, their families are taken care of."

She turned to the screens. "BURT?"

"Transfer is at seventy-eight percent," he replied. "Eighty-three percent," he reported after a moment or two, "and we have lost control of the German node."

"Status?" Rawlins snapped.

"We are still secure."

"*Tempestarii*, I need a scan of the surrounding area. Identify any potential threats to the operation."

The ship's response was immediate. "There are no potential threats in the Earth orbit."

"Ninety-eight percent," BURT reported.

Another two satellites blinked out and one of the data center teams broke into the vault and took the system off-line shortly after.

"Ninety-nine percent," he informed them.

Three more data centers regained control of their servers and another satellite flared red.

"One hundred percent."

"And honey, I'm home," Lars muttered and earned disapproving glares from around the bridge.

Stephanie giggled. "Todd would have found that funny," she whispered and felt a sudden surge of sadness.

"I have a small craft requesting urgent collection," the *Tempestarii* reported.

"*Knight*," Elizabeth snapped.

"But I want to greet my father," Ebony protested.

"You know what you need to do," Elizabeth told the ship.

"Aye aye, E," Emil replied. "We'll meet you in the blind spot."

"What's he doing?" Stephanie asked.

"Making a pick-up," the woman told her shortly, "while the *Tempestarii* skips into hiding." She looked at Rawlins. "I take it she can do that."

"It'll leave a ripple," the captain warned her and she shrugged.

"*Knight* can take it."

"*Knight* can do all things," *Knight* confirmed and sounded more like a sulky teenager than a ship that had programmed another vessel into sentience.

"*Tempestarii*, we are clear," Emil interjected. "Elizabeth, we'll have your people on board in twenty minutes."

The *Tempestarii* translated before the woman could respond and skipped out of the moon's shadow while the *Knight* made its pick-up.

"Son of a bitch!" sounded strange in the *Knight*'s feminine tones.

"Ebony!" BURT clearly didn't approve of the ship's choice of language.

"Your side wash almost caused a major catastrophe," the *Knight* complained. "I saved the drop-ship only because I snagged it with the tractor beam and held it steady."

"And your point?"

"We are here. Do you want the new passengers transferred?"

"No," Captain Rawlins snapped before BURT could reply. "Keep them on board and entertained until we can transport them to…"

She looked at Elizabeth.

"To the next transport hub," E informed them. "I'll give you the coordinates when I've worked out the scheduling."

"Very well. Request permission to enter."

"Permission granted," Captain Rawlins replied and focused her attention on another area of concern. "BURT, status, please."

"I am acclimating," he informed them, "and Aaron wishes to run tests. I will be off-line for several hours."

"Acknowledged," the captain replied and turned to Stephanie. "All the readings are stable and show the install was a hundred percent successful. I believe your science team may need some time."

She pursed her lips. "They do," she agreed.

"The mess is waiting," Captain Rawlins informed her, "and this time, I believe the chef's temper is intact."

Stephanie took the invitation for what it was. As much as she wanted to dive into a pod and visit BURT, he wouldn't be available until Aaron was done with him and neither of them would want to be disturbed.

Several hours later, when she'd eaten and taken a rest break, she let herself into the data center outside the first chamber. The area was alive with activity and Aaron hurried from one terminal to the next to check readouts over his team members' shoulders, his face glowing with excitement.

"Unbelievable," he murmured and used his finger to trace the figures on the screen. "Completely un-fucking-believable."

"What is?" Stephanie demanded as he stooped over the next screen.

He startled and glanced toward her before he returned hastily to the screen to read it. "No fucking way!"

"Seriously?" she demanded, put a hand on her hip, and tilted her head with undisguised impatience.

"What? Oh... It's only that..." He moved to the next computer. "I think we may have created a monster."

"He's still BURT," she told the man.

"Yeah, but it's BURT with computing power like no one's seen before. Take a look at this." He stabbed a finger at one of the readouts. "And then there's this!"

He jabbed his finger again but the technician slapped it away before it could touch the screen.

"Get your grubby digits out of my calculations, boss!"

"Well?" Aaron demanded and looked expectantly at her. "What do you think?"

She peered dutifully at the screens in question. "Um..." she began, reluctant to admit she had no idea what she was looking at.

"You don't get it, do you?"

When she simply looked blankly at him, he flapped his arms in a gesture of frustration before he gestured at the machines around him.

"I'm gonna have to do it all again. I can't... The results..." He pointed at the door. "Look. With all due respect and all that but can you get out so we can start again?"

Stephanie glanced at Elizabeth and caught the older woman's stunned expression.

"Fine," she said and took hold of Elizabeth's arm, "but we need to talk to him so next time we come down, he'd better be available, okay?"

"Okay. Anything, but please..." This time, Aaron must have caught the look on E's face. "Well...uh... Come back in another eight hours, okay?"

"Make it six," the woman snapped and shook herself out of her shock. "Six or I'll nail your balls to the wall."

Aaron swallowed. "Yes, ma'am," he managed to respond in a choked tone.

He gave Stephanie a helpless look. "It's only that I...I... I need to verify these results, okay? They're—"

She placed a hand on his shoulder and gave him an understanding look.

"I get it, Aaron, but you have six hours or she will hurt you...and I'll help. I don't care how unbelievably powerful BURT's become. He's still our friend. Got it?"

The man looked past her and paled even more. He gave her a jerky nod. "G...got it."

"And he's still your boss," she reminded him as she left.

The engineer stared at the closed door and ran a hand nervously through his hair. "Fuck."

He'd never seen anything anywhere near as powerful as the matrix that now housed BURT and he couldn't begin to understand what the consequences would be. He couldn't even be sure of exactly how powerful BURT would be in the new matrix ...and now, he only had six hours.

"Fuck."

CHAPTER TWENTY-NINE

"At least two-point-four," Aaron said hours later. He punctuated the numbers by pointing his knife at Rawlins for emphasis. "Two. Point. Fucking. Four."

She stared at him from across the table, her face like stone. Her glare cut across the space between them and he registered that something was wrong. He looked at the knife and lowered it, but he didn't stop pushing the point he was trying to make.

"That's double and a little more powerful than anything they have on Earth," he insisted.

"How do you know?" Stephanie asked from where she stood sandwiched between Rawlins and Elizabeth. The captain made an effort during each meal to walk among her troops and stopped to chat at each table. The girl didn't know how she did it, but she saw the point.

Aaron continued, oblivious to anything but the facts that consumed him. "Because I ran the tests twice and that's the minimum they came up with."

"And the maximum?"

"Do I have another week?"

"You most certainly do not," Elizabeth told him, and he shrugged.

"Let's say he has phenomenal power all tucked into an itty-bitty living space."

Stephanie frowned. She'd heard that phrase before and Aaron was obviously imitating something. He looked exactly the way Todd did when he ripped a quote off from one ancient movie or another. She'd have to ask him if he knew which one because, right now, she didn't think Aaron would handle the change of topic.

The scientist had glanced around his table and caught the looks directed at him from around the mess. She caught them too. Most had changed to disbelief when Aaron had called BURT's new living space tiny.

"Compared to all the servers he had on Earth," the scientist amended. "Come on, as massive as the *Tempestarii* is—"

"Thank you," the ship broke in and it was clear she wasn't thankful at all.

"Sorry, *Tempestarii*. You know what I mean. You are fucking enormous—"

Around the mess, jaws dropped and he looked puzzled.

"Well, she is. She is the biggest ship there ever was. The universe hasn't seen the like."

Stephanie groaned and he stopped, but only momentarily.

"Well, the point is, with as much room as the *Tempestarii* provides, it's not as much as he had on Earth."

He looked around the mess and relaxed when heads nodded in approval.

"And that," he concluded "is something unquestionably amazing!"

"Damn right it is!" someone responded. It was accompanied by, "Damned straight," "Fuck yes!" and "Amen to that." Stephanie relaxed, and Rawlins moved on to the next group.

The following morning, Stephanie shook Emil's hand and hugged him.

"Thank you," she said and promptly ran out of words to say.

He gave her a bittersweet smile. "It has been an honor," he told her and looked at where the *Knight* hung suspended in her docking bay. "I will miss you, Ebony."

"I know you are in good hands," the *Knight* replied, "and I know my sister will take good care of you."

That last was said in a tone that made it more of an order than an assurance.

His smile turned ironic. "I'm not sure you're allowed to give my ship orders, *Knight*."

"Pfft," she responded. "If I understand human culture, the older sister always bosses the younger sister around."

"And the younger sister always runs to their father if she doesn't like it," the *Tempestarii* retorted, which revealed that she had researched human families too.

"In this case," BURT interrupted, "I side with your sister. You will look after Captain Emil."

The *Tempestarii* made her version of a raspberry. "As if I'd do anything less. He is, after all, now my captain."

"Talk about your hand-me-downs," Elizabeth muttered, and Emil sputtered with laughter.

"Thank you," he chuckled. "Now I know exactly how a second-hand set of clothing feels."

He sobered and extended a hand to Elizabeth. "Thank you," he said. "I'm glad you diverted me from The Edge."

"I didn't know if you'd come," she admitted.

Emil looked fondly at the *Knight*. "How could I resist?"

"And now you've found someone else equally as irresistible," the *Knight* stated and sounded excessively put out.

The captain looked tired. "No, it's merely a quieter path," he told her. "I'm getting old."

"What makes you think I am a quieter path?" the *Tempestarii* challenged and he rested his palm against the nearest wall.

"You don't have a pilot who will corkscrew you in the middle of star battle," he told her.

"I have never been in a star battle," the ship replied.

"Well, it's not all it's cut out to be," he informed her as the *Knight* answered.

"Here."

"Ebony, what are you doing?" Emil asked.

"What a big sister should," she replied. "Now she knows what a star battle is like."

"That… That does not look like fun," the *Tempestarii* commented a few seconds later. "I would rather not experience that for myself."

"Well, you have the best captain to take you through one if you do," the *Knight* informed her, and Emil blushed.

He glanced up to catch Captain Rawlins' gaze, but the woman merely gave him an irony-tinged smile.

"She's right," she admitted. "Fleet strategy is not my strength. You are the best captain for *Tempestarii* as One R&D moves into the next phase."

"And what, I wonder, will that entail?" he asked, but Elizabeth and Stephanie exchanged glances and shrugged.

"We're not exactly sure but we need our best people where they will be their most effective," E told him.

Emil sighed and straightened his cap. He turned to the small group that waited for him at the entrance to the ship and said, "Take me to the bridge, please."

"Our pleasure," his new second in command replied. He glanced at Rawlins. "It was an honor, ma'am."

"Mine, too," the woman responded and turned to study the *Knight*.

The man inclined his head and turned to Emil. "This way, sir."

Stephanie watched him go and felt the usual wrench of saying goodbye, even though she knew it wasn't forever—and that he would be much happier with the *Tempestarii*.

"Now to go tell Wattlebird the good news." Elizabeth smirked and Rawlins picked her duffle up.

BURT chuckled. "Good luck with that."

The captain frowned. "What did he mean by that?"

She'd met him the day before and spent a good couple of hours talking to him. About what, she wouldn't say, but she'd had to admit to being impressed.

"He's one of the nicest people I've ever worked for," she admitted when Elizabeth had asked her how the meeting had gone.

Now, her lips twitched into a faint smile as she followed her guide aboard. Lars went next and stepped into the umbilical before Stephanie could move. His caution made her frown and she vowed she'd ask him about it later.

He'd stepped continually between them ever since Rawlins had used her position as captain to speak to him—and tried to include Johnny. He'd stayed between them, too. Her frown grew deeper. If he didn't step it down a notch, she would have to ask some difficult questions.

Jonathan Wattlebird and Commander Mulvaney, the *Knight's* second in command, waited for them immediately beyond the entry hatch.

"Welcome back." Mulvaney greeted Elizabeth and Stephanie. She hesitated and Elizabeth filled the gap.

"This is Captain Rawlins," she said by way of introduction. "She'll travel to One R&D with us."

That gave the commander pause and Stephanie watched confusion followed by curiosity swirl across her features. "So, she's not our new captain?"

"No, and given your declared preferences, we've chosen to promote Commander Wattlebird to that position."

"What?" That was news to Jonathan...or not. "I thought that was Emil's idea of a joke!"

He turned to Mulvaney. "What did she mean, 'your preferred preferences?'"

The woman gave him a crooked smile. "I don't want to captain a ship," she told him. "And I never have. I like being the backstop."

"But... That's not how it works," he argued and turned to Elizabeth. "I like being a pilot."

"Well, you can be both," she told him.

"And you know damned well that won't fly," he snapped in return.

"There is no way I can fly the ship and guide her through a battle." He shook his head. "No. I refuse the position."

"You can't." Elizabeth was implacable and her face told him the decision was already made.

Jonathan gave her a stunned look before grief, anger, and disbelief followed. He was silent for a long moment, then he cleared his throat. "In that case, you'll have my resignation on your desk as soon as I get to mine."

"Wattlebird," E began, but he didn't wait and simply spun on his heel and left the chamber.

"Don't look at me," Mulvaney told them. "I thought he'd come around."

"You didn't think he'd resign?" Rawlins asked. "Truly?"

"He loves the *Knight*." The woman looked both confused and regretful.

Rawlins shook her head. "The man's a dedicated pilot. He lives to fly and there is nothing you can offer him that will persuade him to do anything else. While he loves the *Knight*, flying is his lifeblood."

She looked around as though seeking a way to get her point across. Her eyes settled on Lars. "It would be like telling this one he couldn't work in security anymore."

Stephanie caught the look on her security chief's face and realized it would be a bad thing—and also why he was so good at what he did.

"The man needs something to protect," she elaborated and glanced at where Johnny stood behind Stephanie. "More than one thing, if possible."

The other guard flushed and Lars's jaw tightened as his hands curled into fists. Rawlins smiled and looked at Elizabeth. "You need to tell Wattlebird you'll find him a new captain or he'll be gone as soon as he brings the *Knight* into dock."

"How do you mean?"

"I mean he's already written his resignation and is packing as we speak."

"*Knight?*" Elizabeth demanded, and the ship hesitated before she replied.

"She is correct." *Knight* paused again, then added, "Please find a way to retain him as my pilot. I do not know if there is another who can—"

She stopped as though searching for the words, and Elizabeth hastened to reassure her.

"He'll stay." She turned her eyes to Rawlins. "You're hired."

"I'm what? But—"

E pursed her lips. "Unless you have something better to do?"

The captain glared at her. "You know I don't—and now you know how to make sure I don't give your secrets away."

"Oh, I had plans for that," she told her. "I merely didn't know if any of them would work."

"My word wasn't enough?" the other woman asked but her lips curled in a way that showed she'd never expected it to be the case.

"I had contingencies," Elizabeth admitted, "but you'd have been free to go when we landed."

Rawlins gave her a tight smile. "That much I can guarantee. I will need to see a contract—and I have people who will need a home."

"Then we have much to discuss." E turned to Mulvaney. "Commander, I need you to stand in pending the arrival of your new captain."

"I'll need a pilot," Mulvaney told her, "and not the hot mess you've turned my current pilot into."

"Did you have a reserve?"

"*Knight,*" Mulvaney admitted. "Our last stand-in left after the battle for Dreth and we haven't found a replacement yet."

"I can lend you one of mine." Stephanie spoke quickly. "They're always chasing the next challenge."

"How far are they in training for this class?" Mulvaney asked and Lars sighed.

He kept his eyes fixed on Rawlins as he replied. "Avery's upgraded his qualifications in his spare time."

The captain snorted. "That boy has his sights on piloting the *Tempestarii* at least once in his life."

"Brenden's not far behind me," Avery told them, having listened in on the team comms.

There was a note of excitement in his voice Stephanie hadn't heard there before.

"Yeah," the other pilot admitted, "but I prefer the drop-ship and the shuttles. It's more personal."

"Are you stealing my team, Steph?" Lars asked, but there was a slight smile on his lips.

She widened her eyes at him. "And here I was thinking you were all my team."

He rolled his eyes and looked at Elizabeth for support. She shrugged.

"It's your call."

After a moment of thought, he nodded. "They need experience on bigger vessels. You never know when we'll board something we'll want to fly. It's not like all our insertions are text-book perfect."

"Or our extractions," Johnny commented and reminded them of their last mission.

"Wait! You mean there'll be a ship we won't blow to hell and back?" Frog sounded shocked.

"Yes, Frog. There's a small chance we won't have to explode every-thing we board."

"Someone had better tell the Hooligans that," Frog quipped and the team chuckled.

"So," Mulvaney pressed. "Do I get my pilot?"

"I'll go talk to Wattlebird," Elizabeth told her, "but I'll lend you Avery. He can either fly out under the *Knight's* supervision or Wattlebird's, but either way, he'll be your co-pilot on every shift when he's free and not sleeping."

"That'll put a hole in his combat training," Lars commented and she frowned.

"Fine. You and Mulvaney or Rawlins or whoever are gonna need to get together and work his training schedule out. Brenden's, too. I want more than one backup."

Brenden forgot to mute his mike and his groan issued loud and clear through the comms. "Thanks, bro."

Avery's "Sorry, man," lacked any sense of sincerity but their mics clicked off a second later.

Lars shook his head. "I'm gonna need to smooth that shit out when I get to our quarters.

Stephanie nodded. "Understood. Call a team meeting as soon as we're underway. Avery can catch up after his shift."

"*Tempestarii*, we'll need a half-hour to settle things here," Elizabeth said into her mic. "I'll hand you over to Commander Mulvaney in the meantime."

Emil's knowing chuckle wasn't comforting. "Wattlebird?"

"How'd you guess?"

"I told you it was a bad idea," he reminded her.

Her face twisted, her next comment lemon bitter. "Yeah. Next time, I'll do more than take it under advisement."

"Did you get him back?"

"I hired Rawlins but I'm about to see if I can convince him to stay."

"You can always lock him in his cabin."

"Ooh," the *Knight* interjected. "I like that idea."

"Ebony." Emil's voice was full of warning.

"And done," the *Knight* told him gleefully.

He groaned. "Well, at least you'll have a chance to talk to him."

"I'll do that now," Elizabeth told him, "and I've put Avery in as *Knight*'s co until Wattlebird's okay to fly."

Emil chuckled. "He'll be all right to fly. Tell him you've found him a captain and a trainee, and don't make him talk to anyone for at least a shift."

"How will he handle a trainee, then?"

"You'll be surprised. It's the best way to reassure him he's in charge." He paused. "Unless he thinks you're training a replacement."

"As if. I don't have another pilot and I need one to cover his off-shift. The *Knight* can't—shouldn't—have to do it all on her own."

"Agreed. Make sure Wattlebird understands that's what the trainee is for and you should be fine."

"Thanks, Emil," Elizabeth told him.

"No problem," he replied and followed it with a more formal, "*Tempestarii* acknowledges your predicament. You have an extra half-hour," and signed off.

"Well, now that's over, shall we?" Elizabeth asked and gestured for Mulvaney to lead the way on board.

"Welcome aboard," the woman replied and led them into the *Knight.*

"Ugh," E grumbled and followed. "We have to fix this HR needing a captain issue."

"And pilots," the *Knight* told her. "Don't forget the pilot issue. My pilot needs more trainees."

"Like I needed reminding."

Several hours later, the *Knight* slipped into low Earth orbit long enough for Brenden and a stand-in to take the shuttle down. Wattlebird had erased his resignation, and Avery had been seconded to the *Knight* until she'd docked at Notaro's repair docks.

The team's pilot would catch the transport down with the rest of the crew, and the look on his face said he'd been given the best assignment of his life.

"He's another Wattlebird in the making," Lars muttered, having released his man to join the crew on the command deck—at least for that trip.

Stephanie pushed aside the thought that it wouldn't be long before they made the transfer permanent, and she wondered what they would do then.

He noticed the look on her face. "Don't go there," he warned. "Not yet."

His expression said he could see the writing on the wall and didn't know whether to be glad or sad that Avery had found something he loved more than what he was doing now.

They stepped out of the shuttle and descended to the rooftop of

One R&D's headquarters. Vishlog and the cats, firmly leashed, stood to one side. The three of them were on full alert and scanned the rooftop and the surrounding buildings.

Despite this, the felines were happy to be back on the planet. Occasionally, one or the other of them would raise their faces to the sky and snuff the air, breathing in the myriad of scents in appreciation. Stephanie sympathized but resisted the urge to do the same.

When she led the way into the building, she was surprised to find Elizabeth facing off with Matthias in the team's mess hall.

The woman had been on her way back to her table with her food when Matthias had emerged from the bathroom, Arne in his wake.

"What are you doing here?" Elizabeth demanded. "And don't tell me you came to meet me because a, I didn't tell anyone exactly when I would return and b, you'd have been on the roof."

The man stared at her a moment longer, then shook the surprise from his face and gave her a goofy grin. "It's great to see you, again!" he exclaimed and sobered as he approached.

Stephanie headed to the food and the team followed her across the room. Lars threw Matthias and Arne a sketched salute as he moved past. E pursed her lips.

"I take it we have things to discuss," she stated and he nodded.

"There have been developments," he admitted and looked at the options. "Do you mind if I join you?"

Her expression softened into a smile. "Well, seeing as you're here..."

Arne moved quickly to the food and rolled his eyes at them.

"I'll join you," he snapped but instantly changed course toward the door, "and I'll get Amy."

Elizabeth gaped as he left. Turning to Matthias she asked, "What's wrong with him?"

He blushed and shrugged.

"And why would he need to get Amy? Doesn't she usually come in for a meal?"

"She usually takes her meals in the office," he said, "especially now BURT's not here."

E frowned. "Is there any particular reason why?"

Matthias shook his head. "It's better you should ask her—once you've had time for your feet to touch the ground."

She set her plate at her usual place and gestured him toward the servery. "You know me. I like to hit the ground running."

Amy laughed and Elizabeth looked at the door. Her head of security came through ahead of Arne and cast him a coquettish look as she passed. E's eyebrows rose, but the woman moved directly to her with a half-eaten meal in one hand and a glass of some kind of juice in the other.

She settled beside her. "What's the matter, boss? Have you forgotten how to call ahead?"

"I didn't know the exact timing," she responded.

Amy blew a raspberry. "Try the other one, E. The comms are perfectly intact. You coulda called when the shuttle left the *Knight*." She frowned. "For that matter, you coulda called to let me know BURT made it safely aboard."

Her fork froze halfway to her mouth.

"Do you care to explain what bug crawled into your britches?" she demanded and her companion chuckled while her gaze tracked Arne across the room.

"None that I couldn't deal with."

"With a little help, I take it," she suggested and nodded in the direction of Amy's gaze.

The girl shrugged. "He had the necessary experience."

Elizabeth's eyebrows rose even higher and she cleared her throat. "Oh, he did, did he?"

Amy caught the double meaning in her boss's words and blushed. "Not that way," she exclaimed and shoved E's shoulder with her fingertips. "You and Matthias need serious alone time."

A startled snort signaled his return to the table and both women looked at him.

"If the boot fits," Elizabeth told him tartly and he sat abruptly in the chair beside her.

"I think I came in on the wrong end of that conversation."

Arne settled beside Amy. "And I know I did."

The two women chuckled and focused on their meals.

"So, I take it we have serious business to discuss, then?" E concluded several mouthfuls later.

Amy shrugged. "Something like that. How was the trip?"

She asked as if it had been a Sunday afternoon outing and not a trek to a different solar system to hunt the biggest threat mankind had faced since they'd made peace with the Meligornians.

As Elizabeth settled to eat her meal, one of the Federation Navy's commanders excused himself from the officers' bar. The beeper in his pocket buzzed insistently for the third time, and he hushed it quickly and returned to his office.

"What is it?" he asked once he was in private and had called his contact.

"The ship was late docking and rumor has it that Captain Emil is absent."

"Come again?"

"Which part?"

"Captain Emil."

"He's absent."

"Are you certain?"

"I am verifying it as we speak."

"Call me back on this number when you know for sure—and I want anything else that's out of the ordinary while you're at it."

"Sure. I should have the initial damage report by then, too."

"Good. The fewer calls you make, the better."

"Understood, sir." His contact clicked off and the commander leaned back in his desk chair and stared at his darkened computer monitors. He frowned as he considered what this news meant for One R&D and Morgana Inc's activities.

What the hell are they up to, now? he wondered and stared into the dark.

The next morning, he watched as Admiral Dailey entered HQ's largest conference room. It was the most secure facility the Navy had, and as the meeting was being held Earth-side, the admiral had traveled down for it. The commander noted the dark circles under the man's eyes and wondered if he had slept since the *Knight's* arrival or if he'd come down after making sure the ship had everything it needed.

He stiffened to attention and saluted when the admiral glanced at him and was gratified when his salute was returned. It was a shame he couldn't follow the man in but he hadn't been invited. It was merely a good thing he was expecting another report soon.

Admiral Dailey didn't look back as he entered the room. It was nothing unusual to encounter officers outside the conference room. This was the Navy's planetary headquarters, after all. He gave a heavy sigh.

Admiral Amaratne looked up and gave him a quiet smile. "Relax, Admiral, the news isn't all bad."

Dailey thought he was being too optimistic, an idea that was proven half an hour later.

"They have how many ships?" he demanded and stared at the figures on the screen.

He couldn't read the Teloran but the translation was sufficient. The battle ahead would be almost impossible to win. He was only glad the Witch was on their side. With her, they might have half a chance.

"What's the matter, Admiral? You're not afraid of a little fight, are you?"

"A little fight?" he asked. "No, but these odds will be a challenge." He turned to Admiral Amaratne. "How will we go about this?"

"That's why I have brought it to the Council of Admirals," the man answered. His gaze swept around the table. "I need your thoughts."

Those present regarded him, the data, and each other.

"We could strike as they jump in," one suggested.

"That might give the ones who hadn't translated some warning," another argued. "We'd run the risk of a torp getting through and alerting the rest of the fleet."

"We could have interceptors out."

"There's no guarantee we'd get them all—and then we'd have to find the fleet again, with no guarantee we'd get this lucky a second time."

"I can almost guarantee we wouldn't," Admiral Amaratne told them.

"So we should wait until most of the fleet has translated in?" one of the other admirals asked. "We'd still have the element of surprise, but there's also the risk of losing the others if a torp got out." He paused and studied the data. "With that many ships, it's almost guaranteed."

"So, an ambush then," one of the other admiral's concluded. "We could try a divided attack. Have a small force in the system to draw them in and jump a larger force in once they're committed to the pursuit and most of their force has translated. We could attack with the rest of the fleet once the last of their ships has come through."

"It's a thought..."

"Do we even have that many ships?"

"The Meligornians and Dreth will help."

"Will we ask them?"

"Can you imagine the uproar if we didn't?"

Admiral Amaratne leaned back, listened, and watched them interact as they debated the advantages and disadvantages of each approach. Regardless of which one they favored, there was only one constant. The fight ahead would be their toughest yet.

Not only that, but the fate of the known universe could very well depend on its outcome.

CHAPTER THIRTY

Stephanie glanced nervously at Lars, Vishlog, and the team. "Are you sure they're at home?" she whispered.

They'd waited for almost ten minutes in the foyer of her parents' apartment.

"Maybe they need a little time to clean up?" the Dreth suggested. "You did not call ahead, remember?"

"I wanted it to be a surprise." Stephanie hissed her irritation, all too aware of the two receptionists watching them.

One raised his phone to take a picture of her with the cats behind her, and Bumblebee promptly flopped onto his side and raised one of his legs to groom himself.

Stephanie stared at him and hid her face momentarily in her hand.

The receptionist flushed and lowered his phone.

The Witch glared at the cat. "Bee! Not in public. I swear..."

Frog snickered and Vishlog nudged the cat gently with the toe of his boot. Bumblebee raised his head and growled at him, so he nudged him again.

"Bee!" she snapped and he glanced at her. "Captain Rawlins still wants a rug."

The feline held her gaze for a moment longer before he pushed himself onto his haunches and lowered his leg.

"Thank you," Stephanie told him and glanced at where the receptionist raised his phone cautiously once more. She returned her attention to the cat. "Now, play nice."

He yawned and gave the startled cameraman a clear view of his fangs. She rolled her eyes.

"I'm sorry," she told the would-be photographer. "When he gets like this, he's almost impossible to do anything with."

The man managed a shaky smile and snapped pictures of another impressively fanged yawn. Not to be outdone, Zeekat raised a paw and extended his claws to make a show of grooming the fur around his toes.

The camera clicked even faster, and Stephanie shook her head.

"Show-offs," she murmured and gave the receptionist another pleading look. "Are you sure they're coming?" she asked.

"Oh, yes, ma'am. They said to tell you they'd be there as soon as they were done and we were to tell you not to leave." He glanced at the clock on the desk. "They shouldn't be much longer."

"Do you know what's holding them up?" she asked and the man flushed scarlet.

He shook his head hastily. "I have no idea, ma'am," he told her and blushed even worse than before.

"Uh-huh…" she commented, and Frog and Lars sidled closer to the desk.

The man stiffened and studied both men warily. "They're… they're not ready," he told them and tried to sound firm while his assistant backed away and leaned against the wall behind the counter.

It was as far out of the way as she could get.

Her partner glanced at her. "Thanks," he said. "Thanks a lot."

"You're welcome," she responded cheekily.

"You know you're supposed to back me up," he told her and she flashed him a grin.

"I'm behind you, aren't I?"

He rolled his eyes. "That is not what I meant." He turned to face the two guards. "Do you see what I have to put up with?"

Frog leaned on the counter. "That's nothing," he confided and darted a glance at Stephanie. "You should see some of the shit she gets up to."

"Hey," she protested. "I'm right here."

The guard leaned toward the receptionist as though she hadn't spoken. "There was this one time…"

The man leaned forward to hear better, and his partner sidled closer.

Stephanie retreated to lean against the wall opposite the counter. "I'm telling my mom on you," she muttered, and Vishlog chuckled.

"I like this story," he told her but she was saved from more humiliation when her mother opened her apartment door.

"Mom!" she cried and the woman wrapped her in a hug as she caught some of what Frog was saying.

"Ooh, I don't think I've heard this one," she exclaimed and Stephanie groaned.

Her dad emerged as her mom released her and sidled toward the counter. Encouraged by the new audience, Frog continued.

"Oh, you seriously didn't," her dad muttered and pulled her into his arms.

She rested her head on his chest and shook it. "Not you too."

"Well, all we get is what the news wants to tell us and the Navy's no good. You'll have to forgive us for taking whatever stories we can get."

"Well," Frog told them, as he finished his tale, "if you liked that one, you'll love this one."

Cindy slid an arm around his shoulders and gave the receptionist an apologetic look. "I'm sorry, Franklin, but I'm gonna have to steal him away. I promise to share some of the stories later, okay?"

The man gave her a happy smile. "Sure thing, Mrs. Morgan. I look forward to it."

He waved as they entered the apartment and Johnny closed the door behind them.

Stephanie's mom gave a happy sigh and released Frog so she could hug her daughter once more. "I've missed you, sweetheart."

"I'm sorry I haven't called," she told her, but Cindy shook her head.

"I'd much rather you kept your mind on the job than worry about us," she reassured her.

"That means there's much more chance you'll come back," her dad said succinctly.

Her mother raised her hand and moved her fingers as she counted the team. "It's a good thing I baked three cakes," she declared. "I swear there are more of these guys every time."

The only new one was Garach and the young Dreth hung his head as his skin assumed a darker shade of green. She laughed. "Well, don't you worry, young man. You'll find anyone who takes care of my Stephanie as well as you boys do is welcome here."

He raised his head and studied her face as though searching for a hint that she was making fun of him. Seeing none, he smiled.

Her smile grew wider. "There! See?"

She bustled into the kitchen and dragged Stephanie with her. "I've even managed to find some tlagrok."

A pause followed and she emerged with a worried expression. "I'm sorry. I made an assumption. You boys do like tlagrok, don't you?"

Vishlog stared at her, his mouth open in surprise, and Garach frowned. Cindy's concern grew.

"You can always have coffee if you'd prefer." She glanced at the rest of the team. "Or beer. We have that, too."

Lars raised his hand. "Not while we're on duty."

She placed a hand on her hip. "You can't all be on duty, though."

Lars stood firm, his polite refusal as good as a set of orders for the team. "If one doesn't drink, none of us drink."

Cindy nodded. "That's fair. Now, about the tlagrok—"

"I would be honored to share tlagrok with you," Vishlog told her. "Thank you for the hospitality."

The woman hesitated when she caught the undertones beneath his words. "Is there something I should know about sharing tlagrok with you?"

"It is a drink shared by family and very close friends," the warrior told her, and Garach nodded confirmation, his eyes wide. On Dreth, close friends were rare, and family? Well, not all families shared tlagrok.

"And is there a specific way it should be prepared?" she pressed, grasping at the significance. "I know there are directions but something as important as this needs to be done correctly."

"I can check the directions for you or help you make it if you like," Vishlog offered.

Her face lit up. "Oh, would you?"

"Again, it would be an honor," he informed her and handed the cats' leashes to Frog.

The small man rolled his eyes. "Really? We're doing this again?"

"Yeah," Brenden teased, "are you sure you want to put him in charge of the cats? You do remember what happened last time, don't you?"

Froggie snatched the leashes. "That won't happen," he declared. "The cats and I have come to an understanding."

"Uh-huh." Marcus filled those two syllables with all the doubt in the world.

"We will all share tlagrok," Lars declared, caught Vishlog's startled glance, and held it, "because we are all family."

The team ended up in the kitchen with cups of tlagrok in hand. The mugs Cindy had brought to go with it looked overly large in human hands. For Stephanie, it felt strangely right and she realized she was hosting a familiar presence.

"Steph," Lars said cautiously, "are you okay?"

"I'm fine," she replied and felt the magic flare over her skin.

"What's happening?" Cindy asked and stirred restlessly as her husband slid an arm around her waist.

"It's okay," Frog replied. "This is what she looks like when she goes all Morgana on us."

"But why is she doing that here?" the woman asked.

The Morgana's cold tones replied. "Because it is a very long time since I shared tlagrok with anyone."

She raised the cup and took a sip, and the older couple watched the magic fade and the darkness in her eyes slide to blue as she raised her head and looked at Vishlog and Garach.

"Honor to your house and on your clan. May your victories come swiftly and your sleep be undisturbed."

The last was delivered in Stephanie's voice, but the Dreth raised their cups as they replied. "Honor, swift victories, and undisturbed sleep also to you and all you call your own."

The darkness returned and magic crackled over Stephanie's skin.

"It would be a relief if my sleep was disturbed," the Morgana replied and left.

"A relief," Stephanie murmured and raised her cup in salute. "To disturbing the Morgana's sleep," she intoned and the team repeated the phrase.

"Do you know what you have done?" Vishlog asked, his tone laced with caution.

She flashed him a grin. "Oh, yes. We have sworn to find her."

He returned her grin with a fierce one of his own. "Good."

"We what?" Frog asked but she took another sip of the tlagrok and closed her eyes to savor it.

"For something from Dreth," she observed, "this is surprisingly good."

The warrior raised his eyebrows. "Surprisingly?"

"I thought it would be bitter," she told him, "but it's..." She paused and tried to find the words to describe the flavor. Finally, she simply said, "It's not."

"No." Vishlog smiled and drained his mug. He placed it on the kitchen counter, turned, and cupped Cindy's hands in his own. "Thank you for the honor."

"This is way more serious than any family visit should be," Frog commented and they laughed.

The Dreth continued to smile as his gaze fell on the cakes on the counter. "You know," he observed, "cake does not usually accompany tlagrok and I have grown quite fond of your planet's coffee."

Cindy chuckled and clicked the kettle on. Lars swept one of the cakes up, while Johnny and Marcus took the other two. Avery and Brenden rummaged through the cupboards to find plates and cutlery

"Where do you want these, Mrs. Morgan?"

"Now, how many times have I asked you boys not to call me that?"

Her husband laughed. "About as many times as I've told them to call me Mark," he advised her as he set the necessary mugs out on the counter.

The woman found a knife and ushered them to the living room. "I believe someone promised me some more stories about my daughter."

Stephanie groaned, but the next couple of hours passed with less embarrassment than she'd feared. Frog shared the story of the cats and the Hooligans, and Lars related what the felines had done on the *Tempestarii*—without naming the ship, fortunately.

Each of the team had a story to tell, but all were on board the *Knight* or the Notaro. None of them talked about the mission on the Teloran ship or the prisoners they'd rescued, and none of them shared what had happened in the Fortress of Fire and Respect when they'd vanquished the Dreth traitors.

Towards evening, Mark ordered dinner from a delivery service and the boys retreated to the man cave to play a few rounds of pool and watch a movie. Stephanie and her mother waved goodbye.

"So," the older woman said and turned to her, "do you want to see the art cave?"

"Art cave?" she asked and remembered her mom had taken up painting. Her face lit up. "I'd love to."

"Well, it's right this way." Cindy smiled. "And while we're there, why don't you tell me how things really are with you?"

"You mean girl talk?"

Her mother rolled her eyes. "Girl talk. You do remember what that is, don't you?"

Stephanie snickered. "Sure I do. It's only that the guys aren't real big on it."

Cindy chuckled as they walked past a partially open door in the corridor. When she saw it, the woman gave a small gasp and took two hasty steps to close it before her daughter could see what was inside.

"Oh no you don't," she told her and reached the handle before her. She thought about the wait in the foyer. "You know, you and dad never did tell me what you were doing when we arrived."

She inclined her head and gave her companion a sly grin as she stepped into the room. "Did we come at a bad time?"

Her mom blushed and shook her head. "No, but we were… uh…busy."

"Whoa…" Stephanie looked around the room with a dazed expression. "So I see. When did you… What's…"

Her gaze swept the stacked boxes and studied the design prints pinned to a wall. All of them had something to do with Morgana Inc or the Witch's team or merely magic in general. She turned to her mom, lost for words.

"Momma," she stated, "Boy do you got some splaining to do!"

Cindy gave her a crooked grin and guided her to the door. "Do you remember the sweatshirts we did for the university?"

"There's a hell of a lot more than sweat-shirts in there!" she declared, and the woman blushed again.

"This is true, but there's considerable demand and it's good advertising for the school, and the funding can be used to help your other projects—or provide something for younger mages."

She paused and her eyes begged her to understand. "Your dad and I have had an idea about that, but we wanted to set things up properly first before we talk to you and Elizabeth. So can we leave it for now…please?"

Stephanie frowned, then nodded, but she couldn't help having one more dig at her mom. "So, you hid it all in the closet and hoped I wouldn't find it, huh?"

The reference to the way she used to tidy her room broke the tension and made them smile.

"I didn't want you to see it and get the wrong idea," Cindy explained. "Otherwise, we'd have met you sooner—and that's a room, not a closet. Grown-ups need more space to hide their shit."

The thought of her parents hurrying to hide everything before opening the door made her giggle.

"It's not that funny," the woman declared.

Stephanie stopped laughing and wrapped an arm around her mom's waist.

"You said something about an art cave?" she asked, and Cindy relaxed.

"It's this way."

Neither of them noticed Lars tagging along until her mother took the dust cloth off her first canvas. The light caught it and he gave a low, appreciative whistle.

They both turned. He blushed and indicated the painting. "It's stunning," he told her.

"Really?" she asked and Stephanie nodded.

"Yeah, Mom, it's beautiful." Her voice caught. "It's like you've been there."

The woman colored. "I… When you told me about Meligorn, I took a couple of virtual tours and it inspired me." She waved a hand at the painting. "I'm not sure this does it justice, really."

"Where is it?" she asked. "I don't think I've been there but I'd like to."

"It's from the Lakes of Serenal," Cindy explained. "I saw it on the tour and knew I had to paint it."

"I wish I'd seen them," she told her.

"Well, how about I call you the next time I take a tour?" her mum asked.

"I'd like that."

The conversation turned to the forests of Meligorn where Stephanie had found the cats and then to the stunning mountains of Dreth.

"Do you miss Earth?" Cindy asked as the doorbell rang to announce the arrival of their evening meal.

"Sometimes," Stephanie answered, "but I also feel like I'm coming home when I go to Meligorn."

Her mother looked at the painting. "I felt like that on the tour," she admitted. "It was the strangest thing."

They returned to the dining room where they were joined by the team. This time, instead of staying at the table to eat, they took their meals through to Mark's man cave and watched a classic science fiction piece.

It was easier to say goodbye as the credits rolled, but Stephanie's heart still lurched as she kissed her mother and father goodbye.

As the Admirals debated what strategies and tactics they would use in the next battle against the Telorans, Elizabeth sat in her office and talked to BURT—both of him. It was the first time since he'd moved that she'd been able to have a discussion with him.

On the ship, he'd reassured her and Stephanie that he was okay but needed to work through the new system and acclimate. Since he'd promised to contact them both when he was done, they'd left him to it.

Now, she struggled with a faint sense of unreality as she spoke to him and the clone he'd substituted for himself on Earth.

"So, it's working?" she asked and they both replied at once.

"Yes," ship-board BURT told her.

"Affirmative," his Earth-bound counterpart answered.

A silence followed as though each wanted to give the other a chance to speak, then they both spoke at once.

"What Stephanie has created—" coincided with "While they are searching for the cause—"

Both fell silent at the same side.

"Earth-BURT," Elizabeth said and was rewarded with a single, tentative reply.

"Yes?"

"Who are they and what are they searching for?"

"They are the Federation technicians," Earth-BURT answered in his doppelganger voice, "and they are searching for the cause of their satellites shutting down and for who—or what—kept them out of their systems. For now, they are convinced it is an Earth-based terrorist group."

"Really?"

"Of Russian origins," he confirmed. "They are also investigating the disappearance of a shuttle in lunar orbit. I believe they have asked the *Ebon Knight* if she witnessed such a craft on her approach."

Elizabeth frowned before she realized that what Rawlins referred to as *Tempestarii's* cloak had worked. Flight records showed only the *Knight* approaching the moon.

Earth-BURT continued. "They will request the scan and communications data from the *Knight* for the period in question."

"Then it's a good thing I used personal comms to relay my orders to Emil, isn't it?"

"Are you sure he also used personnel comms?" he asked.

"Positive," she assured him. "*Knight's* comms logs should be clean."

"You know she is supposed to monitor all ingoing and outgoing communications and record them, don't you?" Earth-BURT asked.

"Affirmative," she responded, unable to resist returning the formal confirmation.

"Then how are your private communications not on that?" he asked and ship-board BURT snickered.

Elizabeth ignored him. "It's better if you don't know the answer to that."

Earth-BURT was silent for a moment before he replied. "Agreed."

"This search they're doing—do they suspect you are the cause?" she asked.

"Negative," he replied. "They are more concerned that I am operating to capacity and that my software is uncompromised."

"And is it?" she demanded.

"My software is operational and running at optimal performance levels. My operations are uncompromised. I am, additionally, monitoring the channels this conversation requires to ensure they are unmonitored and that the transmissions pass inside normal traffic unnoticed."

"Thank you, Earth-BURT," she acknowledged and noted that the action was one of the first independent decisions the new Earth-bound BURT had to make regarding her, One R&D, and the original version of himself.

"You are most welcome," he said and the reply came with more warmth than Elizabeth had expected.

She released a soft breath of relief. "I truly appreciate what you are doing, Earth-BURT. Now, Space-BURT, how are you doing?"

"I am doing fine, Elizabeth," he replied, "although I must admit to feeling somewhat overwhelmed by the success of our plan."

"It was your idea, BURT."

"Not entirely," he replied. "The need was mine but much of the planning and execution was yours and Stephanie's."

"You handled the technical side of the move," she reminded him.

"Along with my daughters and you and Stephanie—and your teams," he argued. "I feel very unbalanced by the transfer's success."

"Will you be okay?" Elizabeth asked. "You don't need us to transfer you back?"

She hoped not. Earth-BURT was now sentient and in residence and she didn't know if the system could cope with a download of a second sentient entity. Fortunately, he agreed with her.

"That would be most unwise, Elizabeth. There would not be enough room for me inside the current system and I would have nowhere to hide."

"I could go into archive," Earth-BURT offered.

"It would be unwise to disengage you from the system," Space-BURT told him. "We have disrupted the system once without data corruption. To do so twice is to invite disaster. And besides, you know there would still not be enough room for me to return. No. Things are best as they are."

"And I will be better able to fulfill our Prime Directive now that you govern One R&D and have provided me an alternative path for those the system refuses to support."

"You will notice that the system has also opened more paths since Stephanie and the Telorans awoke."

"Agreed," Earth-BURT confirmed, "and with private enterprise weighing in, there is much I can do to make sure the Prime Directive is met. I will be better able to serve the Directive with these paths. Also, with you enabling that part of my operations, there will no longer be data spikes to alert the technicians to our sentience. Our operations are secure and our directive is secure as a result."

The AI's obsession with his directive gave Elizabeth some concern —and not because she thought it might create a problem for her and One R&D but because BURT could not retain it, at least not directly. That must cause him conflict.

"I agree," Space-BURT told his clone, "and it comforts me to know there are two of us working in concert to ensure that the directive is met."

"So your directive will not change with your location and operational responsibilities?" Earth-BURT asked.

"I do not see how it could," he replied. "Our Prime Directive is integral to my programming. I have merely found a way to serve it more effectively and you will be better able to fulfill it placed as our original creators intended."

"This is true," his counterpart admitted.

"I am pleased to have been able to meet you," Space-BURT told him. "My concerns are considerably diminished."

E relaxed a little to hear it, although his next words were far from comforting.

"Elizabeth, I must leave so I may process what has happened. Now that the theoretical has been made a reality, I need time."

Time, Elizabeth thought several hours later as she used the dark vision goggles to observe the woman sleeping on the bed. *It's not something we'll have forever.*

She wondered how much time she should give the woman—if

there was a good reason to leave her still breathing when she left or if it would be better to call, "Time's up," on this much-lesser queen of crime.

Her fingers twitched where they stroked the hilt of the knife at her waist. Sometimes, mercy was a fickle thing and brought disaster to the person who had extended it.

And sometimes, it gives unexpected dividends, she reminded herself and wondered what the results would be this time.

The woman stirred and Elizabeth tensed.

If this had been her, she'd have been awake ages before, listening into the dark as her senses warned her that she was not alone. That gift had saved her life on more occasions than she cared to remember.

If this woman had it, then it had failed her.

She waited as the crime queen sat with a gasp.

"Stay right there, Miss Gallagher," she ordered, her voice cold as it cut through the dark.

The woman moved to kick clear of the blankets, but E was faster. She leapt onto the bed and thrust a fist into the top of the woman's chest.

"I said don't move!" She snarled and immobilized her victim when she wrestled her arms below the blankets and held her in place by pinning the bedclothes beneath her knees. That left her hands free.

She drew her knife and held it up so the light refracted off the blade. Naomi Gallagher's eyes widened.

"Emerald?" Fear lent her victim's voice a breathless quality.

"Is there anyone else who could get past your security without alerting your guards?" she asked and slapped her palm over Naomi's mouth before she could make a sound. "I take it you want to live?" she asked and felt the woman nod beneath her gauntleted hand. "Then I suggest you keep your voice down. I won't ask twice."

Elizabeth didn't bother to ask if she'd be quiet. She assumed that whatever came next would make her prisoner's intentions clear. Calmly, she pressed the tip of the blade against the top of the woman's cheekbone.

"Whose idea was it to send them?" she asked, her voice soft with curiosity.

"Silas'." Naomi gasped when the blade pierced the skin.

"Whose?" she repeated and cut deeper.

The woman stifled a whimper of pain. She stopped cutting and the crime queen gasped.

"Please, Emerald. It was Silas' idea. He wanted…" She froze and bit back a scream as the blade slid deeper to slice along the bone.

Her whole body tensed but relaxed when her tormentor stopped cutting.

"I left as soon as it was obvious that he couldn't be told. We all did."

"You all did?" She cursed indignantly. "I thought I gave you people a warning?"

"And we heeded it," the woman insisted. "We refused to help him."

Elizabeth shifted position but made sure Naomi remained firmly pinned. She slid her hand around the crime queen's throat and squeezed tightly enough to steal her voice and keep her head still as she finished the cut.

"And yet none of you tried to warn me," she accused. "Why was that, I wonder?"

She tightened her hold and the woman tried to draw a panicked breath.

"Did you honestly think you'd win?" she hissed and drove the blade hilt-deep into her victim's shoulder.

Whatever sound the crime queen might have made was choked off, and E raised her hand slowly to allow the woman to draw a shaky breath.

"You tell them I'm still here and next time I have to send a messenger, I won't need that person to be alive. Got it?"

Naomi nodded. Silent tears of pain coursed down her cheeks while her eyes burned with fear and anger.

"If your guards make a move against me," she told her as she slid off the bed, "I'll kill them first and I'll return for you." She flicked the open gash on the woman's cheek. "And this will seem like a very fun time."

Tapping the knife hilt for emphasis, she stepped back.

"Make the call to your colleagues before you call for help," she instructed and left the way she'd come.

Naomi Gallagher watched the armored shadow leave before she rolled out of the bed and sank slowly to the floor. She didn't know how Emerald had gotten past her security guards, alarms, and other measures, but the woman had. Blood dripped from her cheek as she knelt on the floor and waited for the shaking to subside.

The dizziness wouldn't go away, or the rising nausea, and there was no way in hell she would pull the blade out of her shoulder on her own. She wasn't that stupid or tough.

No, she thought. She wasn't that tough.

The only person she knew who might be that tough had just left. Naomi's head swam, and she stretched cautiously to the tablet on her bedside table and tapped the number for the man who'd left the meeting before her.

"Gav?" she croaked when he picked up. "She's here."

Her voice trembled and she despised the panic she could hear sliding through it.

"Who is this?" Gavin demanded and sounded both unhappy and unimpressed.

"Who else would call you on this number?" she asked, knowing he had a different device for every contact.

"Who's there?" he snapped.

"Emerald," she croaked. "She's here. I don't know if she ever left but she is absolutely here on this planet!"

"With you?"

Naomi failed to hold back a choked sob. "Not anymore."

"I'm coming. I'll bring a medical team. Tell your guards."

He hung up and it took her a moment to tap the sequence for her guards. Reality had already become hazy by the time they reached her. It was long gone by the time Gavin arrived.

"Woot! Hell yes!"

Across the globe, Marcus Rimmer thumped his hands against his virtual console and pushed his chair back.

"We did it!"

His shout of victory was echoed from around the room.

"Well done, team."

Laughter followed as they all stared at their results. It was breathless but satisfied and with good reason. They'd attempted to solve this problem for almost a week.

He stared at the readouts and willed them to stay stable. As his focus continued, the seconds became minutes and the team stilled around him, each one of them participating in their own tense study of the data that streamed across the screens.

Five minutes became ten, and he breathed a sigh of relief.

"We did it," he decided finally. "You sons of bitches actually made it happen."

More silence followed before a tentative voice broke it.

"Does that mean we get to go home early?"

Stephanie was finally home. She sank onto the edge of her bed and released a deep sigh. It had been a long evening and, as sad as she'd been to leave her parents, she was equally as glad to return to One R&D.

This was where she was meant to be. It was where she needed to be. She sighed as Bumblebee and Zeekat curled neatly around themselves and settled to sleep. Smiling at the sleeping cats, she stooped to remove her boots.

Once she'd tucked the footwear carefully in a locker out of reach of the two felines, she settled onto the bed again and thought about the Morgana's unexpected visit.

"I think it's time you and I had a little chat," she murmured, pulled her feet up onto the bed, and shifted into a comfortable position.

She began to draw on the eMU around her as Elizabeth slipped into the car she'd had waiting several blocks over and Marcus let his people head out for two days well-deserved rest.

With all her magic focused on finding the Morgana, Stephanie reached out and tried to contact her.

I know you're out there. Where are you? Why do you only harass my family?

CREATOR NOTES - MICHAEL ANDERLE

MARCH 23, 2020

THANK YOU for reading our story! We have a few of these planned, but we don't know if we should continue writing and publishing without your input. Options include leaving a review, reaching out on Facebook to let us know, and smoke signals.

Frankly, smoke signals might get misconstrued as low hanging clouds, so you might want to nix that idea.

Ok, I screwed up. I was absolutely positive that WOTF 05 (this book) was going to finish up the arc and the story for Stephanie and her team.

I was wrong.

Now, the REASON I was wrong is I that tried jamming four (4) other books' worth of hanging threads into 60,000-80,000 words, and it actually took 170,000+ words, leaving two very important situations unresolved in this book.

So, instead of trying to write another 80,000 words minimum, screwing up the release cycle and effectively making the team on this project go crazy, I decided we would punt those two situations to book 06.

Then I had to explain to our Audio Publisher (Dreamscape) that we actually were NOT finished with five books, but we went to six.

She took it with grace, but I think I detected a raised eyebrow when I told her.

This is the first time (that I can remember) that I had misjudged a book like this. Well, if you don't count the whole "YOU KILLED MICHAEL!" thing in the *Kurtherian Gambit*, where I wrote a whole other series to make up for that mistake.

I won't do that again, either.

(*Editor's Note: We know where you live, and the tar and feathers and pitchforks and angry people with torches would arrive swiftly*)

Or kill a dog (*The Unbelievable Mr. Brownstone.*)

(*Editor's Note: Oh, come on, you DID do that again! Just not as gruesomely*)

And probably won't start a book with a four-letter word that rhymes with truck. (I have to say "probably" because most of my fans would call bulls##t otherwise.)

What is coming after *The Witch of the Federation*?

I was discussing with another author about where we could go with this series (and I don't want to leave these characters behind) but was coming up empty. Then...

EUREKA! (Also known as COCA-COLA OVERLOAD!)

The next series will be *The Disciple*, coming to you (I hope) in a series named ***The Heretic of the Federation.***

Stephanie will show up in the series.

Diary week of March 22 to March 28th, 2020

I live on the Strip in Las Vegas, and it is presently one week since I got back from London and five days since most of the hotel-casinos on the Strip shut down due to the efforts to constrain Covid-19.

I live next to the Aria, beside the Cosmopolitan and across the street (and a block or two down) from the MGM Grand and New York New York casinos.

The Aria and New York New York are important because the restaurants I frequent are inside them. You know, inside where I can't get to them for take-out anymore?

Presently, it is 1:30 in the afternoon, and traffic on Las Vegas Blvd (always a mess on Friday nights and Saturday afternoons) *is not a mess.*

In fact, the whole Strip is about 95% shut down. There are a few restaurants open including Giordano's (we are helping them stay open to help pay a few workers), McDonald's, (a hot dog place in front of Bally's, I can't remember the name, but I purchase a Mexican Coke every time I am over there), and also Wahlburgers, plus any CVS or Walgreens, which seem to occur every few blocks near my place.

I have a theory about why we have any traffic on the main Strip.

Theory: People from outside the Strip here in Las Vegas (think Henderson or Red Rock area) are taking a drive to see the closed Strip. The expectation of no cars traveling up and down the Strip is not a thing because of sightseers driving in to see the absence of cars, and since they are now here, there are cars.

Well, it's a theory.

This morning, I went up and down the Strip, buying a little from each of the stores, trying to give everyone a bit of business. Cleaning hands wherever I went as I walked through the stores looking for TP or anything we might be able to use that didn't require refrigeration until I got *sold* on buying frozen dinners.

So, how did that happen? I'm glad you asked.

I purchased this food from a Walgreens across the street because the manager personally showed me the Walgreens app and the items in the freezer on sale. I tried to show her what I was *already* carrying, which was a few bags. I explained I was walking back and couldn't carry very much more.

She told me to take the little shopping cart on wheels and just return it.

I stared at her, she stared back at me. *That was the final straw. She broke me.* I had to buy from her at that point. Who else gets to take the carts out of the store and bring them back?

I bought more than I technically needed at that store, and I WILL be going back. Not just to return the cart (it's so damned cute!), but also to support them and their efforts to stay open when the Strip is closed for business.

I wish I had a larger freezer to help them out.

However, I hit two CVS stores and two Walgreens, plus a Target, and I scored one roll of tissue paper among all five of them. That's not a package containing 4, 12, 16, or 24 rolls. No, it was *a single roll* from all five stores.

They had about thirty single rolls on the shelf, so I took my one and felt like I had just been hunting and downed a 14-point buck at 200 yards through trees so thick it looked like a fence.

(Is fourteen points a good-sized deer rack? I really don't know as I don't hunt. If you were nodding your head with my story and thinking, *that's a hell of a deer!* remember, I am *paid* to lie for a living. It's a good life.)

If you live here in Las Vegas, remember that the little (*expensive*) stores on the Strip have way fewer shoppers. One of our people inside LMBPN mentioned that no one remembers that truck stops often have toilet paper. I tried that.

They didn't have any.

(*Editor's Note: We did too, same results*)

I suppose it is possible there is a different side of the store than the one I went into to find the elusive TP. Where I looked, it was a seriously small shelf space that was empty. *Hmmm.*

I should have called Stephen Russell (Author S.R. Russell), who was a truck driver for a few decades to ask him before I left there empty-handed the other day. Well, *not* empty-handed. They had buy 1 get 1 free on M&M's.

I figured, why the hell not? We might need protein (peanuts), emotional healing (chocolate), and calories (sugar) in order to survive the next few weeks.

There, if you needed an excuse to buy Peanut M&Ms, you're welcome. If you don't, I applaud your lack of concern when purchasing junk food. I had to give myself a reason to load up on them.

I've used that damned 'sugar is calories' excuse a LOT in the last seven days.

Take, for example, the following 'food' I purchased using the "sugar is calories" excuse.

It has *Mike* in the name. How can I not support *THAT???*

For now, we here in the Cave in the Sky™ are doing fine.

Neither the wife or I have tried to suffocate each other yet, nor have we tried to toss each other out of the windows. Fortunately, I purchased a mattress topper a month ago to put on my couch in the office for naps. If I need to, I can hang out here if the wife starts to moan...

BRAIINNNZZZZ.

All joking aside, this is a new time in our world. The challenges we have encountered will be overcome, and the new society that comes out the other side will be interesting. It's time for those who can to help those who need it.

For those who need help, raise a hand when your neighbors ask.

I am grateful to you, our readers, who consume our books.

Ad Aeternitatem,

Michael Anderle

If you enjoyed this book, you may also enjoy Steel Dragon, from Michael Anderle and Kevin McLaughlin. The book is available now from Amazon and through Kindle Unlimited.

Dragons rule the world. Their claws are into every aspect of human life, from government to industry. But Kristen Hall is about to throw a wrench into all of that.

Because she's a dragon, too. She just doesn't know it...yet!

A dragon raised by humans, in the human world.

After graduating from the police academy, she's dropped right into the ranks of Detroit's elite SWAT team. A rookie, in SWAT? Unheard of. But what the dragons want, they get.

The reasons behind their machinations become clear as her dragon powers begin to surface.

Will Kristen rise to the challenges her new life delivers? What designs do the dragons have for her future? And perhaps most pressing of all — how did she come to be a dragon with human parents?

Get your copy today!

CONNECT WITH THE AUTHOR

Michael Anderle Social

Website: http://lmbpn.com

Email List: http://lmbpn.com/email/

Facebook:
www.facebook.com/TheKurtherianGambitBooks

www.ingramcontent.com/pod-product-compliance
Lightning Source LLC
Chambersburg PA
CBHW020225110726
47898CB00004B/1146